THE EAGLE OF THE NINTH CHRONICLES

The Eagle of the Ninth Chronicles

Rosemary Sutcliff

OXFORD
UNIVERSITY PRESS

OXFORD
UNIVERSITY PRESS

Great Clarendon Street, Oxford OX2 6DP

Oxford University Press is a department of the University of Oxford.
It furthers the University's objective of excellence in research, scholarship,
and education by publishing worldwide in

Oxford New York

Auckland Cape Town Dar es Salaam Hong Kong Karachi
Kuala Lumpur Madrid Melbourne Mexico City Nairobi
New Delhi Shanghai Taipei Toronto

With offices in

Argentina Austria Brazil Chile Czech Republic France Greece
Guatemala Hungary Italy Japan Poland Portugal Singapore
South Korea Switzerland Thailand Turkey Ukraine Vietnam

Oxford is a registered trade mark of Oxford University Press
in the UK and in certain other countries

'The Eagle of the Ninth' first published 1954
'The Silver Branch' first published 1957
'The Lantern Bearers' first published 1959

First published in this edition 2010

British Library Cataloguing in Publication Data

Data available

ISBN: 978-0-19-278998-3

3 5 7 9 10 8 6 4 2

Printed in Great Britain

Paper used in the production of this book is a natural,
recyclable product made from wood grown in sustainable forests.
The manufacturing process conforms to the environmental
regulations of the country of origin.

Contents

The Eagle of the Ninth 1

The Silver Branch 215

The Lantern Bearers 395

THE EAGLE OF THE NINTH

Foreword

SOMETIME about the year 117 AD, the Ninth Legion, which was stationed at Eburacum where York now stands, marched north to deal with a rising among the Caledonian tribes, and was never heard of again.

During the excavations at Silchester nearly eighteen hundred years later, there was dug up under the green fields which now cover the pavements of Calleva Atrebatum, a wingless Roman Eagle, a cast of which can be seen to this day in Reading Museum. Different people have had different ideas as to how it came to be there, but no one knows, just as no one knows what happened to the Ninth Legion after it marched into the northern mists.

It is from these two mysteries, brought together, that I have made the story of 'The Eagle of the Ninth'.

R.S.

Contents

I	Frontier Fort	5
II	Feathers in the Wind	14
III	Attack!	24
IV	The Last Rose Falls	34
V	Saturnalia Games	41
VI	Esca	53
VII	Two Worlds Meeting	63
VIII	The Healer with the Knife	71
IX	Tribune Placidus	81
X	Marching Orders	89
XI	Across the Frontier	101
XII	The Whistler in the Dawn	108
XIII	The Lost Legion	118
XIV	The Feast of New Spears	130
XV	Venture into the Dark	141
XVI	The Ring-Brooch	154
XVII	The Wild Hunt	166
XVIII	The Waters of Lethe	175
XIX	Tradui's Gift	186
XX	Valedictory	194
XXI	The Olive-Wood Bird	205

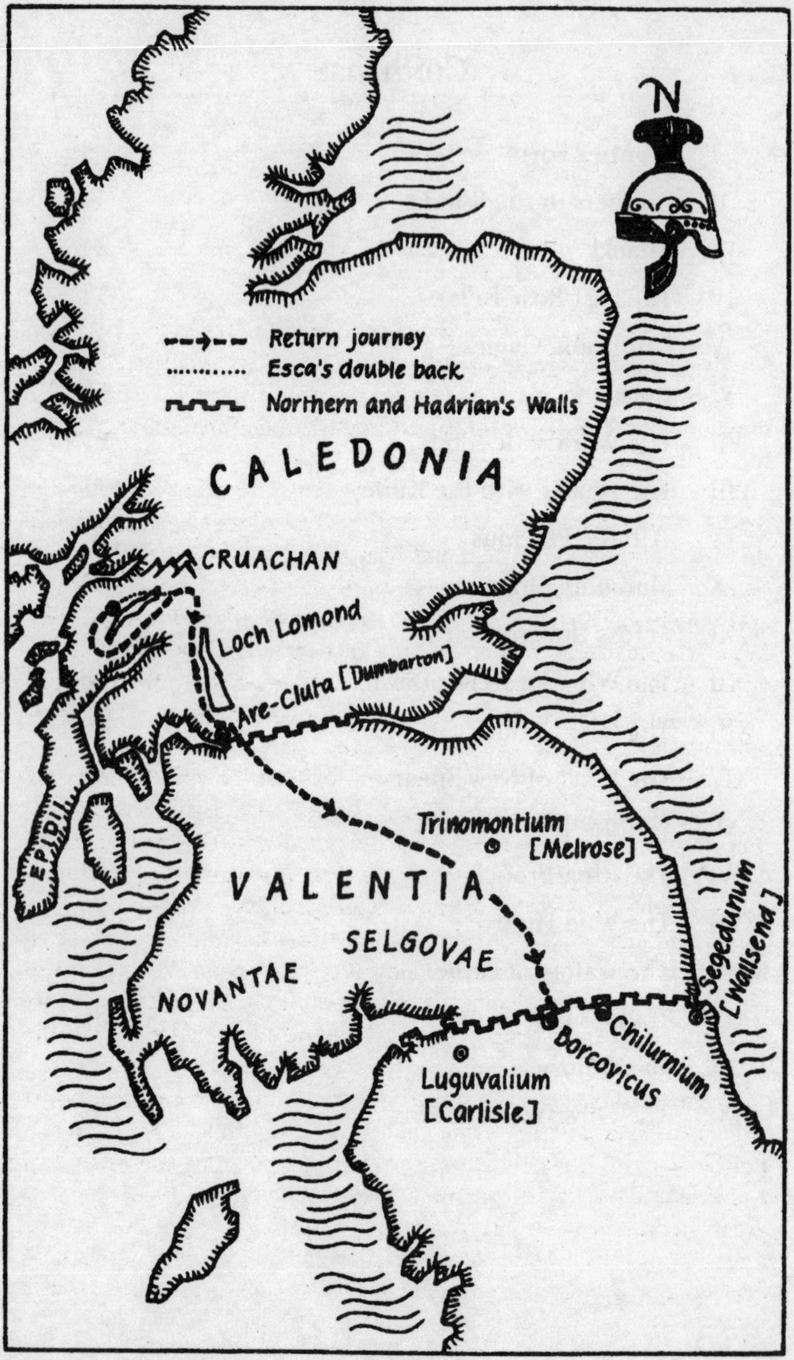
N
Return journey
Esca's double back
Northern and Hadrian's Walls
CALEDONIA
CRUACHAN
Loch Lomond
Are-Cluta [Dumbarton]
EPIDII
Trinomontium
[Melrose]
VALENTIA
SELGOVAE
NOVANTAE
Segedunum
[Wallsend]
Chilurnium
Borcovicus
Luguvalium
[Carlisle]

I
Frontier Fort

FROM the Fosseway westward to Isca Dumnoniorum the road was simply a British trackway, broadened and roughly metalled, strengthened by corduroys of logs in the softest places, but otherwise unchanged from its old estate, as it wound among the hills, thrusting further and further into the wilderness.

It was a busy road and saw many travellers: traders with bronze weapons and raw yellow amber in their ponies' packs; country folk driving shaggy cattle or lean pigs from village to village; sometimes a band of tawny-haired tribesmen from further west; strolling harpers and quack-oculists, too, or a light-stepping hunter with huge wolfhounds at his heel; and from time to time a commissariat wagon going up and down to supply the Roman frontier post. The road saw them all, and the cohorts of the Eagles for whom all other travellers must make way.

There was a cohort of leather-clad auxiliaries on the road today, swinging along at the steady Legion's pace that had brought them down from Isca Silurium at twenty miles a day; the new garrison coming to relieve the old one at Isca Dumnoniorum. On they went, following the road that now ran out on a causeway between sodden marsh and empty sky, now plunged into deep boar-hunted forest, or lifted over bleak uplands where nothing grew save furze and thorn-scrub. On with never a halt nor a change of rhythm, marching century by century, the sun bright on the Standard at their head, and the rolling dust-cloud kicked up over the pack-train behind.

At the head of the column marched the Pilus Prior Centurion, the cohort Commander, the pride that shone from him showing clearly that this was his first command. They were, he had long since decided, a command worthy of anyone's pride; six hundred yellow-haired giants recruited from the tribes of Upper Gaul, with the natural fighting power of mountain cats, drilled and hammered into what he firmly believed to be the finest auxiliary cohort ever to serve with the

Second Legion. They were a newly joined cohort; many of the men had not yet proved themselves in action, and the spearshaft of their Standard had no honours on it, no gilded laurel wreath nor victor's crown. The honours were all to win—perhaps during his command.

The Commander was a complete contrast to his men: Roman to his arrogant finger-tips, wiry and dark as they were raw-boned and fair. The olive-skinned face under the curve of his crested helmet had not a soft line in it anywhere—a harsh face it would have been, but that it was winged with laughter lines, and between his level black brows showed a small raised scar that marked him for one who had passed the Raven Degree of Mithras.

Centurion Marcus Flavius Aquila had seen little of the Eagles until a year ago. His first ten years had been lived quietly with his mother on the family farm near Clusium, while his father soldiered in Judaea, in Egypt, and here in Britain. They had been going to join his father in Britain, but before the time came for them to do so, rebellion had flared up among the northern tribes, and the Ninth Hispana, his father's Legion, had marched north to deal with it, and never came marching back.

His mother had died soon afterwards, leaving him to be brought up in Rome by a rather foolish aunt and the plump and purse-proud official who was her husband. Marcus had loathed the official, and the official had loathed Marcus. They saw everything with different eyes. Marcus came of a line of soldiers—one of those Equestrian families who, when the rest of their kind had turned from soldiering to trade and finance, had kept to the old way of life, and remained poor but held their noses high in consequence. The official came of a line of officials, and his code of life was quite other than Marcus's. Neither of them had a shred of understanding for each other's ideas, and they had both been thankful when Marcus was eighteen and could apply for a centurion's commission.

Marcus, his eyes narrowed into the sun as he marched, smiled to himself a little wryly, as he remembered how almost pathetically thankful that plump official had been. (Tramp, tramp, tramp, said the cohort's feet behind him.)

He had asked to be sent to Britain, though it meant starting in an auxiliary cohort instead of a line-of-battle one, partly because his father's elder brother had settled there when his own years of soldiering were done, but mostly because of his father. If ever anything became known of the lost Legion, it would be known first in Britain, and it might even be that here in Britain he would find out something for himself.

Marching down the Isca Dumnoniorum road in the run-honey evening light, he found himself thinking about his father. He had very vivid memories of a slight, dark man with laughter lines at the corners of his eyes, who had come home from time to time, and taught him to fish, to play 'Flash the Fingers', and throw a javelin. He remembered vividly that last leave of all. His father had just been appointed to command the First Cohort of the Hispana, which meant having charge of the Eagle and being something very like second-in-command of the Legion besides; and he had been like a jubilant boy about it. But his mother had been faintly anxious, almost as if she knew . . .

'If it was any *other* Legion!' she had said. 'You have told me yourself that the Hispana has a bad name.'

And his father had replied: 'But I would not have it any other Legion if I could. I held my first command in the Hispana, and a man's first Legion is apt to hold chief place in his heart ever after, be its name good or bad; and now that I go back to it as First Cohort, we will see whether there is nothing can be done to better its name.' He had turned to his small son, laughing. 'Presently it will be your turn. It has fallen on evil days, but we will make a Legion of the Hispana yet, you and I.'

Looking back across the years, Marcus remembered that his father's eyes had been very bright, like the eyes of a man going into action; and the light had caught suddenly in the great flawed emerald of the signet-ring he always wore, striking from it a spark of clear green fire. Odd how one remembered things like that: little things that somehow mattered.

(Tramp, tramp, tramp, came the sound of the cohort's feet behind him.)

It would be pleasant, he thought, if Uncle Aquila was like his father. He had not met his uncle yet; after learning his foot-drill he had arrived in Britain in the sleety days of late autumn, and been sent straight up to Isca; but he had a rather vague invitation to spend his leave with him at Calleva, when he had any leave to spend. It would be very pleasant if Uncle Aquila was like his father.

Not of course that he and his uncle were likely to have much to do with each other. In a few years' time he would probably be serving in quite a different part of the Empire, since a cohort centurion seldom moved up all the way in the same Legion.

All the way . . . from his present rank right up to his father's rank of First Cohort; and after that? For most of the men who got so far there was nothing after that, but for the outstanding few who went further—as Marcus intended to go further—the ways divided there. One could become a camp commandant, as Uncle Aquila had done, or one could go on, by way of the Praetorian Guard, to try for command of a Legion. Legion Commanders were almost always men of Senator's rank, with no experience of soldiering save a year's service as Military Tribune in their youth; but by long custom the two Egyptian Legions were exceptions to the rule. They were commanded by professional soldiers; and an Egyptian Legion had been Marcus's shining goal for as long as he could remember.

But one day, when he had finished with the Eagles, when he had made an honourable name and become Prefect of his Egyptian Legion, he would go home to the Etruscan hills, and perhaps even buy back the old farm, which the plump official had ruthlessly sold to defray expenses. For a moment he remembered almost painfully the sunlit courtyard flickered over with the shadow of pigeons' wings, and the wild olive-tree in the loop of the stream, on a twisted root of which he had once found a kind of gall growing, that was shaped something like a little bird. He had cut it from the root with the new knife his father had given him, and spent much loving care, all one absorbed summer evening, trimming and carving feathers on it. He had that little bird still.

The road topped a gentle rise, and suddenly Isca Dumnoniorum lay before them, with the fortress-crowned Red Mount dark with shadows against the evening sky; and Marcus came back to the present with a jerk. The farm in the Etruscan hills could wait until he was old and tired and famous; in the present was the glory of his first command.

The British town was spread below the southern scarp of the Mount; a sprawling huddle of reed-thatched roofs, every colour from the gold of honey to the black of dried peat, according to the age of the thatch; with the squared, clean lines of the Roman forum and basilica looking oddly rootless in their midst; and the faint haze of wood-smoke lying over all.

The road led straight through the town and up to the cleared slope beyond, to the Praetorian gate of the fort; here and there, crimson or saffron-cloaked men turned to look at the cohort as it swung by, a look that was reserved rather than hostile. Dogs sat scratching in odd corners, lean pigs rooted among the garbage piles, and women with bracelets of gold or copper on very white arms sat in hut doorways, spinning, or grinding corn. The blue smoke of many cooking-fires curled up into the quiet air, and the savoury smell of many evening meals mingled with the blue reek of wood-smoke and the sharper tang of horse-droppings, which Marcus had by now come to associate with all British towns. Little that was Roman was here as yet, despite the stone-built forum. One day there would be straight streets, he supposed, and temples and bath-houses and a Roman way of life. But as yet it was a place where two worlds met without mingling: a British town huddled under the dominion of the turf ramparts where once the tribe had had its stronghold and now the Roman sentries paced up and down. He looked about him under the curve of his helmet as he marched, knowing that this place would be part of his life for the next year; then looked up to the turf ramparts, and saw a Roman banner drooping in the still air and the tall crest of a sentry burning in the sunset, and heard a trumpet-call ring out, as it seemed, from the fiery sky.

'You have brought clear skies with you,' said Centurion Quintus Hilarion, lounging in the window of the Commander's quarters, and peering into the night. 'But Hercle! you need not expect it to last.'

'As bad as that?' said Centurion Marcus Aquila, who was seated on the table.

'Quite as bad as that! It rains always, here in the west, save when Typhon, the father of all ills, brews up a mist to come between a man and his own feet. By the time you have served your year here you will have toadstools sprouting out of your ears, the same as me, *and* not from the damp alone!'

'From what besides?' enquired Marcus with interest.

'Oh, lack of company, for one thing. I am a sociable soul myself; I like my friends around me.' He turned from the window, and folded up on to a low cushioned bench, hugging his knees. 'Ah well, I am off to rub away the blue mould as soon as I have marched the troops back to Isca.'

'Going on leave?'

The other nodded. 'Long leave, lovely leave, among the flesh-pots of Durinum.'

'Durinum—that is your home?' asked Marcus.

'Yes. My father retired and settled there a few years ago. There is a surprisingly good circus, and plenty of people—pretty girls too. A pleasant enough place to get back to, out of the wilds.' An idea seemed to strike him. 'What shall you do when *your* leave falls due? I suppose, coming out from home, you have no one here to go to?'

'I have an uncle at Calleva, though I have not yet met him,' Marcus said, 'and certainly there is no one at home I should want to spend my leave with.'

'Father and mother both dead?' enquired Hilarion with friendly interest.

'Yes. My father went with the Ninth Legion.'

'Pericol! You mean when they—'

'Disappeared. Yes.'

'So. That is bad!' said Hilarion, wagging his head. 'A deal of ugly stories, there were—still are, for that matter; and of course, they did lose the Eagle.'

Instantly Marcus was up in arms to defend his father and his father's Legion. 'Since not a man of the Legion came back, it is scarcely a matter for wonder that neither did the Eagle,' he flashed.

'Surely not,' agreed Hilarion amicably. 'I was not blowing on your father's honour, so you can keep your feathers on, my Marcus.' He looked up at the other with a wide, friendly grin, and suddenly Marcus, who had been ready to quarrel with him the instant before, found himself grinning back.

It was several hours since Marcus had marched his cohort across the hollow-ringing bridge, answering the sentry's challenge, 'Fourth Gaulish Auxiliaries of the Second Legion, come to relieve this garrison.' Dinner was over, in the officers' mess, with the Quartermaster, the Surgeon, and the double complement of ranker centurions. Marcus had taken charge of the pay-chest keys—in a garrison as small as this there was no paymaster; and for the past hour, here in the Commander's quarters in the Praetorium, he and Hilarion had been going through the office work of the frontier fort. Now, crested helmets and embossed breastplates laid aside, the two of them were taking their ease.

Through the doorless opening Marcus could see almost the whole of the sleeping-cell, the narrow cot piled with gay native rugs, the polished oaken chest, the lamp-bracket high on the bare wall, and nothing more. The outer room held the battered writing-table on which Marcus was sitting, a cross-legged camp-stool, the cushioned bench to represent comfort, another chest for the record rolls, and a bronze pedestal lamp of peculiarly hideous design.

In the little silence that had fallen between them, Marcus looked round him at the austere room in the yellow flood of lamplight, and to him it seemed beautiful. But though it would be his tomorrow, for this one night he was a guest here, and he looked back to his host with a quick smile of apology for having looked too soon at his surroundings with the eye of mastery.

Hilarion grinned. 'You will not be feeling like that this day next year.'

'I wonder,' said Marcus, swinging one sandalled foot and idly watching the swing of it. 'What does one do here, besides growing toadstools? Is there good hunting?'

'Good enough; it is the one thing to be said for this particular corner of the Empire. Boar and wolf in the winter, and the forest swarms with deer. There are several hunters below in the town, who will take you out for the price of the day's work. Unwise to go alone, of course.'

Marcus nodded. 'Have you any advice for me? I am new to this country.'

The other considered. 'No, I think not.' Then he sat up with a jerk. 'Yes, I have, if no one has warned you already. But it has nothing to do with the hunting. It is the priest-kind—the wandering Druids. If one of them appears in the district, or you get the least idea that there is one about, look to your weapons. Good advice, that is.'

'The Druids?' Marcus was surprised and puzzled. 'But surely Suetonius Paulinus dealt with them once and for all, sixty years ago?'

'As an organized priesthood, maybe; but as easily hold off these heathen mists with a palm-leaf umbrella as end the Druids by destroying their stronghold. They spring up still, from time to time, and wherever they do spring up, there is likely to be trouble for the Eagles. They were the heart and soul of British resistance in the early days, and even now, when there is any sign of unrest among the tribes, you can wager your sandals there is a holy man at the bottom of it.'

'Go on,' Marcus prodded, as the other seemed to have finished. 'This becomes interesting.'

'Well, the thing is this. They can preach holy war, and that is ever the most deadly kind, for it recks nothing of consequences.' Hilarion spoke slowly, as though he was thinking the thing out as he went along. 'The frontier tribes are not like those of the south coast, who were half Romanized before ever we landed; they are a wild lot, and superbly brave; but even they have mostly come to think that we are not fiends of darkness, and they have enough sense to see that destroying the local garrison will only mean a punitive expedition and their homes and standing crops burned, and a stronger garrison with a heavier hand thereafter. But let one of their holy men lay hold of them, and all that goes whistling down the wind. They cease to think whether there can be any good come of their rising, cease to think at all. They are keeping faith with their gods by smoking out a nest of the unbelievers, and what happens after is no concern of theirs, for they are going West of the Sunset by the warriors' road. And when you get men into that state there is apt to be trouble coming.'

Outside in the quiet darkness the trumpets sounded for the second watch of the night. Hilarion uncurled himself and stood up. 'We had best do Late Rounds together tonight,' he said, and reached for his sword, slipping the baldrick over his head. 'I am native born,' he added as though in explanation. 'That is how I come to have some understanding of these matters.'

'I imagined that you must be.' Marcus tested a buckle of his own equipment. 'You have had no holy man round here, I suppose?'

'No, but my predecessor had a certain amount of trouble just before I took over, and the trouble-maker slipped through his fingers and disappeared. We lived a month or two on Vesuvius—all the more so as the harvest was bad for the second year running—but it never erupted.'

Footsteps sounded outside, and a red light glimmered at the window; and they went out together to the Duty Centurion, who stood outside with a flaring torch. The clashing Roman salute was exchanged, and they set out on their tour of the darkened fort, from sentry-post to sentry-post along the rampart walk, from guard-point to guard-point, with the low exchange of the password; lastly to the small lighted room in the Praetorium where the pay-chest was kept and the Standard stood against the wall, and between rounds the

Duty Centurion sat with his drawn sword on the table before him, through the night.

Marcus thought: After tonight it will be for me alone to follow the centurion's torch from guard-post to guard-post, from barrack block to horse-lines, seeing that all is well with the frontier of the Empire.

Next morning, after the formal take-over ceremony in the forum, the old garrison marched out. Marcus watched them go, out across the ditch and downhill between the crowding hovels of the native town whose reed-thatched roofs were gold-dusted by the morning sun. Century after Century, marching away up the long road that led to Isca; and at their head the glint of gold and crimson that was the cohort Standard. He narrowed his eyes into the piercing light, and watched that coloured glint till it disappeared into the brightness of the morning. The last driver of the baggage-train dropped out of sight beyond the lift of the road, the rhythmic tramp-tramp-tramp of heavily sandalled feet ceased to pulse through the sunlit air, and Marcus was alone with his first command.

II

Feathers in the Wind

BEFORE many days had passed, Marcus had slipped so completely into the life of the frontier fort that it seemed as though he had never known any other. The plan of all Roman forts was much the same, and the pattern of life lived in them, so that knowing one meant knowing them all, whether it was the stone-built camp of the Praetorian Guard itself, or a baked mud fort on the Upper Nile, or this one at Isca Dumnoniorum, where the ramparts were of rammed turf, and the cohort Standard and the officers were all housed together in one small square of wattle-and-daub buildings round a colonnaded courtyard. But after a few days Marcus began to know the individualities that made every camp different, after all, from every other; and it was these differences, rather than the samenesses, that made him feel at home in Isca. An artist of some long-departed garrison had scratched with his dagger a beautiful leaping wild cat on the bath-house wall, and someone less gifted had scratched a very rude picture of a centurion he had not liked; you could tell that it was a centurion, by the vine staff and the centurion's mark > scored beneath it. There was a martin's nest under the eaves of the shrine where the Standard was housed, and an odd and untraceable smell behind Number Two storehouse. And in one corner of the officers' courtyard, some past commander, homesick for the warmth and colour of the south, had planted a rose-bush in a great stone wine-jar, and already the buds were showing crimson among the dark leaves. That rose-bush gave Marcus a sense of continuance; it was a link between him and those who had been before him, here on the frontier, and the others who would come after. It must have been there a long time, and it was becoming pot-bound; he thought that in the autumn he would see about having a proper bed made for it.

It took him a little while to settle down with his officers. The Surgeon, who appeared, like the Quartermaster, to be a fixture, was a gentle soul, content enough in his backwater so long as it contained sufficient of the fiery native spirit; but the Quartermaster himself was something of a trial, a little red angry man who had missed promotion and grown overfull of his own importance in consequence. Lutorius, who commanded the fort's one squadron of Dacian Horse, spent all his friendliness on his horses and was reserved to the point of sullenness with all men, even his own. Marcus's five ranker centurions were all so much older and more experienced than he was that at first he was uncertain how to deal with them. It was not easy, with less than a year with the Eagles behind him, to tell Centurion Paulus that he was overfond of using his vine-staff on his men's backs; or make Centurion Galba understand that, whatever might be the custom in other cohorts, the centurions of the Fourth Gaulish were not going to take bribes from their men for letting them off fatigues, while he was in command. But he managed it somehow, and the odd thing was that though both Galba and Paulus raged inwardly at the time, and even talked to each other about puppies, there was a better understanding between them and the Cohort Commander afterwards. And between Marcus and his second-in-command there was a good working understanding from the first, which grew to a warm liking as time went by. Centurion Drusillus, like most of his kind, was promoted from the ranks; he was a veteran of many campaigns, full of odd wisdom and hard counsel; and Marcus had need of such, that summer. Day started with the trumpets sounding Cockcrow from the ramparts, and ended with Late Rounds; and between came all the complicated pattern of parades and fatigues, patrols out and in, stables, arms drill. He had to be his own magistrate too; he had to deal with the situation when one of his men claimed that a tribesman had sold him a worthless dog; or a tribesman complained that someone from the fort had stolen his poultry; or when the Dacians and the Gauls fell out over some obscure question of a tribal god whom he had never heard of before.

It was hard work, especially in the earliest days, and he was thankful for Centurion Drusillus; but the work was in his blood, just as farming was, and it was work that he loved. And it was not all work: there was the occasional day's hunting too—good hunting, even as Hilarion had said.

His usual guide and companion on the trail was a Briton not many years older than himself, a hunter and horse-dealer, Cradoc by name. And on a morning of late summer he went down from the fort, carrying his hunting-spears, to pick up Cradoc according to custom.

It was very early, the sun not yet up, and the mist lying like a white sea between the hills. Scent would lie low and heavy on such a morning, and he sniffed the dawn chill like a hound. And yet he could not find his usual pleasure in the fine hunting morning, for he was worried. Not very worried, but enough to take the keen edge off the blade of his enjoyment; turning over in his mind the rumour that had been drifting through the fort for the past day or two—the rumour of a wandering Druid having been seen in the district. Oh, no one had actually seen him themselves; it was much more vague than that. None the less, remembering Hilarion's warning, he had checked up as best he could, without of course the least result. But even if there *were* something in the wind, there would be no result—nothing to be got even from the few men who held official positions from Rome; if their first loyalty was to Rome they would know nothing; if it was to their Tribe they would tell nothing. Probably there was not a scrap of truth in the story; it was just one of those floating rumours that blew up from time to time, like a wind out of nowhere. But he would keep his eyes and ears open, all the same, especially as once again, for the third year running, the harvest was going to be a poor one. You could tell that from the faces of the men and women, as well as you could from their little fields, where the corn stood thin and shrivelled in the ear. A bad harvest was always the time to look for trouble.

As he threaded his way among the crowding huts beyond the forum, it struck Marcus again how untouched this place was by Rome. The tribe found the forum and basilica useful to hold their markets in. One or two men had laid aside their hunting-spears to become Roman officials, occasionally one even saw a Roman tunic. There were wine-shops everywhere, the craftsmen of the town made things to please the garrison, and everybody else sold them dogs, skins, vegetables, and fighting-cocks, while the children scrambled after the auxiliaries for denarii. But all the same, here in Isca Dumnoniorum, Rome was a new slip grafted on to an old stock—and the graft had not yet taken.

He reached the cluster of huts that were Cradoc's, and turned aside at the house-place door, whistling a few bars of the latest tune running in the Legions, with which he was used to announce his arrival. The leather apron over the doorway was drawn aside at once, but instead of the hunter, there appeared a girl with a solemn sunburned baby on her hip. She was tall, as were most British women, and carried herself like a queen; but the thing that Marcus noticed about her was the look on her face: a queer, guarded look, as though she had drawn a veil behind her eyes so that he should not see in.

'My man is out behind with his chariot team. If the Commander goes to look, he will find him,' she said, and stepped back, letting the leather apron fall between them.

Marcus went to look. The sound of the hunter's voice and a horse's soft whinny gave him his direction, and making his way between the wood-pile and a tethered cock whose feathers shone with metallic colours among the duller hens, he reached the doorway of a stable hut, and looked in. Cradoc turned to the doorway as he appeared, and gave him a courteous greeting.

Marcus returned it—by this time he spoke the Celtic tongue fluently, though with an appalling accent—but he was staring into the shadows behind the other man. 'I did not know you drove the Royal Fours in these parts,' he said.

'We are not above learning some lessons from Rome. Have you never chanced to see my team before?'

Marcus shook his head. 'I did not even know you for a charioteer, though I suppose I might have guessed. The British are all charioteers.'

'The Commander is mistaken,' Cradoc said, drawing his hand down a glossy neck. 'The British can all drive after a fashion; not everyone is a charioteer.'

'You, I take it, are a charioteer?'

'I am accounted among the best of my tribe,' Cradoc said with quiet dignity.

Marcus had moved in from the doorway. 'May I see your team?' he asked, and the other stood aside for him without a word.

The four were loose in their stable, and they came to him almost like dogs to sniff enquiringly at his breast and outstretched hands; four superbly matched black chariot ponies. He thought of the Arab team he had sometimes driven in Rome. These were smaller—under fourteen hands, he judged—thicker coated, and for their size a little more heavily built, but in their way they seemed to him without match; the heads that turned to him gentle and intelligent, the ears pricked and delicate as flower petals, the quivering nostrils lined with vivid red, the breasts and haunches deep and powerful. He turned from one to another, moving among them, fondling them, running a practised hand over their lithe bodies from proud crest to sweeping tail.

Before he left Rome, Marcus had been in a fair way to becoming a charioteer, in Cradoc's sense of the word, and now desire woke in him, not to possess this team, for he was not one of those who must be able to say 'Mine' before they can truly enjoy a thing, but to have them out and harnessed; to feel the vibrating chariot floor under him, and the spread reins quick with life in his hands, and these lovely, fiery little creatures in the traces, his will and theirs at one.

Turning, with a soft muzzle against his shoulder, he said, 'Will you let me try your team?'

'They are not for sale.'

'If they were, I could not afford to buy them. I asked that I might try them.'

'The Commander also is a charioteer?' Cradoc said.

At the Saturnalia Games last year, Marcus had been put up to race a borrowed team against a staff officer, reputed to be the finest driver in the Legion; and he had won. 'I am accounted the best in my Legion,' he said.

Cradoc did not seem to think his question answered. 'I doubt if you could handle these black jewels of mine.'

'Will you take a wager on it?' Marcus asked, his eyes suddenly cool and bright, and his mouth smiling.

'A wager?'

'That I will handle your team to your satisfaction, over ground of your own choosing.' Marcus slipped a brooch from the shoulder of his rough cloak, and held it out, the red cornelian with which it was set gleaming faintly in the shadows. 'This fibula against—against one of your hunting spears. Or if that does not suit you, name your own stakes.'

Cradoc did not look at the fibula. He was looking at Marcus, rather as though the young Roman was a horse whose mettle he wished to gauge, and Marcus, facing the cool stocktaking, felt himself flushing. The hunter noticed the angry colour, and the arrogantly raised head, and a queer little twisted smile lifted one side of his mouth. Then, as though satisfied by his scrutiny, he said: 'I will take the wager.'

'When do we put the matter to the test?' asked Marcus, returning the brooch to the shoulder of his cloak.

'I am taking a draft of horses up to Durinum tomorrow; but in eight days I shall be back. We will hold the trial on my return. And now, it is time that we were away.'

'So be it,' said Marcus; and with a final pat to a glossy neck, he turned and followed Cradoc from the stable. They whistled the waiting hounds to heel, collected hunting-spears from the house-place wall where they had been propped, and disappeared into the wilderness.

Cradoc was away longer than he expected, and the harvest, such as it was (there would be many hungry in Isca Dumnoniorum that winter), was gathered in by the time the trial took place. Marcus was turning over in his mind the question of getting in extra grain supplies when he arrived at the appointed meeting ground, a wide stretch of level land in the curve of the river, to find the other waiting for him. Cradoc flung up an arm in greeting as he appeared from the woodshore, and springing into the chariot, turned the team and came thundering towards him through the swaying fern at a gallop. The sun flashed back in spars of light from the bronze ornaments on the breasts and foreheads of the team, and the long hair of the charioteer was flying like the ponies' manes. Marcus stood his ground, though with an uncomfortable tightening of his stomach, until at the last moment the ponies were brought to a rearing halt almost on top of him and the charioteer ran out along the yoke-pole and stood poised against the sky.

'A pretty trick,' said Marcus, grinning up at him. 'I have heard of it before, but never seen it until today.'

The other laughed and stepped back into the chariot, and as he brought the team round, Marcus side-stepped and sprang in beside him. The reins and the many-folded lash changed hands, and Cradoc drew back into the spearman's place, with a hand on the wickerwork side of the chariot. 'Take them across to the dead ash-tree yonder, for a start.'

'All in good time.' said Marcus. 'I am not yet ready.'

The ponies were harnessed Roman fashion, the two inner to the yoke-pole, the two outer by traces to the axles. So far, so good; but the chariot was another matter. Until now his driving had all been done in a Roman racing chariot, a mere cockle-shell with room for no one but the driver; this thing was twice as big, though fairly light, and the open front gave one a sense of being on top of the team which was new to him. To get the best out of chariot and team, certain allowances must be made. Holding the carefully separated reins high, in the approved Colosseum manner, his feet wide planted on the interlaced straps of the chariot bed, he set the fidgeting team in motion; easily at first, getting the feel of them, then steadying them from a trot into a canter, as he headed for the silvery target of the dead ash-tree. Just before it, he wheeled them, obedient to Cradoc's direction, and sent them weaving delicately down the curved row of javelins that the other had stuck upright in the turf before his arrival, in the same way that he had woven the white Arabs between the practice posts on Mars Field, his speed quickening to a gallop, but with never a grazed wheel-hub to disgrace him. He took the team through every trick and test that their master ordered, until the moment came for a final burst of speed, and they were sweeping at full gallop round the mile-wide curve of the woodshore.

To Marcus that moment was always like being born from one kind of life into another. So must an arrow feel when it leaves the bow! It had been hot and sultry in the old life, but in this one the cool wind flowed against him like water, pressing his thin scarlet tunic into his body, singing past his ears above the soft thunder of the ponies' flying hooves. He crouched lower, feeling the chariot floor buoyant and vibrating under his wide-set feet, feeling the reins quick with life in his hands, his will flowing out along them to the flying team, and their response flowing back to him, so that they were one. He called to them in the Celtic tongue, urging them on.

'On, brave hearts! On, bold and beautiful! Thy mares shall be proud of thee, the tribe shall sing thy praises to their children's children! Sweff! Sweff, my brothers!'

For the first time he loosed the lash, letting it fly out and flicker like dark lightning above their ears without ever touching them. The forest verge spun by, the fern streaked away beneath flying hooves and whirling wheels. He and his team were a comet shooting down the bright ways of the sky; a falcon stooping against the sun . . .

Then, on a word from Cradoc, he was backed on the reins, harder, bringing the team to a rearing halt, drawn back in full gallop on to their haunches. The wind of his going died, and the heavy heat closed round him again. It was very still, and the shimmering, sunlit scene seemed to pulse on his sight. Before the wheels had ceased to turn, Cradoc had sprung down and gone to the ponies' heads. After the first plunging moment, they stood quite quiet, their flanks heaving a little, but not over-much.

'Well?' demanded Marcus, rubbing the back of his hand across his wet forehead.

Cradoc looked up at him, unsmiling. 'The Commander begins to be a charioteer,' he said.

Marcus laid by reins and lash, and stepped down to join him. 'I have not driven a team to better these,' he said, and curved his arm over an arched neck. 'Do I win my spear?'

'Come and choose it for yourself, before you go back to the fort,' said the other. He had brought sweet crusts with him in the breast of his tunic, and he held them out on his open palms to the soft questing lips of the ponies. 'These four are the jewels of my heart. They are descended out of the Royal Stables of the Iceni, and there are few could handle them better than the Commander.' And there was a queer note of regret in his voice, for which there seemed no reason; but Marcus was to remember it afterwards.

They drove back slowly, walking the ponies through the summer evening.

'It will not harm them to stand for a little, now that they have cooled off,' Cradoc said, as, after threading their way through the confused huddle of the town, he pulled up before his own house-place. He drew the reins over the ponies' heads and turned to the dark doorway, calling, 'Guinhumara, bring out to me my spears.'

The leather apron had been drawn back to let in what air there was, and the red fire glowed in the centre of the house-place. Marcus saw the tall girl rise without a word—she had been turning wheat cakes among the hot ash for her man's supper—and melt into the darkness of some inner place. Several dogs which had been lying in the piled fern, with the small brown baby sleeping in their midst, came out with waving tails to fawn around their master, but the baby slept on, sucking its thumb. In a few moments the girl came back and joined them in the doorway, carrying a sheaf of spears whose polished blades caught the evening light like so many tongues of flame.

'The Commander and I have laid a wager,' said Cradoc. 'His brooch against one of my hunting-spears. He has won, and now he is come to choose his spear.' As he spoke, he took one from the sheaf and stood leaning on it with a gesture that said quite plainly, 'But not this one.'

Those that were left were fine weapons, beautiful as were all the weapons of the Celts, perfectly balanced and deadly; some light for throwing, some broad-bladed for close work, some for war, some for hunting. The girl handed them to Marcus one by one, and he tested and examined them, finally picking one with a slender, barbed blade and a cross-piece just below the neck. 'This one,' he said. 'It shall be this one, for when I hunt boar with your husband this winter.' He smiled at her, but she did not smile back; her face had the same veiled look that he remembered on it before. She stepped back without a word, and carried the remaining spears with her into the house-place. But Marcus had already turned to the hunter, for that other spear had caught his interest, and been in his mind even while he made his choice. It was to the rest of the sheaf what a king is to his bodyguard; the shaft darkened with much handling, the iron blade perfect in shape as a laurel leaf, engraved with a strange and potent design that swirled like the eddies in running water. The weight of the head was counterbalanced by a ball of enamelled bronze on the butt, and about its neck was a collar of blue-grey heron's feathers.

'I have not seen the like of this before,' Marcus said. 'It is a war spear, is it not?'

Cradoc's hand caressed the smooth shaft. 'It was my father's war spear,' he said. 'It was in his hand when he died—up yonder under our old ramparts where the fortress walls stand now. See, the mark is still upon it . . . his own blood, and the blood of his enemy.' He parted the heron's feathers to show the neck of the shaft blackened by an old stain.

A little while afterwards, carrying his newly-won boar spear, Marcus made his way back towards the Praetorian gate. Children and hounds were playing together in the low sunshine, and here and there a woman in a hut doorway called the evening greeting to him as he passed. It all seemed very peaceful, and yet he was filled with an uneasy feeling that the peace was only a film—a veil like that which the girl Guinhumara had drawn behind her eyes—and that underneath, something very different was stirring. Again he remembered Hilarion's warning.

For the collar of the old war spear had been lately renewed, and the heron's feathers were still bright with the lustre of a living bird.

In all likelihood that spear had been refurbished many times, kept bright by a son in memory of his father; and yet, he wondered suddenly, in how many of these thatched homesteads had an old spear been put in fighting trim? Then he shook his shoulders impatiently, and strode on at a quickened pace up the steep way to the gate. He was simply growing toadstools, even as Hilarion had prophesied. All this because of a few feathers. Yet even a feather might show which way the wind blew.

If only they could have had a good harvest!

III
Attack!

IN the dark hour before the dawn, two nights later, Marcus was roused out of his sleep by the Duty Centurion. A pilot lamp always burned in his sleeping-cell against just such an emergency, and he was fully awake on the instant,

'What is it, Centurion?'

'The sentries on the south rampart report sounds of movement between us and the town, sir.'

Marcus was out of bed and had swung his heavy military cloak over his sleeping-tunic. 'You have been up yourself?'

The centurion stood aside for him to pass out into the darkness. 'I have, sir,' he said with grim patience.

'Anything to be seen?'

'No, sir, but there is something stirring down there, for all that.'

Quickly they crossed the main street of the fort, and turned down beside a row of silent workshops. Then they were mounting the steps to the rampart walk. The shape of a sentry's helmet rose dark against the lesser darkness above the breastwork, and there was a rustle and thud as he grounded his pilum in salute.

Marcus went to the breast-high parapet. The sky had clouded over so that not a star was to be seen, and all below was a formless blackness with nothing visible save the faint pallor of the river looping through it. Not a breath of air stirred in the stillness, and Marcus, listening, heard no sound in all the world save the whisper of the blood in his own ears, far fainter than the sea in a conch-shell.

He waited, breath in check; then from somewhere below came the kee-wick, kee-wick, wick-wick, of a hunting owl, and a moment later a faint and formless sound of movement that was gone almost before he could be sure that he had not imagined it. He felt the Duty Centurion grow tense as a strung bow beside him. The moments crawled by, the silence became a physical pressure on his eardrums. Then the sounds came again, and with the sounds, blurred forms moved suddenly on the darkness of the open turf below the ramparts.

Marcus could almost hear the twang of breaking tension. The sentry swore softly under his breath, and the centurion laughed.

'Somebody will be spending a busy day looking for his strayed cattle!'

Strayed cattle; that was all. And yet for Marcus the tension had not snapped into relief. Perhaps if he had never seen the new heron's feathers on an old war spear it might have done, but he had seen them, and somewhere deep beneath his thinking mind the instinct for danger had remained with him ever since. Abruptly he drew back from the breastwork, speaking quickly to his officer. 'All the same, a break-out of cattle might make good cover for something else. Centurion, this is my first command: if I am being a fool, that must excuse me. I am going back to get some more clothes on. Turn out the cohort to action stations as quietly as may be.'

And not waiting for a reply, he turned, and dropping from the rampart walk, strode off towards his own quarters.

In a short while he was back, complete from studded sandals to crested helmet, and knotting the crimson scarf about the waist of his breastplate as he came. From the faintly lit doorways of the barrack rows, men were tumbling out, buckling sword-belts or helmet-straps as they ran, and heading away into the darkness. 'Am I being every kind of fool?' Marcus wondered. 'Am I going to be laughed at so long as my name is remembered in the Legion, as the man who doubled the guard for two days because of a bunch of feathers, and then turned out his cohort to repel a herd of milch-cows?' But it was too late to worry about that now. He went back to the ramparts, finding them already lined with men, the reserves massing below. Centurion Drusillus was waiting for him, and he spoke to the older man in a quick, miserable undertone. 'I think I must have gone mad, Centurion; I shall never live this down.'

'Better to be a laughing-stock than lose the fort for fear of being one,' returned the centurion. 'It does not pay to take chances on the Frontier—and there was a new moon last night.'

Marcus had no need to ask his meaning. In his world the gods showed themselves in new moons, in seed-time and harvest, summer and winter solstice; and if an attack were to come, the new moon would be the time for it. Holy War. Hilarion had understood all about that. He turned aside to give an order. The waiting moments lengthened; the palms of his hands were sticky, and his mouth uncomfortably dry.

The attack came with a silent uprush of shadows that swarmed in from every side, flowing up to the turf ramparts with a speed, an impetus that, ditch or no ditch, must have carried them over into the camp if there had been only the sentries to bar the way. They were flinging brushwood bundles into the ditch to form causeways; swarming over, they had poles to scale the ramparts, but in the dark nothing of that could be seen, only a flowing up and over, like a wave of ghosts. For a few moments the utter silence gave sheer goose-flesh horror to the attack; then the auxiliaries rose as one man to meet the attackers, and the silence splintered, not into uproar, but into a light smother of sound that rippled along the ramparts: the sound of men fiercely engaged, but without giving tongue. For a moment it endured; and then from the darkness came the strident braying of a British war-horn. From the ramparts a Roman trumpet answered the challenge, as fresh waves of shadows came pouring in to the attack; and then it seemed as if all Tartarus had broken loose. The time for silence was past, and men fought yelling now; red flame sprang up into the night above the Praetorian gate, and was instantly quenched. Every yard of the ramparts was a reeling, roaring battle-line as the tribesmen swarmed across the breastwork to be met by the grim defenders within.

How long it lasted Marcus never knew, but when the attack drew off, the first cobweb light of a grey and drizzling dawn was creeping over the fort. Marcus and his second-in-command looked at each other, and Marcus asked very softly, 'How long can we hold out?'

'For several days, with luck,' muttered Drusillus, pretending to adjust the strap of his shield.

'Reinforcements could get to us in three—maybe two—from Durinum,' Marcus said. 'But there was no reply to our signal.'

'Little to wonder in that, sir. To destroy the nearest signal station is an obvious precaution; and no cresset could carry the double distance in this murk.'

'Mithras grant it clears enough to give the smoke column a chance to rise.'

But there was no sign of anxiety in the face of either of them when they turned from each other an instant later, the older man to go clanging off along the stained and littered rampart walk, Marcus to spring down the steps into the crowded space below. He was a gay figure, his scarlet cloak swirling behind him; he laughed, and made the 'thumbs up' to his troops, calling 'Well done, lads! We will have breakfast before they come on again!'

The 'thumbs up' was returned to him. Men grinned, and here and there a voice called cheerfully in reply, as he disappeared with Centurion Paulus in the direction of the Praetorium.

No one knew how long the breathing space might last; but at the least it meant time to get the wounded under cover, and an issue of raisins and hard bread to the troops. Marcus himself had no breakfast, he had too many other things to do, too many to think about; amongst them the fate of a half Century under Centurion Galba, now out on patrol, and due back before noon. Of course the tribesmen might have dealt with them already, in which case they were beyond help or the need of it, but it was quite as likely that they would merely be left to walk into the trap on their return, and cut to pieces under the very walls of the fort.

Marcus gave orders that the cresset was to be kept alight on the signal roof; that at least would warn them that something was wrong as soon as they sighted it. He ordered a watch to be kept for them, and sent for Lutorius of the Cavalry and put the situation to him. 'If they win back here, we shall of course make a sortie and bring them in. Muster the squadron and hold them in readiness from now on. That is all.'

'Sir,' said Lutorius. His sulks were forgotten, and he looked almost gay as he went off to carry out the order.

There was nothing more that Marcus could do about his threatened patrol, and he turned to the score of other things that must be seen to.

It was full daylight before the next attack came. Somewhere, a war-horn brayed, and before the wild note died, the tribesmen broke from cover, yelling like fiends out of Tartarus as they swarmed up through the bracken; heading for the gates this time, with tree-trunks to serve as rams, with firebrands that gilded the falling mizzle and flashed on the blade of sword and heron-tufted war spear. On they stormed, heedless of the Roman arrows that thinned their ranks as they came, Marcus, standing in the shooting turret beside the Praetorian gate, saw a figure in their van, a wild figure in streaming robes that marked him out from the half-naked warriors who charged behind him. Sparks flew from the firebrand that he whirled aloft, and in its light the horns of the young moon, rising from his forehead, seemed to shine with a fitful radiance of its own. Marcus said quietly to the archer beside him, 'Shoot me that maniac.'

The man nocked another arrow to his bow, bent and loosed in one swift movement. The Gaulish Auxiliaries were fine bowmen, as fine as the British; but the arrow sped out only to pass through the wild hair of the leaping fanatic. There was no time to loose again. The attack was thundering on the gates, pouring in over the dead in the ditch with a mad courage that took no heed of losses. In the gate towers the archers stood loosing steadily into the heart of the press below them. The acrid reek of smoke and smitch drifted across the fort from the Dexter Gate, which the tribesmen had attempted to fire. There was a constant two-way traffic of reserves and armament going up to the ramparts and wounded coming back from them. No time to carry away the dead; one toppled them from the rampart walk that they might not hamper the feet of the living, and left them, though they had been one's best friend, to be dealt with at a fitter season.

The second attack drew off at last, leaving their dead lying twisted among the trampled fern. Once more there was breathing space for the desperate garrison. The morning dragged on; the British archers crouched behind the dark masses of uprooted blackthorn that they had set up under cover of the first assault, and loosed an arrow at any movement on the ramparts; the next rush might come at any moment. The garrison had lost upward of fourscore men, killed or wounded: two days would bring them reinforcements from Durinum, if only the mizzle which obscured the visibility would clear, just for a little while, long enough for them to send up the smoke signal, and for it to be received.

But the mizzle showed no signs of lifting, when Marcus went up to the flat signal-roof of the Praetorium. It blew in his face, soft and chill-smelling, and faintly salt on his lips. Faint grey swathes of it drifted across the nearer hills, and those beyond were no more than a spreading stain that blurred into nothingness.

'It is no use, sir,' said the auxiliary who squatted against the parapet, keeping the great charcoal brazier glowing.

Marcus shook his head. Had it been like this when the Ninth

Legion ceased to be? he wondered. Had his father and all those others watched, as he was watching now, for the far hills to clear so that a signal might go through? Suddenly he found that he was praying, praying as he had never prayed before, flinging his appeal for help up through the grey to the clear skies that were beyond. 'Great God Mithras, Slayer of the Bull, Lord of the Ages, let the mists part and thy glory shine through! Draw back the mists and grant us clear air for a space, that we go not down into the darkness. O God of the Legions, hear the cry of thy sons. Send down thy light upon us, even upon us, thy sons of the Fourth Gaulish Cohort of the Second Legion.'

He turned to the auxiliary, who knew only that the Commander had stood beside him in silence for a few moments, with his head tipped back as though he was looking for something in the soft and weeping sky. 'All we can do is wait,' he said. 'Be ready to start your smother at any moment.' And swinging on his heel, he rounded the great pile of fresh grass and fern that lay ready near the brazier, and went clattering down the narrow stairway.

Centurion Fulvius was waiting for him at the foot with some urgent question that must be settled, and it was some while before he snatched another glance over the ramparts; but when he did, it seemed to him that he could see a little further than before. He touched Drusillus, who was beside him, on the shoulder. 'Is it my imagining, or are the hills growing clearer?'

Drusillus was silent a moment, his grim face turned towards the east. Then he nodded. 'If it is your imagining, it is also mine.' Their eyes met quickly, with hope that they dared not put into any more words; then they went each about their separate affairs.

But soon others of the garrison were pointing, straining their eyes eastward in painful hope. Little by little the light grew: the mizzle was lifting, lifting . . . and ridge behind wild ridge of hills coming into sight.

High on the Praetorium roof a column of black smoke sprang upward, billowed sideways and spread into a drooping veil that trailed across the northern rampart, making the men there cough and splutter; then rose again, straight and dark and urgent, into the upper air. In the pause that followed, eyes and hearts were strained with a sickening intensity towards those distant hills. A long, long pause it seemed; and then a shout went up from the watchers, as, a day's march to the east, a faint dark thread of smoke rose into the air.

The call for help had gone through. In two days, three at the most, relief would be here; and the uprush of confidence touched every man of the garrison.

Barely an hour later, word came back to Marcus from the northern rampart that the missing patrol had been sighted on the track that led to the Sinister Gate. He was in the Praetorium when the word reached him, and he covered the distance to the gate as if his heels were winged; he waved up the Cavalry waiting beside their saddled horses, and found Centurion Drusillus once again by his side.

'The tribesmen have broken cover, sir,' said the centurion.

Marcus nodded. 'I must have half a Century of the reserves. We can spare no more. A trumpeter with them and every available man on the gate, in case they try a rush when it opens.'

The centurion gave the order, and turned back to him. 'Better let me take them, sir.'

Marcus had already unclasped the fibula at the shoulder of his cloak, and flung off the heavy folds that might hamper him, 'We went into that before. You can lend me your shield, though.'

The other slipped it from his shoulder without a word, and Marcus took it and swung round on the half Century who were already falling in abreast of the gate. 'Get ready to form testudo,' he ordered. 'And you can leave room for me. This tortoise is not going into action with its head stuck out!'

It was a poor joke, but a laugh ran through the desperate little band, and as he stepped into his place in the column head, Marcus knew that they were with him in every sense of the word; he could take those lads through the fires of Tophet if need be.

The great bars were drawn, and men stood ready to swing wide the heavy valves; and behind and on every side he had a confused impression of grim ranks massed to hold the gate, and draw them in again if ever they won back to it.

'Open up!' he ordered; and as the valves began to swing outward on their iron-shod posts, 'Form testudo.' His arm went up as he spoke, and through the whole column behind him he felt the movement echoed, heard the light kiss and click of metal on metal, as every man linked shield with his neighbour, to form the shield-roof which gave the formation its name. 'Now!'

The gates were wide; and like a strange many-legged beast, a gigantic woodlouse rather than a tortoise, the testudo was out across the causeway and heading straight downhill, its small, valiant cavalry wings spread on either side. The gates closed behind it, and from rampart and gate-tower anxious eyes watched it go. It had all been done so quickly that at the foot of the slope battle had only just joined, as the tribesmen hurled themselves yelling on the swiftly formed Roman square.

The testudo was not a fighting formation; but for rushing a position, for a break through, it had no equal. Also it had a strange and terrifying aspect that could be very useful. Its sudden appearance now, swinging down upon them with the whole weight of the hill behind it, struck a brief confusion into the swarming tribesmen. Only for a moment their wild ranks wavered and lost purpose; but in that moment the hard-pressed patrol saw it too, and with a hoarse shout came charging to join their comrades.

Down swept Marcus and his half Century, down and forward into the raging battle-mass of the enemy. They were slowed almost to a standstill, but never quite halted; once they were broken, but re-formed. A mailed wedge cleaving into the wild ranks of the tribesmen, until the moment came when the tortoise could serve them no longer; and above the turmoil Marcus shouted to the trumpeter beside him: 'Sound me "Break testudo".'

The clear notes of the trumpet rang through the uproar. The men lowered their shields, springing sideways to gain fighting space; and a flight of pilums hurtled into the swaying horde of tribesmen, spreading death and confusion wherever the iron heads struck. Then it was 'Out swords', and the charge driven home with a shout of 'Caesar! Caesar!' Behind them the valiant handful of cavalry were struggling to keep clear the line of retreat; in front, the patrol came grimly battling up to join them. But between them was still a living rampart of yelling, battle-frenzied warriors, amongst whom Marcus glimpsed again that figure with the horned moon on its forehead. He laughed, and sprang against them, his men storming behind him.

Patrol and relief force joined, and became one.

Instantly they began to fall back, forming as they did so a roughly diamond formation that faced outward on all sides and was as difficult to hold as a wet pebble pressed between the fingers. The tribesmen thrust in on them from every side, but slowly, steadily, their short blades like a hedge of living, leaping steel, the cavalry breaking the way for them in wild rushes, they were drawing back towards the fortress gate—those that were left of them.

Back, and back. And suddenly the press was thinning, and Marcus, on the flank, snatched one glance over his shoulder, and saw the gate-towers very near, the swarming ranks of the defenders ready to draw them in. And in that instant there came a warning yelp of trumpets and a swelling thunder of hooves and wheels, as round the curve of the hill towards them, out of cover of the woodshore, swept a curved column of chariots.

Small wonder that the press had thinned.

The great battle-wains had long been forbidden to the tribes, and these were light chariots such as the one Marcus had driven two days ago, each carrying only a spearman beside the driver; but one horrified glance, as they hurtled nearer behind their thundering teams, was enough to show the wicked, whirling scythe-blades on the war-hubs of the wheels.

Close formation—now that their pilums were spent—was useless in the face of such a charge; again the trumpets yelped an order, and the ranks broke and scattered, running for the gateway, not in any hope of reaching it before the chariots were upon them, but straining heart and soul to gain the advantage of the high ground.

To Marcus, running with the rest, it seemed suddenly that there was no weight in his body, none at all. He was filled through and through with a piercing awareness of life and the sweetness of life held in his hollowed hand, to be tossed away like the shining balls that the children played with in the gardens of Rome. At the last instant, when the charge was almost upon them, he swerved aside from his men, out and back on his tracks, and flinging aside his sword, stood tensed to spring, full in the path of the oncoming chariots. In the breath of time that remained, his brain felt very cold and clear, and he seemed to have space to do quite a lot of thinking. If he sprang for the heads of the leading team, the odds were that he would merely be flung down and driven over without any check to the wild gallop. His best chance was to go for the charioteer. If he could bring him down, the whole team would be flung into confusion, and on that steep scarp the chariots coming behind would have difficulty in clearing the wreck. It was a slim chance, but if it came off it would gain for his men those few extra moments that might mean life or death. For himself, it was death. He was quite clear about that.

They were right upon him, a thunder of hooves that seemed to fill the universe; black manes streaming against the sky; the team that he had called his brothers, only two days ago. He hurled his shield clanging among them, and side-stepped, looking up into the grey face of Cradoc, the charioteer. For one splinter of time their eyes met in something that was almost a salute, a parting salute between two who might have been friends; then Marcus leapt in under the spearman's descending thrust, upward and sideways across the chariot bow. His weight crashed on to the reins, whose ends, after the British fashion, were wrapped about the charioteer's waist, throwing the team into instant chaos; his arms were round Cradoc, and they went half down together. His ears were full of the sound of rending timber and the hideous scream of a horse. Then sky and earth changed places, and with his hold still unbroken, he was flung down under the trampling hooves, under the scythe-bladed wheels and the collapsing welter of the overset chariot; and the jagged darkness closed over him.

IV

The Last Rose Falls

ON the other side of the darkness was pain. For a long time that was the only thing Marcus knew. At first it was white, and quite blinding; but presently it dulled to red, and he began to be dimly aware of the other things through the redness of it. People moving near him, lamp-light, daylight, hands that touched him; a bitter taste in his mouth which always brought back the darkness. But it was all muddled and unreal, like a dissolving dream.

And then one morning he heard the trumpets sounding Cockcrow. And the familiar trumpet-call, piercing through the unreality like a sword-blade through tangled wool, brought with it other real and familiar things: the dawn chill on his face and an uncovered shoulder, the far-off crowing of a real cock, the smell of lamp-smitch. He opened his eyes, and found that he was lying flat on his back on the narrow cot in his own sleeping-cell. Close above him the window was a square of palest aquamarine in the dusky gold of the lamplit wall, and on the dark roof-ridge of the officers' mess opposite was a sleeping pigeon, so clearly and exquisitely outlined against the morning sky that it seemed to Marcus as though he could make out the tip of every fluffed-out feather. But of course that was natural, because he had carved them himself, sitting between the roots of the wild olive-tree in the bend of the stream. And then he remembered that that had been a different bird; and the last shreds of his confusion fell away from him.

So he was not dead, after all. He was faintly surprised, but not very interested. He was not dead, but he was hurt. The pain, which had been first white and then red, was still there, no longer filling the whole universe, but reaching all up and down his right leg: a dull, grinding throb with little sparks of sharper pain that came and went in the dullness of it. It was the worst pain that he had ever known, save for the few blinding moments when the brand of Mithras pressed down between his brows; but he was not much more interested in it than in the fact that he was still alive. He remembered exactly what had happened; but it had all happened so long ago, at the other side of the blackness; and he was not even anxious, because Roman trumpets sounding from the ramparts could only mean that the fort was still safely in Roman hands.

Somebody moved in the outer room and, a moment later, loomed into the doorway. Marcus turned his head slowly—it seemed very heavy—and saw the garrison Surgeon, clad in a filthy tunic, and with red-rimmed eyes and several days' growth of beard.

'Ah, Aulus,' Marcus said, and found that even his tongue felt heavy. 'You look—as if you had not been to bed for a month.'

'Not quite so long as that,' said the Surgeon, who had come forward quickly at the sound of Marcus's voice, and was bending over him. 'Good! Very good!' he added, nodding his vague encouragement.

'How long?' began Marcus, stumblingly.

'Six days; yes, yes—or it might be seven.'

'It seems—like years.'

Aulus had turned back the striped native rugs, and laid a fumbling hand over Marcus's heart. He seemed to be counting, and answered only with a nod.

But suddenly everything grew near and urgent again to Marcus. 'The relief force?—They got through to us, then?'

Aulus finished his counting with maddening deliberateness, and drew the rugs up again. 'Yes, yes. The best part of a cohort of the Legion, from Durinum.'

'I must see Centurion Drusillus—and the—the relief force Commander.'

'Maybe presently, if you lie still,' said Aulus, turning to deal with the smoking lamp.

'No, not presently. Now! Aulus, it is an order: I am still in command of this—'

He tried to crane up on his elbow, and his rush of words ended in a choking gasp. For a few moments he lay very still, staring at the other man, and there were little beads of sweat on his forehead.

'Tch! Now you have made it worse!' scolded Aulus in a slight fluster. 'That is because you did not lie still, as I bade you.' He picked up a red Samian bowl from the chest top, and slipped an arm under Marcus's head to raise him. 'Best drink this. Tch! tch! It will do you good.'

Too weak to argue, and with the rim of the bowl jolting against his teeth, Marcus drank. It was milk, but with the bitter taste in it which always brought back the darkness.

'There,' said Aulus, when the bowl was empty. 'Now go to sleep. Good boy; now go to sleep.' And he laid Marcus's head back on the folded rug.

Centurion Drusillus came next day, and sitting with his hands on his knees and the shadow of his crested helmet blue on the sunlit wall behind him, gave his Commander a broad outline of all that had happened since he was wounded. Marcus listened very carefully; he found that he had to listen very carefully indeed, because if he did not, his attention wandered: to the crack in a roof-beam, to the flight of a bird across the window, to the pain of his wounds or the black hairs growing out of the centurion's nostrils. But when the centurion had finished, there were still things that Marcus needed to know.

'Drusillus, what became of the holy man?'

'Gone to meet his own gods, sir. Caught between the relief force and ourselves. There was a-many of the tribe went with him.'

'And the charioteer?—my charioteer?'

Centurion Drusillus made the 'thumbs down'. 'Dead as we thought you were when we pulled you from the wreck.'

After a moment's silence, Marcus asked, 'Who brought me in?'

'Why, now, that is hard to say, sir. Most of us had our hand in it.'

'I had hoped to gain time for the rest.' Marcus rubbed the back of one hand across his forehead. 'What happened?'

'Nay now, sir, it was all so quick . . . Galba doubled back to you, and the rest with him, and it was a time for desperate measures; so we took down the reserves—'twas not much more than a javelin throw—and brought you off.'

'And got cut to pieces by the chariots in doing it?' Marcus asked quickly.

'Not so badly as we might have been. Your wreck broke the weight of the charge.'

'I want to see Galba.'

'Galba is in the sick-block, with his sword arm laid open,' Drusillus said.

'How bad is the damage?'

'A clean wound. It is healing.'

Marcus nodded. 'You will be seeing him, I suppose? Salute him for me, Centurion. Tell him I shall come and compare scars with him if I am on my feet before he is. And tell the troops I always *have* said the Fourth Gaulish was the finest cohort with the Eagles.'

'I will, sir,' said Drusillus. 'Very anxiously enquiring, the troops have been.' He got up, raised an arm heavy with silver good-conduct bracelets in salute, and tramped off back to duty.

Marcus lay for a long time with his forearm across his eyes, seeing against the blackness of his closed lids picture after picture that Drusillus had left behind him. He saw the relief force coming up the road, tramp-tramp-tramp, and the dust rising behind them. He saw the last stand of the tribesmen crumble and the moon-crested fanatic go down. The British town a smoking ruin and the little fields salted by order of the relief force Commander. (Wattle-and-daub huts were easily rebuilt, and salted fields would bear again in three years, but not all the years in eternity would bring back the young men of the tribe, he thought, and was surprised to find that he cared.) He saw dead men, Lutorius among them; he hoped that there would be horses for Lutorius in the Elysian Fields. Most clearly of all, again and again, he saw Cradoc, lying broken among the trampled bracken of the hillside. He had felt very bitter towards Cradoc; he had liked the hunter and thought that his liking was returned; and yet Cradoc had betrayed him. But that was all over. It was not that Cradoc had broken faith; simply that there had been another and stronger faith that he must keep. Marcus understood that now.

Later, the Commander of the relief force came to see him, but the interview was not a happy one. Centurion Clodius Maximus was a fine soldier, but a chilly mannered, bleak-faced man. He stood aloofly in the doorway, and announced that since everything was under control, he intended to continue his interrupted northward march tomorrow. He had been taking troops up to Isca when the Frontier fort's distress signal had reached Durinum and he had been deflected to answer it. He would leave two Centuries to bring the garrison temporarily up to strength, and Centurion Herpinius, who would take command of the fort until Marcus's relief could be sent from Isca, when no doubt fresh drafts of auxiliaries would be sent with him.

Marcus realized that it was all perfectly reasonable. The Relief Force were Legionaries, line-of-battle troops, and in the nature of things a Legionary Centurion ranked above an auxiliary one; and if he, Marcus, was going to be laid by for a while, a relief would of course have to be sent down to take his place until he was once more fit for duty. But all the same, he was annoyed by the man's highhanded manner, annoyed on Drusillus's account, and on his own. Also, quite suddenly, he began to be afraid. So he became very stiff, and very proud, and for the rest of the short and formal interview treated the stranger with an icy politeness that was almost insulting.

Day followed day, each marked off in its passing by lamplight and daylight, food that he did not want, and the changing shadows that moved across the courtyard outside his window. These, and the visits of Aulus and a medical orderly to dress the spear-gash in his shoulder (he had never felt the blade bite, as he sprang in under the spearman's thrust), and the ugly mass of wounds that seared his right thigh.

There was some delay about the arrival of his relief from Isca, for several cohort centurions were down with marsh fever; and the moon, which had been new when the tribe rose, waxed and waned into the dark, and the pale feather of another new moon hung in the evening sky; and all save the deepest and most ragged of Marcus's wounds were healed. That was when they told him that his service with the Eagles was over.

Let him only be patient, and the leg would carry him well enough, one day, Aulus assured him, but not for a long time; no, he could not say how long. Marcus must understand, he pointed out with plaintive reasonableness, that one could not smash a thigh-bone and tear the muscles to shreds and then expect all to be as it had been before.

It was the thing that Marcus had been afraid of ever since his interview with Centurion Maximus. No need to be afraid now, not any more. He took it very quietly; but it meant the loss of almost everything he cared about. Life with the Eagles was the only kind of life he had ever thought of, the only kind that he had any training for; and now it was over. He would never be Prefect of an Egyptian Legion, he would never be able to buy back the farm in the Etruscan hills, or gather to himself another like it. The Legion was lost to him and, with the Legion, it seemed that his own land was lost to him too; and the future, with a lame leg and no money and no prospects, seemed at first sight rather bleak and terrifying.

Maybe Centurion Drusillus guessed something of all this, though Marcus never told him. At all events he seemed to find the Commander's quarters a good place to spend every off-duty moment, just then; and though Marcus, longing to be alone like a sick animal, often wished him at the other side of the Empire, afterwards he remembered and was grateful for his centurion's fellowship in a bad time.

A few days later, Marcus lay listening to the distant sounds of the new Commander's arrival. He was still in his old quarters, for when he had suggested that he should go across to the sick-block, and leave the two rooms in the Praetorium free for their rightful owner, he was told that other quarters had been made ready for the new Commander, and he was to stay where he was until he was fit to travel—until he could go to Uncle Aquila. He was lucky, he supposed rather drearily, to have Uncle Aquila to go to. At all events he would know quite soon whether the unknown uncle was like his father.

Now that he could sit up, he could look out into the courtyard, and see the rose-bush in its wine-jar, just outside his window. There was still one crimson rose among the dark leaves, but even as he watched, a petal fell from it like a great slow drop of blood. Soon the rest would follow. He had held his first and only command for just as long as the rose-bush had been in flower . . . It was certainly pot-bound, he thought; maybe his successor would do something about it.

His successor: whoever that might be. He could not see the entrance to the courtyard, but quick footsteps sounded along the colonnade and then in the outer room, and a moment later the new Commander stood in the doorway; an elegant and very dusty young man with his crested helmet under one arm. It was the owner of the chariot team which Marcus had driven in the Saturnalia Games.

'Cassius!' Marcus greeted him. 'I wondered if it would be anyone I knew.'

Cassius crossed to his side. 'My dear Marcus; how does the leg?'

'It mends, in its fashion.'

'So. I am glad of that, at all events.'

'What have you done with your bays?' Marcus asked quickly. 'You are not having them brought down here, are you?'

Cassius collapsed on to the clothes-chest and wilted elegantly. 'Jupiter! No! I have lent them to Dexion, with my groom to keep an eye on them, and him.'

'They will do well enough with Dexion. What troops have you brought down with you?'

'Two Centuries of the Third: Gauls, like the rest. They are good lads, seasoned troops; been up on the wall laying stone courses and exchanging the odd arrow now and then with the Painted People.' He cocked a languid eyebrow. 'But if they can give as good an account of themselves in action as your raw Fourth have done, they will have no need to feel themselves disgraced.'

'I think there will be no more trouble in these parts,' Marcus said. 'Centurion Maximus took good care of that.'

'Ah, you mean the burned villages and salted fields? A punitive expedition is never pretty. But I gather from your embittered tone that you did not take warmly to Centurion Maximus?'

'I did not.'

'A most efficient officer,' pronounced Cassius, with the air of a grey-headed Legate.

'To say nothing of officious,' snapped Marcus.

'Maybe if you saw the report he sent in when he got back to Headquarters, you might find yourself feeling more friendly disposed towards him.'

'It was good?' asked Marcus, surprised. Centurion Maximus had not struck him as the type who sent in enthusiastic reports.

Cassius nodded, 'Rather more than good. Indeed, before I marched south there was beginning to be talk of some trifle—say a gilded laurel wreath—to make the standard of the Gaulish Fourth look pretty when it goes on parade,'

There was a short silence, and then Marcus said, 'It is no more than we—than they deserve! Look, Cassius, if anything more than talking comes of it, send me word. I will give you the direction to write to. I should like to know that the cohort won its first honours under my command.'

'Possibly the cohort would like to know it too,' said Cassius gruffly, and lounged to his feet. 'I am for the bath-house. I am gritty from head to foot!' He paused a moment, looking down at Marcus, with his air of weary elegance quite forgotten. 'Do not worry. I shall not let your cohort go to ruin.'

Marcus laughed, with a sudden aching in his throat. 'See that you do not, or I swear I shall find means to poison your wine! They are a fine cohort, the best with the Legion: and—good luck to you with them.'

Outside in the courtyard, the last crimson petals fell in a little bright flurry from the rose-bush in the old wine-jar.

V

Saturnalia Games

UNCLE Aquila lived on the extreme edge of Calleva. One reached his house down a narrow side street that turned off not far from the East Gate, leaving behind the forum and the temples, and coming to a quiet angle of the old British earthworks—for Calleva had been a British Dun before it was a Roman city—where hawthorn and hazel still grew and the shyer woodland birds sometimes came. It was much like the other houses of Calleva, timbered and red-roofed and comfortable, built round three sides of a tiny courtyard that was smoothly turfed and set about with imported roses and gum-cistus growing in tall stone jars. But it had one peculiarity: a squat, square, flat-roofed tower rising from one corner; for Uncle Aquila, having lived most of his life in the shadow of watch-towers from Memphis to Segedunum, could not be comfortable without one.

Here, in the shadow of his own watch-tower, which he used as a study, he was very comfortable indeed, with his elderly wolf-hound Procyon, and the History of Siege Warfare which he had been writing for ten years, for company.

By the dark end of October, Marcus had been added to the household. He was given a sleeping-cell opening on to the courtyard colonnade; a lime-washed cell with a narrow cot piled with striped native blankets, a polished citron-wood chest, a lamp on a bracket high against the wall. Save that the door was differently placed, it might have been his old quarters in the Frontier fort, seven days' march away. But most of his days were spent in the long atrium, the central room of the house, occasionally with Uncle Aquila, but for the most part alone, save when Stephanos, or Sassticca looked in on him. He did not mind Stephanos, his uncle's old Greek body-slave, who now looked after him as well as his master, but Sassticca the cook was another matter. She was a tall and gaunt old woman who could hit like a man, and frequently did when either of her fellow slaves annoyed her; but she treated Marcus as though he were a small sick child. She brought him little hot cakes when she had been baking, and warm milk because she said he was too thin, and fussed and tyrannized over him, until—for he was very afraid of kindness just then—he came near to hating her.

That autumn was a bad time for Marcus, feeling wretchedly ill for the first time in his life, almost always in pain, and face to face with the wreckage of everything he knew and cared about. He would wake in the dark mornings to hear the distant notes of Cockcrow sounding from the transit camp just outside the city walls, and that did not make it any easier. He was homesick for the Legions; he was desperately homesick for his own land; for now that they seemed lost to him, his own hills grew achingly clear, every detail of sight and scent and sound jewel-vivid on his memory. The shivering silver of the olive-woods when the mistral blew, the summer scent of thyme and rosemary and little white cyclamen among the sun-warmed grass, the songs that the girls sang at vintage.

And here in Britain the wind moaned through the desolate woods, the skies wept, and wet gale-blown leaves pattered against the windows and stuck there, making little pathetic shadows against the steamy glass. There had been wild weather often enough in his own country, but that had been the wild weather of home: here was the wind and rain and wet leaves of exile.

It would have gone less hardly with him if he had had a companion of his own age; but he was the only young thing in the house, for even Procyon had grey hairs in his muzzle, and so he was shut in on himself, and though he did not know it, he was bitterly lonely.

There was just one gleam of light for him in the darkness of that autumn. Not long after he came to Calleva, he had word from Cassius that henceforth the Standard of the Gaulish Fourth would have its gilded laurel wreath to carry on parade; and a little later there came to Marcus himself the award of a military bracelet, which was a thing that he had never for an instant expected. This was not, as the various crowns were, purely a gallantry award; rather it was given for the same qualities which had earned for the Second Legion its titles *'Pia Fidelis'*; those titles which were cut deep upon the heavy gold bracelet under the Capricorn badge of the Legion. From the day that it came to him, it was never off Marcus's wrist; and yet it meant rather less to him than the knowledge that his old cohort had won its first laurels.

The days grew shorter and the nights longer, and presently it was the night of the winter solstice. A fitting night for the dark turn of the year, Marcus thought. The inevitable wind was roaring up through the forest of Spinaii below the old British ramparts, driving with it squalls of sleet that spattered against the windows. In the atrium it was warm, for whatever the peculiarities of Uncle Aquila's house, the hypocaust worked perfectly, and for the pleasant look of it rather than for need, a fire of wild-cherry logs on charcoal burned in the brazier hearth, filling the long room with faint, aromatic scent. The light from the single bronze lamp, falling in a golden pool over the group before the hearth, scarcely touched the lime-washed walls, and left the far end of the room in crowding shadows, save for the glim of light that always burned before the shrine of the household gods. Marcus lay propped on one elbow on his usual couch, Uncle Aquila sat opposite to him in his great cross-legged chair; and beside them, outstretched on the warm tessellated floor, Procyon the wolf-hound.

Uncle Aquila was huge; that had been the first thing Marcus noticed about him, and he noticed it still. His joints appeared to be loosely strung together as if with wet leather; his head with its bald freckled top and his bony beautiful hands were big even in proportion to the rest of him, and Authority seemed to hang on him in easy and accustomed folds, like his toga. Even allowing for their twenty years of difference in age, he was not in the least like Marcus's father; but Marcus had long ago ceased to think of him as like, or unlike, anyone. He was simply Uncle Aquila.

The evening meal was over, and old Stephanos had set out a draughts-board on the table between Marcus and his uncle, and gone his way. In the lamplight the ivory and ebony squares shone vividly white and black; Uncle Aquila's men were already in place, but Marcus had been slower, because he was thinking of something else. He set down his last ivory man with a little click, and said: 'Ulpius was here this morning.'

'Ah, our fat physician,' said Uncle Aquila, his hand, which had been poised for an opening move, returning to the arm of his chair. 'Had he anything to say worth the listening to?'

'Only the usual things. That I must wait and wait.' Suddenly Marcus exploded between misery and laughter. 'He said I must have a little patience and called me his dear young man and wagged a scented fat finger under my nose. Fach! He is like the white pulpy things one finds under stones!'

'So,' agreed Uncle Aquila. 'None the less, you *must* wait—there being no help for it.'

Marcus looked up from the board. 'There's the rub. How long can I wait?'

'Hmph?' said Uncle Aquila.

'I have been here two months now, and we have never spoken of the future. I have put it off from one visit of that potbellied leech to the next because—I suppose because I have never thought of any life but following the Eagles, and I do not quite know how to begin.' He smiled at his uncle apologetically. 'But we must discuss it sometime,'

'Sometime, yes: but not now. No need to trouble about the future until that leg will carry you.'

'But Mithras knows how long that will be. Do you not see, sir, I cannot go on foisting myself on you indefinitely.'

'Oh, my good lad, do try not to be such a fool!' snapped Uncle Aquila; but his eyes under their jut of brow were unexpectedly kindly. 'I am not a rich man, but neither am I so poor that I cannot afford to add a kinsman to my household. You do not get in my way; to be perfectly honest, I forget your existence rather more than half the time; you play a reasonably good game of draughts. Naturally you will stay here, unless of course'—he leaned forward abruptly—'is it that you would rather go home?'

'Home?' Marcus echoed.

'Yes. I suppose you still have a home with that peculiarly foolish sister of mine?'

'And with Uncle-by-Marriage Tullus Lepidus?' Marcus's head went up, his black brows twitched almost to meeting point above a nose which looked suddenly as though there was a very bad smell under it. 'I'd sooner sit on Tiber-side and beg my bread from the slum women when they come to fill their water-pots!'

'So?' Uncle Aquila nodded his huge head. 'And now, that being settled, shall we play?'

He made the opening move, and Marcus answered it. For a while they played in silence. The lamplit room was a shell of quiet amid the wild sea-roaring of the wind; the small saffron flames whispered in the brazier, and a burned cherry log collapsed with a tinselly rustle into the red hollow of the charcoal. Every few moments there would be a little clear click as Marcus or his uncle moved a piece on the board. But Marcus did not really hear the small peaceful sounds, nor see the man opposite, for he was thinking of things that he had been trying not to think of all day.

It was the twenty-fourth evening of December, the eve of the winter solstice—the eve of the birth of Mithras; and quite soon now, in camps and forts wherever the Eagles flew, men would be gathering to his worship. In the outposts and the little frontier forts the gatherings would be mere handfuls, but in the great Legionary Stations there would be full caves of a hundred men. Last year, at Isca, he had been one of them, newly initiated at the Bull-slaying, the brand of the Raven Degree still raw between his brows. He ached with longing for last year to be given back to him, for the old life and the comradeship to be given back to him. He moved an ivory man a little blindly, seeing, not the black-and-white dazzle of the board before his eyes, but that gathering of a year ago, filing out by the Praetorian gate and downhill to the cave. He could see the crest of the centurion in front of him up-reared blackly against the pulsing fires of Orion. He remembered the waiting darkness of the cave; then, as the trumpets sounded from the distant ramparts for the third watch of the night, the sudden glory of candles, that sank and turned blue, and sprang up again; the reborn light of Mithras in the dark of the year . . .

A great gust of wind swooped against the house like a wild thing striving to batter its way in; the lamplight jumped and fluttered, sending shadows racing across the chequered board—and the ghosts of last year were once more a year away. Marcus looked up, and said, as much for the sake of shutting out his own thoughts as for anything else, 'I wonder what possessed you to settle here in Britain, Uncle Aquila, when you could have gone home?'

Uncle Aquila moved his piece with meticulous care before he answered with another question. 'It seems very odd to you, that anyone free to go home should choose to strike his roots in this barbarous country?'

'On a night like this,' said Marcus, 'it seems odd almost past believing.'

'I had nothing to take me back,' said the other, simply. 'Most of my service years were spent here, though it was in Judaea that my time fell due for parting with the Eagles. What have I to do with the South? A few memories, very few. I was a young man when first I saw the white cliffs of Dubris above the transport galley's prow. Far more memories in the North. Your move. . . '

Marcus moved an ivory man to the next square, and his uncle shifted his own piece. 'If I settled in the South, I should miss the skies. Ever noticed how changeful British skies are? I have made friends here—a few. The only woman I ever cared a denarius for lies buried at Glevum.'

Marcus looked up quickly. 'I never knew—'

'Why should you? But I was not always old Uncle Aquila with a bald head.'

'No, of course not. What was—she like?'

'Very pretty. She was the daughter of my old Camp Commandant, who had a face like a camel, but she was very pretty, with a lot of soft brown hair. Eighteen when she died. I was twenty-two.'

Marcus said nothing. There seemed nothing to say. But Uncle Aquila, seeing the look on his face, gave a deep chuckle. 'No, you have it all quite wrong. I am a very selfish old man, perfectly well content with things as they are.' And then, after a pause, he harked back to an earlier point in their discussion. 'I killed my first boar in Silurian territory; I have sworn the blood brotherhood with a painted tribesman up beyond where Hadrian's Wall stands now; I've a dog buried at Luguvallium—her name was Margarita; I have loved a girl at Glevum; I have marched the Eagles from end to end of Britain in worse weather than this. Those are the things apt to strike a man's roots for him.'

Marcus said after a moment, 'I think I begin to understand.'

'Good. Your move.'

But after they had played a few more moves in silence, Uncle Aquila looked up again, the fine wrinkles deepening at the corners of his eyes. 'What an autumnal mood we have wandered into! We need livening up, you and I.'

'What do you suggest?' Marcus returned the smile.

'I suggest the Saturnalia Games tomorrow. We may not be able to compete quite on equal terms with the Colosseum, here at Calleva; but a wild-beast show, a sham fight with perhaps a little blood-letting—we will certainly go.'

And they went, Marcus travelling in a litter, for all the world, as he remarked disgustedly, like a Magistrate or a fine lady. They arrived early, but by the time they were settled on one of the cushioned benches reserved for the Magistrates and their families (Uncle Aquila was a Magistrate, though he had not come in a litter), the amphitheatre just outside the East Gate was already filling up with eager spectators. The wind had died down, but the air struck cold, with a clear, chill tang to it that Marcus sniffed eagerly while he pulled the folds of his old military cloak more closely round him. After being so long within four walls, the sanded space of the arena seemed very wide; a great emptiness within the encircling banks up which the crowded benches rose tier on tier.

Whatever else of Rome the British had not taken to, they seemed to have taken to the Games with a vengeance, Marcus thought, looking about him at the crowded benches where townsfolk and tribesmen with their womenfolk and children jostled and shoved and shouted after the best places. There was a fair sprinkling of Legionaries from the transit camp, and Marcus's quick glance picked out a bored young tribune sitting with several British lads all pretending to be equally Roman and equally bored. He remembered Colosseum crowds, chattering, shouting, quarrelling, laying bets and eating sticky sweets. The British took their pleasures a little less loudly, to be sure, but on almost every face was the same eager, almost greedy look that the faces of the Colosseum crowds had worn.

A small disturbance near him drew Marcus's attention to the arrival of a family who were just entering their places on the Magistrates' benches a little to his right. A British family of the ultra-Roman kind, a large, good-natured-looking man, running to fat as men do who have been bred to a hard life and take to living soft instead; a woman with a fair and rather foolish face, prinked out in what had been the height of fashion in Rome two years ago—and very cold she must be, Marcus thought, in that thin mantle; and a girl of perhaps twelve or thirteen, with a sharply pointed face that seemed all golden eyes in the shadow of her dark hood. The stout man and Uncle Aquila saluted each other across the heads between, and the woman bowed. All Rome was in that bow; but the girl's eyes were fixed on the arena with a kind of horrified expectancy.

When the new-comers were settled in their places, Marcus touched his uncle's wrist, and cocked an enquiring eyebrow.

'A fellow Magistrate of mine, Kaeso by name, and his wife Valaria,' Uncle Aquila said. 'Incidentally, they are our next-door neighbours.'

'Are they so? But the little maiden; she is no bud of their branch, surely?'

But he got no answer to his question then, for at that moment a great crashing of cymbals and a fanfare of trumpets announced that the Games were about to begin. All round the crowded circus there was a sudden quietness and a craning forward. Again the trumpets sounded. The double doors at the far side were flung open, and out from their underground lodgements a double file of gladiators came marching into the arena, each carrying the weapons he would use later in the show. Shout on shout greeted their appearance. For a small colonial circus they seemed rather a good lot, Marcus thought, watching them as they paraded round the arena; too good, maybe, though probably they were all slaves. Marcus was something of a heretic where the Games were concerned; he liked well enough to see a wild-beast show, or a sham fight if it were well done, but to put up men—even slaves—to fight to the death for a crowd's amusement, seemed to him a waste.

The men had halted now, before the Magistrates' benches; and in the few moments that they stood there, Marcus's whole attention was caught by one of them: a sword-and-buckler man of about his own age. He was rather short for a Briton, but powerful. His russet-brown hair, flung back by the savage pride with which he carried his head, showed the clipped ear that branded him for a slave. Seemingly he had been taken in war, for his breast and shoulders—he was stripped to the waist—were tattooed with blue warrior patterns. But it was none of these things that Marcus saw, only the look in the wide-set grey eyes that strained back at him out of the gladiator's young sullen face.

'This man is afraid,' said something deep in Marcus. 'Afraid—afraid,' and his own stomach cringed within him.

A score of weapons flashed in the wintry light as they were tossed up with a shout and caught again, and the gladiators wheeled and strode on down the wide curve that led back to their starting point. But the look he had seen in the young swordsman's eyes remained with Marcus.

The first item on the programme was a fight between wolves and a brown bear. The bear did not want to fight, and was driven into battle by the long curling whip-lashes of the attendants. Presently, amid a great shouting from the onlookers, it was killed. Its body was dragged away, and with it the bodies of two wolves it had slain; the others were decoyed back into their wheeled cage for another time, and attendants spread fresh sand over the blood in the arena. Marcus glanced, without quite knowing why, at the girl in the dark hood, and saw her sitting as though frozen, her eyes wide and blank with horror in an ashy face. Still oddly shaken by that queer moment of contact with the young gladiator who was so very much afraid, he was filled with a sudden unreasoning anger against Kaeso and his wife for bringing the little maiden to see a thing like this, against all Games and all mobs who came to watch them with their tongues hanging out for horrors, even against the bear for being killed.

The next item was a sham fight, with little damage done save a few flesh wounds. (In the back of beyond, circus masters could not afford to be wasteful with their gladiators.) Then a boxing match in which the heavy cestus round the fighters' hands drew considerably more blood than the swords had done. A pause came, in which the arena was once again cleaned up and freshly sanded; and then a long gasp of expectancy ran through the crowd, and even the bored young tribune sat up and began to take some notice, as, with another blare of trumpets, the double doors swung wide once more, and two figures stepped out side by side into the huge emptiness of the arena. Here was the real thing: a fight to the death.

At first sight the two would seem to be unequally armed, for while one carried sword and buckler, the other, a slight dark man with something of the Greek in his face and build, carried only a three-pronged spear, and had over his shoulder a many-folded net, weighted with small discs of lead. But in truth, as Marcus knew only too well, the odds were all in favour of the man with the net, the Fisher, as he was called, and he saw with an odd sinking of the heart that the other was the young swordsman who was afraid.

'Never did like the net,' Uncle Aquila was grumbling. 'Not a clean fight, no!' A few moments earlier, Marcus had known that his damaged leg was beginning to cramp horribly; he had been shifting, and shifting again, trying to ease the pain without catching his uncle's notice, but now, as the two men crossed to the centre of the arena, he had forgotten about it.

The roar which greeted the pair of fighters had fallen to a breathless hush. In the centre of the arena the two men were being placed by the captain of the gladiators; placed with exquisite care, ten paces apart, with no advantage of light or wind allowed to either. The thing was quickly and competently done, and the captain stepped back to the barriers. For what seemed a long time, neither of the two moved.

Moment followed moment, and still they remained motionless, the centre of all that great circle of staring faces. Then, very slowly, the swordsman began to move. Never taking his eyes from his adversary, he slipped one foot in front of the other; crouching a little, covering his body with the round buckler, inch by inch he crept forward, every muscle tensed to spring when the time came.

The Fisher stood as still as ever, poised on the balls of his feet, the trident in his left hand, his right lost in the folds of the net. Just beyond reach of the net, the swordsman checked for a long, agonizing moment, and then sprang in. His attack was so swift that the flung net flew harmlessly over his head, and the Fisher leapt back and sideways to avoid his thrust, then whirled about and ran for his life, gathering his net for another cast as he ran, with the young swordsman hard behind him. Half round the arena they sped, running low; the swordsman had not the other's length and lightness of build, but he ran as a hunter runs—perhaps he had run down deer on the hunting trail, before ever his ear was clipped—and he was gaining on his quarry now. The two came flying round the curve of the barrier towards the Magistrates' benches, and just abreast of them the Fisher whirled about and flung once more. The net whipped out like a dark flame; it licked round the running swordsman, so intent on his chase that he had forgotten to guard for it; the weight carried the deadly folds across and across again, and a howl burst from the crowd as he crashed headlong and rolled over, helplessly meshed as a fly in a spider's web.

Marcus wrenched forward, his breath caught in his throat. The swordsman was lying just below him, so near that they could have spoken to each other in an undertone. The Fisher was standing over his fallen antagonist, with the trident poised to strike, a little smile on his face, though his breath whistled through widened nostrils, as he looked about him for the bidding of the crowd. The fallen man made as though to raise his hampered arm in the signal by which a vanquished gladiator might appeal to the crowd for mercy; then let it drop back, proudly, to his side. Through the fold of the net across his face, he looked up straight into Marcus's eyes, a look as direct and intimate as though they had been the only two people in all that great amphitheatre.

Marcus was up and standing with one hand on the barrier rail to steady himself, while with the other he made the sign for mercy. Again and again he made it, with a blazing vehemence, with every atom of will-power that was in him, his glance thrusting like a challenge along the crowded tiers of benches where already the thumbs were beginning to turn down. This mob, this unutterably stupid, blood-greedy mob that must somehow be swung over into forgoing the blood it wanted! His gorge rose against them, and there was an extraordinary sense of battle in him that could not have been more vivid had he been standing over the fallen gladiator, sword in hand. Thumbs up! *Thumbs up!* you fools! . . . He had been aware from the first of Uncle Aquila's great thumb pointing skyward beside him; suddenly he was aware of a few others echoing the gesture, and then a few more. For a long, long moment the swordsman's fate still hung in the balance, and then as thumb after thumb went up, the Fisher slowly lowered his trident and with a little mocking bow, stepped back.

Marcus drew a shuddering breath, and relaxed into a flood of pain from his cramped leg, as an attendant came forward to disentangle the swordsman and aid him to his feet. He did not look at the young gladiator again. The moment was shame for him, and Marcus felt that he had no right to witness it.

That evening, over the usual game of draughts, Marcus asked his uncle: 'What will become of that lad now?'

Uncle Aquila moved an ebony piece after due consideration. 'The young fool of a swordsman? He will be sold in all likelihood. The crowd do not pay to see a man fight, when once he has been down and at their mercy.'

'That is what I have been thinking,' Marcus said. He looked up from making his own move. 'How do prices run in these parts? Would fifteen hundred sesterces buy him?'

'Very probably. Why?'

'Because I have that much left of my pay and a parting thank-offering that I had from Tullus Lepidus. There was not much to spend it on in Isca Dumnoniorum.'

Uncle Aquila's brows cocked enquiringly. 'Are you suggesting buying him yourself?'

'Would you give him house-room?'

'I expect so,' said Uncle Aquila. 'Though I am somewhat at a loss to understand why you should wish to keep a tame gladiator. Why not try a wolf instead?'

Marcus laughed. 'It is not so much a tame gladiator as a body-slave that I need. I cannot go on overworking poor old Stephanos for ever.'

Uncle Aquila leaned across the chequered board. 'And what makes you think that an ex-gladiator would make you a suitable body-slave?'

'To speak the truth, I had not thought about it,' Marcus said. 'How do you advise me to set about buying him?'

'Send down to the circus-master, and offer half of what you expect to pay. And sleep with a knife under your pillow thereafter,' said Uncle Aquila.

VI

Esca

THE purchase was arranged next day, without much difficulty, for although the price that Marcus could afford was not large, Beppo, the master of the circus slaves, knew well enough that he was not likely to get a better one for a beaten gladiator. So, after a little haggling, the bargain was struck, and that evening after dinner Stephanos went to fetch home the new slave.

Marcus waited for their return alone in the atrium, for Uncle Aquila had retired to his watch-tower study to work out a particularly absorbing problem in siege warfare. He had been trying to read his uncle's copy of the Georgics, but his thoughts kept wandering from Virgil on bee-keeping to the encounter before him. He was wondering for the first time—he had not thought to wonder before—why the fate of a slave gladiator he had never before set eyes on should matter to him so nearly. But it did matter. Maybe it was like calling to like; and yet it was hard to see quite what he had in common with a barbarian slave.

Presently his listening ear caught the sound of an arrival in the slaves' quarters, and he laid down the papyrus roll and turned towards the doorway. Steps came along the colonnade, and two figures appeared on the threshold. 'Centurion Marcus, I have brought the new slave,' said Stephanos, and stepped discreetly back into the night; and the new slave walked forward to the foot of Marcus's couch, and stood there.

For a long moment the two young men looked at each other, alone in the empty lamplit atrium as yesterday they had been alone in the crowded amphitheatre, while the scuff-scuffling of Stephanos's sandals died away down the colonnade.

'So it is you,' the slave said at last.

'Yes, it is I.'

The silence began again, and again the slave broke it. 'Why did you turn the purpose of the crowd yesterday? I did not ask for mercy.'

'Possibly that was why.'

The slave hesitated, and then said defiantly, 'I was afraid yesterday; I, who have been a warrior. I am afraid to choke out my life in the Fisher's net.'

'I know,' Marcus said. 'But still, you did not ask for mercy.'

The other's eyes were fixed on his face, a little puzzled. 'Why have you bought me?'

'I have need of a body-slave.'

'Surely the arena is an unusual place to pick one.'

'But then, I wished for an unusual body-slave.' Marcus looked up with the merest quirk of a smile into the sullen grey eyes fixed so unswervingly on his own. 'Not one like Stephanos, that has been a slave all his life, and is therefore—nothing more.'

It was an odd conversation between master and slave, but neither of them was thinking of that.

'I have been but two years a slave,' said the other quietly.

'And before that you were a warrior—and your name?'

'I am Esca, son of Cunoval, of the tribe of Brigantes, the bearers of the blue war-shield.'

'And I am—I was, a centurion of auxiliaries with the Second Legion,' Marcus said, not knowing quite why he made the reply, knowing only that it had to be made. Roman and Briton faced each other in the lamplight, while the two statements seemed to hang like a challenge in the air between them.

Then Esca put out a hand unconsciously and touched the edge of the couch. 'That I know, for the goaty one, Stephanos, told me; and also that my Master has been wounded. I am sorry for that.'

'Thank you,' Marcus said.

Esca looked down at his own hand on the edge of the couch, and then up again. 'It would have been easy to escape on my way here,' he said slowly. 'The old goaty one could not have held me back if I had chosen to break for freedom. But I chose to go with him because it was in my heart that it might be you that we went to.'

'And if it had been another, after all?'

'Then I should have escaped later, to the wilds where my clipped ear would not betray me. There are still free tribes beyond the Frontiers.' As he spoke, he drew from the breast of his rough tunic, where it had lain against his skin, a slender knife, which he handled as tenderly as if it had been a thing living and beloved. 'I had this, to my release.'

'And now?' Marcus said, not giving a glance to the narrow, deadly thing.

For a moment the sullenness lifted from Esca's face. He leaned forward and let the dagger fall with a little clatter on to the inlaid table at Marcus's side. 'I am the Centurion's hound, to lie at the Centurion's feet,' he said.

So Esca joined the household and, carrying the spear that marked him for a personal slave and superior to mere household slaves, stood behind Marcus's couch at meals to pour wine for him, fetched and carried and saw to his belongings, and slept on a mattress across his door at night. He made a very good body-slave, so good that Marcus guessed him to have been somebody's armour-bearer in the days before his ear was clipped; a father's, or an elder brother's, perhaps, after the custom of the tribes. He never asked about those days, nor how Esca had come into the Calleva arena, because something about his slave, some inner reserve, warned him that to ask would be an intrusion, a walking in without leave. One day, perhaps, Esca would tell him freely, but not yet.

The weeks went by, and suddenly the rose-bushes in the courtyard were gemmed with swelling leaf-buds, and the air had a sense of quickening that was the first distant promise of spring. Slowly, very slowly, Marcus's leg was mending. It no longer woke him with a stab of pain every time he turned in the night, and he could hobble round the house more and more easily.

As time passed, he got into the way of leaving his stick behind him and walking with a hand on Esca's shoulder instead. It seemed natural to do that, for without quite realizing it, he was slipping more and more often from the master to the friend in his dealings with Esca; though, after that first night, Esca never for an instant forgot the slave in his dealings with Marcus.

That winter there was a lot of trouble with wolves in the district. Driven out from their fastnesses by hunger, they hunted under the very walls of Calleva; and often Marcus would hear their long-drawn cry in the night, setting every dog in the town baying in that frenzy that was half hate and half longing, half enemy hurling defiance at enemy, half kin calling to kin. In the outlying farms of the forest clearings, lambing pens were attacked, and anxious men kept the wolf-guard every night. At a village a few miles away a pony was killed, at another a baby was taken.

Then one day, Esca, going into the town on an errand for Marcus, returned with news of a country-wide wolf hunt planned for next day. It had started simply among the outlying farms, desperate to save their lambing ewes, then gathered to itself professional hunters, and a couple of young officers from the transit camp out for a day's sport; and now it seemed that half the countryside was out to end the menace. He poured it all out to Marcus. The hunters were to meet at such a place, two hours before sunrise; at such another place they were going to drive the thickets with dogs and torches; and Marcus laid aside the belt he was mending, and listened to him as eager to hear as his slave was to tell.

Listening, he longed to be off on that wolf hunt and run the spring fret out of his bones; and he knew that the same longing was hot in his slave. For him, it did not seem likely that there would be any more hunting, but that was no reason why there should be none for Esca. 'Esca,' he said abruptly, when the other had told all that there was to tell. 'It would surely be a good thing if you joined this wolf hunt.'

Esca's whole face lit with eagerness, but after a moment he said, 'It would mean maybe a night and a day that the Centurion must do without his slave.'

'I shall do well enough,' Marcus told him. 'I shall borrow half of Stephanos from my uncle. But what will you do for spears? I left my own for the man who came after me at Isca, else you could have had those.'

'If my Master is sure, really sure, I know where I can borrow spears.'

'Good. Do you go and borrow them now.'

So Esca borrowed the spears he needed, and in the pitch dark of that night, Marcus heard him get up and collect them from the corner where they had been stacked. He turned on his elbow and spoke into the darkness. 'You are going now?'

A light footfall and a sense of movement told him that Esca was standing at his side. 'Yes, if the Centurion is still sure—quite sure?'

'Perfectly sure. Go and spear your wolf.'

'It is in my heart that I wish the Centurion came too,' Esca said in a rush.

'Maybe I'll come another year,' Marcus said sleepily. 'Good hunting, Esca.'

For an instant a dark shape showed in the lesser darkness of the doorway, and then it was gone, and he lay listening, not at all sleepily now, to the quick, light footfall dying away along the colonnade.

In the grey of the next dawn, he heard the footfall returning, a little heavier than at the setting out, and the dark shape loomed again into the cobweb pallor of the doorway.

'Esca!—How went the hunting?'

'The hunting was good,' Esca said. He stacked the spears with a slight clatter against the wall, and came and bent over the cot; and Marcus saw that there was something curled in the crook of his arm, under the rough cloak. 'I have brought back the fruits of my hunting for the Centurion,' he said, and set the thing down on the blanket. It was alive, and being disturbed, it whimpered: and Marcus's gently exploring hand discovered that it was warm and harshly furry.

'Esca! A wolf cub?' he said, feeling a scrabble of paws and a thrusting muzzle.

Esca had turned away to strike flint and steel and kindle the lamp. The tiny flame sank and then sprang up and steadied; and in the dazzle of yellow light he saw a very small grey cub, who staggered to uncertain paws, sneezing at the sudden light, and pushed in under his hand with the nuzzling thrust of all very young things. Esca came back to the cot and dropped on one knee beside it. And as he did so Marcus noticed that there was a hot look in his eyes, a brightness that he had not seen there before, and wondered with an odd sense of hurt if his return to bondage, from a day and night of freedom was the cause.

'In my tribe, when a she-wolf with whelps is killed, we sometimes take the young ones to run with the dog-pack,' Esca said. 'If they are like this one, little, little, so that they remember nothing before; so that their first meat comes from their master's hand.'

'Is he hungry now?' Marcus asked, as the cub's muzzle poked and snuggled into his palm.

'No, he is full of milk—and scraps. Sassticca will not miss them. See, he is half asleep already; that is why he is so gentle.'

The two of them looked at each other, half laughing; but the queer hot look was still in Esca's eyes; while the cub crawled whimpering into the warm hollow of Marcus's shoulder, and settled there. His breath smelled of onions, like a puppy.

'How did you get him?'

'We killed a she-wolf in milk, so I and two others went to look for the whelps. They killed the rest of the litter, those fools of the South; but this one, I saved. His sire came. They are good fathers, the wolf kind, fierce to protect their young. It was a fight: aie! a good fight.'

'It was taking a hideous risk,' Marcus said. 'You should not have done it, Esca!' He was half angry, half humbled, that Esca should have taken such a deadly risk to know what the hazard was in robbing a wolf's lair while the sire still lived.

Esca seemed to draw back into himself on the instant. 'I forgot it was my Master's property that I risked,' he said, his voice suddenly hard and heavy as stone.

'Don't be a fool,' Marcus said quickly. 'I didn't mean that, and you know it.'

There was a long silence. The two young men looked at each other, and there was no trace of laughter now in their faces.

'Esca,' Marcus said at last, 'what has happened?'

'Nothing.'

'That is a lie,' Marcus said. 'Someone has been working mischief.'

The other remained stubbornly silent.

'Esca, I want an answer.'

The other moved a little, and some of the defiance went out of him. 'It was my own fault,' he began at last, speaking as though every word was dragged out of him. 'There was a young Tribune; one of those from the transit camp, who I think is taking troops up to Eboracum—a very splendid young Tribune, smooth as a girl, but a skilled hunter. He was one of us who went into the lair; and after the old dog-wolf was dead, and we had come away, and I was cleaning my spear, he laughed and said to me, "So, that was a noble thrust!" And then he saw my clipped ear, and he said, "For a slave." I was angry, and I let my tongue run away from me. I said: "I am body-slave to the Centurion Marcus Flavius Aquila; does the Tribune Placidus (that was his name) see any cause therein that I should be a worse hunter than himself?"' Esca broke off for a moment, drawing a harsh breath. 'He said: "None in the world; but at least the Tribune Placidus's life is his own to hazard as he wills. Your Master, having paid good money for his slave, will not thank you for leaving him with a carcass that he cannot even sell to the knacker's yard. Remember that when next you thrust your head into a wolf's lair." And then he smiled, and his smile is a sickness in my belly, still.'

Esca had been speaking in a dull, hopeless monotone, as though he had the bitter lesson by heart; and as he listened, Marcus was filled with a cold anger against the unknown Tribune; and the light of his rage suddenly made clear to him certain things that he had never thought of before.

Abruptly he reached out his free hand and grasped the other's wrist. 'Esca, have I ever, by word or deed, given you to believe that I think of you as that six-month soldier evidently thinks of his slaves?'

Esca shook his head. His defiance was all gone from him, and his face in the paling lamplight was no longer set and sullen, but only wretched. 'The Centurion is not such a one as the Tribune Placidus, to show the whip-lash without need to his hound,' he said drearily.

Marcus baffled, hurt, and angry, suddenly lost his temper. 'Oh, curse Tribune Placidus!' he burst out, his grasp tightening fiercely on the other's wrist. 'Does his word strike so much deeper with you than mine, that because of it you must needs talk to me of hounds and whip-lashes? Name of Light! Do I have to tell you in so many words that I really do not imagine a clipped ear to be the dividing-line between men and beasts? Have I not shown you clearly enough all this while? I have not thought of equal or unequal, slave or free in my dealings with you, though you were too proud to do the same for me! Too *proud*! Do you hear me? And now'—forgetful for the moment of the sleeping cub, he made a sudden movement to get on to his elbow, and collapsed again, exasperated but half laughing, his fury gone like a pricked bubble, holding up a bleeding thumb. 'And now your gift has bitten me! Mithras! His mouth is full of daggers!'

'Then you had best pay me a sesterce for the lot of them,' said Esca, and suddenly they were both laughing, the quick light laughter of breaking strain that has very little to do with whether or not there is anything to laugh at, while between them on the striped native blanket the small grey wolf-cub crouched, savage, bewildered, but very sleepy.

The household varied a good deal in their reactions to the sudden appearance of a wolf-cub in their midst. Procyon was doubtful at the first meeting; the new-comer had the wolf smell, the outland smell, and the great hound walked round him on stiff legs, the hair on his neck rising a little, while the cub squatted like a hairy malignant toad on the atrium floor, ears laid back and muzzle wrinkled in his first attempt at a snarl. Uncle Aquila scarcely noticed his arrival, being at the moment too deeply absorbed in the siege of Jerusalem; and

Marcipor, the house slave, and Stephanos looked on him rather askance—a wolf-cub that would one day be a wolf, roaming at large about the house. But Sassticca was unexpectedly an ally. Sassticca, her hands on her hips, told them roundly that they should be ashamed of themselves. Who were they, she demanded shrilly, with two sound legs apiece, to begrudge the young Master a pack of wolf-cubs if he wanted them? And she finished her baking in a state of high indignation, and presently brought Marcus three brown honey-cakes in a napkin, and a chipped bowl of castor ware with a hunting scene on it, which she said he might have for the little cub's feeding-bowl.

Marcus, who had overheard her championship—she had a loud voice—accepted both gifts with becoming gratitude, and when she had gone, he and Esca shared the cakes between them. He no longer minded Sassticca quite so desperately as he had done at first.

A few days later, Esca told Marcus about the days before his ear was clipped.

They were in the bath-house when it happened, drying themselves after a cold plunge. The time that he spent in the plunge-bath each day was one of Marcus's greatest pleasures, for it was big enough to splash about in and swim a few strokes; and while he was in the water, unless he was very careless, he could forget about his lame leg. It was a little like his old sense of being born from one kind of life into another, that he had been used to know in his charioteering days. But the likeness was the kind that a shadow bears to the real thing, and this morning as he sat up on the bronze couch, drying himself, he was suddenly sick with longing for the old splendour. Once more, just once more, to know that burst of speed as the team sprang forward, the swoop and the strength of it, and wind of his going singing by.

And at that moment, as though called up by the intensity of his longing, a swiftly driven chariot came whirling up the street beyond the bath-house wall.

Marcus reached out and took his tunic from Esca, saying as he did so, 'Not often that we hear anything but a vegetable cart in this street.'

'It will be Lucius Urbanus, the contractor's son,' Esca said. 'There is a back way from his stables which comes through behind the temple of Sull-Minerva.' The chariot was passing the house now, and evidently the driver was having trouble, for the crack of a whip and the loud burst of swearing reached them through the bath-house wall, and

Esca added with disgust, 'It should be a vegetable cart and drawn by an ox. Listen to him! He is not worthy to handle horses!'

Marcus pulled the folds of fine wool over his head and reached for his belt. 'So Esca also is a charioteer,' he said, fastening it.

'I was my father's charioteer,' Esca said. 'But that was a long time ago.'

And suddenly Marcus realized that he could ask Esca, now, about the time before his ear was clipped. It would no longer be walking in without leave. He shifted a little, making a quick gesture towards the foot of the couch, and as the other sat down, he said: 'Esca, how did your father's charioteer come to be a gladiator in the Calleva arena?'

Esca was buckling his own belt; he finished the task very deliberately, and then, locking his hands round one updrawn knee, sat silent for a moment, staring down at them. 'My father was a Clan Chieftain of the Brigantes, lord of five hundred spears,' he said at last. 'I was his armour-bearer until such time as I became a warrior in my own right—with the men of my tribe that happens after the sixteenth summer. When I had been a year or more a man among men and my father's charioteer, the Clan rose against our overlords, for the lust for freedom that was in us. We have been a thorn in the flesh of the Legions since first they marched north; we, the bearers of the blue war-shield. We rose, and we were beaten back. We made our last stand in our strong place, and we were overwhelmed. Those of the men's side who were left—there were not many—were sold as slaves.' He broke off, jerking up his head to look at Marcus. 'But I swear before the gods of my people, before Lugh the Light of the Sun, that I was lying for dead in a ditch when they took me. They would not have taken me, else. They sold me to a trader from the South, who sold me to Beppo, here in Calleva; and you know the rest.'

'You alone of all your kin?' Marcus asked after a moment.

'My father and two brothers died,' Esca said. 'My mother also. My father killed her before the Legionaries broke through. She wished it so.'

There was a long silence, and then Marcus said softly: 'Mithras! What a story!'

'It is a common enough story, still. Was it so very different at Isca Dumnoniorum, do you suppose?' But before Marcus could answer, he added quickly. 'None the less, it is not good to remember too closely. The time before—all the time before—that is the good time to remember.'

And sitting there in the thin March sunshine that slanted down through the high window, without either of them quite knowing how it happened, he began to tell Marcus about the time before. He told of a warrior's training; of river-bathing on hot summer days when the midges danced in the shimmering air; of his father's great white bull garlanded with poppies and moon flowers for a festival; of his first hunt, and the tame otter he had shared with his elder brother . . . One thing led to another, and presently he told how, ten years before, when the whole country was in revolt, he had lain behind a boulder to watch a Legion marching north, that never came marching back.

'I had never seen such a sight before,' he said. 'Like a shining serpent of men winding across the hills; a grey serpent, hackled with the scarlet cloaks and crests of the officers. There were queer tales about that Legion; men said that it was accursed, but it looked stronger than any curse, stronger and more deadly. And I remember how the Eagle flashed in the sun as it came by—a great golden Eagle with its wings arched back as I have seen them often stoop on a screaming hare among the heather. But the mist was creeping down from the high moors, and the Legion marched into it, straight into it, and it licked them up and flowed together behind them, and they were gone as though they had marched from one world into—another.' Esca made a quick gesture with his right hand, the first two fingers spread like horns. 'Queer tales there were, about that Legion.'

'Yes, I have heard those tales,' Marcus said. 'Esca, that was my father's Legion. His crest will have been the scarlet hackle next after the Eagle.'

VII
Two Worlds Meeting

FROM the open end of Uncle Aquila's courtyard, two shallow steps flanked by a bush of rosemary and a slender bay-tree led down into the garden. It was a rather wild garden, for Uncle Aquila did not keep a full-time garden slave, but a very pleasant one, running down to the crumbling earthworks of British Calleva. In some places the fine stone-faced city walls were already rising. One day they would rise here too, but as yet there was only the curved wave-break of old quiet turf, glimpsed between the branches of wild fruit-trees; and where the bank dipped, stray glimpses over mile upon mile of forest country rolling away into the smoke-blue distance where the Forest of Spinaii became the Forest of Anderida, and the Forest of Anderida dropped to the marshes and the sea.

To Marcus, after being cooped within doors all winter long, it seemed a wonderfully wide and shining place when he reached it for the first time some days later; and when Esca had left him to go off on some errand, he stretched himself out on the bench of grey Purbeck marble, under the wild fruit-trees, his arms behind his head, gazing upwards with eyes narrowed against the brightness, into the blown blue heights of heaven, which seemed so incredibly tall after roof-beams. Somewhere in the forest below him, birds were singing, with that note of clear-washed surprise that belongs to the early spring; and for a while Marcus simply lay letting it all soak into him, the wideness and the shine and the bird-song.

Close beside him, Cub lay curled into a compact ball. Looking at him now, it was hard to believe what a small fury he could be, crouched over his food-bowl with laid-back ears and bared milk-teeth, Marcus thought. Then he took up the task that he had brought out with him. He was one of those people who need something to do with their hands at all times, even if it is only a stick to whittle; and something of the craftsman in him demanded always to have an outlet. If he had not been wounded, he would have turned that craftsmanship to the making of a happy and efficient cohort; things being as they were, he had turned it this spring to overhauling and renovating the Celtic weapons which were the only ornament Uncle Aquila allowed on his walls. Today he had brought out the gem of the small collection, a light cavalry buckler of bull's hide faced with bronze, the central boss exquisitely worked with red enamel; but the straps must have been in a poor state when Uncle Aquila came by it, and now they were ready to tear like papyrus. Laying out his tools and the leather for the fresh straps beside him on the broad seat, he set to work to cut away the old ones. It was a delicate task, needing all his attention, and he did not look up again until he had finished it, and turned to lay the outworn straps aside.

And then he saw that he was no longer alone with Cub. A girl was standing among the wild fruit-trees where the hedge ran up into the slope of the old earthwork, and looking down at him. A British girl, in a pale saffron tunic, straight and shining as a candle-flame; one hand raised to thrust back heavy masses of hair the colour of red baltic amber, which the light wind had blown across her face.

They looked at each other in silence for a moment. Then the girl said in clear, very careful Latin, 'I have waited a long time for you to look up.'

'I am sorry,' Marcus said stiffly. 'I was busy on this shield.'

She came a step nearer. 'May I see the wolf-cub? I have not seen a tame wolf-cub before.'

And Marcus smiled suddenly, and laid aside his defences with the shield he had been working on. 'Surely. Here he is.' And swinging his feet to the ground, he reached down and grabbed the sleeping cub by the scruff of his neck, just as the girl joined him. The wolfling was not fiercer than most hound puppies, save when annoyed, but being bigger and stronger for his age, he could be very rough, and Marcus was taking no chances. He set Cub on his feet, keeping a restraining hand under his small chest. 'Be careful; he is not used to strangers.'

The girl gave him a smile, and sat down on her heels, holding out her hands slowly to Cub. 'I will not startle him,' she said. And Cub, who at first had crouched back against Marcus, ears flattened and hairs bristling, seemed very slowly to change his mind. Warily, ready to flinch back or snap at any sign of danger, he began to smell at her fingers; and she held her hands quite still, to let him. 'What is his name?' she asked.

'Just Cub.'

'Cub,' she said crooningly. 'Cub.' And as he whimpered and made a little darting thrust towards her, against Marcus's guarding hand, she began to caress the warm hollow under his chin with one finger. 'See, we be friends, you and I.'

She was about thirteen, Marcus imagined, watching her as she played with Cub. A tall, thin girl, with a pointed face wide at the temples and narrow at the chin; and the shape of her face and the colour of her eyes and hair gave her a little the look of a young vixen. If she were angry, he thought, she would probably look very like a vixen indeed. He had the glimmering of an idea that he had seen her before, but he could not remember where.

'How did you know about Cub?' he asked at last.

She looked up. 'Narcissa, my nurse, told me—oh, about a moon ago. And at first I did not believe it, because Nissa so often gets her stories wrong. But yesterday I heard a slave on this side of the hedge call to another, "Oh worthless one, thy Master's wolf-whelp has bitten my toe!" And the other called back, "Then the gods grant that the taste of it will not make him sick!" So I knew that it was true.'

Her imitation of Esca and Marcipor the house slave was unmistakable, and Marcus flung up his head with a crow of laughter. 'And it did!—at all events, something did.'

The girl laughed too, joyously, showing little pointed teeth as white and sharp as Cub's. And as though their laughter had unlocked a door, Marcus suddenly remembered where he had seen her before. He had not been interested enough in Kaeso and Valaria to remember that they lived next door, and although he had noticed her so vividly at the time, he had not remembered the girl he had seen with them, because Esca, coming immediately afterwards, had been so much more important; but he remembered her now.

'I saw you at the Saturnalia Games,' he said. 'But your hair was hidden under your mantle, and that was why I did not remember you.'

'But I remember you!' said the girl. Cub had wandered off after a beetle by that time, and she let him go, sitting back and folding her hands in her lap. 'Nissa says you bought that gladiator. I wish you could have bought the bear too.'

'You minded very badly about that bear, didn't you?' said Marcus.

'It was cruel! To kill on the hunting trail, that is one thing; but they took away his freedom! They kept him in a cage, and then they killed him.'

'It was the cage, then, more than the killing?'

'I do not like cages,' said the girl in a small hard voice. 'Or nets. I am glad you bought that gladiator.'

A little chill wind came soughing across the garden, silvering the long grass and tossing the budding sprays of the wild pear- and cherry-trees. The girl shivered, and Marcus realized that her yellow tunic was of very thin wool, and even here in the shelter of the old earthworks it was still very early spring.

'You are cold,' he said, and gathered up his old military cloak which had been flung across the bench. 'Put this on.'

'Do you not want it?'

'No. I have a thicker tunic than that flimsy thing you are wearing. So. Now, come and sit here on the bench.'

She obeyed him instantly, drawing the cloak around her. In the act of doing so, she checked, looking down at the bright folds, then up again at Marcus. 'This is your soldier's cloak,' she said. 'Like the cloaks the centurions from the transit camp wear.'

Marcus made her a quick mocking salute. 'You behold in me Marcus Aquila, ex-Cohort Centurion of Gaulish Auxiliaries with the Second Legion.'

The girl looked at him in silence for a moment. Then she said, 'I know. Does the wound hurt you still?'

'Sometimes,' Marcus said. 'Did Nissa tell you that too?'

She nodded.

'She seems to have told you a deal of things.'

'Slaves!' She made a quick, contemptuous gesture. 'They stand in doorways and chatter like starlings; but Nissa is the worst of them all!'

Marcus laughed, and a small silence fell between them; but after a little while he said: 'I have told you my name. What is yours?'

'My aunt and uncle call me Camilla, but my real name is Cottia,' said the girl. 'They like everything to be very Roman, you see.'

So he had been right in thinking she was not Kaeso's daughter. 'And you do not?' he said.

'I? I am of the Iceni! So is my Aunt Valaria, though she likes to forget it.'

'I once knew a black chariot team who were descended out of the

Royal Stables of the Iceni,' Marcus said, feeling that perhaps Aunt Valaria was not a very safe subject.

'Did you? Were they yours? Which strain?' Her face was alight with interest.

Marcus shook his head. 'They were not mine, and I only had the joy of driving them once; it was a joy too. And I never knew their strain.'

'My father's big stallion was descended from Prydfirth, the beloved of King Prasutogus,' said Cottia. 'We are all horse-breeders, we of the Iceni, from the King downward—when we had a king.' She hesitated, and her voice lost its eager ring. 'My father was killed, breaking a young horse, and that is why I live with my Aunt Valaria now.'

'I am sorry. And your mother?'

'I expect that all is well with my mother,' Cottia said, matter-of-factly. 'There was a hunter who had wanted her always, but her parents gave her to my father. And when my father went West of the Sunset, she went to the hunter, and there was no room in his house for me. It was different with my brother, of course. It is always different with boys. So my mother gave me to Aunt Valaria, who has no children of her own.'

'Poor Cottia,' Marcus said softly.

'Oh no. I did not wish to live in that hunter's house; he was not *my* father. Only . . . ' Her voice trailed into silence.

'Only?'

Cottia's changeable face was suddenly as vixenish as he had guessed it could be. 'Only I hate living with my aunt; I hate living in a town full of straight lines, and being shut up inside brick walls, and being called Camilla; and I hate—hate—*hate* it when they try to make me pretend to be a Roman maiden and forget my own tribe and my own father!'

Marcus was quickly coming to the conclusion that he did not like Aunt Valaria. 'If it is any consolation to you, they seem to have succeeded very ill so far,' he said.

'No! I will not let them! I pretend, outside my tunic. I answer when they call me Camilla, and I speak to them in Latin: but underneath my tunic I am of the Iceni, and when I take off my tunic at night, I say, "There! That rids me of Rome until the morning!" And I lie on my bed and think—and think—about my home, and the marsh birds flighting down from the north in the Fall of the Leaf, and the brood mares with their foals in my father's runs. I remember all the things that I am not supposed to remember, and talk to myself inside my head in my own tongue—' She broke off, looking at him in quick surprise. 'We are talking in my tongue now! How long have we been doing that?'

'Since you told me about your real name being Cottia.'

Cottia nodded. It did not seem to strike her that the hearer to whom she was pouring out all this was himself a Roman: and it did not strike Marcus either. For the moment all he knew was that Cottia also was in exile, and his fellowship reached out to her, delicately, rather shyly. And as though feeling the touch of it, she drew a little nearer, huddling the scarlet folds more closely round her.

'I like being inside your cloak,' she said contentedly. 'It feels warm and safe, as a bird must feel inside its own feathers.'

From beyond the hedge at that moment there arose a voice, shrill as a pea-hen before rain. 'Camilla! Ladybird! Oh, my Lady Camilla!'

Cottia sighed in exasperation. 'That is Nissa,' she said. 'I must go.' But she did not move.

'Camilla!' called the voice, nearer this time.

'That is Nissa again,' said Marcus.

'Yes, I—must go.' She got up reluctantly, and slipped off the heavy cloak. But still she lingered, while the screeching voice drew nearer. Then with a rush, 'Let me come again! Please let me! You need not talk to me, nor even notice that I am here.'

'Oh, my Lady! Where are you, child of Typhon?' wailed the voice, very near now.

'Come when it pleases you—and I shall be glad of your coming,' Marcus said quickly.

'I will come tomorrow,' Cottia told him, and turned to the old rampart slope, carrying herself like a queen. Most British women seemed to carry themselves like that, Marcus thought, watching her drop out of sight round the hedge; and he remembered Guinhumara in the hut doorway at Isca Dumnoniorum. What had happened to her and the brown baby, after Cradoc lay dead and the huts were burned and the fields salted? He would never know.

The shrill voice was raised in fond scolding on the far side of the hedge; and footsteps came across the grass, and Marcus turned his head to see Esca coming towards him.

'My Master has had company,' Esca said, laying spear-blade to forehead in salute, as he halted beside him.

'Yes, and it sounds as though she is getting a sharp scolding from her nurse on my account,' Marcus said a little anxiously, as he listened to the shrill voice fading.

'If all I hear be true, scolding will not touch that one,' Esca said. 'As well scold a flung spear.'

Marcus leaned back, his hands behind his neck, and looked up at his slave. The thought of Guinhumara and her baby was still with him, standing behind the thought of Cottia. 'Esca, why do all the Frontier tribes resent our coming so bitterly?' he asked on a sudden impulse. 'The tribes of the south have taken to our ways easily enough.'

'We have ways of our own,' said Esca. He squatted on one heel beside the bench. 'The tribes of the south had lost their birthright before ever the Eagles came in war. They sold it for the things that Rome could give. They were fat with Roman merchandise and their souls had grown lazy within them.'

'But these things that Rome had to give, are they not good things?' Marcus demanded. 'Justice, and order, and good roads; worth having, surely?'

'These be all good things,' Esca agreed. 'But the price is too high.'

'The price? Freedom?'

'Yes—and other things than freedom.'

'What other things? Tell me, Esca; I want to know. I want to understand.'

Esca thought for a while, staring straight before him. 'Look at the pattern embossed here on your dagger-sheath,' he said at last. 'See, here is a tight curve, and here is another facing the other way to balance it, and here between them is a little round stiff flower; and then it is all repeated here, and here, and here again. It is beautiful, yes, but to me it is as meaningless as an unlit lamp.'

Marcus nodded as the other glanced up at him. 'Go on.'

Esca took up the shield which had been laid aside at Cottia's coming. 'Look now at this shield-boss. See the bulging curves that flow from each other as water flows from water and wind from wind, as the stars turn in the heaven and blown sand drifts into dunes. These are the curves of life; and the man who traced them had in him knowledge of things that your people have lost the key to—if they ever had it.' He looked up at Marcus again very earnestly. 'You cannot expect the man who made this shield to live easily under the rule of the man who worked the sheath of this dagger.'

'The sheath was made by a British craftsman,' Marcus said stubbornly. 'I bought it at Anderida when I first landed.'

'By a British craftsman, yes, making a Roman pattern. One who had lived so long under the wings of Rome—he and his fathers before him—that he had forgotten the ways and the spirit of his own people.' He laid the shield down again. 'You are the builders of coursed stone walls, the makers of straight roads and ordered justice and disciplined troops. We know that, we know it all too well. We know that your justice is more sure than ours, and when we rise against you, we see our hosts break against the discipline of your troops, as the sea breaks against a rock. And we do not understand, because all these things are of the ordered pattern, and only the free curves of the shield-boss are real to us. We do not understand. And when the time comes that we begin to understand your world, too often we lose the understanding of our own.'

For a while they were silent, watching Cub at his beetle-hunting. Then Marcus said, 'When I came out from home, a year and a half ago, it all seemed so simple.' His gaze dropped again to the buckler on the bench beside him, seeing the strange, swelling curves of the boss with new eyes. Esca had chosen his symbol well, he thought: between the formal pattern on his dagger-sheath and the formless yet potent beauty of the shield-boss lay all the distance that could lie between two worlds. And yet between individual people, people like Esca, and Marcus, and Cottia, the distance narrowed so that you could reach across it, one to another, so that it ceased to matter.

VIII
The Healer with the Knife

MARCUS had said 'Come when you like,' and Cottia had said, 'I will come tomorrow.' But it was not so simple as that, after all. Kaeso would have made no particular difficulty, for he was an easy-going and kindly man, very eager to stand well with his Roman fellow-Magistrate. But Aunt Valaria, always so careful to follow the custom of what she called 'civilized Society', was very sure that it was not the custom for gently nurtured Roman maidens to take themselves into other people's gardens and make friends with the total strangers they found there. It was not as though Aquila had ever shown himself in the least friendly.

Marcus of course knew nothing of this; he only knew that Cottia did not come tomorrow, nor the day after. And he told himself that there was no reason why she should. It had been to see Cub that she came in the first place, and having seen him, why should she come again? He had thought that perhaps she wanted to be friends, but it seemed that that had been a mistake, and it did not much matter.

And then on the third day, when he had sworn to himself that he would not look for her coming any more, he heard her calling his name, softly and urgently, and when he looked up from the spear-blade that he had been burnishing, there she was, standing where he had first seen her, among the wild fruit-trees.

'Marcus! Marcus, I could not get free of Nissa before,' she began breathlessly. 'They say that I must not come again.'

Marcus laid down the spear, and demanded, 'Why?'

She glanced quickly over her shoulder into her own garden. 'Aunt Valaria says it is not seemly for a Roman maiden to do as I have done. But I am not a Roman maiden; and oh, Marcus, you must make her let me come! You *must*!'

She was hovering on the edge of flight, even while she spoke, and clearly it was no time for needless talk or long explanations. 'She *shall* let you come,' Marcus said quickly, 'but it may take time. Now go, before they catch you.' He made her a swift half-laughing obeisance, palm to forehead, and she turned and dropped out of sight.

Marcus returned to his burnishing. The whole incident had come and gone as quickly as the flight of a bird across the garden, but behind it he was suddenly happier than he had been for three days.

That evening, after talking it over with Esca, he laid the whole problem before Uncle Aquila.

'And what,' enquired Uncle Aquila when he had finished, 'do you suggest that I should do about it?'

'If you could make a few neighbourly remarks to the Lady Valaria the next time you cross her path, I think it would help.'

'But Jupiter! I scarce know the woman, save to bow to her as Kaeso's wife.'

'Which is exactly why a few neighbourly remarks seem indicated.'

'And what if she becomes neighbourly in return?' demanded Uncle Aquila in blighting tones.

'She cannot invade you here in your stronghold, at all events, since there are no womenfolk to receive her,' Marcus pointed out, quite unblighted.

'There is truth in that, admittedly. Why do you want the chit to come?'

'Oh—because she and Cub understand each other.'

'And so I am to be thrown to the lions in order that Cub may have his playmate?'

Marcus laughed. 'It is only one lion, or rather lioness.' And then the laughter left him. 'Uncle Aquila, we do need your help. I would contrive to play Perseus for myself, but at this stage nothing I could do would in the least avail to rescue Andromeda. It is a job for the head of the household.'

'It was peaceful in this house before you came,' said Uncle Aquila with resignation. 'You are an unutterable nuisance, but I suppose you must have your own way.'

Marcus was never quite sure how it was brought about. Certainly Uncle Aquila never appeared to bestir himself at all in the matter, but from that time forward there began to be more of surface friendliness between the two houses, and before the woods below the old ramparts had thickened into full leaf, Cottia had become a part of life in the Aquila household, and came and went as it pleased her, and as it pleased Marcus.

Esca, who was by nature silent and withdrawn with anyone save the young Roman, was somewhat prone at first to stand on his dignity as a slave, where she was concerned; but he lowered his barriers to her little by little, so far as it was in him to lower them to anyone who was not Marcus. And Marcus tyrannized over and laughed at her, and was content in her company; he taught her to play 'Flash the Fingers', a game beloved of Legionaries and gladiators; and told her long stories about his old home in the Etruscan hills. Telling Cottia about it, conjuring up for her the sights and sounds and smells, seemed somehow to bring it all nearer and ease the ache of exile; and as he told about it, he would catch again that first glimpse of the farmstead from the corner of the hill track where the wild cherry-trees grew. 'There were always a lot of pigeons strutting and fluttering about the courtyards and the roofs, and their necks would catch the sunlight and shine iridescent green and purple; little white stock-doves, too, with coral-pink feet. And when you came into the courtyard they would all burst upwards with a great deal of fuss, and then come circling down again round your feet. And then old Argos would come out of his kennel and bark and wag his tail at the same time; and there would be a wonderful smell of whatever was for supper—grilled river trout, perhaps, or fried chicken if it was a special occasion. And when I came home in the evening, after being out all day, my mother would come to the door when she heard Argos barking . . . '

Cottia never tired of hearing about the farm in the Etruscan hills, and Marcus, homesick as he was, never tired of telling her. One day he even showed her his olive-wood bird.

But towards the summer's end he began to have more and more trouble with the old wound. He had grown so used to the dull ache of it that often he could forget about it altogether, but now there was a jangling sharpness in the old ache, that could not be forgotten, and sometimes the scars were hot to touch and reddened and angry to the sight.

Matters came to a head on a hot August evening, when Marcus and his uncle had just played out their usual game of draughts. It had been a blazing day, and even out here in the courtyard there seemed no air. The evening sky was drained of all colour by the day's heat, a bleached and weary sky, and the scent of the roses and cistus in the courtyard jars hung heavy in the air, as smoke hangs in misty weather.

Marcus had been feeling sick with pain all day, and the heavy sweetness of the flowers seemed to stick in his throat. He had played a thoroughly bad game, and he knew it. He could not lie still. He shifted a little in search of an easier position, and then shifted again, pretending that he had only moved to look at Cub—half grown now, and superbly handsome lying sprawled on the cooling turf beside Procyon, with whom he had long ago made friends.

Uncle Aquila was watching a yellow wagtail on the bath-house roof, and Marcus shifted yet again, hoping that he would not notice.

'Wound troublesome tonight?' enquired Uncle Aquila, his eye still following the yellow wagtail as it scuttled after flies on the warm tiles.

Marcus said, 'No, sir. Why?'

'Oh, I merely wondered. You are quite sure?'

'Perfectly.'

Uncle Aquila brought his eye down from the yellow wagtail, and fixed it on Marcus. 'What a liar you are,' he remarked conversationally. Then, as Marcus's mouth tightened, he leaned forward, crashing a huge hand on the draughts-board and scattering the pieces broadcast. 'This has been going on long enough! If that fat fool Ulpius does not know his craft, I have an old friend in practice at Durinum who does. Rufrius Galarius. He was one of our field surgeons. He shall come and take a look at that leg.'

'I should not think for a moment that he will,' Marcus said. 'It is a long way from Durinum.'

'He will come,' said Uncle Aquila. 'He and I used to hunt boar together. Oh yes, he will come.'

And come he did.

Rufrius Galarius, one-time field surgeon of the Second Legion, was a blue-jowled Spaniard with a merry eye, close curling black hair scarcely touched with grey, and a chest like a barrel. But his blunt wrestler's hands were very sure and gentle, Marcus found, a few evenings later, when he lay on his narrow cot while his uncle's friend examined the old wounds.

It seemed a long time before he had finished; and when he had, he replaced the rug, straightened his back and strode swearing up and down the little cell. 'Who in the name of Typhon searched this wound?' he demanded at last, swinging round on him.

'The camp surgeon at Isca Dumnoniorum,' Marcus said.

'Been there twenty years, and drunk as a mule-driver at Saturnalia, every night of them,' snapped Galarius. 'I know these passed-over camp surgeons. Butchers and assassins, every one!' He made an indescribable and very vulgar noise.

'Not every night, and he was a very hard-working soul,' said Marcus, doing his best for the shaggy and rather pathetic old man whom he remembered with liking.

'Puh!' said Galarius. Then his manner changed abruptly, and he came and sat himself down on the edge of the cot. 'The thing is that he did not finish his work,' he said.

Marcus ran the tip of his tongue over uncomfortably dry lips. 'You mean—it is all to do again?'

The other nodded. 'You will have no peace until the wound has been re-searched.'

'When—' Marcus began, and checked, trying desperately to steady the shameful flinching at the corner of his mouth.

'In the morning. Since it must be done, the sooner it were done the better.' He put a hand on Marcus's shoulder, and kept it there.

For a moment Marcus lay rigid under the blunt, kindly hand, then he drew a long, uneven breath, and relaxed, with a rather crooked attempt at a smile. 'I beg your forgiveness. I think I—am rather tired.'

'It seems possible,' agreed the surgeon. 'You have had rough marching lately. Oh yes, I know. But soon you will have it behind you and better things ahead. I promise you that.'

For a while he sat there, talking of matters that were a long way from tomorrow morning, drifting from the flavour of native oysters to the iniquities of provincial tax-gatherers, yarning about the early days on the Silurian frontier, and long-ago boar hunts with Uncle Aquila. 'We were great hunters, your uncle and I; and now we grow stiff in our joints and set in our ways. Sometimes I think I will pack up and go on my travels again, before it is too late and I am utterly rusted into my socket. But I chose the wrong branch of my calling for that. A surgeon's craft is none so easily picked up and carried about the world. An oculist's, now, that is the craft for a follower of Aesculapius with the itch to wander! Here in the north, where so many have the marsh-blindness, an oculist's stamp is a talisman to carry a man safely where a Legion could not go.' And he launched out into an account of the adventures of an acquaintance who had crossed the Western

Ocean and plied his trade through the wilds of Hibernia, a few years before, while Marcus listened with about half his attention, little guessing that the time was to come when that story would be tremendously important to him.

Presently Galarius got up, stretching until the little muscles cracked behind his bull-shoulders. 'Now I go to talk hunting with Aquila until bedtime. Do you lie still, and sleep as well as may be, and I shall be back early in the morning.'

And with a brusque nod, he turned and strode out into the colonnade.

With him, most of Marcus's hard-held courage seemed to go too. He was horrified to find that he was shivering—shivering at the smell of pain as a horse shivers at the smell of fire. Lying with his forearm pressed across his eyes, he lashed himself with his own contempt, but found no help in it. He felt cold in his stomach and very alone.

There came a sudden pattering across the floor, and a cold muzzle was thrust against his shoulder. He opened his eyes to see Cub's grinning head within a few inches of his own. 'Thanks, Cub,' he said, and shifted a little to catch the great head between his hands as Cub put his fore-paws on the cot and blew lovingly in his face. It was near to sunset, and the light of the westering sun was flooding into the cell, splashing like quivering golden water on walls and ceiling. Marcus had not seen it come, and it seemed to break singing on his sight, as a fanfare of trumpets breaks upon the ear. The light of Mithras, springing out of the dark.

Esca, who had come hard behind Cub, appeared in the doorway, sending a great thrust of shadow up the sunlit wall as he came to Marcus's side. 'I have spoken with Rufrius Galarius,' he said.

Marcus nodded. 'He will need your help in the morning. You will do that for me?'

'I am the Centurion's body-slave; who but I should do it?' Esca said, and bent to disentangle the blanket.

As he did so, sounds of a scuffle arose somewhere in the courtyard. Stephanos's old bleating voice was raised in protest, and then a girl's, high, clear, and hard. 'Let me pass. If you do not let me pass, I'll bite!' The scuffle seemed to be resumed, and an instant later a howl of anguish from Stephanos told all too clearly that the threat had been carried out. As Marcus and Esca exchanged questioning glances, flying feet came along the colonnade, and Cottia burst into the doorway, a burnished, warlike figure, with the setting sun making a nimbus round her.

Marcus raised himself on one elbow. 'You little vixen! What have you done to Stephanos?'

'I bit his hand,' said Cottia, in the same clear, hard voice. 'He tried to keep me out.'

The scuff-scuff of hurrying sandals sounded behind her even while she spoke, and Marcus said urgently, 'Esca, in the name of Light, go and keep him out of here!' He felt suddenly that he could not deal with a righteously indignant Stephanos at this moment. Then, as Esca strode out to do his bidding, he turned on Cottia. 'And what is it that you suppose you are doing here, my Lady?'

She came close, thrusting in beside Cub, and stood looking down at him accusingly. 'Why did you not tell me?' she demanded.

'Tell you what?' But he knew what.

'About the Healer with the Knife. I saw him come in a mule carriage, through the storeroom window, and Nissa told me why he came.'

'Nissa talks too much,' Marcus said. 'I did not mean that you should know until it was all over and done with.'

'You had no right not to tell me,' she said stormily. 'It was mine to know!' And then in an anxious rush, 'What will he do to you?'

Marcus hesitated an instant, but if he did not tell her, the unspeakable Nissa undoubtedly would. 'I am to have the wound cleaned up. That is all.'

Her face seemed to grow narrower and more sharply pointed while he looked at it. 'When?' she asked.

'In the morning, very early.'

'Send Esca to tell me when it is over.'

'It will be *very* early,' Marcus said firmly. 'You will scarcely be awake by then.'

'I shall be awake,' Cottia said. 'I shall be waiting at the bottom of the garden. And I shall wait there until Esca comes, whoever tries to take me away. I can bite others besides Stephanos, and if anyone tries to take me away, I will, and then I shall be beaten. You would not like to know that I had been beaten because you would not send Esca, would you, Marcus?'

Marcus recognized defeat. 'Esca shall come and tell you.'

There was a long pause. Cottia stood very still, looking down at him. Then she said, 'I wish it could be me instead.'

It was a thing more easily said than meant, but Cottia did mean it. Looking at her, Marcus knew that. 'Thank you, Cottia. I shall remember that. And now you must go home.'

She drew back obediently, as Esca reappeared in the doorway. 'I will go home. When may I come again?'

'I do not know,' Marcus said. 'Esca shall come and tell you that also.'

Without another word she turned and walked out into the golden light. At a sign from Marcus, the slave fell in behind her, and their steps sounded fainter and fainter along the colonnade.

Marcus listened to them until they faded into silence, lying quiet, with the familiar rough warmth of Cub's head under his hand. He was still unpleasantly cold in the pit of his stomach, but he no longer felt alone. In some way that he did not understand, Cub and Esca and Cottia had comforted and steadied him for what was coming.

The golden light was fading, and into the quietness stole a shimmering thread of bird-song, the thin, regretful autumn song of a robin in the wild pear-tree; and he realized that summer was nearly over. Suddenly he knew, with a sense of discovery, that it had been a good summer. He had been homesick, yes, dreaming night after night of his own hills, and waking with a sore heart; but none the less, it had been a good summer. There had been the day that Cub discovered how to bark. Marcus had been almost as surprised as Cub. 'But wolves never bark,' he said to Esca; and Esca had said: 'Rear a wolf with the dog-pack and he will do as the dog-pack does in all things.' And Cub, proud of his new accomplishment, had filled the garden with his shrill puppy clamour for days. Other small sharp-edged memories sprang to meet him: twists of hot pastry brought out by Sassticca and eaten by the four of them as a feast; the hunting-bow which he and Esca had built between them; Cottia holding his olive-wood bird in cupped hands.

A kind summer, a kingfisher summer; and suddenly he was grateful for it.

He slept that night quietly and lightly as a hunter sleeps, and woke to the call of distant trumpets sounding Cockcrow from the transit camp.

It was so early that the gossamer still lay thick and dew-grey over the courtyard grass and the smell of the day-spring was cold and fresh in the air when Rufrius Galarius returned; but Marcus had been waiting his coming for what seemed a long time. He returned the surgeon's greeting, and explained, 'My slave is gone to shut up the wolf-cub. He should be back at any moment.'

Galarius nodded. 'I have seen him. He is also fetching sundry things that we shall need,' he said, and opening the bronze case that he had brought with him he began to set out the tools of his trade on the chest top.

Before he had finished, Esca was back, carrying hot water and new linen, and a flask of the native barley spirit which Galarius considered better than wine, though fiercer, for cleansing a wound. 'There will be more hot water when you need it,' he said, setting the things down on the chest top beside the instrument case; and came to stand over Marcus, a little as Cub might have done.

Galarius finished his preparations, and turned. 'Now, if you are ready?'

'Quite ready,' Marcus said, tossing off the blanket, and shut his teeth for what was coming.

A long while later he drifted out of the darkness that had come roaring up over him before the work was finished, to find himself lying under warm rugs, with Rufrius Galarius standing beside him with a square hand set over his heart, as old Aulus had stood in that other waking, just a year ago. For one confused moment he thought that it was still that other waking and he had dreamed in a circle; and then, as his sight and hearing cleared somewhat, he saw Esca standing just behind the surgeon, and a huge shadow in the doorway that could only be Uncle Aquila, and heard the despairing howls of Cub shut in the storeroom: and came back to the present like a swimmer breaking surface.

The ache of the old wound was changed to a jangling throb that seemed to beat through his whole body with a sickening sense of shock, and involuntarily he gave a little moan.

The surgeon nodded. 'Aye, it strikes sharp at first,' he agreed. 'But it will ease presently.'

Marcus looked up rather hazily into the blue-jowled Spaniard's face. 'Have you done?' he mumbled.

'I have done.' Galarius drew up the blanket. There was blood on his hand. 'In a few months' time you will be a sound man again. Lie still and rest now, and this evening I will come back.'

He gave Marcus's shoulder a small brisk pat, and turned to gather up his instruments.

'I leave him in your hands. You can give him the draught now,' he said to Esca, over his shoulder as he went out. Marcus heard him speak to someone in the colonnade. 'Enough splinters to quill a porcupine; but the muscles are less damaged than one might expect. The boy should do well enough now.'

Then he found Esca beside him, holding a cup. 'Cottia—and Cub—' he stammered.

'I will see to them soon, but first you must drink this.'

Esca dropped to one knee beside the cot, and Marcus found that he was lying with his head on his slave's shoulder and the rim of the cup was cool against his mouth as he drank. He remembered the bitter taste from last year. Then, as the cup was withdrawn, he turned his head contentedly on Esca's arm. There was a pinched greyness in the other's face, he realized, an odd wryness about his mouth, like the look of a man who wishes to be sick but has nothing in his stomach to be sick with.

'Was it as bad as that?' he asked with a weak attempt at laughter.

Esca grinned. 'Go to sleep.'

IX
Tribune Placidus

A MILE or two south of Calleva, where the forest opened suddenly to a steep drop of bracken-clad hillside, two men were standing: a Roman and a Briton; and between them, head up and muzzle quivering into the wind, a young brindled wolf.

Abruptly, the Roman stooped to unbuckle the heavy bronze-studded collar from the wolf's neck. Cub was full grown now, though not yet come to his full strength, and the time had arrived when he must have his choice of returning to the wild. You could tame a wild thing, but never count it as truly won until, being free to return to its own kind, it chose to come back to you. Marcus had known that all along, and he and Esca had made their preparations with infinite care, bringing Cub to this spot again and again; that he might be sure of the way home if he wished to take it. If he wished to take it. With his fingers on the buckle, Marcus wondered whether he would ever feel the hairy living warmth of Cub's neck again.

The collar was off now, and he thrust it into the breast of his tunic. For a lingering moment he fondled the pricked ears. Then he stood erect. 'Go free, brother. Good hunting.' Cub looked up into his face, puzzled; then, as a fresh burst of woodland smells reached his quivering nose, trotted off down the woodshore.

The other two watched him go in silence, a brindled shadow slipping away into the undergrowth. Then Marcus turned and made for the trunk of a fallen birch-tree a little way down the slope, moving quickly but awkwardly over the rough ground with a sideways lurch of the shoulders at every step. Rufrius Galarius had done his work well, and now, some eight months later, Marcus was to all intents and purposes as sound as ever, just as the surgeon had promised. He would carry the scars to his dying day, and a twisted leg that would bar him from the Legions, but that was all; indeed, after a winter spent with Esca's help in training as though for the arena, he was now as hard as a gladiator. He reached the fallen tree-trunk and sat down on it, and an instant later Esca was squatting at his feet.

This was a favourite vantage point of theirs. The tree-trunk made a convenient seat, and the steep drop of the hillside gave a clear view of wooded hills and the blue lift of the downs beyond. He had seen these rolling woods in their winter bareness, dappled like a partridge's breast. He had seen the first outbreaking of the blackthorn foam; and now the full green flame of spring was running through the forest and the wild cherry-trees stood like lit candles along the woodland ways.

The two in their vantage point sat talking lazily, with long silences between, of many things under the sun, including the guest whom Uncle Aquila was expecting that evening; no less a person than the Legate of the Sixth Legion on his way down from Eburacum to Regnum, and thence to Rome.

'He is a very old friend of your uncle's?' asked Esca idly.

'Yes. I believe they served together in Judaea when my uncle was First Cohort of the Fretensis and this man was doing his year as a Tribune on the Staff. He must be a great deal younger than Uncle Aquila.'

'And now he goes home, to his own place?'

'Yes, but only on some business with the Senate, Uncle Aquila says; then back to the Eagles again.'

After a time they fell silent altogether, each busy with his own thoughts. Marcus's were mainly concerned, as they had been for some time past, with the question of what he was going to do with himself and his life, now that he was well again. The Legions were closed to him, and that left just one other way of life that he would have turned to as a bird flies home. Farming was in the blood of most of his race, from the Senator with his estate in the Alban Hills to the time-expired Legionary with his pumpkin patch; and to Marcus, born and bred as he had been, farming and soldiering were yoke-mates, the two natural ways of life. But to start anything of that sort, one needed money. It was all right for the time-expired Legionary with his government grant of land. It would have been all right for Marcus if he had served his twenty years—even though he never became Prefect of an Egyptian Legion—and had savings from his pay and a centurion's gratuity behind him. But as it was, he had nothing. He might have turned to Uncle Aquila for help, he knew, but he would not do that. His uncle, although he had sufficient for his needs, was not a rich man, and had done enough for him already. He should have set about finding some way to earn his living before now, he supposed, but there were so few ways open to a free man, and the frightful conviction was growing on him that he would end up as somebody's secretary. There were people who preferred a free secretary to a slave, here—or even at home in Etruria. But even as that thought touched his mind, he knew that for him to drift home, rootless, and without any stake in the country that had bred him, nor any hope of such, would be only the shadow and none of the substance of homecoming. He would have carried his exile with him into his own hills and spoiled them; and that was all. No, he must look for his secretaryship here in Britain.

Only this morning he had made up his mind to lay the secretary idea before Uncle Aquila tonight, but the Legate's message had arrived, and now of course it would have to wait until the sudden guest had gone on his way. And part of him—a part of which he was rather ashamed—caught at the delay as a breathing-space; one day's grace in which something might happen, though what was likely to happen he would have been hard put to it to say.

In their silence, the wild had drawn close in to the two in the vantage point. Presently a red glint slipping through the uncurling bracken and young foxgloves at the lower end of the clearing told them where a vixen passed. She paused an instant in full view, her pointed muzzle raised, the sun shining with almost metallic lustre on her coat; then she turned in among the trees. And watching the russet glint of her flicker out of sight, Marcus found himself thinking of Cottia.

The closer friendliness between her house and his had continued. He knew Kaeso quite well now, and even Valaria a little; Valaria, plumpish and prettyish and foolish, floating with pale-coloured mist-linen, clanking with bracelets, her hair closely curled as a ram's fleece. He was for ever meeting her in her litter, as he came and went about Calleva, to the baths or the gymnasium or the Golden Vine, from whose stables he and Esca had lately hired ponies once or twice for a trip into the outback; and always he had to stop and talk. But of Cottia herself, he suddenly realized, he had seen less and less as the months went by.

With life opening to him again, he had had less need of her, and she had drawn back little by little, without a shadow of reproach. Yet he did not feel in the least guilty, and all at once, realizing how very easily Cottia could have made him feel guilty if she had chosen to, he felt a quick rush of warmth towards her. The odd thing was that now he came to think of it he did need Cottia as much as ever; he often forgot her altogether with the surface of his mind, but he knew that if he were never to see her again he would be very unhappy, perhaps as unhappy as he would if Cub never came back . . .

And would Cub ever come back? Would the call of his own kind prove stronger than the tie that bound him to his master? Either way, Marcus hoped that it would be quick and easy and final; no tearing of the heart in two, for Cub. He stirred, and looked down at Esca. 'We have been roosting here long enough.'

The other tipped back his head, and for a moment their eyes met. Then Esca got up, and reached a helping hand to Marcus. 'Let the Centurion whistle once, in case he is near; then we will go home.'

Marcus gave the shrill, broken whistle he had always used to summon Cub, and stood listening. A magpie, startled by the sound, scolded sharply from the woods behind them, and nothing more. After a few moments he whistled again. Still no answering bark, no brindled shape trotting out of the wood-shore.

'He is out of hearing,' said Esca. 'Well, he knows the way home, and there'll be no harm come to him.'

No, there would be no harm come to Cub. He was well known in and around Calleva, and since he had long since lost his wolf-smell, the dog-pack accepted him for one of themselves, and one to be respected. No harm would come to him from his own kind, either, for save when man took a hand, there was little war between wolf-pack and dog-pack, who indeed mated together often enough to make it sometimes hard to tell which was which. Only, if he went back to his own kind, the day might come when men would hunt Cub as they had hunted his mother.

Marcus longed to look back once, as they turned in among the hazel scrub of the forest verge, in case, even now, Cub might be coming uphill at a canter. But looking back was not in the bargain, and with his slave beside him he turned resolutely homeward.

They came to the South Gate of Calleva and passed through, Esca immediately falling the usual three paces to the rear. They made their way round by the short cut behind the temple of Sull-Minerva and entered the house by the nearest door, which gave on to the slaves' quarters and the garden. Cub, if he came at all, would likely come over the old earthworks at the foot of the garden, for he was used to that road, but Marcus had had word with the City gatekeepers in case he came the other way.

They reached the courtyard without meeting anyone, and while Esca went to set out a fresh tunic for his master, Marcus turned off along the colonnade towards the atrium. As he neared the doorway, a strange voice sounded behind it. The guest had arrived already, then.

'You are sure?' said the voice, a harsh, clipped voice, but pleasant. 'It would be a simple matter to send him up to the transit camp.'

And Uncle Aquila's voice replied: 'When I have not the space to lodge two guests at the same time, I will tell you. You are a fool, Claudius.'

There were two strangers in the long room with Uncle Aquila, both in uniform: one, resplendent under his coating of dust in the gilded bronze of a Legate; the other, standing a little behind him, evidently a Staff Officer. It seemed that they had only just arrived, for they had done no more than lay aside cloak and crested helmet. That much Marcus saw as he hesitated an instant on the threshold before his uncle looked round and saw him.

'Ah, you are back, Marcus,' said Uncle Aquila; and then, as he came forward to join the group, 'Claudius, I present to you my nephew Marcus. Marcus, this is my very old friend Claudius Hieronimianus, Legate of the Sixth Legion.'

Marcus raised his hand in salute to his uncle's friend, and found himself looking into a pair of long, jet-black eyes that seemed to have the sun behind them. The Legate was an Egyptian, and, he judged, of the old strain, for there was none of the Syrian softness in his face that he had seen so often in the faces of the men of the Nile. 'I am very much honoured to meet the Legate of Victrix,' he said.

The Legate's face crinkled into a smile that sent a thousand fine lines deepening about his mouth and eyes. 'And I am very glad to meet a kinsman of my ancient friend, all the more so because until today he might have been hatched out of a turtle's egg in the sand, for all the kith and kin that he had to my knowledge.' He indicated his companion. 'I make known to you Tribune Servius Placidus, of my staff.'

Marcus turned to the young officer, and instantly became painfully conscious of his twisted leg. Once or twice before he had met people who made him feel like that, and he did not find that it endeared them to him. The two greeted each other as custom demanded, but without warmth. The Staff Officer was about Marcus's own age, an extremely beautiful young man, with the graceful carriage, the oval face, and clustering hair that suggested Athenian ancestry. Smooth as a girl, Marcus thought with quick dislike; and the phrase seemed vaguely familiar. So did the name, Placidus, for that matter; but it was a common enough name, and anyhow, this was no time to be trailing marsh-light memories. Marcus supposed that until the guests went to wash off the dust of the journey, it was for him to hold the Tribune in conversation, leaving Uncle Aquila free to talk to his old friend.

Marcipor had brought in wine for the travellers, and when it had been poured, the two young men turned from their elders and drifted over to a sunlit window. For a while they made casual small-talk to each other; but as the moments went by, Marcus found it harder and harder to think of anything to say, while the Tribune appeared to have been born bored. At last Marcus, at his wits' end for another word, asked: 'You return to Rome with the Legate, or only as far as Regnum?'

'Oh, to Rome. Praise be to Bacchus, I am done with Britain once and for all when I board the galley in two days' time.'

'You have not, I take it, found Britain much to your taste?'

The other shrugged, and took a gulp of his wine. 'The girls are well enough, and the hunting. For the rest—Roma Dea! I can bear to leave it behind me!' A doubt seemed to strike him. 'You are not native born to this benighted province?'

'No,' Marcus said. 'I am not native born.' And then, feeling that he had been over abrupt, he added: 'Indeed, I have been out less than three years.'

'What possessed you to come out at all? You must have found the long journey very trying.'

There was nothing so very much in the words, but the tone in which they were spoken made Marcus, who was rather on edge because of Cub, feel his hackles rising. 'I came out to join my Legion,' he said coldly.

'Oh.' Placidus was slightly put out. 'A wound, then?'

'Yes.'

'I do not think that I have ever met you in the Tribune's Club, at home?'

'It would be strange if you had. I was a mere cohort centurion.' Marcus smiled, but all the contempt that the professional soldier could feel for the aristocrat playing at soldiers for a year was politely but thinly veiled behind his quiet words.

Placidus flushed a little. 'Really? Do you know, I should scarce have guessed it.' He returned the thrust, with the silken suggestion in his tone that really Marcus seemed almost civilized. 'Do I salute a brother of the Victrix? Or was it Capricorn or the charging boar with you?'

Before Marcus could answer, a low chuckle came from the Legate, whose back was towards them. 'For one who considers himself—I believe not without the right—a somewhat skilled hunter, you can be singularly unobservant of small things, my Placidus.' He said over his shoulder, 'I have mentioned the fact to you before. You will find the Signum of his Legion on his left wrist,' and he returned to his conversation with Uncle Aquila.

At his words, something had clicked in Marcus's mind, and as the Tribune's glance jerked down to the heavy gold bracelet that he always wore, he remembered. 'Smooth as a girl, but a skilled hunter,' Esca had said; and the name had been Placidus. His mouth felt dry with disgust, and the flicker of discomfiture—yes, and something very like envy—that showed for an instant in the other's face, gave him a quick satisfaction that was on Esca's account rather than his own.

Placidus recovered himself at once, and looked up with his faintly supercilious air. 'See what it is to serve under a Legate renowned for his appreciation of his junior officers,' he murmured. 'My dear Marcus, I do congratulate—' His eyes widened suddenly, and the soft, drawling voice sharpened into life. 'Roma Dea! A wolf!'

Before the words were out, Marcus had swung round. There in the colonnade doorway stood a brindled shape, savage head alertly raised, and eyes wary of the strangers within, whose unfamiliar scent had halted him on the threshold.

'Cub!' Marcus called. 'Cub!' and crouched down as, with a joyful bark, the brindled shape hurled itself upon him, fawning against his breast and singing as a crock sings on the boil. Cub's flanks were heaving with the speed that he had made to find his master, and he was frantically apologetic for having somehow lost him. And Marcus caught the great head in his hands, rubbing his thumbs into the hollows behind the pricked ears. 'So you have come back, brother,' he said. 'You have come back, Cub.'

'It is a wolf! It really is a wolf—and the brute behaving like a puppy!' said Placidus, in tones of disgusted unbelief above him.

'It seems that we are witnesses to a reunion. Surely we have come in a happy hour,' said the Legate.

Marcus freed himself from Cub's embraces and got to his feet. 'A reunion—yes, you could call it so,' he said.

Then Cub did a thing that he had never done before. He thrust his lowered head between Marcus's knees, as a dog will sometimes do with someone he perfectly trusts; and stood there contentedly, in the one position in which he was utterly defenceless and at his master's mercy.

And while he stood like that with slowly swinging tail, Marcus brought out the bronze-studded collar from the breast of his tunic, and bent to put it round his neck again.

'How long have you had him?' Placidus asked, watching with a gleam of interest as, his collar safely buckled on again, the young wolf shook himself violently, and sat down with lolling tongue and eyes half closed, propped against his master's leg.

'Since he was a very small cub, more than a year ago,' Marcus said, fondling a twitching ear.

'Then, if I am not mistaken, I saw him taken from the lair after his dam was killed! The painted barbarian who fetched him out claimed to be slave to a Marcus Aquila. I remember now.'

'You are not mistaken,' Marcus said quietly. 'The painted barbarian told me that story.'

Rather fortunately Stephanos appeared at that moment hovering in the doorway; and Uncle Aquila took the Legate's empty wine-cup from him. 'You will be wishing to soak off the dust of the road,' he said. 'We may live at the world's end, but the bath-water could not be hotter in Rome itself. Your own slaves will be awaiting you in your quarters, no doubt. That is so, Stephanos? Good. I look forward to our next meeting at dinner.'

X
Marching Orders

PRESENTLY, having bathed and changed, the four came together again in the small dining recess which opened from the atrium. This room was as austere as the rest of the house; the lime-washed walls bare of ornament save for the bronze-faced cavalry buckler with a pair of crossed javelins behind it, hanging opposite the entrance; the three couches about the table spread with beautifully dressed deer-skins instead of the usual quiltings and embroideries. And, ordinarily, the meals which Marcus and his uncle ate there were as austere as the room. But tonight was an occasion, and Sassticca had bestirred herself to produce a dinner worthy of it.

To Marcus, because Cub had come back, the whole room seemed to shimmer with a faint air of festival, as he glanced about him by the soft yellow light of the palm-oil lamps on the table. The future and the question of finding a livelihood could wait for the moment; he was pleasantly tired after a long day in the open; he had had a cold plunge and changed his rough tunic for one of soft white wool; and he was prepared even to keep a truce with Placidus, since Esca had only laughed when told of his arrival.

The main part of dinner was over. Uncle Aquila had just poured the second libation to the household gods, whose little bronze statues stood with the salt-cellars at the corners of the table; and Esca and the other slaves had gone their way. The soft, uncertain lamplight cast a delicate web of radiance over the table, making the red Samian bowls glow like coral, turning the withered yellow apples of last year's harvest to the fruit of the Hesperides, casting here a bloom of light over the fluted curve of a glass cup, kindling there a pointed scarlet flame in the heart of a squat flask of Falernian wine, strangely intensifying the faces of the men who leaned each on a left elbow round the table.

So far the two older men had had most of the conversation to themselves, talking over old days, old skirmishes, old frontier camps, old friends and enemies, while Marcus and Placidus put in a word from time to time, spoke to each other occasionally—the truce was holding quite well—but for the most part ate their dinner in silence.

And then, splashing water into the Falernian in his cup, Uncle Aquila asked, 'Claudius, how long since you left the Fretensis?'

'Eighteen years in August.'

'Jupiter!' said Uncle Aquila, reflectively. Suddenly he glared at his old friend. 'Eighteen years in August since you and I last sat at meat in the same mess; and yet you have been in Britain almost three, and made no attempt—not the faintest attempt—to come near me!'

'Nor you to come near me,' said Claudius Hieronimianus, helping himself to one of Sassticca's honey cakes and topping it with a cluster of raisins. He looked up from his plate, his strange face breaking into a winged, eager smile. 'Is it not most often so, when we follow the Eagles? We make a friend here and there, in Achaea, in Caesarea or Eburacum; and our ways part again, and we take remarkably few pains to keep in touch one with another. But if the gods who rule the destinies of men bend our paths to cross again—why then . . . '

'Why then we take up the old threads very much where we laid them down,' said Uncle Aquila. He raised his re-charged cup. 'I drink to the old threads. No, I don't. It is only old men who look backward all the time. I drink to the *renewing* of old threads.'

'Do you come and renew them at Eburacum, after I return,' said the Legate, as he set down his own cup.

'It may be that I will even do that—one day. It is all of five-and-twenty years since I was last at Eburacum, and I should be interested to see the place again.' Suddenly, bethinking himself of his manners, Uncle Aquila turned to include the young Tribune. 'I took a contingent of the Second up there in one of the Troubles; it was thus that I came to know the Station a little.'

'So?' Placidus contrived to sound bored and polite at the same time. 'That would be in the Hispana's time, of course. You would scarce recognize the Station now. It is really almost habitable.'

'The new generally build in stone where the old cleared the forest and built in wood,' said Uncle Aquila.

The Legate was staring reflectively into the heart of his wine. 'Sometimes at Eburacum it seems to me that the foundations of that old building lie uneasy beneath the new,' he said.

Marcus turned on him quickly. 'You mean, sir?'

'Eburacum is still—how shall I put it?—still more than a little ghost-ridden by the Ninth Legion. Oh, I do not mean that their spirits have wandered back from the fields of Ra, but the place is haunted, none the less. By the altars to Spanish gods that they set up and worshipped at; by their names and numbers idly scratched on walls; by British women whom they loved and children with Spanish faces whom they fathered. All this lying, as it were, like a sediment under the new wine of another Legion. Also they linger strongly, almost terrifyingly, in the minds of the people.' He made a small gesture with his open hand. 'It sounds little enough, put into words, and yet it can create an atmosphere which is unpleasantly strong. I am not an imaginative man, but I tell you that there have been times, when the mist comes down from the high moors, when I have more than half expected to see the lost Legion come marching home.'

There was a long silence, and a little shiver ran through the room like a little wind through long grass. Uncle Aquila's face was unreadable. Placidus's showed clearly his opinion of such vapourings. Then Marcus said: 'Have you any idea—any theory—as to what became of the Hispana, sir?'

The Legate looked at him shrewdly. 'Their fate has some importance for you?'

'Yes. My father was their First Cohort—Uncle Aquila's brother.'

The Legate turned his head. 'Aquila, I never knew that.'

'Oh yes,' said Uncle Aquila. 'Did I never mention him to you? He never came much in my way; we were at opposite ends of the family, with twenty years between us.'

The Legate nodded, and after seeming to consider a moment, gave his attention back to Marcus. 'There is, of course, the possibility that somewhere they were cut off and annihilated so completely that no survivors were left to carry back word of the disaster.'

'Oh, but surely, sir,' put in Placidus with a great show of deference, 'in a Province the size of Valentia, even in the whole of Caledonia, upward of four thousand men could not be destroyed without trace? Is it not far more likely that having had their fill of the Eagles, they merely butchered such of their officers as would not join with them, and deserted to the Tribes?'

Marcus said nothing; the Tribune was his uncle's guest; but his mouth shut into a hard, hot line.

'No, I do not think it particularly likely,' said the Legate.

But Placidus had not yet finished planting his sting. 'I stand corrected,' he said silkily. 'I was led to think it was the only possible explanation to the mystery, by the extremely unsavoury reputation the Hispana left behind them. But I am happy to find that I was at fault.'

'I am sure you are,' said the Legate, with a glint of humour.

'But you do not find the ambush theory a very likely one, either, I think, sir?' Marcus helped himself carefully to a cluster of raisins which he did not want.

'I do not greatly care to believe that any Legion of the Empire could have fallen so low, could have become such rotten fruit, as the other explanation would prove them.' The Legate hesitated, and his face seemed to grow keener; no longer the face of a man enjoying a pleasant meal, Marcus thought, but that of a soldier. He began to speak again, abruptly. 'There has been a rumour quite lately, along the Wall—incidentally giving me cause to wish profoundly that the Senate had not chosen this moment to recall me, though I leave behind a Camp Commandant and a First Cohort both knowing more of the game than I shall ever do—a rumour which, if it were true, would suggest that the Hispana did indeed go down fighting. Only market talk, but in such there is often a core of truth. The story runs that the Eagle has been seen; that it is receiving divine honours in some tribal temple in the far north.'

Uncle Aquila, who had been playing with his wine-cup, set it down so sharply that a drop splashed over on to his hand. 'Go on,' he said, as the other halted.

That is all; there is no more to add, no more to work on, which is the cursed part of it. But you take my point?'

'Oh yes, I take your point.'

'But I am afraid that I do not, not with any clearness,' Marcus said.

'A Legion which went rogue would probably hide its Eagle or hack it to pieces, or simply topple it into the nearest river. It would be most unlikely to have either the wish or the chance to set it up in the temple of some local godling. But an Eagle taken in war is in a very different case. To the Outland Tribes it must seem that they have captured the god of the Legion: and so they carry it home in triumph, with many torches and perhaps the sacrifice of a black ram, and house it in the temple of their own god to make the young men strong in war and help the grain to ripen. You see now?'

Marcus saw. 'What do you intend doing about it, sir?' he asked, after a moment.

'Nothing. For all the evidence that I can gather, there may be no shred of truth in the story.'

'But if there is?'

'There is still nothing that I can do about it.'

'But, sir, it is the Eagle; the Hispana's lost *Eagle*!' Marcus said, as though trying to drive an idea into the head of one half-witted.

'Eagle lost—honour lost; honour lost—all lost,' the Legate quoted. 'Oh yes, I know.' The regret in his voice sounded very final.

'More than that, sir.' Marcus was leaning forward, almost stammering in his sudden desperate eagerness. 'If the Eagle could be found and brought back, it—it might even mean the re-forming of the Legion.'

'That also I know,' said the Legate. 'And I know a thing which interests me even more. If trouble were to break out again in the north, a Roman Eagle in the hands of the Painted People might well become a weapon against us, owing to the power it would undoubtedly have to fire the minds and hearts of the Tribes. The fact remains that on a mere wind-blown rumour, I can take no action. To send an expeditionary force would mean open war. A whole Legion would scarcely win through, and there are but three in Britain.'

'But where a Legion could not get through, one man might; at least to find out the truth.'

'I agree, if the right man came forward. It would have to be one who knew the Northern Tribes and would be accepted by them and allowed to pass; and it would have, I think, to be one who cared very deeply for the fate of the Hispana's Eagle, else he would not be madman enough to thrust his head into such a hornets' nest.' He set down the cup that he had been turning between his fingers while he spoke. 'If I had had such a one among my young men, I would have given him his marching orders. The matter seems to me serious enough for that.'

'Send me,' Marcus said deliberately. His glance moved from one to another of the men round the table; then he turned to the curtained entrance and called, 'Esca! Hi! Esca!'

'Now by the—' began Uncle Aquila, and broke off, for once at a loss for words.

No one else spoke.

Quick footsteps came through the atrium, the curtain was drawn aside, and Esca appeared on the threshold. 'The Centurion called?'

In as few words as might be, Marcus told him what was toward. 'You will come with me, Esca?'

Esca moved forward to his master's side. His eyes were very bright in the lamplight. 'I will come,' he said.

Marcus turned back to the Legate. 'Esca was born and bred where the Wall runs now: and the Eagle was my father's. Between us we fulfil your conditions finely. Send us.'

The queer silence that had held the other men was shattered abruptly as Uncle Aquila banged an open hand on the table. This is lunacy! Sheer, unmitigated lunacy!'

'No, but it is not!' Marcus protested urgently. 'I have a perfectly sane and workable plan. In the name of Light, listen to me.'

Uncle Aquila drew breath for a blistering reply, but the Legate put in quietly, 'Let the boy speak, Aquila,' and he subsided with a snort.

For a long moment Marcus stared down at the raisins on his plate, trying to get the rough plan in his head into some sort of order. Trying also to remember exactly what Rufrius Galarius had told him that would help him now. Then he looked up and began to speak, eagerly, but with great care and long pauses, rather as though he were feeling his way, as indeed he was.

'Claudius Hieronimianus, you say that it would have to be one whom the Tribes would accept and allow to pass. A travelling oculist would be such a one. There are many sore eyes here in the north, and half the travellers on the roads are quack-salvers. Rufrius Galarius, who used to be a field surgeon with the Second,' (he glanced at his uncle with a half smile), 'once told me of a man well known to him, who even crossed the Western Waters and plied his trade through the length and breadth of Hibernia, and came back with a whole hide to tell the tale. And if an oculist's stamp will carry a man safely through Hibernia, of a surety it will carry Esca and me through what was once, after all, a Roman Province!' He sat up on the couch, almost glaring at the two older men. Placidus he had forgotten. 'It may be that we shall not be able to bring back the Eagle; but the gods willing, we will at least find out the truth or untruth of your rumour for you.'

There was a long pause. The Legate was looking at Marcus searchingly. Uncle Aquila broke the silence. 'An enterprising plan, but with one trifling objection to it, which you would appear to have overlooked.'

'And what is that?'

'You know rather less than an addled egg about the doctoring of sore eyes.'

'The same could be said for three out of four quacksalvers on the roads; but I shall go on a visit to Rufrius Galarius. Oh yes, he is a surgeon and not an oculist, I have not forgotten that; but he will know enough of the craft to put me in the way of getting a few needful salves, and give me some idea how to use them.'

Uncle Aquila nodded, as conceding the point.

And then, after a moment, the Legate asked abruptly, 'How serviceable is that leg of yours?'

Marcus had been expecting the question. 'Save that it would not do for the parade ground, very near as serviceable as ever it was,' he said. 'If we should have to run for it, it would load the dice against us, I grant you, but in strange country we should not stand a dog's chance on the run, anyway.'

Again the silence settled. And he sat with his head up, gazing from the Legate to his uncle and back again. They were summing up his chances, and he knew it: his chances of coming through, his chances of doing the thing that he went out to do. Moment by lengthening moment it became more desperately urgent to him that he should win his marching orders. The very life or death of his father's Legion was at stake; the Legion that his father had loved. And because he had loved his father with all the strength of his heart, the matter was a personal quest to him and shone as a quest shines. But beneath that shining lay the hard fact of a Roman Eagle in hands that might one day use it as a weapon against Rome; and Marcus had been bred a soldier. So it was in no mood of high adventure alone, but in a soberer and more purposeful spirit that he awaited the verdict.

'Claudius Hieronimianus, you said just now that had you had the right man among your young men, you would have sent him,' he said at last, able to keep silent no longer. 'Do I get my marching orders?'

It was his uncle who answered first, speaking to the Legate as much as to Marcus. 'The gods of my fathers forbid that I should hold back any kinsman of mine from breaking his neck in a clean cause, if he has a mind to.' His tone was distinctly caustic; but Marcus, meeting the disconcertingly shrewd eyes under his fierce jut of brow, realized that Uncle Aquila knew and understood very much more of what all this was meaning to him than he would somehow have expected.

The Legate said, 'You understand the position? The Province of Valentia, whatever it once was, whatever it may be again, is not worth an outworn sandal-strap today. You will be going out alone into enemy territory, and if you run into trouble, there will be nothing that Rome can or will do to help you.'

'I understand that,' Marcus said. 'But I shall not be alone. Esca goes with me.'

Claudius Hieronimianus bent his head. 'Go then. I am not your Legate, but I give you your marching orders.'

Later, after certain details had been thrashed out round the brazier in the atrium, Placidus said an unexpected thing. 'I almost wish that there was room for a third in this insane expeditionary force! If there were, Bacchus! I would leave Rome to fend for itself awhile, and come with you!'

For the moment his face had lost its weary insolence, and as the two young men looked at each other in the lamplight Marcus was nearer to liking him than he had been since they first met.

But the faint fellowship was short-lived, and Placidus killed it with a question. 'Are you sure that you can trust that barbarian of yours in a venture of this kind?'

'Esca?' Marcus said in surprise. 'Yes, quite sure.'

The other shrugged. 'Doubtless you know best. Personally I should not care to let my life hang by so slender a thread as the loyalty of a slave.'

'Esca and I—' Marcus began, and broke off. He was not going to make a circus show of his innermost feelings and Esca's for the amusement of such as Tribune Servius Placidus. 'Esca has been with me a long time. He nursed me when I was sick; he did everything for me, all the while that I was laid by with this leg.'

'Why not? He is your slave,' said Placidus carelessly.

Sheer surprise held Marcus silent for a moment. It was a long time since he had thought of Esca as a slave. 'That was not his reason,' he said. 'It is not the reason that he comes with me now.'

'Is it not? Oh, my Marcus, what an innocent you are; slaves are all—slaves. Give him his freedom and see what happens.'

'I will,' said Marcus. 'Thanks, Placidus, I will!'

When Marcus, with Cub at his heels, entered his sleeping-quarters that night, Esca, who was waiting for him as usual, laid down the belt whose clasps he had been burnishing, and asked: 'When do we start?'

Marcus closed the door and stood with his back against it. 'Probably the morn's morning—that is, for myself, at least. The details can wait awhile; but first you had best take this,' and he held out a slim papyrus roll he had been carrying.

Esca took it with a puzzled glance at his face, and unrolling it, he held it to the lamplight. And watching him, Marcus remembered suddenly and piercingly the moment that afternoon when he had taken off Cub's collar. Cub had come back to him; but Esca?

Esca looked up from the papyrus, and shook his head. 'Capitals are one thing,' he said, 'but I can make nothing of this script. What is it?'

'Your manumission—your freedom,' Marcus said. 'I made it out this evening, and Uncle Aquila and the Legate witnessed it. Esca, I ought to have given it to you long ago; I have been a completely unthinking fool, and I am sorry.'

Esca looked down to the thing in his hands once more, and again back to Marcus, as though he was not sure that he understood. Then he let the roll spring back on itself, and said very slowly: 'I am free? Free to go?'

'Yes,' Marcus said. 'Free to go, Esca.'

There was a long dragging silence. An owl cried somewhere afar off, with a note that seemed at once desolate and mocking. Cub looked from one to the other, and whined softly in his throat.

Then Esca said, 'Is it that you are sending me away?'

'No! It is for you to go, or stay, as you wish.'

Esca smiled, the slow grave smile that always seemed to come a little unwillingly to his face. 'Then I stay,' he said, and hesitated. 'It is perhaps not only I who think foolish thoughts because of the Tribune Placidus.'

'Perhaps.' Marcus reached out and set both hands lightly on the other's shoulders. 'Esca, I should never have asked you to come with me into this hazard when you were not free to refuse. It is like to prove a wild hunt, and whether or no we shall come back from it lies on the knees of the gods. No one should ask a slave to go with him on such a hunting trail; but—he might ask a friend.' He looked questioningly into Esca's face.

Esca tossed the slender papyrus roll on to the cot, and set his own hands over Marcus's. 'I have not served the Centurion because I was his slave,' he said, dropping unconsciously into the speech of his own people. 'I have served Marcus, and it was not slave-service . . . My stomach will be glad when we start on this hunting trail.'

Next morning, promising to pay his old friend another visit on his way north again in the autumn, the Legate departed with Placidus, escorted by half a squadron of Cavalry. And Marcus watched them ride away down the long road to Regnum and the waiting galleys, without quite the heart-ache that the sight would once have given him, before he set about his own preparations.

Esca's freedom caused less interest, and certainly less ill-feeling in the household than might have been expected. Sassticca, Stephanos, and Marcipor had all been born slaves, the children of slaves; and Esca, the freeborn son of a free chieftain, had never been one with them, even while he ate at their table. They were old and well content with things as they were; they had a good master, and slavery sat easy on them, like an old and familiar garment. Therefore they did not greatly begrudge freedom to Esca, accepting it as something that was likely to have happened one day or another—he and the young master having been, as Sassticca said, the two halves of an almond these many moons past, and only grumbled a little among themselves, for the pleasure of grumbling.

And anyhow, with Marcus going off—as the household had been told—about some sudden business for his uncle next day, and Esca going with him, no one, including Esca, had much time for raising difficulties or even for feeling them.

That evening, having made the few preparations that were needful, Marcus went down to the foot of the garden and whistled for Cottia. Lately she had always waited to be whistled for; and she came out to him among the wild fruit-trees under the old ramparts, with one end of her damson-coloured mantle drawn over her head against the heavy spring shower that had come with her.

He told her the whole story as briefly as might be, and she heard him out in silence. But her face seemed to grow sharper and more pointed in the way that he knew of old, and when he had finished, she said, 'If they want this Eagle back; if they fear that it may harm them, where it is, let them send someone else for it! Why need *you* go?'

'It was my father's Eagle,' Marcus told her, feeling instinctively that

that would make sense to her as the other reasons behind his going would never do. A personal loyalty needed no explaining, but he knew that it was quite beyond him to make Cottia understand the queer, complicated, wider loyalties of the soldier, which were as different from those of the warrior as the wave-break curve of the shield-boss was from the ordered pattern of his dagger sheath. 'You see, with us, the Eagle is the very life of a Legion; while it is in Roman hands, even if not six men of the Legion are left alive, the Legion itself is still in being. Only if the Eagle is lost, the Legion dies. That is why the Ninth has never been re-formed. And yet there must be more than a quarter of the Ninth who never marched north that last time at all, men who were serving on other frontiers, or sick, or left on garrison duty. They will have been drafted to other Legions, but they could be brought together again to make the core of a new Ninth. The Hispana was my father's first Legion, and his last, and the one he cared for most of all the Legions he served in. So you see . . . '

'It is to keep faith with your father, then?'

'Yes,' Marcus said, 'amongst other things. It is good to hear the trumpets sounding again, Cottia.'

'I do not think that I quite understand,' Cottia said. 'But I see that you must go. When will you start?'

'Tomorrow morning. I shall go down to Rufrius Galarius first, but Calleva will not come in my way again as I go north.'

'And when will you come back?'

'I do not know. Maybe, if all goes well, before winter.'

'And Esca goes with you? And Cub?'

'Esca,' Marcus said. 'Not Cub. I leave Cub in your charge, and you must come and see him every day and talk to him about me. In that way neither of you will forget about me before I come back.'

Cottia said, 'We have good memories, Cub and I. But I will come every day.'

'Good.' Marcus smiled at her, trying to coax a smile in return. 'Oh, and Cottia, do not mention the Eagle to anyone. I am supposed to be going on business for my uncle; only—I wanted you to know the truth.'

The smile came then, but it was gone again at once. 'Yes, Marcus.'

'That is better. Cottia, I cannot stay any longer, but before I go, there is one thing else that I want you to do for me.' As he spoke he pulled off the heavy gold bracelet with its engraved signum. The skin showed almond white where it had been, on the brown of his wrist. 'I cannot wear this where I am going; will you keep it safe for me until I come back to claim it?'

She took it from him without a word, and stood looking down at it in her hands. The light caught the Capricorn badge and the words beneath. '*Pia Fidelis*.' Very gently she wiped the rain-drops from the gold, and stowed it under her mantle. 'Yes, Marcus,' she said again. She was standing very straight and still, very forlorn, and with the darkness of her mantle covering her bright hair as it had done when he first saw her.

He tried to think of something to say; he wanted to thank her for the things that he was grateful for; but with everything that was in him reaching out to what lay ahead, somehow he could not find the right words, and he would not give Cottia words that meant nothing. At the last moment he would have liked to tell her that if he never came back, she was to keep his bracelet; but maybe it were better that he told Uncle Aquila. 'You must go now,' he said. 'The Light of the Sun be with you, Cottia.'

'And with you,' said Cottia. 'And with you, Marcus. I shall be listening for you to come back—for you to come down here to the garden foot and whistle for me again, when the leaves are falling.'

Next instant she had put aside a dripping blackthorn spray and turned from him; and he watched her walking away without a backward glance, through the sharp thin rain.

XI
Across the Frontier

FROM Luguvallium in the west to Segedunum in the east, the Wall ran, leaping along with the jagged contours of the land; a great gash of stone-work, still raw with newness. Eighty miles of fortresses, mile-castles, watch-towers, strung on one great curtain wall, and backed by the vallum ditch and the coast-to-coast Legionary road; and huddled along its southern side, the low sprawl of wine shops, temples, married quarters, and markets that always gathered in the wake of the Legions. A great and never-ceasing smother of noise: voices, marching feet, turning wheels, the ring of hammer on armourer's anvil, the clear calling of trumpets over all. This was the great Wall of Hadrian, shutting out the menace of the north.

On a morning in early summer, two travellers who had been lodging for some days in a dirty and dilapidated inn close under the walls of Chilurnium presented themselves at the Praetorian gate of the fortress, demanding to pass through to the north. There was not much coming and going across the frontier, save for the military patrols; but such as there was, hunters for the most part, or trappers with chained wild beasts for the arena, or a stray fortune-teller or quack-salver, had all to pass through the great fortresses of the Wall.

They were a faintly disreputable couple, mounted on small ex-cavalry mares of the Arab type which had certainly seen better days. The Legions could always find a steady market for their old mounts, cheap and well trained, and with several years of working life in them. They were to be seen everywhere along the Empire's roads, and there was nothing about these two to suggest that they had been bought, not for money, but by a few words signed by the Legate of the Sixth Legion, on a sheet of papyrus.

Esca had made very little real difference to his appearance, for he had no need; he had returned to the dress of his own people, and that was all. But with Marcus it was quite otherwise. He also had taken to British dress, and wore long bracco of saffron wool, cross-gartered to the knee, under a tunic of faded and distinctly dirty violet cloth. Bracco were comfortable in a cold climate, and many of the wandering herbalists and suchlike wore them. But the dark cloak flung back over his shoulders hung in folds that were foreign and exotic, and he wore a greasy Phrygian cap of scarlet leather stuck rakishly on the back of his head. A small silver talisman shaped like an open hand covered the brand of Mithras on his forehead, and he had grown a beard. Being little over a month old, it was not a very good beard; but such as it was, he had drenched it in scented oils. He looked much like any other wandering quack-salver, though somewhat young, despite the beard; and there was certainly no trace about him of the centurion of the Eagles he had once been. His box of salves, provided for him by Rufrius Galarius, was stowed in the pack behind Esca's saddlepad, and with it his oculist's stamp, a slab on which the hardened salves were ground, which proclaimed in engraved letters round the edge, 'The Invincible Anodyne of Demetrius of Alexandria, for all kinds of defective eyesight'.

The sentries passed them through without trouble into the fortress of Chilurnium, into the world of square-set barrack lines, and life ordered by trumpet calls that was familiar as a home-coming to Marcus. But at the Northern Gate, as they reached it, they met a squadron of the Tungrian Cavalry Cohort that formed the garrison coming up from exercise. They reined aside and sat watching while the squadron trotted by; and that was when the pull of long-familiar custom laid hold of Vispania, Marcus's mare, and as the tail of the squadron passed she flung round with a shrill whinny, and tried to follow. Because of the old wound, Marcus had little power in his right knee, and it was a few trampling and sweating moments before he could master her and swing her back to the gate, and when he finally managed it, it was to find the decurion of the gate guard leaning against the guardhouse wall, holding his sides and yelping with laughter, while his merry men stood grinning in the background.

'Never bring a stolen cavalry nag into a cavalry barracks,' said the decurion amiably, when he had had his laugh out. 'That's good advice, that is.'

Marcus, still soothing his angry and disappointed mare, demanded with a cool hauteur that Aesculapius himself could scarcely have bettered, had he been accused of being a horse-thief, 'Do you suggest that I, Demetrius of Alexandria, *the* Demetrius of Alexandria, am in the habit of stealing cavalry horses? Or that if I were, I should not have had the wisdom to steal a better one than this?'

The decurion was a cheerful soul, and the small grinning crowd that had begun to gather spurred him on to further efforts. He winked. 'You can see the brand on her shoulder, as plain as a pilum shaft.'

'If you cannot also see as plain as a pilum shaft that the brand has been cancelled,' Marcus retorted, 'then you must be in dire need of my Invincible Anodyne for all kinds of defective eyesight! I can let you have a small pot for three sesterces.'

There was a roar of laughter. 'Better have two pots, Sextus,' somebody called out. 'Remember the time you didn't see that Pict's legs sticking out from under the furze bush?'

The decurion evidently did remember the Pict's legs, and would rather not, for though he laughed with the rest, his laughter rang a trifle hollow, and he made haste to change the subject. 'Are there not enough sore eyes for your salving in the Empire, that you must needs go jaunting beyond the Pale to look for more?'

'Maybe I am like Alexander, in search of fresh worlds to conquer,' said Marcus modestly.

The decurion shrugged. 'Every man to his own taste. The old world is good enough for me—with a whole hide to enjoy it in!'

'Lack of enterprise. That is the trouble with you.' Marcus sniffed. 'If I had been so lacking, should I now be *the* Demetrius of Alexandria, the inventor of the Invincible Anodyne, the most celebrated oculist between Caesarea and—'

'*Cave!* Here's the Commander,' somebody said. Instantly such of the group who had no business there melted away, and the rest straightened themselves on their feet and became painfully efficient. And Marcus, still discoursing loudly on his own importance and the healing powers of the Invincible Anodyne, was hustled out through the dark crowded arch of the gate-house, with Esca, solemn-faced, in his wake.

The Frontier was behind them, and they rode out into the one-time Province of Valentia.

Chilurnium must be a pleasant place for the garrison, Marcus thought, as his quick glance took in the shallow wooded vale, the quiet river. There would be fishing and bathing here—when no trouble was brewing—and good hunting in the forest; a very different life from that of the upland fortresses further west, where the Wall crossed bare moorland, leaping from crest to crest of the black hills. But his own mood just now was for the high hills, the tearing wind, and the curlews crying, and as soon as Chilurnium was well behind, he was glad to swing westward following the directions given them by a hunter before they set out, leaving the quiet vale for the distant lift of damson-dark uplands that showed through a break in the oakwoods.

Esca had ranged up alongside him, and they rode together in companionable silence, their horses' unshod hooves almost soundless on the rough turf. No roads in the wilderness and no shoe-smiths, either. The country south of the Wall had been wild and solitary enough, but the land through which they rode that day seemed to hold no living thing save the roedeer and the mountain fox; and though only the man-made wall shut it off from the south, the hills here seemed more desolate and the distances darker.

It was almost like seeing a friendly face in a crowd of strangers when, long after noon, they came dipping down over a shoulder of the high moors into a narrow green glen through which a thread of white water purled down over shelving stones, where the rowan-trees were in flower, filling the warm air with the scent of honey. A good place to make a halt, it seemed to them, and they off-saddled accordingly, and having watered the horses, and seen them begin to graze, they drank from their cupped hands and sprawled at their ease on the bank. There was wheaten biscuit and dried fish in the saddle-pack, but they left it there, having long since learned—Marcus on the march and Esca on the hunting trail—that morning and evening were the times for food.

Esca had stretched himself full length, with a sigh of content, under the leaning rowan-trees; but Marcus lay propped on one elbow to watch the little torrent out of sight round the shoulder of the glen. The silence of the high hills was all about them, made up of many small sounds: the purling of the water, the murmur of wild bees among the rowan blossom overhead, the contented cropping of the two mares. It was good to be up here, Marcus thought, after the long contriving of ways and means, the days of hanging along the Wall, kicking one's heels and listening for the faintest breath of a rumour that had evidently died as a stray wind dies, since it came to the Legate's ears. Up here in the silence of the hills, the strivings and impatiences of the past few weeks that had seemed to web him round all fell away, leaving him face to face with his task.

They had worked out a rough plan of campaign weeks ago, in Uncle Aquila's study, which now seemed a whole world away. It was very simple: merely to work their way north in a series of casts that would take them from coast to coast each time, in the manner of a hound cutting across a scent. In that way they must cut the trail of the Eagle—and the Legion, too, for that matter—at every cast; and surely somewhere, if they kept their eyes and ears open, they must pick it up. It had all seemed fairly simple in Uncle Aquila's study, but out here in the great emptiness beyond the Frontier it seemed a gigantic task.

And yet its seeming hopelessness was a challenge that he took up joyously. For the moment he forgot the sober facts of his search, and remembered only the personal quest. And sitting there in the little sun-warmed glen, his heart lifted suddenly and almost painfully to the crowning moment when he would carry the lost Eagle back into Eburacum, knowing that his father's Legion would live again, its name clean before the world; and surely, surely, no god worth the serving would be so unjust as not to see that his father knew that he had kept faith.

Esca broke the silence presently. 'So the contriving is done with,' he said, speaking apparently into the bee-loud rowan branches above his head, 'and the hunting is begun at last.'

'The hunting-ground is a wide one,' Marcus said, and turned to look down at his companion. 'And who knows into what strange covers the hunt may lead us? Esca, you know this sort of country better than I do, and if the people are not of your tribe, at least they are nearer to you than to me. They are people of the shield-boss, and not of the pattern on my dagger sheath. Therefore, if you tell me to do a thing, I will do it, without clamouring to know why.'

'There may be wisdom in that,' Esca said.

Presently Marcus shifted, looking up at the sun. 'Soon we must be moving on, I suppose, lest we sleep in the woods tonight, seeing that we have not yet found this village that the man at the inn spoke of'; for even south of the Wall one did not go to a strange village after dark, unless one was tired of life.

'We shall not have far to seek,' Esca said, 'if we follow the stream downward.'

Marcus quirked an eyebrow at him. 'What tells you that?'

'Smoke. Over the shoulder of the hill yonder; I caught the blur of it against the birch-trees, a while back.'

'It could be heath fire.'

'It was hearth fire,' Esca said with simple conviction.

Marcus relaxed again on the grass. Then, as though on a sudden impulse, he drew his dagger and fell to cutting small square turfs from the fine burnside grass, loosening and lifting them with infinite care. Having cut as many as he wanted, he drew the arching briars and the hemlock leaves back over the scars, and shifting further up the bank, began to build them one a-top the other.

'What is it that you do?' Esca asked, after watching him in silence for a while.

'I build an altar,' Marcus said, 'here in the place of our first halt.'

'To what god?'

'To my own god. To Mithras, the Light of the Sun.'

Esca was silent again. He did not offer to help with this altar to Marcus's god, who was not his; but he drew closer and sat hugging his knees and looking down at the work. Marcus went on trimming and shaping the sods; the crumbling soil was faintly warm under his fingers, and a low-hanging rowan branch cast ring-streaked shadows over his intent hands. When the altar was finished and squared to his satisfaction, he cleaned and sheathed his dagger, and brushed away the scatter of loose soil from the surrounding grass with his palms. Then with scraps of birch bark and dry sticks and sprigs of dead heather—Esca helped him gather these—he built a small fire on the altar top. He built it very carefully, hollowing it slightly in the middle, as though to make a nest for something that he loved, and breaking a creamy curd of blossom from the rowan spray, nipped floweret from floweret, and scattered them all over. Lastly, he took from the breast of his tunic his olive-wood bird—his olive-wood bird. It was polished smooth and dark with years of carrying; rather a clumsy and ridiculous little bird, now that he came to look at it, but dear to him; and its dearness made it a fitting sacrifice. It had been part of his life, something that continued back from him to the wild olive-tree in the loop of the stream, and the life and places and things and people that the wild olive-tree belonged to. And suddenly, as he laid it in the hollow among the tiny stars of the rowan blossom, it seemed to him that with it—in it—he was laying the old life down too.

He held out his hand to Esca for the flint and steel which he always carried on him.

The golden sparks that he struck out dropped on to the tinder-dry scraps of birch bark, and hung there an instant like jewels; then, as he blew on them, nursing them to life, they flared up into crackling flame; a flower of flame with the olive-wood bird sitting at its heart like a dove on her nest.

He fed the fire carefully, with bits of wood from a fallen branch that Esca brought him.

XII
The Whistler in the Dawn

ALL that summer Marcus and Esca wandered through the abandoned Province of Valentia, crossing and recrossing from coast to coast, and making steadily northward. They ran into no serious trouble, for Rufrius Galarius had spoken the truth when he said that the oculist's stamp was a talisman that would carry its owner anywhere. In Valentia, as in the rest of Britain, there were many people with marsh ophthalmia, and Marcus did his best for those who came to him for help, with the salves which the old field surgeon had shown him how to use. They were good salves, and Marcus had common sense and gentle hands and the craftsman's dislike of a job ill done, and so he succeeded better than most of the few quack-salvers who had passed that way. The tribesmen were not exactly friendly; it was not in them to be friendly towards men not of their own tribe, but they were certainly not unfriendly. There was generally somebody in each village who would give them food and shelter at the day's end; and always, if the way was difficult to find or dangerous to follow, a hunter from one village would act as their guide to the next. They would have paid well, too, for Marcus's skill, with a palmful of jet beads, a fine javelin-head or a dressed beaver skin—things which would have fetched many times the value of the salves, south of the Wall. But Marcus was not in this adventure to make a fortune, nor did he wish to jingle round the country loaded like a trader, and he shelved the difficulty by saying to each offer, 'Keep it for me until I come again on my way south.'

Late summer came, and the rowan-trees that had been in new flower when Marcus built his altar in the glen of their first halt were heavy now with flaming bosses of berries; and on an August noon they sat side by side, looking down through the birchwoods to the great firth which half cut Valentia from what lay beyond. It was a day like a trumpet blast, the wooded hills swimming in the heat, and at their backs the mares stamped and fretted, swishing their tails against the cloud of flies that beset them. Marcus sat with his hands locked round his updrawn knees and stared out across the firth. The sun was hot on the nape of his neck, scorching his shoulders through the cloth of his tunic, and he would have dearly liked to copy Esca, lying on his stomach beside him, who had discarded his tunic altogether and now went stripped to the waist like the Painted People. But to ride round the country in his bracco would have been beneath the dignity of Demetrius of Alexandria, and he supposed that he must continue to stew in his woollen tunic.

He heard the bees zooming among the bell-heather of the clearing, smelled the warm aromatic scents of the sun-baked birch-woods overlaying the cold saltiness of the sea; singled out one among the wheeling gulls and watched it until it became lost in a flickering cloud of sun-touched wings. But he was not really conscious of any of these things.

'We have missed the trail somehow,' he said abruptly. 'It is in my mind that we have come too far north. We are all but up to the old frontier now.'

'The Eagle is surely more likely to be found beyond the northern wall,' said Esca. 'The tribesmen would scarcely leave it in territory that was even in name a Roman province. They will have carried it away into one of their holy places.'

'I know,' Marcus said. 'But the traces should be in Valentia; and if the accounts of Caledonia that we have heard are true, we stand small chance of sighting our quarry among the mountains, unless we have some trail to follow. We shall simply wander up through Caledonia until we fall into the sea off the northernmost headland.'

'A holy place is apt to spread signs of itself abroad, for those, having eyes to see, who come even a little near,' Esca suggested.

Marcus sat silent for a moment, still hugging his knees. Then he said, 'When there is nothing, nothing at all, to guide a man in his choice, then it is time to lay the choice on the gods,' and fishing in the breast of his tunic, he brought out a small leather bag, and from the bag, a sesterce.

Esca rolled over and sat up, the blue warrior patterns moving on arms and breast as the muscles slid under his brown skin.

The disc of silver lay in Marcus's palm, showing the head of Domitian crowned with laurel; a small thing to hold their destinies. 'Heads we push on, ships we try a cast back,' Marcus said, and sent the coin spinning into the air. He caught it on the back of his hand, clapping the other over it, and for an instant their eyes met, questioningly. Then Marcus lifted the covering hand and they looked down at the winged victory on the obverse side of the coin, which had been called 'Ships' from the days of the Republic, when the design had been the prow of a galley.

'We turn south again,' Marcus said.

Turn south they did; and a few nights later they encamped in the old fort which Agricola had raised at Trinomontium, the Place of Three Hills.

Thirty years ago, when Valentia was a Roman province in more than name, before Agricola's work had been all undone by meddling from the Senate, Trinomontium had been a busy fort. A double cohort had drilled in the wide forum and slept in the barrack rows; there had been many horses in the stables, cavalry manoeuvres on the gentle southern slope below the ramparts, with the riders crested with tossing yellow plumes, the usual baths and wineshops and the turf bothies of the women's quarters; and over all, the crested sentries marching to and fro. But now the wild had flowed in again; grass covered the cobbles of the streets, timber roofs had fallen in, and the red sandstone walls stood gaunt and empty to the sky. The wells were choked with the debris of thirty autumns, and an elder-tree had taken root in one corner of the roofless shrine where once had stood the cohort's standard and the altars of its gods, and had thrust a jagged gap in the wall to make room for itself. In all that desolation the only living creature that Marcus and Esca found as they wandered through it in the heavy stillness of the summer evening, was a lizard basking on a fallen block of stone, which darted off like a whip-lash at their approach. Looking down at the stone, Marcus saw roughly carved on it the charging boar of the Twentieth Legion. Somehow the sight brought the desolation home to him very sharply.

'If ever the Legions come north again, they will have a fine building job on their hands,' he said.

The hoof-beats of their led mounts sounded unnaturally loud in the silence; and when they halted at a crossways, the silence that came rushing in on them seemed almost menacing.

'It is in my heart that I wish we had pushed on to the next village,' Esca said, half under his breath. 'I do not like this place.'

'Why not?' Marcus asked. 'You did not mind when we were here before.' For they had turned aside to look at the derelict fort on their way north, hoping against hope that it might hold some clue for them.

'That was at noon. Now it is evening, and soon the light will go.'

'We shall do well enough with a fire,' Marcus said in surprise. 'We have slept out time and again since we started on this venture, and had no trouble while the fire burned. And surely the only creatures likely to lair in these ruins are wild pig, and we have seen no signs of any such.'

'I have not been a hunter since first I could hold a spear without growing used to sleeping in the wild,' Esca said, in the same suppressed voice. 'It is not the forest folk that make me cold between my shoulders.'

'What, then?'

Esca laughed, and broke off his laughter midway. 'I am a fool. Maybe the ghosts of a lost Legion.'

Marcus, who had been gazing out over the grass-grown forum, looked round quickly. 'It was a cohort of the Twentieth that served here, never the Ninth.'

'How do we know where the Ninth served,' Esca said, 'after they marched into the mist?'

Marcus was silent for a moment. He came of a breed that did not trouble unduly about ghosts, but he knew that with Esca it was quite otherwise. 'I do not think that they would bring us any harm, if they did come,' he said at last. 'It seemed to me that this would be a good place to sleep, especially with the curlews calling rain as they are this evening; but if you say the word, we will find a sheltered place among the hazel woods, and sleep there.'

'I should be ashamed,' Esca said simply.

Marcus said, 'Then we had best set about choosing our quarters.'

They settled finally on one end of a barrack row, where the roof had not fallen in, and the few feet of timber and rotten thatch made a shelter from the coming rain. There they unloaded the mares, rubbed them down and turned them loose in the long building, in the British fashion; after which Esca went off to gather a few armfuls of fodder, and bracken for bedding, while Marcus collected a stock of the rotten timber which lay about, and got a fire going, watched with close attention by Vipsania and Minna.

Later that evening the tumble-down shelter bore a much more

cheerful aspect; a small fire burned brightly at its entrance, the smoke finding its own way round the bat-wing edge of the rotten thatch, into the darkening sky; and the piled bracken in the far corner spread with the sheepskins which by day were folded to serve as saddles. Marcus and Esca ate some of the food which they had brought with them from last night's village, coarse barley bannock and strips of strong part-smoked deer meat, which they broiled over the fire; and afterwards Esca lay down at once to sleep.

But Marcus sat for a while beside the fire, watching the sparks fly upward, hearing nothing but the occasional shifting of the mares in the further shadows. From time to time he bent forward to put more wood on the fire; otherwise he sat quite unmoving, while, on the piled bracken against the wall, Esca slept the quiet, light sleep of the hunter. Looking at him, Marcus wondered whether he would have had the courage to lie quietly down to sleep on what he believed to be haunted ground. With the full dark, the rain came up, soft, heavy swathes of rain; and the swish and whisper of it on the rotten thatch seemed to deepen the utter desolation of this place that had once been living and was now dead. Marcus found himself listening with straining ears to the silence, his thoughts growing full of crowding ghosts that came and went along the rampart walls and through the forsaken forum, until it was all he could do to make himself bank the fire and lie down beside Esca.

Normally when they camped in the wild they took turns to sit up and keep the fire in while the other slept, but here, with four walls round them and a pile of thorn branches across the door to keep the horses in, there could be no need for that. For a while he lay wakeful, every nerve jumping with a queer expectancy; but he was tired, and the spread skins and the fragrant, high-piled bracken were very comfortable. And before long he fell asleep, and dreamed that he was watching Legionaries at pilum practice, quite ordinary Legionaries, save that between their chin-straps and the curves of their helmets—they had no faces.

He woke to a sense of light, steady pressure below his left ear, woke quietly and completely as people roused in that way always do, and opened his eyes to see that the fire had sunk to a few red embers and Esca was crouching beside him in the first faint pallor of the dawn. The evil taste of the dream was still in his mouth. 'What is it?' he whispered.

'Listen.'

Marcus listened and felt a small unpleasant chill trickling up his spine. His own eerie fancies of last night returned to him uncomfortably. Maybe Esca had been right about this place, after all. For somewhere in the abandoned fort, somebody—or some *thing*—was whistling the tune of a song that he knew well. He had marched to it more than once, for though an old song, it was a favourite with the Legions, and for no particular reason had outlived many and many that they picked up and marched to for a few months and then forgot.

Oh when I joined the Eagles,
(As it might be yesterday)
I kissed a girl at Clusium
Before I marched away.

The familiar words joined themselves to the tune in Marcus's head, as he rose silently, and stood getting his stiffened leg into marching order. The whistling was drawing nearer, becoming every moment more clearly recognizable:

A long march, a long march, and twenty years in store,
When I left my girl at Clusium, beside the threshing-floor.

There were many more verses, all describing girls that the maker of the song had kissed in different parts of the Empire; but as Marcus went purposefully to the doorway, and Esca stooped to drag aside the thorn branches, the whistling ceased, and a voice—a husky voice with a queer, brooding quality in it, as though the singer's thoughts were turned inward and backward—took up the song at the last verse of all:

The girls of Spain were honey-sweet,
And the golden girls of Gaul:
And the Thracian maids were soft as birds
To hold the heart in thrall.
But the girl I kissed at Clusium
Kissed and left at Clusium,
The girl I kissed at Clusium
I remember best of all.

A long march, a long march, and twenty years behind,
But the girl I kissed at Clusium comes easy to my mind.

Rounding the end of the barrack row, they came face to face with the singer, who was standing in the Sinister Gate. Marcus had not known what he had expected to see—perhaps nothing, which would have been worst of all. But what he did see pulled him up in astonishment, for the man—it was no ghost—standing with his hand on the bridle of a rough-coated pony, was one of the Painted People, such as he had lived among all summer.

The man had checked at sight of Marcus and Esca, and stood looking at them warily, with upflung head, like a stag when it scents danger; his hunting-spear held as though for instant attack. For a moment they surveyed each other in the dawn light, then Marcus broke the silence. By now he could make himself understood without much trouble in the dialect of the Northern Tribes. 'It has been a good hunting, friend,' he said, pointing to the carcass of a half-grown roe-buck that was slung across the pony's back.

'Good enough until I can do better,' said the man. 'There is none to spare.'

'We have food of our own,' Marcus said. 'Also we have a fire, and unless it seems good to you to build your own or eat your meal raw, you are welcome to share it.'

'What do you here, in the Place of Three Hills?' asked the man suspiciously.

'Camp for the night. Not knowing how far we might be from a village, and judging that rain was on the way, it seemed to us a better sleeping-place than the open moor. Is not the Place of Three Hills free to all, or only to the raven and the lizard—and yourself?'

For an instant the man did not answer, then slowly and deliberately he reversed the spear in his hand, so that he was carrying it with head trailing, as a man carries his spear when he comes in peace. 'I think that you will be the Healer of sore eyes, of whom I have heard?' he said.

'I am.'

'I will come and share your fire.' He turned and whistled, and in answer to the summons, two swift brindled hunting dogs came springing up through the bracken to join him.

A few moments later they were back in their shelter, and the small, shaggy pony, free of his burden now, was hitched to a fallen beam beside the door. Esca threw a birch branch on to the red embers, and as the silver bark blackened and flared up, Marcus turned for a better look at the stranger. He was a middle-aged man, lean and powerful, his eyes wary and a little furtive under the wild hair that was coarse and grey as a badger's pelt; he wore nothing but an ochre-coloured kilt, and in the light of the fire his body and arms were covered all over with bands of tattooing, after the manner of the Painted People. Even on his cheeks and forehead and the wings of his nostrils the blue curves and spandrils showed. The dogs were nosing at the body of the deer which lay at his feet, and as their master stooped to cuff them away, the firelight fell strongly slantwise across his forehead, throwing into relief the scar of a curiously shaped brand, just between the brows.

Esca squatted down by the fire and put more strips of smoked meat to broil in the hot ash, then sat with his arms across his knees and his spear within easy reach, watching the stranger under his brows; while the stranger, kneeling over the flattened carcass of the buck—which had been gralloched already—began to skin it with the long hunting-knife which he drew from his raw-hide belt. Marcus also watched him, though less obviously. He was puzzled. The man seemed a tribesman like any other of his kind; yet he had sung 'The Girl Kissed at Clusium' in good Latin; and at some time, years ago to judge by the faintness of the scar, he had been initiated into the Raven Degree of Mithras.

He might of course have learned the song from the Legionaries who had served here; he was fully old enough for that. Mithras sometimes found followers in unexpected places. But taking the two things together, it was unusual, to say the least of it, and Marcus had been looking for something unusual all summer.

The hunter had laid back a large flap of hide from the flank and haunch of the buck. He cut thick collops of meat from it, and a shapeless lump with the hair still on, which he flung to the dogs who crouched beside him. And while they fought over it, snarling and worrying, he heaved up what remained of the carcass and flung it across a half-rotten tie-beam, where it hung, the dangling legs out of reach of the hounds. He put the collops that he had cut for his own eating to broil in the hot ash, rubbed his hands on his kilt, for they were juicy, and sitting back on his heels, peered from Marcus to Esca and back again with a strange intent look, as though their faces—Marcus's at all events—had some meaning for him which he could not fathom.

'I thank you for the heat of your fire,' he said, speaking less roughly than he had done before. 'It is in my heart that I might have been swifter to reverse my spear; but I had not thought to find any before me, here in the Place of Three Hills.'

'I can well believe that,' Marcus said.

'Aye, in all the years that I have come here on the hunting trail, never until now have I found any man here before me.'

'And now you have found two. And since we share the same fire,' said Marcus with a smile, 'surely we should know each other's names. I am Demetrius of Alexandria, a travelling oculist, as you seem to know, and this, my friend and spear-bearer, is Esca Mac Cunoval, of the tribe of the Brigantes.'

'The Bearers of the blue war-shield. You have heard maybe of my tribe, if not of me,' added Esca, and his teeth flashed white in his tanned face as he lifted his head and smiled.

'I have heard of your tribe—a little, yes,' said the stranger, with, as it seemed to Marcus, a hint of grim amusement in his voice, though there was no amusement in his gaunt face, as he blinked at the fire. 'For myself, I am called Guern, and I am a hunter, as you see. My rath lies upwards of a day's trail to the west, and I come here sometimes for the sake of the fat deer to be had in the hazel woods yonder.'

Silence fell between the three, while the daylight grew around them, and the dogs snarled and tussled over their lump of meat. Then Marcus, idly peeling a bit of stick, began half under his breath to whistle the tune that had so startled him an hour before. Out of the corner of his eyes he was aware that Guern had started and looked towards him. For a few moments he continued with the peeling and the whistling, and then, seeming suddenly to tire of his pastime, tossed the stick into the fire and looked up. 'Where did you learn that song, friend Guern the Hunter?'

'Where else but here?' said Guern. For an instant his face took on a look of blank stupidity, but Marcus had an idea that behind it he was thinking furiously. 'When this was a Roman fort there were many Roman songs sung here. That one I learned from a centurion who used to hunt boar with me. I was only a boy, but I have a good memory.'

'Did you pick up any Latin, other than the words of the song?' Marcus shot at him, speaking in that language.

The hunter made as if to answer, checked, and looked at him an instant slantwise, under down-twitched brows. Then he spoke in Latin, very slowly, like a man fumbling back across the years for a speech that comes half-forgotten to his tongue. 'A few words I remember still, such words as soldiers use.' Then, dropping back into the Celtic speech, 'Where did *you* learn that song?'

'I have followed my trade in fortress towns before now,' Marcus said, 'and ones that were not deserted to the wild boar, as the Place of Three Hills. I have a quick ear for a tune.'

Guern leaned forward to turn the cooking meat with his hunting-knife. 'Yet surely you can have been but a short while at this trade you practise. There are not many years under that beard of yours.'

'Maybe there are more than there seem,' Marcus said, and stroked the beard tenderly. It had grown well in the months since he came north, though it was still very clearly a young beard. 'Moreover, I began early, following my father's footsteps in the way of sons . . . And talking of this trade of mine, are there any that have sore eyes in your village?'

Guern poked experimentally at the meat. He seemed to be making up his mind about something; and after a few moments he looked up as though he had made it. 'I am an outdweller, living to myself and my family,' he said, 'and we have no sore eyes for your healing. None the less, if you wait until my hunting is done, you are very welcome to come with me; and we will eat salt together, and later I will set you on your way to another village. That is for the place that you have given me at your fire.'

For an instant, Marcus hesitated; then, with the instinct still strong upon him that this man was not what he seemed, he said, 'All ways are alike to us. We will come, and gladly.'

'There is more flesh on my kill than I had thought,' said Guern, suddenly and shamefacedly, and stood up, knife in hand.

So the three of them ate fresh broiled buck together, in good fellowship; and a day later, when Guern's hunting was done, they set out, Marcus and Esca riding, and the hunter leading his own pony, across whose back was bound the carcass of a great red stag, and the dogs cantering ahead. Swishing through the rain-wet bracken they went, over the heathery shoulder of three-headed Eildon and away into the west, leaving the red sandstone fort deserted once again to the creatures of the wild.

XIII
The Lost Legion

GUERN'S homestead, when they reached it, proved to be a bleak huddle of turf huts high among the dark moors. A small boy herding wild-eyed cattle up from the drinking-pool to the night-time shelter of the cattle-yard greeted their appearance with a kind of fascinated dismay. Evidently strangers were not in his scheme of things, and while stealing constant sly peeps at them, he took care to keep the great herd bull, which he managed with casual pokes and slaps, between him and danger, as they went on towards the rath together.

'This is my house,' said Guern the Hunter, as they reined in before the largest of the huts. 'It is yours for so long as it pleases you.'

They dismounted, while the yelling small boy and the lowing herd pelted by in the direction of the cattle-yard, and, tossing the reins over a hitching-post, turned to the doorway. A girl child of perhaps eighteen months old, wearing nothing but a red coral bead on a thong round her neck to ward off the Evil Eye, sat before the door, busily playing with three dandelions, a bone, and a striped pebble. One of the hounds poked a friendly muzzle into her face as he stalked past her into the darkness, and she made a grab at his disappearing tail, and fell over.

The doorway was so small that Marcus had to bend double under the heather thatch, as he stepped over the little sprawling figure and followed his host steeply down into the firelit gloom. The blue peat-smoke caught him by the throat and made his eyes smart, but he was used to that by now: and a woman rose from beside the central hearth.

'Murna, I have brought home the Healer of sore eyes and his spear-bearer,' said Guern. 'Do you make them welcome while I tend to their horses and the fruits of my hunting.'

'They are very welcome,' said the woman, 'though praise be to the Horned One, there are no sore eyes here.'

'Good fortune on the house, and on the women of the house,' Marcus said courteously.

Esca had followed their host out again, trusting no one but himself to see to the mares, and Marcus sat down on the roe deerskin that the woman spread for him on the piled heather of the bed-place, and watched her as she returned to whatever she was cooking in the bronze cauldron over the fire. As his eyes grew used to the peat-smoke and to the faint light which filtered down through the narrow doorway and the smoke-hole in the roof, he saw that she was much younger than Guern: a tall, raw-boned woman with a contented face. Her tunic was of coarse reddish wool, such as only a poor woman would have worn in the south; but clearly she was not a poor woman, or rather her husband was not a poor man, for there were bracelets of silver and copper and blue Egyptian glass on her arms, and the mass of dull-gold hair knotted up behind her head was held in place with amber-headed pins. Above all, she was the proud possessor of a large bronze cauldron: Marcus had been long enough in the wilderness to know that a bronze cauldron, more than anything else, brought a woman the envy of her neighbours.

After a short while footsteps sounded outside, and Esca and Guern came ducking in, followed almost at once by the small herdsman and an even younger boy, both very like Guern in face, and already tattooed as he was, against the day when they would be warriors. They watched the strangers warily under their brows, and drew back against the far wall of the hut, while their mother brought bowls of black pottery from some inner place, and served the steaming stew to the three men sitting side by side on the bed-place. She poured yellow mead for them into the great ox-horns, and then went to eat her own meal on the far side of the fire, the women's side, with the small girl child in her lap. The younger boy sat with her, but the elder, suddenly overcoming his distrust, came edging round to examine Marcus's dagger, and finished up by sharing his bowl.

They were a pleasant small family, yet oddly isolated in a land where most people lived in groups for greater safety; and it seemed to Marcus that here was another hint of the unusual to add to the song and the brand of Mithras . . .

It was next morning that he got the final proof of his suspicions.

That morning, Guern decided to shave. Like many of the British tribesmen, he went more or less clean shaven save for his upper lip, and he was certainly in need of a shave. As soon as he announced his intention, preparations began as though for a solemn festival.

His wife brought him a pot of goose-fat to soften his beard, and the whole family gathered to watch their lord and master at his toilet; and so, amid an enthralled audience of three children and several dogs, sitting in the early light before the hut-place door, Guern the Hunter set to work, scraping away at his chin with a heart-shaped bronze razor. How little difference there was between children, all the world over, Marcus thought, looking on with amusement, or fathers, or shaving, for that matter; the small patterns of behaviour and relationship that made up family life. He remembered the fascination of watching his own father on such occasions. Guern squinted at his reflection in the polished bronze disc his patient wife was holding for him, cocked his head this way and that, and scraped away with an expression of acute agony, that made Marcus look forward with foreboding to the day when he and Esca would have to rid themselves of their own beards.

Guern had begun to shave under his chin, tipping his head far back, and as he did so, Marcus saw that just under the point of his jaw, the skin was paler than elsewhere, and had a thickened look, almost like the scar of an old gall. It was very faint, but still to be seen; the mark made by the chin-strap of a Roman helmet, through many years of wearing it. Marcus had seen that gall too often to be mistaken in it, and his last doubt was gone.

Something forbade him to tax Guern with his old life, here at the heart of the new life that he had made. And so a little later, while preparing to take the trail once more, he reminded the hunter of his promise, to set them on their way to the next village. He had a mind to go westward, he said, and Guern replied willingly enough, that since westward there were no more villages for two days' trail, if they were set on going that way, he would ride with them the first day and share their camp that night.

So presently they set out. And in the long-shadowed evening, many miles to the west, the three of them ate their evening meal in the curved lee of a rocky outcrop, and afterwards sat together round their small fire. Their three mounts, each hobbled by a rein from the head to the left foreleg to prevent them straying, cropped contentedly at the short hill-turf that spread here and there like green runnels among the bell-heather. Below them the hills rolled away north-westward, falling gradually to a blue haze of low ground, maybe forty miles away, and Marcus followed the fall of them with his eyes, knowing that somewhere in that blueness the wreck of Agricola's northern wall slashed across the land, severing Valentia from the country beyond that the Romans called Caledonia and the Celts Albu; knowing that somewhere beyond the blueness was the lost Eagle of his father's Legion.

In all the world there seemed no sound but the dry soughing of the wind through the heather, and the sharp yelp of a golden eagle circling the blue spirals of the upper air.

Esca had drawn back a little into the heather, and sat polishing his spear, and Marcus and Guern were alone by the fire, save for the hunter's favourite hound, who lay, nose on paws, with his flank against his master's thigh. Presently Marcus turned to his companion. 'Soon, very soon now, our ways part,' he said, 'but before you go your way and I go mine, there is a question that I have in my heart to ask you.'

'Ask, then,' said the other, playing with his dog's ears.

Marcus said slowly, 'How did you come to be Guern the Hunter who once served with the Eagles?'

There was a sudden flicker in the other's eyes; and then for a long moment he became very still, with a sullen stillness, peering at Marcus under his brows, in the way of the Painted People. 'Who told you such a thing?' he asked at last.

'No one. I go by a song, and the scar between your brows. But most of all by the gall-mark under your chin.'

'If I were—what you say,' Guern growled, 'what need have I to tell you of it? I am a man of my tribe, and if I was not always so, there is none among my sword-brethren who would speak of that to a stranger. What need, then, have I to tell?'

'None in the world,' said Marcus, 'save that I asked you in all courtesy.'

There was another long silence, and then his companion said, with a queer mingling of sullen defiance and a long-forgotten pride, 'I was once Sixth Centurion of the Senior Cohort of the Hispana. Now go and tell it to the nearest Commander on the Wall. I shall not stop you.'

Marcus took his time, sitting quiet and searching the fierce face of the man before him. He was looking for any trace that might be left under the painted hunter of the Roman centurion of twelve years ago; and presently he thought he had found it. 'No patrol could reach you, and you know it,' he said. 'But even if it were not so, still there is a reason that I should keep my mouth shut.'

'And that reason?'

Marcus said, 'That I bear on my forehead a mark which is brother to the mark that you bear on yours,' and with a quick movement he freed the crimson riband that bound the silver talisman in place, and jerked it off. 'Look!'

The other bent forward swiftly. 'So,' he said lingeringly. 'Never before have I known one of your trade who made his evening prayer to Mithras.' But even as he spoke, his gaze narrowed into a new intentness, became like a dagger-thrust. 'Who are you? What are you?' he demanded; and suddenly his hands were on Marcus's shoulders, wrenching him round to face the last windy gold of the sunset. For a long moment he held him so, kneeling over him and glaring into his face; while Marcus, with his lame leg twisted under him, stared back, his black brows frowning, his mouth at its most disdainful.

The great hound crouched watchfully beside them, and Esca got quietly up, fingering his spear; both man and hound ready to kill at a word.

'I have seen you before,' said Guern in a rasping voice. 'I remember your face. In the Name of Light, who are you?'

'Maybe it is my father's face that you remember. He was your Cohort Commander.'

Slowly Guern's hands relaxed and dropped to his side. 'I should have known,' he said. 'It was the talisman—and the beard. But none the less, I should have known.' He sat rocking himself a little, almost as if he were in pain, his eyes never leaving Marcus's face. 'What is it that you do, your father's son, here in Valentia?' he said at last. 'You are no Greek of Alexandria, and I think that you are no eye doctor.'

'No, I am no eye doctor. Nevertheless, the salves that I carry are good, and I was shown how to work with them by one skilled in their use. When I told you that I had followed my father's trade, that at least was the truth. I followed it until I got me this leg and my discharge, two years ago. As to what I do, here in Valentia—' he hesitated, but only for an instant. He knew that in this one matter, at least, he could trust Guern utterly.

And so, very briefly, he told him what it was he did in Valentia, and why. 'And when it seemed to me that you were not as the other hunters of the Painted People,' he finished, 'it seemed to me also that from you I might learn the answer to my questions.'

'And could you not have asked me at the first? Because I was drawn to you, not knowing why, and because you spoke the Latin tongue that I had not heard these twelve years, I brought you to my own place, and you slept under my roof and ate of my salt; with this hidden in your heart concerning me. It would have been better that you asked me at the first!'

'Much better,' Marcus agreed. 'But all that I had in my heart concerning you was a guess, and a wild guess enough! If I had spoken out to you without first being sure, and found too late that you were, after all, no other than you seemed, would there not have been Ahriman the Dark One to pay?'

'What is it that you want to know?' Guern said dully, after a moment.

'What became of my father's Legion. Where is the Eagle now?'

Guern looked down at his own hand, on the head of the great dog who was once more lying quiet beside him; then up again. 'I can answer the first of your questions, at least in part,' he said, 'but it is a long story, and first I will mend the fire.'

He leaned forward as he spoke, and fed the sinking flames from the pile of thorn branches and heather snarls beside him. He did it slowly, deliberately, as though holding off the moment when he must begin his story. But even when the flames sprang up again, he still squatted silent on his haunches, staring into the smoke.

Marcus's heart had begun to race, and suddenly he felt a little sick.

'You never knew your father's Legion,' Guern began at last. 'No, and if you had, you would have been too young to read the signs. Too young by many years.' He had changed his tongue to Latin, and with the change, all that was of the tribes in him seemed to have dropped away. 'The seeds of death were in the Hispana before ever it marched north that last time. They were sown sixty years ago, when men of the Legion carried out the procurator's orders to dispossess the Queen of the Iceni. Boudicca her name was; maybe you have heard of her? She cursed them and their whole Legion, it is said, for the treatment that she had at their hands, which was hardly just, for they had their orders: if she was minded to curse anyone, it had better have been the Procurator himself. But a woman who thinks herself wronged is seldom over particular where her thrust lands, so that it draws blood. Me, I am not one to set much store by cursings, or I was not in the old days. But be that as it may, the Legion was cut to pieces in the rising that followed. When at last the rising failed, the Queen took poison, and maybe her death gave potency to her cursing.

'The Legion was re-formed and brought up to strength again, but it never prospered. Perhaps if it had been moved elsewhere it might have been saved, but for a Legion to serve year after year, generation after generation, among tribes who believe it to be accursed is not good for that Legion. Small misfortunes bloat into large ones, outbreaks of sickness are set down to the working of the curse, instead of the marsh mists; the Spaniards are a people quick to believe in such things. So it became harder to find recruits, and the standard of those taken grew lower, year by year. It was very slow at first—I have served with men no older than myself, who remembered the Ninth when it was only a little rough and run to seed. But at the last it was terribly swift, and when I joined the Legion as a centurion, two years before the end—I was promoted from the ranks of the Thirtieth, which was a proud Legion—the rind seemed sound enough, but the heart was rotten. Stinking rotten.'

Guern the Hunter spat into the fire.

'I strove to fight the rot in my own Century at first, and then—the fighting grew to be too much trouble. The last Legate was a hard and upright man without understanding—the worst man to handle such a Legion—and soon after his coming the Emperor Trajan withdrew too many troops from Britain for his everlasting campaigns; and we who were left to hold the Frontier began to feel the tribes seethe under us like an over-ripe cheese. Then Trajan died, and the tribes rose. The whole North went up in flames, and barely had we settled with the Brigantes and the Iceni when we were ordered up into Valentia to hammer the Caledonians. Two of our cohorts were serving in Germany; we had suffered heavy casualties already, and leaving a cohort to garrison Eburacum and be cut to shreds by the Brigantes if they happened to feel like it, that left well under four thousand of us to march north. And when the Legate took the omens in the usual way, the sacred chickens had gone off their feed and would not touch the pulse he threw to them. After that we gave ourselves up for doomed, which is a bad state of mind for a Legion to march in.

'It was autumn, and almost from the start the mountain country was blanketed in mist, and out of the mist the tribesmen harried us. Oh, it never came to a fight; they hung about our flanks like wolves; they made sudden raids on our rearguard and loosed their arrows into us from behind every tuft of sodden heather, and disappeared into the mist before we could come to grips with them; and the parties sent out after them never came back.

'A Legate who was also a soldier might have saved us; ours had seen no more of soldiering than a sham fight on Mars Field, and was too proud to listen to his officers who had, and by the time we reached Agricola's old headquarters on the Northern Wall, which was to be our base, upward of another thousand of us had gone, by death or desertion. The old fortifications were crumbling, the water supply had long since given out, and the whole North had gathered in strength by then. They sat round the walls and yelled, like wolves howling to the moon. We stood one attack in that place. We rolled the dead down the scarp into the river; and when the tribes drew off to lick their wounds, we chose a spokesman and went to the Legate and said: "Now we will make what terms we can with the Painted People, that they may let us march back the way we came, leaving Valentia in their hands, for it is no more than a name, and a name that tastes sour on the tongue at that." And the Legate sat in his camp chair, which *we* had had to carry for him all the way from Eburacum, and called us evil names. Doubtless we deserved the names, but they did not help. Then more than half of us mutinied, many of my own Century among them.'

Guern turned from the fire to face Marcus. 'I was not one of them. Before the Lord of the Legions I swear it. My full shame was not yet come upon me and I held the few men left to me in leash yet awhile. Then the Legate saw where his mistake had lain, and he spoke more gently to his Legion in revolt than ever he had done before, and that was not from fear. He bade the mutineers lay down the arms that they had taken up against their Eagle, and swore that there should be no summary punishment, even of the ringleaders; swore that if we did our duty from thenceforth, he would make fair report of it, the good with the bad, on our return. As though we should ever return! But even had the way back been clear, it was too late for such promises. From the moment that the cohorts mutinied it was too late. There could be no turning back for them, knowing all too well what the word of the Senate would be.'

'Decimation,' Marcus said quietly, as the other halted.

'Aye, decimation. It comes hard, to draw lots out of a helmet, knowing that one in every ten means death by stoning to the man who draws it.

'So the thing ended in fighting. That was when the Legate was killed. He was a brave man, though a fool. He stood out before the mob, with his hands empty, and his Eagle-bearer and his beardless Tribunes behind him, and called on them to remember their oath, and called them curs of Tiber-side. Then one struck him down with a pilum, and after that there was no more talking . . .

'The tribesmen came swarming in over the barricades to help the red work, and by dawn there were barely two full cohorts left alive in the fort. The rest were not all dead, oh no; many of them went back over the ramparts with the tribesmen. They may be scattered about Caledonia now, for all I know, living even as myself, with a British wife, and sons to come after them.

'Just after dawn, your father called together the few that were left in the open space before the Praetorium, and there, every man with his sword ready in his hand, we took hurried counsel, and determined to win out of the old fort, which was become a death-trap, and carry the Eagle back to Eburacum as best we might. It was no use by then to think of making terms with the tribesmen, for they had no longer any cause to fear us. And besides, I think there was the thought in all of us that if we won through, the Senate could scarcely count us as disgraced. That night the fools feasted—so low had we sunk in their contempt—and while they drank, baying to the moon, we got out, all that were left of us, by the southern scarp, and passed them by in the darkness and the mist—the first time ever the mist had seemed our friend—and began the forced march back, heading for Trinomontium.

'The tribes picked up our trail at dawn and hunted us as though it had been for sport. Have you ever been hunted? All that day we struggled on, and the sorest wounded, who dropped out, died. Sometimes we heard them die, in the mist. Then I dropped out too.' Guern rubbed his left flank. 'I had a wound that I could put three fingers in, and I was sick. But I could have gone on. It was being hunted—the being—hunted. I took my chance at dusk, when the hunters drew off a space; I slipped into some long furze-cover, and hid. One of the Painted People nearly trod on me presently, but they did not find me, and after dark, when the hunt had passed far away, I stripped off my harness and left it. I look like a Pict, do I not? That is because I am from Northern Gaul. Then I suppose I wandered all night. I do not know, but in the dawn I came to a village and fell across the door-sill of the first hut.

'They took me in and tended me. Murna tended me. And when they found that I was a Roman soldier, they did not greatly care. I was not the first of my kind to desert to the tribes; and Murna spoke for me, like a lioness whose cub is threatened.' For an instant, a glint of laughter sounded in his voice, and then it grew harsh and heavy again. 'A few nights later I saw the Eagle carried by on its way north again, with a great triumph of torches following behind.'

There was a long, strained silence. Then Marcus said in a quiet, hard voice, 'Where did they make an end?'

'I do not know. But they never reached Trinomontium. I have looked there again and again, and found no sign of fighting.'

'And my father?'

'He was with the Eagle when I dropped out. There were no captives with it when they carried it north again,'

'Where is the Eagle now?'

Guern reached out and touched the dagger in the other's belt, looking at him steadily. 'If you are minded to die, here is the means to your hand. Save yourself the further journey.'

'Where is the Eagle now?' Marcus repeated his question, as though the other had not spoken.

For a moment he held the hunter's eyes with his own; then Guern said, 'I do not know. But tomorrow, when there is light to see by, I will give you what direction I can.'

And Marcus realized suddenly that he was seeing the other's face by firelight, and all beyond him was blurred into the blue dusk.

He did not sleep much that night, but lay rigid with his head in his arms. All these months he had followed a dream; in a way, he realized now, he had followed it since he was eight years old. It had been bright and warm, and now it was broken, and without it he felt very cold, and suddenly older than he had been a few hours ago. What a fool he had been! What a blind fool! Clinging to the stubborn faith that because it had been his father's, there had been nothing much wrong with the Ninth Legion, after all. He knew better now. His father's Legion had been putrid, a rotten apple that fell to pieces when it was struck by a heel. And God of the Legions! what his father must have suffered!

Out of the ruin, one thing stood up unchanged: that the Eagle was still to be found and brought back, lest one day it became a menace to the Frontier. There was something comforting about that. A faith still to be kept.

Next morning when the early meal had been eaten, and the fire quenched and scattered, Marcus stood beside his mare, looking away north-west, along the line of Guern's pointing finger. The light wind whipped his face, and his morning shadow ran away downhill as though eager to be off before him, and he heard the wild, sweet calling of the green plover that seemed to be the voice of the great loneliness.

'Yonder where the vale opens,' Guern was saying. 'You will know the ford by the leaning pine that grows beside it. You must cross there, and follow the right bank, or you will find yourself at the last with the whole broad Firth of Cluta between you and Caledonia. Two days' march, three at the most, will bring you to the old northern line.'

'And then?' Marcus said, not turning his narrowed gaze from the blue hazed distance.

'I can tell you only this: that the men who carried the Eagle north were of the tribe of the Epidaii, whose territory is the deep firths and the mountains of the west coast, running from the Cluta.'

'Can you hazard any guess as to where in this territory their holy place may be?'

'None. It may be that if you find the Royal Dun, you will find the Holy Place not far off; but the Epidaii is divided into many clans, so I have heard, and the Royal Clan may not be the guardians of the Holy Place and the holy things of the tribe.'

'You mean—it might be some quite small and unimportant clan?'

'Not unimportant; it would be as powerful as the Royal Clan, maybe more so. But small, yes. There is no more help that I can give you.'

They were silent a moment until there sounded behind them the faint jink of a bridle-bit, as Esca brought up the other mare. Then Guern said hurriedly, 'Do not follow that trail; it leads into the mouth of death.'

'I must take my chance of that,' Marcus said. He turned his head. 'And you, Esca?'

'I go where you go,' said Esca, busy with a buckle.

'Why?' Guern demanded. 'Now that you know the truth? They will not re-form the Legion. Why should you go on? Why?'

'There is still the Eagle to be brought back,' Marcus said.

Another silence, and then Guern said almost humbly, 'You have said nothing about all this that I have told you; no more than if it had been a story told to while away an idle evening.'

'What should I say?'

The other laughed, shortly and harshly. 'Mithras knows! But my belly would be the lighter if you said it.'

'Last night I felt too sick in my own belly to care over much for yours,' Marcus said wearily. 'That is passed now, but if I cursed the Hispana with every foul Tiber-side word that I could lay my tongue to, it would not serve my father, nor sweeten the stink of the Legion's name.' He looked for the first time at the man beside him. 'As for you, I have never been hunted, and the Lord of the Legions forbid that I should be your judge.'

The other said defiantly, 'Why did you come? I was happy with my woman; she is a good woman to me. I am a great man in my tribe, though an outdweller. Often I forget—almost—that I was not born into my tribe, until once again Trinomontium draws me back for a little while. And now I shall be ashamed to my dying day, because I let you go north on this trail alone.'

'No need that you should carry a new shame,' Marcus said. 'This is a trail that three can follow better than four, and two better than three. Go back to your tribe, Guern. Thank you for your salt and your shelter, and for answering my questions.'

He turned away to mount his horse, and a few moments later was heading down the stream-side with Esca close behind.

XIV
The Feast of New Spears

ON an evening more than a month later, Marcus and Esca reined in to breathe their tired horses, on the crest of a steep ridge above the Western Ocean. It was an evening coloured like a dove's breast; a little wind feathered the shining water, and far out on the dreaming brightness many scattered islands seemed to float lightly as sleeping sea-birds. In the safe harbourage inshore, a few trading-vessels lay at anchor, the blue sails that had brought them from Hibernia furled as though they, too, were asleep. And to the north, brooding over the whole scene, rose Cruachan, sombre, cloaked in shadows, crested with mist, Cruachan, the shield-boss of the world.

Mountain and islands and shining sea were all grown familiar to Marcus. For a month now he had seldom been out of sight of one or other of them, as he came and went among the mist-haunted glens where the Epidaii had their hunting grounds. It had been a heart-breaking month. So often, since he crossed the northern line, it had seemed to him that he was at last on the trail of what he sought, and always he had been wrong. There were so many holy places along the coast. Wherever the Ancient People, the little Dark People, had left their long barrows, there the Epidaii, coming after, had made a holy place at which to worship their gods; and the Ancient People had left so many barrows. Yet nowhere could Marcus hear any whisper of the lost Eagle. These people did not speak of their gods, nor of the things which had to do with their gods. And suddenly, this evening, looking out over the shining sea, Marcus was heart-sick and not far from giving up hope.

He was roused from his bleak mood by Esca's voice beside him. 'Look, we have companions on the road.' And following the direction of his friend's back-pointing thumb, he turned to look down the deer-path by which they had come, and saw a party of hunters climbing towards them. He wheeled Vipsania, and sat waiting for them to come up. Five men in all, two of them carrying the slung carcass of a black boar; and the usual pack of wolfish hounds cantering among them. How different they were from the men of Valentia: darker and more slightly built. Maybe that was because the blood of the Dark People ran more strongly in them than in the lowland tribes; less outwardly fierce than the lowlanders too, but in the long run, Marcus thought, more dangerous.

'The hunting has been good.' He saluted them as they came up at a jog-trot.

'The hunting has been good,' agreed the leader, a young man with the twisted gold torque of a chieftain round his neck. He looked enquiringly at Marcus, forbidden by courtesy to ask his business, but clearly wondering what this stranger, who was not one of the traders from the blue-sailed ships, was doing in his territory.

Almost without thinking, Marcus asked him the question which had become a habit with much asking. 'Are there any in your dun who have the eye sickness?'

The man's look grew half eager, half suspicious. 'Is it that you can cure the eye sickness?'

'Can I cure the eye sickness?—I am Demetrius of Alexandria. *The* Demetrius of Alexandria,' said Marcus, who had long since learned the value of advertisement. 'Speak my name south of the Cluta, speak it in the Royal Dun itself, and men will tell you that I am indeed a healer of all sickness of the eye.'

'There are several that I know of in the dun, who have the eye sickness,' said the man. 'None of your trade ever came this way before. You will heal them?'

'How should I know, even I, until I see them?' Marcus turned his mare into the way. 'You are for the dun now? Let us go on together.'

And on they went, Marcus with the Chieftain loping at his horse's shoulder, then Esca and the rest of the hunting party with the slung boar in their midst and the hounds weaving to and fro among them. For a while they followed the ridge, then turned inland, and came looping down through thin birch-woods towards a great loch that lay, pearl-pale with evening, among the hills. Marcus and Esca knew that loch—they had touched its further shores more than once. The Loch of Many Islets it was called, from the little islands scattered in it, some of them steep and rocky, or low and willow-fringed where the herons nested.

It was twilight when they reached the dun on its hill shoulder above the still waters of the loch; the soft mulberry twilight of the west coast, through which the firelit doorways of the living-huts bloomed like yellow crocus flowers dimly veined with red. The cluster of huts that made up the rath of the Chieftain was at the head of the dun, in a sharp curve of the turf ramparts, and they turned aside to it, while the other hunters, after arranging for the sharing of the boar, scattered to their own houses.

At the sound of their arrival, a lad who Marcus took to be the Chieftain's brother ducked out from the firelit doorway and came running to meet them. 'How went the hunting, Dergdian?'

'The hunting was good,' said the Chieftain, 'for see, besides a fine boar, I have brought home a healer of sore eyes; also his spear-bearer. Look to their horses, Liathan.' He turned quickly to Marcus, who was rubbing his thigh. 'You are saddle-stiff? You have ridden over-far today?'

'No,' said Marcus. 'It is an old hurt which still cramps me sometimes.'

He followed his host into the great living-hut, ducking his head under the low lintel. Inside it was very hot, and the usual blue peat-reek caught at his throat. Two or three hounds lay among the warm fern. A little, wizened woman, evidently a slave, bent over the raised hearth, stirring the evening stew in a bronze cauldron, and did not look up at their coming in; but a gaunt old man who sat beyond the fire peered at them through the eddying peat-smoke with bright, masterful eyes. That was in the first instant; then the curtain of beautifully worked deerskins over the entrance to the women's place was drawn aside, and a girl appeared on the threshold; a tall girl, dark even for a woman of the Epidaii, in a straight green gown, clasped at the shoulder with a disc of red-gold as broad and massive as a shield-boss. She had been spinning, it seemed, for she still carried a spindle and distaff.

'I heard your voice,' she said. 'Supper is ready and waiting.'

'Let it wait a while longer, Fionhula my heart,' said Dergdian the Chieftain. 'I have brought home a healer of sore eyes; therefore do you bring out to him the little cub.'

The woman's long dark eyes moved quickly, with a kind of startled hope in them, to Marcus's face, then back to the Chieftain's. She turned without a word, letting the curtain fall behind her, and a few moments later she was back, holding a little boy of about two in her arms. A brown pleasant infant, dressed in the usual coral bead, but as the light fell on his face, Marcus saw that his eyes were so swollen and red and crusted that they would scarcely open.

'Here is one for your healing,' said the Chieftain.

'Yours?' Marcus asked.

'Mine.'

'He will be blind,' said the old man by the fire. 'All along, I have said that he will be blind, and I am never wrong.'

Marcus ignored him. 'Give the little cub to me,' he commanded. 'I will not hurt him.' He took the little boy from his mother with a quick reassuring smile, and slipped down awkwardly on to his sound knee beside the fire. The child whimpered, turning away from the fire; evidently the light hurt him. Not blind already, then. That was something. Very gently, he turned the little boy's face back to the firelight. 'There, cubling, it is but for a moment. Let me look. What is this you have been putting in the child's eyes?'

'Toad's fat,' said the old man. 'With my own hands I salved them, though it is women's work, for my grandson's wife is a fool.'

'Have you found it do any good?'

The old man shrugged his gaunt shoulders. 'Maybe not,' he said grudgingly.

'Then why use it?'

'It is the custom. Always our womenfolk put toad's fat on such places; but my grandson's wife—' The old man spat juicily to express his opinion of his grandson's wife. 'But all along, I have said the child will be blind,' he added, in the satisfied tone of a true prophet.

Marcus heard the girl behind him catch her breath in agonized protest, and felt his own temper flash up in him, but he had the sense to know that if he made an enemy of the old devil he might as well give up any hope of saving the child's sight. So he said peaceably enough, 'We will see. Toad's fat is doubtless good for sore eyes, but since it has failed, this time, I shall try my own salves; and it may be that they will do better.' And before the old man could get in another word he turned to Fionhula. 'Bring me warm water and linen rags,' he said, 'and light a lamp. I must have light to work by, not this flickering fire-glow. Esca, do you bring in my medicine box.'

And there and then, while the mother held the sick child in her lap, he set to work, bathing, salving, bandaging, by the light of the lamp which the slave woman deserted the stew to hold for him.

Marcus and Esca remained many days in the dun of Dergdian. Always before, Marcus had merely started the good work, left a lump of salve and instructions how to use it, and moved on. But this time it was different. The child's eyes were worse than any that he had had to tend before, and there was grandfather and his toad fat to be reckoned with. This time he would have to stay. Well, he might as soon stay here as in any other place, since he was as likely, or as unlikely, to be near finding the Eagle here as anywhere else.

So he stayed, and a weary stay it seemed. The days went very slowly, for he had long empty stretches of time on his hands, and after the first sharp battle for the cub's sight had been won, and it was only a question of waiting, they seemed to crawl more slowly still.

Most of the time he sat in the hut-place doorway, watching the womenfolk at work, or grinding sticks of dried salves for the small leaden pots that needed replenishing, while Esca went off with the hunters, or joined the herdsmen in the steep cattle-runs. In the evening he talked with the men round the fire; exchanged travellers' tales with the dark Hibernian traders who came and went through the dun (for there was a constant trade in goldwork and weapons, slaves and hunting dogs, between Hibernia and Caledonia); listening patiently to old Tradui, the Chieftain's maternal grandfather, telling interminable stories of seal hunts when he and the world were young and men and seals stronger and fiercer than they were now.

But all the while, listen as they might, neither he nor Esca heard anything to suggest that the place and the thing they were looking for was nearby. Once or twice, during those days, Marcus glimpsed a black-cloaked figure passing through the dun, remote from the warm and crowded humanity of the tribe and seeming to brood over it as Cruachan brooded over the land. But Druids were everywhere, up here beyond the reach of Rome, just as holy places were everywhere. They did not live among the people, but withdrawn into themselves, in the misty fastnesses of the mountains, in the hidden glens, and among the forests of birch and hazel. Their influence lay heavy on the duns and villages, but no one spoke of them, any more than they spoke of their gods and the prowling ghosts of their forefathers. Neither did anyone ever speak of a captured Eagle. But still Marcus waited, until he knew that the little cub's sight was safe.

And then one evening, returning with Esca from a plunge in the deep water below the dun, he found the Chieftain squatting in his hut-place doorway with his hunting dogs around him, lovingly burnishing a heavy war-spear with a collar of eagles' feathers. Marcus folded up beside him and watched, vividly remembering another war-spear whose collar had been the blue-grey feathers of a heron. Esca stood leaning one shoulder against the rowan-wood doorpost, watching also.

Presently the Chieftain looked up and caught their gaze. 'It is for the Feast of New Spears,' he said. 'For the warrior dancing that comes after.'

'The Feast of New Spears,' Marcus echoed. 'That is when your boys become men, is it not? I have heard of such a feast, but never seen it.'

'You will see in three nights from now; on the Night of the Horned Moon,' Dergdian said, and returned to his burnishing. 'It is a great feast. From all over the tribe, the boys come, and their fathers with them. If it were the King's son, still he must come to us, when it is time for him to receive his weapons.'

'Why?' Marcus asked, and then hoped that he had not sounded too eager.

'We are the keepers of the Holy Place, we, the Seal People,' said Dergdian, turning the spear on his knee. 'We are the guardians of the Life of the Tribe.'

After a long pause, Marcus said casually, 'So. And it is allowed to anyone to witness this mystery of the New Spears?'

'Not the mystery, no; that is between the New Spears and the Horned One, and none save the priest-kind may and live; but the ceremonies of the forecourt, they are for any who choose to be there. They are not hidden, save from the women's side.'

'Then with your leave I shall most assuredly choose to be there. We Greeks—we are born asking questions,' Marcus said.

Next day began a bustle of preparation that reminded Marcus of his own Etruscan village on the eve of Saturnalia; and by evening the first inflow of the New Spears had begun; boys and their fathers from the furthest fringes of the tribal lands, riding fine small ponies, wearing their brightest clothes, and many of them with their hounds cantering along beside. Odd, he thought, watching them, odd that people so poor in many ways, hunters and herdsmen who do not till the soil, and live in mud hovels in acute discomfort, should enrich the bridles of their superbly bred ponies with silver and bronze and studs of coral, and clasp their cloaks with buckler-brooches of red Hibernian gold. There was an in-swarming of another kind too, of merchants and fortune-tellers, harpers and horse-dealers, who encamped with the tribe on the level shores of the loch until the whole stretch below the dun was dark with them. It was all warm and gay and human, a market crowd on a large scale, and nowhere any sign of the strangeness that Marcus had expected.

But there was to be strangeness enough before the Feast of New Spears was over.

It began on the second evening, when suddenly the boys who were to receive their weapons were no longer there. Marcus did not see them go; but suddenly they were gone, and behind them the dun was desolate. The men daubed their foreheads with mud; the women gathered together, wailing and rocking in ritual grief. From within the dun and from the encampment below the ramparts the wailing rose as the night drew on, and at the evening meal a place was left empty and a drinking-horn filled and left untouched for every boy who had gone, as for the ghosts of dead warriors at the feast of Samhain; and the women made the death chant through the long hours of darkness.

With morning, the wailing and the lamentation ceased, and in its place there settled on the dun a great quietness and a great sense of waiting. Towards evening the tribe gathered on the level ground beside the loch. The men stood about in groups, each clan keeping to itself. Wolf Clan to Wolf Clan, Salmon to Salmon, Seal to Seal; skin-clad or cloaked in purple or saffron or scarlet, with their weapons in their hands and their dogs padding in and out among them. The women stood apart from the menfolk, many of the young ones with garlands of late summer flowers in their hair: honeysuckle, yellow loosestrife, and the wild white convolvulus. And men and women alike turned constantly to look up into the south-western sky.

Marcus, standing with Esca and Liathan, the Chieftain's brother, on the outskirts of the throng, found himself also looking again and again to the south-west, where the sky was still golden, though the sun had slipped behind the hills.

And then, quite suddenly, there it was, the pale curved feather of the new moon, caught in the fringes of the sunset. Somewhere among the women's side a girl saw it at the same instant, and raised a strange, haunting, half-musical cry that was caught up by the other women, then by the men. From somewhere over the hills, seaward, a horn sounded. No braying war-horn, but a clearer, higher note that seemed perfectly akin to the pale feather hanging remote in the evening sky.

As though the horn had been a summons, the crowd broke up, and the men moved off in the direction from which it had sounded; a long, ragged train of warriors moving quietly, steadily, leaving the dun to the women, to the very old, and the very young. Marcus went with them, keeping close to Liathan, as he had been told, and suddenly very glad to know that Esca was walking at his shoulder in this strange multitude.

They climbed steadily to the mountain saddle, and came dropping down on the seaward side. They traversed a steep glen and swung out along a ridge. Down again, and another steep climb, and suddenly they were on the lip of a wide upland valley running at an angle to the sea. It lay at their feet, already brimmed with shadows under a sky still webbed and washed with light that seemed to burst upward from the hidden sun; but at its head a great turf mound rose steeply, catching still a faint glow from the sunset on its thorn-crowned crest and the tips of the great standing stones that ringed it round like a bodyguard. Marcus had seen the long barrows of the Ancient People often enough before, but none had caught and held his awareness as this one did, at the head of its lonely valley, between the gold of the sunset and the silver of the new moon.

'Yonder is the Place of Life!' said Liathan's voice in his ear. 'The Life of the Tribe.'

The many-coloured throng had turned northward, winding along the valley towards the Place of Life. The great mound rose higher on their sight, and presently Marcus found himself standing among the Seal People, in the shadow of one of the great standing stones. Before him stretched the emptiness of a wide, roughly paved forecourt, and beyond the emptiness, in the steep mass of the bush-grown mound, a doorway. A doorway whose massive uprights and lintel were of age-eaten granite. A doorway from one world into another, Marcus thought with a chill of awe, closed seemingly by nothing but a skin apron enriched with bosses of dim bronze. Was the lost Eagle of the Hispana somewhere beyond that barbaric entrance? Somewhere in the dark heart of this barrow that was the Place of Life?

There was a sudden hiss and flare of flame, as somebody kindled a torch from the fire-pot they had brought with them. The fire seemed to spread almost of its own accord from torch to torch, and several young warriors stepped out from the silent waiting crowd, into the vast emptiness within the standing stones. They carried the flaming brands high above their heads, and the whole scene, which had begun to blur with the fading light, was flooded with a flickering red-gold glare that fell most fiercely on the threshold of that strange doorway, showing the uprights carved with the same curves and spirals that swirled up the standing stones, flashing on the bronze bosses of the sealskin apron so that they became discs of shifting fire. Sparks whirled upward on the light, sea-scented wind, and by contrast with their brightness, the hills and the dark thorn-crowned crest of the mound seemed to sink back into the sudden twilight. A man's shape showed for an instant high among the thorn-trees, and again the horn sounded its high clear note; and before the echoes had died among the hills, the sealskin curtain was flung back, its bronze discs clashing like cymbals.

A figure stooped out under the low lintel into the torchlight. The figure of a man, stark naked save for the skin of a grey dog-seal, the head drawn over his own. The Seal Clan greeted his coming with a quick, rhythmic cry that rose and fell and rose again, setting the blood jumping back to the heart. For an instant the man—Seal-priest or man-seal—stood before them, receiving their acclamation, then with the clumsy scuffling motion of a seal on dry land, moved to one side of the doorway; and another figure sprang out of the darkness, hooded with the snarling head of a wolf. One after another they came, naked as the first had been, their bodies daubed with strange designs in woad and madder, their head-dresses of animal pelts or bird-feathers, the wings of a swan, the pelt of an otter with the tail swinging behind the wearer's back, the striped hide of a badger shining black and white in the torchlight. One after another, prancing, leaping, shuffling; men who were not merely playing the part of animals, but who in some strange way, impossible of understanding, actually *were* for the moment the animals whose skin they wore.

One after another they came, until for every clan of the tribe, a totem priest had joined the grotesque dance—if dance it could be called, for it was like no dance that Marcus had ever seen before, and none that he wanted ever to see again. They had swung into a chain, into a circle, hopping, scuffling, bounding, the animal skins swinging behind them. There was no music—indeed music of any sort, however weird, however discordant, seemed worlds away from this dancing; but there seemed to be a pulse beating somewhere—perhaps a hollow log being struck with an open palm—and the dancers took their time from it. Quicker and quicker it beat, like a racing heart, like the heart of a man in fever; and the wheel of dancers spun faster and faster, until, with a wild yell, it seemed to break of its own spinning, and burst back to reveal someone—something—that must have come unnoticed into its midst from the blackness of that doorway in the barrow.

Marcus's throat tightened for an instant as he looked at the figure standing alone in the full red glare of the torches, seeming to burn with its own fierce light. An unforgettable figure of nightmare beauty, naked and superb, crested with a spreading pride of antlers that caught the torch-light on each polished tip, as though every tine bore a point of flame.

A man with the antlers of a stag set into his head-dress so that they seemed to grow from his brow—that was all. And yet it was not all; even for Marcus, it was not all. The people greeted him with a deep shout that rose and rose until it was like a wolf-pack howling to the moon; and while he stood with upraised arms, dark power seemed to flow from him as light from a lamp. 'The Horned One! The Horned One!' They were down on their faces, as a swathe of barley going down before the sickle. Without knowing that he did so, Marcus stumbled to his knee; beside him Esca was crouching with his forearm covering his eyes.

When they rose again, the priest-god had drawn back to the threshold of the Place of Life, and was standing there, his arms fallen to his sides. He burst into a spate of speech, of which Marcus could understand just enough to gather that he was telling the tribe that their sons who had died as boys were now reborn as warriors. His voice rose into pealing triumph, passing little by little into a kind of wild chant in which the tribesmen joined. Torches were springing up all along the close-packed throng, and the standing stones were reddened to their crests and seemed to pulse and quiver with the crashing rhythm of the chant.

When the triumphal chanting was at its height, the priest-god turned and called, then moved from before the doorway; and again someone stooped out from the darkness of the entrance into the glare of torches. A red-haired boy in a chequered kilt, at sight of whom the tribesmen sent up a welcoming shout. Another followed, and another, and many more, each greeted with a shout that seemed to burst upward and break in a wave of sound against the standing stones, until fifty or more New Spears were ranged in the great forecourt. They had a little the look of sleep-walkers, and they blinked dazzled eyes in the sudden blaze of torches. The boy next to Marcus kept running his tongue over dry lips, and Marcus could see the quick panting of his breast, as though he had been running—or very much afraid. What had happened to them in the dark, he wondered, remembering his own hour, and the smell of bull's blood in the darkened cave of Mithras.

After the last boy, came one last priest, not a totem priest, as the others had been. His head-dress was made of the burnished feathers of a golden eagle, and a long roar burst from the crowd, as the curtain dropped clashing into place behind him. But to Marcus everything seemed for the moment to have grown very still. For the last comer was carrying something that had once been a Roman Eagle.

XV

Venture into the Dark

A man stepped out from the ranks of the tribe, stripped and painted as for war, and carrying shield and spear; and at the same instant a boy started forward. The two—they were clearly father and son—came together in the centre of the open space, and the boy stood with shining pride to take shield and spear from his father's hand. Then he turned slowly on his heel, showing himself to the tribe for their acceptance; turned to the place where Cruachan was hidden by the darkness; turned last of all to the new moon, which had strengthened from a pale feather to a sickle of shining silver in a deep-green sky; and brought his spear crashing down across his shield in salute, before following his father, to stand for the first time among the warriors of his tribe.

Another boy stepped out, and another, and another; but Marcus was aware of them only as moving shadows, for his eyes were on the Eagle; the wreck of the Ninth's lost Eagle. The gilded wreaths and crowns that the Legion had won in the days of its honour were gone from the crimson-bound staff; the furious talons still clutched the crossed thunderbolts, but where the great silver wings should have arched back in savage pride, were only empty socket-holes in the flanks of gilded bronze. The Eagle had lost its honour, and lost its wings; and without them, to Demetrius of Alexandria it might have seemed as commonplace as a dunghill cock; but to Marcus it was the Eagle still, in whose shadow his father had died; the lost Eagle of his father's Legion.

He saw very little of the long-drawn ritual that followed, until at last the Eagle had been carried back into the dark, and he found himself part of a triumphal procession led by the New Spears, heading back for the dun: a comet-tail of tossing torches, a shouting like a victorious army on the homeward march. As they came down the last slope they were met by the smell of roasting meat, for the cooking-pits had been opened. Great fires burned on the open turf below the dun, flowering fiercely red and gold against the remote, sheeny pallor of the loch below, and the women linked hands and came running to join their returning menfolk and draw them home.

Only a few men who were not of the tribe had cared to go with the warriors to the Place of Life. But now the ceremonies were over and it was time for feasting; and traders and soothsayers and harpers had thronged in from the encampment, a party of seal-hunters from another tribe, even the crews of two or three Hibernian ships; they crowded with the warriors of the Epidaii around the fire and feasted nobly on roast meat, while the women, who did not eat with their lords, moved among them with great jars of fiery yellow metheglin, to keep the drinking-horns brimming.

Marcus, sitting between Esca and Liathan at the Chieftain's fire, began to wonder if the whole night was going to be spent like this, in eating and drinking and shouting. If it was, he should go raving mad. He wanted quiet; he wanted to think; and the joyous uproar seemed to beat inside his head, driving all thought out of it. Also he wanted no more metheglin.

Then quite suddenly the feasting was over. The noise and the vast eating and deep drinking had been, maybe, only a shield raised against the too-potent magic that had gone before. Men and women began to draw back, leaving a wide space of empty turf amid the fires; dogs and children were gathered in. Again torches flared up, casting their fierce light on to the empty space. Again there came that sense of waiting. Marcus, finding himself beside the Chieftain's grandfather, turned to the old man, asking under his breath, 'What now?'

'Dancing now,' said the other without looking round. 'See . . . '

Even as he spoke, the flaming brands were whirled aloft, and a band of young warriors sprang into the torch-lit circle and began to stamp and whirl in the swift rhythm of a war-dance. And this time, strange and barbaric as it might be, Marcus found this was dancing as he understood the word. Dance followed dance, blending into each other so that it was hard to tell where one ended and another began. Sometimes it would seem that the whole men's side was dancing, and the ground would tremble under their stamping heels. Sometimes it would be only a chosen few who leapt and whirled and crouched in mimic hunting or warfare, while the rest raised the terrifying music of the British before battle by droning across their shield-rims. Only the women never danced at all, for the Feast of New Spears had nothing to do with womenkind.

The moon had long since set, and only the fierce fight of fire and torches fit the wild scene, the twisting bodies and brandished weapons, when at last two rows of warriors stepped out on to the trampled turf and stood facing each other. They were stripped to the waist like the rest of the men's side, and carried shield and feathered war spear; and Marcus saw that one rank was made up of the boys who had become men that day, and the other of their fathers who had armed them.

'It is the Dance of the New Spears,' Esca told him as the two lines swept together with upraised shields. 'So, we dance it, too, we the Brigantes, on the night our boys become men.'

On his other side Tradui leaned towards him, asking 'Do not your people hold the Feast of New Spears?'

'We hold a feast,' Marcus said, 'but it is not like this. All this is strange to me, and I have seen many things tonight that make me wonder.'

'So?—and these things?' The old man, having got over his first annoyance with Marcus over the toad's fat, had gradually become more friendly as the days went by; and tonight, warmed still further by the feasting and the metheglin, he was eager to enlighten the stranger within his gates. 'I will explain them to you, these things at which you wonder; for you are young and doubtless wish to know, and I am old and by far the wisest man in my tribe.'

If he went warily, Marcus realized, here might be a chance to gather certain information that he needed. 'Truly,' he said, 'wisdom shines from Tradui the Chieftain's grandsire, and my ears are open.' And he settled himself, with a most flattering show of interest, to ask and listen. It was slow work, but little by little, drawing the old man on with all the skill he possessed, listening patiently to a great deal that was of no use to him whatever, he gathered the scraps of knowledge that he needed. He learned that the priest-kind had their living-place in the birchwoods below the Place of Life, and that no guard was kept over the holy place, no watch of attendant priests.

'What need?' said the old man when Marcus showed surprise at this. 'The Place of Life has guardians of its own, and who would dare to meddle with that which is of the Horned One?' He broke off, abruptly, as though catching himself in the act of speaking of forbidden things, and stretched out an old thick-veined hand with the fingers spread hornwise.

But presently he began to talk again. Under the influence of the metheglin and the torch-light and the dancing, he, too, was remembering his own night: the long-ago night when he had been a New Spear, and danced for the first time the warrior dances of the tribe. Never taking his eyes from the whirling figures, he told of old fights, old cattle-raids, long-dead heroes who had been his sword-brothers when the world was young and the sun hotter than it was now. Pleased at finding an attentive listener who had not heard the story before, he told of a great hosting of the tribes, no more than ten or twelve autumns ago; and how he had gone south with the rest—though some fools had said that he was too old for the war-trail, even then—to stamp out a great army of the Red Crests. And how, having given them to the wolf and to the raven, they had brought back the Eagle-god that the Red Crests carried before them, and given it to the gods of his own people in the Place of Life. The Healer of sore eyes must have seen it tonight when it was carried out and shown to the men's side?

Marcus sat very still, his hands linked round his updrawn knees, and watched the sparks fly upward from the whirling torches.

'I saw it,' he said. 'I have seen such Eagle gods before, and I wondered to see it here. We are always curious, we Greeks; also we have small cause to love Rome. Tell me more of how you took this Eagle-god from the Red Crests; I should like to hear that story.'

It was the story that he had heard once already, from Guern the Hunter; but told from the opposite side; and where Guern's story had ended, this one went on.

Much as he might tell of a bygone hunting that had been good, the old warrior told how he and his sword-brethren had hunted down the last remnants of the Ninth Legion, closing round them as a wolf-pack closes round its prey. The old man told it without a shadow of pity, without a shadow of understanding for the agony of his quarry; but with a fierce admiration that lit his face and sounded in every word.

'I was an old man even then, and it was my last fight, but *what* a fight! Ayee! Worthy to be the last fight of Tradui the Warrior! Many a night when the fire sinks low, and even the battles of my youth grow thin and cold, I have kept warm thinking of that fight! We brought them to bay at last in the bog country a day north of the place they call the Three Hills; and they turned like a boar at bay. We were flushed with easy triumph, for until that day it had been very easy. They crumbled at a prick, but that day it was not so. Those others had been but the flakings of the flint, and these were the core; a small core, so small . . . They faced outward all ways, with the winged god upreared in their midst; and when we broke their shield-wall, one would step over his fallen brother, and lo, the shield-wall would be whole as before. We pulled them down at last—aye, but they took a goodly escort of our warriors with them. We pulled them down until there were left but a knot—as many as there are fingers on my two hands—and the winged god still in their midst. I, Tradui, I slew with my last throw-spear the priest in the spotted hide who held the staff; but another caught it from him as he fell, and held it so that the winged god did not go down, and rallied the few who were left, yet again. He was a chieftain among the rest, he had a taller crest, and his cloak was of the warrior scarlet. I wish that it had been I who killed him, but one was before me . . .

'Well, we made an end. There will be no more Red Crests going to and fro in our hunting grounds. We left them to the raven and the wolf, and also to the bog. Bog country is swift to swallow the traces of fighting. Yes, and we brought back the winged god; we, the Epidaii, claiming it as our right because it was the warriors of the Epidaii who were First Spear at the killing. But there was heavy rain later, and the rivers coming down in spate; and at a ford the warrior who carried the god was swept away, and though we found the god again (three lives it cost us, in the finding), the wings, which were not one with it but fitted into holes in its body, were gone from it, and so were the shining wreaths that hung from its staff; so that when we brought it to the Place of Life it was as you saw it tonight. Still, we gave it to the Horned One for tribute, and surely the Horned One was well pleased, for have not our wars gone well for us ever since, and the deer waxed fat in our hunting runs? And I will tell you another thing concerning the Eagle-god; it is ours now, ours, the Epidaii's; but if ever the day comes when we host against the Red Crests again, when the Crantara goes out through Albu, calling the tribes to war, the Eagle-god will be as a spear in the hands of all the tribes of Albu, and not of the Epidaii alone.'

The bright old eyes turned at last, consideringly, to Marcus's face. 'He was like you, that Chieftain of the Red Crests; yes. And yet you say that you are a Greek. Surely that is strange?'

Marcus said, 'There are many of Greek blood among the Red Crests.'

'So. That might be it.' The old man began to fumble under the shoulder-folds of the chequered cloak he wore. 'They were truly warriors, and we left them their weapons, as befits warriors . . . But from that chieftain I took this for the virtue in it, as one takes the tush from a boar who was fierce and valiant above others of his kind; and I have worn it ever since.' He had found what he wanted now, and slipped a leather thong from about his neck. 'It will not go on my hand,' he added, almost fretfully. 'It must be that the Red Crests had narrower hands than we have. Take it and look.'

A ring swung on the end of the thong, sparkling faintly with green fire in the torch-light. Marcus took it from him and bent his head to examine it. It was a heavy signet-ring; and on the flawed emerald which formed the bezel was engraved the dolphin badge of his own family. He held it for a long moment, held it very gently, as if it were a living thing, watching the torch-light play in the green heart of the stone. Then he gave it back into the old man's waiting hand with a casual word of thanks, and turned his attention again to the dancers. But the fierce whirl of the dance was blurred on his sight, for suddenly, across twelve years and more, he was looking up at a dark, laughing man who seemed to tower over him. There were pigeons wheeling behind the man's bent head, and when he put up his hand to rub his forehead, the sunlight that rimmed the pigeons' wings with fire caught the flawed emerald of the signet-ring he wore.

All at once, with over much finding-out for one day, Marcus was tired to the depths of his soul.

Next morning, sitting on an open hill-shoulder where they could not be overheard, Marcus laid his plans very carefully with Esca.

He had already told the Chieftain that he was for starting south again next day, and the Chieftain, and indeed the whole dun, were loath to let him go. Let him stay until spring; maybe there would be more sore eyes for him to salve.

But Marcus had remained firm, saying that he wished to be in the south again before the winter closed in, and now, with the great gathering for the Feast of New Spears breaking up and going its separate ways, was surely the time for him to be going too. The friendliness of the tribesmen gave him no sense of guilt in what he was going to do. They had welcomed and sheltered him and Esca, and in return Esca had hunted and herded with them, and he had doctored their sore eyes with all the skill that he possessed. In all that there was no debt on either side, no room for guilt. In the matter of the Eagle, they were the enemy, an enemy worthy of his steel. He liked and respected them; let them keep the Eagle if they could.

That last day passed very quietly. Having laid their plans and made what few preparations were needful, Marcus and Esca sat in the sun, doing—to all outward seeming—nothing in particular, save watch the delicate flight of the sandpipers above the still waters of the loch. Towards evening they bathed; not their usual plunge and splash about for pleasure, but a ritual cleansing in readiness for whatever the night might bring. Marcus made his sunset prayers to Mithras, Esca made them to Lugh of the Shining Spear; but both these were Sun Gods, Light Gods, and their followers knew the same weapons against the dark. So they cleaned themselves for the fight, and ate as little as might be at the evening meal, lest a full stomach should blunt their spirits within them.

When the time came for sleep, they lay down as usual with Tradui and the dogs and Liathan in the great living-hut; lay down in the places nearest to the door, which also was usual with them, for they had always had it in mind that a time might come when they would wish to leave quietly in the night. Long after the rest were asleep, Marcus lay watching the red embers of the fire, while every nerve in his body twanged taut as an overdrawn bowstring; and beside him he could hear Esca breathing quietly, evenly, as he always breathed in sleep. Yet it was Esca, with a hunter's instinct for the passing of the night, who knew when midnight was gone by—the time at which the priest-kind would be making the nightly offering—and the Place of Life would be deserted again; and told Marcus so with a touch.

They got up silently, and slipped out of the hut. The hounds raised no outcry, for they were used to night-time comings and goings. Marcus dropped the deerskin apron silently into place behind him, and they made for the nearby gateway. They had no difficulty in getting out, for with the dun full of guests and so many of the tribe encamped outside, the thorn-trees that usually blocked the gate at night had not been set in place. They had counted on that.

Turning away from the camp-fires, the sleeping men, and the familiar things of this world, they struck off uphill, and the night engulfed them. It was a very still night, with a faint thunder haze dimming the stars, and once or twice as they walked a flicker of summer lightning danced along the sky-line. The moon had long since set, and in the darkness and the brooding quiet the mountains seemed to have drawn closer than by day; and as they dropped downward into the valley of the Place of Life, the blackness rose around them like water.

Esca had brought them into the valley from its head, behind the Place of Life, where the sun-dried turf would make no sound at their passing, and carry no track afterwards. But in one place the heather came down almost to the foot of the standing-stones, and he stooped and broke off a long switch of it, and thrust it into the strap about his waist. They reached the lower end of the temple, and stood for what seemed a long time to listen for any sound; but the silence was like wool in their ears; not a bird cried, even the sea was silent tonight. No sound in all the world save the quickened drubbing of their own hearts. They passed between the standing stones and stood in the paved forecourt.

The black mass of the barrow rose above them, its crest of thorn-trees upreared against the veiled stars. The massive granite uprights and lintel were a faint pallor against the surrounding turf; it swelled on their sight as they walked towards it. They were on the threshold.

Marcus said softly but very clearly, 'In the Name of Light,' and feeling for the edge of the sealskin curtain, lifted it back. The bronze discs on it grated and chimed very faintly as he did so. He ducked under the low lintel, Esca beside him, and the curtain swung back into place. The black darkness seemed to press against his eyes, against his whole body, and with the darkness, the atmosphere of the place. The atmosphere: it was not evil, exactly, but it was horribly personal. For thousands of years this place had been the centre of a dark worship, and it was as though they had given to it a living personality of its own. Marcus felt that at any moment he would hear it breathe, slowly and stealthily, like a waiting animal . . . For an instant sheer panic rose in his throat, and as he fought it down, he was aware of a rustle and a faint glow, as Esca fetched out from under his cloak the fire-pot and glim they had brought with them. Next instant a tiny tongue of flame sprang up, sank to a spark, and rose again, as the wick in its lump of beeswax caught. Esca's bent face grew suddenly out of the dark as he tended the little flame. As it steadied, Marcus saw that they were in a passage, walled, floored, and roofed with great slabs of stone. How long it might be there was no guessing, for the little light could find no end to it. He held out his hand for the glim. Esca gave it to him, and holding it high he walked forward, leading the way. The passage was too narrow for two to walk abreast.

A hundred paces, the darkness giving back unwillingly before them, crowding hungrily in behind, and they stood on the threshold of what must once have been the tomb chamber, and saw, set close before them on the slightly raised flagstone at the entrance, a shallow and most beautifully wrought amber cup filled to the brim with something that gleamed darkly and stickily red in the light of the glim. Deer's blood, maybe, or the blood of a black cock. Beyond, all was shadow, but as Marcus moved forward with the light, past the midnight offering, the shadows drew back, and he saw that they were standing in a vast circular chamber, the stone walls of which ran up out of the candle-light and seemed to bend together high overhead into some kind of dome. Two recesses at either side of the chamber were empty, but there was a third in the far wall, opposite the entrance. In it, too far off for any spark of light to catch its gilded feathers, something was propped a little drunkenly, blotted dark against the stones; that must surely be the Eagle of the Ninth Legion.

Otherwise the place was empty, and its emptiness seemed to add a hundredfold to its menace. Marcus did not know what he had expected to find here, but he had not expected to find nothing—nothing at all, save that in the exact centre of the floor lay a great ring of what appeared to be white jadite, a foot or more across, and a superbly shaped axehead of the same material, arranged so that one corner of the blade very slightly overlapped the ring.

That was all.

Esca's hand was on his arm, and his voice whispering urgently in his ear: 'It is strong magic. Do not touch it!'

Marcus shook his head. He was not going to touch it.

They made their way round the thing, and reached the recess in the far wall. Yes, it was the Eagle all right.

'Take the glim,' Marcus whispered.

He lifted it from its place, realizing as he did so that the last Roman hand to touch the stained and battered shaft had been his father's. An odd, potent link across the years, and he held to it as to a talisman, as he set about freeing the Eagle from its staff.

'Hold the light this way—a little higher. Yes, keep it so.'

Esca obeyed, steadying the shaft with his free hand that Marcus might have both hands free to work with. It would have been easier to have lain the thing on the ground and knelt down to it, but both of them had a feeling that they must remain on their feet, that to kneel down would put them at a disadvantage with the Unknown. The light fell on the heads of the four slim bronze pegs that passed through the Eagle's talons, securing them through the crossed thunderbolts to the shaft. They should have drawn out easily enough, but they had become corroded into their holes, and after trying for a few moments to shift them with his fingers, Marcus drew his dagger, and began to lever them up with that. They came, but they came slowly. It was going to take some time—some time here in this horrible place that was like a crouching animal waiting to spring at any moment. The first peg came out, and he slipped it into his belt and began on the second. Panic began to whimper up from his stomach again, and again he thrust it down. No good hurrying; once he started to hurry he would never get these pegs out. For a moment he turned over in his mind the idea of taking the whole standard outside and finding some hide-out among the heather, and doing the job in the clean open air. But the job would have to be done, for the whole standard was too big to hide in the place that they had in mind; time was limited, and he could not work quickly without light, and light, anywhere outside, might betray them, however carefully they shielded it. No, this was the one place where they might be safe from interruption (for unless something went wrong, the priest-kind would not return until the next midnight)—from the interruption of men, that was.

Marcus began to feel that he could not breathe. 'Quietly,' he told himself. 'Breathe quietly; don't hurry.' The second pin came out, and he thrust it into his belt with the other; and as Esca turned the shaft over, began on the third. It came more easily, and he had just started on the fourth and last, when it seemed to him that he could not see as clearly as he had done a few moments ago. He looked up, and saw Esca's face shining with sweat in the upward light of the glim; but surely the glim was giving less light than it had done? Even as he looked, the tiny flame began to sink, and the dark came crowding on.

It might be only bad air, or a fault in the wick—or it might not. He said urgently, 'Think Light! Esca, *think Light*!' And even as he spoke, the flame sank to a blue spark. Beside him he heard Esca's breath, whistling through flaring nostrils; his own heart had begun to race, and he felt not only the many-fingered dark, but the walls and roof themselves closing in on him, suffocating him as though a soft cold hand was pressed over his nose and mouth. He had a sudden hideous conviction that there was no longer a straight passage and a leather curtain between them and the outer world, only the earth-piled mountain high over them, and no way out. No way out! The darkness reached out to finger him, softly. He braced himself upright against the cold stones, putting out his will to force the walls back, fighting the evil sense of suffocation. He was doing as he had told Esca to do, thinking Light with all the strength that was in him, so that in his inner eye, the place was full of it: strong, clear light flowing into every cranny. Suddenly he remembered the flood of sunset light in his sleeping-cell at Calleva, that evening when Esca and Cub and Cottia had come to him in his desperate need. He called it up now, like golden water, like a trumpet call, the Light of Mithras. He hurled it against the darkness, forcing it back—back—back.

How long he stood like that he never knew, until he saw the blue spark strengthen slowly, sink a little, and then lick up suddenly into a clear, small flame. It might have been only a fault in the wick . . . He realized that he was breathing in great shuddering gasps, and the sweat was running down his face and breast. He looked at Esca, and Esca returned his look; neither of them spoke. Then he started again on the fourth pin. It was the most stubborn of the lot, but it yielded at last, and Eagle and thunderbolts came loose in his hands. He lifted them off with a long, shaken breath, and sheathed his dagger. Now that it was done, he wanted to fling the staff aside and make a blind dash for the open air, but he schooled himself to take the staff from Esca and return it to its place in the recess, to lay the thunderbolts and the four bronze pegs on the floor beside it, before he turned at last to go, carrying the Eagle in the crook of his arm.

Esca had taken the branch of heather from his belt, and, still carrying the glim, followed him, moving backward to brush out any recognizable tracks they might have left in the dust. His own tracks, Marcus knew, were all too easily recognizable, because, however hard he tried not to, he dragged his right leg a little.

It seemed a long way round to the other side of the tomb chamber, and every few instants Esca glanced hastily aside to the ring and the axehead, as though they were a snake about to strike. But they gained the mouth of the entrance passage at last, and began to make their way down it; Esca still switching out their trail. Marcus moved sideways along the wall, guarding his own back and his friend's. Esca's crouching figure blotted out most of the light from the glim he carried, save where it fell on the dusty flag-stones and the flicking heather-switch, and his shadow swallowed up their way, so that every step Marcus took was into the edge of the darkness. The passage seemed much longer than it had done when they followed it inward; so long that a new nightmare grew on Marcus that either there were two passages and they had chosen the wrong one, or the only one had ceased, since their coming in, to have an end.

But the end was still there. Suddenly Esca's giant shadow ran on to the sealskin curtain, and they had reached it.

'Get ready to douse the light,' Marcus said.

The other glanced round without a word. Marcus's hand was on the curtain when they were plunged in darkness. He drew it back slowly, with infinite care, ears and eyes straining for any hint of danger, and the two of them ducked out under the lintel. He let the curtain ease back into place behind them, and stood with his hand on Esca's shoulder, drawing in great gasps of the clean night air with its scent of bog myrtle and its salt tang of the sea, and gazing up at the veiled stars. It seemed to him that they had been many hours in the dark; but the stars had swung only a little way on their courses since he saw them last. The summer lightning was still flickering along the hills. He realized that Esca was shuddering from head to foot, like a horse that smells fire, and tightened his hand on his friend's shoulder.

'We are out,' he said. 'We are through. It is over. Steady, old wolf.'

Esca answered him with a shaken breath of laughter. 'It is that I want to be sick.'

'So do I,' Marcus said. 'But we have no time, just now. This is no place to wait in until we are discovered by the priest-kind. Come.'

Some while later, having recrossed the hills and fetched a wide half-circle round the dun and encampment, they emerged from the steeply falling woods on to the bleak shores of the loch, just where a spit of rough turf and boulders laced together with alder scrub ran out from the grey shingle beach. Just above the beach they halted, and Esca hurriedly stripped. 'Now give me the Eagle.' He took it, handling it reverently, though it had been no Eagle of his; and a moment later Marcus was alone. He stood with one hand on a low-hanging rowan branch, and watched the pale blur that was Esca's body slip down through the alder scrub, and come out on the spit of land below. There was the tiniest splash as of a fish leaping, then silence; only the water lapping on the lonely shore, and then the faint mutter of thunder a long way off, and a night bird cried eerily in the heavy silence. For what seemed a long time, he waited, eyes straining into the darkness, and then suddenly a pale blur moved again on the spit, and a few moments later Esca was beside him once again, wringing the water out of his hair.

'Well?' Marcus murmured.

'It fits into the place under the bank like a nut into a nutshell,' Esca told him. 'They might search till the loch runs dry, and never find it; but I shall know the place when I come again.'

The next danger was that their absence would have been noticed; but when they came to the dun again, and passed unseen through the gateway, all was quiet. They were none too soon. The sky was still black—blacker than at their setting out, for the cloud had thickened, blotting out the stars. But the smell of the day-spring was in the air, unmistakable as that other smell of thunder. They slipped in through the hut-place doorway. In the darkness only the embers of the fire glowed like red jewels, and nothing moved. Then a dog growled, half sleepily, green-eyed in the gloom, and there was a sudden stirring and an equally sleepy murmur of enquiry from Liathan, who lay nearest to the door.

'It is only I,' Marcus said. 'Vipsania was restless; it's the thunder in the air. Always makes her restless.'

He lay down. Esca also lay down, curled close to the fire, that he might not have damp hair to explain in the morning. Silence settled again over the sleeping-hut.

XVI
The Ring-Brooch

A FEW hours later Marcus and Esca took their leave of the Dun, and started out, riding through a world that was clear-washed and as deeply coloured as a purple grape, after the thunderstorm which had finally broken over them at dawn. Southwards they went at first, following the shores of the loch to its foot, then north-east by a herding path through the mountains that brought them down towards evening to the shores of another loch, a long sea-loch this time, loud with the crying of shore-birds. That night they slept in a village that was no more than a cluster of turf bothies clinging to the narrow shore between the mountains and the grey water, and next morning set out again for the head of the loch, where there was a village through which they had passed before.

All that day they rode easily, breathing the horses often. Marcus was eager to be out of this land of sea lochs, through which one had to zigzag like a snipe, in which one could so easily become trapped and entangled, but it was no good getting too far from the Place of Life before the next move in the game could be played. The loss of the Eagle would have been discovered at midnight, when the priest went to renew the offering, and suspicion, though it would be widespread over all outside the tribe who had gathered to the Feast of New Spears, would certainly fall most heavily on himself and Esca. So the tribe would be up and after them long before now. Knowing the way that they had taken, Marcus reckoned that their pursuers could be up with them not long after noon if they crossed the loch by coracle and commandeered ponies on the near shore, as they undoubtedly would do. But he had forgotten to allow for the difficulties of the few mountain passes, and it was much later than he had expected when at last his ear caught the soft drumming of unshod hooves a long way off; and looking back, he saw a ragged skein of six or seven horsemen coming at break-neck speed down a steep side-glen towards them. He drew a quick breath that was almost of relief, for it had been a nerve-racking business waiting for them. 'Here they come at last,' he said to Esca; and then as a distant yell echoed down the mountain-side, 'Hear how the hounds give tongue.'

Esca laughed quietly, his eyes bright with the excitement of danger. 'Sweff! Sweff!' he encouraged them softly. 'Do we ride on, or rein in and wait for them?'

'Rein in and wait,' Marcus decided. 'They will know that we have seen them.'

They wheeled the mares, and sat waiting while the skein of wild riders swept towards them, the ponies sure-footed as goats among the rocks of the steep glen. 'Mithras! What cavalry they would make!' Marcus said, watching them. Vipsania was uneasy; she fidgeted and side-stepped, blowing down her nose, her ears pricked forward, and he patted her neck reassuringly. The tribesmen had reached the low ground now, and swung into the long curve of the lochside; and a few moments later they were up with the two who waited for them, and reining back their ponies in full gallop, dropped to the ground.

Marcus looked them over as they crowded in on him, seven warriors of the tribe, Dergdian and his brother among them. He took in their ugly looks, and the war-spears they carried, and his face was puzzled and enquiring. 'Dergdian? Liathan? What is it that you want with me, in so much haste?'

'You know well enough what it is that we want with you,' Dergdian said. His face was set like a stone, and his hand tightened on the shaft of his spear.

'But I fear that I do not,' Marcus said in a tone of rising annoyance, pretending not to notice that two of the tribesmen, leaving their own mounts standing, had gone to Vipsania's and Minna's heads. 'You will have to tell me.'

'Yes, we will tell you,' an older hunter cut in. 'We come to take back the winged god; also for blood to wash out the insult that you have put upon us and upon the gods of our tribe.'

The others broke into a threatening outcry, pressing in on the two, who had by now dismounted also. Marcus faced them with a pucker of bewilderment between his black brows. 'The winged god?' he repeated. 'The Eagle-god that we saw carried at the Feast of New Spears? Why, you—' Light seemed to dawn on him. 'You mean that you have lost it?'

'We mean that it is stolen, and we are come to take it back from those who robbed us,' Dergdian said very softly; and the softness was as though a cold finger gently stroked Marcus's spine.

He looked into the other's face with slowly widening eyes. 'And it must needs be I who stole it?' he said, and then flared out at them. 'Why in the name of the Thunderer should I want a wingless Roman Eagle?'

'You might have had your reasons,' said the Chieftain in the same soft voice.

'I cannot think of any.'

The tribesmen were growing impatient; there were shouts of 'Kill! kill!' And they crowded closer; fierce, rage-darkened faces were thrust into Marcus's and a spear was shaken before his eyes. 'Kill the thieves! There has been enough of talking!'

Startled by the angry turmoil, Vipsania was flinging this way and that, showing the whites of her eyes, and Minna squealed, going up in a rearing turn as she tried to break from the man who held her, and was forced down again by a blow between the ears.

Marcus raised his voice above the tumult. 'Is it the custom of the Seal People to hunt down and slay those who have been their guests? Well do the Romans call the men of the North barbarians.'

The shouting sank to a sullen, menacing mutter, and he went on more quietly.

'If you are so sure that we have stolen the Red Crests' god you have but to search our gear, and you will surely find it. Search, then.'

The muttering grew fiercer, and Liathan had already turned to Esca's mare, stretching out his hand to the fastening of the pack. Marcus moved distastefully aside, and stood watching. Esca's hand tightened for an instant on the shaft of his spear, as though he longed to use it; then he shrugged, and swung away to join Marcus. Together they watched their few possessions tumbled on the grass; a couple of cloaks, a cooking-pot, some strips of smoked deer-meat flung out with rough haste. The lid of the bronze medicine box was wrenched back, and one of the hunters began to rummage inside like a little dog after a rat. Marcus said quietly to the Chieftain, who stood beside him with folded arms, also looking on, 'Will you bid your hounds be less rough with the tools of my trade. It may be that there are still sore eyes in Albu, though your small son's eyes are well.'

Dergdian flushed at the reminder, and glanced aside at him for an instant, with a kind of sullen half-shame; then he spoke sharply to the man who was delving among the salves. 'Softly, you fool; there is no need that you should break the medicine sticks.'

The man growled, but handled the things more carefully thereafter. Meanwhile the others had unfolded and shaken out the sheepskin saddle-pads, and all but torn the bronze ring-brooch out of a violet-coloured cloak by their rough handling.

'Are you satisfied now?' Marcus asked, when everything had been turned inside out, and the tribesmen stood about, baffled and empty-handed, staring down at the chaos they had made. 'Or is it that you would search us to the skin?' He held out his arms, and their eyes ran over him, over Esca. It was perfectly obvious that they could have nothing a tenth the size and weight of the Eagle hidden on them.

The Chieftain shook his head. 'We must cast our net wider, it seems.'

The tribesmen were all known to Marcus, at least by sight; they looked bewildered, sullen, a little shamed, and they found it hard to meet his eyes. At a gesture from the Chieftain they began to gather up the scattered objects and bundle them, with the torn cloak with its dangling ring-brooch, into the pack-cloth. Liathan stooped to the disembowelled medicine box, glancing up at Marcus, and then away again.

They had offended against their own laws of hospitality. They had hunted down two who had been their guests, and not found the winged god, after all. 'Come back with us,' said the Chieftain. 'Come back with us, lest our hearths are shamed.'

Marcus shook his head. 'We are for the south, before the year closes in. Go and cast your net wider for this wingless winged god of yours. We shall remember that we have been your guests, Esca and I.' He smiled. 'The rest we have already forgotten. Good hunting to you on the game trails this winter.'

When the tribesmen had whistled up their own ponies, who had stood quietly by all this while with their reins over their heads, and, remounting, set off back the way they had come, Marcus did not move at once. He stood gazing after the dwindling specks up the glen, with a queer regret, while his hand mechanically soothed and fondled his upset and angry mare.

'Do you wish the Eagle yet in the place we took it from?' Esca asked.

Marcus was still watching those dwindling specks, almost out of sight now. 'No,' he said. 'If it were yet in the place we took it from, it would be still a danger to the Frontier—a danger to other Legions. Also it was my father's Eagle and none of theirs. Let them keep it if they can. Only it is in my heart that I wish we need not have made Dergdian and his sword-brethren ashamed.'

They saw to their gear, tightened the ponies' belly-straps, and rode on.

Presently the loch began to narrow, and the mountains to crowd in on it, rising almost sheer from the water's edge; and at last they caught sight of the village; the distant huddle of turf bothies at the head of the loch, cattle grazing up the steep glen behind, and the straight blue smoke of cooking-fires rising pale against the sombre browns and purples of the mountains that towered above them.

'It is time that I sickened of the fever,' said Esca, and without more ado he began to sway from side to side, his eyes half closed. 'My head!' he croaked. 'My head is on fire.'

Marcus reached out and took the reins from him. 'Slump a little more and roll a little less; it is fever, not metheglin, that lit the fire, remember,' he directed, beginning to lead the other horse with his own.

The usual crowd of men and women, children and boys gathered to meet them as they entered the village, and here and there, people called out a greeting to them, glad in their remote way to see them back again. With Esca slumped over Minna's neck beside him, Marcus singled out the ancient headman, greeted him with due courtesy, and explained that his servant was sick and must rest a few days; two days, three at the most. It was an old sickness that returned from time to time, and would last no longer, given proper treatment.

The headman replied that they were welcome to share his fireside, as they had done when they passed that way before. But to that, Marcus shook his head. 'Give us some place to ourselves; it matters not how rough, so long as it will keep out the weather. But let it be as far from your living-huts as may be. The sickness of my servant is caused by devils in his belly, and to drive them out it is needful that I use strong magic.' He paused, and looked round at the questioning faces. 'It will do no harm to this village, but it cannot be looked upon safely by any who have not the signs for protection. That is why we must have lodging apart from the living-huts.'

They looked at each other. 'It is always dangerous to look upon forbidden things,' said a woman, accepting the story without surprise. There could be no question of refusing them shelter; Marcus knew the laws of the tribes. They talked the matter over quickly among themselves, and finally decided that Conn's cow-byre, which was not now in use, would be the best place.

Conn's cow-byre proved to be the useful turf bothy, exactly like the living-huts, save that it was not set so far below ground-level, and there was no hearth in the centre of the trampled earthern floor. It was well away from the main rath, with its doorway at an angle that would make it possible to slip out and in without showing up too clearly to any watchers among the living-huts. So far, so good.

The villagers, feeling perhaps that a man who could conjure out devils was best treated kindly, did their best for the two returned strangers; and by dusk the mares had been taken in charge, fresh fern stacked inside the hut for bedding, an old skin rug skewered up over the doorway; and the women had brought broiled boar's flesh for Marcus, and warm ewe's milk for Esca, who lay on the piled bracken, moaning and babbling most realistically.

Later, with the deerskin rug drawn close across the door, and the villagers crowded about their own hearths with faces and thoughts carefully turned from the outlying bothy and the magic that would be a-making there, Marcus and Esca looked at each other by the faint light of a floating reed-wick in a shell of rancid seal oil. Esca had eaten the lion's share of the meat, for he would need it most; and now, with a few strips of smoked deer meat thrust into the middle of a rolled-up cloak, he stood ready to go.

At the last moment, Marcus said savagely, 'Oh, curse this leg of mine! It should be me going back, not you.'

The other shook his head. 'That leg of yours makes no difference. If it were as sound as mine, still it would be better, quicker, and safer that I should go. You could not leave this place and return to it in the dark, without rousing the dogs; but I can. You could not find your way through the passes that we have traversed only once before. It is work for a hunter—a hunter born and bred, not a soldier who has learned a little forest-craft.' And he reached up to the little stinking lamp hanging from the roof tree, and pinched it out.

Marcus drew back a fold of the rug and peered out into the soft darkness of the mountains. Away to the right, a solitary glint of gold shone from the chink in a deerskin apron over a distant doorway. The moon was behind the mountains, and the waters of the loch were only a lesser darkness, without spark or lustre.

'All is clear,' he said. 'You are sure you can find the way?'

'Yes.'

'Good hunting, then, Esca.'

A dark shadow slipped past him, and was gone into the night. And he was alone.

He stood for a while in the bothy doorway, ears stretched for any sound to break the silence of the mountains, but heard only the wet whisper of falling water where the swift stream came tumbling into the loch, and a long while later, the belling of a stag. When he was sure that Esca had got clear away, he dropped the rug. He did not re-light the lamp, but sat for a long time on the piled bracken in the pitchy darkness, with his arms across his knees, thinking. His one comfort was the sure knowledge that if Esca ran into trouble, he himself would very soon share it.

For three nights and two days Marcus kept guard over an empty hut. Twice a day one of the women, with face averted, would bring broiled meat and fresh ewe milk, sometimes herrings, once a golden lump of wild honeycomb, and set them on a flat stone a little way off, and Marcus would collect them and later take back the empty bowls. After the first day there were only women and children in the village; evidently the men had gone to answer some call from the dun. He wondered whether he ought to provide noises for the benefit of the village, but decided that silence would probably be more effective; so save for a little muttering and moaning when he thought someone was near enough to hear, just enough to keep it in their mind that there were two people in the bothy, he remained silent. He slept when he could, but he did not dare to sleep much, for fear that trouble should blow up suddenly when he was not on the alert for it. Most of his time, day or night, was spent sitting just within the doorway watching, through a back-drawn chink in the rug, the grey waters of the loch and the sheer, boulder-strewn upward thrust of the mountains towering so high above him that he had to tip his head far back to see their jagged crests where the mist-rags trailed among the peaks and the high corries.

Autumn had come to the mountains almost overnight, he thought. A few days ago, summer had still lingered, though the heather was past its flowering and the flaming rowan berries long since gone. But now it was the Fall of the Leaf; one could smell it in the wind, and the trees of the glen grew bare and the brawling stream ran gold with yellow birch leaves.

Some while ago after moonset on the third night, without any warning, a hand brushed across the skin rug at the entrance, and as Marcus tensed in the close darkness, he heard the faintest ghost of a whistle: the broken, two-note whistle that he had always used to summon Cub. A sudden wave of relief broke over him, and he echoed the whistle. The rug was drawn aside and a black shape slipped through.

'Is it well?' Esca whispered.

'It is well,' Marcus returned, striking flint and steel to kindle the lamp. 'And with you? How went the hunting?'

'The hunting was good,' Esca said, as the tiny flame sprang up and steadied, and he stood and set down something closely bundled in the cloak.

Marcus looked at it. 'Was there any trouble?'

'None, save that I pulled the bank down a little in landing with the Eagle. It must have been rotten, I suppose—but there is nothing in a bank slip to set anyone thinking.' He sat down wearily. 'Is there anything to eat?'

Marcus had made a habit of saving each meal that he was given, and eating it only when the next one came, so that he always had a meal in hand, packed into the old cooking-pot. He produced it now, and sat with his hand resting on the bundle that meant so much to him, while he watched the other eat, and listened to the story of the last three days, told in low snatches between mouthfuls.

Esca had cut back across the mountains without much difficulty, but by the time he reached the Loch of Many Islets it had been near to dawn, and he had had to lie up in the dense hazel-woods through the day. Twice during the day parties of warriors had passed close to his hiding-place, carrying coracles, and evidently bound, like himself, for the dun by the short way across the loch. Also they had been carrying war-spears, he said. As soon as it was dark, he had set out once again to swim the loch. It was little more than a mile across at the place he chose, and that, too, had not been difficult. He had worked his way down the far shore until he came to the spit of land that marked the place where they had hidden the Eagle; found it, and landed again, pulling down the bank a little in doing so, and bundled it in the wet cloak that he had carried bound to his shoulder. Then he had returned the way he came as fast as might be, for the dun was thrumming like a disturbed bees' nest. Of a certainty the tribe was hosting. It had all been very easy—almost too easy.

Esca's voice was growing blurred towards the close of the story. He was blind weary, and the instant he had finished eating, he stretched out on the piled bracken and sleep took him like a tired hound after a day's hunting.

But before the sun was above the mountains next day they were on their way once more, for though they were now clear of suspicion, it was no time for lingering. The village had shown no signs of surprise at Esca's sudden recovery; presumably when the devils were no longer in his belly the man was whole again. They had given the travellers more of the eternal smoked meat, and a boy—a wild, dark-faced lad too young for the hosting and sulking in consequence—to guide them on the next stage of their journey, and bidden them good hunting and let them go.

That day they had gruelling travelling; no level loch-side to follow, but a steep thrust northward into the heart of the mountains, and then east—so far as they could hold to any course—by narrow passes between sheer heather-washed crags of black rock, skirting wide mountain shoulders, traversing bare ridges, across what seemed to be the roof of the world; until at last the lie of the country turned them south again into the long downward sweep that ended afar off in the marshes of the Cluta. Here the boy parted from them, refusing to share their camp for the night, and set off back the way he had come, tireless as a mountain buck among his native glens.

They watched him go, easily, not hurrying, at the long, springing mountaineer's stride. He would walk like that through the night and arrive home before dawn, not much tired. Marcus and Esca were both hillmen, but they could never have equalled that, not among these crags and passes. They turned their back on the last glimpse of Cruachan, and set off southward, making for more sheltered country, for once again there was storm in the air, not thunder this time, but wind—wind and rain. Well, that would not matter much; mist was the one thing that would matter, and at least an autumn gale would keep the autumn mists away. Only once before had weather meant as much to Marcus as it did now: on the morning of the attack at Isca Dumnoniorum when mizzle rain had kept the signal smoke from rising.

In the last flush of the evening they came upon the ruins of a broch, one of those strange, chambered towers built by a forgotten people, perched like a falcon's eyrie on the very edge of the world. They made camp there, in company with the skeleton of a wolf picked bare by ravens.

Thinking it best not to light a fire, they simply knee-hobbled the mares, gathered fern for bedding, and after filling the cooking-pot at the mountain stream, which came leaping down through its own narrow gorge nearby, sat down with their backs to the crumbling stones of the entrance, to eat leathery shavings of dried meat.

Marcus stretched out thankfully. It had been a gruelling march; most of the day they had had to trudge and scramble, leading Vipsania and Minna, and his lame leg was aching horribly, despite the ready help that he had had from Esca. It was good to rest.

Before their feet the land swept away southward over ridge after ridge into the blue distance, where, a thousand feet below and maybe two days' march away, the old frontier cut Valentia from the wilderness. Far below them, among dark ranks of pine-trees, the northern arm of a great loch reflected back the flame of the sunset; and Marcus greeted it as a familiar friend, for he and Esca had followed its shores on their way north, almost two moons ago. A straight journey now, no more sniping to and fro among sea-lochs and mist-wrapped mountains, he thought; and yet there was a queer superstitious feeling in him that it had all been too easy—a queer foreboding of trouble to come. And the sunset seemed to echo his mood. A most wonderful sunset; the whole western sky on fire, and high overhead, torn off, hurrying wind clouds caught the light and became great wings of gold that changed, even while Marcus watched them, to fiery scarlet. Stronger and stronger grew the light, until the west was a furnace banked with purple cloud, and the whole world seemed to glow, and the upreared shoulder of the mountain far across the loch burned crimson as spilled wine. The whole sunset was one great threat of coming tempest; wind and rain, and maybe something more. Suddenly it seemed to Marcus that the crimson of that distant mountain shoulder was not wine, but blood.

He shook his shoulders impatiently, calling himself a fool. He was tired, so was Esca and the horses for that matter, and there was a storm on the way. That was all. A good thing that they had found shelter for the night; with any luck it would have blown itself out by morning. It struck him that he had not so much as looked at the Eagle. It had seemed better not to, in the village they had left that morning; but now . . . It lay beside him, and on a swift impulse he picked up the bundle and began to unroll it. The dark folds of the cloak as he turned them back caught a more brilliant colour from the sunset, warming from violet to Imperial purple. The last fold fell away, and he was holding the Eagle in his hands; cold, heavy, battered, burning red-gold in the sunset. 'Euge!' he said softly, using the word he would have used to praise a victory in the arena, and looked up at Esca. 'It was a good hunting, brother.'

But Esca's suddenly widened eyes were fixed on one corner of the cloak, outflung towards him, and he did not answer; and Marcus, following the direction of his gaze, saw the cloth at that corner torn and ragged.

'The ring-brooch!' Esca said. 'The ring-brooch!'

Still holding the Eagle in the curve of his arm, Marcus was hastily flinging the folds this way and that, but he knew that it was useless. The brooch had been in that corner. With sudden sharp-eyed vividness, now that it was too late, he remembered that scene by the loch-side, the threatening faces of the tribesmen gathered round, the gear tumbled on the coarse grass, the cloak with its dangling brooch all but torn out of the cloth by their furious handling. Fool that he was, it had gone completely out of his mind; out of Esca's, too, it seemed.

'It may have fallen at any time—even while you were in the water,' he said.

'No,' Esca said slowly. 'It rang on the pebbles when I dropped the cloak before I dived for the Eagle.' He rubbed the back of one hand across his forehead, thinking back. 'When I picked up the cloak, it caught for an instant on an alder root; you know how the alders grow right down to the water's edge. I remember now, but at the time I scarcely noticed.'

He dropped his hand and they sat quite still, staring at each other. The ring-brooch was a cheap bronze one, but its design was rather unusual, and the tribesmen must often have seen Demetrius of Alexandria wearing it. Also, to judge by the state of that jagged corner, there was probably a wisp of violet cloth caught in it, to help their memories.

Marcus was first to break the silence. 'If they find it, they will know that one of us has been back since they searched our gear, and there could be but one reason for that.' As he spoke, he began methodically to wrap up the Eagle once more.

'When they speak with the warriors from the village we left this morning, they will know that it was I who went back,' Esca said hurriedly, and checked. 'No, that will not serve, for they will know that I went with your knowledge . . . Listen, Marcus. You must push on alone. If you take Vipsania and go now, you may stand a chance. I will put myself in their way. I will tell them that we quarrelled for possession of the Eagle; we fought for it down yonder, and you went into the loch, and the Eagle with you.'

'And Vipsania?' Marcus said, his hands still busy with the folds of the cloak. 'And what will they do to you when you have told them this story?'

Esca said very simply, 'They will kill me.'

'I am sorry, but I do not think much of that plan,' Marcus said.

'There is the Eagle to be taken into account,' Esca urged.

Marcus made a quick, impatient gesture. 'The Eagle will serve no useful purpose when we get it home. I know that well enough. So long as it does not fall again into the tribesmen's hands to be a weapon against Rome, it will lie as worthily in a Caledonian bog as on a Roman scrap-heap. If the worst comes to the worst, we will find means to dispose of the Eagle before they take us.'

'It seems strange that you have not cast a thing of so little worth into the loch before this. Why trouble to carry it south at all?'

Marcus was already drawing his legs under him; but he checked an instant, his gaze holding Esca's. 'For an idea,' he said. He got up stiffly. 'We are in this together, and we will win clear together, or not at all. It may be days before that accursed brooch is found, none the less the sooner we get down to Valentia the better.'

Esca got up also, saying nothing. There was no more to be said, and he knew it.

Marcus glanced up at the wild clouds; hurrying clouds like wind-driven birds. 'How long have we before the storm breaks?'

The other seemed to be smelling the weather. 'Long enough to get down to the loch-side, anyway; there will be some shelter from the wind down there among the pine-woods. We might make a few more miles tonight.'

XVII
The Wild Hunt

TWO mornings later, Marcus lay full length in a hollow of the lowland hills and looked down through the parted bracken fronds. Grey and tawny marshes lay below him, rising to the blue heights of Valentia to the south, and through the flatness of them wound the silver Cluta, spreading westward into its firth: with Are-Cluta, once a frontier town, still a meeting-place and market for all the neighbouring tribes, squatting within turf ramparts on its northern bank. There were coracles on the river, looking, from this distance, like tiny water-beetles; one or two larger vessels with blue sails furled, riding at anchor below the dun, from which the smoke of many cooking-fires rose towards a high grey sky; a sky that was gentle with exhaustion after the autumn gale, Marcus thought, while he lay looking back over the past two days as it might be over a wild dream.

The storm had broken over them towards midnight, the wild westerly gale swooping at them down the shoulder of the mountains like a wild thing that wanted to destroy them; whipping the waters of the loch into racing white-caps, bringing with it the bitter, hissing rain to drench them through and through. They had passed the greater part of the night crouching with the two frightened mares under a steep overhang of rock, wrapped about with a shrieking turmoil of wind and rain and darkness. Towards dawn the storm had abated a little, and they had pushed on again until long past noon, when they had found a sheltered hollow under the bole of an uprooted pine, knee-hobbled the mares, and crawled under the upreared mass of torn roots, and slept. When they awoke it was well into the night, and the rain was falling softly before a dying wind that sobbed and roared through the pines but no longer beat against them like a live thing. They had eaten what was left of the smoked meat, and pushed on again through the dying storm, until, in the spent calm of the day-spring, with the wet oak-woods waking to the song of chaffinch and robin and wren, they had halted at last, here in the low hills above the Cluta.

As soon as it grew light, Esca had gone on down to Are-Cluta, to sell the mares. The parting was hard for all of them, for they had grown fond of each other, Marcus and Vipsania, Esca and Minna, in the months that they had been together; and the mares had known perfectly well that it was goodbye. A pity they could not have kept the mares, but with the old cavalry brand on their shoulders they were much too easily recognizable, and there was nothing for it but to trade them for others. But at least they would be sure of a good master, for the tribesmen loved their horses and hounds, using them hard but only as they used themselves hard, treating them as members of the family.

All would be well with Vipsania and Minna, Marcus told himself firmly. He stretched. It was good to lie here on the soft turf of the woodshore, to feel his tunic drying on him, and rest his aching leg, knowing that however fast the hunt came on their trail, they were past the last point where they could be cut off by men pouring down any side glen that linked loch with loch in the misty maze that was behind them. But how was it going with Esca, down there in the dun? Always it was Esca who had the extra task to do, the extra risk to run. It was bound to be so, for Esca, who was British, could pass unnoticed where Marcus, with his olive skin, his darkness that was of quite a different kind from that of the tribesmen, would be suspect at once. He knew that, but it infuriated him, none the less; all his relief began to ebb away, and as the morning dragged on he grew restless and yet more restless. He began to feel sickeningly anxious. What was happening down there? Why was Esca so long? Had word of the Eagle reached Are-Cluta ahead of them?

It was near to noon when Esca suddenly appeared in the glen below him, riding a shaggy mouse-coloured pony and leading another. Relief flooded over Marcus, and as the other glanced up towards his hiding-place he parted the bracken fronds more widely and flung up a hand. Esca returned the signal, and a few moments later, having joined Marcus in the little hollow, he dropped from the back of the shaggy creature he rode, with an air of duty well and truly done.

'Do you call these mossy-faced objects ponies?' Marcus enquired with interest, rolling over and sitting up.

Esca was busy with the bundle he had taken from one of them. For an instant his slow, grave smile lifted the corners of his mouth. 'The man who sold them to me swore they were sired out of the stables of the High King Eriu.'

'Did you by any chance believe him?'

'Oh no,' said Esca. He had looped the reins of both ponies over a low branch and sat down beside Marcus with the bundle. 'I told the man I sold ours to, that they were sired out of the stables of Queen Cartimandua. He did not believe me, either.'

'They were game little brutes, whoever sired them. You found them a good master?'

'Yes, and the same master for both; a little fox of a man, but he had the right hands. I told him my brother and I were taking ship for Eriu. It was a good enough reason for selling the mares, and if anyone should ever ask him, it may serve to start a false trail. We haggled for a long time, because the mares were near foundering. I had to tell him a long story about wolves, to account for that, and so of course he swore their wind was broken, which was obviously a lie. But I sold them to him at last, for a fine sealskin rug and two enamelled war-spears, and a bronze cooking-pot and a sucking pig. Oh, and three fine amber bracelets.'

Marcus flung up his head with a croak of laughter. 'What did you do with the sucking pig?'

'It was a little black pig, very shrill,' said Esca reflectively. 'I sold it to a woman, for this.' He had been busy with the bundle while he spoke, and now shook out a hooded cloak of shaggy cloth that seemed to have once been chequered blue and red, but was now grease-stained and weather-faded to a universal mud-colour. 'Even a small thing will help to change the look of a whole company—at least from a distance . . . Also for dried meat. Here it is. Then I went back to the horse market and bought these two, with their head-gear on them, for the war-spears and all the other things. The other man had the best of the bargain; ill luck go with him! But there was no help for that.'

'We are in no case to drive a hard bargain,' Marcus agreed with his mouth full. They were both eating by that time. 'I should have liked to have seen you with that piglet,' he added thoughtfully.

Neither of them wasted more time on words. They ate quickly, and not over much, since there was no knowing how long the food would have to last them; and by noon they had loaded their few belongings into the yellow pack-cloth, flung the sheepskin saddle-pads across the backs of their shaggy little mounts, tightened the belly-straps, and were on their way once more.

Marcus wore the cloak for which Esca had traded the black piglet, the hood pulled well over his forehead, for he had laid aside the hand-shaped talisman which was too distinctive to serve him any longer; and under the greasy, evil-smelling folds, he carried the lost Eagle. He had contrived a kind of sling for it, with strips torn from the cloak in which it was closely bundled, so as to have both hands free, but as he rode he cradled it in the crook of his bridle arm.

They fetched a wide half-circle around Are-Cluta, and reached the river again where it swung south-eastward into the heart of Valentia. Their return journey was very different from the outward one. Then, they had wandered openly from village to village, with a meal and a place by somebody's fire at the day's end. Now they were fugitives, lying up in some remote glen through the day, making southward through the night, and somewhere behind them, the hunt was up. For three days they had no sign that it was so, but they knew it in their hearts, and they pushed on grimly, listening always for sounds behind them. They made good speed, for the ponies, though not beautiful, were game little brutes, bred in the mountains, tough as whip-cord and sure-footed as goats, and they were able to ride much of the time. Presently, they knew, they might have to let the ponies go, and take to the heather on foot. Meanwhile they pushed on in desperate haste, that they might be as far south as possible before that time came.

The fourth evening found them on their way again, after a day spent lying-up in a thicket of thorn-trees. A murky evening, closing in under a low grey sky. In the low country at their backs it was dusk already, but up here on the high moors the daylight still lingered, reflected back by many little silver tarns among the brown heather.

'Three more days,' Marcus said suddenly. 'Three more days by my reckoning, and we should reach the Wall!'

Esca looked round to answer, and then suddenly his head went up with a jerk, as though he heard something. An instant later, Marcus heard it too, very faint and far behind: a hound giving tongue.

They had reached the crest of a long ridge of moorland, and looking back, they saw a cluster of dark specks cresting a lesser ridge behind them; a long way behind, but not too far to be recognized for what they were: men on horseback and many hounds. And in that instant another hound took up the cry.

'I spoke too soon,' Marcus said, and his voice jumped oddly in his own ears.

'They have sighted us.' Esca laughed sharply in his throat. 'The hunt is up with a vengeance. Ride, brother quarry!' And even as he spoke, his little mount leapt forward, snorting, from the jab of his heel.

Marcus urged his own pony into a tearing gallop at the same instant. The ponies were fairly fresh, but both fugitives knew that in the open it was only a matter of time before they were ridden down by the better-mounted tribesmen—pulled down by the yelling hounds as by a pack of wolves. And with one accord they swung a little in their course, heading for the higher ground ahead; broken country by the look of it, in which they might be able to shake off their pursuers.

'If we can keep the lead till dark,' Esca shouted above the drumming hooves and the wind of their going, 'we've a chance among the glens yonder.'

Marcus did not answer, but settled down to ride as he had never ridden before. The dark heather streaked backward under his pony's thudding hooves, the long harsh hairs of its mane sprayed back over his wrists, and the wind sung past his ears. For one flashing instant there rose in him the exultancy of speed, the surge and splendour that he had once thought never to know again. The instant passed, swift as the darting flight of a kingfisher. He was riding for his life with the dark hunt in full cry behind him, putting out all his skill to keep clear of hidden pitfalls, the hummocks and snags and snarls among the heather that might bring disaster, grimly aware that he could not grip strongly with his right knee, and if the pony stumbled at this flying gallop, he would go clean over its head. On and on they hurtled, now skirting a reed-fringed upland pool, now swerving from a patch of bog luminously green in the fading light; uphill and down, through bronze tides of dying heather, startling here a flock of plover, there a stray curlew from the bents, and always, behind them, the hunt drawing nearer. Marcus could hear the hounds giving tongue above the soft thunder of the ponies' hooves, nearer, steadily nearer; but there was no time for looking back.

On and on. Now the ponies were tiring. Marcus could feel the panting of his little mount's flanks, and foam flew back from its muzzle, spattering against him. He leaned far forward over its neck to ease it; he talked to it, sang and shouted, fondled its sweating neck and dug in his heels, urging it on by every means in his power, though indeed the poor brute was already winged by terror to its utmost speed, knowing as well as its rider the meaning of those sounds behind.

The land was rising under them, and the light fading moment by moment; the little glens and the hazel woods were very near; but so was the hunt. Snatching one glance over his shoulder, Marcus glimpsed a flying blur of horsemen and low-running hounds, smudged out of all clear shape by the twilight, streaking across the open turf, the leading hound scarce a bowshot away.

Near to their last gasp, and with the clamour of the hunt swelling in their ears, they struggled desperately over the crest of another ridge, and saw below them through the dusk the pale streak of running water. Very faintly, an unexpected scent drifted up to them, a sweet, heavy scent like musk, and Esca let out a sound that was halfway between a laugh and a sob. 'Down to the stream before they top the ridge, and we've a chance yet.'

Only half understanding, but content to trust to the other's better knowledge of the wild, Marcus drove his heel again and again into his pony's sobbing flank, urging it to one last effort. Shivering and sweating, the foam that flew from its muzzle blood-flecked now, it plunged forward in one last frantic burst of speed. Neck and neck they hurtled down through the tall bracken, the scent of musk growing every instant stronger; down and down towards the trampled hollow beside the stream, from which two battling, antlered shapes broke at their approach and went crashing away down the glen. Esca was already half off his pony, and in the musk-reeking hollow where only the instant before two great stags had been fighting for lordship of the herd, Marcus half fell, half flung himself from his own mount. His friend's arm was round him almost before he touched the ground. 'Into the water, quick!' Esca gasped, as, snorting with terror, the two ponies plunged on riderless into the dusk.

They dived through the alder scrub and scrambled headlong down the bank, Esca still with his arm round Marcus to help him, and slipped into the ice-cold, swift-running water, just as the first wave of the hunt topped the rise behind them. Crouching under the steep overhang, they heard the ponies crashing away downstream in terrified stampede, heard the hunt sweep down towards them, the check, the baying and the trampling and the sudden splurge of voices; and crouched lower yet, the water flowing almost to their nostrils.

It seemed an eternity that they crouched so, listening to the turmoil just above their heads, and praying that the dusk would hide the traces of their swift descent through the alder scrub, and that the hounds, having been set on to follow horses, would not concern themselves to pick up and follow the scent of men. But in reality it could have been only a few moments before a triumphant yell told them that the movement of the stampeding ponies had been picked up. The hounds were already away yelling on the hot scent of stags or ponies, or both. There was a fresh burst of shouts and trampling, the shrill, angry squeal of a horse, and with the confused speed of a dissolving nightmare, men, hounds, and horses were off in full cry after the flying shadows.

A little further down, the glen curved, bringing them for an instant into full view of the two who crouched under the bank and stared after them with straining eyes, a shadow chase, sweeping down the dusk-sodden glen, the wild clamour of their passing growing fainter with every beat of flying hooves; swiftly come, and passed, and gone, as though they had been the Wild Hunt, the hunters of souls.

The dusk swallowed them; the last, long-drawn cry of a hound drifted back on the night wind, and that was all. No sound now, but a curlew somewhere, and the racing of their own hearts.

Esca rose quickly to his feet. 'They will go like the wind for a while,' he said. 'Lightened of our weight, and terrified as they are; but they will be run down before long, and then the hunt will be back looking for us, so the sooner we are away from here, the better.'

Marcus was making sure he still had the Eagle safe in its sling. 'I feel sick about those ponies,' he said.

'There will be no harm come to them, unless their wind is broken. Those were hunting-dogs, trained to run down and bring to bay, and not to kill until the word is given. With us, I think the word would have been given, but the wanton waste of a horse is not in these hunters unless their tribe be different from all the other tribes of Britain.' Esca had been feeling about under the bank as he spoke, and now brought up his spear with a satisfied grunt. 'Better keep to the stream for a while, and break the trail,' he said, and put out a steadying hand to Marcus.

For what seemed an interminable time they struggled upstream, now wading knee deep through the shifting shallows, now plunged to the waist in the deep, swift flow where the stream narrowed. It was a fight every yard of the way, against the thrust of the water and the shifting footholds, against time, with every nerve on the stretch for the long-drawn cry of a hound that might rise at any moment above the soft rush of the stream.

It was quite dark now, for the moon was hidden by low cloud; and the hills closed round them, rising, blackly on every hand. The stream began to lead them too far eastward, and anyway, they dared not stick to it too long; and at last, where a narrow side glen opened to the south, they scrambled out, chilled to the bone, and thankful to be done with icy water. They shook themselves like dogs, wrung as much water as they could from their clothes, and set off again.

Presently, coming over a steep rise, they dropped down into another glen, wooded with hazel and rowan, through which another burn fell in steep slides and cascades of white water. Indeed, one never seemed out of the sound of running water in these hills. And stumbling at last on a jagged hollow left by a landslip that the rain had torn away, they more or less fell into it, and sat there, huddled close together for warmth, to get their breath and take stock of the situation.

The little food that they had left had gone with the ponies, and from now on they would have to march empty, since they certainly could not stop to trap for food as they went. They were still at least two full marches from the nearest station on the Wall, and must cover the distance on foot, through unfamiliar country with the wild hunt on their trail. All in all, their prospects did not look very bright.

Marcus sat rubbing his leg, which was aching intolerably, and staring at the white water through the dark blur of the hazels. The sense of being hunted was heavy on him, and he knew that it was on Esca, too. The very countryside seemed to have grown hostile and menacing, as though not only men were on their trail, but the whole land up and hunting, the dark hills themselves closing in to the kill. And yet the Wild had stood their friend once tonight, he told himself, setting a pair of battling stags in their way, just in the moment of their direst need.

They sat silent a short while longer, snatching a breathing space before pushing on again; but they dared not rest long, for they must be much further from the place where they had taken to the water, and in a much surer hiding, before dawn. Marcus sighed, and was actually drawing his legs under him to rise, when he became aware of Esca grown suddenly tense beside him, and then, above the soft wet rush of the stream, of someone, or something, moving far down the glen. Marcus crouched where he was, frozen, his head turned to listen, and gradually the sounds drew nearer: a queer confusion of sounds that might be one man or several, a great brushing and rustling through the hazel scrub. It came slowly up the glen towards them, while they crouched motionless in their hiding-place, nearer and louder until it seemed almost on top of them; and Marcus, peering up through the overhanging screen of rowan and hazel, made out a pale blur and a dark one. Of all homely and unexpected things, a man leading a cow.

Furthermore, the man was whistling softly between his teeth as he came up the burnside; so softly that it was not until he was within a few feet, that the tune broke through. A catchy tune.

'Oh when I joined the Eagles,
(As it might be yesterday)
I kissed a girl at Clusium
Before I marched away.'

Marcus reached up and parted the drooping rowan branches. 'Well met, Guern the Hunter,' he said in his own tongue.

XVIII
The Waters of Lethe

THERE was a sudden pause; the white cow, startled by the unexpected voice, fidgeting and blowing, with lowered horns; the man, who had checked with a grunt, peering down through the rowan branches. Then the soft growling of the old dog, which Marcus had not at first noticed, rose suddenly to a sing-song snarl, and was checked by a backward thrust of the hunter's heel.

'Well met, Demetrius of Alexandria.'

There was no time to waste in surprise and explanation. Marcus said quickly, 'Guern, we need your help.'

'Aye, I know that well enough. You have brought away the Eagle, and the Epidaii are up after you,' Guern said. 'The word went by at sunset, and the Dumnonii and my tribe at least will join spears with them.' He came a step nearer. 'What would you have me do?'

'We want food—and a false trail, if you can provide one.'

'Food is easily managed, but it is more than a false trail you will need to get you in one piece to the Wall. Every pass to the south will be guarded by now, and there is but one way known to me that is likely to be left open.'

'Tell us how to find it.'

'Telling is not enough. It is a way that is death without a guide. That is why the tribesmen will not trouble to guard it.'

'And you know this way?' Esca spoke for the first time.

'Yes, I know the way. I—will take you by it.'

'How if you are caught with us?' Marcus said. 'How if you are missed from your own place, and any think to wonder where you are?' .

'I shall not be missed from my own place, for there will be many out hunting these next few days. If any come upon us together I can always knife one of you, and claim the honour of being First Spear among the hunters.'

'It is a pleasant thought,' said Marcus. 'Do we come with you now?'

'Yes. It is best that you come the first part of the way now,' Guern decided. 'We shall have to take the cow; ill luck to her. She is for ever straying.'

Marcus laughed, and got up, catching his breath as his over-taxed leg twinged under him. 'At least her straying has stood us in good stead tonight. Give me your shoulder, Esca, this place is—somewhat—steep.'

Many steep glens and moorland ridges lay between them and the place of the fighting stags, and it was near dawn when Guern at last led them down into an old sandstone quarry that had not been worked since the Eagles flew from Valentia. He thrust them into the crumbling cave or gallery of some sort that seemed to have been the occasional lair of wild pig, and bidding them be quiet until he came again, departed with the cow, who seemed very weary. 'It may be that this will teach you not to wander again, oh daughter of Ahriman!' they heard him say as he hauled her by the horns up the rough slope.

Left to themselves, Marcus and Esca drew the hanging curtain of bramble and dog-rose across the mouth of their hole, and lay down as comfortably as they could. 'If the roof doesn't cave in and the pigs do not come back to challenge our presence, we look like having a quiet day,' Marcus said, pillowing his head on his arms.

Neither of these things happened, and the day dragged slowly by, while Marcus and Esca slept fitfully, trying to forget the emptiness of their stomachs. Beyond the bushes at the entrance the light grew golden and then faded. It was after dusk when Guern the Hunter returned, bringing with him, besides the inevitable strips of leathery smoked meat, a lump of fresh broiled venison. 'Eat the fresh meat now,' he said, 'and quickly.'

They did as he bade them, while he stood leaning on a spear in the cave mouth, with the great dog lying at his feet, and before it was full dark outside they were on their way again. They made slow marching at first, for Marcus's leg was stiff after the day's rest but the way was easier than it had been last night, running mostly downhill, and little by little the stiffness wore off, and he was able to make better going. Silent as shadows, they followed Guern, by ways that only the hunter and the deer knew, with never a spoken word between them. But Marcus was puzzled as the hours went by, for so far there had been no real difference between this and any other march that they had made among the hills; no sign of this unguarded way which it was death to travel without a guide.

And then, as they came down a gentle slope, the air seemed to change, and with it, the feel of the ground under their feet; and suddenly he understood. Bog! Bog with presumably some hidden path across it for those who knew the secret. They came to the edge of it almost as abruptly as to the edge of a pool, and the queer rooty smell of it was all around them. Guern was casting about like a hound cutting across a scent. Suddenly he halted, and his dog with him.

'Here. It is here,' he said, speaking under his breath for the first time since their setting out. 'From now on we must go behind one another. Follow me exactly, and do not halt for so long as a heart-beat; even on the secret way the ground is soft. Do as I bid you and you will cross safely; disobey me, and you will sink.' It was as simple as that.

'Understood,' Marcus murmured back. It was no time or place for needless talk: Mithras alone knew how near the scouting tribesmen might be.

With the dog pressed against them, Guern turned outward to the bog. Marcus moved into place behind him, and Esca brought up the rear. The ground felt spongy under their feet, sucking at them gently at every step that seemed taken only just in time to keep from sinking; and they had gone only a short way when Marcus noticed that a faint mist had begun to rise. At first he took it for no more than the breath of the bog, but soon he realized that it was more than that. Higher and higher it rose, wreathing upward in faint gauzy swathes that closed together overhead. Looking up, he could still see the moon shining, but faintly, through mist-wreathes in a glimmering sky. Mist; the weather of all others that they had cause to dread! And that it should come now! There could be no turning back; yet how was it possible for any man to find such a way as they were following, in this murk? And if they lost it? But that was not good to think about.

The mist was thickening steadily. Soon they were walking almost blind, their world made up of a few feet of sodden turf and tufted bog-cotton, and the occasional glint of water, dissolving into a nothingness of glimmering mist; and there was no sign of any path. But Guern seemed never at a loss, walking lightly and steadily forward, changing his course from time to time, and the other two followed. The dank, rooty smell grew always stronger, colder; the moon was sinking low and the mist losing itself in darkness, and still Guern the Hunter walked on. On and on. It was very silent, only a bittern boomed somewhere to their right, and there came small, evil, sucking noises from the bog.

Marcus had long since got over his first unpleasant doubts of Guern's ability to find the secret way in the mist, but now he was beginning to wonder how much longer he could keep on at this light, unvarying stride; and then suddenly it seemed to him that the ground was growing firmer underfoot. A few more steps, and he was sure of it. They were drawing up out of the quag. The mist smelled different, chill as ever, but lighter and sweeter. Soon the secret way was behind them, like an evil dream.

By that time dawn was near, and the mist was growing out of the darkness again, no longer glimmering, but dully grey as the ash of a long-dead fire. In the growing light, clear of the last pocket of bog, they halted thankfully in the lee of a clump of ancient thorn-trees and turned to face each other, while the dog lay down at their feet.

'I have brought you as far as I can,' Guern said. 'Every man to his own hunting grounds, and from now on the land is strange to me.'

'You have brought us clear through the guard of our enemies, and we can fend for ourselves now,' Marcus said quickly.

Guern shook his ragged head doubtfully. 'They may be drawing these hills also, for all I know. Therefore travel by night and lie up by day; and if you do not go astray in the mist, nor fall into the hands of the tribesmen, you should reach the Wall some time in the second night from now.' He hesitated, tried to speak, and hesitated again. At last he said with a kind of half-angry humility: 'Before our trails divide, it is in my heart that I would see the Eagle once again. It was my Eagle once.'

For answer, Marcus slipped the closely wrapped bundle from its sling, and turning back the folds, laid bare the lost Eagle. It was dark and lustreless in the grey dawn murk; a mere bird-shaped lump of battered metal. 'It has lost its wings,' he said.

Guern reached out eagerly as though to take it, then checked, and dropped his hands back to his sides. The betraying gesture tore harshly at something deep in Marcus's chest, and suddenly he could have howled like a dog. For a long moment he held the Eagle, while the other stood with rigidly bent head, looking down at it, unspeaking. Then as Guern stepped back, he folded the dark cloth once more over it, and returned it to its place under his cloak.

Guern said, 'So. I have seen the Eagle once more. Maybe after today I shall not look on a Roman face nor hear my own tongue spoken again . . . It is time that you were on your way.'

'Come with us,' Marcus said on a sudden impulse.

Guern's ragged head went up, and he stared at Marcus under his brows. For an instant he actually seemed to be considering the idea. Then he shook his head. 'My welcome might be an over-warm one. I have no yearning after death by stoning.'

'Tonight's work would alter that. We owe our lives to you, and if we get the Eagle back to its own place, that will be your doing.'

Guern shook his head again. 'I am of the Selgovae. I have a woman of the tribe to wife, and she is a good wife to me. I have sons, born into the tribe, and my life is here. If ever I was—something else, and my life was elsewhere, all that lies in another world and the men I knew in it have forgotten me. There is no way back through the Waters of Lethe.'

'Then—good hunting to you on your own trails,' Marcus said after a silence. 'Wish us well, between here and the Wall.'

'I will wish you well; and it is in my heart that I will wish myself with you. If you win through, I shall hear of it, and be glad.'

'You will have played no small part in it, if we do,' Marcus said, 'and neither of us will forget. The Light of the Sun be with you, Centurion.'

They looked back when they had gone a few paces, and saw him standing as they had left him, already dimmed with mist, and outlined against the drifting mist beyond. A half-naked, wild-haired tribesman, with a savage dog against his knee; but the wide, well-drilled movement of his arm as he raised it in greeting and farewell was all Rome. It was the parade-ground and the clipped voice of trumpets, the iron discipline and the pride. In that instant Marcus seemed to see, not the barbarian hunter, but the young centurion, proud in his first command, before ever the shadow of the doomed legion fell on him. It was to that centurion that he saluted in reply.

Then the drifting mist came between them.

As they turned away, Marcus found himself hoping that Guern would get back safely to the new life that he had made for himself, that he would not have to pay for the faith that he had kept with them. Well, the mist would give him cover on his homeward way.

Almost as though he had heard his friend's unspoken thoughts and was answering them, Esca said: 'He will hear if we come with our lives out of this, but we shall never hear whether he does.'

'I wish that he had chosen to come with us,' Marcus said. But even as he spoke, he knew that Guern the Hunter was right. There was no way back through the Waters of Lethe.

Two dawns later, Marcus and Esca were still a long way from the Wall. The mist that had met them on the secret way had haunted them ever since; a patchy and treacherous mist that was sometimes no more than a faint blurring of the more distant hills, and at others swooped down on them, blotting out all landmarks in a swirling greyness in which the very ground seemed dissolving away. They would have become lost over and over again but for the hunter's sense of direction that made Esca able to smell the south as a townsman might smell garlic. And even with that to help them, they could only struggle on with maddening slowness, covering what distance they could when the mist thinned, and lying up wherever they happened to be when it grew too thick to push on any further. Once or twice they came very near to disaster; many times they had to cast back for a way round some pitfall that the mist had hidden from them, and Marcus, who was leaving the route to Esca as usual was having anxieties of his own. His lame leg, which had carried him well enough through the forced marches and weary scrambles of their way south, was beginning to let him down, and let him down badly. He held on doggedly, but he was growing clumsy, and when he stumbled the jar of it made him set his teeth.

That dawn brought them their first warning that the enemy were indeed, as Guern had said, drawing these hills also, when the fitful mist rolled back to show them the figure of a mounted man, evidently on watch, high on a hill-shoulder not more than a bowshot away. Luckily he was not looking their way, and they fell flat among the heather, and spent a bad few moments watching him ride slowly along the ridge, until the mist closed down again.

They spent part of that day lying up in the lee of a great boulder, but started out again while there were still several hours of daylight left. While the mist hung about them, they had had to abandon their plan of travelling only by night, and push on when and how they could.

'How far have we still to go, by your reckoning?' Marcus asked, as he stood trying to rub the stiffness out of his leg.

Esca tightened his rawhide belt, which had become too loose for him, collected his spear and brushed up, as well as he could, the flattened grass where they had been lying.

'It is hard to judge,' he said. 'It has been slow travelling in this murk, but I think that I have not brought us greatly out of our way. By the fall of the land, I should say twelve or fourteen of your Roman miles. There; if any hunter comes close to this place, he will see that we have lain there, but from a few paces distant, it will not show.'

They set out once more on the long march south.

Towards evening a faint wind began to stir; and before it, the mist, which had been thick all day, grew ragged as a beggar's cloak.

'If the wind rises, we may lose this witches' brew at last,' said Marcus, as they halted at the curve of a narrow glen to make sure of their direction.

Esca lifted his head and sniffed, like an animal grown suddenly wary. 'Meanwhile it is in my heart that we should do well to find ourselves a fox-hole until dusk.'

But they had left the finding of their fox-hole too late. The words were scarcely out of his mouth when the mist seemed to curl back on itself. It spread sideways like blown smoke; the brown heather and golden bracken across the burn warmed suddenly through the drifting swathes, and next instant a cry, high and carrying and oddly triumphant, pierced upward from the far side of the glen, and a saffron-kilted figure started from cover and ran, crouching low, for the hill-crest. Esca's spear followed him, but it was too far for a throw. In six racing heart-beats he had reached the sky-line and dropped out of sight, crying his summons as he ran.

'Downhill,' Esca said harshly. 'Into the woods.'

They swung in their tracks, towards the nearest tongue of the birch woods that were spreading like a stain through the ragged mist, but even as they did so, the signal cry rose from among the golden trees in answer. There was no escape that way; and as they turned again, from far up the glen behind them the same cry went up, thin as a bird's call. Only one way lay open for them, and they took it; straight uphill to their right, and what lay over the hill-crest only the Lord of the Legions knew.

They gained the crest somehow, Marcus was never sure how, and as they hesitated an instant on the bare ridge, the cry—it was changing its quality now, becoming a hunting cry—rose again behind them, and was answered and flung up out of the mist below, closing in. They must have blundered into a large band of the hunters. Southward along the ridge, a dark mass of furze seemed to offer a certain amount of cover, and they dived into it like hunted animals going to ground, and began to work their way forward into its heart.

After that all was a blurred confusion of mist and jagged furze branches, and a chaos of dark islands swirled through by tawny tides of bracken and bilberry; of lying rigid among the dagger-sharp furze-roots with a suffocating reek of fox in their throats and the horror of the hunted in their racing hearts, while death with many heron-tufted war-spears stalked them through the dark maze. There were men all round them, on horseback, on foot, thrusting heedless of torn skin through the spiney branches, leaping high on stiff legs like hunting dogs who seek their quarry in long grass, giving tongue like hunting dogs too, now on this side, now on that. Once a probing spear struck like a snake within a span of Marcus's shoulder. And then quite suddenly they realized that against all seeming possibility, the hunt had missed them. It had swept over them and was no longer all around them, but behind!

They began to work forward on their stomachs again, with slow, agonizing caution. They could not tell where they were going, save that it was away from the enemy behind them. A dark and evidently much-used tunnel in the furze opened to them, and they slid into it, Esca leading. The reek of fox grew stronger than ever. The tunnel curved, leading them slightly downhill, and there was nothing to do but follow it, no breaking out through the dense furze that walled and roofed it in. It ended suddenly on the edge of the cover, and before them a spur of rocky, bush-grown turf ran out at an angle from the main ridge. Swathes of mist, drawn up out of the deep glen, were still drifting across it before the rising wind, but at the furthest point, upward of a bowshot away, something that might be a broch loomed through the greyness. It did not look promising, but they could not stay where they were, for it seemed to them that the sounds of the hunt were drawing nearer again, and there could be no turning back.

So they struck out into the open, getting what cover they could from the rocks and scrub, in search of some way down. But it seemed that there was no way down. The north-western slope would have been easy enough, but as they crouched among the bushes at the edge of it, the jink of a pony's bridle-bit came up to them, and the movement of men waiting. That way was securely stopped up. The south-eastern scarp dropped practically sheer into drifting mist-wreaths, out of which rose the indefinable sense and smell of deep water. There might be a way out for the Eagle, there, but there was certainly none for Marcus. Driven on by the sound of the hunt questing through the furze behind them like hounds after a lost scent, they struggled on a few steps, then checked, panting and desperate, looking this way and that, with eyes that strained to find some way of escape. But Marcus was almost done, and Esca had his arm round him. They could go no further even if the way were clear; they were trapped, and they knew it. The building that they had glimpsed through the mist was quite clear now; not a broch at all, but an old Roman signal-tower. They gathered themselves together and made for it.

It was a very obvious hiding-place, so obvious that it offered a bare chance of safety, or at all events respite, because the hunters might well have searched it already. At the worst it would give them a chance to put up some sort of fight; and there was always the dark coming.

The narrow archway, doorless now, gaped blackly in the wall, and they stumbled through into a small courtyard where grass had long since covered the cobbles. Another empty doorway faced them, and Marcus made for it. They were in the guardroom now. Dead leaves rustled to and fro on the floor, and the milky light filtering from a high window embrasure showed them the foot of a stairway in the wall. 'Up here,' he gasped.

The steps were of stone and still in good condition, though slippery with damp, and they stumbled upward, the sound of their feet seeming very loud in the silence of the stone shell where a little Roman garrison had lived and worked, keeping watch over the border hills, in the short years when the province of Valentia was more than a name.

They ducked out through a low door under the signal platform, on to the flat roof of the tower, into daylight as translucent as a moon-stone after the dark below. As they did so, Marcus was almost blinded by a thrashing of great black wings past his face, and a startled raven burst upward uttering its harsh, grating alarm cry, and flew off north-ward with slow, indignant wing-beats, caaking as it went.

Curse! That will announce our whereabouts clearly to all who may be interested, Marcus thought, but was suddenly too tired to care very much. Utterly spent, he lurched across to the far side of the roof, and looked down through a crumbling embrasure. Below him the ground dropped sheer from the tower foot, and through the last filmy rags of the mist he caught the darkness of deep water, far below, a still and sombre tarn brooding on its own secrets, between the spur and the main ridge. Yes, there would be a way out for the Eagle.

On the landward side, Esca was crouching beside a broken place in the parapet, where several large stones had fallen, leaving a gap. 'They are still beating the furze,' he muttered as Marcus joined him. 'It is well for us that there are no dogs with this band. If they do not come before dusk, we may escape them yet.'

'They will come before dusk,' Marcus murmured back. 'The raven has made sure of that. Listen . . . ' A sound came up to them from below the northern side of the spur, a confused, formless splurge of excitement, faint with mist and distance, that told them all too clearly that the waiting man had understood the raven's message. Marcus lowered himself stiffly on to his sound knee beside the other, slipped into an easier position, and stretched out sideways, leaning on one arm, his head hanging low. After a few moments he looked up. 'I suppose I should feel guilty about you, Esca. For me, there has been the Eagle; but what had you to win in all this?'

Esca smiled at him, a slow grave smile. There was a jagged tear in his forehead where a furze root had caught him, Marcus noticed, but under it his eyes looked very quiet. 'I have been once again a free man amongst free men. I have shared the hunting with my brother, and it has been a good hunting.'

Marcus smiled back. 'It has been a good hunting,' he agreed. The soft beat of unshod hooves on turf came drumming up from the mist below; the unseen hunters of the furze cover were casting back towards the open spur, beating as they came, making sure that their quarry did not again slip through them. They would be here soon, but the riders from below would be first. 'A good hunting; and now I think that is ended.' He wondered if any word of that ending would one day drift south across the Wall, would reach the Legate Claudius, and through him, Uncle Aquila; would reach Cottia in the garden under the sheltering ramparts of Calleva. He should like them to know . . . it had been a good hunting, that he and Esca had had together. Suddenly he knew that, despite all outward seeming, it had been worth while.

There was a great quietness in him. The last of the mist was blowing clear away as the wind freshened; something that was almost sunshine brushed fleetingly across the old signal-tower, and he noticed for the first time that a clump of harebell had taken root in a cranny of the fallen parapet close to him, and, late in flowering because of the place in which it grew, still carried one fragile bell aloft on an arching thread-slender stem. It swayed as the wind blew over, and regained its place with a tiny, defiant toss. It seemed to Marcus that it was the bluest thing he had ever seen.

Up over the edge of the spur, three wild horsemen appeared heading for the gateway.

XIX
Tradui's Gift

AS they dropped from their ponies in the courtyard below, Marcus and Esca drew back from the parapet. 'Only three, so far,' Marcus whispered. 'Don't use your knife unless you have to. They may be of more use to us living than dead.'

Esca nodded, and returned his hunting-knife to his belt. Life and the urgency of doing had taken hold of them again. Flattened against the wall on either side of the stairhead they waited, listening to their pursuers questing through storehouse and guard-room. 'Fools!' Marcus breathed, as a shout told them that the stairway had been spotted; and then came a rush of feet that checked at the floor below and then came on, storming upward.

Marcus was a good boxer, and much practice with the cestus last winter had made Esca something of a boxer also; together, weary though they were, they made a dangerous team. The first two tribesmen to come ducking out through the low doorway went down without a sound, like poled oxen: the third, not so completely caught unawares, put up more of a fight. Esca flung himself upon him, and they crashed down several steps together, in a flailing mass of arms and legs. There was a short, desperate struggle before Esca came uppermost, and staggering clear, heaved an unconscious man over the doorsill.

'Young fools,' he said, stooping for a fallen spear. 'A hound puppy would have known better than that.'

Two of the tribesmen—they were all very young—lay completely stunned where they had fallen; but one was already stirring; and Marcus bent over him. 'It is Liathan,' he said. 'I'll see to him. Do you tie up and gag the other two.'

The young warrior groaned, and opened his eyes to find Marcus kneeling over him with his own dagger to his throat, while close by, Esca was hastily trussing and gagging the two unconscious men with strips torn from the cloak of one of them. 'That was a mistake,'

Marcus said. 'You should have kept with the rest of the hunt, not come thrusting in here on your own.'

Liathan lay looking up at him. His black eyes were hard with hate; blood trickled from the corner of his mouth. 'Maybe we saw the raven and we sought to be First Spear, lest a lowland tribe claim the Eagle-god for its own,' he said between shut teeth.

'I see. It was a brave thing to do, but extremely stupid.'

'Maybe; but though we fail, there will be others here soon.' There was a gleam of savage triumph in the black eyes.

'So,' Marcus nodded. 'When they come, these others, you will tell them that we are not here; that we must after all have slipped by in the mist; and you will send them back the way they came, over the main ridge yonder, towards the sunrise.'

Liathan smiled. 'Why will I do these things?' He glanced for a contemptuous instant at the dagger in Marcus's hand. 'Because of that?'

'No,' said Marcus. 'Because when the first of your friends sets foot on the stair, I shall send the Eagle—here it is—into the tarn which lies below this place. We are still a long way from the Wall, and you will have other chances—you or others of the hunt—before we reach it; but if we die here, you will lose whatever chance you have of retaking the Red Crests' god.'

For a long moment Liathan lay staring up into Marcus's face; and in that silent moment there grew a light smother of hoof-beats and a distant burst of shouting. Esca rose quickly and crossed, half crouching, to the broken parapet. 'The hunt is up,' he said softly. 'They have done with the furze cover. Aiee! Like a wolf-pack, they close in.'

Marcus withdrew the dagger, but his eyes never left the young tribesman's face. 'Choose,' he said, very quietly. He got up and moved backward to the far parapet, unwrapping the Eagle as he did so. Liathan had risen also, and stood swaying a little on his feet, looking from Marcus to Esca and back again. Marcus saw him swallow, saw him lick the cut on his lip. He heard the sounds of the in-closing hunt, very near now, the men giving tongue like excited hounds; and from the emptiness at his back, only the plaintive cry of a marsh bird in the wind-haunted silence. He let the last violet fold fall from the Eagle, and held it up. The evening light, spreading as the mist thinned, struck on the savage, gilded head.

Liathan made a queer gesture of defeat. He turned and strode rather shakily to the broken parapet, and leaned over. The first of the hunt was almost at the gateway, and a shout from under the walls greeted his appearance. Liathan called down to them: 'They are not here, after all. They must have slipped through the other way in this accursed mist.' He pointed wildly, and his voice broke like the crying of a storm bird. 'Try the woods yonder; they will likely have bolted that way.'

A confusion of fierce voices answered him and a pony whinnied shrilly; he drew back from the parapet as though coming hot-foot to follow his words, and as the hunt flung back on itself, turned once more to Marcus.

'It was well done, was it not?'

Marcus nodded without speaking. Through one of the embrasures he was watching the hunt streaming back along the spur and into the furze cover of the main ridge, men on ponies and men on foot, calling to each other, gathering others as they went; dissolving into the last shreds of the mist. He brought his gaze back to the young tribesman. 'Truly it was well done,' he said, 'but keep the head down, lest any straggler should look back and think it strange to see you still here.'

Liathan lowered his head obediently—and sprang. Sprang like a wild cat. But Marcus, warned by some flicker of his eyes an instant before, flung himself sideways, half falling, with the Eagle under him, and as he did so, Esca was upon the highlander and brought him crashing down.

'You fool,' Marcus said a moment later, staggering to his feet and looking down at Liathan, who lay squirming under Esca's knees. 'You young fool; there are two of us and only one of you.'

He crossed to the two bound men, and after satisfying himself that all was well with them, tore off some more strips from the cloak that lay beside one of them, and returned to Esca. Between them they bound the hands and feet of the young warrior, who had ceased to struggle and lay rigid with his face turned from them.

'We can leave the gag for the moment,' Marcus said when it was done. He picked up the Eagle and began to fold it close once more. 'Esca, do you go and make sure the ponies are safe. We shall need them.'

When Esca was gone, he got up stiffly and turned to the southern parapet. The upland tarn lay clear and dark now beneath the steep fall of the spur. The hills were blown almost clear of the mist, though it still scarfed the glen with white; and the evening was coming swiftly,

swiftly. And somewhere southward beyond those hills, not far now, surely, was the Wall.

'Why did you come among us, calling yourself a healer of sore eyes, to steal from us the winged god?'

Marcus swung round in answer to the furious voice behind him. 'In the first place, am I so lacking as a healer of sore eyes? At least your brother's son will not be blind.' He leaned one shoulder wearily against the parapet, and stood gazing down reflectively at his captive. 'In the second, I came to take back—not to steal, for it was never yours—*take back* the winged god, because it was the Eagle of my father's Legion.' Instinctively he knew that with Liathan, as with Cottia, that was the part that would make sense; knew also that it was better for the peace of the frontier that the thing be kept a private feud between himself and the tribes.

There was a queer little flicker in Liathan's dark eyes. 'So my grandfather was right,' he said.

'Was he? Tell me about this rightness of his.'

'When the priest-kind found the winged god was gone,' Liathan said, with a kind of defiant willingness to talk, 'my grandfather swore it was you who had taken it. He said you had the face of that Chieftain of the Red Crests he had seen killed under the wings of the god, and that he had been blind and doting not to know you for his son. But when we had followed you and searched your gear and found nothing, we said among ourselves that the grandfather grew old and fanciful. Then Gault the fisherman found your ring-brooch by the shore of the loch, and the bank pulled down and a hollow place under the waterline. And later, we heard a strange tale from the rath where your sword-brother was taken sick; and we knew. And my grandfather said, "I was right, after all, who am never wrong," and he sent for me, for my brother had been savaged by a seal and was too sick of the wound to go to the Hosting. He sent for me, and said: "It may be that it is you who will hunt him down, for there is a link of fate between his line and ours. If it be so, kill him if you can, for he has put shame on the gods of the tribe; but also give him his father's ring, for he is his father's son in more than blood."'

There was an instant's complete silence; and then Marcus said: 'You have it now?'

'On a thong round my neck,' Liathan said sullenly. 'You must take it for yourself, since my hands are bound.'

Marcus lowered himself on to his sound knee, and slipped a hand warily under the shoulder-folds of the other's cloak. But it was no trick; he found the ring, which had worked round to the back, and drawing it out, cut the thong, and slipped it on to his bare signet finger. The light was beginning to fade, and the great stone that had been full of green fire when he saw it last, was cooly dark as ilex leaves, lit only by a faint surface reflection of the sky. 'If the fortunes of war had gone otherwise, and Esca and I had fallen to your spears, you would have had small chance to give me my father's ring. How, then, would you have carried out your grandfather's bidding?' he asked curiously.

'You should have had the ring to take with you, as a man takes his weapons and his favourite hound.'

'I see,' said Marcus. From the ring he looked back to Liathan, suddenly half smiling. 'When you go back to your own place, say to Tradui that I thank him for the gift of my father's ring.'

Esca's step sounded on the stairs and a moment later he ducked out into the evening light. 'All is well with the ponies,' he said. 'Also I have looked round a little, and seen that our way lies down the glen westward. That way there is birch cover almost from the first, and moreover the hunt went toward the sunrise.'

Marcus glanced up at the sky. 'The light will be gone in the half of an hour, but much can happen in that time, and it is in my heart that we will go now.'

Esca nodded, reaching him a steadying hand as he rose; and in so doing, saw the flawed emerald, and gave him a quick, questioning glance.

'Yes,' said Marcus. 'Liathan has brought me my father's ring as a gift from his grandfather.' He turned to look down at the tribesman. 'We shall take two of your ponies, Liathan, to carry us to the Wall, but we will turn them loose when we have done with them, and with good fortune you will find them again—later. I hope you do, because you brought me my father's ring . . . See to the gag, Esca.'

Esca saw to it.

Meeting the furious eyes above the gag, Marcus said, 'I am sorry, but we can ill afford to have you shouting the moment we are gone, lest there be someone within hearing. It will assuredly not be long before your sword-brethren return and find you, but to make all safe I will see that word of your whereabouts reaches the tribesmen, when *we* have reached the Wall. That is the best that I can do.'

They crossed to the stairhead. Esca paused to collect the tribesmen's weapons from the place where he had stacked them, and sent them—all save one spear, which he kept to replace his own—over the parapet into the tarn below. Marcus heard them take the water in a stutter of faint splashes, while he bent over the other two captives, both conscious and hating hard by this time, to make sure that they had not yet contrived to slacken their bonds. Then they ducked through the doorway into the descending darkness.

The strain of their escape had taxed Marcus to the uttermost, and the respite in the signal-tower, short as it had been, had been long enough to let the old wound begin to stiffen. He had to nerve himself to every step, and there seemed a great many more steps on the way down than there had been on the way up. But they reached the bottom at last, and came out into the little courtyard, where three ponies stood with their reins over their heads.

They chose the two of them, a black and a dun, who seemed the freshest and, hitching the reins of the third one over a fallen timber to prevent him following, led them out through the narrow gateway. 'The last lap,' Marcus said, drawing a hand caressingly down the neck of the black pony. 'We will break fast in one of the Wall stations tomorrow morning.'

Esca helped him to mount, before he himself swung on to the back of the dun. For a few moments Marcus had all he could do to master his mount, for the fiery little brute objected strongly to an unfamiliar rider, snorting and plunging like an unbroken colt, until, seeming suddenly to tire of the fight, it answered to his hand and set off at a canter, shaking its head and spilling foam over its chest and knees.

Esca ranged alongside on the dun, and they swung over the steep scarp of the spur, and headed downhill for the woods below them. 'Praise be to Lugh, they are yet fairly fresh; for we've a hard ride before us.'

'Yes,' said Marcus, rather grimly; and shut his teeth on the word. That plunging tussle with his mount had taken most of the endurance that was left in him.

The light was going fast, as they swung into the long southward curve of the glen. The wind was surging through the birch and hazel of the woods, and overhead the sky between the hurrying clouds was kindling yellow as a lantern.

A long while later, a sentry on the northern ramparts of Borcovicus thought that in a lull of the tearing wind he heard the beat of horses' hooves somewhere far below him. He checked his pacing to look down, far down where the burn cut through its wild glen a hundred feet below the fortress walls, but a racing, silver-fringed cloud had come across the moon, and the glen was a black nothingness below him, and the wind swooped back, blowing away all sound. Curse the wind! There was always a wind—save where there was mist—up here on the highest lift of the Wall; nothing to hear all day and all night but the wind and the peewits calling. It was enough to make a man hear worse than horses' hooves inside his head. The sentry spat disgustedly down into the dark abyss, and continued his measured pacing.

Some while later still, the guard on duty at the North Gate was surprised by a most imperious beating on the timbers and shout of 'Open in Caesar's name!' So might a bearer of dispatches announce his arrival, if it were at any other gate; but the few who came from the north—horse-dealers, hunters, and the like—did not hammer on the gate as though they were the Legate himself demanding entrance in the name of the Emperor. It might be a trick of some kind. Leaving his gate-guard turned out and standing ready, the Optio clanked up to the look-out above the gateway.

The moon rode clear of the clouds now, and faintly, by its reflected light, the Optio could pick out two figures directly below him in the shadow of the arch. The sheer drop of the hillside was in shadow, but there was enough light to show it empty of men, clear down to the white streak of the burn. Not a trick, then.

'Who demands entrance in Caesar's name?'

One of the figures looked up, his face a pale blur in the darkness. 'Two who have urgent business with the Commander and would fain keep whole skins if possible. Open up, friend.'

The Optio hesitated an instant, then turned and clattered down the few steps. 'Open up,' he ordered.

Men sprang to obey him, the heavy oaken valve swung smoothly outward on its stone socket, and in the opening, clearly lit now by the yellow light from the guard-room doorway, appeared two wild, bearded figures, who might have been born of the autumn gale. One of them was leaning heavily on the shoulder of the other, who seemed to be supporting him by an arm round his waist; and as they stumbled forward, the Optio, who had begun curtly, 'Now what—' went kindly enough to steady him on the other side, saying, 'Run into trouble, eh?'

But the other laughed suddenly, his teeth showing white in the dark tangle of his beard; and staggering clear of his friend's supporting arm, propped himself against the guardroom wall, and drooped there, breathing hard and fast through widened nostrils. Clad in filthy rags, gaunt as famine and well-nigh as dirty, scratched and blood-smeared as though from contact with many furze bushes, he was as villainous an object as the Optio had seen for a long time.

As the gate clanged shut behind him, this apparition said in the cool, clipped accents of a cohort centurion, 'Optio, I wish to see the Commanding Officer immediately.'

'Ugh?' said the Optio, and blinked.

Presently, after a queer confusion of changing faces, of brusque soldiers' voices and clanging footsteps, and long wavering alleyways between buildings whose corners never seemed to be quite where he expected them, Marcus found himself standing on the threshold of a lamp-lit room. It flowered suddenly golden on his sight, out of the windy dark; a small room, white-walled, and almost filled by a battered writing-table and records chest. He blinked at it with a queer, dream-like sense of unreality. A square-built man in half uniform rose from the camp-chair, and turned enquiringly to the door. 'Yes, what—' he began, much as the Optio had done.

As the door closed behind him, Marcus looked at the stocky familiar figure, the square face with the dark hairs growing out of the nose, and felt no surprise. He had come back to a familiar world, and it seemed only natural that he should find old friends in it. 'Good evening to you, Drusillus,' he said. 'My congratulations on—your promotion.'

The centurion's face was puzzled, and his head went up a little stiffly.

'Do you not know me, Drusillus?' Marcus said almost pleadingly. 'I am—'

But light had already dawned on his old centurion, and the bewilderment in his square brown face became blank astonishment and then lit into incredulous delight. 'Centurion Aquila!' he said. 'Yes, sir, I know you, I would know you in Tartarus itself, now that I come to look at you!' He came tramping round the table. 'But what in the name of Thunder brings you here?'

Marcus set his bundle carefully on the table. 'We have brought back the Hispana's lost Eagle,' he said, rather muzzily, and very quietly crumpled forward on top of it.

XX
Valedictory

TOWARDS evening of a day in late October, Marcus and Esca came riding up the last lift of the Calleva road. Having learned at Eburacum that the Legate Claudius was not yet returned, they had pushed on south, knowing that they could not miss him by the way, to wait for him at Calleva.

They were rid of their beards and reasonably clean once more, and Marcus had had his hair clipped short again in the Roman manner; but still clad in the tatterdemalion clothes of their adventuring, still gaunt and hollow-eyed and disreputable, they had more than once needed the permit provided by Drusillus to save them from the awkward charge of having stolen the army post-horses on which they rode.

They were tired, bone tired, and without any glow of triumph to warm the leaden chill of their tiredness; and they rode with the reins loose on their horses' necks, in silence save for the strike of shod hooves on the metalled road and the squeak of wet leather. But after many months in the wild aloofness of the north, this gentler and more friendly countryside seemed to Marcus to hold out its arms to him, and it was with a sense of homecoming that he lifted his face to the soft grey mizzle, and saw afar off, beyond the rolling miles of dappled forest, the familiar and suddenly beloved outline of the South Downs.

They rode into Calleva by the North Gate, left the horses at the Golden Vine for return to the transit camp next day, and set out on foot for the house of Aquila. In the narrow street, when they turned into it, the poplar trees were already bare, and the way slippery with shrivelled wet leaves. The daylight was fading fast, and the windows of Uncle Aquila's watch-tower were full of lemon-pale lamp-light that seemed somehow like a welcome.

The door was on the latch, and they pushed it open and went in. There was an air of most unwonted bustle in the house, as though someone had lately arrived or was expected to arrive at any moment. As they emerged from the narrow entrance closet, old Stephanos was crossing the atrium towards the dining recess. He cast one glance at them, uttered a startled bleat, and all but dropped the lamp he was carrying.

'It is all right, Stephanos,' Marcus told him, slipping off his wet cloak and tossing it over a convenient bench. 'It is only the Golden Vine that we are sprung from, not the realms of Hades. Is my uncle in his study?'

The old slave's mouth was open to reply, but nobody ever heard what he said, for his voice was drowned by a frenzied baying that rose on the instant. There was a wild scurry of paws along the colonnade, and a great brindled shape sprang over the threshold and came streaking across the floor, skidding on the smooth surface, ears pricked and bush tail flying. Cub, lying dejectedly in the colonnade, had heard Marcus's voice and come to find him.

'Cub!' Marcus called, and sat down hurriedly on top of his cloak, just in time to save himself from being bowled over liked a stoned hare as Cub landed with a flying leap on his chest.

They slid together off the bench with a resounding thump. Marcus had his arms round the young wolf's neck, and Cub thrust against him, whining and yelping, licking his face from ear to ear with frantic joy. But by now news of their return had burst through the house, and Marcipor came scuttling with dignified haste to one door while Sassticca ran in through another, still clutching a large iron spoon; and somehow, between Cub's joyful onslaughts, Marcus was turning from one to the other, greeting and being greeted. 'You have not got rid of us, you see, Marcipor! Sassticca, it is like the flowers in spring to see you! The nights that I have dreamed of your honey cakes—'

'Ah, I thought I heard your voice, Marcus—among others.'

There was a sudden hush; and Uncle Aquila was standing at the foot of the watch-tower stairs, with old grey-muzzled Procyon at his side, and behind him, the dark, austere figure of Claudius Hieronimianus.

Marcus got up slowly, one hand still on the great savage head that was pressed against his thigh. 'It seems that we have timed our arrival well,' he said. He started forward at the same instant as his uncle strode to meet him, and next moment they had come together in the middle of the atrium, and Marcus was gripping both the older man's hands in his.

'Uncle Aquila! Oh, it's good to see you again. How goes it with you, sir?'

'Strangely enough, it goes the better for seeing you safely home once more, even in the guise of a Tiber rat,' said Uncle Aquila. His glance went to Esca and back again. 'In the guise of two Tiber rats.' And then after an instant's pause, very quietly, 'What news?'

'I have brought it back,' Marcus said, equally quietly. And that was all for the moment on the subject of the lost Eagle. The four of them were alone in the atrium, the slaves having slipped out to their own duties when the master of the house appeared, and Uncle Aquila gathered both young men after him with an imperious gesture to where the Legate, who had drawn aside from their meeting, was quietly warming himself at the brazier. In the general shifting Cub circled for an instant to thrust his muzzle into Esca's hand in greeting, then returned to Marcus again. Procyon greeted nobody, he was a one-man-dog to the point of seldom appearing conscious that other men existed.

'He has done it!' Uncle Aquila was announcing in a kind of triumphant grumble. 'He has done it, by Jupiter! You never thought he would, did you, my Claudius?'

'I am—not sure,' said the Legate, his strange black eyes resting on Marcus consideringly. 'No, I am not—at all sure, my Aquila.'

Marcus saluted him, then drew Esca forward from the outskirts of the group. 'Sir, may I bring to your remembrance my friend Esca Mac Cunoval?'

'I already remember him very well,' said Claudius with a quick smile to the Briton.

Esca bent his head to him. 'You witnessed my manumission papers, I believe, sir,' he said in a dead-level tone that made Marcus glance at him anxiously, realizing suddenly that there had been no real homecoming for Esca in this return to a house in which he had been a slave.

'I did. But I generally remember men by other things than the papers I may have witnessed for them,' the Legate said gently.

An exclamation from Uncle Aquila cut across the little exchange, and looking round, Marcus found the other staring at his left hand, which he had unconsciously curved about the precious bundle which he still carried in its sling. 'That ring,' said Uncle Aquila. 'Show it to me.'

Marcus slipped off the heavy signet-ring and passed it to him. 'Of course you recognize it?'

His uncle stood for a few moments examining it, his face unreadable. Then he gave it back. 'Yes,' he said. 'Yes, by Jupiter, I do recognize it. How came you by your father's ring?'

But with Sassticca's voice rising near at hand, and one or other of the slaves likely at any moment to come through the atrium about their preparations for dinner, Marcus could not bring himself to start on that story. Slipping the ring back on to his finger, he said, 'Uncle Aquila, could we leave that—with all the rest, for a fitter place and season? It is a long story, and there are many doors to this room.'

Their eyes met, and after a pause, Uncle Aquila said, 'Aye, well. Both matters have waited long enough for an hour to make little difference. You agree, Claudius?'

The Egyptian nodded. 'Most assuredly I agree. In your watch-tower, after we have eaten, we shall be safe from interruption. Then Marcus shall make his full report.' Suddenly his face crinkled into a thousand-creased smile, and with a swift change of manner that seemed to draw a silken curtain over the whole affair of the lost Eagle, shutting it decently from view until the time came to take it out again and deal with it, he turned to Marcus. 'It seems always that I visit this house at a happy hour. The last time, it was Cub who came back, and this time it is you, but the reunion remains the same.'

Marcus looked down at Cub, who was leaning against him, head up and eyes half closed in ecstasy. 'We are glad to be together, Cub and I,' he said.

'So it seems. It is almost past believing that a wolf should be so much a friend. Was he greatly more difficult than a hound, in the making?'

'I think he was more stubborn; certainly fiercer to handle. But it was Esca rather than I who had the making of him. He is the expert.'

'Ah, of course.' The Legate turned to Esca. 'You come of the Brigantes, do you not? More than once I have seen Cub's brethren running among the dog-packs of your tribe, and wondered how—'

But Marcus heard no more. He had stooped quickly, and was running an exploring hand over the young wolf, suddenly aware of something that he had not really taken in, in the first flush of homecoming. 'Uncle Aquila, what have you done to Cub? He is nothing but skin and bone.'

'We have done nothing to Cub,' said Uncle Aquila in accents of acute disgust. 'Cub has been breaking his own wilful heart for his own amusement. Since you left, he has refused food from any but that chit Cottia, and since her going, he has preferred to starve. That brute has been deliberately dying in our midst with the entire household buzzing round him like blowflies round a stranded fish.'

Marcus's caressing hand had checked on Cub's neck, and something seemed to twist and turn cold inside him. 'Cottia,' he said. 'Where has Cottia gone?' He had scarcely thought of her, save twice, in all the months that he had been away; but it seemed a long, long time before his uncle answered.

'Only to Aquae Sulis for the winter. Her Aunt Valaria discovered a need to take the waters, and shifted the whole household, a few days ago.'

Marcus let go the breath that he had been holding. He began to play with Cub's ears, drawing them again and again through his fingers. 'Did she leave any word for me?'

'She came to me in a fine flaming passion, the day before she was swept away, to bring back your bracelet.'

'Did you tell her—about keeping it?'

'I did not. Some things are best unsaid until the need comes for saying them. I told her that since you had left it in her charge, it seemed to me best that she keep it until she came back in the spring and could give it into your hands. I also promised to tell you that she would guard it well through the winter.' He held one great blue-veined hand to the warmth of the brazier, and smiled at it. 'She is a vixen, the little one, but a faithful vixen.'

'Yes,' said Marcus. 'Yes . . . sir, with your leave I will take the Cub and feed him now.'

Esca, who had been answering the Legate's questions about the taming of wolf-cubs, said quickly, 'I will take him.'

'Maybe if we both take him, we can wash off some of the journey while we are about it. We have time for that, Uncle Aquila?'

'Time and to spare,' said his uncle. 'Dinner will doubtless be put back to Jupiter knows what hour, while Sassticca ransacks her store shelves for your benefit.'

Uncle Aquila was perfectly right. For Marcus's benefit, Sassticca ransacked her store shelves with joyful abandon; and the sad thing was that it was all as good as wasted. To Marcus at all events, that dinner was completely unreal. He was so tired that the soft light of the palm-oil lamps seemed a golden fog, and he tasted nothing of what he ate and scarcely even noticed the handful of rain-wet autumn crocuses which Sassticca, proud of her knowledge of Roman ways, had scattered on the table. It seemed odd, after so many meals eaten in the open or squatting beside peat fires, to eat at a civilized table again, to see the clean-shaven faces of the other men, and the tunics of soft white wool that they wore—Esca's a borrowed one of his own—to hear the quiet, clipped voices of his uncle and the Legate when they spoke to each other. Very odd, like something out of another world; a familiar world, grown suddenly unfamiliar. He had almost forgotten what to do with a napkin. Only Esca, clearly finding it strange and uncomfortable to eat while reclining on his left elbow, seemed real in the queer brittle unreality.

It was an uneasy meal, eaten without lingering and almost in silence, for the minds of all four were on one subject, carefully shut away behind its silken curtain, but making it hopeless to try to talk of something else. A strange home-coming meal, with the shadow of the lost Eagle brooding over it; and Marcus was thankful when at last Uncle Aquila set down the cup after pouring the final oblation, and said, 'Shall we go up to my study now?'

Following the two older men, and once again carrying the Eagle, Marcus had mounted four or five of the watch-tower steps before he realized that Esca was not coming up behind, and looking back, he saw him still standing at the foot of the stairs.

'I think that I will not come,' Esca said.

'Not come? But you must come.'

Esca shook his head. 'It is between you and your uncle and the Legate.'

Followed as ever by Cub, Marcus came down the few steps again. 'It is between the four of us. What maggot has got into your head, Esca?'

'I think that I should not go to your uncle's private sanctum,' Esca said stubbornly. 'I have been a slave in his house.'

'You are not a slave now.'

'No, I am your freed-man now. It is strange. I never thought of that until this evening.'

Marcus had never thought of it either, but he knew that it was true. You could give a slave his freedom, but nothing could undo the fact that he had been a slave; and between him, a freed-man, and any free man who had never been unfree, there would still be a difference. Wherever the Roman way of life held good, that difference would be there. That was why it had not mattered, all these months that they had been away; that was why it mattered now. Suddenly he felt baffled and helpless. 'You did not feel like this before we went north. How is it altered now?'

'That was at the beginning. I had not had time to—understand. I knew only that I was free—a hound slipped from the leash; and we were going away from it all in the morning. Now we have come back.'

Yes, they had come back, and the thing had got to be faced, and faced at once. On a sudden impulse Marcus reached out his free hand and caught his friend's shoulder, not at all gently. 'Listen to me,' he said. 'Are you going to live all the rest of your life as though you had taken a whipping and could not forget it? Because if you are, I am sorry for you. You don't like being a freed-man, do you? Well, I don't like being lame. That makes two of us, and the only thing we can do about it, you and I, is to learn to carry the scars lightly.' He gave the shoulder a friendly shake, and dropped his hand. 'Come up with me now, Esca.'

Esca did not answer for a moment. And then slowly his head went up, and his eyes wore the dancing look they always wore in action. 'I will come,' he said.

When they emerged into Uncle Aquila's watch-tower, the two older men were standing over the wrought-iron brazier that glowed red in its alcove at the far side of the room. They looked round as Marcus and Esca entered, but nobody spoke; only the rain whispered softly, delicately, against the narrow windows. The small lamplit room seemed very remote from the world, very tall above it. Marcus had a sense of immense depths dropping away beneath him in the darkness, as though, if he went to the window, he might look down and see Orion swimming like a fish below him.

'Well?' said Uncle Aquila at last; and the word fell sharply into the silence, like a pebble dropping into a pool.

Marcus crossed to the writing-table and set his bundle down upon it. How pathetic and shapeless it seemed; a bundle that might contain boots or washing. 'It has lost its wings,' he said. 'That is why it bulks so small.'

The silken curtain had been drawn back now, and with it was gone the brittle surface of ordinariness that they had kept all evening. 'So the rumour was a true one,' the Legate said.

Marcus nodded, and began to undo the shapeless mass. He turned back the last fold, and there, amid the tumble of tattered violet cloth, the lost Eagle stood, squat and undignified, but oddly powerful, on its splayed legs. The empty wing sockets were very bleak in the lamplight which kindled its gilded feathers to the strong yellow of gorse flowers. There was a furious pride about the upreared head. Wingless it might be, fallen from its old estate, but it was an Eagle still; and out of its twelve-year captivity, it had returned to its own people.

For a long moment nobody spoke, and then Uncle Aquila said, 'Shall we sit down to this?'

Marcus folded up thankfully on one end of the bench which Esca had drawn to the table, for his unsound leg had begun to shake under him. He was warmly aware of Cub's chin settling contentedly on his foot, and Esca sitting beside him, as he began to make his report. He made it clearly and carefully, abating nothing of the stories told him by Guern the Hunter and by old Tradui, though parts of them were hard in the telling. At the appropriate places he handed over to Esca, to speak for himself. And all the time, his eyes never left the Legate's intent face.

No one moved or spoke at once when the report was finished. Marcus himself sat very still, searching into the long black eyes for their verdict. The rain sharpened to a little impatient spatter against the window. Then Claudius Hieronimianus shifted, and the spell of stillness was broken. 'You have done well, both of you,' he said; and his gaze moved from Marcus to Esca and back again, drawing them both in. 'Thanks to you, a weapon which might one day have been used against the Empire, will never be so used. I salute two very courageous lunatics.'

'And—the Legion?'

'No,' said the Legate. 'I am sorry.'

So Marcus had his verdict. It was 'thumbs down' for the Ninth Legion. He had thought that he had accepted that from the night when he had heard Guern's story. Now he knew that he had never quite accepted it. In his heart of hearts he had clung, against all reason, to the hope that his own judgement was wrong, after all. He made one desperate appeal for his father's Legion, knowing as he did so, that it was hopeless.

'Sir, there were upward of three cohorts who were not with the Legion when it marched North. Many Legions have been re-formed from fewer survivors than that—if the Eagle was still in Roman hands.'

'Those cohorts were broken up twelve years ago, and distributed among other Legions of the Empire,' the Legate said very kindly. 'By now more than half the men will have finished their military service, and those that have not, will have changed their allegiance to their new Eagles, long ago. On your own showing, the name and number of the Ninth Hispana is no heritage for a new Legion to carry. It is better that it be forgotten.'

'There is no way back through the Waters of Lethe.' Behind the Legate's words, Marcus seemed to hear Guern the Hunter. 'No way back through the Waters of Lethe—no way back—!'

Uncle Aquila crashed up from the table. 'And what of their last stand, that Marcus has just told us of? Is not *that* a heritage fit for any Legion?'

The Legate turned a little in his chair, to look up at him. 'The conduct of a few score men cannot counterbalance the conduct of a whole Legion,' he said. 'You must see that, Aquila, even though one of them was your brother.'

Uncle Aquila grunted savagely, and the Legate turned back to Marcus. 'How many people know that the Eagle has been brought back?'

'South of the Wall, we four, your own Camp Commandant, who I gather knew of the matter from yourself, and the Commander of the garrison at Borcovicus. He was my old Second at Isca Dumnoniorum, and gained his cohort for his defence of the fort after I was wounded. We took pains that no one else in Borcovicus should know what it was all about; and he will say nothing unless I give him leave. Rumour may come down from the North, of course, but if so, I imagine that it will die out as the earlier rumour did.'

'Well enough,' said the legate. 'Naturally I shall lay the whole matter before the Senate. But I have no doubt of their verdict.'

Uncle Aquila made a small, expressive gesture, as though screwing something up and tossing it into the brazier. 'What do you suggest becomes of this?' he nodded to the defiant, squatting Eagle.

'Give it honourable burial,' said the Legate.

'Where?' Marcus demanded huskily, after a moment.

'Why not here in Calleva? Five roads meet here, and the Legions are for ever passing by, while the place itself is the territory of no particular Legion.'

He leaned forward to brush the gilded feathers lightly with one finger, his face thoughtful in the lamplight. 'So long as Rome lasts, the Eagles will pass and re-pass under the walls of Calleva. What better place for it to lie?'

Uncle Aquila said, 'When I had this house built, there had lately been a flare-up of unrest hereabout, and I had a small hiding-place made under the floor of the shrine, to take my papers in case of further trouble. Let it lie there and be forgotten.'

Very much later that night, the four of them stood together in the small alcove shrine at the end of the atrium. The slaves had long since gone to their own quarters, and they had the house and the silence of the house to themselves. A bronze lamp on the altar sent up a long tongue of flame the shape of a perfect laurel leaf; and by its light the household gods in their niches in the lime-washed walls seemed to look down, as the four men were looking down, into the small square hole in the tessellated floor, just before the altar.

Marcus had brought the Eagle down from the watch-tower, carrying it as he had carried it so many miles and slept with it so many nights, in the crook of his arm. And while the others watched in silence, he had knelt down and laid it in the small square cist that reached down through the hypocaust into the dark earth beneath. He had laid it—no longer bundled in tattered violet cloth—on his old military cloak, and drawn the scarlet folds closely over it with a gentle hand. He had been very proud to wear that cloak; it was fitting that his father's Eagle should have it now.

The four men stood with bent heads; three who had served with the Eagles in their different times, one who had suffered slavery for taking up arms against them; but in that moment there was no gulf between them. The Legate stepped forward to the edge of the square hole, looking down to where the scarlet of Marcus's cloak was all but lost in the depths beyond the reach of the lamplight. He raised one hand, and began, very simply, to speak the Valedictory, the Farewell, as he might have spoken it for a dead comrade.

Suddenly, to Marcus's tired mind, it seemed that there were others besides themselves in the little lamplit shrine; notably two: a slight, dark man, with an eager face beneath the tall crest of a First Cohort

Commander; and a shock-headed tribesman in a saffron kilt. Yet when he looked at the tribesman, he was gone, and in his place the young centurion he had once been.

'Here lies the Eagle of the Ninth Legion, the Hispana,' the Legate was saying. 'Many times it found honour in the wars, against foes abroad and rebellion at home. Shame came to it; but at the end it was honourably held until the last of those who held it died beneath its wings. It has led brave men. Let it lie forgotten.'

He stepped back.

Esca looked questioningly to Uncle Aquila, then at a sign from him, stooped to the segment of solid-moulded tessera which stood upreared against the wall, and fitted it carefully back into place over the hole. It had been well contrived, this hiding-place that Uncle Aquila had had made for his papers; with the segment replaced and the pattern completed, no trace of it remained, save for one all but invisible chink just wide enough to take a knife-blade.

'Tomorrow we will seal it up,' said Uncle Aquila, heavily.

Faintly into the silence, down the soft wet wind, stole the long-drawn, haunting notes of the trumpets from the transit camp, sounding for the third watch of the night. To Marcus, still gazing down blindly at the place where the square hole had been, it seemed that they were sounding with unbearable sadness for the lost Eagle, and for the lost Legion that had marched into the mist and never come marching back. Then, as the distant trumpets quickened into the shining spray of notes that ended the call, suddenly his sense of failure dropped from him like a tattered cloak, and he knew again, as he had known in the ruined signal-tower while the hunt closed in below, that it had all been worth while.

He had failed to redeem his father's Legion, since it was past redeeming, but the lost Eagle was home again, and would never now be used as a weapon against its own people.

He raised his head at the same time as Esca, and their eyes met. 'A good hunting?' Esca seemed to be asking.

'It was a good hunting,' Marcus said.

XXI
The Olive-Wood Bird

THAT winter was not an easy one for Marcus. For months he had mercilessly overtaxed his lame leg, and when the strain was over, it quite suddenly took its revenge. He did not much mind the pain it gave him, save when it kept him awake at night, but he did most bitterly mind finding himself shackled by the old wound again, when he had thought that all that was over. He felt ill, and he was wildly impatient, and he missed Cottia through the dark winter days as he had never missed her before.

Also there was the old nagging question of the future still to be settled. For Esca, the future was simpler—simpler as to the outward things at all events. 'I am your armour-bearer, though I am no longer your slave,' he said when they discussed the question. 'I will serve you, and you shall feed me, and between whiles maybe I will turn hunter, and that will bring in a sesterce from time to time.' Even before the year turned Marcus had spoken to his uncle about his old idea of becoming somebody's secretary; but Uncle Aquila had disposed of his capabilities to be anybody's secretary in a few well-chosen and blistering words, and when he proved stubborn in the plan, finished up by making him promise to wait at least until he was strong again.

The year drew on to spring, and slowly Marcus's leg began to strengthen under him once more. March came, and the forest below the ramparts was flushed with rising sap, and the many thorn-trees which gave it its name began to feather the wooded hills with white. And quite suddenly the House of Kaeso woke up. For a few days slaves came and went, scurrying about it; hangings were shaken out of doors, and the fumes of the freshly lit hypocaust fire blew into the slaves' quarters of Uncle Aquila's house and created unpleasantness between the two households. Then one evening, returning from the baths, Marcus and Esca met a hired mule-carriage being driven away empty from the house of Kaeso, and glimpsed a mass of luggage being carried indoors. The family had returned.

Next morning Marcus went down to the foot of the garden, and whistled for Cottia, as he had been used to do. It was a wild day of blustering wind and thin, shining rain, and the little native daffodils in the rampart curve tossed and streamed before the gusts like points of wind-blown flame, with the shrill sunshine slanting through their petals. Cottia came with the wind behind her, up round the end of the swaying hedge, to join him under the bare fruit-trees.

'I heard you whistle,' she said, 'and so I came. I have brought your bracelet back to you.'

'Cottia!' Marcus said. 'Why, Cottia!' and stood looking at her, making no move to take the bracelet that she held out to him. It was almost a year since their last meeting, but he had expected her to wait as she had been then. And Cottia had not waited. She stood before him much taller than she had been, with her head up, and returned his look, suddenly a little uncertain. Her soft golden-green mantle was swathed closely round her over the straight white folds of her tunic; one end of it, which had been drawn over her head, had fallen back, and her flaming hair that had been used to blow wild, was braided into a shining coronal so that she seemed more than ever to carry her head like a queen. Her lips were touched with red, and her eyebrows darkened, and there were tiny gold drops in her ears.

'Why, Cottia,' he said again, 'you have grown up,' and felt suddenly a little ache of loss.

'Yes,' said Cottia. 'Do you like me grown up?'

'Yes—yes, of course,' Marcus said. 'Thank you for looking after my bracelet for me. Uncle Aquila told me how you came to see him about it before you went away.' He took the heavy gold bracelet from her and sprang it on to his wrist, still looking at her as he did so. He found that he did not know how to talk to her, and as the silence lengthened, he asked with desperate politeness, 'Did you like Aquae Sulis?'

'*No!*' Cottia spat the word between little pointed teeth, and her face was suddenly bright with fury. 'I hated every moment of Aquae Sulis! I never wanted to go there; I wanted to wait for you because you told me you might be home before the winter closed in. And all winter I have had no word of you save one little—*little* message in some silly letter your uncle sent mine about the new town water supply; and I have waited, and waited, and now you are not at all glad to see me! Well, neither am I at all glad to see you!'

'You little vixen!' Marcus caught her wrists as she turned to run, and swung her round to face him. Suddenly and softly he laughed. 'But I am glad to see you. You do not know how glad I am to see you, Cottia.'

She was dragging away from him, wrenching at her wrists to free them, but at his words she checked, looking up into his face. 'Yes, you are now,' she said wonderingly. 'Why were you not, before?'

'I did not recognize you, just at first.'

'Oh,' said Cottia, a little blankly. She was silent a moment, and then asked with sudden anxiety: 'Where is Cub?'

'Making love to Sassticca for a bone. He is growing greedy.'

She drew a deep breath of relief. 'All was well with him, then, when you came home?'

'He was very thin; he would not eat after you left. But all is well with him now.'

'I was afraid of that; that he would fret, I mean. It was one of the things that made me not want to go to Aquae Sulis; but I could not take him with me, truly I could not, Marcus. Aunt Valaria would never have allowed it.'

'I am very sure she would not,' Marcus said, his mouth quirking as he thought of the Lady Valaria confronted with the suggestion that she should take a young wolf to a fashionable watering-place.

By this time they were sitting side by side on Marcus's cloak spread on the damp marble bench, and after a few moments Cottia asked: 'Did you find the Eagle?'

He looked round at her, his arms resting across his knees. 'Yes,' he said at last.

'Oh, Marcus, I *am* so glad! So very glad! And now?'

'Nothing now.'

'But the Legion?' She searched his face, and the sparkle died in her own. 'Will there not be a new Ninth Legion, after all?'

'No, there will never be a Ninth Legion again.'

'But, Marcus—' she began, and then checked. 'No, I will not ask questions.'

He smiled. 'One day, maybe, I will tell you the whole story.'

'I will wait,' said Cottia.

For a while they sat there, talking by fits and starts, but silent for the most part, glancing at each other from time to time with a quick smile, and then away again, for they were unexpectedly shy of each other. Presently Marcus told her about Esca, that he was no longer a slave. He had expected her to be surprised, but she only said, 'Yes, Nissa told me, just after you went away, and I was glad—for you both.' And then they were silent again.

Behind them, in the bare swaying branches of the wild pear-tree, a blackbird with a crocus-coloured bill burst into song, and the wind caught and tossed the shining notes down to them in a shower. They turned together to look up at the singer, swaying against the cold blown blue of the sky. Marcus narrowed his eyes into the thin dazzle of sunlight and whistled back, and the blackbird, bowing and swaying on the wind-blown branch, its throat swelling with an ecstasy of song, seemed to be answering him. Then a cloud came sailing across the sun, and the bright world was quenched in shadow.

At the same moment they heard a horse coming down the street, its hoof-beats ringing on the wet roadway. It stopped before the house, or before the next one; Marcus could not be sure which.

The blackbird was still singing, but when he turned to look at Cottia, a shadow that was not merely the passing cloud seemed to have touched her. 'Marcus, what is it that you will do now?' she asked suddenly.

'Now?'

'Now that you are strong again. You are strong again, aren't you?' Then swiftly: 'No, I do not believe you are, you were limping more, just now, than you were when I saw you last.'

Marcus laughed. 'I have been lying up like a sick badger all winter, but I am mending fast now.'

'That is the truth?'

'That is the truth.'

'Then—what will you do? Will you go back to the Legions?'

'No. I should do well enough in a skirmish, maybe, but I could not march my cohort down from Portus Itius to Rome at twenty miles a day, and I should certainly be no use on the parade ground.'

'The parade ground!' Cottia said indignantly. 'I have seen them on the parade ground through the gates of the transit camp. They march about in straight lines with all their legs working together, and make silly patterns of themselves while a man with a voice like a bull shouts at them. What has *that* to do with the fighting of wars?'

Marcus hastily gathered his wits together to make Cottia understand what it had to do with the fighting of wars, but he did not have to struggle with the explanations, for she hurried on without waiting for an answer. 'Then if you cannot go back to the Legions, what *will* you do?'

'I am not—quite sure.'

'Perhaps you will go home,' she said; and then seemed suddenly to realize her own words, and her eyes grew frightened. 'You will go back to Rome, and take Cub and Esca with you!'

'I do not know, Cottia, truly I do not know. But I do not suppose for a moment that I shall ever go home.'

But Cottia did not seem to hear him. 'Take me too.' Suddenly her voice broke almost into a wail. 'They will build the city wall round here soon, and you could not leave me in a cage! You could not! Oh, Marcus, take me too!'

'Even if it were to Rome?' Marcus said, remembering her old wild hatred of all things Roman.

Cottia slipped from the bench, and turned to him as he got up also. 'Yes,' she said. 'Anywhere at all, if only it was with you.'

Two distinct waves of feeling swept over Marcus, so close upon each other that they were almost one. The first was the joyful surprise of finding, and the second the desolation of losing again . . . How was he to explain to Cottia that possessing nothing in the world, without even a trade to his hands, he could not take her with him?

'Cottia,' he began wretchedly. 'Cottia, my heart—it is no use—'

But before he could get any further, he heard Esca calling, with a note of excitement in his voice. 'Marcus! Where are you, Marcus?'

'Down here. I am coming,' he shouted back, and caught Cottia's hand. 'Come with me now, anyway.'

Rain had begun to spatter round them, but the sun was out again and the rain shone as it fell. Cub met them at the courtyard steps, circling about them and barking joyously, his straight bush of a tail streaming out behind. And hard behind Cub, was Esca. 'This has just come for you,' he said, holding out a slim, sealed papyrus roll.

Marcus took the roll from him, raising his brows at the sight of the Sixth Legion's signum on the seal; while Cottia and Esca and Cub all greeted each other after their fashion. In the act of breaking the thread he glanced up to see Uncle Aquila stalking towards them.

'Curiosity is one of the privileges of extreme old age,' said Uncle Aquila, towering over the group in the entrance to the colonnade.

Marcus unrolled the crackling papyrus sheet. He was half blind with the dazzle of the day outside and the written words seemed to float in the midst of red and green clouds. 'To Centurion Marcus Flavius Aquila, from Claudius Hieronimianus, Legate of the Sixth Victrix, Greeting,' the letter began. He skimmed the few close lines to the end, then glanced up and met Cottia's wide golden eyes fixed on him. 'Are you a witch out of Thessaly, to draw down the moon in a net of your hair? Or is it only the Other Sight that you have?' he said; and returned to the letter in his hand.

He began to read it a second time, more carefully, taking it in, as he had scarcely been able to do at first, and giving them the gist of it as he went along. 'The Legate has laid that matter before the Senate, and their ruling is as we knew it must be. But he says that "in just recognition of service to the State, which is none the less real that it must remain unpublished . . ." He looked up quickly. 'Esca, you are a Roman citizen.'

Esca was puzzled, almost a little wary. 'I am not sure that I understand. What does it mean?'

It meant so much; rights, and duties. It could even, in a way, mean the cancelling of a clipped ear, for if a man were a Roman citizen, that fact was stronger than the fact that he had been a slave. Esca would find that out, later. Also, in Esca's case, it was his honourable quittance, the wooden foil of a gladiator who had won freedom with honour in the arena; the settlement of all debts. 'It is as though they gave you your wooden foil,' he said; and saw Esca, who had been a gladiator, begin to understand, before he returned again to his letter.

'The Legate says that for the same service, I am to be awarded the gratuity of a time-expired cohort centurion—paid in the old style, part sesterces, part land.' A long pause, and then he began to read word for word. 'Following the established custom, the land-grant will be made over to you here in Britain, as the province of your last military service; but a good friend of mine on the Senate benches writes to me that if you so wish, there should be no difficulty in working an exchange for land in Etruria, which I believe is your own country. The official documents will be reaching both of you in due course, but since the wheels of officialdom are notoriously slow, I hope that I may be the first to give you the news . . .'

He stopped reading. Slowly the hand which held the Legate's letter dropped to his side. He looked round at the faces that crowded him in: Uncle Aquila's wearing the look of someone watching with detached interest the result of an experiment; Esca's face with an alert and waiting look in it; Cottia's, grown all at once very pointed and white; Cub's great head upraised and watchful. Faces. And suddenly he wanted to escape from them all; even from Cottia, even from Esca. They were part of all his plans and calculations, they belonged to him and he to them, but for this one moment, he wanted to be alone, to realize what had happened without anyone else entering in to complicate it. He turned away from them and stood leaning against the half wall beside the courtyard steps, staring away down the rain-wet garden where the little native daffodils were a myriad points of dancing flame under the wild fruit-trees.

He could go home.

Standing there with the last cold spattering of the shower blowing in his face, he thought, I can go home, and saw behind his eyes the long road leading south, the Legion's road, white in the Etruscan sunlight; the farmsteads among their terraced olive-trees, and the wine-darkness of the Apennines beyond. He seemed to catch the resiny, aromatic smell of the pine forests dropping to the shore, and the warm mingling of thyme and rosemary and wild cyclamen that was the summer scent of his own hills. He could go back to all that now, to the hills and the people among whom he had been bred, and for whom he had been so bitterly home-sick, here in the North. But if he did, would there not be another hunger on him all his life? For other scents and sights and sounds; pale and changeful northern skies and the green plover calling?

Suddenly he knew why Uncle Aquila had come back to this country when his years of service were done. All his life he would remember his own hills, sometimes he would remember them with longing; but Britain was his home. That came to him, not as a new thing, but as something so familiar that he wondered why he had not known it before.

Cub thrust a cold muzzle under his hand, and he drew a long breath and turned once again to the others. Uncle Aquila stood still with arms folded and huge head a little bent, looking on with that air of detached interest.

'My congratulations, Marcus,' he said. 'It is by no means everyone for whom my friend Claudius will sweat as he must have sweated to drag justice out of the Senate.'

'I could lay my head on his feet,' Marcus said softly. 'It is a new beginning—a new beginning, Esca.'

'Of course, it will take a little time to work the exchange,' said

Uncle Aquila, thoughtfully. 'But I imagine that you should be back in Etruria by autumn.'

'I shall not be going back to Etruria,' Marcus said. 'I shall take up my land here in Britain.' He looked at Cottia. She was standing just as she had stood ever since he began to read the Legate's letter, still and waiting as a winter-bound withy.

'Not Rome, after all; but you did say, "Anywhere", did you not, Cottia sweet,' he said, holding out a hand to her.

She looked at him for an instant, questioningly. Then she smiled, and making a little gesture to gather her mantle as though she were quite prepared to come now, anywhere, anywhere at all, put her hands into his.

'And now I suppose that I shall have to arrange matters with Kaeso,' said Uncle Aquila. 'Jupiter! Why did I never realize how peaceful life was before you came!'

That evening, having written to the Legate for both of them, Marcus had wandered up to join his uncle in the watch-tower, while Esca went to arrange about getting the letter sent. He was leaning at the high window, his elbows propped on the sill, his chin in his hands, while behind him Uncle Aquila sat squarely at the writing-table, surrounded by his History of Siege Warfare. The high room held the fading daylight as in a cup, but below in the courtyard the shadows were gathering, and the rolling miles of forest had the softness of smoke, as Marcus looked out over them to the familiar wave-life of the Downs.

Down country: yes, that was the country for farming. Thyme for bees, and good grazing; maybe even a southern slope that could be terraced for vines. He and Esca, and what little labour they could afford, little enough that would be at first; but they would manage. Farming with free or freed labour would be an experiment, but it had been done before, though not often. Esca had given him a distaste for owning human beings.

'We have been talking it over, Esca and I; and if I have any choice in the matter, I am going to try for land in the Down Country,' he said suddenly, still with his chin in his hands.

'I imagine that you should not have much difficulty in arranging that with the powers that be,' said Uncle Aquila, searching for a mislaid tablet among the orderly litter on his table.

'Uncle Aquila, did you know about this—beforehand, I mean?'

'I knew that Claudius intended bringing your names before the Senate, but whether any result would come of it was quite another matter.' He snorted. 'Trust the Senate to pay its debts in the old style! Land and sesterces; as much land and as few sesterces as may be; it comes cheaper that way.'

'Also one Roman citizenship,' said Marcus, quickly.

'Which is a thing apart from price, though not costly in the giving,' agreed Uncle Aquila. 'I think they need not have economized on your gratuity.'

Marcus laughed. 'We shall do well enough, Esca and I.'

'I have no doubt about it—always supposing that you do not first starve. You will have to build and stock, remember.'

'Most of the building we can do ourselves; wattle and daub will serve until we grow rich.'

'And what will Cottia think of that?'

'Cottia will be content,' Marcus said.

'Well, you know where to come when you need help.'

'Yes, I know.' Marcus turned from the window. 'If we should need help—really need it, after three bad harvests—I will come.'

'Not until then?'

'Not until then. No.'

Uncle Aquila glared. 'You are impossible! You grow more and more like your father every day!'

'Do I?' Marcus said, with a glint of laughter, and hesitated; there were some things that it was never easy to say to the older man. 'Uncle Aquila, you have done so much for Esca and me already. If I had not had you to turn to—'

'Bah!' said Uncle Aquila, still searching for his missing tablet. 'No one else to turn to me. No son of my own to plague me.' He found the tablet at last, and began with delicate precision to smooth the used wax with his quill pen, evidently under the impression that it was the flat end of his stylus. Suddenly he looked up under his brows. 'If you had applied for that exchange, I believe I should have been rather lonely.'

'Did you think I would be away back to Clusium on the first tide?'

'I did not think so, no,' said Uncle Aquila slowly, looking with surprised disgust at the wreck of his quill, and laying it down. 'You have now made me ruin a perfectly good pen and destroy several extremely important notes. I hope you are satisfied . . . No, I did not think so, but until the time came, and the choice was between your hands, I could not be sure.'

'Nor could I,' Marcus said. 'But I am sure now.'

All at once, and seemingly for no particular reason, he was remembering his olive-wood bird. It had seemed to him as the little flames licked through the pyre of birch-bark and dead heather on which he had laid it, that with the childhood treasure, all his old life was burning away. But a new life, a new beginning, had warmed out of the grey ash, for himself, and Esca, and Cottia; perhaps for other people too; even for an unknown downland valley that would one day be a farm.

Somewhere a door slammed, and Esca's step sounded below in the colonnade, accompanied by a clear and merry whistling.

> 'Oh when I joined the Eagles,
> (As it might be yesterday)
> I kissed a girl at Clusium
> Before I marched away.'

And it came to Marcus suddenly that slaves very seldom whistled. They might sing, if they felt like it or if the rhythm helped their work, but whistling was in some way different; it took a free man to make the sort of noise Esca was making.

Uncle Aquila looked up again from mending the broken pen. 'Oh, by the way. I have a piece of news that may interest you, if you have not heard it already. They are rebuilding Isca Dumnoniorum.'

THE SILVER BRANCH

Historical Note

MORE than a hundred years went by after the time of this story, before Rome fell; before the last of the Legions were withdrawn from Britain and Rutupiae Light went out and the Dark Ages had begun. But already the great days were over. Rome was harassed by the barbarians all along her frontiers, while at home generals fought to become Emperors and rival Emperors struggled among themselves for power.

Marcus Aurelius Carausius was a real person; so were Allectus the Traitor and the Legate Asklepiodotus; and so of course was the Caesar Constantius, whose son Constantine was the first Christian Emperor of Rome. For the rest: the body of Saxon warrior buried with his weapons was found in one of the ditches of Richborough Castle, which was Rutupiae in the days of the Eagles. The Basilica at Calleva was burned down towards the end of the Roman occupation and later roughly rebuilt, and the Eagle which I have already written about in another story was discovered during excavations in the ruins of one of the courtrooms behind the Main Hall. At Calleva also—Silchester as it is now—there was found a stone with a man's name carved on it in the script of ancient Irish; and the name was Evicatos, or Ebicatos, which means 'Spear Man'.

Contents

I	The Saxon Shore	219
II	A Whisper Down the Wind	230
III	The House on the Cliffs	238
IV	The Sea Wolf	246
V	Nightshade!	256
VI	Evicatos of the Spear	262
VII	'To the Fates, that They May Be Kind'	270
VIII	The Feast of Samhain	281
IX	The Sign of the Dolphin	292
X	The *Berenice* sales for Gaul	303
XI	The Shadow	314
XII	A Sprig of Broom	323
XIII	The Silver Branch	335
XIV	An Ancient Ensign	347
XV	Return of the Legions	356
XVI	'Carausius! Carausius!'	365
XVII	Eagle in the Flames	372
XVIII	Triumphal Garlands	385

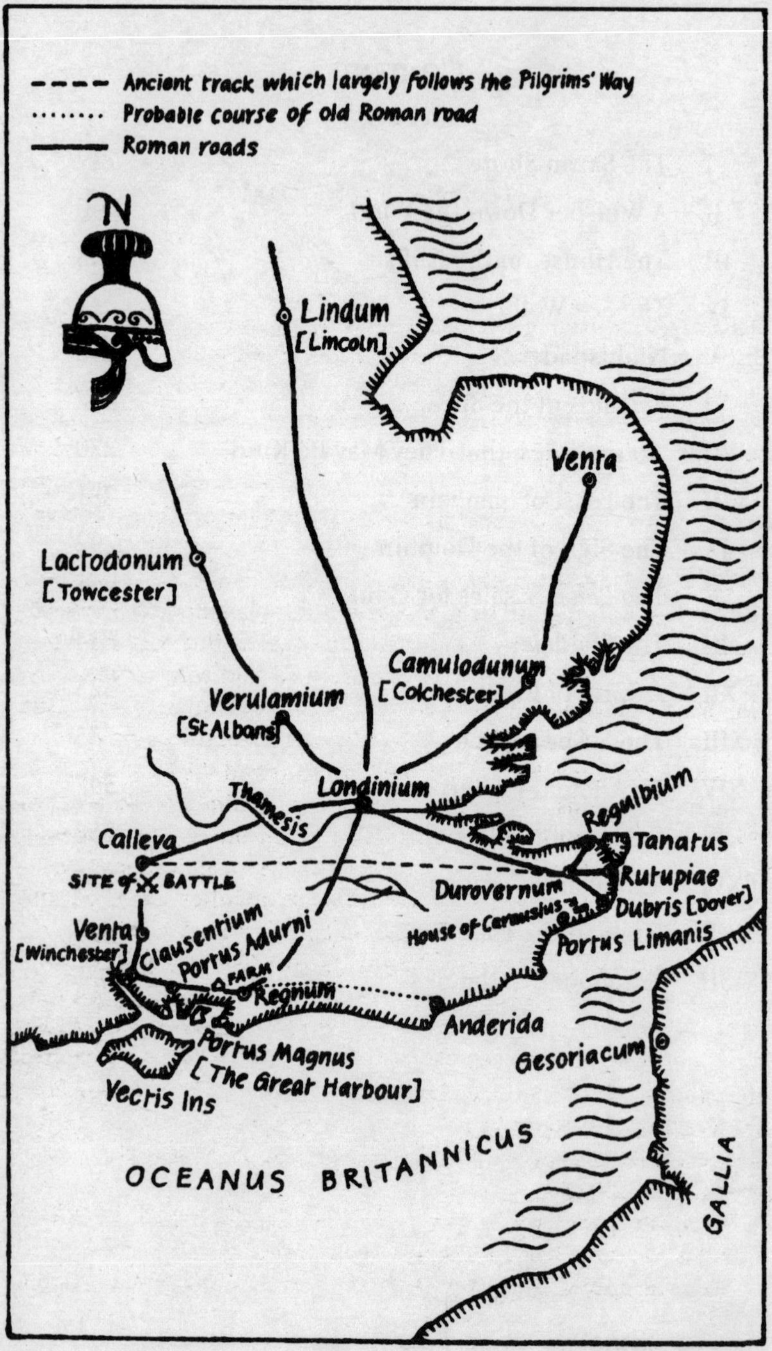

Ancient track which largely follows the Pilgrims' Way
Probable course of old Roman road
Roman roads
N
Lindum
[Lincoln]
Venta
Lactodonum
[Towcester]
Camulodunum
[Colchester]
Verulamium
[St Albans]
Londinium
Thamesis
Regulbium
Calleva
Tanatus
SITE of BATTLE
Rutupiae
Durovernum
Dubris [Dover]
House of Carausius
Venta
[Winchester]
Clausentium
Portus Adurni
Portus Limanis
FARM
Regnum
Anderida
Portus Magnus
[The Great Harbour]
Gesoriacum
Vectis Ins
OCEANUS BRITANNICUS
GALLIA

I
The Saxon Shore

ON a blustery autumn day a galley was nosing up the wide loop of a British river that widened into the harbour of Rutupiae.

The tide was low, and the mud-banks at either hand that would be covered at high tide were alive with curlew and sandpiper. And out of the waste of sandbank and sour salting, higher and nearer as the time went by, rose Rutupiae: the long, whale-backed hump of the island and the grey ramparts of the fortress, with the sheds of the dockyard massed below it.

The young man standing on the fore-deck of the galley watched the fortress drawing nearer with a sense of expectancy; his thoughts reaching alternately forward to the future that waited for him there, and back to a certain interview that he had had with Licinius, his Cohort Commander, three months ago, at the other end of the Empire. That had been the night his posting came through.

'You do not know Britain, do you?' Licinius had said.

Justin—Tiberius Lucius Justinianus, to give him his full name as it was inscribed on the record tablets of the Army Medical Corps at Rome—had shaken his head, saying with the small stutter that he could never quite master, 'N-no, sir. My grandfather was born and bred there, but he settled in Nicaea when he left the Eagles.'

'And so you will be eager to see the Province for yourself.'

'Yes, sir, only—I scarcely expected to be sent there with the Eagles.'

He could remember the scene so vividly. He could see Licinius watching him across the crocus flame of the lamp on his table, and the pattern that the wooden scroll-ends made on their shelves, and the fine-blown sand-wreaths in the corners of the mud-walled office; he could hear distant laughter in the camp, and, far away, the jackals crying; and Licinius's dry voice:

'Only you did not know we were so friendly with Britain, or rather, with the man who has made himself Emperor of Britain?'

'Well, sir, it does seem strange. It is only this spring that Maximian sent the Caesar C-Constantius to drive him out of his Gaulish territory.'

'I agree. But there are possible explanations to these postings from other parts of the Empire to the British Legions. It may be that Rome seeks, as it were, to keep open the lines of communication. It may be that she does not choose that Marcus Aurelius Carausius should have at his command Legions that are completely cut away from the rest of the Empire. That way comes a fighting force that follows none but its own leader and owns no ties whatsoever with Imperial Rome.' Licinius had leaned forward and shut down the lid of the bronze ink-stand with a small deliberate click. 'Quite honestly, I wish your posting had been to any other Province of the Empire.'

Justin had stared at him in bewilderment. 'Why so, sir?'

'Because I knew your father, and therefore take a certain interest in your welfare . . . How much do you in fact understand about the situation in Britain? About the Emperor Carausius, who is the same thing in all that matters?'

'Very little, I am afraid, sir.'

'Well then, listen, and maybe you will understand a little more. In the first place, you can rid your mind of any idea that Carausius is framed of the same stuff as most of the six-month sword-made Emperors we have had in the years before Diocletian and Maximian split the Purple between them. He is the son of a German father and a Hibernian mother, and that is a mixture to set the sparks flying; born and bred in one of the trading-stations that the Manopeans of the German sea set up long since in Hibernia, and only came back to his father's people when he reached manhood. He was a Scaldis river-pilot when I knew him first. Afterwards he broke into the Legions—the gods know how. He served in Gaul and Illyria, and under the Emperor Carus in the Persian War, rising all the time. He was one of Maximian's right-hand men in suppressing the revolts in eastern Gaul, and made such a name for himself that Maximian, remembering his naval training, gave him command of the fleet based on Gesoriacum, and the task of clearing the Northern Seas of the Saxons swarming in them.'

Licinius had broken off there, seeming lost in his own thoughts, and in a little, Justin had prompted respectfully, 'Was not there a t-tale that he let the Sea Wolves through on their raids and then fell on them when they were heavy with spoil on their h-homeward way?'

'Aye—and sent none of the spoil to Rome. It was that, I imagine, that roused Maximian's ire. We shall never know the rights of that tale; but at all events Maximian ordered his execution, and Carausius got wind of it in time and made for Britain, followed by the whole Fleet. He was ever such a one as men follow gladly. By the time the official order for his execution was at Gesoriacum, Carausius had dealt with the Governor of Britain, and proclaimed himself Emperor with three British Legions and a large force from Gaul and Lower Germany to back his claim, and the sea swept by his galleys between him and the executioner. Aye, better galleys and better seamen than ever Maximian could lay his hands to. And in the end Maximian had no choice but to make peace and own him for a brother Emperor.'

'But we have not k-kept the peace,' Justin had said bluntly after a moment.

'No. And to my mind Constantius's victories in North Gaul this spring are more shame to us than defeat could have been. No blame to the young Caesar; he is a man under authority like the rest of us, though he will sit in Maximian's place one day . . . Well, the peace abides—after a fashion. But it is a situation that may burst into a blaze at any hour, and if it does, the gods help anyone caught in the flames.' The Commander had pushed back his chair and risen, turning to the window. 'And yet, in an odd way, I think I envy you, Justin.'

Justin had said, 'You liked him, then, sir?'

And he remembered now how Licinius had stood looking out into the moonlit night. 'I—have never been sure,' he said, 'but I would have followed him into the mouth of Erebos itself,' and turned back to the lamp.

That had been almost all, save that at the last Licinius had stayed him in the doorway, saying, 'If you should at any time have speech with the great man himself, salute him from me, and ask him if he remembers the boar we killed below the pine-woods at the third bend of the Scaldis.'

But it was scarcely likely, Justin thought, that a Junior Surgeon would have the chance to give any message to the Emperor Carausius.

He came back to the present with a jerk, to find that they had entered a world of stone-and-timber jetties, ringed round with sail-lofts and armourers' shops and long-boat sheds, threading their way among the galleys that lay at anchor in the sheltered water. The mingled reek of pitch and salt-soaked timber and hot metal was in his nostrils; and above the beat of the galley's oars and the liquid rush of water parting under the bows, he could hear the mingled myriad beehive hum of planes and saws and hammers on anvils that was the voice of a dockyard all the world over. And above him towered the ramparts of Rutupiae; a grey prow of ramparts raw with newness, from the midst of which sprang the beacon-crested tower of the Light.

A while later, having landed and reported to the Commandant and to the Senior Surgeon, having left his kit in the lime-washed cell in the officers' block that had been assigned to him, and set out in search of the bath-house and lost his way in the crowded unfriendly immensity of the huge fortress, Justin was standing close before that tower.

The thing was no match for the Pharos at Alexandria, but seen at close quarters it was vast enough to stop one's breath, all the same. In the centre of the open space rose a plinth of solid masonry four or five times the height of a man, and long as an eighty-oar galley, from the midst of which a tower of the same grey stone-work soared heavenward, bearing on its high crest the iron beacon brazier that seemed to Justin, staring giddily up at it, almost to touch the drifting November skies. The gulls rose and fell about it on white wings, and he heard their thin, remote crying above the busy sounds of the fortress; then, with his head beginning to swim, brought his gaze down as far as the top of the plinth. Curved ramps for the fuel-carts led up to it at either end, and from them roofed colonnades ran in to the base of the tower itself; and now that he had got over the stupendous size of the thing enough to take in the details, he saw that the columns and cornices were of marble, enriched with statues and splendid carvings, but that they were broken and falling into decay, which was strange, here in the midst of a fortress so new that in places they were still at work on the walls. But there was broken marble everywhere, some of it roughly stacked as though for use at a future time, some clinging yet to the stark grey walls that it had once covered. A small piece that must have fallen from its fellows when being carried away lay almost at his feet and, stooping to pick it up, he saw that it was part of a sculptured laurel-wreath.

He was still holding the fragment of marble and gazing up at the great tower from which it had fallen, when a voice behind him said, 'Pretty, isn't it?' and he swung round to find standing at his elbow a very dusty young man in Centurion's uniform, with his helmet under one arm; a stocky, red-haired young man with a thin, merry face and fly-away eyebrows, who seemed friendly.

'It is half ruined,' Justin said, puzzled. 'What is it? I mean, I can see it is a pharos, b-but it looks as though it was meant to be something else as well.'

A shadow of bitterness crept into the young Centurion's voice. 'It *was* a triumphal monument as well—a triumphal monument to the might of Imperial Rome and her conquest of Britain. Now it is just a pharos, and we break up the fallen marble for rubble in the walls that we build to keep the Saxons out . . . There's a moral somewhere in that, if you like morals.'

Justin glanced down at the fragment of marble laurel-wreath in his hand, then tossed it aside. It fell with a little sharp clatter, raising a puff of dust.

'Would you be looking for anyone or anything?' enquired his new acquaintance.

'I was looking for the bath-house,' Justin told him; and then, by way of giving an account of himself, 'I am the new Junior Surgeon.'

'Are you so? Well, truth to tell, I thought you might be.' The other glanced at the uniform without armour, which Justin wore. 'You have reported to the Commandant?'

'And to the Senior Surgeon,' Justin said, with his rather hesitating smile. 'He called me a fledgling butcher and turned me off until an hour before sick parade tomorrow.'

The young Centurion's eyes had become dancing slits. 'Vinicius must be in rather a mellow mood; he called your predecessor a ham-fisted assassin and threw a pitch-pot at his head, so I've heard. I wasn't here myself then . . . Well, if it's a bath you want, you had best come with me. I'm just going to shed this harness, and then I'm for the bath-house myself. We'll just have time for a plunge and a splash about before dinner if we're quick.'

Retracing his steps with his new acquaintance, between the busy workshops and crowded barrack rows, it seemed to Justin that the great fortress had all at once put on a more friendly face; and he looked about him with a quickened interest. 'This place seems very big and busy to me,' he said. 'I spent my year as a surgeon's Cub at Beersheba, and that is a single Cohort fort. It could g-get lost in this one.'

'They're all monsters, these new Saxon shore fortresses,' said his companion. 'They have to be; they are fort and shipyard and naval base in one. You'll grow used to it after a while.'

'Are there many of them, then? Great new forts like this?'

'A good few, from the Metaris round to the Great Harbour; some of them altogether new, and some built over old ones, like Rutupiae. They are all part of Carausius's defences against the Sea Wolves.'

'Carausius,' Justin said, with a touch of awe in his tone. 'I suppose you will have seen Carausius often?'

'Zeus! Yes! This is his headquarters, though of course he's all over the province too, in between whiles. Not one to let the turf smoulder under his feet, our little Emperor. You'll see him yourself this evening, in all likelihood; he most often feeds in Mess with the rest of us.'

'You mean—he's here now?'

'Surely. And so are we. Come up and sit on the bed. I shall be but a few moments.'

And so, a short while later, Justin was sitting on the edge of the cot in a limewashed cell exactly like his own, while his newfound acquaintance laid aside sword and helmet and set to work on the straps of his breastplate, whistling softly and very cheerfully through his teeth as he did so. Justin sat and watched him. He was a friendly soul himself, but he was always gratefully surprised at any sign of friendliness from other people, and with his gratitude, his liking went out, hesitant but warm, to the red-headed Centurion.

The other slipped the last buckle free, and broke off his whistling. 'So you're from Beersheba, are you? A long march, you have had. Ah, thanks.' (This as Justin reached and took the heavy breastplate from him.) And his next words were muffled in the folds of his leather harness-tunic as he dragged it over his head. 'And where before that? What part of the Empire do you spring from?'

'Nicaea, in southern Gaul.'

'So this is your first sight of Britain?'

'Yes.' Justin laid the breastplate down on the cot beside aim. 'But my people are from Britain, and I have always had a mind to c-come back and see it for myself.'

The young Centurion emerged from the leather folds, and stood up in his uniform tunic of fine crimson wool, looking, with his red hair on end, suddenly much more of a boy and less of a grown man. 'What part of Britain?'

'The South. Somewhere in the Down Country towards C-calleva, I believe.'

'Famous! All the best people are from the Down Country; the best people and the best sheep. I am myself.' He eyed Justin with frank interest. 'What is your name?'

'Justin.—Tiberius Lucius Justinianus.'

There was a moment's silence, and then his companion said very softly, 'Justinianus.—*Is* it so?' And with a swift gesture pulled something off his left hand and held it out to Justin. 'Have you ever seen anything like that before?'

Justin took the thing and bent his head over it. It was a heavy and very battered signet ring. The flawed emerald which formed the bezel was darkly cool, holding the surface reflection of the window as he turned it to catch the light, and the engraved device stood out clearly. 'This Dolphin?' he said, with a dawning excitement. 'Yes, I have, on—on the ivory lid of an old cosmetic box that belonged to my grandmother. It was the badge of her family.'

'That proves it!' said the young Centurion, taking back his ring. 'Well, of all the—' He began to do strange calculations on his fingers, then abandoned the attempt. 'Nay, it is beyond me. There have been more marryings than one between your house and mine, and it would take my Great Aunt Honoria to unsnarl such a tangled skein,—but we are undoubtedly cousins of some kind!'

Justin said nothing. He had risen from the cot, and stood watching the other's face as though suddenly unsure of his welcome. It was one thing to take casual pity on a stranger and bring him back to one's quarters on the way to the bath-house, but it might be quite another to find oneself saddled with him for a kinsman.

That unsureness, though he did not know it, was one of the things that years of being a disappointment to his father had done to him. He had always been miserably aware of being a disappointment to his father. His mother, whom he could scarcely remember, had been beautiful; but Justin, always unfortunate, had continued to be both very like her and very ugly, with a head too large for his thin shoulders, and ears that stuck out defiantly on either side of it. He had spent a good deal of his childhood being ill, and as a result, when the time came for him to go into the Legions, as the men of his family had always done, he had failed to come up to the needful standard of fitness for the Centuriate. He had not minded for himself, because he had always wanted to be a surgeon; but he had minded deeply for his father's sake, knowing himself more than ever a disappointment; and became even more unsure of himself in consequence.

And then it dawned on him with delight that the red-headed young man was every whit as glad of the astonishing discovery as he was himself.

'So, we are kinsmen,' he said. 'And that is good. And I am Tiberius Lucius Justinianus—but still I do not know by what name to call you.'

'Flavius,' said the red-headed Centurion. 'Marcelus Flavius Aquila.' He reached out and caught Justin by the shoulders, half laughing, half incredulous still. 'Oh, but this is most wonderful that you and I should meet like this on your first day on British soil! It must be that the fates mean us to be friends, and who are we to fly against the fates?'

And suddenly they were both talking together, in breathless, laughing half-sentences, holding each the other at arm's length the better to look at each other, caught up in delight at the thing that had happened, until Flavius broke off to catch up the fresh tunic which the orderly had left for him on the foot of the cot. 'This is a thing that we must celebrate royally by and by; but if we aren't quick we shall neither of us get a bath before dinner—and I don't know about you, but I've been on wall building duty all day and I'm gritty from head to heel.'

The Mess Hall was already crowded when Justin and Flavius entered it, and men stood talking idly in groups, but as yet nobody had taken their seats at the long tables. Justin had been rather dreading his entry alone into a hall full of strangers. But with Flavius's arm across his shoulders he was swept at once into a group of young officers. 'Here's our new Junior Surgeon—what Vinicius has left of him, and he's a kinsman of mine!' And immediately appealed to to take sides in an argument about oysters, the plunge was over almost before he knew it.

But soon after, the hum of talk in the long room fell abruptly silent, as steps and a quick voice sounded outside in the Colonnade, and as every man straightened himself on his feet, Justin looked with eager expectancy towards the door.

At first sight the man who entered with his Staff Officers behind him was a disappointment. A short, thick-set man of immensely powerful build, with a round head set on a neck of extraordinary thickness, and crisp brown hair and beard as curly as a ram's fleece. A man who looked as though he would have been more at home in leather frock and seaman's bonnet than the fine linen he wore, and who advanced into the hall with the unmistakable rolling step of a man used to a heaving deck under his feet.

But I have seen the like of this man a score of times—a hundred times before, Justin thought. You can see him on the deck of any galley in the Empire.

The Emperor had halted at the upper end of the room, his gaze moving over the faces of the men gathered there; and his eyes under their thick bar of brows met Justin's. 'Ah, a new face among us,' said the Emperor, and crooked a finger. 'Come here, boy.'

He heard the Camp Commandant speak his name and position quickly to Carausius. Then he was saluting before the man who had risen from a Scaldis river pilot to be Emperor of Britain; and suddenly he knew that he had been wrong. He had never seen the like of this man before.

Carausius set a hand on his shoulder and turned him—for it was dusk by now—to get the lamp-light on his face. After a long unhurried scrutiny, he said, 'So you are our new Junior Surgeon.'

'Yes, Caesar.'

'Where did you serve your Cubhood?'

'With the third Cohort of the Fretencis, at Beersheba in Judea,' Justin said. 'Fulvius Licinius, who commands the garrison, bade me salute you from him, and ask you if you remember the boar that you and he killed below the pine-woods at the third bend of the Scaldis.'

Carausius was silent a moment. Then he said, 'I remember that boar, yes—and Licinius. And so he's in Judea, is he? He was senior to me in those days; and now he commands the garrison at Beersheba, while I wear this'—touching the mantle of Imperial Purple that he wore clasped by a huge ruby at the shoulder. 'There's naught so odd as life. Maybe you haven't noticed that yet, but you will, you will, if you live long enough . . . So my brother Emperors send me a Junior Surgeon from the Fretencis. There have been several postings from overseas to the Legions here in Britain, lately. Almost like old times.—Yet they showed themselves none so friendly this spring, as I remember.' Voice and manner were musing, nothing more, the hand on Justin's shoulder barely tightened its grip, there was no change in the blunt, straight-featured face so near his own, save that perhaps for a moment the eyes seemed to grow a little paler, as the sea whitening before a rain-squall; and yet suddenly Justin was cold afraid. 'Can you read me the riddle, I wonder?'

Somehow he held his ground under the light, deadly hand on his shoulder, and gave back the Emperor's look, without wavering.

A voice—a pleasantly cool voice with a laugh in it—protested lazily, 'Excellency, you are too hard on the boy. It is his first night among us, and you will put him off his dinner.'

Carausius paid not the faintest attention. For a few moments he continued that terrible raking stare; then a slow, straight-lipped smile spread over his face. 'You are so right, my dear Allectus,' he said; and then to Justin, 'No, you have not been sent to play the spy, or if you have, you do not know it.' His hand slipped from the young surgeon's shoulder, and he glanced about him. 'Shall we begin dinner, my friends?'

The man who had been called Allectus caught Justin's eye as he turned away, and smiled. Justin returned the smile, grateful as always for kindness, and slipped back through the crowd to Flavius, who greeted him half under his breath with a swift 'Eugé! That was well done!' which warmed him still further.

And a little later he was sitting between Flavius and another Centurion at the foot of the table. His right-hand neighbour was too busy eating to have any conversation, and he was free to give his whole attention to the highly irreverent account of the great ones at the upper end of the table, with which Flavius was favouring him under cover of the general hum of talk.

'You see that one with the sword-cut down his cheek?' said Flavius, dealing with pickled herring. 'That's Arcadius, the captain of the *Caleope*, our biggest three-bank galley. He came by that mark in the arena. A bright lad, Arcadius, in his young days. Oh, and the melancholy fellow beside him is Dexion, a Centurion of Marines. Never,' said Flavius, wagging his head, '*never* shake the dice with him unless you want to lose the tunic off your back. I don't say he doesn't play square, but he throws Venus more often than any mere mortal has a right to.'

'Thanks for the warning,' Justin said. 'I'll remember.'

But his eyes strayed with an odd fascination, as they had done more than once before, to the man whom the Emperor had called Allectus, who now sat among Carausius's staff officers near the head of the table. He was a tall man with a cap of shining fair hair greying a little at the temples; a man with a rather heavy face that would have been good to look at but that it was too pale; everything about him just a little too pale—hair, skin, and eyes. But even as Justin watched, the man smiled at something his neighbour had said, and the smile, swift and completely charming, gave to his face all that it lacked before.

'Who is the tall very fair man?' he murmured to Flavius. 'The Emperor called him Allectus, I think.'

'Carausius's Finance Minister and general right-hand man. He has a vast following among the troops, as well as the merchants and moneyers, so that I suppose after Carausius he's the most powerful man in Britain. But he's a good enough fellow, in spite of looking as though he'd been reared in a dark closet.'

And then, a few moments later, something happened; something so slight and so ordinary that afterwards Justin wondered if he had simply let his imagination run away with him—and yet he could never quite forget it, nor the sudden sense of evil that came with it. Roused perhaps by the warmth rising from the lamps, a big, soft-winged night-moth had come fluttering down from the rafters to dart and hover and swerve about the table. Everyone's attention was turned towards the Emperor, who was at that moment preparing to pour the second Libation to the gods. Everyone, that is, save Justin and Allectus. For some unknown reason, Justin had glanced again at Allectus; and Allectus was watching the moth.

The moth was circling wildly nearer and nearer to one of the lamps which stood directly before the Finance Minister, its blurred shadow flashing about the table as it swooped and spun in dizzy spirals about the bright and beckoning flame, closer and closer, until the wild, ecstatic dance ended in a burst of shadows, and the moth spun away on singed wings, to fall with a pitiful, maimed fluttering close beside Allectus's wine-cup. And Allectus, smiling faintly, crushed out its life under one deliberate finger.

That was all. Anybody would crush a singed moth—it was the obvious, the only thing to do. But Justin had seen the pale man's face as he watched the dancing moth, waiting for it to dance too near, seen it in the unguarded instant as he stretched out the precise forefinger to kill.

II
A Whisper Down the Wind

AS the days went by, Justin grew used to the great fortress that was the heart and headquarters of Carausius's defence against the Saxons. Under the tall grey pharos that had once been triumphant with bronze and gleaming marble, the galleys and the merchantmen came and went; and all day behind the noises of the fortress, behind the parade-ground voices and the trumpets and the tramp of marching feet, sounded the ring and rasp of adze and hammer from the dockyard below the rampart walls. And behind the hum of the busy dockyard sounded always the sea.

Three times that autumn, before winter closed the sea-ways, there were brushes between the British fleets and the black-sailed ships of the Saxons; and Justin had much practice for his skill when the wounded were brought in, and won grudging praise from the irascible Senior Surgeon, which made him happy.

That was a good autumn for him in other ways too, and for Flavius, with whom he spent a good deal of his off-duty times. The quick liking of their first meeting had grown into a close and enduring friendship. They were drawn together by a common loneliness; for Flavius, brought up by a widowed Great-Aunt after the death from pestilence of both his parents, had loneliness behind him also. That autumn and the winter that followed they hunted boar together in the Great Forest, and took their birding bows out after wild-fowl in the marshes, and poked about the fishing village that considered itself a town, with its added huddle of shops and temples and beersellers' bothies beneath the fortress walls.

One place that they haunted a good deal was a shop close under the North bastion, kept by one Serapion, a little withered man, half British, half Egyptian, with jewel-bright eyes and pointed fingers like a lizard. A veritable dog-hole of a shop, viewed from outside, but inside, filled with delights; with little bundles of dried herbs and pots and jars of unnamed substances, with fragrant oils in little crystal flasks, and dried and shrivelled things that one did not care to guess at too closely. It was a shop much frequented by the garrison; here one might buy scented oils and unguents for oneself, or a stick of perfume for a girl.

Flavius went there for the sake of Serapion's rubbing-oil, which was good when one was stiff and tired from the hunting trail, and for some unguent which he vainly hoped would make his hair lie down; Justin went because Serapion's concoctions interested him, and the man's talk of healing and harming herbs and the influence of the stars interested him still more.

On an evening just after Saturnalia, Justin and Flavius turned in through the low doorway of Serapion's shop, to find the little Egyptian serving another customer; and by the light of the small hanging lamp, recognized Allectus. Justin had seen him many times, by now, in the Emperor's train; this tall man with the ashy-fair head and the heavy face that lightened so pleasantly at his ready smile, who was, after Carausius, the most powerful man in Britain. He had never told Flavius about the moth—after all, what was there to tell, when one came to put it into words? 'I saw him kill that moth, and he enjoyed doing it.' That was all. And as time went by he had almost, though never quite, forgotten the whole thing.

Allectus looked round at their entrance, with that swift, pleasant smile of his. 'Ah, I trust you are not pressed for time. I fear I am lamentably slow to make my choice, this evening.' Then he turned back to the matter in hand, which seemed to be the choice of a phial of perfume. 'Something out of the common—something that will be at once a gift and a compliment, for the lady's birthday.'

Serapion bowed, smiled, touching with one pointed finger the fine alabaster flask that he had set on the table before his noble customer. 'This is the perfume that I blended especially to your order last time, Excellency. Was the lady not pleased?'

'Yes, but this is a different lady,' said Allectus, with that cool note of laughter in his voice; then tossing the words casually over his shoulder to the two young men in the gloom behind him, 'Never give the same perfume to two different women at the same time—they may meet. That is a thing for you to remember, my young cockerels.'

'Ah, now I understand, Excellency.' The little Egyptian bowed again. 'If your Honour could give me until tomorrow to blend something worthy of the lady whom Allectus honours with his gift—'

'Do I not tell you her birthday is tomorrow, and I must send it tonight? Show me something that you have here ready blended.'

Serapion was still a moment, considering, then turned, and moved, silent as a cat, into the farthest shadows, to return holding something between his cupped hands. 'I have this,' he said—'this, the perfume of perfumes. Blended by myself, ah yes, as I alone can blend the precious essences into one exquisite whole.' He set the thing down on the table, and it stood there, a small crystal flask, glowing under the lamp like a green-gold jewel.

'It is a charming flask,' said Allectus, taking it up and turning it in strong white fingers.

'A charming flask, ah, but the fragrance within—the flowering essence of a thousand summers caught in amber! Wait now, I will break the seal and you shall judge.'

He took back the tiny flask, and with a sharp thumbnail peeled away the film of wax about the neck, and withdrew the stopper; then dipped in a thin glass rod, and touched Allectus on the back of the hand he held out for the purpose. Instantly, as the drop of precious liquid ran on to the man's warm skin, a wonderful scent arose, strong but delicate, engulfing the other odours of the place.

Allectus held his hand to his nostrils. 'How much?'

'A hundred sesterces, Excellency.'

That is a great price for a very small flask of perfume.'

'But such perfume, Excellency! The cost of such ingredients is very great, and I assure you a hundred sesterces allows me but a very small reward for my time and skill.'

'So. I still think it a great price, but I'll take it. Seal it up for me again.'

'Allectus is most good and gracious.' Serapion bowed, and continued his plaint as he warmed the stick of wax he had taken up, and again sealed the neck of the flask. 'Aye, aye, costly they are indeed, such ingredients as these—sheer liquid gold. And on so many of them one must pay a king's ransom in duty, to bring them into the province. Ah me, they come hard upon a poor man, these new taxes of the Emperor's.'

Allectus laughed softly. 'Maybe you should lay the taxes at my door, friend. Who else should take the blame if not the Emperor's Finance Minister?'

'Why of course, your Excellency. See, here is the perfume.' Serapion handed it over, glancing up under his thin lids as though to judge how far he might venture. 'But is an Emperor always guided by his Finance Minister? They say in the market-place that sometimes a Finance Minister might be—not altogether at one with his Emperor in all things; that the taxes might be less harsh if—'

'It is generally foolish to listen to market-place talk,' said Allectus. 'And generally foolish to repeat it.' He slipped the flask into the breast of his fine woollen tunic, shaking his head with smiling impatience at the Egyptian's protestation that he meant no harm. 'Nay, man, we all let our tongues run away with us at times. Here, take your hundred sesterces.' And with a courteous goodnight, which included the two young men, he gathered the folds of his cloak about him and was gone into the wintry darkness.

Serapion the Egyptian stood looking after him, with an expression of sly understanding in his little bright eyes. Then he turned back to the two young men, with a face empty of everything except willingness to oblige.

'And now, young sirs—I regret that you have been kept waiting. Is it some more of the muscle oil?—or maybe a gift for the ladies at home? I hear that you go on leave together in a few days' time.'

Justin was startled, for it was only that morning that Flavius had managed an exchange with another Centurion, so that they could take their leave at the same time.

Flavius laughed. 'Does ever anyone sneeze in Rutupiae that you don't know about it within the hour? No, just the muscle oil.'

They made the purchase, thinking no more of the little scene that was just past, and returned to barracks. And a few days later, when their leave fell due, set out together on the long two days' ride westward, to spend it at the old farm in the Down Country that was Flavius's home.

'It is no good pushing on to Calleva,' said Flavius, 'because Aunt Honoria will be at Aquae Sulis taking the waters, at this time of year. So we'll head along the chalk to the farm, and descend on Servius. He'll be glad to see us—and so will the farm.'

And then, as Justin looked at him sideways, he grinned, but said seriously enough, 'The farm is always pleased to see the people it is fond of, and who are fond of it. You can feel it being pleased—like an old wise hound.'

And when, towards dusk on the second day, with the frost crisping in the ruts of the wagon-way, they came through a little wood of oak and birch and wild cherry, and saw the house with its farm buildings at the head of the long downland valley, Justin knew what he meant. He felt the welcome reaching out to them, and knew that it was for him also, as though, stranger as he was, the place knew him for one of its own, and was glad of his coming.

Presently there were other welcomes: from Servius the old steward who had been an optio under Flavius's father; from Gutha his wife, and Kyndylan his son when he came up from the cattle; from the other farm-hands, free men and women, all of them. 'Aunt Honoria has a few old slaves,' Flavius said. 'But we have always farmed with free labour. It makes it difficult at times, but we manage. Couldn't change.'

They spent five days at the farm, and it was during those five days that Justin first really discovered Britain. The bare winter woods dappled like a partridge's breast, the slow, broad voices of the farm-hands, the lapwings on the winter ploughland; the low, long house itself, built on to by succeeding generations but holding still at its heart the smoke-blackened atrium, used as a storeroom now, that had been the original houseplace, built by another Marcus Flavius Aquila making a home for himself and his British wife and the children that came after—these were all Britain to Justin.

He had that other Marcus Flavius Aquila much in mind during those days while, with Flavius, he poked happily about the byres and barns, or helped old Buic the shepherd in the lambing-pens. It was as though, because he also was of Marcus's blood, the old house, the whole downland valley was a link between them.

He was thinking about that Marcus the last evening of all as he and Flavius leaned side by side on the wall that kept the Downs from sliding into the vine terraces on the warm southern slope. From where they were, they could see the whole farm lying clear down to the shores of the forest that closed the valley at last, all quenched and quieted in the first faint thickening of the winter twilight.

'It is queer, you know, Justin,' Flavius said suddenly, 'I've never been here for more than a few weeks at a time, since—since I was very small; but ever since I can remember it has been home to me.' He propped himself more comfortably against the old dry-stone wall. 'The place looks well enough, all things considered.'

'What particular things?' Justin asked.

'Me being away with the Eagles, for one thing,' Flavius said. 'I ought really to have stayed at home and helped Servius run the farm. But you know how it is with us; the old Service is in all our blood; look at you, you're a surgeon, but you couldn't break away from the Eagles, even so. Luckily Servius is a better farmer than I could ever be—but it isn't an easy world for farmers and the small estates nowadays. Things must have been so much simpler when my namesake first cleared this valley and made his home here.'

They were silent a few moments, and then Flavius added, 'You know, I've so often wondered what lay behind the starting of our farm.'

'How do you mean?'

Flavius hesitated a moment. 'Well, see now,' he said at last. 'He—Marcus—was only a very junior Centurion, if family accounts be true, when he was lamed in some tribal rising or other, and invalided out; and yet the Senate gave him the full land grant and gratuity for a time-expired Centurion. That isn't like the Senate.'

'Maybe he had a powerful friend on the Senate benches,' Justin suggested. 'Such things do happen.'

Flavius shook his head. 'I doubt it. We aren't a family that collects powerful friends.'

'A reward, a special p-payment of some kind, then?'

'That seems more likely. The question is, what was it for?'

Justin found that the other had turned his head to look at him, clearly hesitating on the edge of saying something. 'You have an idea about that?'

'I'm—not sure.' Flavius most unexpectedly flushed up to the roots of his fiery hair. 'But I've always wondered whether it could have been anything to do with the Ninth Legion.'

'The Ninth Legion?' Justin said, a little blankly. 'The one that was ordered up into Valentia in the troubles, and was never seen again?'

'Oh, I know it sounds far-fetched. I wouldn't speak of it to anyone but you. But his father disappeared with the Ninth Legion, remember; and there's always been a vague story in the family of some sort of an adventure in the North in his wild young days before he married and settled down. It's just that, and a sort of—feeling I have—you know.'

Justin nodded. He knew. But he said only, 'I wonder . . . You know most of this is quite new to me. You must have the family history at your finger-tips.'

Flavius laughed, the odd seriousness of the moment dropping from him as swiftly as seriousness generally did. 'It is not me. It is Aunt Honoria. Nobody sneezed in the family for two hundred years that our Aunt Honoria doesn't remember all about it.' He leaned forward to call to Servius, who had appeared on the lowest of the three vine terraces. '*Sa ha!* Servius, we're up here.'

The old man looked up and saw them, and altered course towards them, marching up between the trained vines with a long legionary swing that seemed to carry with it the unheard jingle of accoutrements. 'I see you.' He halted just below them. 'Cutha has the supper almost ready.'

Flavius nodded. 'We are coming,' but he made for the moment no move, lingering as though unwilling to abandon his vantage point and come indoors on this last evening of his leave. 'We were saying that the farm looks good,' he said alter a moment.

'Aye, none so bad, all things considered.' Servius unconsciously echoed Flavius's words of a short while before. 'But it is in my mind that we are falling behind the times. I'd like fine to see one of those new-fashioned water-mills down below the pool; we've enough head of water to turn the wheel.'

'I'd like it too,' Flavius said. 'But it cannot be done.'

'And well I know it. With the corn tax gone up to where it is, it is as much as we can do to hold our own, let alone rise to any new thing that we can do without.'

Flavius said soberly, 'Don't grudge the corn tax. If we are to have a fleet and coastwise forts to keep the Saxons out, we must pay for them. Do you remember before Carausius took command, summer nights when we saw the coastwise farms burning, and wondered how much further inland the Sea Wolves would come?'

'Aye,' Servius growled. 'I remember well enough; no need that you remind me. Nay then, I'm not complaining at the corn tax, for I see the need of it—though mind you they do say that the right-hand man of the Emperor's who sees to such things is none so much of the Emperor's mind in the matter of taxes, and would find ways to ease them if he might.'

'Who says?' Flavius said quickly.

'Folks. One of the tax-gatherers himself was talking about it at Venta a week or so back.' Servius pushed himself off from the wall. 'See, Cutha has lit the lamp. I'm away down to my supper, if you aren't.'

And he went swinging off into the softly gathering dusk, towards the light that had sprung up marigold-coloured in the houseplace window.

The two cousins watched him for a moment in silence, then turned, as by common consent, to look at each other. There it was again, that vague half suggestion that Allectus and not Carausius was the man to follow, the man who had the people's good at heart.

Justin, with a little cleft deepening between his brows, was the first to speak. 'That's the second time,' he said.

'Yes,' Flavius said. 'I was just thinking that. But he shut Serapion up firmly enough.'

Justin was thinking back over that little unimportant scene in the shop under the walls of Rutupiae, realizing something that he had not noticed at the time. 'He did not deny it, though.'

'Maybe it was true.'

'I don't see that that makes any d-difference,' said Justin, who had his own rigid code of loyalty.

Flavius looked at him a moment. 'No, you're right, of course it does not,' he said slowly at last. And then in sudden exasperation, 'Oh Hell and the Furies! We are getting as fanciful as a pair of silly maidens up here in the dusk! First it was the Ninth Legion; and now . . . Come on, I want my supper.'

He shook himself off from the wall and went striding down the steep path through the vine terraces towards the light in the window below.

Justin followed, forbearing to point out that it was not he who had had the idea about the Ninth Legion.

III
The House on the Cliffs

DURING their time at the farm, the weather had been gentle, green winter weather shot through with the promise of spring, but no sooner were they on the road than winter swooped back with the snow on its wings. That meant hard travelling, but there were still two hours of daylight left when, on the second day, Justin and Flavius changed horses at Limanis and set out on the last stage. The road skirted the forest of Anderida, and they rode with their ears full of the deep-sea roaring of the wind in the branches, heads down against the stinging sleet. And when, a couple of miles further on, the road dipped to a paved ford beside which squatted a little forest smithy, the red glow of the forge fire seemed a kind of shout of warmth and colour amid the grey moanings of the storm-lashed woods.

Through the sleet scurry they could make out a small group of dismounted cavalry before the smithy; and Flavius said, 'Someone's horse has cast a shoe, by the look of things.' And then with a low whistle, 'Name of Thunder! It's the Emperor himself!'

The Emperor it was, sitting very composedly on a fallen tree trunk beside the way, with the sleet in his beard and the eagle-feathers of his helmet crest, and sleet whitening the shoulders of his purple cloak; and a small cavalry escort standing by, holding their horses, while Nestor, his big roan stallion, slobbered at the shoulder of the smith, who held one great round hoof between his leather-aproned knees.

The Emperor looked up as the two young men drew rein, and raised thick brows under his helmet rim. 'Ah, Centurion Aquila and our Junior Surgeon. What brings you riding these wintry roads?'

Flavius had already swung down from his horse, slipping his arm through the rein. 'Hail, Caesar. We are on our way back from leave. Can we be of any service, sir?'

'Thank you, no. Nestor has cast a shoe, as you see, but Goban here has the matter well in hand.'

A stinging blast of sleet whipped their faces, making every man shiver in his cloak, and causing the horses to swerve sideways, turning their heads from the gust. And the Decurion in command of the escort said beseechingly, 'Excellency, will you not take one of my men's horses and ride on? The man can bring Nestor after us.'

Carausius settled more comfortably on his tree trunk, drawing the shoulder folds of his cloak about his ears. 'A little sleet will not shrink me,' he said, and eyed the Decurion with distaste. 'Possibly, however, it is not so much my health that concerns you as that of your men—or possibly even yourself.' And ignoring the poor man's stuttering denial of the charge, turned his gaze back under a cocked eyebrow to the two cousins. 'Are you two due in Rutupiae tonight?'

'No, Caesar,' Flavius said. 'We allowed an extra day, but we have not needed it.'

'Ah, an extra day for a winter journey, that is always a wise precaution. And this is certainly the most wintry of winter journeys.' He seemed to consider for a moment, then nodded as though in full agreement with himself. 'Surely it would be a cruel thing to drag ten men on a needless ten mile ride in such weather as this . . . Decurion, you may remount and take your men back to Limanis. I shall remain quietly here until Nestor is re-shod, and then ride on with these two of my Rutupiae officers. They will be all the escort that I shall need.'

Justin, who had dismounted also by this time, and stood holding his horse on the fringe of the group, cast a somewhat startled glance at Flavius, who was staring straight before him as though he were on parade. The Decurion stiffened. 'You—you are dismissing your escort, Caesar?'

'I am dismissing my escort,' agreed Carausius.

The Decurion hesitated an instant, swallowing. 'But Excellency—'

'I bid you farewell, Decurion,' said Carausius. His tone was gentle, but the Decurion whipped to the salute, and turned away in desperate haste, with the order to his men to mount.

It was not until the little escort had swung on to their horses and were clattering away with the wind and sleet behind them down the Limanis road, that the Emperor turned back to the two young men, who stood by, holding their mounts. 'I fear that I forgot to ask you whether you would accompany me,' he said.

Flavius's lip twitched. 'Does one refuse to ride with an Emperor?'

'If one is wise, one does not.' Carausius's blunt seaman's face answered the laughter for an instant, harshly. 'Also, observe; the wind is rising, Rutupiae is all of fifteen miles away, and my house, for which I was bound when Nestor cast his shoe, rather less than five, and once there I can offer you an open fire, and better wine than any they keep in Rutupiae.'

And so some two hours later, fresh from a hot bath, Justin and Flavius were following a slave across the courtyard of a great house on the cliff edge high above the sea, to the chamber in the North Wing where the Emperor waited for them.

The great square chamber was bright with lamps in tall bronze stands, and a fire of logs burned British fashion on a raised hearth, so that all the room was full of the fragrance of burning wood. Carausius, who had been standing by the fire, turned as they entered, saying, 'Ah, you have washed the sleet out of your ears. Come you now, and eat.'

And eat they did, at a small table drawn close before the hearth; a good meal, though an austere one for an Emperor, of hard-boiled duck eggs and sweet downland mutton broiled in milk, and wine that was better, as Carausius had promised, than anything they had at Rutupiae; thin yellow wine that tasted of sunshine and the south, in flasks of wonderful coloured glass, iridescent as the feathers of a pigeon's neck, and wound about with gold and inset jewels.

They were served by soft-footed table slaves of the usual kind, but behind Carausius's chair, to serve him personally, stood a creature whom they had glimpsed once or twice before, distantly, at his lord's heel, but never seen at close quarters.

He was a very small man, lightly built as a mountain cat, his legs sheathed in close-fitting dark hose, his body in a woollen tunic of many coloured chequer that clung to him like a second skin. Straight black hair hung in heavy locks about his cheeks and neck, and his enormous eyes were made to seem still larger and more brilliant in his narrow, beardless face by the fine blue lines of tattooing that rimmed them round. About his waist was a broad strap of crimson leather set with bright bronze studs like a hound's collar, and into this was thrust a musical instrument of some kind, a curved rod of bronze from which hung nine silver apples that gave out a thin and very sweet chiming as he moved. But the strangest thing about him only appeared when he turned away to take a dish from another slave, and Justin saw that hanging from his belt behind, he wore a hound's tail.

The odd creature served his master with a kind of proud and prancing willingness, a slightly fantastic flourish that was very different from the well-trained impersonal bearing of the other slaves. And when the third course of dried fruits and little hot cakes had been set on the table, and Carausius dismissed the serving slaves, the creature did not go with them, but laid himself down, hound-wise, before the fire. 'When the Lord of the House is away, Cullen sleeps in the warm cook-place. When the Lord of the House comes home, Cullen sleeps beside his lord's fire,' he said composedly, stretching himself out on one elbow.

The Emperor glanced down at him. 'Good Hound, Cullen,' he said, and taking a cluster of raisins from the red samian dish, tossed it down to him.

Cullen caught it with a swift and oddly beautiful gesture of one hand, his strange face splitting into a grin which reached from ear to ear. 'So! I am my Lord's hound, and my Lord feeds me from his own table.'

The Emperor, turning again in his chair, one hand out to the wine-flask, caught Justin's fascinated and puzzled gaze on the little man, and said with that straight, wide-lipped smile of his, 'The High King of Erin has his Druth, his Household Fool, and should the third-part Emperor of Rome lack what the High King of Erin has?'

Cullen nodded, eating raisins and spitting the pips into the fire. 'Wherefore my Lord Curoi bought me from the slavers up yonder on the coast of the Western Sea, that he might not lack what the High King of Erin has in his Halls at Tara;—and also, it is in my mind, because I was from Laighin, even as my Lord. And I have been my Lord's hound these seven summers and winters past.' Then, spinning over and coming to his knee in a single kingfisher flash of movement, he took from his belt the instrument that Justin had noticed before.

Sitting cross-legged now beside the fire, while above him the talk drifted on to other matters, he tipped the thing with a curious flick of the wrist, and a kind of ripple of bell-notes ran from the smallest apple at the tip to the greatest just above the thick enamelled handle and up again, in a minor key. Then, very quietly, and clearly for his own pleasure, he began to play—if playing it could be called, for there was no tune, only single notes, falling now soft, now clear, as he flicked each silver apple with knuckle or nail; single notes that seemed to fall from a great height like shining drops distilled out of the emptiness, each perfect in itself.

It was a strange evening; an evening that Justin never forgot. Outside, the beat of the wind and the far-down boom of the sea, and within, the scent of burning logs, the steady radiance of the lamps, and the stains of quivering coloured light cast upon the table by the wine in its iridescent flasks. He held his hand in one such pool, to see it splashed with crimson and emerald and living peacock-blue; and wondered suddenly whether these wonderful flasks, whether Carausius's great gold cup and the hangings of thick Eastern embroideries that shut off the end of the room, and the coral-studded bridle-bit on the wall behind him, had all known the hold of a black-winged Saxon longship. Outside, the wild wings and the voices of the storm; and within, the little flames flickering among the logs, and facing each other around the table, Flavius and himself and the little thick-set seaman who was Emperor of Britain; while the strange slave Cullen sprawled hound-wise beside the fire, idly touching the apples of his Silver Branch.

It had been for little more than a despot's whim, Justin knew, that Carausius had dismissed his escort and ordered the two of them to ride with him instead; but far down within him he knew also that after this evening, though they never met again like this, there would be something between them that was not usually between an Emperor and two of his most junior officers.

Yes, a most strange evening.

Carausius had most of the talk, as was fitting, while the two young men sat with their cups of watered wine before them, and listened. And indeed it was talk worth listening to, for Carausius was not merely an Emperor, he had been a Scaldis river pilot, and the commander of a Roman Fleet, a Centurion under Carus in the Persian War, and a boy growing up in Laighin, three days south from Tara of the Kings. He had known strange places, and done strange things, and he could talk of them so that they came to life for his hearers.

And then, as though suddenly tired of his own talk, he rose and turned to the curtained end of the room. 'Ah, but I have talked enough of yesterday. I will show you a thing that is for today. Come here, both of you.'

Chairs rasped on the tesserai, and Justin and Flavius were close at his shoulder as he flung back the hangings glimmering with peacock and pomegranate colours, and passed through. Justin, the last to follow, was aware of a grey, storm-lashed window and a sense of the wild night leaping in on them with a shout, and stood an instant holding the rich folds back, uncertain whether they might need the light of the room behind them for whatever it was that they were going to see. But Carausius said, 'Let the curtains fall. Can't see with the lamplight dancing in the panes.' And he let the dark hangings swing across behind him.

As he did so, and the lamplight was cut off, the world outside sprang out of the darkness into a hurrying, moonshot clarity. They were standing in the bay of a great window such as Justin had never seen before, that swole out with the curve of a drawn bow; a window that was a veritable watch-tower, a falcon's eyrie, clinging as it seemed to the very edge of the cliff.

A ragged sky of grey and silver went racing by, the moon swinging in and out of the storm-scuds, so that one moment the whole sweep of the coast was flooded with swift silver radiance, and the next, all would be blotted out by a curtain of driving sleet. Far below them the white-capped waves charged by, rank on rank, like wild white cavalry. And far away to the eastward, as Justin looked along the coast, a red petal of fire hung on the dark headland.

'This is my look-out,' Carausius said. 'A good place to watch my shipping come and go, with Dubris light and Limanis and Rutupiae lights to guide them safely in their coming and their going.' He seemed to sense the direction of Justin's gaze. That is the pharos at Dubris on the headland. Limanis light one can see from the hill behind the house. Now look out to sea—yonder on the edge of the world south-eastward.'

Justin looked, and as a sleet-squall passed away from the sea, leaving the distance clear, saw, very far off, another spark of light on the skyline.

'That is Gesoriacum,' said Carausius.

They were silent a moment, remembering that last winter Gesoriacum had been within the territory of the man beside them. And in that silence, above the mingled voices of wind and sea, the ripple of Cullen's Silver Branch sounded in the room behind them, faint and sweet and somehow mocking.

Flavius said quickly, as though in answer to that silver mocking of bells, 'Maybe we are the better off without Gesoriacum. An outlying post is always something of a liability.'

Carausius gave a harsh bark of laughter. 'It is a bold man who seeks to console his Emperor for past defeat!'

'I did not mean it as consolation,' Flavius said levelly. 'I spoke what I believe to be true.'

'So? And you believe rightly.' Justin could hear that straight, wide-lipped smile of Carausius's in his voice. 'Yet it is truth that wears one face for him who seeks to make a single province strong, and quite another for him who would strengthen and enlarge his own hold on the Purple.'

He fell silent, his face turned towards that spark of light, dimming already as another sleet-squall came trailing across the sea. And when he spoke again, it was broodingly, more than half to himself. 'Nay, but whichever it be, either or—both, the true secret is in sea-power, which is a thing that Rome has never understood . . . In greater fleets, manned by better seamen. Legions we must have, but above all, sea-power, here with the sea all about us.'

'Some sea-power we have already, as Maximian found to his cost,' Flavius said, leaning a shoulder against the window frame and looking down. 'Aye, and the black-sailed fleets of the Sea Wolves also.'

'Yet the Wolves gather,' Carausius said. 'Young Constantius would be hard put to it to take his troops from the German Frontier *this* spring to drive me from Gesoriacum . . . Always, everywhere, the Wolves gather on the frontiers, waiting. It needs only that a man should lower his eye for a moment, and they will be in to strip the bones. Rome is failing, my children.'

Justin looked at him quickly, but Flavius never moved; it was as though he had known what Carausius would say.

'Oh, she is not finished yet. I shall not see her fall—my Purple will last my life-time—and nor, I think, will you. Nevertheless, Rome is hollow rotten at the heart, and one day she will come crashing down. A hundred years ago, it must have seemed that all this was for ever; a hundred years hence—only the gods know . . . If I can make this one province strong—strong enough to stand alone when Rome goes down, then something may be saved from the darkness. If not, then Dubris light and Limanis light and Rutupiae light will go out. The lights will go out everywhere.' He stepped back, dragging aside the hanging folds of the curtains, and stood framed in their darkness against the firelight and the lamplight behind him, his head yet turned to the scudding grey and silver of the stormy night. 'If I can steer clear of a knife in my back until the work is done, I will make Britain strong enough to stand alone,' he said. 'It is as simple as that.'

As they turned back to the lamplight room, Flavius said swiftly and urgently, 'Caesar knows that for all the worth that there is in us, we are Caesar's men for life or death, Justin and I.'

Carausius stood for an instant, the curtain still in his hand, and looked at them. 'Caesar knows,' he said at last. 'Aye. Caesar knows that, my children,' and let the dark folds fall between the lamplight and the scudding moon.

IV
The Sea Wolf

SEVERAL times as that winter drew on to spring, Justin and Flavius went out together after wild fowl in the marshes: the strange border country between land and sea, that had for Justin the magic of all halfway things.

Their usual hunting ground was Tanatus, the great marsh island across the shipping lane from Rutupiae, but about mid March there were reports of a Saxon ship hovering in the seaways that had somehow eluded the patrol galleys, and Tanatus was put out of bounds to the fortress because of the ease with which stray, wild-fowling Legionaries might be cut off there by the Sea Wolves. And so, in the dark of a certain March morning, Justin and Flavius made their way out to the forsaken fisher village at the southernmost tip of the mainland marshes.

And now they were crouching among the reeds in the lee of the old dyke that had once served to keep back the sea from the village, their bows ready strung, and the small birding bolts stuck barb-down in the turf before them.

The dawn was coming. It was in the smell of the little knife-edged wind that shivered and sang through the hairy grasses and about the crumbling turf walls of the abandoned village; in the calling of curlew and sandpiper; in the faint, sheeny paleness creeping up the eastern sky and the fading of the red iris-bud of flame that was Rutupiae light. Slowly the light gathered and grew; any moment now they would hear the wing-beats of the duck rising into the wind; the steady throb of wings that was the beginning of the dawn flight.

But before it came, another sound caught their straining ears; a sound so faint and so swiftly still that it might have been almost anything, or nothing at all. Yet there was about it a suggestion of being human and a suggestion of stealth that made it alien among the other sounds of the marsh.

Flavius stiffened, staring away to his left through the thin curtain of reeds that they had left between themselves and the outer world.

'What is it?' Justin whispered. And the other made a quick gesture for silence; then, timing the movement of his hand with a gust of wind, swayed back a few of the tall reeds. And Justin saw.

A man was standing not more than a spear-throw from them, his head turned to watch another who had that moment emerged from the willow-break further inland. The water-cool light, growing every moment stronger, showed them the round buckler between his shoulders, and the wiry yellow gold of his hair and beard; and his sword-side being towards them, they could see the saex, the short Saxon thrusting-sword, in its wolf-skin sheath at his belt. And as the second man drew nearer, Flavius gave a long, soundless whistle. 'Name of Thunder!' he whispered. 'It is Allectus!'

Justin, crouching frozen beside him, was without any surprise. It was as though he had known.

Allectus had come up with the other man now. The Saxon said something in a low, angry growl, and he replied more loudly, 'Aye, I know it is dangerous after cock-light. If I could have come sooner I would have done so—for my own skin's sake. After all, it is I who run the chief risk. You have but to lie hid until the *Sea Witch* puts in for you . . . Now this is what I have to say to your lords who sent you.' But even as he spoke, the two men had turned away together, and their voices sank to a formless murmuring.

Justin strained every sense to catch what they were saying, but could make nothing of the low mutter. Indeed he had a feeling that they had abandoned Latin and were speaking in a tongue that he did not know. He scanned the ground ahead of him, searching desperately for some means of getting closer without being seen, but once out of the reeds there was no cover for a curlew, let alone a man.

And then suddenly it seemed that the two men had reached the end of whatever it was that they had to say to each other. The Saxon nodded, as though in answer to some order; and Allectus turned away in the direction from which he had come. The Saxon stood a few moments looking after him, then, with a shrug, turned himself about and bending low so as not to break the skyline, set off along the old thorn windbreak, heading westward for the wildest and most solitary part of the marsh.

Among the reeds Justin and Flavius took one look into each other's faces. There was no time to think, no time to weigh one thing against another and decide what was best to do. They must make an instant decision, and abide by it wherever it led them.

'Wait till he rounds the end of the windbreak,' Flavius muttered, his eyes narrowed as he stared out through the parted reeds. 'If we go after him now, and he cries out, it will warn friend Allectus.'

Justin nodded. From where he was he could no longer see the retreating Saxon, and so he watched Flavius crouching with a knee drawn under him like a runner poised for the start of a race, watched him grow tense on the edge of movement . . .

'Now,' Flavius breathed.

They were out from the reeds like an arrow from a bow, running low for the end of the windbreak. By the time they reached it the man had disappeared from sight, but a few moments later, as they checked uncertain, he came into view again at the curve of a dry dyke, and glancing once behind him, struck out into the open over the tawny levels.

'He's probably got a hideout somewhere among the dunes,' Flavius said. 'Come on!'

And again they were out after him. There was no possibility now of keeping under cover—when he looked back he was bound to see them, and it would be a matter of speed against speed, and nothing else. At least they must be well out of earshot of Allectus by this time.

They had almost halved the distance between them when, on the edge of a clump of wind-twisted thorn trees the Saxon checked and glanced back, as they had known he must before long. Justin saw him freeze for one instant into intense stillness, like an animal that scents the hunter; then his hand flew to his sword-hilt, and next instant he had sprung away, running like a hare with the two young Romans on his trail.

As though realizing the danger of such country, lacking all shelter, and veined by wandering arms of the sea that might cut him off at any moment, the Saxon changed course almost at once, and began to swing away from the coast, heading inland for the forest fringe; knowing that once he gained the trees they would almost certainly lose him, Justin and Flavius lengthened their stride, straining every nerve to come up with him before he reached shelter. Flavius was drawing slowly away from his kinsman, slowly nearer to the desperate quarry, while Justin, who was not much of a runner, came pounding doggedly along in the rear. The smoke-grey shoreline of the bare woods was very near now, and Justin was far behind snatching at his breath in great gasps. He felt horribly sick, and he was deaf with the drubbing of his own heart; but the only thing in his mind was that away ahead of him, Flavius with only a little dagger was alone on the heels of a desperate man running with a naked sword in his hand.

On and on, the two figures in front were running almost as one now. They were into the furze and blackthorn scrub, when suddenly—he could not see quite what happened, he was too blind with his own running—the foremost figure seemed to stumble, and instantly the other was upon him. Justin saw them go down together, and put on one last heart-tearing burst of speed. Flavius and the Saxon were locked together in a struggling mass as he reached them; and through the buzzing haze before his eyes he caught the gleam of the naked blade upon the tawny grass, and Flavius's hand gripping white-knuckled about the Saxon's sword-wrist. He dropped upon it, twisted the sword out of the man's grasp and sent it spinning sideways. Flavius, with a hand now to spare, drew it back and hit the Saxon cleanly under the ear, and the fight went out of him in one gasp.

'So—that is better,' Flavius panted. 'Now help me bind his hands. The spare bow-strings will serve.'

They got his arms behind him and lashed his wrists together with the thin, strong bow-string which Justin, still sobbing for breath, dragged out from his belt; and rolled him over on his back. Flavius had struck only hard enough to quieten the man for the moment, and he was coming to himself already. His eyes opened, and he lay staring up at them stupidly, then his lips parted in a snarl, his teeth showing little and pointed in the gold of his beard, and he began to fight like a wild beast at his bonds.

Flavius had a knee on his chest, and slipping the dagger from his belt, held it to his throat. 'No use to struggle, my friend,' he said. 'Never wise to struggle with a handspan of cold iron against your windpipe.'

Justin, still feeling very sick, but with the breath beginning to come back into him, crossed to the Saxon's sword where it had fallen among the roots of a gorse-bush. He picked it up and turned again to the other two. The Saxon had ceased to struggle and lay glaring at his captor.

'Why do you set on me?' he demanded at last, speaking in Latin, but with a thick and guttural accent that made it almost unintelligible. 'I do no harm—I am from the Rhenus Fleet.'

'And you with the gear and weapons of a Saxon pirate on you,' Flavius said softly. 'Go tell that tale to the seamews.'

The man was silent a moment, then he said with sullen pride, '*Sa*; I will tell it to the seamews. What do you want with me?'

'What passed between you and the man you met back yonder by the ruined fisher-huts?'

'That is a thing between the man and me.'

Justin said quickly, 'It doesn't m-matter much for now. Whatever his orders or his message are, he won't be passing them on, and someone else can get the truth out of him later. Our job is to get him up to the fortress.'

Flavius nodded, his eyes never leaving the Saxon's face. 'Yes, you are in the right of it. The main thing is to get him back; otherwise it is but our word against Allectus's.' He lifted his knee from the man's chest. 'Up, you.'

Rather more than an hour later, they stood before the Commandant in his office, their captive between them, his eyes darting and sliding from side to side in search of a way of escape.

Mutius Urbanus, Commandant of Rutupiae, was a thin, stooping man with a long, grey face a little like a tired old horse's; but his eyes were shrewdly alert as he leaned back in his chair surveying the three before him. 'So, one of the Sea Wolves,' he was saying. 'How did you come by him?'

'We were out on the marshes by the old fisher-huts, sir,' Flavius said, 'lying up among the reeds for the duck, and we saw a meeting between this man and—a man of our own. After they parted we gave chase to this one, and—here he is.'

The Commandant nodded. 'And this man of our own. Who was he?'

There was a silence, and then Flavius said deliberately, 'We did not know him, sir.'

'How then did you know him for a man of our own?'

Flavius never blinked an eyelid. 'He was in uniform, sir.'

'Centurian Aquila,' said the Commandant, 'I am not sure that I believe you.'

'I am sorry, sir.' Flavius looked him straight in the eye, and pressed on to the next thing. 'Sir. I believe the Emperor is expected this evening? Will you apply for us—Justin and myself—to have speech with him as soon as may be after his arrival, and meanwhile have this man bestowed in the Guard-house to await his coming?'

Urbanus raised his brows. 'I scarcely think that this is such a matter as need go to Caesar.'

Flavius came a step nearer and set a hand on the littered table, desperate urgency in both face and voice. 'But it is, sir, I swear to you that it is. If it doesn't go to Caesar, and that quickly, and without anyone else meddling with it first, the gods alone know what the consequences may be!'

'So?' The Commandant's gaze turned on Justin. 'And you also are of that opinion?'

'I also,' said Justin.

'And you do not know who the other man was. More than ever I am not sure that I believe you, Centurion Aquila.' The Commandant tapped his nose gently with the butt end of his stylus, a trick of his when thoughtful. Then he said abruptly, 'So let it be; you shall have your speech with the Emperor. But your reason for this mystery, whatever it may be, had better be a good one, for if it is not, and you make me look a fool, the gods may have mercy on you, but I'll have none.' He raised his voice to the Optio of the Guard standing at the door. 'Optio, take this man down to the cells. You two had best go and see him safely under lock and key. After that I suggest that you change into uniform. I will send for you when you may speak with the Emperor.'

'Thank you, sir. At once, sir.' Flavius drew himself up and saluted, followed by Justin; and behind the two Legionaries of the Guard who had appeared to take their places on either side of the captive, marched out from the Commandant's office across the Praetorium Courtyard into the parade-ground of the fort. They were just crossing the Via Principia when they met a party of horsemen clattering up it from the main gate and the Londinium road; and drawing aside to give them the crown of the way, Justin saw that the tall man in civilian dress riding in their midst was Allectus.

He glanced down at them as he passed, and his glance lighted on the face of the Saxon captive—and seemed to hang there an instant before it moved on; and to Justin it seemed that his face stiffened for that instant into a mere smiling mask. But he gave no sign, and rode by without a second glance; and the little party moved forward again, hobnailed sandals ringing on the cobbles, down between the workshops where the armourers were busy, and so to the Guard-house by the gate.

'It is a most hideous piece of ill fortune that Allectus saw him,' Flavius said, as they recrossed the parade ground toward their quarters. 'I suppose he has come on ahead of Carausius—leastwise it's meant to look like that.'

'He can't know for sure that we saw him with the Saxon,' Justin said. 'We might have come on the man afterward. And anyway, there can be little enough that he can do about it without b-betraying himself still more completely.'

'I don't know. I can't think of anything; but then—I'm not Allectus.' And Justin saw that his kinsman was very white in the thin March sunlight.

In the pressure of work that waited for him in the hospital that day, Justin had little more leisure to think about Allectus, even when he heard in the distance the clatter of hooves and the sound of trumpets that heralded the Emperor's arrival. He was measuring a draught for one of his patients when at last the Commandant's summons reached him, and he finished the task with great care and exactness before he went clattering down the stone stairway after the messenger, hastily making sure that nothing was amiss with his uniform tunic and the clasp of his belt was dead centre.

Outside he met Flavius hurrying to answer the same summons and they went on together.

The two young tribunes on duty in the Ante-room of the Emperor's quarters looked at them with interest. Clearly the story of their having brought in a Saxon captive that morning had gone the rounds. And one of them rose and disappeared into the inner chamber, returning in a few moments to stand aside, leaving the door open. 'Go in now, the Emperor will see you.'

Carausius had done no more than lay aside crested helmet and heavy mud-sparked cloak before turning himself to his writing-table, on which various papers awaited his attention. He was standing beside it now, an open scroll in his hands; he looked up as they entered. 'Ah, you two again. The Commandant tells me that you would speak to me on a matter of urgency. Surely it must be a matter of very great urgency that even at this late hour it cannot wait for the morning.'

'Caesar, it is a matter of very great urgency,' Flavius said, saluting, as the door closed behind them. His gaze went past the Emperor to the tall figure lounging in the farther shadows. 'Caesar, we would have speech with you alone.'

'If the matter be indeed as urgent as you appear to think it, speak and have done,' Carausius said. 'You can scarcely expect that I shall dismiss the chief among my ministers like a dog to his kennel at your behest.'

Justin, standing at Flavius's shoulder, felt him stiffen, felt the resolve take shape and harden in him. 'Be it as you say, Caesar; I will speak and have done. This morning we two were lying up in the reeds by the old fisher-huts, waiting for the duck. There we saw—though we could make out little of what passed—a meeting between one of the Sea Wolves and a certain man of our own camp.'

Carausius let the scroll he was holding roll back on itself with a snapping sound. 'That much I have already gathered from the Commandant Urbanus,' he said. 'What was the little that you made out to pass between them?'

'Nothing to much purpose. The Saxon seemed to protest at the other man's lateness, and the other said, "I know it is dangerous after daylight. I would have come earlier if I could, for my own skin's sake. I run the chief risk; you have but to lie hid until the *Sea Witch* puts in for you." That is as near as I can remember it. And then he said, "Now this is what I have to say to your Lords who sent you," and after that they turned away together and we could hear no more.'

'And this—certain man of our own camp. You told the Commandant that you did not know who he was. Was that the truth?'

The split moment of silence seemed to tingle. Then Flavius said, 'No, Caesar, it was not.'

'Who was he, then?'

'The chief among your ministers, Allectus,' Flavius said.

His words seemed to fall into the stillness like a pebble in a pool, and Justin had a vivid awareness of them spreading out and out like ripples across the waiting silence, until they burst and shattered as Allectus sprang up from the couch on which he had been lounging, with an exclamation between rage and sheer amazement.

'Roma Dea! If this be a jest—'

'It is no jest,' Flavius flung back at him. 'I give you my word of that.'

And then Carausius's voice came like a naked blade between them.

'Let me be clear about this thing. With what, exactly, do you charge my chief minister Allectus?'

'With holding secret converse with the Sea Wolves, who are our enemies,' Flavius said.

'So, that is clear at all events.' Carausius turned a bleak stare upon Justin. 'You make the same charge?'

With his mouth uncomfortably dry, Justin said, 'I saw what Flavius my kinsman saw. I make the same charge.'

'And what defence has Allectus my chief minister to set against that?'

Allectus seemed to have got over his first astonishment and to be now merely angry. 'The thing is so—so outrageous that I scarce know what to say. Am I to seriously defend myself from such a preposterous charge?'

Carausius gave a mirthless bark of laughter. 'I scarcely think so.'

Flavius took an impulsive step forward. 'Caesar, the matter does not rest on our word alone. The Saxon is held captive in the Guard-house at this moment; let him be brought face to face with Allectus, and assuredly the truth may be laid bare!'

'So—it seems that you have plotted this thing with remarkable care!' Allectus exclaimed; but Carausius's voice drowned the sentence.

'Centurion Aquila, will you open the door behind you and summon me a tribune?'

Flavius did as he was bid, and a moment later the tribune stood saluting on the threshold. 'Excellency?'

'I wish the prisoner in—' Carausius turned to Flavius, who replied to the unspoken question, 'Number five cell.'

'Ah, the prisoner in number five cell brought here immediately, Tribune Vipsanius.'

Tribune Vipsanius saluted again, and withdrew. They heard his clipped footsteps through the Ante-room, and voice as he issued an order outside.

In the Emperor's quarters an utter silence settled; a silence that was complete and oppressive, as though they were inside a giant gong. Justin, standing with Flavius near the door, was staring straight before him, seemingly at nothing. Yet he was aware of all kinds of details that he remembered afterwards. The perfect shadow of Carausius's great helmet—every eagle-feather of the crest sharply distinct—thrown on the lamplit wall; a little muscle twitching in the angle of Flavius's set jaw; the colour of the evening sky beyond the window, peacock blue, filmed with a kind of murky gold-dust haze by the great pharos beacon. And then a sound grew in the stillness, a small insistent rapping and drumming; and turning his eyes in the direction from which it came, he saw that Allectus, still standing by the couch from which he had risen, had begun to beat a tattoo with long, strong fingers on the wooden couch-head beside him. His face, pale as always in the lamplight, showed nothing but the set mouth and frowning brows of anger with difficulty held in check. Justin wondered what was going on behind the pale, angry mask; was it the fear and fury of the trapped?—or only a cool brain making or changing plans? The tattoo seemed to grow louder and louder in the stillness, and then it was joined by another sound: the urgent beat of footsteps, half marching, half running. The footsteps of two men, Justin thought, not more.

A few moments later Tribune Vipsanius again stood in the doorway, and with him the Centurion of the prison guard breathing heavily through his nose.

'Excellency,' said Tribune Vipsanius, 'the prisoner in number five cell is dead.'

V

Nightshade!

JUSTIN had a physical sensation as if he had been jolted in the stomach, and yet in an odd way he knew that he was not surprised. Allectus had ceased his drumming. Carausius set down the scroll on the table, very softly and exactly, and demanded, 'How comes that about?'

The Tribune shook his head. 'I do not know, Caesar; he's just—dead.'

'Centurion?'

The Centurion stared straight before him. 'The prisoner was well enough, though dumb sullen, when his evening food went in to him an hour or so since; and now he's dead, same as the Tribune said. That's all I know, Caesar.'

Carausius stood away from the table. 'It seems that I must come and see for myself.' Then to Justin and Flavius, 'You will accompany me.'

As the little group turned to the doorway, Allectus stepped forward. 'Caesar, since this is a matter that concerns me somewhat closely, with your leave I also will accompany you.'

'In Typhon's name come then,' Carausius said, and strode out with the rest behind him.

The Guard-house seemed disturbed and excited. In the first cell a drunken legionary was singing.

Oh why did I join the Eagles
The Empire for to roam?
Oh why did I leave me pumpkin patch
And me little dun cow at home?

Their footsteps rang hollow down the flagged passageway. The pale blur of a face appeared at the barred squint of a door, and hastily disappeared again as they went by. The voice of the singer fell more faintly behind them.

They said I'd rise to Emperor
As sure as sure could be.
If I left me little pumpkin patch
And sailed across the sea.

The door of the furthest cell was ajar, and a sentry who stood before it moved aside to make way for them. The cell was in darkness save for the reflection of the pharos beacon shining down through the high barred window, and the red square of light striped with the shadows of the bars fell full across the figure of the Saxon lying face down on the floor.

'Bring a light, somebody,' Carausius said, without raising his voice.

Justin, the surgeon in him suddenly uppermost, had pushed through the rest, and was already kneeling beside the fallen man as the Centurion brought the Guard-room lantern. There was nothing to be done for the Saxon, and one look at him in the lantern light told Justin all he needed to know. 'Nightshade,' he said. 'He's been poisoned.'

'How?' Carausius snapped.

Justin did not answer at once, but picked up the pottery bowl that lay beside the man and sniffed the few thick drops of broth remaining in it. He tasted gingerly, and then spat. 'Probably in his supper broth. Quite simply.'

Away down the passage the singer had begun again, in a tone of deep melancholy.

So I upped and joined the Eagles,
And I left me little cow,
And I may be Emperor one of these days,
But Mother, just *look* at me now!

Justin had a sudden insane desire to laugh—to laugh and laugh, until he was sick. But the sight of Flavius's face steadied him,

It was Allectus who spoke first. 'Then it must have been one of the prison guard. No one else could have been sure in which bowl to put the poison.'

'No, sir,' the Centurion contradicted respectfully. 'That isn't so, sir. There are only three other men in detention at this moment, and they are all on bread and water for their sins. Easy enough, 'twould be, for anyone to find that out and act according.'

Flavius cut in—Flavius with very bright eyes in a fierce white face. 'What matter for the moment how the poison came into the man's bowl? The thing that matters is *why*, and the answer to that is plain. Alive, he could tell who it was that he met on the marshes this morning, and what passed between them. Therefore he has died. Caesar, does the proof suffice?'

'It is both chilly and depressing in this place,' said Carausius. 'Shall we return to my quarters?'

And not until they were back in the lamplit office, and the door shut behind them, did he speak again, as though Flavius had but that moment asked his question. 'The Saxon you caught this morning in the marshes did indeed have dealings with *someone* in Rutupiae. For that, the proof suffices. No more.' Then as Flavius made a quick gesture of protest, 'Nay, hear me out. Had I, or the Camp Commandant or the bath-house sweeper had dealings with this Saxon, we should have had but two courses open to us after he was taken: to contrive his escape, or to kill him before he was questioned. And of the two, the second would be the surer and simpler method.'

Flavius spoke in a dead-level voice that somehow gave all the more desperate earnestness to his words. 'Caesar, I beg you to listen to us. We were no more than a spear-throw from our men, it was more than half light, and neither of us is blind. We could not have been mistaken. If indeed the other man was not Allectus, then it must be that for some purpose of our own we deliberately bear false witness against him. Do you accuse us of that?'

Allectus himself answered first, with the quickness of anger. 'That is assuredly the most likely explanation of your behaviour. What you yourself have to gain by this I cannot imagine—it may be that your cousin has influenced you in some way—but as for our Junior Surgeon,' he turned to Carausius, 'I remember that when first he was posted here, you yourself, Caesar, were not too sure of his good faith. This is surely some plot of Maximian's, to cast doubt and suspicion between the Emperor of Britain and the man who, however unworthily, serves him to the best of his ability as chief minister.'

Justin stepped forward, his hands clenched at his sides. 'That is a foul lie,' he said, for once without a trace of his stutter. 'And you know it, Allectus; none better.'

'Will you grant me also a space to speak?' Carausius said quietly, and silence fell like a blight on the lamplit chamber. He looked round at all three of them, taking his time.

'I remember my doubts, Allectus. I remember also that the dawn-light can be uncertain, and that there are in Rutupiae more tall fair-haired men than one.—They will all be questioned in due course.—I believe that this has been an honest mistake.' He turned his attention to the two young men. 'However, I, Carausius, do not tolerate such mistakes, and I have no further use for the men who make them. Tomorrow you will receive fresh postings; and it may be that life on the Wall will keep you better occupied and save your over-active fancies from leading you into such mistakes again.' He picked up the scroll that he had been studying when they first entered. 'You may go now. I have no more to say.'

For one instant neither of the two made any move. Then Flavius drew himself rigidly to attention, and saluted. 'It is as Caesar commands,' he said, and opened the door and walked stiffly out.

Justin followed him, carefully closing the door at his back. On the far side of it, he heard Allectus's voice beginning, 'Caesar is too lenient—' and the rest was lost.

'Come to my sleeping-cell,' Flavius demanded, as they crossed the parade-ground under the great pharos.

'I will come by and by,' Justin said dully. 'There are men needing me in the hospital. I must see to them first.'

Tomorrow they would be no affair of his, those men; but tonight he was the surgeon on duty, and it was not until he had made his round of the men in his care, that he went to join Flavius.

Flavius was sitting on the edge of his cot, staring straight before him; his red hair ruffled like the feathers of a bird with the wind behind it, his face, in the light of the wall lamp overhead, drawn and white and angry. He looked up as Justin entered, and jerked his head towards the clothes-chest.

Justin sat down, his arms across his knees, and for a while they looked at each other in silence. Then Flavius said, 'Well, so that is that.'

Justin nodded, and the silence settled again.

And again it was Flavius who broke it. 'I'd have staked all I possess that the Emperor would have given us a fair hearing,' he said moodily.

'I suppose coming out of a clear sky, it would be hard to believe that someone you trusted could betray you,' Justin said.

'Not for Carausius,' Flavius returned with certainty. 'He is not the blindly trusting kind.'

Justin said, 'If the *Sea Witch* puts in again to pick up that Saxon, maybe our galleys will get her, and the truth will come out that way.'

The other shook his head. 'Allectus will find means to warn her not to come.' He stretched, with an angry and miserable laugh. 'Well, no good to yelp about it. He did *not* believe us, and that's all there is to it. We did our best, and there's nothing more that we can do;—and if one day, in some stinking little Auxiliary outpost of the Wall, we hear that Allectus has led a Saxon invasion and made himself Emperor, I hope we both find that very comforting.' He got up, stretching still. 'The Emperor's done with us. We're broke, my lad, broke, and to no purpose. Get off that clothes-chest. I want to start packing.'

The sleeping-cell was looking as though it had been hit by a whirlwind, when a while later the tramp of feet came up the stair, and there was a rap on the door.

Justin, who was nearest, opened it to find one of the Commandant's messengers standing there. 'For the Centurion Aquila,' said the man; and then, recognizing Justin, 'For you also, sir, if you will take it here.'

A few moments later he had disappeared into the night, and Flavius and Justin turned to look at each other, each with a sealed tablet in his hand.

'So he could not even wait for tomorrow to give us our marching orders,' Flavius said bitterly, snapping the crimson thread under the seal.

Justin broke the thread of his own, and opened out the two leaves of the tablet, hastily scanning the few lines of writing scored on the wax inside. A half-made exclamation from his cousin made him look up in enquiry. Flavius read out slowly, 'To proceed at once to Magnis on the Wall, to take over command of the Eighth Cohort of the Second Augustan Legion.'

'We are to be posted together, then,' Justin said. 'I am to report as Surgeon to the same Cohort.'

'The Eighth,' Flavius said, and sat down on his cot. 'I don't understand—I simply don't understand.'

Justin knew what he meant. It scarcely seemed a likely moment to be getting promotion; and yet it was promotion for both of them. Nothing spectacular, just the step up that should have come to them before long, in the normal way of things, but promotion, all the same.

Outside in the tawny half-light that was all Rutupiae ever knew of darkness, the trumpets sounded for the second watch of the night. Justin gave up the attempt to understand. 'I'm going to get some sleep,' he said. 'We must needs make an early start in the morning.' In the doorway he turned. 'C-could it be that Carausius knows he was there, that he was there by his orders, for some purpose best not brought into the daylight?'

Flavius shook his head. 'That wouldn't account for the Saxon's death.'

They were silent a moment, looking at each other. The terrible little Emperor would most certainly not allow one man's life—and he an enemy—to stand between him and his plans, but just as surely, he would have found another way, not poison. Justin would have staked his own life on that without hesitation.

'Maybe he is using Allectus for his own ends, without Allectus knowing,' he suggested. That would still leave the poisoning where he was convinced that it belonged, at Allectus's door.

'I simply—don't know,' Flavius said: and then suddenly explosive: 'I don't know and I don't care! Go to bed.'

VI
Evicatos of the Spear

'YOU have come to the world's end,' said Centurion Posides. The three of them were in the Commander's quarters of Magnis on the Wall, where Flavius had just taken over from the man who would now be his Number Two. 'I hope you like it.'

'I don't very much,' Flavius said frankly. 'But that is beside the point. I also don't like the way the garrison bears itself on parade, Centurion Posides, and that is very much to the point.'

Centurion Posides shrugged; he was a big man with a little, crumpled, bitter face. 'You'll see no better anywhere else along the Wall. What can you expect from a mob of Auxiliaries, the sweepings of every breed and colour in the Empire?'

'The Eighth happens to be a legionary Cohort,' Flavius said.

'Aye, and here come you straight from your fine new fortress at Rutupiae, under the Emperor's eye, and think all legionary Cohorts are the same,' said Centurion Posides. 'Well, there was a time when I thought the like. You'll mend your ideas in time.'

'Either that, or the garrison of Magnis will mend its ideas,' Flavius said, standing with his feet apart and his hands behind his back. 'I rather think that it will be the garrison, Centurion Posides.'

But at first it seemed that he was mistaken in that. Everything that could be wrong with Magnis, was wrong with Magnis. Fort and garrison alike were dirty and unkempt, the bath-house smelt, the cooks were stealing the rations and selling them outside the walls. Even the catapults and skeins of the battery covering the North Gate were in ill repair.

'How often do you have catapult practice?' Flavius demanded when he came to the battery on his first inspection.

'Oh, not for a good while past,' said Posides carelessly.

'So I should judge. If you loosed off Number Three she'd fly to pieces, by the look of her.'

Posides grinned. 'So long as they look all right to the little painted devils. We don't need to use them these days, with the Emperor's fine treaty holding the Picts down.'

'That is no reason why we should not be able to use them if need arises,' Flavius said sharply. 'Look at this thing! The wood is rotten here, and the collar eaten up with rust.—Have Number Three taken down to the workshop for major repairs, Centurion, and let me know when the job is finished.'

'The work could be carried out just as well up here, without dismounting the thing.'

'And have every native hunter who passes Magnis see to what a shameful state our armament has fallen?' Flavius snapped. 'No, Centurion, we'll have her down to the repair shop.'

Number Three Catapult went down to the repair shop, the bath-house was scrubbed, and the fear of the gods put into the thieving cooks; and after the first three days the men no longer slouched on parade with their tunics dirty and their belts undone. But it was all no more than an unwilling gloss of saluting and heel-clicking under which the spirit of Magnis was not changed at all, and the new Commander said wearily to his Cohort Surgeon at the end of the first week, 'I can make them stand up straight on parade, but that alone won't make them into a decent Cohort. If only I could reach them. There must be a way but I can't find it.'

Oddly enough, it was Number Three Catapult that was to find the way for him, a few days later.

Justin saw the whole thing happen. He was clearing up after morning Sick Parade when he heard a creaking and trundling outside, and strolling to the door of the little hospital block, saw that they were bringing the catapult back from the repair shop. From where he stood, he could see the battery by the North Gate, and he lingered a few moments, watching the great weapon being urged that way, trundling and lurching along on its rollers with its sweating team of legionaries hauling in front and pushing behind. He saw Flavius appear from the doorway of the Praetorium and walk forward to join the group about it, as it reached the foot of the temporary ramp that led up to the shoulder-high battery platform; saw the thing lurch like a ship in a gale as it began to climb. Its straining team were all around it, hauling, pushing, handling the rollers from either side. He heard the hollow rumble of it on the ramp, the orders of the Centurion in charge, 'Heave!—Heave!—Once more—he-eave!'

It was almost at the top when something happened; he never saw quite what, but he heard the creak of slipping timbers and a warning cry. There was a swift movement among the men, an order shouted by the Centurion, and a slithering clatter as one of the ramp-timbers went down. For a split moment of time the whole scene seemed frozen; and then, amid a splurge of shouting, the great catapult heeled over and side-slipped with a splintering crash, bringing down the rest of the ramp with it.

Justin saw men scattering outward, and heard a sharp, agonized cry. He called back to his orderly behind him, and in the same instant was running towards the scene of the crash. The great engine lay like a dead locust on its side among the fallen ramp-timbers, partly on the ground and partly supported by the stone kerb of the battery platform. The dust of the crash still hung on the air, but already men were heaving at the wreckage beneath which one of their comrades lay trapped; and as Justin, thrusting through the rest, slithered in under the splintered framework to the man's side, he found someone before him, crouching braced under the weight of the beam which had come down across the legionary's leg, and saw without really looking that it was Flavius with the crest ripped from his helmet and blood trickling from a cut over one eye.

The injured man—it was Manlius, one of the hardest cases in all Magnis—was quite conscious, and the young surgeon heard him gasp, 'It's my leg, sir, I can't move—I—'

'Don't try,' Flavius said, breathing quickly; and there was an odd gentleness in his tone that Justin had never heard before. 'Hold still, old lad; we'll have you clear of this before you can sneeze . . . Ah, here you are, Justin.'

Justin was already busy with the injured legionary, as hands appeared out of nowhere to help Flavius with the great beam. He called over his shoulder, 'Can you get this lot shifted away? I don't want to drag him out if I can help it.'

He was scarcely aware of the clatter of beams being dragged aside, and his own voice saying, 'Easy now, easy; you're all right,' and the straining, cursing moments as the framework of the great catapult was urged up and over, and toppled sideways away from them; until Flavius straightened, cherishing a bruised shoulder, and demanded, 'Is he going to be all right?'

And looking up from the work of his hands, he realized with surprise that it was all over, and the legionaries who had been straining at the wreckage were now standing round looking on, while his orderly knelt beside him steadying the injured man's leg. 'Yes, I think so, but he's got a bad break and he's bleeding like a pig, so the sooner we get him into the hospital and deal with it properly, the better.'

Flavius nodded, and remained squatting beside the man as he lay silent and sweating, until they were ready to move him, then helped to shift him on to the stretcher, and gripped his shoulder for a moment with a quick 'Good luck', before he turned away, wiping the blood from his eyes with the back of his hand, to see how bad was the damage to the catapult.

Number Three Catapult was almost past repair. But by evening word of what had happened had gone round the fort and along the Watch-towers and Mile Castles on either side, and the odd thing was that the new Commander of Magnis had very little more trouble with his garrison.

The weeks passed, and on an evening well into the spring, Justin was packing up after his day's work, when one of his orderlies appeared in the doorway with the news that a native hunter had come in with a wolf-bite to be dealt with.

'All right, I'll come,' Justin said, abandoning his hope of getting a bath before dinner. 'Where have you put him?'

'He's out in the parade-ground, sir; he wouldn't come any further,' said the orderly, with a grin.

Justin nodded. By this time he was growing used to the ways of the Painted People, for it was not the first time that wolf-bitten hunters had come up to the fort, wary and distrustful as wild animals, yet demanding that the Cohort Surgeon should make them well. He went out into the evening light, and there, leaning against the sun-washed wall, found a man naked save for a wolf-skin belted about his hips, and with a shoulder swathed in stained and bloody rags; a man much taller than was usual with his kind, with a mane of hair as thick and proudly tawny as a lion's and eyes in his head like a pretty girl's. 'You are the Healer with a Knife?' he said, with the simple and direct dignity of wild places. 'I come to you that you may heal my shoulder.'

'Come you into the Healing-Place, and show it to me,' said Justin.

The man looked up at the low range of the hospital block beside him. 'I like not the smell of this place, but I will come, because you bid me,' he said, and followed Justin through the doorway. In the surgery,

Justin made him sit down on a bench under the window, and began to undo the filthy rags about his arm and shoulder. When the last of them came away, he saw that the man had been only lightly mauled in the first place, but that with neglect the wounds had become sick, and now his whole shoulder was in a bad way.

'This was not done an hour ago,' Justin said.

The man looked up, '*Na*, half a moon since.'

'Why did you not come here when the harm was new?'

'Nay, I would not come for so small a matter as a wolf-bite; but the wolf was old and his teeth bad, and the bite does not heal.'

'*That* is a true word,' Justin said.

He brought fresh linen and salves, and a flask of the native barley spirit that burned like fire in an open wound. 'Now I am going to hurt you,' he said.

'I am ready.'

'Hold still, then; your arm like that—so.' He cleansed the wounds with searching thoroughness, while the hunter sat like a stone under his ruthless surgery; then salved them and bound the man's shoulder with strips of linen. 'That is done for today. Only for today, mind; you must come back tomorrow—every day for many days.'

In the doorway of the hospital block they parted. 'Come back at the same hour tomorrow, friend,' Justin said, and watched him go with the long, light step of the hunter across the parade-ground towards the gate, and scarcely expected to see him again. So often they did not come back.

But next evening at the same hour the man was once again leaning against the wall of the hospital block. And every day after that he appeared, sat like a stone to have his wounds dressed, and then disappeared until the same time next day.

On the seventh evening Justin had started to change the dressing as usual, when a shadow darkened the door and Flavius appeared on his way to look in, as he often did, on the legionary Manlius, who was still cot-bound with his broken leg. He looked in passing at the two under the window, and then checked, with his eyes on the man's shoulder, drawing in his breath in a hiss.

'It was looking worse than this a few days since,' Justin said.

Flavius peered more closely. 'It looks ugly enough now. Wolf?'

The hunter looked up at him. 'Wolf,' he agreed.

'How did it happen?'

'Nay, whoever knows how these things happen? They are too swift in the happening for any man to know. But it will be a while and a while before I hunt with the Painted People again.'

'The Painted People,' Flavius said. 'Are you not, then, one of the Painted People?'

'I? Am I blue from head to heel, that I should be one of the Painted People?'

That was true; painted he was, with blue warrior patterns on breast and arms, but not as the Picts with their close-set bands of tattooing all over their bodies. He was taller and fairer than most of the Picts, also, as Justin had thought when he first saw him leaning against the hospital wall.

'I am of the people of the firths and islands of the west coast up yonder, beyond the old Northern Wall; the people that were from Erin in the old times.'

'A Dalriad,' Flavius said.

The hunter seemed to draw himself together a little under Justin's hands. 'I was a Dalriad—a Scot of the tribe of . . . Nay, but I am a man without tribe or country now.'

There was a small stillness. Justin, to whom words never came easily in the things that mattered, went on salving the wolf-bites in the man's shoulder. Then Flavius said quietly, 'That is an ill thing to be. How does it come about, friend?'

The hunter threw up his head. 'When I was in my sixteenth year, I all but slew a man at the Great Gathering, the three-yearly gathering of the Tribes. For that—even for carrying weapons upon the Hill of Gathering when the Council Circle is set up—the price is death or outlawry. Because I was but a boy who had taken Valour only that spring, and because the man had put an insult on my house, the King spoke the word for outlawry and not for slaying. Therefore these fifteen years and more I hunt among the Painted People, forgetting my own kind as much as may be.'

After that it became a habit with Flavius to stroll across to the hospital on his way to see Manlius at about the time when he knew that Justin would be dressing the hunter's shoulder. And little by little there grew up a fellowship between the three of them, so that the hunter who had at first been so silent and withdrawn, came to speak more and more freely to the two young Romans; while little by little the wolf-wounds in his shoulder cleared and healed, until the day came when Justin said, 'See, it is finished. There is no more need for salves and linen.'

Squinting at the pinkish scars of the wolf's teeth that were all that was left, the hunter said, 'It would have been another story if I had met my wolf a year—a few moons ago.'

'Why so?' Justin asked. 'I am not the first healer here at Magnis on the Wall.'

'*Na*, and the Centurion is not the first Commander here at Magnis on the Wall. "Out dogs, to your dung-heap," that was the last Commander. *We* could never have come near the healer, even had we sought to.' He looked from Justin to Flavius lounging in the doorway. 'It is in my mind that Carausius your Emperor chooses his cubs well.'

Flavius said harshly, 'You are mistaken, my friend. It was not for our worth that Carausius posted us to this godforsaken outpost.'

'So?' The hunter studied them thoughtfully. 'Yet it is not, I think, always that one may clearly see what lies behind the deeds of High Kings.' He rose, and turned to something that he had brought in with him half hidden under the plaid he had been wearing. '*Sa, sa,* that is as may be . . . You were saying, a day since, that you had never seen one of our great war-spears; therefore I have brought mine, a queen among war-spears, that you may see what I would not show in peace to any other of your breed.'

He turned to the light of the high window. 'See now, is she not fair?'

The great spear which he laid in Justin's hands was the most beautiful weapon Justin had ever seen; the blade long and slender as a flame, a darkly silver flame in the cool evening light; butt weighted by a bronze ball as big as an apple most wonderfully worked with blue-and-green enamel, and about its neck, just below the blade, a collar of wild-swan's feathers. Beautiful and deadly. He tested it in his hand, feeling it unusually heavy, but so perfectly balanced that one would scarcely notice the weight in use. 'It is indeed a queen among spears!' and gave it into the eager hand that Flavius was holding out for it.

'Ah, you beautiful!' Flavius said softly, testing it as Justin had done, running a finger along the blade. 'To carry this in battle would be to carry the lightning in one's hand.'

'Aye so. But I have not carried her in battle since I followed your little Emperor south, seven summers ago. Aye, aye, I keep her furbished, a fresh collar of wild swan's feathers every summer. But it is seven collars since the white feathers changed to red.' The hunter's tone was regretful, as he took back his treasure.

Flavius's head had gone up with a jerk, his fly-away brows twitching together. 'So? You have marched with Carausius? How came that to pass?'

'It was when he first landed. Over yonder among the mountains south and west, between Luguvalium and the Great Sands.' Leaning on his spear, the hunter all at once kindled to his story. 'A little man, a very great little man! He called together the Chieftains of the Painted People and the Chieftains of the Coastwise Dalriads, and the Chieftains out of Erin also; called them all together there among the mountains, and talked with them long and deeply. And at first the Chieftains and we who followed them listened to him because he was of our world, Curoi the Hound of the Plain, before ever he returned to his father's people and became Carausius and part of Rome; and then we listened to him because he was himself. So he made a treaty with the Kings of my people and the Kings of the Painted People. And when he turned south with the Sea Warriors from his fleet, many of us followed him. Even I followed him, among the Painted People. I was with him when he met with the man Quintus Bassianus who they said was Governor of Britain, at Eburacum of the Eagles. It was a great fight! *Aiee!* a most great fight; and when the day ended, Quintus Bassianus was food for the ravens and no more Governor of Britain, and Carausius marched on south, and those that were left of Quintus Bassianus's soldiers marched with him gladly enough; and I and most of my kind went back to our own hunting trails. But we heard from time to time—we hear most things among the heather—how Carausius was become Emperor of Britain, and then how he was become one with the Emperor Maximian and the Emperor Diocletian in the ruling of Rome—and we remembered that very great little man, among the mountains—and we did not wonder at these things.'

He broke off, and half turned towards the open doorway, then checked, looking from Justin to Flavius and back again, with a slow-grave inclination of the head. 'If you should wish to go hunting at any time, send word into the town for Evicatos of the Spear. It will reach me, and I will surely come.'

VII

'To the Fates, that They May be Kind'

SEVERAL times that summer and autumn, Flavius and Justin hunted with Evicatos of the Spear; and on a morning in late autumn they took their hunting-spears and went out by the North Gate under the tall grasshopper heads of the catapults, and found him with his hounds and the three shaggy ponies waiting for them in their usual meeting-place at the foot of the steep northern scarp. It was a raw morning with the mist lying low and heavy like smoke among the brown heather, and the rooty tang of bog and the bitter-sweetness of sodden bracken hanging in the air.

'A good hunting day,' Flavius said, sniffing the morning with satisfaction, as they joined the waiting hunter.

'Aye, the scent will lie long and heavy in this mist,' Evicatos said; but as they mounted their ponies, Justin had a feeling that the hunter was thinking of something far removed from the day's hunting; and an odd chill of foreboding fell for an instant like a shadow across his path. But as they moved off down the burnside with the hounds loping about them, he forgot it in the promise of the day.

They got on the track of an old dog wolf almost at once, and after a wild chase, brought him to bay far up among the rolling border hills; and Flavius, dismounted now, slipped in low among the yelling hounds, with shortened spear, and made the kill.

By the time they had skinned the great grey brute under Evicatos's direction, it was drawing on to noon, and they were ravenously hungry.

'Let's eat here. My stomach's flapping against my backbone,' Flavius said, stabbing his knife into the turf to clean it.

Evicatos was making the raw skin into a bundle, while the dogs snarled and tore at the flayed carcass. 'It is good to eat when the belly is empty,' he said, 'but first we will go a short way south from here.'

'Why?' Flavius demanded. 'We have made our kill, and I want to eat now.'

'So do I.' Justin seconded him. 'It is as good a spot as any. Let's stay here, Evicatos.'

'I have a thing to show you, further south,' Evicatos said, and rose to his feet with the bundled skin. 'Oh foolish one, have you never carried a baled wolf-skin before?' (This to the snorting and sidling pony.)

'Will it not keep till we are full?' Flavius demanded.

Evicatos got the wolf-skin settled to his entire satisfaction across the pony's withers before he answered. 'Did I not say to you when first we hunted together, that among the heather you should obey me in all things, because among the heather I am the hunter and the man who knows, and you are no more than children?'

Flavius touched palm to forehead in mock salute. 'You did—and we promised. So be it then, oh most wise of hunters. We will come.'

So they whipped the hounds off the carcass, and leaving it to the ravens that were already gathering, south they went, until, some while later, the hunter brought them dipping over a bare shoulder of the hills, to a burn of white water brawling down over shelving stones. Further down, the glen narrowed in on itself, clothed in harsh willow-scrub, but here the hills rose bare on either side, clothed in short grass instead of heather; a great tawny bowl of hills running up to the tumbled autumn sky, empty save for a peregrine swinging to and fro along the further slopes.

Evicatos checked his pony beside the burn, and the others with him, and as the sounds of their own movement ceased, it seemed to Justin that the silence and solitude of the high hills came flowing in on them.

'See,' said Evicatos. 'Here is the thing.'

The two young men followed the line of his pointing finger, and saw a dark lump of stone that rose stark and oddly defiant from the tawny burnside grass.

'What, that boulder?' Flavius said, puzzled.

'That boulder. Come closer now, and look, while I make ready the food.'

They dismounted and knee-hobbled the ponies, then made their way down the burn; and while Evicatos busied himself with the meal-bag, Flavius and Justin turned their attention to the thing that they had been brought to see. It seemed to be part of an outcrop of some kind, for small ledges and shelves of the same rock broke through the bank below it, half hidden in the grass; but looking more closely, they saw that it had been roughly squared, as though maybe it had always been rather square, and someone had decided to improve on nature. Also, as they examined it, there seemed to be carving of some sort on the stone. 'I believe it is an altar!' Justin said, dropping on one knee before it, while Flavius bent over him hands on knees. 'Look, here are three figures!'

'You're right,' Flavius said, with awakening interest. 'Furies—or Fates—or maybe it is the Great Mothers. The carving is so rough and weather-worn you can't really see. Scrape off some of this lichen down below, Justin. It looks as though there's something written there.'

A short space of work with Justin's hunting-knife and the ball of his thumb, and they were sure of it. 'Here's a name,' Justin said. ' "S-Y-L-V-Sylvanus Varus".' He worked on steadily, crumbling away the lichen from the crudely carved letters, while Flavius, squatting beside him now, brushed away fallen debris, until in a little, the thing was clear.

'To the Fates, Sylvanus Varus, standard-bearer of the fifth Tungrian Cohort with the Second Augustan Legion, raised this altar, that they may be kind,' Flavius read aloud.

'I wonder if they were,' Justin said after a pause, crumbling the golden lichen-dust from his fingers.

'I wonder what he wanted them to be kind *about*.'

'Maybe he just wanted them to be kind.'

Flavius shook his head with decision. 'You wouldn't make an altar just because you wanted the Fates to be kind in general, only if you needed their kindness badly, now, for some particular thing.'

'Well, whatever it was, it was all over a l-long time ago . . . How long since we pulled out of Valentia the last time?'

'Not sure. About a hundred and fifty years, I think.'

They were silent again, looking down at those three crudely carved figures and the shallow ill-made letters beneath.

'So there are words there too. Was it worth seeing?' said Evicatos's voice behind them.

Flavius, still squatting before the stone, looked up at him, smiling. 'Yes. But as worth seeing on a full stomach as an empty one.'

'The food is ready,' Evicatos said. 'Let you turn about and fill your bellies now.'

Clearly he had some reason in all this, but equally clearly he was not going to declare it save in his own good time. And it was not until the three of them were sitting round the pot of cold stir-about, and already well on with the buttered bannock and strips of smoked deer-meat, that he broke silence at last. 'As for this carved stone, one excuse serves as well as another. It was needful that I bring you to this place and show reason for doing so, to—any who might be interested.'

'Why?' Flavius demanded.

'Because even a Pict cannot hide in ankle-high grass, nor hear across the distance from the willow-scrub yonder to this stone. There are few places in Albu where one can be sure that there is no little Painted Man behind a rock or under the heather.'

'Meaning that you have something to tell us that must not be overheard?'

'Meaning that I have this to tell you—' Evicatos cut a gobbet from the dried meat and tossed it to his favourite hound. 'Listen now, and hear. There are emissaries of the man Allectus on the Wall and North of the Wall.'

Justin checked in the act of putting a piece of bannock into his mouth, and dropped his hand back to his knee. Flavius gave a startled exclamation. 'Here?—What do you mean, Evicatos?'

'Go on eating; sight carries further than sound, remember. I mean what I say; there are emissaries of the man Allectus in Albu. They make talk of friendship with the Picts; they make promises—and ask for promises in return.'

'And these p-promises?' Justin said softly, cutting a shaving from his dried meat.

'They promise that Allectus will help the Painted People against us, the Dalriads, if first the Painted People will help him to overthrow the Emperor Carausius.'

There was a long silence pin-pricked by the sharp cry of the peregrine now high above the glen. Then Flavius said with quiet, concentrated fury, 'So we were right about Allectus. We were right, up to the very hilt, all the time!'

'So?' Evicatos said. 'I know nothing of that. I know only that if he succeeds in this thing, there will be death for my people.' He checked as though to listen to what he had just said, with a kind of half-wondering interest. 'My people.—I that am a man without tribe or country. But it seems that my faith reaches back to my own kind, after all.'

'Will the Painted People agree?' Justin asked.

'It is in my heart that they will agree. Always there has been distrust and ill blood between the Picts and my people, until Carausius made his treaty. For seven years, under the treaty, there has been peace. But the Painted People fear us because we are different from them, and because we begin to grow strong among the Western islands and the coastwise mountains; and where the Pict fears, there the Pict hates.'

'He fears and therefore hates the Eagles also,' Justin said. 'And you say that he will make a promise with Allectus?'

'Aye, he fears the Eagles and he fears the Dalriads,' Evicatos agreed simply. 'He would as lief join with us and drive the Eagles into the sea; but he knows that even together, we are not strong enough. Therefore if he can, he will join with the Eagles and drive us. Either way he is rid of one enemy.'

'Allectus is not the Eagles,' Flavius said quickly.

'He will be, with Carausius dead.' Evicatos looked from one to the other. 'You know the Wall, and the Cohorts of the Wall; they will shout for whoever wears the Purple, so that he pays them with wine enough. Can you be sure that the Eagles elsewhere are of a different breed?'

No one answered for a moment; and then Flavius said, 'Your own people know of all this?'

'I do not speak with my own people, these fifteen years past, but assuredly they know. Yet, knowing, what can they do? If they make war on the Painted People while there is still time, that is to break the treaty; and whether Carausius or Allectus wears the Purple, we, the little people, shall go down before the wrath of Rome.' Evicatos leaned forward as though to dip into the stir-about. 'Warn him! Warn this Emperor of yours; it is in my mind that he may listen to you. (We hear things, among the heather.) That is why I bring you to this place, and tell you these things that are death to speak of—that you may warn Carausius of the wind that blows!'

'Can a blackbeetle warn Almighty Jove? The blackbeetle tried it once, and was trodden on for his pains,' Flavius said bitterly. His head was tilted back, and his eyes gazing out beyond the far rim of hills that dropped southward to the Wall. 'How are we going to get word to him?'

'There isn't much sickness in the fort,' Justin heard his own voice saying. 'And there's always the field surgeon at L-Luguvalium if one should be needed. I'll go.'

Flavius looked round at him quickly, but before he could speak,

Evicatos cut in: '*Na, na,* if either one of you go, it is deserting, and there will be questions asked. No man will ask questions after me. Write him word of all this that I have told you, and give me the writing.'

'You mean—you would carry it south yourself?' Flavius said.

'Aye.'

'Why should you be running your head into a wolf-trap on this trail?'

Evicatos, fondling the ears of the great hound beside him, said: 'Not for the love of your Emperor, but that it may not be death for my own people.'

'You would do so much—risk so much, for the people that cast you out?'

'I broke the laws of my kind, and I paid the agreed price,' Evicatos said. 'There is no more to it than that.'

Flavius looked at him a moment without speaking. Then he said: 'So. It is your trail also.' And then, 'You know what mercy there will be for you if you fall into the hands of Allectus's creatures with the writing on you?'

'I can guess,' said Evicatos with a small, grim smile. 'Yet since your names must be on the writing, clear for all to read, that will be a risk fairly shared among us, after all.'

Flavius said, 'So be it, then,' and leaned forward to the stir-about pot in his turn. 'But there is no time to lose. The letter must be on its way tonight.'

'That is a simple matter. Let one of you come down tonight to watch the cock-fighting in the Vallum ditch. One of your Optios has challenged all comers with his red cock; did you know? There will be many there, British and Roman, and if maybe you and I should speak together among the rest, none will think it strange.'

'Pray the gods he believes us this time!' Flavius said, softly and very soberly.

Justin swallowed his last mouthful of bannock without tasting it, and got to his feet, tightening his belt which he had slackened for ease when he sat down. His gaze fell again on the rough altar, on the worn figures and the uneven lettering from which they had scraped the moss.

Flavius, glancing up at him, caught the direction of his gaze, and turned his own the same way. Abruptly he took a silver sestercia from his belt, and pressed it into the turf before the altar. 'Surely we also have sore need that the Fates be kind,' he said.

Behind them, Evicatos was gathering up the remains of the food, tying up the neck of the meal-bag, as he had done after the other hunting meals that they had eaten together. On the fringe of the scrub, downstream, a feathering of vivid colour caught at Justin's eyes, where a tangle of dogwood had burst into its autumn flame. He walked down the burnside to the thicket, made careful selection, and broke off a long spray on which the leaves were scarlet as a trumpet-call. Something rustled among the deeper shadows as he did so; something that might be only a fox, but as he turned away he had a feeling of watching eyes behind him that were not the eyes of fox or wild cat.

The other two were waiting for him with the ponies, when he rejoined them twisting the spray into a rough garland; and he stopped on to one knee and laid it on the weather-worn altar. Then they turned away and mounted, whistling the dogs to heel, and rode with Evicatos of the Spear down the burnside, leaving the bare bowl of the hills empty once more, save for the wheeling peregrines and the thing that had rustled in the shadows of the scrub.

And behind them Justin's dogwood garland was bright as blood upon the lichened stone, where an unknown soldier of their Legion had made his own desperate appeal to the Fates, a hundred, two hundred years ago.

In the Commander's quarters that evening they wrote the letter between them, their heads bent together in the pool of lamplight, over the tablets open on the table.

It was just finished and the tablet sealed, when a knock came at the door. Their eyes met for an instant, then Justin swept up the tablet into the flat of his hand, as Flavius bade the visitor enter, and the Quartermaster appeared. 'Sir,' said the Quartermaster, saluting, 'I have brought the new supply lists. If you could spare me an hour, we could get them settled.'

Justin had risen, also saluting. In public he kept up very carefully the formalities between the Cohort Surgeon and the Cohort Commander. 'I will not take up any more of your time, sir. Have I your permission to leave camp for an hour or so?'

Flavius looked up at him under red, fly-away brows. 'Ah yes, the cocking main. Put something on our man's bird for me, Justin.'

The great Vallum that had been the frontier before the Wall was built, had become of late years a vast, unsavoury ditch choked with tattered and stinking hovels, small dirty shops and temples, garbage piles, and the dens of the legionaries' hunting dogs. The smell of it met Justin like a fog as he crossed the coast-to-coast road and dropped into it by the steps opposite the Praetorian Gate of Magnis. In an open space a spear-throw from the foot of the steps a crowd was already gathered, jostling round the makeshift arena and thronging the steep slopes of the Vallum on either side; shadowy in the autumn dusk save for the glow of a brazier here and there among them, and the splashing yellow light of one big lantern in their midst. Justin made his way towards it, shouldering through the noisy, shifting throng.

He could see no sign of Evicatos as yet; not that it would be easy to pick out one man from that shifting, shadowy crowd. But on the edge of the lantern light he found Manlius, who had returned to full duty only a few days before, and checked beside him. 'Well, Manlius, how is the leg?'

Manlius looked round, grinning in the lantern-light. 'Good as new, sir.'

Justin's heart warmed to him, because it had been a long fight and a hard one to mend that leg, and now it was as good as new. Anyone who had been hurt or ill under his hands always called out that humble and surprised warmth in Justin. It was one of the things, though he did not know it, that made him a good surgeon. 'So. That makes fine hearing,' he said, and the warmth was in his voice.

Manlius said rather gruffly, as though he were ashamed, 'If it hadn't been for you, sir, I'm thinking I'd be out of the Eagles now, with one leg to hobble on.'

'If it hadn't been for yourself also,' Justin said after a moment. 'It takes two, you know, Manlius.'

The legionary glanced at him sideways, then straight ahead again. 'I see what you mean, sir. None the less, I don't forget all you done for me; nor I don't forget the Commander with his face all over blood, hauling that cursed great beam off me when I thought I was about done for.'

They were silent then, among the noisy crowd, neither of them skilled in words, and neither with the least idea what to say next. Finally Justin said, 'Do you back our man and the red cock?'

'Of course, sir—and you?' Manlius replied with obvious relief.

'Assuredly. I have a wager with Evicatos of the Spear. Also I want to ask him about the skin of the wolf that the Commander killed today. Have you seen him anywhere in this crowd?'

'No, sir, can't say I have.'

'Ah well, he'll be somewhere about.' Justin nodded, friendly-wise, and side stepped between two legionaries, emerging on the lantern-lit edge of the arena. Somebody provided him with an upturned pail to sit on, and he sat, huddling his cloak around him for warmth. Before him stretched an open space covered with rush matting, in the centre of which a yard-wide ring daubed in chalk shone white in the light of the lantern rigged overhead. Above the lantern, the sky was still barred with the last fading flare-streaks of the sunset, but down here in the Vallum it was already almost dark, save where the light of the lantern fell on eager faces thronged about that shining chalk circle.

And now two men had pushed out from their fellows in the arena, each carrying a large leather bag which wriggled and bounced with the angry life inside it. And instantly a solid roar went up from the crowd. 'Come on, Sextus, show 'em what the red can do!—Ya-ah! Call that dunghill rooster a fighting cock?—Two to one on the tawny devil!—Give you three to one on the red!'

One of the men—it was the Magnis Optio—was undoing the neck of his bag now, bringing out his cock, and there was a redoubled burst of voices as he handed it to a third man who stood by to see fair play. The bird he held up was indeed worth shouting for: red and black without a pale feather anywhere, slim and powerful, very much a warrior stripped for battle, with his close-cut comb, clipped wings, and square docked tail. Justin saw the lantern-light play on his quivering wings, the fierce head in which the black, dilating eyes were brilliant as jewels, the deadly iron spurs strapped about his ankles.

The third man handed him back to his owner, and the other cock was produced in his turn. But Justin took less notice of him, for just as he was held up to view, Evicatos appeared on the far side of the arena, while at the same instant somebody edged through the crowd into the vacant space at his side, and the voice of Centurion Posides said, 'All the world is here, it seems, even to our Cohort Surgeon. I did not know that you were one for the fighting cocks, my Justin.—Nay, no need to shy like a startled horse, or I shall think you have an unquiet conscience.' For Justin had indeed jumped slightly at the sound of his voice.

Centurion Posides was friendly enough, these days, but Justin had never come to like him. He was a man with a grudge against the world—a world that had denied him the promotion he thought it owed him. Justin was sorry for him; it must be hard to go through life bearing it a grudge, but he certainly did not want him at his shoulder just now. However, it would be a while yet before he need do anything about passing on the letter under his cloak: 'I am n-not, usually,' he said, 'but I have heard so much about this red cock that I felt I must c-come and judge his fighting p-powers for myself.' (Oh, curse that stutter, it would have to betray him now, just when he most needed to seem completely at ease!)

'We must be very healthy just now, up at the fort, that our Surgeon can spend the evening at a cocking main after a whole day's hunting,' said Posides in the faintly aggrieved tone that was usual with him.

'We are,' Justin said quietly, mastering his stutter with a supreme effort, 'or I should not be here.' He had meant to add 'Centurion Posides', but he knew that the P would be his undoing, so he left it; and turned his attention firmly to what was passing on the matting before him.

The tawny cock had been returned to its owner, and to the accompaniment of much advice from rival supporters, the two men had taken their places and set their cocks down at opposite sides of the chalk circle. Now, suddenly as their owners loosed them, the birds streaked forward, and the fight was on.

It did not last long, that first fight, though it was fierce enough while it lasted. It ended with a lightning strike of the red's spurs, and a few feathers drifting sideways on the matting, and the tawny cock lying a small dead warrior, where he had fallen.

His owner picked him up, shrugging philosophically, while the other man took up his crowing and triumphant property. Bets were being settled, and quarrels breaking out in a score of places at once, as generally happened at a cock-fight, and under cover of the noise and the shifting of the crowd, Justin murmured something about speaking to Evicatos of the Spear about the Commander's wolf-skin, and getting up, made his way round to the far side of the ring. Evicatos was waiting for him, and as they came together, close-jammed in the crowd, the sealed tablet passed between them under cover of their cloaks.

The thing was done so easily that Justin, his ears full of his own voice talking somewhat at random about the wolf-skin, could have laughed aloud in sheer relief.

The quarrels were sorting themselves out, and another cock had been brought in and set opposite to the red, as he turned back to the Arena. This time the fight was long drawn and uncertain, and before the end of it, both cocks were showing signs of distress: the open beak, the wing dragging on the blood-stained matting. Only one thing seemed quite unquenched in them, their desire to kill one another. That, and their courage. They were very like human gladiators, Justin thought, and suddenly he sickened, and did not want to see any more. The thing that he had come to do was done, and Evicatos of the Spear, when he looked for him, was already gone. He slipped away too, and made his way back to the fort.

But as he went, Centurion Posides, on the far side of the ring, looked after him with an odd gleam in his eyes. 'Now I wonder,' murmured Centurion Posides, 'I wonder, my very ill-at-ease young friend, if it really *was* only the wolf-skin? With your previous record, I think that we will take no chances,' and he rose and slipped off also, but not in the direction of the fort.

VIII
The Feast of Samhain

TWO evenings later, Justin was making ready to leave the hospital block after late rounds, when Manlius appeared in the surgery doorway with a bloody rag twisted round one hand. 'Sorry to trouble you, sir, but I hoped I might find you here. I've chopped my thumb and I can't stop it bleeding.'

Justin was about to call the orderly who was cleansing instruments nearby and bid him deal with it, when he caught the urgent message in the Legionary's eyes, and changed his mind. 'Come over to the lamp,' he said. 'What has happened this time? Another catapult on top of you?'

'No, sir, I've been chopping wood for my woman. I was off duty—and I chopped it.'

The man moved after him, pulling off the crimson rag; and Justin saw a small but deepish gash in the base of his thumb from which the blood welled up as fast as he wiped it away.

'Orderly—a bowl of water and some bandage linen.'

The man dropped what he was doing and brought the water. 'Shall I take over, sir?'

'No, c-carry on cleaning those tools.'

And Justin set about bathing and dressing the cut, while Manlius stood staring woodenly into space. In a little, the orderly took the burnished instruments into an inner room, and instantly Manlius's eyes flew to the door after him, then back to Justin's face, and he muttered, 'Where's the Commander, sir?'

'The Commander? In the P-Praetorium, I imagine. Why?'

'Get him. Get all the money you have, anything of value, and go both of you to my woman's bothie in the town. It is the last bothie in the street of the Golden Grasshopper. Don't let any see you enter.'

'Why?' Justin whispered. 'You must tell me what you mean; I—'

'Don't ask questions, sir; do as I tell you, and in Mithras's name do it at once, or I've gashed my thumb to no purpose.'

Justin hesitated an instant longer. Then with the footsteps of the returning orderly already at the door, he nodded. 'Very well, I'll trust you.'

He finished his task, tied off the bandage, and with a casual 'Goodnight' to both men, strolled out into the autumn dusk, picking up in passing the slim, tube-shaped case that held his own instruments from the table on which it lay.

A few moments later he was closing the door of Flavius's office behind him. Flavius looked up from the table at which he was working late on the week's duty roster. 'Justin? You look very solemn.'

'I feel very solemn,' Justin said, and told him what had happened.

Flavius gave a soundless whistle when he had finished. 'One of the bothies of the town, and take all the money we have. What do you suppose lies behind this, brother?'

'I don't know,' Justin said. 'I'm horribly afraid it has to do with Evicatos. But I'd trust Manlius to the world's end.'

'Or *at* the world's end. Yes, so would I.' Flavius was on his feet as he spoke. He began to move quickly about the room, clearing the tablets and papyrus rolls from the table and laying them away in orderly fashion in the record chest. He locked the chest with the key which never left its chain about his neck, then turned to the small inner room that was his sleeping-cell.

Justin was already next door in his own cell, delving under the few garments in his clothes-chest for the leather bag containing most of his last month's pay. He hadn't anything else of value except his instrument case. He picked that up again, stowed the small leather bag in his belt, and returned to the office just as Flavius came out from the inner room flinging on his cloak.

'Got your money?' Flavius said, stabbing home the brooch at his shoulder.

Justin nodded. 'In my belt.'

Flavius cast a look round to see that all was in order, and caught up his helmet. 'Come on, then,' he said.

They went down through the fort in the darkness and the mist that was creeping in from the high moors; and with a casual word to the sentries at the gate, passed through into the town.

The town that, though its name changed with every fort along its length—Vindobala, Aesica, Chilurnium—was in truth one town eighty miles long, strung out along the Wall and the coast-to-coast legionary road behind it. One long, teeming, stinking maze of wine-shops and baths and gaming-houses, stables and granaries, women's huts and small dirty temples to British and Egyptian, Greek and Gaulish gods.

The last bothie in the narrow, winding alley-way that took its name from the Golden Grasshopper wine-shop at the corner was in darkness as they drew near. A little squat black shape with the autumn mists creeping about the doorway. Almost as they reached it, the door opened silently into deeper blackness within and the pale blur of a face showed in the opening. 'Who comes?' a woman's voice demanded softly.

'The two you wait for,' Flavius murmured back.

'Come, then.' She drew them into the houseplace, where the red embers of a fire shone like a scatter of rubies on the hearth but left the room in wolf darkness, and instantly closed the door behind them. 'There will be light in a moment. This way. Come.'

For the one moment it seemed very like a trap, and Justin's heart did undignified things in his throat. Then, as he moved forward after Flavius, the woman pulled aside a blanket over an inner doorway, and the faint gleam of a tallow dip came to meet them. Then they were in an inner room where the one tiny window-hole under the thatch had been shuttered close against prying eyes; and a man who had been sitting on the piled skins and native rugs of the bed-place against the far wall raised his head as they entered.

The woman let the heavy curtain fall again behind them, as Flavius whispered, 'Evicatos! Ye gods, man! What does this mean?'

Evicatos's face was grey and haggard in the uncertain light, and the purple smudge of a great broken bruise showed on one temple. 'They caught and searched me,' he said.

'They found the letter?'

'They found the letter.'

'Then how do you come to be here?'

'I contrived to break free,' Evicatos said in a swift undertone. 'I laid them a trail that might serve—for a little—to make them think that I was still heading south. Then I doubled back to Magnis and slipped in at twilight, but I dared not come up to the fort after you, for all our sakes.'

'So he came here.' The woman took up the tale. 'Knowing Manlius was one he could trust, and I was Manlius's woman. And the gods so willed it that Manlius was at home—and the rest you know, or you would not be here.'

Justin and Flavius looked at each other in an utter silence that seemed to clamp down on the little back room. Then Flavius said, 'Well, the Cohort records are in good order for whoever takes them over.'

Justin nodded. There was only one thing to be done now. 'We must get to Carausius ourselves, and quickly.'

'It is going to be a race against time—and against Allectus—with the hunt up for the three of us,' Flavius said. 'Stirring days we live in.' His voice was hard, and his eyes very bright, and he was slipping free the great brooch at his shoulder as he spoke. He shook off the heavy folds of his military cloak, and stood forth in the bronze and leather of a Cohort commander. 'Manlius's wife, can you find us a couple of rough tunics, or cloaks to cover our own?'

'Surely,' the woman said. 'Food also you will need. Wait and you shall have both.'

Evicatos rose from the bed place. 'You have brought your money?'

'All that we had about us.'

'*Sa.* Money is good on a journey, especially if one would travel swiftly . . . I go now to fetch the ponies.'

'You ride with us?' Flavius said, as Justin took his sword from him and set it beside the crested helmet on the bed-place.

'Surely. Is not this my trail also?' Evicatos checked with a hand on the blanket over the door. 'When you leave this place, go out past the temple of Serapis, and make for the place of three standing stones, up the Red Burn. You know the spot. Wait for me there.' And he was gone.

The woman came back almost at the same instant, carrying a bundle of clothes, which she set down on the bed-place. 'See, here are two tunics of my man's, and one of them is his festival best, and rawhide shoes for the Commander—those mailed sandals will betray you a mile off; your dagger also, therefore I bring you a hunting-knife in its place. There is but one cloak, and the moth in the hood of that one; but take this rug from the bed; it is thick and warm, and will serve well enough with your brooch to hold it. Change quickly while I get the food.'

When she returned again, Justin was securing the chequered

native rug at his shoulder with his own brooch; and Flavius, standing ready in the cloak with its moth-eaten hood pulled forward on his face, was thrusting the long hunting-knife into his belt. His military harness lay stacked on the bed-place, and he jerked his head towards it as she appeared. 'What of these? They must not be found in your keeping.'

'They will not be,' she said. 'They will be found—presently—in the Vallum ditch. Many things are found, and lost, in the Vallum ditch.'

'Be careful,' Flavius said. 'Don't bring yourself or Manlius to grief for our sakes. Tell us what we owe you for the clothes and food.'

'Nothing,' she said.

Flavius looked at her for a moment as though he were not sure whether to press the matter. Then he said, a little stiffly because he was very much in earnest, 'Then we can only thank you, both on our own behalf, and on behalf of the Emperor.'

'Emperor? What do we care for Emperors?' the woman said, with soft scornful laughter. '*Na na*, you saved my man in the spring, and we remember, he and I. Go now, quickly. Save this Emperor of yours if you can, and take care.' Suddenly she was almost crying as she pushed Flavius past her into the dark outer room. 'You're only boys, after all.'

Justin caught up the food bundle, and turned to follow him, but checked at the last moment on the edge of the dark, smitten with his usual inability to find the words he wanted when he wanted them badly. 'The gods be kind to you, Manlius's wife. Tell Manlius to k-keep his thumb clean,' he managed, and was gone.

A long while later—it seemed a long while later—they were squatting huddled together for warmth, with their backs against the tallest of the three standing stones by the Red Burn. Just before they reached it, Flavius had taken the key of the record chest from about his neck, and dropped it into the pool where the burn grew still and deep under the alders. 'They can get another key made when there is another Commander at Magnis,' he had said. And to Justin it seemed that the tiny splash, small as the sound of a fish leaping, was the most terribly final sound he had ever heard.

Up till now there had been no time for thinking; but now, crouching here in the solitude of the high moors with the mist thickening about them, the smell of it cold as death in their nostrils, and the slow moments dragging by without bringing Evicatos, there was too much time. Time to realize just how big and how bad the things that had happened were; and Justin was cold to the pit of his stomach and the depth of his soul. It was like the mist, he thought, the creeping, treacherous mist that made everything strange, so that you could not be sure of anything or anybody, so that you could not go to the Commander of the Wall and say 'It is thus and it is thus. Now therefore give me leave to go south with all speed.' Because the Commander himself might be one of Them.

The mist was creeping closer, wreathing like smoke through the sodden heather and around the standing stones. He shivered, stirred abruptly to cover it, and so felt the thing that he had carried out of Magnis along with the food-bundle under his cloak. His instrument-case. He had scarcely been aware of bringing it away with him, it was so much a part of himself; but here it was, and it belonged to the good things of life, the clean and the kindly things—something constant and unchanging to hold on to. He lifted the slim tube of metal and laid it across his knee.

Flavius glanced round. 'What is it?'

'Only my instrument-case,' Justin said, and then as the other gave a sudden splutter of laughter, 'Why is that funny?'

'Oh, I don't know. Here we are on the run, with the hunt up behind us and the world falling into shards around our ears, and you bring your instrument-case away with you.'

'I am still a surgeon, you see,' Justin said.

There was a moment's pause, and then Flavius said, 'Of course. That was stupid of me.'

Even as he spoke, from far down the burn came the unmistakable jink of a bridle bit, and as they listened with suddenly strained attention, it was followed by a high shaken whistle that might well have been the call of some night bird.

'It is Evicatos!' Justin said, with a quick surge of relief, and threw up his head and whistled back.

The jinking came again, and with it the soft beat and brush of horses coming up through the heather; nearer and nearer yet, until a solid knot of darkness loomed suddenly through the mist, and Flavius and Justin rose to their feet as Evicatos rode up past the lowest of the standing stones, with the two led ponies behind him.

He reined in at sight of them, and the ponies stood with their breath smoking into the mist.

'All well?' Flavius said.

'Well enough so far, but I think that we are none too soon. There is a stirring in the fort, and the word runs already along the Wall that the Commander of Magnis and his healer are nowhere to be found. Mount now, and ride.'

It was just before dusk on the third day that they came down into the head of a widening dale, and saw before them a farm lost in the wilderness.

Until now they had kept clear of the haunts of men, but their meal-bag was empty, and since on this desperate forced march south they could not spend precious time in hunting, they must get more supplies from somewhere. It was a risk, but it had to be taken, and they turned the ponies' heads down in the dale, Evicatos reversing his great war-spear that he had brought with him, to show that they came in peace. In the lonely vastness of the surrounding hills, the cluster of bracken-thatched huts within the ring fence seemed no larger than a palmful of brown beans, but as they drew nearer they saw that it was a big farm, as such places went, and that it was full of a great coming and going, both of men and cattle.

'Are they expecting an attack, that they drive all the cattle in among the steading huts?' Flavius said.

Evicatos shook his head. '*Na na*, it is the feast of Samhain, when they bring the sheep and cattle down from the summer pasture and pen them close for the winter. I had lost count of the days. Yet it will only make our welcome the most sure.'

And so indeed it proved, for at Samhain all doors stood open, and before it was full dusk the three strangers had been accepted without question, their ponies stabled, and they themselves brought in and given places on the men's side of the fire, among the others gathering there.

The fire burned on a raised hearth in the midst of the great houseplace, and at the four corners of the hearth four whole tree-trunks stood to uphold the crown of the bracken-thatched roof high overhead, and on every side the shadows ran away into the dark. The people gathering about the fire—he supposed that they were all one family—were roughly clad, the men for the most part in the skins of wolf and red deer, the women in rough woollen cloth, as though they were less skilled in spinning and weaving than the women of the

South; but it seemed that they were prosperous in their way, and not cut off from the world, for among the pots in which the women were making ready the evening meal were some fine red Roman pottery; and the lord of the house himself, an immensely fat man clad in the skin of a wolf over his rough plaid breeks, had a necklace of yellow amber beads that shone here and there through the grey tangle of his beard. And when the woman of the house rose in her place, and brought the Guest Cup to the three strangers, it was an ox horn mounted in red Hibernian gold.

'It is good to have a stranger within the gates at Samhain,' said the woman, smiling.

'It is good to be the stranger who comes within such gates as these, at the day's end,' Flavius said, and took the cup, and drank, and gave it back to her.

There was much food and much drink, and the party waxed more and more uproarious as the heather-beer went round, and old stories were told and old songs chanted, for winter was the time for such things, and Samhain was the start of winter. But Justin noticed that through it all, the men kept a place empty among themselves, and no man touched the beer-cup that had been set before it.

Flavius it seemed had noticed it, too, for presently he turned to the lord of the house, and asked, 'Are you expecting another guest tonight?'

'Why should we be expecting another guest?'

'Because you keep his place for him.'

The fat man glanced in the direction he had indicated. '*Na*, how should you know, being as I think Romans? Samhain is the feast of home-coming; we bring the cattle safe home out of the wild weather until spring comes again, and should we deny a like shelter to the ghosts of our own dead? For them also it is home-coming for the winter, and we set their beer-cup by the hearth to bid them welcome. Therefore Samhain is also the feast of the dead. That place is for a son of mine that carried his spear after the Emperor Curoi, and died down yonder at Eburacum of the Eagles, seven summers ago.'

'Curoi!' Flavius said swiftly, and then, 'I beg you forgive me. I should not have asked.'

'Nay, he was a fool that he went at all,' said the old man grumblingly. 'I care not if he hears me say it now, for I said it to him at the time.' He took a long pull at the beer-pot and set it down, smacking his lips. Then he shook his head. 'Yet it was a waste, for he was the best hunter of all my sons. And now there is another Emperor in Britain after all.'

Justin had an odd sensation, as though all the blood in his body had leapt back to his heart; and suddenly everything seemed to go both still and slow. He shot one sideways glance at Flavius, and saw the hand that had been hanging relaxed across his knee clench slowly, very slowly, into a fist, and then relax again. Nothing else moved. Then Evicatos said, '*Sa*, that is news indeed. Is it the man they call Allectus?'

'Aye. Did you not know then?'

'We have been long away from men's tongues. How did it come about?'

'I will tell you as it was told me by a Hibernian merchant that was here yester night. It was the Sea Wolves that struck the blow. They slipped in past the ships of the Romans that were against them, in the mist and darkness, and ran their dragon keels ashore below Curoi's houseplace where Curoi was. They say that this Allectus gave them the signal, and was with him that night and opened the door to them; but that is a thing that matters little either way, for all men know who stands behind the Sea Wolves. They overcame his guards and slew them, and cried to Curoi to come out to them from his great chamber where he was; and he went out to them unarmed, and they cut him down on the threshold.' He ended his tale and reached again for his beer-pot, glancing sideways under his brows at the three strangers, as though half afraid that he had said too much.

Flavius said in a curious dead-level voice, 'Nay, we be none of us Allectus's men . . . When was this thing done?'

'Six nights since.'

'*Six nights?* Such news travels fast, but this must have had the wings of the wind. Surely it can be no more than some wild rumour?'

'Nay.' It was Evicatos who answered, with quiet certainty, his eyes on the lord of the house. 'It is no rumour. It is news that runs by the old ways that you and your people have forgotten.'

And something in his own heavy certainty made certainty for the other two also. No use, all this forced marching, Justin thought, no use pushing on. They were too late, after all. Too late. Suddenly he was seeing that lamplit room on the cliffs, just as he had seen it on a wild winter's night nearly a year ago with the logs burning on the hearth, and the great window looking toward Gesoriacum Light; and the terrible little Emperor who had held Britain and the seaways of Britain safe in a ruthless yet loving hand. He saw the red gleam of fire in the courtyard and heard the cries and the clash of weapons; and the voices shouting for Carausius. He saw the short, square-built figure walk out by the courtyard door, unarmed, to meet death. The drifting sea-mist gilded by the torches, and the fierce barbarian faces; men who were seamen even as the man who faced them was a seaman, and kin to him in blood. He saw the wide-lipped, contemptuous smile on the Emperor's face, and the flash of the saex blades as they cut him down . . .

But it was only a half-burned birch falling into the red heart of the fire; and the beer-jar was coming round again, and the talk had swung away from the change of Emperors to the prospects of the winter's hunting. A change of rulers, after all, meant little up here in the mountains. The deer were as fleet of foot and a cow carried her calf as many days, no matter who wore the Purple.

The three had no chance to speak to each other apart until far into the night, when, having been out to see that all was well with the ponies, they stood together in the thorn-closed doorway of the steading, looking away down the widening sweep of the dale towards the lopsided hunters' moon shaking clear of the dark fells.

Flavius was the first to break the silence. 'Six nights since. So it was already too late by a night and a day when we wrote that letter.' He looked round at the other two, and in the moonlight his eyes were like black holes in his face. 'But why should Allectus seek the help of the Painted People against the Emperor if he meant to murder him before their help could come? Why, why, why?'

'Maybe he did not mean it to happen so, when he sent his emissaries north,' Evicatos said. 'Then maybe Curoi began to suspect, and he dared wait no longer.'

Flavius said, 'If we could have made him believe us, back in the spring. If *only* we could have made him believe us!' And his voice was shaking. After a few moments he steadied it, and went on, 'Since Allectus has seized the Purple without aid of the Painted People, and will have, moreover, sundry other matters to attend to, it seems that at least for a while your people are saved, Evicatos of the Spear.'

'For a while, yes,' Evicatos said, smiling at the great spear on which he leaned. A little chill wind ruffled the swan's feathers, and Justin noticed how white they shone in the moonlight. 'Presently, in a few years, if Allectus still wears the Purple, the danger will come back; but nevertheless, for this while, my people are saved.'

'And therefore this is your trail no longer.'

Evicatos looked at him. 'This is my trail no longer. So I will go north again, in the morning, to my hounds that I left with Cuscrid the smith and my own hunting runs; yet taking care, I think, that men do not see me on the Wall again. And maybe I shall watch a little, and listen a little, among the heather . . . And you? What trail do you follow now?'

'Southward still,' Flavius said. 'There is one thing for us to do now—to make our way somehow across to Gaul, and thence to the Caesar Constantius.' He threw up his head. 'Maximian and Diocletian had no choice but to make peace with our little Emperor, but they'll not stomach his murderer in his place. Sooner or later they will send the Caesar Constantius to end the thing.'

Justin spoke for the first time, his eyes still on the wind-stirred swan's feathers about the neck of Evicatos's great war-spear. 'It is a strange thing—Carausius began to make of us something more and—and greater than a p-province among other provinces; and now, in the bare time that it takes to kill one man, that is undone, and all that we can hope for is that the Caesar Constantius will come and take back his own.'

'Better for Britain to take her chance with Rome than fall into ruin under Allectus's hand,' Flavius said.

IX
The Sign of the Dolphin

WINTER had come, and a snow-wind was blowing up through the bare trees of Spinaii Forest, when at last Justin and Flavius entered Calleva with the market-carts as soon as the gates were open one morning.

They had made for Calleva because in spite of having sold the ponies, in spite of having lived lean all those weary weeks on the trail south, they had not as much money left as they would certainly need to get them across to Gaul. 'I do not want to go to the farm,' Flavius had said some days before, when they talked the thing over. 'Servius would raise the money somehow, but it would take time, and already most of the shipping will be beached for the winter. No, we'll go to Aunt Honoria—with any luck she won't have gone to Aquae Sulis yet. She'll lend us what we need, and Servius can pay her back how and when he can. Besides, it is in my mind that once we get to Gaul it may be a long time before we get back, and so I would not go without saying farewell.'

Just inside the East Gate, by which they had entered, Flavius said, 'This is where we turn off,' and leaving the trundling and lowing stream of market traffic, they plunged away to the left through a fringe of shops, into the gardens of some big houses, quiet save for the little hushing wind in the winter dawn; and presently, with many garden hedges behind them, emerged close to the back quarters of a house rather smaller than the rest.

'Round here,' Flavius whispered. 'Lie up behind the wood stack and spy out the land. Don't want to run into any of the slaves and have to explain ourselves.'

They circled the dark huddle of out-buildings, and a little later were lying up in the lee of the brushwood pile, while before them, across the narrow courtyard of the slaves' quarters, the house gradually awoke. A light showed in a window. A voice sounded scoldingly, and as the light broadened into a bar of cold daffodil behind the roof ridge a stringy little woman with her head tied up in a crimson kerchief began sweeping the dust and small refuse of the kitchen out into the yard, humming softly to herself the while.

It was full daylight when an immensely fat woman with a saffron-coloured mantle drawn forward over her grey hair appeared from the house-doorway, and stood looking round her at the bleak morning. At sight of her, Flavius let out a soft breath of satisfaction. 'Ah, the Aunt is in residence.'

'Is that her?' Justin whispered. Somehow she was not what he expected.

Flavius shook his head, his face alight with laughter. 'That is Volumnia. But where Volumnia is, Aunt Honoria is also . . . Now if I can catch her attention.'

The enormously fat woman had waddled out into the courtyard to get a better view of the weather; and as she halted, Flavius picked up a pebble and tossed it towards her. She glanced towards the tiny sound, and as she did so, he whistled very softly, an odd, low-pitched call on two notes, at sound of which she started as though a horse-fly had stung her. Justin saw her stand a moment, staring towards their hiding-place. Then she came waddling towards them. Flavius slithered back, swift as a snake, and Justin followed him, so that they were well out of sight of the house when she came panting round the brushwood pile and found them.

She had both hands to her enormous bosom, and she was wheezing half under her breath as she came. 'Is it—is it yourself then, my Flavius, my dearie?'

Flavius said softly, 'Don't tell me anyone else has ever called you in just that way, Volumnia.'

'Nay—I knew it must be you the moment I heard it. Many's the time you've called to me like that, and you out when you should have been in your bed, and wishful to be let in quiet like. But oh, my honey, what are you doing here behind the wood-stack when we thought you was on the Wall? And you so ragged, and so lean as any wolf in a famine winter—and this other with you—and—'

'Volumnia dear,' Flavius cut her short, 'we want to speak with Aunt Honoria; can you get her for us? And Volumnia, we don't want anyone else to know.'

Volumnia sat down on a pile of logs and clasped her bosom as though it was trying to escape. 'Oh my dear, is it as bad as that?'

Flavius grinned at her. 'It isn't bad in the way you mean, at all. We haven't been stealing apples. But we do need to speak with my aunt—can you contrive it?'

'Why, as to the Lady Honoria, that's easily done. Do you go down to the arbour and wait there till I send her to you. But, my dearie dear, what *is* all this? Can't you tell your own Volumnia as used to bake you pastry-men, and saved you many and many a smacking when you was little?'

'Not now,' Flavius said. 'There isn't time. If you bide much longer round here we shall have one of the others coming to see that you haven't been carried off by the Sea Wolves. Aunt Honoria will tell you, I don't doubt. And Volumnia'—he laughed, and slid an arm round where her waist would have been if she had had one, and gave her a kiss—'that is for the pastry-men, and all those smackings that you saved me.'

'Get along with you,' wheezed Volumnia. She surged to her feet and stood an instant looking down at him and pulling her veil about her head. 'You're a bad boy, and you always were!' she said, 'and the gods alone know what you are up to this time. But I'll send My Lady down to the arbour to you.'

Justin, who had stood silent against the brushwood pile throughout, watched her waddle away, and heard her voice upraised distressfully from the house a few moments later. 'Something did ought to be done about those rats! There was one round by the woodpile just now; I heard it scuffling, and when I went to look, there it was—a big grey one, and sat up and stared at me so bold as a wolf—with all its teeth and whiskers—'

'We had one of that sort,' he said softly. 'My mother's old nurse. She was the best thing in my childhood, but she's d-dead now.'

A little later, working their way down through the dark tangle of privet and juniper that divided the garden from its neighbour, they had reached the arbour and settled themselves again to wait, seated very coldly on the grey marble bench within.

But they had not long to wait before they heard someone coming, and Flavius, peering through the screening ivy, said softly, 'It is her.'

Justin, doing the same, saw a woman muffled close in a mantle so deeply and brilliantly crimson that its colour seemed to warm the whole grey morning, coming across the grass from the house.

She came slowly, turning aside to look at this and that, as though she had no particular aim, only a stroll in the garden. And then she was round the tangle of bushes, shielded from sight of the house, and they rose to their feet as she appeared in the opening of the arbour.

A thin old woman with a proud beak of a nose and very bright eyes, brown and wrinkled as a walnut and painted like a dancing-girl—save that no dancing-girl would have put the paint on so badly. Yet even with the stibium smeared along her eyelids, and a valiant slash of mouth-paint sliding up towards one ear, she seemed to him more worth looking at than any other woman he had ever met, because her face was so much more alive.

She was looking from Flavius to him and back again, with her thin brows raised a little. 'I greet you, Great-Nephew Flavius.—And this? Who is this with you?' Her voice was husky, but clear-cut as a gem, and there was no surprise in it. Justin thought suddenly that she would never waste time in being surprised, whatever the emergency.

'Aunt Honoria, I salute you,' Flavius said. 'I think he's another great-nephew of yours—Justin. Tiberius Lucius Justinianus. I told you about him when I wrote to you from Rutupiae.'

'Ah yes, I know.' Great-Aunt Honoria turned to Justin, holding out a hand that felt dry and light in his when he took and bent over it. 'Yes, you have good manners, I am glad to see. I should intensely dislike to have an ill-mannered great-nephew.' She looked at him appraisingly. 'You must be Flavia's grandson. She married an extremely plain man, I remember.'

It was so obvious that she meant, though she did not say, 'That accounts for it,' that Justin felt himself reddening to the tips of his unfortunate ears. 'Yes, I—I am afraid she d-did,' he said ruefully, and became aware of the understanding and the glint of laughter in his great-aunt's eyes.

'Yes, that of course was very rude of me,' said Aunt Honoria. 'It's I who should be blushing, not you.' She turned back to Flavius, saying abruptly, 'Now what is it that brings you here when we all thought you were on the Wall?'

Flavius hesitated; Justin saw him hesitate, wondering just how much to tell her. Then, very briefly, he told her the whole story.

Halfway through it Aunt Honoria seated herself composedly on the grey marble bench, setting down beside her something folded in a napkin that she had been carrying under her mantle; otherwise she made neither sound nor movement from beginning to end. When it was finished, she gave a small decisive nod. 'So. I wondered whether it had to do with this most sudden change of Emperors. It is an ill story, all of it a very ill story . . . And now you would make your way overseas to join the Caesar Constantius.'

'There'll be a good few following that road in the next few months, I'm thinking,' Flavius said.

'So I suppose. These are evil days, and it is in my mind that they will grow more evil.' She looked up at him swiftly. 'And to join the Caesar Constantius you will need money, and so you come to me.'

Flavius grinned. 'We do need money. Also—once we get across the seas we may be gone a long time, therefore I come to take my leave, Aunt Honoria.'

Her face flashed up in a smile. 'I am honoured, my dear Flavius. We will deal with the money question first. Now see—it was in my mind, when Volumnia came to me a while since, that if you were in trouble you would need money; but I have not much ready money in the house. *So*—' She laid a small silken purse on top of the napkin-covered bundle, 'I bring you what I can for your immediate needs, and also, I have dressed for the occasion.'

As she spoke she unclasped first one and then the other of a pair of bracelets from her thin brown wrists, and held them out to Flavius; narrow golden bracelets set with opals in which the fires came and went, rose and green and peacock blue in the wintry light.

Flavius took them into his own hands, and stood looking down at her. 'Aunt Honoria, you're wonderful,' he said. 'We'll give you another pair one day.'

'No,' said Aunt Honoria. 'They are not a loan, they are a gift.' She rose to her feet and stood looking at them. 'If I were a man, and a young man, I should be taking your road. As it is, my trinkets must serve instead.'

Flavius made her a little unconscious bow. 'Thank you for your gift then, Aunt Honoria.'

Aunt Honoria made a swift gesture with her hands, as though to dismiss the whole thing. 'Now—Volumnia is heartstricken that we cannot bring you in and feast you; but short of that we have done what we can.' She touched the bundle in the napkin. 'Take it with you and eat on the road.'

'We will,' Flavius said. 'We will indeed; for we're both of us as empty as wine-skins after Saturnalia.'

'So. I think that is all that needs to be said; and now you must go. And in these ill and uncertain days, who shall say when you will come back—though indeed I believe with you that the Caesar Constantius will come one day. And so—the gods be with you, my nephew Flavius . . . and you—' She turned to Justin and most unexpectedly put up her hands and took his face between them, and looked at him again. 'You are not at all like your grandfather—I never liked him over much. You're a surgeon, Flavius tells me, and, I *think*, a good one. The gods be with you, too, my silent other nephew Justin.'

She dropped her hands, and drawing the glowing folds of her mantle once more close about her, turned and walked away.

The two lean and ragged young men stood in silence a moment, looking after her. Then Justin said, 'You never told me she was like that.'

'I think I had forgotten myself until just now. Or maybe I didn't know,' Flavius said.

They walked out of Calleva by the South Gate, broke their fast on the edge of the forest, and took the road south through the forest and over the downs to Venta. And the second day had scarcely turned towards evening when they trudged into Portus Adurni, and saw the massive grey ramparts of just such another fortress as Rutupiae standing four square among the marshes and the vast maze of winding water that made up Portus Magnus, the Great Harbour.

But it was not under the fortress walls that they were likely to find their transport across to Gaul; and they turned their steps towards the poorer part of the town, where mean wine-shops mingled with fish-drying sheds, and the hovels of seafaring folk straggled out along the low shore, and the craft drawn up along the tide-line were all kinds from small trading-vessels to native dug-out canoes.

That evening they got into conversation with several owners of small, hopeful-looking vessels on the pretext of looking for a kinsman who they thought was in the wine trade in those parts. But everybody seemed either to have just laid up for the winter or to be just going to do so, while one little slim sea-captain with a blue faience drop in one ear showed signs of knowing someone of the name that Flavius had invented for the kinsman, which might have been awkward if Flavius had not thought to ask what colour the man's hair was, and on being told red, said that in that case it could not be the same one because his kinsman was as bald as an egg. And they were no further forward with their plans when, in the winter dusk, cold, tired, and hungry, and both of them feeling rather more desperate than they dared to admit, they found themselves close by a wine-shop on the foreshore. It was a wine-shop like any other—and there were many in Portus Adurni—but daubed on a rough piece of board over the doorway was something green, with an arched back and a round rolling eye at sight of which Flavius said with a spurt of weary laughter, 'Look, it's the family dolphin! This is the place for us!'

The wind was rising, swinging the lantern before the doorway to and fro so that the painted dolphin seemed to dive and leap, and the shadows about the threshold ran like wild things. And in the confusion of wind and dusk and lantern-light, neither of them saw the little man with the blue faience ear-drop strolling by, who turned after they had gone in, and slipped away into the deepening shadows.

They found themselves in a place that would be a small open courtyard in summer, roofed in now with what looked like an old striped sail or ship's awning spread above the bare vine-trellis. A charcoal brazier glowed red at either end of the place, and though it was yet early, a good many men were gathered about them or lounging at the small tables round the walls, eating, drinking, or dicing. The babel of voices and the beat of the wind in the striped awning, the warmth of the braziers and the smell of broiling meat and crowding humanity made the whole place seem so bulging full that Justin thought the walls must be straining apart at the seams, like a garment too tight for the person inside it.

They found a corner well out of the way, gave their order for supper to a big man with the stamp of the legions clear upon him—half the wine-shops in the Empire, Justin thought, were kept by ex-legionaries—and settled down, stretching out their weary legs and slackening their belts.

Looking about them as they waited, Justin saw that the customers were for the most part seafarers of some sort, and a few traders, while about the nearest brazier a knot of Marines from the Fleet were playing dice. Then the master of the place dumped a bowl of steaming stew between Justin and Flavius, with a platter of little loaves and a jug of watered wine. And for a while they were too busy eating to spend much more attention on their surroundings.

But they had got over their first hunger when a newcomer ambled in through the foreshore doorway.

There had been a good deal of coming and going all the while, but this man was of a different kind from the others, and after one casual glance Justin put him down as a government clerk or maybe a small tax-gatherer. He hesitated, glancing about the crowded place, then came drifting in their direction; and a few moments later was standing beside them in their corner. 'The Dolphin is very full tonight. Will you allow me to join you? It seems that there is—ahem—nowhere else.'

'Sit, and welcome,' Justin said, and moved to make room on the narrow horseshoe bench, and the man seated himself with a grunt of satisfaction, crooking a finger for the shopkeeper.

He was a small man, not fat exactly, but flabby, running to paunch, as though he ate too much and too quickly and didn't take enough exercise. 'My usual cup of wine—your best wine,' he said to the shopkeeper; and then, as the man went to fetch it, turned to the other two with a smile. 'The best wine here is very good indeed. That is why I come. It is—ahem—scarcely the kind of place I should frequent otherwise.' The smile puckered his plump, clean-shaven face rather pleasantly, and Justin saw with sudden liking that he had the eyes of a small, contented child.

'You come here often?' Flavius asked, clearly trying to shake off his depression and be friendly.

'No, no, just sometimes, when I am in Portus Adurni. My—ahem—my work takes me about a good deal.'

Flavius pointed to the wrought-iron pen-case and inkhorn that hung at the man's girdle. 'And your work is—that?'

'Not altogether, no. I was a government clerk at one time; now I have various interests. Oh yes indeed.' The wide, quiet gaze wandered from Justin to Flavius and back again. 'I buy a little here and sell a little there, and I play an—ahem—a small but I trust useful part in the handling of the Corn Tax.' He took up the wine cup which the master of the place had just set down at his elbow. 'Your health.'

Flavius raised his own cup, smiling, and echoed the toast, followed by Justin.

'And you?' said the little tax-gatherer. 'I think I have not seen you here before?'

'Nay, we come seeking a kinsman who was to have settled

hereabouts, but it is in my mind that he must have moved on after all, for we can get no word of him.'

'So?—What is his name? Maybe I can help you.'

'Crispinius. He's in the wine trade,' said Flavius, keeping the question of his kinsman's hair in case it should be needed.

But the other shook his head regretfully. 'Nay, I fear I cannot call to mind anyone of that name.' His gaze seemed caught and held a moment by Flavius's left hand as it curved about his wine-cup on the table; and Justin, glancing the same way, saw that it was the signet ring with the intaglio dolphin that had caught his interest. Flavius became aware of it at the same instant, and drew his hand back on to his knee under the table. But already the little tax-gatherer's gaze had drifted away to the knot of Marines round the brazier, who had wearied of dice and betaken themselves to loud-voiced argument.

'What's the odds?' a long, lean man with the white seam of an old sword-cut on his forehead was demanding. 'Any man who gives me free wine to drink his health in and a fistful of sesterces can be Emperor for all I care.' He spat juicily into the brazier. 'Ah, but it had better be a big fistful this time, and it had better come quick.'

'Trouble is there's a sight too many Emperors all at the same time,' said a sad-looking individual in the sea-green tunic of the scouting galleys. 'And maybe the other two aren't going to like the Divine Allectus in the Purple. How if we have the Caesar Constantius a-top of us one of these fine days?'

The first man took another drink, and wiped his mouth with the back of his hand. 'The Caesar Constantius has got plenty to keep him happy where he is. Every fool knows the tribes are heaving like a maggoty cheese along the Rhenus defences.'

'Maybe you're right at that, and maybe you're wrong,' said the pessimist darkly. 'I've served under that lad, and despite his wey face he's the best soldier in this tired old Empire, and I'd not put it past him to settle the Germans yet, and then come settle *us*.'

'Let him come then!' roared the man with the sword-cut in sudden defiance. 'Let him come; that's all *I* say! We settled the Emperor Maximian when he tried that game, and I reckon we can settle his pup if need be!' He teetered backwards, recovered himself with a slight stagger, and crooked a finger for the shopkeeper. 'Hi! Ulpius, more wine.'

'When we settled the Emperor Maximian we had a whole heart

and a whole belly in the business.' It was a third man who spoke, with a savagery that somehow jarred like the clash of weapons in that crowded place. 'We haven't, now.'

'Speak for your own belly,' somebody said, and there was a general laugh.

'So I will then—I'm sick of all these brave doings, to the pit of my own belly!'

The man with the scarred forehead, his wine-cup refilled, swung round on him. 'You shouted loud enough with the rest of us when we swore allegiance to the new Emperor a while back.'

'Aye, I shouted loud enough with the rest of you curs. I swore my allegiance; by Jupiter I did, by Thundering Jove I did! And how much do you suppose my oath is worth if it comes to that? How much is *yours* worth, my friend?' He wagged a finger in the other's face, his eyes brilliant in the light of the swinging lantern. One of the other men tried to silence him, but he only raised his voice a little higher. 'If I were Allectus I wouldn't trust us a pilum's length, I wouldn't, Legion or Fleet, lest we shout for another Emperor tomorrow.—And what sort of use is an army and a fleet that you can't trust a pilum's length when it comes to fighting? Just about as much use as an Emperor you can't trust a pilum's length either!'

'Be quiet, you fool!' The wine shopkeeper had joined the group. 'You're too drunk to know what you're saying. Go back to barracks and sleep it off.'

'Yes, you want to get rid of me—you're afraid I'll get your wretched little dog-hole of a wine-shop into trouble.' The man's voice rose in reckless mockery. 'Phuh! What a country! Anybody give me a nice dark corner below decks in a ship making the crossing, and I'll go further than back to barracks—I'll be off to Gaul tonight, and never once look back. Meanwhile I'll have another cup of wine.'

'You will not,' said the shopkeeper. 'You'll go back to barracks, and you'll go now.'

By this time the silence that had laid hold of the rest of the company was breaking up into an ugly splurge of voices, and men were on their feet, moving in on the group. A wine-cup fell with a clatter and rolled across the floor; and Justin, who had been listening with an almost painful attention to what went forward, for it was the first time that he had heard the Legion themselves on the change of Emperors, suddenly realized that the little tax-gatherer was leaning towards them with a murmured 'Best, I think, to get out of here.'

Flavius said uncompromisingly, 'Why?'

'Because,' said the tax-gatherer, 'the man nearest to the door has slipped out. At almost any moment now there is going to be trouble—and trouble spreads.' He smiled apologetically behind a plump hand. 'It is never wise to get mixed up in such things if one has oneself—ahem—anything that one does not wish the Watch to know.'

X

The *Berenice* Sails for Gaul

JUSTIN'S eyes flew to the man's face, then to his cousin's. Flavius had turned a little and was looking at their new acquaintance with a startled frown; then he got up without a word, felt in his belt, and laid some money on the table.

Justin rose also, his hand going instinctively to his instrument-case in the shoulder-sling that he had made for it. Their eyes met, questioningly, then Flavius gave a suspicion of a shrug, and turned towards the door on to the foreshore. But the little tax-gatherer shook his head. 'No, no, no, this way—much better,' and opened another door close beside them but so lost in shadows that they had not noticed it before. They followed him through, hearing behind them a sudden bellow of rage and the crash of a table going over. Then Justin let the ramshackle door close softly, and the swelling uproar fell away behind it.

They were in a passage-way of some sort, and a few moments later, another door closing behind them, they emerged into a narrow street with the harbour glimmering at one end of it; a street dark and empty, quiet save for the wind that fretted the garbage to and fro.

'And now,' Flavius demanded in a swift undertone, standing stock still in the deserted roadway, 'what makes you think that we have anything we would not wish the Watch to know?'

'My dear young man,' said their companion reasonably, 'do you think that the open street is quite the place to discuss that?'

'Where shall we discuss it, then?'

'I was about—ahem—to ask you to come home with me.'

There was a moment's surprised silence, and then Flavius asked, 'Can you give us any good reason why, supposing that we *had* something to hide, we should trust you?'

'No, I fear I cannot. It is most awkward—most awkward; but I assure you that you may.' The little man sounded so genuinely bothered that somehow they found themselves believing him.

Flavius said with a sudden breath of laughter, 'Well, of course, if you say so—'

They moved off up the street, the plump little tax-gatherer trotting in front, muffled so close in his cloak that Justin thought he looked like an enormous pale cocoon. Were they being complete fools? he wondered. No, somehow he was sure that they were not: this odd little man was to be trusted. Then, as they passed a narrow lane leading down to the foreshore, the wind swooping up it brought the quick tramp of mailed sandals as a patrol of the Watch hurried by in the direction of the wine-shop they had so lately left; and he said urgently, 'There they go. Isn't there anything we can do about that poor fool? It's d-dreadful to just abandon him.'

The cocoon looked over its plump shoulder as it scurried. 'Abandon him? Oh dear me, we haven't abandoned him. No need to worry. No, no; no need at all,' and dived into another dark alleyway.

Justin had lost all sense of direction by the time they came up a gash of a blind alley, and found at the end of it a door in a high wall. 'I ask your forgiveness for bringing you in the back way,' said the tax-gatherer, opening it. 'I generally come in this way myself because it isn't overlooked. My neighbours are, I fear, rather prone to—ahem—overlooking.' And so saying he led them through into a narrow courtyard.

It was not a dark night, and there was enough light in the courtyard, with its lime-washed walls, to show them the raised well-head in the centre, and the small tree growing beside it. The cocoon said bashfully, 'I call this my garden. It is just the one apple-tree, but it is the best little apple-tree in the Empire. There's something about an apple-tree that—ahem—to my mind no other tree possesses; "The apple-tree, the singing, and the gold"—you know your Euripides?'

Still burbling gently, he led the way across to a door on the far side, and opening it, ushered them through into a darkness that smelled pleasantly warm and lived in, with a suggestion of the last meal about it. 'Home again. I always like to get home at the day's end. This is the kitchen, if you will just come through here into my living-room.—Ah, Myron has left a nice bit of fire in the brazier; very nice, very nice indeed.' He was bustling about like a house-proud hen as he spoke, kindling a twig at the low red glow of the charcoal, lighting the lamp, putting fresh logs on the brazier. And as the light strengthened, Justin saw that they were in a small, cheerful room, with bands of colour on the walls, piles of gay native rugs on the two low couches by the fire, and a set of household gods in brightly painted plaster standing in niches round the walls. It was all so ordinary, so far away from the wild journey south and the scene in the wine-shop, that suddenly he wanted to laugh, and wasn't sure why. 'We shall not be disturbed,' said their host, testing the shutter over a high window to make sure that there was no chink. 'I don't keep slaves, I like to be quite free; and Myron goes out in the evenings.'

Flavius, standing in the middle of the floor, his feet a little apart and his hands behind his back, said: 'And now that we are no longer in the open street, will you tell us what lies behind all this?'

'Ah yes, you asked what made me think that you had anything to hide.' The little man held his fingers to the warmth. 'It is—ahem—difficult to explain. A good friend of mine, whom you spoke to on the foreshore this evening, was not quite sure that you were what you seemed. You—if I may say so—should try to slouch rather more. The Legionary carriage does not—ahem—altogether go with the rest of your appearance. He saw you into the Dolphin, and then came and reported to me. So I went down to the Dolphin, to see for myself, feeling that you might be in trouble. And then of course I could scarcely help noticing that ring, which is also—ahem—somewhat out of keeping.'

'And then you made up your mind, with no more than that to go on?'

'Oh, no, no, I was not sure until I suggested to you that it would be as well to come away if one had anything to hide—and you came.'

Flavius looked at him blankly. 'Oh, yes, it sounds quite simple when you put it like that.'

'Quite,' said their host. 'Now tell me what I can do for you.'

Justin's desire to laugh returned to him. Because he was so tired, his laughter did not seem under very good control, and nor did his legs. 'May I—may I sit down?' he asked.

The plump face of his host was instantly distressful. 'Of course; why, of course! What am I thinking of, that I leave my guests standing? See now, sit here, close to the brazier.' With the little man fussing round him like a hen, Justin smiled gratefully, and folded up on to the foot of the couch, holding out his hands to the warmth.

Flavius shook his head impatiently, and remained standing. He was frowning into the fire where the little new flames were beginning to lick up round the logs. Suddenly his brows quirked up to their most fly-away, and he laughed. 'Well, we have got to put our lives into somebody's hands, or we shall get no further until the Greek Calends. We want to get across to Gaul.'

'Ah, I thought it might be that.'

'Can you do anything about it, beyond thinking?'

'I—ahem—have arranged something of the kind before now.' The little tax-gatherer sat himself down, and fixed his wide, serene gaze on Flavius's face. 'But first I should require to know something more of your reasons. You must forgive me, but I dislike handling unknown cargoes.'

'Could you be sure of knowing more, however much we told you? We could tell you a string of lies.'

'You could try,' said their host limpidly.

Flavius looked at him very hard for a moment. Then he told him the whole story, much as he had told it yesterday to Great-Aunt Honoria.

When he had finished, the little man nodded. 'Under the circumstances your desire for foreign travel seems most reasonable. *Most* reasonable. Yes, I think we can help you, but it may not be for a few days yet. There are certain arrangements to be made, you see, arrangements and—ahem—and so on.'

'As to payment—' Flavius began.

'Oh, it isn't a matter of payment—no, no, no,' said their host cosily. 'In this kind of business, men who need buying are too dear at any price.'

There was a little silence, and then Flavius said, 'I ask your pardon.'

'No need, not the least need in the world, my dear young man. Now, as to present plans—you will of course accept my hospitality for the next few days. Though indeed I fear that the only quarters I can offer you are somewhat close and primitive. You will understand that I cannot safely keep you in the house.' He smiled apologetically, and rose to his feet. 'In fact, if you will not mind, I will take you to your quarters now. There may be work for me later in connection with—ahem—our rash friend of the Dolphin; and I should like to see you safely bestowed before I go forth again.'

'We are under your orders,' Flavius said, with a smile.

Back they went across the kitchen, and into what seemed to be a storeroom beyond. They heard the little tax-gatherer moving boxes and baskets in the darkness, and sensed rather than saw, that a hole had opened in the opposite wall. 'Through here. There was a larger door once, filled in long ago. I—er—adapted it, oh quite a while since. Mind your heads.'

The warning seemed scarcely necessary, as the hole was about half man high, and they followed him through on all fours. Beyond the hole there was a steep and much-worn flight of steps leading up into the darkness, and at the head of it a space of some kind smelling strongly of dust and mildew.

'What is this place?' Flavius said.

'It is part of the old theatre. Alas, no one ever thinks of going to a play now, and there are no more actors left; and the place has become a veritable slum since it fell from its original use, and the populace moved in.' Their host was panting slightly from the stairs. 'I fear I cannot give you a light; there are too many chinks for it to shine through. But there are plenty of rugs here in the corner—clean and dry—yes, yes: and I suggest that you go to sleep. When there is nothing else to do, go to sleep; it passes the time.'

They heard him pause at the stairhead. 'I shall be back in the morning. Oh, there are some loose boards in the wall just to the right of the stairway here: I would suggest that you do not take them out and crawl through to see what is on the other side. The floor is quite rotten beyond them, and if you go through it, you will not only break your own necks, but—ahem—betray this very useful little hiding-place of mine.'

They heard his footsteps on the steep stair, and then the baskets and boxes being stacked over the entrance hole again.

They did not discuss the situation when they were alone; somehow there did not really seem anything to say; and they were too blind weary to say it, even if there had been. They simply took their host's advice, and groping their way over to the pile of rugs in the corner, crawled in and fell asleep like a couple of tired dogs.

Justin woke with a crash to find the first greyness of the morning filtering in through a chink of a window high above his head, and the sound of footsteps on the stair, and for a moment he could not remember where he was. Then he tumbled out after Flavius from among the rugs, shaking the sleep out of his eyes, as their host loomed into the doorway.

'I do trust I did not disturb you,' he said, ambling forward to set something he was carrying on the bench below the window. 'I have brought you your morning meal—only bread and cheese and eggs, I am afraid.' He gave that little apologetic cough that they were coming to know. 'Also my library, to help you pass the time; just the first roll of my "Hippolytus", you know.—I think I mentioned Euripides to you last night; and I fancied from your manner that neither of you had read him . . . I always think one values a thing more if one has had to make—ahem—a certain amount of sacrifice for it. The "Hippolytus" cost me a great many meals and visits to the Games when I was one of Carausius's Under-Secretaries, and—ahem—not over well paid. I know that I need not ask you to treat it gently.'

'Thank you for trusting it to us,' Justin said.

And at the same instant Flavius said quickly, 'You were one of Carausius's Secretaries, then?'

'Yes—oh, a long time ago, when he was first—ahem—raised to the Purple. Quite a temporary measure, but it suited both of us at the time.'

Flavius nodded, and asked after a moment, 'What happened to that fool at the Dolphin?'

'Our rash friend? We—er—picked him up before the Watch Patrol could do so, the wine shopkeeper being somewhat of a friend of mine—which was as well for him; Allectus does not encourage wild talk of that kind.' They heard him smile. 'Our friend is a sober and a very scared man this morning, and more than ever eager to be away to Gaul.'

'Where is he now?' Flavius asked.

'Quite safe. There are more hiding-places than one in Portus Adurni; so we did not put him in here. You have all you want? Until this evening, then.'

They were very hungry, and they cleared the food to the last crumb, while slowly the daylight grew, and around and below them Portus Adurni woke to life. The cold light filtering in through the chink of window showed them that they were in a narrow slip of a room, whose sloping rafters, high on the side where the window was, came down on the other side almost to the level of the uneven floor. And when they investigated, they found that from the window, by standing on the bench to reach it, they could look down through the withering leaves of a creeper into the trim, lime-washed courtyard where grew the best little apple-tree in the Empire. And by lying on the floor opposite, and shutting one eye to squint down through the gap where some tiles had fallen, they could catch a glimpse of the old, elegant ruins of the theatre, and the squalid turf roofs of the slum bothies that had come crowding in among the fallen columns.

They seemed perched between two worlds; and the odd-shaped chamber was as fantastic as its situation, derelict, half ruined, the uneven planks of the floor blotched with livid fungus where the rain had beaten in, the corners grey with cobwebs that hung down, swaying in the wind that rustled the dead creeper leaves to and fro along the floor. Yet with one wall still showing traces of the frescoes it had once worn, faded ghosts of garlands hanging on the painted columns that had long since flaked away, even a little Eros hovering on azure wings.

Justin spent that day in trying to read Euripides, mainly because he felt that if he lent someone a thing that he loved as their plump host loved his Euripides, and they did not use it, he should be hurt. But he made poor progress with it. He had always hated and feared being shut up in any place from which he could not get out at will—that was from the day when the wine-shed door had swung to on him, when he was very small, and held him prisoner in the dark for many hours before anyone heard him. Last night he had been so drugged with weariness that nothing could have come between him and sleep. But now his consciousness of being caged in the narrow secret chamber, as surely as though the piled baskets over the entrance hole were a locked door, came between him and the story of Hippolytus, and took all the power and the beauty out of what he read.

At evening their host returned, and remarked that as it was now dark and they were not likely to be disturbed, it might be, that they would give him the pleasure of their company at supper. And after that, each night save once, when their supper was brought to them early by a boy with a sharply eager face and two front teeth missing, who introduced himself as 'Myron that saw to everything', they supped with the tax-gatherer behind closed shutters in the little house that backed on to the wall of the old theatre.

Those winter evenings in the bright commonplace room, with Paulinus, as they found their host to be called, were completely unreal, but very pleasant. And for Justin they were a respite from the cage.

For the small secret chamber was increasingly hard to bear. He began to be always listening, listening for voices in the courtyard and blows against the house door; even at night, when Flavius slept quietly with his head on his arm, he lay awake, staring with hot eyes into the darkness, listening, feeling the walls closing in on him like a trap . . .

The only thing that made it bearable was knowing that one day quite soon—surely very soon now—Gaul lay at the end of it, like daylight and familiar things at the end of a strange dark tunnel.

And then at last, on the fifth evening, when they were gathered as usual in the pleasant room behind its closed shutters, Paulinus said, 'Well now, I am happy to tell you that moon and the tide both serving, everything is settled for your journey.'

They seemed to have waited for it so long that just at first it did not sink in. Then Flavius said, 'When do we go?'

'Tonight. When we have eaten we shall walk out of here, and at a certain place we shall take up our friend of the Dolphin. The *Berenice*, bound for Gaul with a cargo of wool, will be waiting for us two miles westward along the coast, at moonset.'

'So simple as that,' Flavius said, with a smile. 'We are very grateful, Paulinus. There doesn't seem much that we can say, beyond that.'

'Hum?' Paulinus picked up a little loaf from the bowl at the table, looked at it as though he had never seen such a thing before, and put it back again. 'There is—ahem—a thing that I should very much like to ask you.'

'If there is a thing—anything—that we can do, we will,' Flavius said.

'Anything? Will you, both of you—for I think that you count as one in this—let the *Berenice* sail for Gaul with only our friend of the Dolphin on board?'

For a moment Justin did not believe that he had really heard the words; then he heard Flavius say, 'You mean—stay behind, here in Britain? But why?'

'To work with me,' Paulinus said.

'*Us*. But Roma Dea! what use should we be?'

'I think that you would have your uses,' Paulinus said. 'I have taken my time, to be sure, and it is because of that that I can leave you so little time to decide . . . I need someone who can take command if anything happens to me. There are none of those linked with me in this—ahem—business whom I feel could do that.' He was smiling into the red glow of the brazier. 'We are doing really very good business. We have sent more than one hunted man out of Britain in these past few weeks; we can send word out of the enemy camp of such things as Rome needs to know; and when the Caesar Constantius comes, as I believe most assuredly he will, we may have our uses as—ahem—a friend within the gates. It would be sad if all that went down the wind because one man died and there was no one to come after him.'

To Justin, staring at the flame of the lamp, it seemed bitterly hard. Gaul was so near now, so very near, and the clean daylight and familiar things; and this little fat man was asking him to turn back into the dark. The silence lengthened, began to drag. Far off in the night-time hush he heard the beat of mailed sandals coming up the street, nearer, nearer: the Watch patrol coming by. Every evening at about this time it came; and every evening at its coming, something tightened in his stomach. It tightened now, the whole bright room seemed to tighten, and he was aware, without looking at them, of the same tension in the other two—tightening and tightening and then going out of them like a sigh, as the marching feet passed by without a check. And it would always be like that, always, day and night; the hand that might fall on one's shoulder at any moment, the footsteps that might come up the street—and stop. And he couldn't face it.

He heard Flavius saying, 'Look for somebody else, sir; somebody better suited to the task. Justin is a surgeon and I am a soldier; we have our worth in our own world. We haven't the right kind of make-up for this business of yours. We haven't the right kind of courage, if you like that better.'

'I judge otherwise,' Paulinus said; and then, after a little pause, 'It is in my mind that when the Caesar Constantius comes, you may be of greater worth in this business than you would had you gone back to the Legions.'

'Judge? How can you judge?' Flavius said desperately. 'You have talked with us a little, on four or five evenings. No more.'

'I have—ahem—something of a knack in such things. I find I am very seldom mistaken in my judgements.'

Justin shook his head, miserably. 'I'm sorry.'

And Flavius's voice cut across his in the same instant. 'It's no good, sir. We—must go.'

The tax-gatherer made a small gesture with both hands, as one accepting defeat; but his plump pink face lost none of its kindliness. 'I also am sorry . . . Nay then, think no more of it; it was unfair to put you to such a choice. Now eat; see now, time passes, and you must eat before you go.'

But to Justin, at all events, the food which should have had the taste of freedom in it tasted like ashes, and every mouthful stuck in his throat and nearly choked him.

Some two hours later they were standing, Justin and Flavius, the tax-gatherer and the Marine from the Dolphin, on the edge of a clump of wind-twisted thorn-trees, their faces turned seaward towards the small vessel that was nosing in under oars. The moon was almost down, but the water was still bright beyond the darkness of the sand dunes; and the little bitter wind came soughing across the dark miles of the marshes and low coast-wise grasslands, making a faint Aeolian hum through the bare and twisted branches of the thorn-trees. A gleam of light pricked out low down on the vessel's hull, marigold light in a world of black and silver and smoky grey; and the tension of waiting snapped in all of them.

'Ah, it is the *Berenice*, safe enough,' said Paulinus.

And the time for going was upon them.

The Marine, who had been subdued and completely silent since they took him up at the agreed meeting-place, turned for a moment, saying ruefully, 'I know not why you should have taken so great pains on my account; but I'm grateful. I—I don't know what to say—'

'Then don't waste time trying to say it. Get along, man. Now get along, do,' said Paulinus.

'Thank you, sir.' The other flung up his hand in leave-taking, and, turning, strode away down the shore.

Flavius said abruptly, 'May I ask you something, sir?'

'If you ask it quickly.'

'Do you do this for adventure?'

'Adventure?' Paulinus sounded quite scandalized in the darkness. 'Oh dear me, no, no, no! I'm not at all the adventurous kind; too—ahem—much too timid, for one thing. Now go quickly; you must not keep your transport waiting, with the tide already on the turn.'

'No. Goodbye, then, sir; and thank you again.'

Justin, a hand on his instrument-case, as usual, murmured something that sounded completely unintelligible, even in his own ears, and turned in behind Flavius, setting his face down to the shore.

They overtook the Marine from the Dolphin, and together made their way down between the sand dunes to the smooth, wave-patterned beach below. The boat was waiting, quiet as a sea-bird at rest. At the water's edge, Justin checked, and looked back. He knew that he was lost if he looked back, yet he could not help himself. In the very last of the moonlight he saw the stout little figure of Paulinus standing solitary among the thorn-trees, with all the emptiness of the marshes behind him.

'Flavius,' he said desperately, 'I am not going.'

There was a little pause, and then Flavius said, 'No, nor I, of course.' Then, with a breath of a laugh, 'Did not Paulinus say that we counted as one in this?'

The Marine from the Dolphin, already foot-wet, looked back. 'Best hurry.'

'Look,' said Flavius. 'It is all right. We are not coming. Tell them on board that the other two are not coming. I think they'll understand.'

'Well, it's your own affair—' began the other.

'Yes, it's our own affair. Good luck, and—best hurry.' Flavius echoed him his own words.

In the silence the tide made small, stealthy noises around their feet. They watched him take to the water, wading deeper and deeper until he was almost out of his depth as he reached the waiting vessel. They saw by the light of the lantern that he had been pulled on board. Then the lantern was quenched, and in complete silence the sails were set and the little vessel gathered way and slipped seaward, like a ghost.

Justin was suddenly very much aware of the lap and hush of the ebbing tide, and the wind-haunted, empty darkness of the marshes behind him. He felt very small and defenceless, and rather cold in the pit of his stomach. They could have been slipping out to sea now, he and Flavius; by dawn they could have been at Gesoriacum; back once more to the daylight and the life they knew, and the fellowship of their own kind. And instead . . .

Flavius shifted abruptly beside him, and they turned without a word and went trudging back through the soft dune-sand towards the figure waiting by the thorn-trees.

XI
The Shadow

THEY handed one of Great-Aunt Honoria's opal bracelets over to Paulinus for use, as it might be needed. They would have given him both, but he bade them keep the other against a rainy day; and Flavius took off the battered signet ring which was out of keeping with the sort of characters that they would be henceforth, and hung it on a thong round his neck, inside his tunic. And a night or two later, Justin asked Paulinus for leave to write to his father. 'If I might write, once, to warn him that he will hear no more of me for a while.—I will g-give you the letter to read, that you may be sure I have betrayed nothing.'

Paulinus considered a moment, and then gave a brisk nod. 'Yes, there is wisdom in that; it may well save—ahem—awkward enquiries.'

So Justin wrote his letter, and found it unexpectedly hard to do. He knew that it might quite likely be the last letter that ever he would write to his father, and so there were many things that he wanted to say. But he did not know how to say them. 'If it should come to your ears that I left my post at Magnis,' he wrote finally, after the bare warning, 'and if that, and this letter, should be the last that ever you hear of me, please do not be ashamed of me, father. I have done nothing to be ashamed of, I swear it.' And that was almost all.

He gave the open tablet to Paulinus, according to his word, and Paulinus cast one vague glance in its direction and handed it back to him. And in due course it went off by a certain trader making the crossing in the dark; and Justin, feeling as though he had cut the last strand that held him to familiar things, turned himself, with Flavius, full face to this other, stranger life in which they found themselves.

A strange life it proved to be, and full of strangely assorted company. There was Cerdic the boat-builder, and the boy Myron who had originally been caught by Paulinus trying to steal his purse; and Phaedrus of the *Berenice*, with his blue faience ear-drop; there was a government clerk in the Corn Office at Regnum, and an old woman who sold flowers outside the temple of Mars Toutate at Clausentium, and many others. They were linked together by nothing more definite than a snatch of tune whistled in the dark, or a sprig of common rye-grass tucked into a brooch or girdle-knot. Many of them, even those who lived in Portus Adurni, did not know the secret of the hole behind the lumber in Paulinus's store-room, nor that other way—'the Sparrow's Way' Paulinus called it when he showed it to Justin and Flavius—that started behind a low wall near the main entrance to the old theatre, and ended at those loose boards in the wall of the room where the painted Eros was. Yet in their odd way they were a brotherhood, none the less.

Justin and Flavius lodged with Cerdic the boat-builder, earning their living at any kind of job that they could pick up around the town and the repair yards. That is, they did so when they were at Portus Adurni; but often, that winter, they were at Regnum, at Venta, at Clausentium. Justin, though not Flavius, who would have been too easily recognized even in his present guise, pushed as far north as Calleva more than once. Five great roads met at Calleva, and the Cohorts of the Eagles were forever passing and re-passing through the transit camp outside the walls; and in all the province of Britain there could have been no better place for keeping one's eyes and ears open.

Winter wore away, and Paulinus's apple-tree was in bud. And upward of a score of men had been sent safely overseas; men who came to the Dolphin or to one or other of the meeting-places, wearing a sprig of rye-grass somewhere about themselves, saying, 'One sent me.'

Spring turned to summer, and the best apple-tree in the Empire shed its pink-tipped petals into the dark water of the courtyard well. And from his chief city of Londinium, the Emperor Allectus was making his hand felt. Those corn and land taxes, heavy but just in Carausius's day, which men had expected would be lightened under Allectus, became heavier than ever, and were levied without mercy for the Emperor's private gain. And before midsummer news was running from end to end of Britain that Allectus was bringing in Saxon and Frankish Mercenaries, bringing in the brothers of the Sea Wolves, to hold his kingdom down for him. Britain was betrayed indeed! Men said little—it was dangerous to say much—but they looked at each other with hot and angry eyes; and the trickle of those who brought their sprig of rye-grass to the Dolphin increased as the weeks went by.

The first time Portus Adurni saw anything of the hated Mercenaries was on a day in July when Allectus himself came to inspect the troops and defences of the great fortress.

All the town of Adurni turned out to throng the broad, paved street to the Praetorium Gate, drawn by curiosity and the exciting prospect of seeing an Emperor, even an Emperor they were coming to hate, and by the fear of Imperial displeasure if they did not make enough show of rejoicing.

Justin and Flavius had found good places for themselves right against the steps of the little temple of Jupiter, where the Emperor was to sacrifice before entering the fortress. In the July sunlight the heat danced like a cloud of midges above the heads of the crowd—a great crowd—all in their best clothes and brightest colours. The shops had hung out rich stuffs and gilded branches for a sign of rejoicing, and the columns of the temple were wreathed with garlands of oak and meadow-sweet, whose foam of blossom, already beginning to wilt, mingled its honey sweetness with the tang of garden marigolds and the sour smell that rose from the close-packed crowd. But over the whole scene, despite the festival garments, the bright colours and the garlands, there was a joylessness that made it all hollow.

The two cousins were close against the Legionaries on street-lining duty; so close to the young Centurion in charge that when he turned his head they could hear the crimson horsehairs of his helmet-crest rasp against his mailed shoulders. He was a dark, raw-boned lad with a jutting galley-prow of a nose, and a wide, uncompromising mouth; and for some reason, perhaps because he was someone very much of their own kind, Justin took particular note of him.

But now, far off up the Venta road, a stir arose, and expectancy rippled through the crowd before the temple. Nearer and nearer, a slow, hoarse swell of sound rolled towards them like a wave. All heads were turned one way. Justin, crushed against a particularly craggy Legionary, with a fat woman breathing down his neck, saw the cavalcade in the distance, swelling larger and clearer moment by moment. Saw the tall, gracious figure of the new Emperor riding in the van, with his ministers and staff about him, and the Senior Officers of the fortress garrison; and, behind him, the Saxons of his bodyguard.

Allectus the Traitor was within a few feet of them now, riding up between the swaying crowd; a still, white man, whose eyes and skin seemed all the paler in the sunlight by contrast with the glowing folds of the Imperial Purple that fell from his shoulders over the gilded bronze of his armour. He turned with the old charming smile to speak to the Camp Commandant at his side; he looked about him with interest, acknowledging the acclamation of the crowd with a bend of the head and a gesture of one big white hand, seeming unaware of the hollow ring to the cheering. And after him crowded the Saxons of his bodyguard; big, blue-eyed, yellow-haired tribesmen out of barbarian Germany, sweating under their back-flung wolf-skin cloaks, with gold and coral at their throats and serpents of red gold above the elbows, who laughed and made their guttural talk among themselves as they rode.

Now they were dismounting before the temple portico, the horses wheeling out in all directions to spread confusion among the close-jammed crowd. Over the Legionary's shoulder, Justin saw the tall figure in the Purple turn on the flower-strewn steps, with an actor's gesture to the populace; and was seized with such a blinding rage that he scarcely saw what happened next until the thing was half over.

An old woman had somehow slipped under the guard of the Legionaries, and ran forward with hands outstretched to cast herself at the Emperor's feet with some plea, some petition. What it was, nobody ever heard. One of the Saxons stooped and caught her by the hair and hurled her backwards. She went over with a scream, and they were all round her. They pricked her to her feet with the tips of their saexes, laughing, for the sport of seeing her scuttle. A stupefied hush had descended on the crowd; and then, as the old woman stumbled and all but fell again, the Centurion strode forward, sword in hand, and stepped between her and her tormentors. Quite clearly in the sudden hush Justin heard him say, 'Get back quickly, old mother.' Then he turned to face the Saxons, who seemed momentarily quelled by his air of authority, and said, 'The game is finished.'

Allectus, who had turned again on the steps to see what was happening, gestured to one of his staff officers. Somehow the thing was sorted out; the Saxons were whistled off like hounds, and the old woman had gathered herself together and scuttled weeping back into the crowd, the Legionaries parting their crossed pilums to let her through.

When Justin, who had been watching her, looked round again, the young Centurion was standing on the temple steps before Allectus. Justin was within a spear's length of them, half shielded by a garland-hung column; and he heard Allectus say very gently, 'Centurion, no man interferes with my bodyguard.'

The Centurion's hands clenched at his sides. He was very white, and breathing rather quickly. He said in a tone as gentle as Allectus's own, 'Not even when they turn their dirks on an old woman for amusement, Caesar?'

'No,' said Allectus, still more gently. 'Not even then. Go back to your duties, Centurion, and another time remember not to step beyond them.'

The Centurion drew himself up and saluted, then turned and marched back to his place, with a face that might have been cut from stone. And Allectus, smiling his very charming smile, turned and went, with the senior officers about him, into the temple.

The whole thing had passed so swiftly that it was over before half the crowd had realized what was happening. But Justin and Flavius were to remember it afterwards; to remember—of all unexpected things—the narrow, pointed face of Serapion the Egyptian, starting out of the ranks of those in attendance on the Emperor, his dark, darting gaze fixed on the young Centurion.

In the great fortress that night, the Commandant's quarters, made over to the Emperor for his visit, bore a very different aspect from their usual one. Soft Eastern rugs and embroideries of delicate colours from the Emperor's baggage-train had made the place more like a suite of chambers for a queen; and the air was heavy with the sweetness of the perfumed oil burning in a silver lamp beside the couch on which Allectus reclined. The evening garland of white roses which he had just taken off lay wilting beside him, and he was amusing himself by delicately pulling the flowers to pieces. His rather heavy face was satisfied as a great white cat's, as he smiled at the Egyptian seated on a stool at his feet.

'Caesar should have a care to that young Centurion,' Serapion was saying. 'He looked as though he would have knifed Caesar for a denarius this morning, and this evening he excused himself from attending the banquet in Ceasar's honour.'

'Bah! He was angry at being called to account before the world, no more.'

'Nay, I think that it was more than that. It was a pity that Caesar's bodyguard thought fit to amuse themselves as they did this morning.'

Allectus shrugged indifferently. 'They are barbarians, and they behave as such; but they are loyal, so long as I pay them.'

'Nevertheless, it was a pity.'

Allectus's smile faded a little. 'Since when has Serapion the Egyptian been Caesar's counsellor?'

'Since Serapion the Egyptian furnished Caesar with enough nightshade to kill a man,' said the other smoothly.

'Hell and the Furies! Am I never to hear the last of that? Have I not paid you well enough? Have I not made you one of my personal staff?'

'And am I not a good servant?' Serapion cringed, his dark eyes downcast. 'Nay, but I did not seek to remind Caesar of—unpleasant things . . . Yet I served Caesar well in that matter. It would have been better had Caesar used my services again—for a greater occasion.'

The other laughed softly. 'Nay, man, you set too much store by secrecy and the dark. In these days no Emperor troubles overmuch to hide the hand that slew the Emperor before him. Besides, it was politic to get the Saxons deeply involved, that I might be sure of a good supply of Saxon Mercenaries thereafter.'

Serapion cast up his eyes. 'Caesar thinks of everything! None the less, it is in my mind that while we are here at least, I will have an eye to that young Centurion and his affairs.'

The big, pale man on the couch turned to look at him more closely. 'What is in that crooked mind of yours, little poison-toad?'

'One was telling me that of late months on this part of the coast more than one man who had no cause to love Caesar has—disappeared from under the noses of Caesar's Authorities. And it is in my mind that by watching that young Centurion one might just possibly—find out how.'

At about the same time next night, Justin was sitting in the shadowy corner at the Dolphin. It was a still, close summer evening, and the old striped awning had been rolled back, so that the narrow, lantern-lit courtyard was roofed with a luminous darkness of night sky above the leafy interlacings of the trellised vine. The wine-shop was not very full tonight, and he had the dark corner to himself and his thoughts.

He had got the news that he had come for, and when he had finished his cup of wine—not too quickly, lest anyone should be watching—he would be on his way back to Paulinus with word that the latest man to be shipped to Gaul had been safely landed. Flavius would be there, and Phaedrus coming later when he had finished unloading a cargo of wine from the *Berenice*. They had some plans to discuss for shortening the time that it took to get a man out of the province; plans that needed a good deal of thought. Justin tried to think about them, but for the most part his mind was taken up with that startling glimpse of Serapion the Egyptian among Aliectus's personal attendants yesterday. Why should Allectus take the little perfume-seller into his train? Something in the back of his mind whispered that there was, there always had been, a strong link between such things as Serapion sold, and poison. The Sea Wolf who could have told too much had died of poison . . . Well, whatever the truth of the matter, there could be no menace for them in the man's reappearance, for, thank the gods, he had not seen them. And yet Justin could not clear his mind of an odd uneasiness; something that was almost foreboding.

Someone strolled in from the dark foreshore; and Justin glanced up to see a young man in a shaggy homespun cloak, with ruffled dark hair above a pockmarked forehead, and a great bony beak of a nose, who hesitated an instant in the doorway, glancing about him. Lacking harness and helmet, he looked very different from the last time Justin had seen him, but with his thoughts already hovering around yesterday's scene on the temple steps, he knew him instantly.

The man seemed to make up his mind, and crooking a finger for the keeper of the place, came to sit not far from where Justin was watching. As he did so, a shadow moved in the darkness beyond the doorway; but there was nothing unusual in that, many people came and went along the foreshore. Justin went on watching the young Centurion. The wine came, but he did not drink it, only sat forward, his hands across his knees, playing with something between his fingers. And Justin saw that it was a sprig of rye-grass.

He picked up his own wine-cup, rose, and crossed over to the newcomer. 'Why, this is a pleasant and unexpected thing. I greet you, friend,' he said in the manner of one joining a chance-found acquaintance, and placing his wine-cup on the table, sat down. The other had looked up quickly at his coming, and was watching him guardedly, his face carefully non-committal, as Justin studied it in his turn. There was always a risk about this moment, always the chance that the sprig of rye-grass had found its way into the wrong hands. But he was sure enough of this man, remembering that scene yesterday on the steps of the Temple of Jupiter; besides, his pleasant, craggy face was not the face of an informer, and had in it something strained and a little desperate.

'It is very hot tonight,' Justin said, and loosed the folds of his light cloak, revealing the sprig of rye-grass thrust through the bronze clasp at the neck of his tunic.

The other saw it, and there was a kind of flicker in his face, instantly stilled. He leaned a little towards Justin, saying in a quick undertone, 'It was told me by—someone—that if I came to this wine-shop wearing a certain token, it might be that I should find those who would help me.'

'So? That depends on the help,' Justin murmured, watching lantern-light and leaf-shadows mingle in his cup.

'The same help as others have found before me,' said the man, with a quick, strained smile that barely touched his eyes. 'Let us lay aside the foils. See, I set myself in your hands. I do not wish to serve longer under such an Emperor as Allectus.'

'That is since yesterday?'

'You know about yesterday?'

'I was c-close by, among the crowd before the Temple of Jupiter.'

'Yesterday,' murmured the young man, 'was the last straw that breaks the camel's back. What do we do now?'

'Drink our wine slowly, and try to look a little less like c-conspirators,' said Justin, with a flicker of laughter.

They sat on for a while, quietly drinking their wine, and talking of the prospect of fair weather for the harvest, and kindred subjects, until presently Justin crooked a finger for the wine shopkeeper. 'Now I think that it is time we were moving.'

The other nodded without a word, pushing away his empty cup. They paid each their own score, and rising together, passed out, Justin leading and the other at his shoulder, into the still summer night.

None of those who came and went after dark to the little house or the secret chamber in the old theatre ever travelled straight, lest they should be followed; and tonight, because of the uneasiness that the sight of Serapion had left with him, Justin led his companion by ways even more roundabout than usual. Yet when at last they came down the narrow gash of darkness to the courtyard door, a shadow that had been behind them all the way from the Dolphin was still behind them. Justin paused by the courtyard door, listening, as always, for any sound of their being followed. But there was no sound, nothing moving in the crowding gloom of the alley-way. Yet as he lifted the latch and slipped through with the young Centurion, letting the latch fall silently again behind them, one of the shadows shook free of the rest, and darted lizard-swift across the door.

The little courtyard was in darkness, but the light of a late-rising moon just past the full was whitening the crest of the old theatre wall above them, and the upper branches of the little apple-tree by the well were touched with silver, so that the half-grown apples were like the apples on Cullen's beloved Silver Branch. Justin paused again, listening with strained intensity born of that odd uneasiness that he could not shake off. But the shadow in the alley-way made no more sound than a shadow makes, and with a murmured 'This way' he drew his companion across to the house door.

It was unbolted as the courtyard door had been, ready for Phaedrus coming later, and he opened it and led the way through.

The courtyard door opened a crack behind them, then closed again as silently as it had opened. Nothing moved in the courtyard but a silver night-moth among the silver branches of the apple-tree.

XII
A Sprig of Broom

A CRACK of light showed primrose pale under the door ahead of them, and the little room seemed very bright as Justin raised the latch and went in. Flavius was there with Paulinus, and a chess-board set out on the table between them showed how they had been whiling away the time as they waited for Phaedrus of the *Berenice*.

'Ah, you are back,' Paulinus greeted him, and then, seeing the figure behind him, 'And who is this that you bring with you?'

'Another to go by the usual road,' Justin said.

'So? Well, we must see what can be done.' Paulinus moved his piece a little absent-mindedly. 'What news of the last one?'

'Safely landed.'

Flavius was watching the newcomer. 'It was you who fell foul of the Divine Allectus outside the temple of Jupiter yesterday,' he said suddenly, and rose to his feet, rocking the chessboard so that a pained expression flitted for a moment across Paulinus's face.

The newcomer smiled, that quick, strained smile. 'You also were among the crowd?'

'I was,' Flavius said. 'I hope I'd have had the courage to do the same, if it had been my Cohort on street-lining duty yesterday.'

For a moment they stood looking at each other across the lamp on the table; Flavius in his rough workman's clothes, hairy and none too clean. And yet the newcomer said with only half a question in his tone, 'You speak, I think, as one of the brotherhood.'

'This time last year I commanded a Cohort on the Wall.'

Paulinus, who had been watching the newcomer, gave a little grunt of approval. 'I have heard the story of this falling foul of the Emperor. Unwise, my dear young man; but on the whole—ahem—creditable, very creditable indeed. And so now you feel Gaul to be a fitter place for you than Britain?'

'Can you arrange that for me?'

'I can arrange it,' said Paulinus tranquilly, 'if you will have patience for a few days, during which you will be my guest in—ahem—slightly close quarters, I fear.' And so saying he heaved himself to his feet and began one of his soft, hen-like fusses. 'But why do I keep you all standing here? Sit down, do sit down. There will be one more of us presently, and when he comes, if you will forgive me, I will show you up to those same close quarters. In this business it is best for no one to know more than they need. No, no, no. Meanwhile, have you supped? A cup of wine, then?—and do pray sit down.'

The newcomer wanted neither wine nor supper, but he sat down. They all sat down round the table, and after a moment's pause he said, 'I feel that the thing to do is to ask no questions, and therefore I will ask none . . . Will you not go on with your game?'

Paulinus beamed at him. 'Well, well if you are sure you will not think it discourteous. There will be no more time for chess when our—ahem—friend arrives, and I confess I do hate to leave a game unfinished, especially when I am winning. Flavius, I believe that it is your move.'

It was very hot in the small bright room with the shutters closed, very quiet behind the buzzing of a bluebottle among the rafters, and the faint click of the pieces as they were moved on the board. The young Centurion sat with his arms across his knees, staring soberly before him. Justin, watching the game, began to be very sleepy, so that the pieces danced a little on the blurred black-and-white chequer, and the click as they were moved seemed to be going further and further away . . .

But that game of chess was never to be finished, after all.

Suddenly Justin was broad awake again, to the sound of lumber being thrust aside in the storeroom, and next instant Phaedrus the ship-master burst in upon them, bringing with him a desperate urgency, a smell of deadly danger that had them all on their feet even before he gasped out his warning.

'The Barbarian Guard are all round the house. In the street—and the courtyard is full of them! I all but blundered into them, but by the grace of the gods I saw them in time and cast back for the Sparrow's Way.'

The little silence that followed could have lasted no more than a heart-beat, but it seemed to Justin to swell out and out like a gigantic bubble; a bubble of utter stillness. And from the midst of the stillness, Paulinus said quietly, 'Justin and Flavius, will you oblige me by barring the outer doors?'

They sprang to do his bidding; only just in time, for even as Justin dropped the bar of the courtyard door—an unusually strong bar for a private house—into place, a crash of blows came against it, making the timber jar and vibrate under his hand, and a roar of guttural voices arose outside. 'Open up! Open up, or we break the doors down! Open up, man who harbours traitors, or we fire the roof and smoke you out!'

Well, the bar would hold for a little while though the end was sure. He swung back into the living-room, still bright and commonplace, with its half-played game of chess on the table and its painted household gods in their niches on the walls, just in time to hear the Centurion saying, 'This is my doing. Someone must have followed me. I'll go out to them, sir.'

And Paulinus answered, 'No, no, it was liable to happen at any time, and as for going out to them: my good boy, do you think they would be content with you?'

Justin shut the living-room door and stood with his back to it. Flavius was standing in the same way against the door that led directly into the street, and behind him also the wolf-pack uproar rose. Paulinus glanced quickly at one after another of his companions and gave a little brisk nod. 'Yes, you're all of you slight and active—a mercy it's you, Phaedrus, and not that giant Cerdic. Out by the Sparrow's Way, all four of you, and make for Cerdic's boat-yard.'

'And you?' Flavius snapped.

'Have I the figure for the Sparrow's Way? Go now; wait for me, at the boat-yard, and I'll join you when I can.'

'How?' Justin demanded bluntly, standing his ground, his hand on the dagger in his belt. 'I think we'll stay with you, sir, and fight it out t-together.'

The blows had spread to the high, shuttered window now, and from street and courtyard the wolf-pack yelling rose. 'I have another way out,' Paulinus said quickly; 'one that I have always kept for myself because I am too fat and too old for the other. But it can only be used alone. Will you waste all our lives?'

'Is that the truth?' Flavius said.

'The truth. Listen; the door will go any moment now. *Get out!* That's an order.'

'Very well, sir,' Flavius saluted, as to a superior officer, and turned towards the door into the kitchen before which Justin stood.

Justin, the last of the four to go, looked back once, and saw Paulinus standing beside his unfinished game of chess. His face was very pink in the heat, and he looked, as always, faintly ridiculous; a plump, commonplace little man in a plump, commonplace little room, looking after them. Remembering that moment afterwards, it always seemed to him odd that Paulinus should still have looked ridiculous. He should have looked—Justin was not sure how, but not ridiculous; and there should have been a shiningness about him that did not come from the lamp.

With the thunder of blows and the guttural voices in their ears, they made for the crowded darkness of the storeroom. 'You go first; you know the way best of all of us,' Flavius whispered to the little seaman. 'I'll do rearguard.'

'Right.' The whisper came back out of the blackness, and one after another they ducked through into the stairway. Justin heard Flavius draw a couple of store-baskets over the hole behind them—not that that would be much use when the tide of barbarians broke in. In the dark well of the stairway the menacing uproar was muffled, but as they gained the upper chamber it came bursting up to them full force, and Justin saw the red glare of torches reflected up from below mingled with the white light of the moon as he dropped on his stomach and wormed after the young Centurion through the gap in the wall.

There was a halt, while Flavius replaced the loose boards, which were so worked that they could be dealt with from either side; and then they set out in good earnest. The Sparrow's Way was never pleasant, and to Justin, who had no head for heights, it was very unpleasant indeed, even when it did not have to be negotiated above the heads of a mob of yelling Saxon Mercenaries, along ledges flickering with reflected torchlight, where an unwary handhold or the slip of a foot on a sloping roof might bring the hunt all round them at any moment.

But they made it safely; and a very long while later, as it seemed, swung themselves over the last low ledge, and landed soft in a garbage pile behind the tumbledown entrance of the theatre.

Later still, with Cerdic the boat-builder in their midst, the four of them were gathered in a waiting knot about the doorway of the turf-roofed bothie just outside the town, where Justin and Flavius had lodged all these months.

They were quite silent, stunned by the suddenness of what had happened, their strained gaze going out to a red glow that had sprung up in the sky over Portus Adurni. Justin shivered a little in the cool marsh air. Had the Saxons fired the place? Or was it something to do with Paulinus's way of escape? How long would it be before Paulinus came?—or—would he ever come? No, he must not think like that; he pushed the thought away in a hurry. Paulinus had sworn that there was another way out . . .

Flavius, frowning into the moonlight, said abruptly, 'Phaedrus, have you ever heard of this other way out before? This way that can only be taken alone?'

The seaman shook his head. 'Nay—but he said that it was one that he had kept for himself. Happen we should none of us have heard of it.'

'I hope you're right,' Flavius said. 'I hope to the gods you're right.'

Almost as he spoke, something moved in the shadow of the dunes, and Justin's heart gave a little lurch of relief. 'Here he comes now!'

And then, as the moving thing swayed out into the moonlight, stumbling in the soft, drifted sand, they saw that it was not Paulinus, but the boy Myron.

Flavius whistled softly, and the boy looked up and saw them and came on at an increased speed; and as he drew nearer they could hear him gasping, half sobbing as he ran.

'Name of Thunder! What's happened?' Flavius said under his breath, starting to meet him.

And somehow they were all down into the soft sand, and in their midst the boy Myron was gasping out in a broken jumble that at first they could scarcely understand. 'Oh, thank the gods you are here! The whole town's full of those devils, and I couldn't do nothing—I—I—' And he fell to gusty weeping.

Flavius caught him by both shoulders. 'Time enough for that later, if need be. Tell us what has happened.'

'Paulinus!' The boy drew a shuddering breath. 'They've killed Paulinus—I see them do it.'

Justin couldn't speak; he heard Phaedrus make a harsh sound in his throat, and then Flavius said in a hard, level voice, 'What have you seen?'

'I went back early because I'd forgot to fill the lamps, and he hated to have them run dry in the middle of the evening. And I was almost there when I heard the shouting and saw the flames. And I crept closer to look—right up to the courtyard door—and the courtyard was full of those Saxon devils with firebrands, and the roof was on fire and all—and just as I got there, the house door opened and—Paulinus walked out—just walked out into the middle of them, and they killed him—like killing a badger.'

There was a long, long silence. No sound in all the world but the sighing, singing, air-haunted stillness of the marsh under the moon. Not even a bird calling. Then Flavius said, 'So there wasn't another way out, after all—or, if there was, something went wrong and he couldn't use it.'

'There was another way out—and that was it,' Justin said slowly.

The young Centurion, who had been completely still throughout, said very softly, as though to himself, 'Greater love hath no man—' and Justin thought it sounded as though he were quoting someone else.

The boy Myron was crying desolately, repeating in a snuffling whisper over and over again, 'I couldn't do nothing—I couldn't—'

'Of course you couldn't.' Justin put an arm round his shoulders. And then, 'It was we who left him.'

Flavius made a harsh gesture of denial. 'We did not leave him. He ordered us out, that we might carry on the work after him. It was for that that he took us in the first place. So now we carry on the work.' Then, seeming for the first time to remember the stranger among them, he turned to him saying, 'I am sorry, but your jaunt to Gaul will have to wait awhile.'

The young Centurion had turned seaward, his head up into the faint breath of night wind. 'May I change my mind about Gaul?'

'It is too late to go back,' Flavius said.

'I do not ask to go back. I ask to join this team of yours.'

'Why?' Flavius demanded bluntly, after a small, startled pause.

'I—do not speak of paying my debts: there are debts that cannot be paid. I ask to join it because it seems to me worth joining.'

By dawn, Paulinus's neat little house was a gutted ruin, the secret chamber torn open to the sky, the apple-tree in the courtyard hacked to pieces in the sheer wanton joy of destruction; and Allectus's barbarians were questing like hounds into every corner of Portus Adurni, in search of they did not quite know what.

And crouching in the lee of Cerdic's boat-shed, with the faint mist rising about them as the night drew towards dawn, Flavius spoke straightly to those of the band whom they had been able to gather, with an arm over Justin's shoulder as he spoke, as though to make it clear that the two of them were one in the leadership that had fallen upon them with Paulinus's death. 'You all know the thing that has happened; talking won't mend it. Now we have to make plans for carrying on the work in the future.'

There was a ragged murmur of agreement from the dark, huddled shapes, and the keeper of the Dolphin said, 'Aye, and the first thing we'll be wanting is a new headquarters. And I'd suggest that after tonight's work, Portus Adurni will be no place for it for a while and a while to come.'

'Somewhere inland a bit,' said another man briefly.

Flavius glanced over them in the low moonlight. 'That same thing is in my mind also,' he said.

'Anywhere to suggest?' That was Phaedrus, leaning forward, with his arms round his up-drawn knees.

'Yes,' Flavius said, and Justin felt the arm across his shoulders tighten a little. 'As Paulinus used his own home for the purpose, so I have it in mind—unless any among you find reason against the plan—to use mine.'

It was the first Justin had heard of it, but he knew instantly that it was right; the whole feel of the plan was right, and fitting.

'And whereabouts might your home be?' Cerdic the boat-builder asked in the deep rumble that seemed always to come from somewhere far down in his barrel chest.

'Up into the chalk, north-east of here, ten or twelve miles. It's a good strategic position, as near to Clausentium as we are now, nearer to both Regnum and Venta. Easy of access over the Downs or by the old track from Venta; and the forest for cover in case of trouble.'

There was a certain amount of urgent and low-voiced talk before the thing was settled, but none of the men gathered there had any particular fault to find with the plan, and indeed after some discussion and argument they found it good. The house by the theatre had never really been a meeting-place, rather it had been the spot where the threads were gathered together. And so long as they were gathered together somewhere reasonably near to the centre of the web, it made very little difference exactly where.

'So: it is a good plan, and we will abide by it,' Phaedrus said at last. 'Show us now how we may find this place.'

And so, in the misty moonlight and the first cobweb greyness of the dawn, Flavius made them a relief map in the sand, that they might know how to find it. The great curved ridge of the Downs, rising a handspan high among marsh grasses, with the soft moon-shadows in its tiny valleys; and the furrow of a finger trailed through the sand for the great roads and the tracks that had been old before the roads were new. And for the farm itself, a sprig of broom with the sand between its leaves, and one spark of blossom.

And when each of them had carefully memorized the map, he smoothed it all away. 'So. That is all. Justin and I go inland now to make arrangements, but we shall be back in two days at the latest. The newest recruit comes with us, I think. He will be too well known in these parts.'

Justin glanced towards a small desolate figure, huddled against the boat-shed wall, and said quickly, half under his breath, 'Myron, too. He has nowhere and no one belonging to him in Portus Adurni—and he's in no fit state to be seen by our enemies.'

Flavius nodded. 'Yes, you're right. We can't leave him here. Myron too, then.'

The light was growing, and it was time to break up, but at the last moment he stayed them. 'Wait; there's one thing more. Better after this that we change the token. There may be others now beside ourselves on the look-out for sprigs of rye-grass.'

'What shall it be, then?' said Phaedrus.

It was Justin, in the act of turning away to fetch his beloved instrument-case from the bothie, who picked up the sprig of broom that had been used to mark the position of the farm and shook the sand out of it. 'How about this? It is easily come by, and all men know it.'

'So: that will serve,' Flavius said. 'Pass the word along the coast, Phaedrus.'

At noon, far up on the crest of the downs, Flavius halted them for a few hours, not wishing to walk into the farm, where doubtless he and Justin were thought to be in Gaul, unheralded and in broad daylight.

There were harebells in the tawny downland grass, and the blue butterflies of chalk country dancing in the sunshine, the turf was warm to the touch, and thyme-scented; and it seemed to Justin unbearable that it should be like that after last night—after Paulinus. Paulinus was in all their thoughts, he knew—that timid little man who had made sure of the safety of his followers, and then walked quietly out to his own death—but they did not speak of what had happened. It was as Flavius had said, 'You all know what has happened. Talking won't mend it.' They did not talk of anything. They had not known while they were on the march that they were tired; but now that they were halted, they were suddenly weary to the bone. The boy Myron, who seemed completely dazed, simply pitched down where he stood, and was asleep almost before he touched the ground; and the other three, taking turns to keep watch, followed his example.

Justin had the last watch, and by the time it came the warm noontide was long past, and the sunlight was thickening into an amber glow over the hills. Now that he had slept, the crowding beastliness of last night had drawn back a little, and he could say to something accusing within himself, 'No, I took all the care that anyone could take, to be sure that none followed me. Whoever it was, was cleverer than I am. That is all.' And he could know that it was true. But the thing within him went on accusing, all the same, so that he had to go over it all in his mind round and round, until his head ached almost as much as his heart. At last, desperate for something to do with his hands that might stop him thinking, he slipped free the worn shoulder-sling of his instrument-case, ranged the contents on the grass beside him, and with the soft cloth in which they had been muffled, fell to burnishing the tools of his trade. Not that they needed burnishing, for he had kept them bright as glass all these long months, as though by doing so he was keeping faith with something in himself—something that was for healing and creating and making whole again, in a world that seemed to be all destroying.

Presently he became aware that Anthonius the young Centurion was no longer asleep, but had turned his head on his arms to watch him. 'Is it a rust spot, that you rub—and rub—and rub so desperately?' the Centurion asked, as their eyes met.

Justin said slowly, 'I think I try to rub away the knowing that—it was I who led the wolves to P-Paulinus's door last night.'

'Far more likely it was I. I found that little Egyptian shadow of Allectus's watching me more than once, after that business on the temple steps. It should have put me more on my guard.'

The Egyptian shadow, Justin thought; yes, that fitted Serapion perfectly. He had been right to smell danger at the sight of the creature in Allectus's train. Danger and death; it had come swiftly.

'Yet, whichever one of us it was they followed, it was still I who led the way,' he said miserably, unable to slip out so easily from under the blame and leave it on the other's shoulders.

'Paulinus blamed neither of us,' Anthonius said quietly. 'He knew that it was a thing that might happen any day, through no fault of any man within the team. It was a risk he was prepared to run, just as—you run it, from now on.'

And somehow those last most uncomforting words comforted Justin a little, as nothing else could have done. He laid down the instrument he had been burnishing, and took up another.

The young Centurion watched him in silence for a while, then he said: 'I wondered what was in that case that you carry with such care.'

'The tools of my trade.'

'Ah. So you're a surgeon?'

Justin looked at his hands, seeing them hardened and calloused after nine months in the shipyards and rope-walks of Adurni, cut to pieces and ingrained with pitch; feeling the finger-tips no longer sensitive as they had used to be. 'I—was a surgeon, when Flavius was a C-Cohort Commander,' he said.

Anthonius took up one of the little bright instruments and looked at it, then laid it down again among the dwarf thyme. 'You're lucky,' he said. 'You're wonderfully lucky. Most of us can only break things.'

Presently Flavius woke up also, and with the sun sinking low behind Vectis, roused Myron, who had not stirred since he first fell asleep, and got them all to their feet again. 'If we start now, we shall just about make the farm at dusk . . . Look how the Island is rearing up out of the sea. It's going to rain at last.'

Rain it did, and that night in the Atrium of the old farmhouse, they could hear it hushing and pattering on the roof and among the broad leaves of the fig-tree outside; and the little breath of air from the open door that scarcely stirred the flame of the lamp on the table bore with it that most wonderful of all smells, the throat-catching heart-catching scent of rain on a hot and thirsty earth.

They had stayed their empty stomachs with curds and bannock and fried downland mutton, and left Myron asleep once more before the low fire in the steward's quarters, and now here they were in the old Atrium, with the folk of the farm about them in obedience to Flavius's summons. Justin, looking about him at the men gathered in the faint lamplight, found them little changed since that leave he had spent among them a year and a half ago. Servius himself, seated on the one stool by right of his position as steward; Kyndylan with his broad pleasant face half lost in a fuzz of golden beard; Buic the old shepherd, crinkle-eyed from a long lifetime of looking into the distance after his sheep, with his crook beside him and his wall-eyed sheep-dog against his knee; Flann the ploughman, and the rest, all seated comfortably on the store-chests and the baled wool yet remaining of the last clip. Two or three women also, gathered about Cutha near the door. The first startled excitement of their arrival had died down, and the company sat looking to the master of the place with no more than mild enquiry; a quiet attention that seemed somehow one with the unchanging quietness of the Downs themselves.

Flavius sat sideways on the table by the lamp, swinging a muddy foot as he looked round on them. He said, 'You'll be wondering what all this is about, and why Justin and I are not in Gaul, and I can't tell you. At least, I'm not going to tell you—for the present, anyway. But I need your help. You've none of you ever failed me before, and I'm trusting you not to fail me now, so you've got to trust me. There'll be odd things happening, strangers coming and going about the farm. Mostly they'll be wearing a sprig of broom somewhere about them, like this—' He shook back the fold of his rough cloak, and showed the little green sprig with its one spark of blossom still clinging to it, stuck in the shoulder-pin. 'Justin and I will be coming and going too; and there must be no word of all this outside the farm—not one word. That is life and death. I am depending on your loyalty to me, and to Justin, who is one with me in this.' He looked round on them with a grin. 'That is really all I wanted to say.'

There was a long silence while the company thought this over; and the sound of the rain came into the room. Justin had expected Servius to speak for the rest, by the same right as he sat on the one stool; but it was Buic the shepherd, by right of age, who spoke up for his fellows, in the soft speech of his own people that came to his tongue more readily than the Latin did. 'We've knowed your father, my dear, and we've knowed you since the third day after you was born, and *I* knowed your grandfather pretty well, too. So I reckon we'll trust you, and no questions asked; and I reckon we won't fail you.'

When steward and farm-folk were all gone, and the three of them were alone in the smoke-darkened Atrium, they gathered to the small fire that Cutha had lit for them on the hearthplace, for with the rain the evening was turning chilly. Anthonius, who had stood by, watching the scene in silence, said suddenly, 'You are fortunate to be able to trust your people so completely.' And after a moment, 'They are none of them, I think, slaves?'

Flavius looked at him in surprise. 'Slaves? Oh no, there are no slaves on the farm; there never have been. Those were all free men and women and—rather dear friends.'

'So? It is in my mind that this must be a happy place,' Anthonius said. He looked from one to the other, leaning a little sideways, his right hand moving idly across his knee to trace something in the white ash on the hearthstone.

And Justin, watching, saw that the thing he drew was a fish.

He had seen that sign before, in Judea. It was something to do with a man called the Christos—a man who had been executed more than two hundred years ago: but it seemed that he still had followers. You would need to be a good leader, Justin thought suddenly, for people to follow you still, two hundred years afterwards: not just priests out for what they could get, or silly women; but men like Anthonius.

The young Centurion's eyes caught and held his for a moment, with a shadow of a question in them; then moved to Flavius, who was making some adjustment to his shoulder-pin and did not seem even to have noticed. Then he brushed his hand across the hearth, and the fish was gone again.

XIII

The Silver Branch

THAT summer the Sea Wolves, slipping past the slackened guard of the Galleys, came raiding far up the south-coast rivers, burning and harrying far into the Downs and the Weald. It was as it had been before Carausius came; worse, for now Allectus's Saxon Mercenaries were loose in the land. Pirates and Mercenaries fought to the death when they met, like two wolf-packs hunting the same territory. But for the hunted there was often enough little difference between one pack and the other.

The farm, lost in its downland valley, somehow escaped. Summer passed, and they harvested the cornland below the Downs, and the work that Paulinus had died for went on. But as summer turned to autumn, the sprig of broom was coming to mean something wider than it had done at first.

It began with three young brothers from the Otter's Ford, their farm burned over their heads by a band of drunken Mercenaries, who came to Flavius for refuge and a chance by and by to repay their debt to Allectus.

'If you take them,' Servius said on a note of warning, 'you'll have a legion before you know where you are.'

And Flavius, with his red brows at their most fly-away, replied: 'So be it, then. We'll have a legion!'

By the time it was the season for salting down the winter's meat supply, the legion numbered upward of a score, including the boy Myron; men dispossessed, men with wrongs to avenge, fugitives of all kinds, with a couple of legionaries gone wilful-missing to toughen the whole, who made their hide-outs in the forest for miles around—the forest that was ever the friend of wanted men. Later, Kyndylan came to Flavius with three of the younger farm-hands behind him, and said: 'Sir, my father, your steward, is old now, and too stiff from old wounds to be of use to you; but we four, who are the young men of the farm, we would have you know that our spears are ready, and when you have need of us, we also are your hounds.'

And only a few days after that, Justin added a derelict gladiator to the growing band.

He found him at Venta on the day of the Games, standing in the shadow of the main entrance to the amphitheatre; a gaunt and tattered creature, pressed back from the rest of the throng, with his head turned towards the distant glimpse of the arena, and on his face a look of absolute despair that seemed to Justin to take all the shine out of the gleamy autumn day.

His first instinct had been to say, 'What is it? Is there anything—anything at all—that I can do to help?' but something about the man warned him against that. 'There's a good bill today,' he said after a while. 'A Libian tiger isn't to be seen every day in these parts. Going in?'

The man started and glanced round. 'No,' he said, and defiance came up like a shield over the naked despair in his face.

From somewhere below them, beyond the barred gates of the wild beasts' den, a wolf began to howl, the wild and mournful note rising above the uproar of the crowded benches. The man said, 'Aye, even the wolves feel it.'

'Feel it?'

'The thing that's running through the dens down there. But what should you know of that?' The man glanced contemptuously at Justin again. 'How should you know what it's like, the last moments of waiting before the trumpets sound? You test your weapons again, though you tested them not a hundred heart-beats ago; and may be your sword-hand grows a little sticky, so you rub it in the sand to give you a better chance of life. You take your place in the file that's forming up, ready to march into the arena; and you hear the crowd gathering, a thousand, twenty thousand strong, it makes no matter—as many as the place will hold—and you know that they've come to watch *you*. And the bread and onions you ate this morning tasted better than any feast to a man who expects to eat again. And the sun through the grilles overhead is brighter for you than for any man who thinks to see it rise tomorrow; because you know that, like as not, you're going to die, out there in the sand with twenty thousand people looking on . . . If not this fight, then the next, or the hundredth after that. But there's always the chance that you'll gain your wooden foil.'

'Ave Caesar, those about to die salute you,' Justin said quietly. 'B-but for you, it was the wooden foil.'

The man looked at him quickly, clearly startled to realize how completely he had betrayed himself. 'Aye, they gave me my wooden foil last winter, at the Games in honour of the new Emperor—up yonder at Londinium,' he said after a moment.

'And so now you are free.'

'Free?' said the other. 'Aye, I'm free. Free of all that, free to starve in a ditch, free to follow my own road. And all roads are flat and grey.'

Justin was silent, borne down by that terrible 'All roads are flat and grey', and his own inability to do anything about it.

The other looked at him, and broke into a jeering laugh. 'That's it. Now make helpful suggestions. Here's a denarius; go and buy myself something to eat. They want men at the dye-works, why don't I go there and ask for work? I don't want your denarius, and I'm not the sort for steady work. Can you give me the sort of work I'm good for? Can you give me a risk to run? A gamble with life and death hanging on the fall of the dice? If so—'

And suddenly Justin saw light, 'I am not sure,' he said. 'But I think it may be that I can.'

As spring wore on, the rumours that had been rife in Britain all winter gathered substance and certainty. The Caesar Constantius had begun building transports at Gesoriacum. The Emperor Maximian himself was coming north to take over the Rhenus defences! The transports were ready to sail—a great fleet of transports and escort galleys waiting at Gesoriacum and in the mouth of the Sequana! And then, a little after sheepshearing, the news came down by the ways of the wilderness that Allectus, who was massing his forces along the south-east coast, with his headquarters at Rutupiae, had withdrawn more than half the troops from the Wall.

It was a few nights later that the next news came. They were in Calleva, Justin and this time Flavius too, in search of weapons for their tattered legion. There had been many recruits in the past few weeks, and though some had weapons of their own, others had come in with nothing but a light hunting-spear that would be little use in battle. An ambushed Saxon here and there had done something to increase their stock of war-gear, but they were still badly under-armed, and so the second of Great-Aunt Honoria's opal bracelets, carefully saved against a sudden need, had been sold to a jeweller in Clausentium; and in the past few days several swordsmiths and armourers in that town, in Regnum and Venta, and now in Calleva, had received visits from a couple of strangers who bought here a plain but serviceable sword, there a heavy spear-head. Now the thing was finished, and earlier that evening Justin and Flavius had seen the last of their purchases packed in lamp-oil jars, ready for loading on to a pair of pack-mules lent them by a good friend near the South Gate. They had had a hasty meal in an eating-house just behind the Forum kept by an ex-legionary with one eye, and were actually setting out to pick up the mules, when a man passed them half running, who called out to them in passing, 'Have you heard?—Constantius's sails have been seen off Tanatus!' and hurried on to spread the news elsewhere.

'It looks as though we have got our lamp-oil none too soon,' Flavius said when he had gone, and then, 'I'm glad Aunt Honoria is safe in Aquae Sulis—whatever happens, they should be well out of it down there.' For they had passed the Aquila house earlier that day, and seen it shuttered close, and obviously empty of life.

In the wide street that ran straight as a pilum-shaft from the Forum to the South Gate, a few people were abroad, despite the lateness of the hour, and the mizzle rain that had begun to fall, standing in little half-anxious, half-eager groups in shop doorways and at street corners, with an air of waiting, like people waiting for a storm to break.

They were halfway down the street when, with a sudden hubbub of shouts and flying feet, out from a dark side-street just ahead of them bounded a small fantastic figure with a knot of howling Saxons on its heels. The fugitive was swift and light as a cat, but the hunters were almost upon him, and even as he gained the street, with a yell of triumph, the foremost of them had him round his neck, bringing him half down, and instantly they were all around him. For an instant, as they pulled him down, Justin caught the little man's desperate upturned face in the light of a lantern over a shop doorway; a narrow, beardless face with enormous eyes. And in the same instant he heard Flavius cry, 'Ye gods! It's Cullen!'

Then they were running. 'Hold on, Cullen; we're coming!' Flavius shouted, and the next instant they were into the fight. There were four of the Saxons, but surprise was on the side of the rescuers, and Cullen himself fought like a mountain cat. Flavius threw one man across his hip—a gymnasium throw—and he came down with a stunning crash, bringing another with him. A knife flashed in the lantern light, and Justin felt the wind of it on his cheek as he side-stepped and sprang in under the Saxon's guard . . . And then somehow—quite how the break-away came, he never knew—the three of them were running for their lives down the dark side-street, with the pounding feet of their pursuers hard behind.

'Round here,' Flavius panted, and they swung left into a gash of darkness that opened between the houses. Up one narrow way and down another they dived, bursting through the hedges of quiet gardens, doubling and turning in their tracks, with always the clamour of pursuit swelling behind them. Flavius was trying to make for the northern part of the town, in the hope of shaking off their pursuers and being able to get down to the mules and the precious oil-jars again from the other side. But when they came upon a street leading in the right direction, there were more Saxons with torches a little way up it, and as they swerved back into the dark gap between the two shops, a redoubled yelling told them that they had been seen.

It was not so much that they were being chased now, as hunted. From all quarters of Calleva, it seemed, the Saxons were up and hunting, part in deadly earnest, part in sport that would be just as deadly, closing in on them, driving them further and further into the south-east angle of the old ramparts. And, to make matters worse, poor little Cullen, who had been hard hunted before they came upon him, was almost done. The dark shape of a temple loomed ahead of them, and they rounded it and dived into the thick shadows under the colonnade, crouching frozen for a few tingling moments, as the hunt came yowling by; then they were up again, and running, almost carrying Cullen between them, heading for the dark mass of evergreens and neglected roses behind the place. Into it they dived, worming their way forward into the deepest heart of the tangle, and lay still.

At any moment the hunt would be back on its tracks, but now, for this little space of time, there was respite; the clamour of the hunt dying into the distance, only the hushing of the wind through the evergreen branches all around them, and the dark brown smell of old dry leaves and exposed roots, even the mizzle rain shut out. Little Cullen lay flat on his belly, his flanks heaving like the flanks of some small hunted animal. Justin lay straining his ears to catch any sound of the hunt returning, above the sickening drub of his own heart. Any moment now . . . Well, the cover was dense enough, anyway; they might stand a chance.

And then suddenly the hounds were giving tongue again, ahead of them now as well as behind, from a score of places at once; and Justin, tensing under the holly tangle, caught the red flare of a torch, and then another; and heard Flavius draw a harsh breath. 'Fiends and Furies! They've called in all their friends to beat us out!'

So that was that, Justin thought quite calmly, I suppose this is the end. It will be for us as it was for Paulinus—as it was for the Emperor himself; the torch-light and the naked saex blades, I wonder what it will really be like.

But Flavius was crouching over them, whispering urgently, 'Come—we've one more chance. Up, Cullen; it's the last lap—you can do it, you've got to!' And beside him Cullen was drawing his legs under him again, with a hoarse sob of sheer exhaustion. And somehow they were on the move once more, belly-snaking down through the bushes towards the old ramparts.

'Where?' whispered Justin urgently.

'Our house—empty—' he caught, and the rest was lost in the wind through the holly branches and the cries of the hunt behind.

Torches were flaring in the street beyond the houses, and the hunt was closing in through the gardens of the temple of Sul Minerva, as they gained the shelter of the thick-growing things at the foot of the Aquila garden and headed for the house.

A few moments later they were into the colonnade, and the wing of the dark and silent house was between them and the distant torches, reaching out like a protecting arm to hold back the danger and gain them a little time. 'There's a way in—through the bath-house if they haven't—had the shutter mended,' Flavius panted, starting along the colonnade.

'If they're beating—this cover for us—they'll beat the house, too,' Justin objected swiftly.

'The odds are they'll miss the hypocaust—they don't warm their houses in that way beyond the Rhenus. Come on.'

And then the Atrium door opened, letting out into the courtyard a soft flood of lamplight to set the white roses of the colonnade shining, and Aunt Honoria appeared, evidently drawn by the nearing uproar, and prepared if need be to do something about it, for she held in one hand a small flower-shaped lamp, and in the other an old uniform dagger.

Her gaze fell with the lamplight on the three tattered and panting fugitives, and she stiffened, her eyes widening a little. But Justin had been right in his judgement of her at their first meeting. She would never waste time in surprise or useless questions. She said in that husky, jewel-cut voice of hers, 'So, my Great-Nephews—and another.' Then, with a flick of her dagger-hand towards the clamour that rose with the unmistakable note of a hunt giving tongue, 'Is that for you?'

Justin nodded dumbly, his breath too thick in his throat for speech. Flavius said, 'Yes, Saxons.'

'Inside with you.' She stepped back, and next instant they were in the Atrium, and the door shut and barred behind them. 'The hypocaust,' said Aunt Honoria. 'Thank the gods it is summer and there's no fire.'

'You and I always thought alike,' said Flavius, with a breathless croak of laughter, his back against the door. 'But we thought the house was empty. Better put us out again through the slaves' quarters and let us run for it. We shall bring danger on you if we stay.'

'Flavius dear, there isn't time to be noble,' said Aunt Honoria, and her bright glance flicked to the little Fool drooping between the other two. 'Besides, one of you at least is past running. Quick now.' And somehow while she was yet speaking, without any of them but herself quite knowing how it happened, she had swept them after her through the door at the end of the Atrium into a passage-way beyond, then by an outer door, down three steps into the narrow, windowless stoke-house. The light of the little lamp showed logs and charcoal stacked against the lime-washed wall, and the square iron door of the stoke-hole. The clamour of the hunt sounded no nearer; probably they were still beating the temple gardens or had turned to one of the other houses. Flavius stooped and pulled open the little iron doors.

'You first, Justin.'

And suddenly Justin's old horror of enclosed places, places from which he could not get out again at will, had him by the throat, and it was all he could do to force himself down on hands and knees and through that square of darkness that was like the mouth of a trap, the mouth of a tomb.

'You next,' Flavius said, and he heard little Cullen coming after him, and then Flavius's voice again, in a hurried undertone, 'Aunt Honoria, I'll stay outside where I can come to your help if need be—and take my chance.'

'Do you really want to kill us all?' said Aunt Honoria crisply. 'Get in after the others, and don't any of you try to get out again until I come for you.'

And then the three of them were together in the enclosed space. The iron door shut behind them, and they were in darkness such as Justin had never known existed. Black darkness that pressed against one's eyeballs like a pad. Faintly they heard Aunt Honoria piling logs against the door. 'Get forward a bit,' Flavius whispered.

Justin could sense that they had come out into a wider space. They must be right under the floor of the Atrium, here. He put out a hand and felt one of the fire-brick pillars on which the floor rested, strong pillars so short that if one tried to sit up, the floor would be against one's shoulders. Justin tried not to think of that. He tried listening instead. He heard Aunt Honoria's footsteps overhead, and women's voices somewhere. He could hear the hunt too, very close now. It was odd to hear so much, when one seemed to be miles down below the world of living men. The sounds must come down the wall-flues, he supposed, like the air. Plenty of air coming down the wall-flues; no need to feel as though one couldn't breathe. 'Don't be such a fool,' he told himself angrily. 'You can breathe perfectly well; you're just a bit winded with the running, that's all; and the Atrium floor isn't sinking down on top of you either. Breathe slowly—*slowly*. You can't panic in here, Justin, you miserable coward; it's bad enough for the other two without that.'

How long he lay sweating, with the darkness turned soft and loathsome and suffocating about him, he had no idea; but it could not have been long, because little Cullen's exhausted panting had scarcely quieted away when there was a furious pounding on one or other of the Atrium doors, and a crash, and then the tramp of feet almost overhead and a ragged splurge of voices, so many and so guttural that it came down to the three in hiding only as a confused roar. Then Aunt Honoria's voice, raised a little from its usual quietness, clear-cut and imperious. 'Will someone among you tell me what is the meaning of this?'

A deep voice, almost unintelligible in its thickness, answered her. 'Ja, we seek three men that ran this way. Maybe you hide them here?'

'Three men?' said Aunt Honoria coolly. 'There are none here but myself and these my slaves, four old women, as you see.'

'So you say, old woman—old thin cow! Now we look.'

It was at that moment Justin realized that Cullen was no longer beside him. Well, there was nothing to be done about that now save pray that the little man was not doing anything foolish.

Aunt Honoria's voice sounded again, cool as ever. 'Look then, but I tell you beforehand that if you would find these men, whoever they be, then you must search elsewhere.'

There was a growl of voices and rough laughter, and the swift tramp of feet overhead again. And in the same instant, from somewhere before him in the darkness of the hypocaust itself, came a faint grating sound, a sound that Justin could give no name to save that it was like something shifting. What in the name of Esculapius was Cullen doing? He tensed, waiting for the next thing, but no other sound came out of the darkness. A woman squealed shrilly; and then suddenly the footsteps were everywhere, and a guttural snarl of voices calling to each other, laughing, savage. And after a while Justin felt little Cullen slipping back to his side.

The steps went to and fro across the Atrium floor, dulled and muffled into a kind of thunderous padding in the enclosed space underneath, dying away and pounding back again as the Saxons scattered questing through the house, like hounds drawing a dense cover. There was a crash somewhere, and a roar of laughter; and a rising babble of other voices, shrill and scared, that must be the household slaves. Once again Aunt Honoria's voice sounded. But the three listening with straining ears in the dark could make out little of what was passing.

And then, quite suddenly, it seemed that it was over.

The distant distressful babble of women's voices still reached them faintly, but the guttural tones of the Saxons had blurred into the night, and the padding footsteps sounded no more overhead. The scared voices of the slaves sank away little by little into quiet; and again they waited.

And then, faintly through the iron door, they heard the logs being shifted. The iron door opened; lamplight burst in upon them in a dazzling beam, and Aunt Honoria's voice said, 'I'm sorry to have left you here so long. It has taken me all this while to soothe my silly women and get them safely back to their own quarters.'

A few moments later the three of them, covered with ash and charred brick-dust, were standing in the stoke-house; and in the blessed sense of space above his head and air to breathe, Justin stood drawing in great gasps of breath as though he had been running. Flavius said quickly, 'You are not scathed, Aunt Honoria?'

'I am not scathed. I have had a somewhat anxious time; no more.'

The Atrium, when they were back in it a few moments later, bore testimony to the Saxons' passing, in broken furniture and hangings torn down, mud trampled across the tesserae, and the painted plaster of one wall scored across and across as with a dagger, in the sheer wanton pleasure of breaking and marring. Aunt Honoria wasted no look on the damage, as she crossed to the shrine of the household gods and set the flower-shaped lamp on the altar.

'What a good thing our household gods are only bronze,' she said. 'The altar lamp was silver.' Then she turned to the tattered and grimy figures behind her. 'When did you return from Gaul?'

'We have not been in Gaul,' Flavius said. 'We put your bracelets to a better use this side of the water, Aunt Honoria.'

She searched his face with those beautiful eyes, so bright under the wrinkled lids and the eye-paint. 'So you have been in Britain all this while? A year and the half of a year? And could you not have found means to send me word, just once, or twice, in all that time?'

Flavius shook his head. 'We have been busy, Justin and I and some others; busy on the sort of work you do not risk dragging your family into.'

'So,' Aunt Honoria said, and her gaze went to little Cullen in his tattered motley on the edge of the lamplight. 'And here is one of those others?'

Justin and Flavius turned to look at the little Fool as though becoming truly aware of him for the first time. Somehow, after that first startled moment of unbelief when the lantern-light showed them his face as he struggled with his captors, there had been nothing to spare for surprise. But now all at once they realized the astonishing thing that had happened. That this was Cullen the Fool of Carausius, whom they had never once thought of as amongst the living, since his lord was dead.

It was Cullen himself who answered first. '*Na*, Lady, I am Cullen that was hound to Curoi the Emperor. And though for long and long I have been seeking these two, it was not until tonight, by all the wheeling stars of the sky, that I found them again in my need.'

'You have been seeking us?' Flavius said.

The little man nodded vehemently. 'Seeking and seeking, because my Lord Curoi bade me.'

'The Emperor bade you? When—what is it that you mean?'

'Two years ago last seed-time he wrote a letter, and when it was written, he gave it to me, and bade me take it to you if he should—die. He gave it to me because he knew that he could trust me; he said I was the most faithful of hunting dogs. But when he was slain'—Cullen showed his teeth as a hound shows them—'they caught and held me captive a while and a long while to make them laugh. And when at last I broke free, I went North—my Lord said I should find you on the Wall.' He sounded reproachful. 'But you were gone, and I could get no word of you for another long while, until a woman in the street of the Golden Grasshopper at Magnis told me you were gone South on the road to Gaul. Then South I came—and this evening, those who held me captive aforetime knew me again in the streets of Calleva.'

Flavius nodded. 'And the letter? Have you the letter yet?'

'Should I have come without it?' Cullen said. From the breast of his tattered motley he brought out something long and curved, muffled close in rags, and unwinding it gently as a woman loosing her babe from its swaddling bands, laid bare his Silver Branch.

Justin wondered at its silence in his hands until he saw the wisp of sheep's wool sticking through the opening of the largest apple, and realized that, as well as the outer wrappings, each apple had been packed with wool to silence it. 'Other things I have carried for Curoi my Lord in this hiding-place. It is a good hiding-place,' Cullen was saying. He did something to the end of the enamelled hand-piece, and drew out from it a roll of papyrus not much thicker than a man's finger. 'Sa, here it is, safe where it has lain these more than two years past.'

Flavius took and unrolled it with great care, turning to the little lamp on the altar. The papyrus was so thin that the flame shone through it pinkish until he tipped it to catch the light on the surface. Justin, looking over his shoulder, saw Carausius's bold writing flash up blackly from the fragile sheet.

'To Centurion Marcelus Flavius Aquila, and to Tiberius Lucius Justianus, Cohort Surgeon, from Marcus Aurelius Carausius, Emperor of Britain, Greeting,' he read. 'If ever you read this it will be that the man of whom you sought to warn me has slipped beneath my guard in the end. And—as though it mattered—if I should have no more speech with you in this world, I would not have you think I sent you from me in anger. You young fools, if I had not sent you to the Wall as being of no further use to me, you would have been dead men within three days. I salute you, my children. Farewell.'

There was a long silence. Only the faint whisper of the rain and the distant night-time sounds of the city. The noise of the hunt had quite died away. Flavius let the thin papyrus roll up on itself, very gently. Justin was staring at the flame of the lamp; a slender, spear-shaped flame, blue at the heart, exquisite. There was a small aching lump in his throat, and somewhere below it, a small aching joy.

'So he d-did believe us,' he said at last. 'He knew, all the time.'

'A great man, our little Emperor,' Flavius said huskily, and slipped the roll into the breast of his ragged tunic.

XIV
An Ancient Ensign

AS he did so, from somewhere just beneath their feet came a thud, followed by a rustle as of falling plaster.

'What is that?' Flavius said, after a moment's startled hush.

Little Cullen squirmed slightly, as a dog squirms in apology when he knows he has been doing what he should not. 'Maybe it is the stone that moved in one of the pillars that hold up the floor. When we were down there I crept forward to hear better what went on, and it moved under my hand as I felt before me in the dark. It might be that I disturbed something.'

So that was what the sound in the darkness of the hypocaust had been.

'Ah well, better the house falling down than more Saxons,' Flavius said, and put out a hand to the lamp on the altar. 'Aunt Honoria, may I take this? Better perhaps that I go see what *has* happened. Cullen, come you and show me.'

Aunt Honoria, who had seated herself in the one unbroken chair, rose. 'While you are gone I'll see to some food for you.'

Justin went with neither his Great-Aunt nor Flavius. There was no point in his going with either, and he was possessed suddenly of an odd stillness, a certainty that something very strange was coming. And he stood beside the little altar, waiting for it to come. With the lamp gone, it was almost as dark as it had been in the hypocaust. He heard the wind and the rain, and the waiting silence of the poor scarred house. He heard the other two moving below the floor, a grunt that was unmistakably Flavius, the soft, formless sound of something being shifted, followed by a muffled exclamation; and in a little the sounds of movement drawing away towards the door.

And then the other two were back, the shadows circling and racing before the lamp in Cullen's hand. Flavius carried something else, a shapeless bundle of some sort, and as Cullen set the lamp once more on the altar, and the light steadied, Justin, casting a questioning glance at his cousin, was struck by the look of hushed excitement on his face.

'All's well?' he asked.

Flavius nodded. 'The house isn't falling down. The side had come out of an old hiding-place in one of the hypocaust pillars—the plaster must have crumbled away. And inside was—this.'

'What is it?'

'I—do not know yet.' Flavius turned to the lamp, and began very carefully to turn back the dark, musty-smelling folds of cloth in which the thing was wrapped. 'The wool is rotten as tinder,' he said. 'But look at these inner folds, where the lamplight falls. Look, Justin, you can see that it has been scarlet!'

Justin looked; and then put out his hands to take the mass of tindery cloth as the last folds fell away—scarlet: scarlet for a military cloak.

Flavius was holding an eagle of gilded bronze. Greenstained with verdigris where the gilding was gone, battered, mutilated—for where the great back-swept silver wings should have sprung from its shoulders were only empty socket-holes staring like blind eyes; but defiant in its furious pride, unmistakably an Eagle still.

Justin drew a long breath. 'But it is an Eagle!' he whispered unbelievingly. 'I mean—it is the Eagle of a Legion.'

'Sa, it is the Eagle of a Legion,' Flavius said.

'But—only one such Eagle was ever lost in Britain.'

They looked at the thing in silence, while little Cullen, with an air of being very well pleased with himself, after all, stood swinging his hound's tail behind him with little flicks of his rump, and looking on. The lost Ninth Legion, the lost Hispana that had marched into the Northern mists and never returned . . . 'But how could it be that one?' Justin whispered at last. 'Who could have brought it South again? None of them ever got back.'

'I don't know,' Flavius said. 'But Marcus's father disappeared with the Ninth, remember, and there was always that story in the family about an adventure in the North . . . Maybe he went to find out the truth and bring back the Eagle. A Roman Eagle in the hands of the Painted People would be a powerful rallying point. Justin, do you remember once—one evening at the farm, we were wondering how it all started; why he got that gratuity and land-grant from the Senate? Don't you see it all fits?'

'But—but if he brought it back, why should it have been hidden here? Why was the L-Legion never reformed?'

'It wasn't exactly hidden, it was buried before the altar,' Flavius said. 'Maybe it was disgraced. We shall never know. But there could have been reasons.' In the circle of lamplight, a soft yellow rose of lamplight in the darkened house, they looked at each other with growing excitement and certainty; while little Cullen stood by, swinging his hound's tail behind him. 'And I'd wager all I have that this is the Ninth's lost Eagle!'

Aunt Honoria, who, unnoticed by any of them, had returned a little before, set down the bundle of food on a nearby table, and said, 'So, you have found a lost Eagle, under the floor. At another time I will wonder and care and be amazed, but now it seems to me that it is not the time to be discovering lost Eagles. Here is food—the hunt may rouse up again at any moment, it will be dawn in an hour, and after this disturbance the Fates alone know how soon Volumnia and the rest will be stirring—let you take it, and go.'

Flavius did not seem to hear the last part of this speech. His head was up and his eyes suddenly blazing bright under the red fly-away brows. He held the battered thing against his breast. 'But it is the time of all others to be discovering lost Eagles! We have our dunghill legion—and now the gods send us a standard to follow, and who are we to refuse a gift of the gods?'

'So, take it with you. Only take it now, and go!'

Flavius had turned from her to the shrine, the Eagle still held against his breast, looking to the tiny crocus-flame of the lamp, or to the little bronze figures of the household gods in their niches, Justin was not sure which; or through them to something beyond. 'I take it for the old Service again,' he said.

And as though in answer, far off and faintly down the wind came the long-drawn, haunting notes of Cockcrow sounding from the transit camp without the Walls.

'Flavius dear,' said Aunt Honoria very gently, 'I have had a rather trying night, and I feel my temper none too sure within me. Will you please go, before I lose it and box all your ears?'

And so a few moments later they stood ready to depart; Flavius with the Eagle once more wrapped in the remains of what had once been a military cloak, Justin with the food bundle under his arm. Aunt Honoria had taken the lamp into another room, that it might not outline them in the doorway, and slipped out first herself to see that all was quiet, before she beckoned them after her. At the last moment, as they stood in the Atrium doorway with the soft rain blowing in their faces, Flavius said, 'You have heard the news, that Constantius's sails have been sighted off Tanatus?'

'Yes, I have heard. Who has not?'

'We thought you were at Aquae Sulis, safely out of the way.'

'But, then, I have always hated to be out of the way when things happen.'

'Well, there's likely to be plenty happening soon,' Flavius said, and kissed her gravely on the cheek. 'The gods keep you when they start happening, you and Volumnia.'

Justin, going out last of all, hesitated, then bent also, and gave her a kiss that was clumsy with shyness, and at which she laughed on an unexpectedly soft and young note, as she closed the door behind them.

They found their friend who lived near the South Gate waiting anxiously with the mules ready loaded up, and when the gates opened at first light, passed out without any trouble, leading the beasts, little Cullen between them with his head coyly down-bent and the folds of a woman's mantle drawn close over his motley rags which he had refused to change.

And two evenings later they stood on the crest of the Downs, where their way turned down to the farm. The wind that had been blowing off and on for several days had strengthened and was blowing hard from the south-west, driving before it the mist-scurries and low cloud as a dog drives sheep. Soft rain blew in their faces—rain that tasted faintly salt on their lips—and already the light was fading; but Justin, straining his eyes into the blurred and drifting distance, could make out no sign of Vectis Light.

His gaze going out in the same direction, Flavius said, 'Dirty weather out round the Island. The Vectis fleet would have its work cut out to intercept anything that tries to get through on this part of the coast tonight, I'm thinking.'

And they turned their backs on the sea and went on down the last home stretch, urging the tired mules ahead of them. Anthonius met them at the lower end of the vine-terraces, followed by the boy Myron, who was seldom willingly apart from him. 'All well?' he asked.

'All well, though there were exciting moments. And here?'

'We've had nine new recruits in the past few days, and several of the old lot from Regnum and Adurni have come in. More than ever the "lamp-oil" will be welcome, especially if half the rumours flying through the forest be true.'

Young Myron had come forward to take charge of the mules, and as he led them away, Flavius said, 'Here is another for the brotherhood. One that was Carausius's hound and has no love for Allectus.'

'So. We grow more to a full Legion every hour,' Anthonius said. And then, 'Pandarus and I have already called the band in and camped them about the farm. We thought it best not to wait for your orders, lest there be too little time to spare for mustering them later.'

Flavius nodded. 'Good. Then let's go and eat. I've forgotten what food looks like.'

Anthonius turned back beside them. 'There's a man waiting for you up at the houseplace—been there since yesterday, and won't tell his errand to anyone.'

'What sort of man?'

'A hunter. Big, rather splendid-looking fellow with a great spear.'

Justin and Flavius glanced at each other in the dusk, with one swift unspoken thought between them. Then Flavius said, 'Sa, we will go up and see this hunter. Anthonius, take Cullen and feed him; we'll be down for some food ourselves by and by.'

'We'll keep you some deer-meat,' said Anthonius. 'Come, Cullen, hound of Carausius.'

And so while Anthonius and the little Fool turned off towards the farm-garth below the terrace, where a deer shot by Kyndylan was being baked, Flavius and Justin made their way up to the houseplace in search of the stranger with the spear.

A dark figure squatting on the terrace before the houseplace shook clear of the shadows as they drew near, and stood out into the faint glow of a doorway that shone coppery on his lion's mane of hair and touched with palest moony gold the collar of white swan's feathers about the neck of the great spear on which he leaned.

'It *is* Evicatos!' Flavius said, voicing the thing that had been unspoken in both their minds. 'Evicatos, by the gods!' And he started forward. 'In the name of all that is most wonderful, what brings you down here?'

Justin did not feel any particular surprise. After Cullen, it seemed natural and fitting, somehow; a gathering together of those who had been caught up in the thing at the outset, now that the end of it was in sight.

'Allectus has withdrawn half the garrison from the Wall, and there is talk, much talk, among the heather,' Evicatos said. 'So I left my hounds again with Cuscrid the smith, and came south with my spear, to share the last fight, that nothing may be left of Allectus to join with the Picts one day against my people.'

'So. But how did you know where to find us? How did you know that we were not in Gaul?'

'One hears things,' said Evicatos vaguely. 'One hears things, among the heather.'

'Well, however you found the trail, glad we are to see you!' Flavius said, with a hand on the hunter's shoulder. 'You and your great spear. But you had an over-long wait after a long trail, and they are baking a deer down yonder. Afterwards we will talk of many things; but now—come you and eat.'

But before he himself sat down to eat with the rest of the band, Flavius fetched a new white-ash spear-shaft from the store; and after the meal was over he went and routed out old Tuan the shoesmith and bade him blow up the forge fire and make him a cross-bar of iron with a socket to fit on to the head of the spearshaft, and four bronze pegs. And later that night, when all the rest of the band had lain down to sleep in the byres and barns and the wing-rooms of the houseplace, he took all these things into the Atrium. And there, crouching over the low fire, with Little Cullen, who had refused to be parted from them, curled hound-wise in a corner, his Silver Branch, freed now of its muffling sheep's wool, shining in his hand, Flavius and Justin mounted the battered bronze Eagle on its spear-shaft, driving home the bronze pegs through the peg-holes in the gripping talons to make all secure.

Justin had had complete faith from the first that the Eagle was what Flavius had guessed it to be, but if he had had doubts, they would have left him that night as he worked in the sinking firelight with the soft sou-wester filling the night outside. The thing was strangely potent under his hands. What things it must have seen—bitter and dark and glorious things—this maimed bird of gilded bronze that was the life and the honour of a lost Legion. And now, he thought, it must feel that the old days were back. Again there came to him as he worked that sense of kinship with the young soldier who had made a home in this downland valley, the young soldier who surely had brought the lost Eagle of a lost Legion home to its own people, so that Eagle and farm were linked, and it was fitting that the ancient standard should go out from here to its last fight. The feeling of kinship was so strong that when, just as they had finished their task, someone loomed into the open doorway, he looked up almost expecting to see the other Marcus standing there with the windy dark behind him.

But it was Anthonius who came in, shaking the rain from his rough, dark hair.

'There's a light—a fire of some kind, burning up on the Chalk,' Anthonius said. 'Come and have a look.'

The night was clearer than it had been, and from the corner of the sheep-fold above the steading, when they reached it, they could see a red petal of fire on the crest of the Chalk far over towards the south-east.

'Yes,' Flavius said. 'Chance fire, or signal beacon? That's the question.' He put up his hand and thrust the hair back from his eyes. 'Well, there's nothing we can do to find out; that blaze is upward of a day's march away.'

Justin, straining his eyes eastward, caught another spark, away beyond the first, infinitely small and faint, but surely there. 'Signal beacon,' he said. 'There another. It's a chain of beacons.'

The fire had sunk to red embers and the Atrium was almost in darkness when they returned, but the faint glow from the hearth was enough to show the Eagle on its spear shaft, as Flavius took it up and held it for Anthonius to see.

Anthonius looked closely and in silence. Then he said: 'A standard for tomorrow?'

'A standard for tomorrow.' Flavius was smiling a little.

The other looked from him to the thing he held, and back again. 'And one, I think, that comes out of yesterday—out of a long-ago yesterday,' he said at last. 'Nay, then, I will ask no questions, and nor shall the others, though I think—some of us may guess . . . We have a standard to follow, and that is good. That is always good.'

Turning to go, he flung up a hand in salute, as a soldier in the presence of his Eagle.

In the grey of the dawn, Justin woke with a crash to hear the flying hoof-beats of a horse coming at full gallop down from the Chalk towards the farm. He tossed off the rug and scrambled to his feet.

Flavius was before him at the door, and others were already at their heels as they plunged out into the mizzle rain. A moment later a rider on a lathered pony swung into the farmyard and, reining his mount back on its haunches, dropped to the ground.

The pony stood where it had slithered to a stop, with hanging head and heaving flanks; and Phaedrus of the *Berenice* was calling out to them almost before his feet touched the ground. 'It's come, lads! It's come at last!'

Men were starting out of the half-light in all directions, to throng around him. He turned to Flavius and Justin, breathing hard. 'Constantius and his legionaries are here! They must have slipped in past the Vectis Fleet in last night's murk. I watched them run the transports aground at the head of Regnum Harbour about midnight, with a screen of galleys to cover them!'

Justin remembered the beacons in the night. Signal beacons they had been, all right. Sails off Tanatus, and now a landing in Regnum Harbour. What did that mean? An attack from two points? Maybe from many points? Well, they would know soon.

There was a moment's silence; men looked at each other almost uncertainly. The years of waiting were over. Not merely drawing to a close, but *over*, finished. And just for the first few moments they could not quite take it in.

Then they went wild. They were all round Phaedrus, round Flavius, giving tongue like a hound-pack. 'The Caesar Constantius! Caesar is come! What are we waiting for? Lead us out to join him, Flavius Aquila!' Bucklers were shaken, spears were tossed in the grey dawn-light. Suddenly Justin turned and shouldered out of the throng, back to the houseplace. He caught up the Wingless Eagle from its corner among the storechests and stacked farm implements, laughing, almost weeping, and strode out again, holding it high above his head. 'See now, my hearts! M-march we shall, and here's a standard for our following!'

He stood above them on the edge of the terrace steps, holding high the battered Eagle on its spear-shaft. He was aware of Flavius and Anthonius suddenly beside him, of faces looking up; a wild sea of faces. Men who had marched too long with the Eagles not to recognize the standard for what it was, to whom it meant lost honour and old habits of service; men to whom, without understanding, it was a thing to rally round and shout for. A reckless, tatterdemalion throng, of legionaries gone wilful-missing, farmers and hunters with wrongs to right; a sneak thief, a ship-master, a gladiator, an Emperor's Fool . . . The roar of voices beat up to him in a solid wave of sound, crashing about him so that he seemed engulfed in it.

But Flavius had flung up his arm and was shouting down the uproar. '*Sa, sa, sa!* The waiting is over, and we go to join the Caesar Constantius; but first we will eat. I want to eat, if you don't! Softly! Softly, lads! We march in an hour.'

Gradually the tumult sank, and men began to break away, making for the food-store. Pandarus the gladiator checked to break a small yellow rose from the bush below the terrace, grinning up at them. 'When I was a sword-fighter before my wooden foil, I ever liked to have a rose for the Arena!' and stuck it in the shoulder-pin of his cloak as he swaggered after the rest.

Flavius watched them go with suspiciously bright eyes. 'Ye gods, what a rabble!' he said. 'A lost Legion, sure enough! A legion of broken men. It is fitting that we should follow a wingless Eagle!' And his laughter cracked a little.

Anthonius said very gently, 'Would you change them for the finest Cohort of the Praetorian Guard, if you could?'

'No,' Flavius said. 'No, by the gods I wouldn't. But that does not explain why I should want to cry like a girl-child.' He flung a heavy arm across Justin's shoulder. 'That was nobly done, old lad. You brought the Eagle out at the one perfect moment, and they'll follow it through Tophet fires now, if need be . . . Come on, let's get some food.'

XV

Return to the Legions

THE mizzle rain had finally cleared, and the wind fallen; and the skies were breaking up as the tatterdemalion warband crossed the coast road and set their faces to the last low wooded ridge between them and the sea. At the crest of the ridge the wind-shaped oaks and thorn-trees ceased abruptly, and before them the land fell gently away to the seaward marshes; and far to the westward, where the ground rose a little clear of the saltings, uncompromisingly square among the blurred and flowing lines of the marsh, the outline of a Roman Camp, with beyond it, like a school of stranded sea-beasts along the tide-line, the dark shapes of the transports, and beyond again, anchored well out into the harbour, the screening galleys. Justin, scanning the oily sea that still heaved uneasily off-shore, could just make out, away, beyond the harbour mouth, the dark flecks of two patrol galleys on guard, he supposed, against the fleet of Allectus.

'There they are,' Flavius said. 'There—they—are!' And a deep murmur ran through the tattered band behind him.

About a hundred paces from the Dexter Gate of the camp they were halted by pickets with levelled pilums. 'Who comes?'

'Friends, in Caesar's name,' Flavius shouted back.

'Two of you may advance.'

'Wait here,' Flavius said to the rest of the band, and he and Justin went forward together.

By the turf horseshoe of the picket post the Optio met them, demanding their business.

'We are reinforcements,' Flavius said, with superb assurance. 'And must speak with the Caesar Constantius.'

The Optio looked past him and goggled slightly. 'Reinforcements, are you? Then we're sure of victory.' He brought his gaze back to Flavius's face. 'But as to the Caesar Constantius—you've got the wrong army. We're the Western Force.'

'So? Who commands here, then?'

'Asklepiodotus, his Praetorian Prefect.'

'Then we must speak with Asklepiodotus.'

'Must you?' said the Optio. 'Well, I don't know so much about that,' and then, after studying them both again, and taking another long stare at the men behind them, 'Well, you can take that robber band of yours up to the Gate, anyway. I'll send one of my men with you.'

At the Gate they were confronted by the Optio of the Gate guard, who goggled in his turn, and sent for his Centurion, who sent for one of the Tribunes; and at last they were passed through under the raised locust heads of the catapult battery covering the gateway.

Within the strongly manned stockade—clearly the camp was prepared to withstand an attack at any moment—was an ordered activity that seemed actually to throb. Bands of men working under their Optios were stacking rations and war supplies; field armourers were at work, and horses still groggy from the voyage were being got up from the stranded galleys and picketed within the seaward gate, and the smoke of many cooking-fires rose into the morning air; while here, there, and everywhere came and went the crimson crests of the Centurions overseeing all. But amidst all this, the Via Principia was almost empty as they marched up it. A broad, straight street of trampled turf, along which, supported in strands of lashed spears, stood the Cohort and Century standards, blue and violet, green and crimson, stirring a little in the light wind that still sighed across the marshes. And close beside the tent of the Commander himself, as they halted before it, the spreadwinged Eagle of the Legion.

The Tribune spoke to the staring sentry at the tent-opening, and passed within; and they were left to wait. Justin looked up at the great gilded Eagle, reading the number and titles of the Legion. The Thirtieth, Ulpia Victrix; a Lower Rhenus Legion that had come under Carausius's influence at one time, and closely flanking it—this was evidently a mixed force, drawn from more legions than one—a Vexhilation standard bearing the number and Centaur badge of a Gaulish legion that had followed the little Emperor in the early days. Somehow that seemed fitting.

The Tribune had returned now. 'The two leaders may enter.'

Flavius glanced quickly at Anthonius, saying very much in earnest beneath the laughter, 'Keep them in good order for the god's sakes!' And to Justin, 'Now for it!'

They advanced together, past the sentry into the brown-shadowed interior of the tent, and halted with drilled precision, head up and heels together, just within the entrance. A large pink-and-gold man seated at a camp table, with a papyrus list in one hand and a half-eaten radish in the other, looked up as they did so, and said in a tone of mild enquiry that reminded Justin a little of Paulinus, 'You wish to speak with me?'

The two young men came to attention and saluted; and Flavius, the spokesman as usual said, 'Sir, in the first place we would bring you word, if you have it not already, that the Caesar Constantius's sails were sighted several days since, off Tanatus; and that last night beacon-fires were burning along the Chalk.'

'As signalling the news of our landing, you mean?' said the large man, with gentle interest.

'I think so, yes.'

The large man nodded once, deeply. 'The first of these things we have heard; the second we have not heard. What else is there that you would say to me?'

'We have brought in a band of'—Flavius hesitated for a flicker of time over the word—'of allies, sir, to serve with you in this campaign.'

'So?' Asklepiodotus considered them quietly. He was a very large man, tall and stooping and beginning to be fat, with an air of gentle sloth about him which they learned later was deceptive. 'Supposing—just as a start to negotiations—that you tell me who and what in Typhon's name you are—beginning with you.'

'Marcelus Flavius Aquila,' Flavius said. 'A year and a half ago I was Cohort Centurion of the Eighth Cohort of the Second Augustan, stationed at Magnis on the Wall.'

'H'mm,' said the Commander, and his heavy-lidded eyes moved to Justin.

'Tiberius Lucius Justinianus, Surgeon to the same C-Cohort at the same time, sir.'

Asklepiodotus raised his brows. 'So? This is all very surprising. And this past year and a half?'

Briefly and levelly, with the air of one making a formal report, Flavius accounted for the past year and a half, while the Praetorian Prefect sat and gazed at him as one lost in a gentle reverie, the radish still in his hand.

'So the occasional intelligence and—reinforcements—that have reached us from time to time from this province were of your providing?'

'Some of them, anyway, sir.'

'Most interesting. And this band—how many does it number, and what is it made up of?'

'Something over sixty. Tribesmen for the most part, with a stiffening of legionaries gone wilful-missing.' Suddenly Flavius was grinning. 'Another Cohort Centurion, and an ex-gladiator and Carausius's tame Fool for good measure . . . Oh, it's a thundering fine Legion, sir. But we all know how to fight, and most of us have something to fight for.'

'So. Show it to me.'

'If you come to the tent opening you will see it in all its glory.'

Asklepiodotus laid his half-eaten radish back in the dish of little loaves and cheese from which he had been making a belated morning meal when they arrived, laid the papyrus sheet neatly and exactly on top of another, and got up. His bulk almost completely filled the tent-opening, but Justin, peering anxiously from behind him, could catch a wedge-shaped glimpse of the band drawn up outside. Anthonius rigidly erect as any Cohort Centurion of the Empire on parade; Pandarus with his yellow rose and the desperado swagger of his old calling in every line of him; little Cullen with his Silver Branch in the girdle of his tattered motley, holding the wingless Eagle proudly upright, but standing himself on one leg like a heron, which somewhat spoiled the effect; Evicatos beside him, leaning on his great war-spear, whose collar of white swan's feathers stirred and ruffled in the light wind. And behind them, the rest—the whole tattered, reckless, disreputable crew.

Asklepiodotus looked them over, seemed to ruminate for a few moments on the battered Eagle, and turned back to the mule-pack on which he had been sitting. 'Yes, I see what you mean.' He took up the radish again, looked at it for a moment as though he were going on with his breakfast, and then seemed to change his mind. Suddenly he opened both eyes wide upon the two young men before him, and it was as though for an instant the bare blade glinted through the furry sheath. 'Now, give me proof that you are what you claim to be. Give me proof that there is so much as a mustard seed of truth in this story that you have been telling me.'

Flavius said a little blankly, 'What proof can we give you? What else could we be?'

'For all that I know, you may be no more than a band of robbers and renegades in search of easy plunder. Or—you may even be a Trojan horse.'

Complete silence descended on the brown shadowed tent; and around it even the great camp was silent with one of those odd hushes that fall sometimes for no reason on a busy place. Justin could hear the faint, uneasy sounding of the sea, and the mocking ripple of bells beyond the tent-flap, as Cullen changed from one weary leg to the other. There must be a right thing to say or do, he was thinking. There must be *some* answer. But if Flavius can't think of it, there's not much chance for me.

And then footsteps sounded outside, and someone loomed into the opening of the tent. A thin, brown man in the uniform of a Senior Cohort Centurion entered and saluted, laying some tablets on the table before the Commander. 'List complete, sir. I suppose you are aware that there's some kind of comic warband with what looks remarkably like the remains of a Roman Eagle tied to a spear-shaft paraded in the Forum?' Then, as his quick glance took in the two young men standing in the deeper shadows, he gave a startled exclamation. 'Light of the Sun! Justin!'

Justin's gaze had been fixed on the newcomer from the first instant of his appearing. That makes three—, he was thinking. Cullen and Evicatos and now . . . Things always go in threes—things and people. Oh, but this is wonderful; most wonderful all the same!

'Yes, sir!' he said.

'Do you know these two, Centurion Licinius?' interposed the Commander.

Licinius had already caught Justin's hand. 'I know this one, anyway, though he does seem to have grown into a hairy barbarian. He was cub to my Cohort Surgeon at Beersheba. Roma Dea! Boy, are you one of that band of cut-throats outside?'

Justin's wide mouth was curling up at the corners, and his deplorable ears were bright pink with pleasure. 'I am, sir. And this my k-kinsman also.'

'So?' Licinius looked Flavius over, and nodded brusquely as he saluted.

'When you have finished your reunion,' said Asklepiodotus, 'tell me this, Primus Pilus: would you trust these two?'

The lean brown Centurion looked down at his Commander with a faint smile in his eyes. 'The one I know, I would trust anywhere, and in any circumstances. If he vouched for the other, as seems to be the case, then I would trust him too.'

'So be it, then,' said Asklepiodotus. 'We could do with scouts who know the countryside; also with more cavalry. Was there ever a time when the Legions could not do with more cavalry?' He drew tablets and stylus towards him, and scratched a few words on the soft wax. 'March this cut-throat band of yours down to the horse-lines, and take over the mounts and equipment of the two squadrons of Dacian horse that came in last night from the Portus Adurni garrison; here is your authorization. Then hold yourselves ready for orders.'

'Sir.' Flavius took the tablets, but stood his ground.

'Something more?'

'Leave to lodge our Eagle in the Via Principia with the rest, sir.'

'Ah yes, this Eagle,' said Asklepiodotus reflectively. 'How did you come by it?'

'It was found in a hiding-place beneath the shrine of my family's house in Calleva.'

'So? You know, of course, what it is?'

'It is what remains of a Legionary Eagle, sir.'

Asklepiodotus picked up the list which his Senior Centurion had laid on the table. 'Only one such Eagle has ever been lost in this province.'

'That also I know. One of my line was lost with it. I—think the Senate knew about its coming back, at the time.'

They looked at each other steadily. Then Asklepiodotus nodded. 'The sudden reappearance of a lost Eagle is a serious matter, so serious that I propose to know nothing about it . . . Permission granted, on condition that the thing is—shall we say "missing" again when all be over.'

'Agreed, and thank you, sir,' Flavius said, saluting.

They had turned to the opening of the tent when the Commander halted them again. 'Oh, and Centurion Aquila, I have called a Council to meet here at noon. As men who know the country, and as—er—leaders of an allied force, I shall expect you both to attend.'

'At noon, sir,' Flavius said.

They found the Decurion in charge at the horse-lines, showed him the Commander's authorization, and duly took over the fine little part-arab cavalry mounts of the Dacian Horse. The bow-legged

Auxiliary who was told off to show them the equipment stores and fodder stacks was a friendly soul, fortunately more interested in talking himself than in asking questions. In common with about half the camp, he was not yet over the rough crossing.

'My *head*!' said the bow-legged Auxiliary. 'Like an armourer's shop. Bang—bang—bang! And the ground heaving almost as bad as the deck of that cursed transport. It would be my luck to be in the Western force, with the long crossing all up from the Sequana—and me the worst sailor in the Empire!'

Flavius, more interested in troop movements than in the bow-legged Auxiliary's sufferings, said, 'I suppose the Caesar Constantius and the Eastern force sailed direct from Gesoriacum?'

'Aye—Constantius sailed before we did, so they say; and the galleys with him to scout ahead and cover the transports coming on after; so I do suppose *he'll* have been at sea as long as us or longer—but his transports will have had maybe only a few hours of it, and it's transports I'm interested in . . .'

Altogether, Justin and Flavius were a good deal wiser as to the general situation when, at noon, they found themselves in the exalted company of half a dozen staff Tribunes, several Senior Centurions, and the Legate of the Ulpia Victrix, gathered round the makeshift table before the Commander's tent.

Asklepiodotus opened the proceedings, sitting with his hands clasped peacefully on his stomach. 'I believe you know, all of you, that Constantius's sails were seen off Tanatus several days ago. You will not, I believe, know that in all probability Allectus has already been warned of our landing by beacon chain. You will agree that this makes it imperative that we march on Londinium without delay.' He turned to the Senior Centurion. 'Primus Pilus, how soon can you have us in marching order?'

'You must give us two days, sir,' said Licinius. 'We've had a foul crossing and both men and horses are in poor shape.'

'I had a feeling you were going to say that,' said Asklepiodotus plaintively. 'I can't think *why* people will be seasick.' (Here the Legate of the Ulpia Victrix, still faintly green, shuddered visibly.) '*I* never am.'

'The rest of us have not your strength of mind, sir,' said Licinius, with a quirk of laughter in his hard face. 'We need two days.'

'Every hour's delay adds to the danger, amongst other things, of our being attacked while still in camp. I'll give you one day.'

There was a moment's silence, and then Licinius said, 'Very good, sir.'

The Council went on, following the usual way of such Councils, while the short noontide shadow of the Ulpia Victrix's Eagle crept slowly across the group before the Commander's tent. And Justin and Flavius had no part in it until Asklepiodotus brought up the question of routes. 'There are two roads possible for our advance; and the choice of them we have left until now, since it is a matter depending on circumstances. Now it is time that we considered the matter; but before we make choice of either road, I feel that we should hear what one who knows the country well has to say,' and he crooked a plump finger at Flavius, who with Justin stood silent on the outskirts of the group.

Flavius's head went up with a jerk. 'Me, sir?'

'Yes, you. Come here and give us your counsel.'

Flavius moved forward into the circle, to stand beside the makeshift table; and suddenly very much the Cohort Centurion under his barbarian outer-seeming, suddenly very sober and rather white as he looked round him at the grave-faced men in the bronze and crimson of the higher command. It was one thing to lead the kind of outlaw band that he had brought in that day to serve in the ranks of Rome; quite another to be called on suddenly to give advice which, if it were taken and proved wrong, might lead an army to destruction.

'There are, as the Prefect says, two roads from here to Londinium,' Flavius said, after that one moment's pause: 'One from Regnum about two miles east of here, one through Venta and Calleva. I would choose the Venta and Calleva road, though it may be a few miles longer.'

Licinius nodded. 'Why?'

'For this reason, sir: that after the first day's march, over the Chalk, the road from Regnum runs into the Forest of Anderida. Dense wild country, ideal for ambush, especially for such as Allectus's mercenaries, used to forest warfare in their own land. And you'll have that with you right up to where the scarp of the North Chalk rises like a rampart only a day's march before Londinium. The Venta road, on the other hand, runs into wooded downland almost at once, and the chief danger of ambush lies in the first forty miles—the part furthest from Allectus's main force, and therefore least open to attack.'

'And after that first forty miles?' asked Asklepiodotus.

'Calleva,' Flavius said. 'And once half a march past Calleva, you are well down into the Thamesis Valley. That is forest too, in part, but open forest; big trees, not damp-oak scrub—and open cornland. And you will be in the very heart of the province, where it will be hard indeed for any defence to stand against you.'

'Yes, you have a good eye for country,' Asklepiodotus said, and there was silence. One or two of the men about the table nodded as though in agreement. Then the Commander spoke again. 'Thank you, Centurion; that is all for now. If we have further need of you, I will send for you again.'

And there the thing rested.

But when the Western Force marched out for Londinium next morning, it was by the Venta and Calleva road.

Flavius, knowing the country as he did, had been sent for to ride with Asklepiodotus, leaving Justin and Anthonius to command the two squadrons of ragged cavalry that the band had now become; and looking round at them, Justin felt that, all things considered, tattered and disreputable as they were, they made a good showing, finely mounted, properly armed now with long cavalry swords—all save Evicatos, who had refused any weapon but his beloved spear, and little Cullen, who was their Eagle-bearer. His glance rested for a moment on the Fool riding in the forefront of their company, managing his mount one-handed with surprising ease, while with the other he steadied aloft the wingless Eagle, its spear-shaft now adorned with a wreath of yellow broom hung there by Pandarus in a mood of reckless mockery, to imitate the gold wreaths and medallions of the Ulpia Victrix.

Gradually the ground began to rise, and they were clear of the marsh when an exclamation from Anthonius, riding knee to knee with him, made Justin glance back over his shoulder towards the deserted camp behind them. Fire met his gaze; red, hungry fire leaping heavenward from the stranded transports, and dark smoke drifting aside on the sea-wind.

It was as though the Prefect Asklepiodotus said to his Legions, 'Forward now, to victory. Victory it must be, for there's no sounding the Retreat in *this* campaign.'

XVI

'Carausius! Carausius!'

NEWS met them on the march, news brought in by the scouts, by native hunters, by deserters from the usurper's army; and some of it was not good. The transports of the Eastern Force had failed to make contact with Constantius in the foul weather; and knowing that the young Caesar could not force a landing without his troops, Allectus was staking everything on a wild attempt to finish with Asklepiodotus before the moment came to turn at bay against the other. He was hurrying westward along the ancient track from Durovernum under the scarp of the North Chalk, straining every nerve to reach the pass in the downs before the avenging forces of Rome could do so, and with him every fighting man that he could lay hands on. Twelve thousand men or more, said the reports: mercenaries and marines for the most part. Not more than six or seven Cohorts of the regular Legions. The Cohorts of the Wall had not reached him yet, and even if they did so in time, there was so much disaffection among the Legions that it seemed very doubtful if he would dare to use them.

That was to the good, anyway, Justin was thinking, casting up good and bad as he sat two nights later looking out over the camp-fires of the army massed in the shallow downland pass where the old track came up to cross the Calleva road. He did not really doubt the outcome of tomorrow's battle, he had faith in Asklepiodotus and the power of the Legions. But the fact remained that since Constantius had failed to land, they were going to have only half their forces tomorrow, to handle everything that Allectus could bring against them; and he realized soberly that they would have no easy victory.

The army had come up at full pace, covering the fifteen miles from Venta in three hours, a gruelling business in June, for men in heavy marching order. But they had done it, and now they waited—a long flat waiting—around their bivouac fires, while Allectus, beaten in that desperate race for the strategic pass, had made camp also, a couple of miles away, to rest his weary host, and maybe also in the hope of tempting the forces of Rome from their strong position.

Asklepiodotus, not finding himself tempted, had used the time to make strong defence works of felled thorn-trees across the mouth of the pass from which to base tomorrow's operations. And now the camp was complete; the bivouac fires glowed red in the moon-washed darkness, and around them the men took their ease, each with his sword buckled on and his shield and pilum to his hand, waiting for tomorrow. From where he sat with the rest of the Lost Legion round their own fire a little above the main camp, Justin could look out to the silver snail-trail that was the moon on the metalled road to Calleva, six miles away. But that other, more ancient way, coming up from the lower ground, was hidden by the rising mist—mist which already lay like the ghost of a forgotten sea over the low ground of the Thamesis Valley; over the great camp where Allectus waited with his host.

Figures came and went like shadows between him and the fires, low voices exchanged a password. The horses stamped and shifted from time to time, and once he heard the scream of an angry mule. But the night itself was very still, behind the sounds of the camp. A wonderful night, up here above the mist; the bracken of the hillside frozen into silver stillness below the dark fleece of thorn-scrub that covered the higher slopes on either side, the moon still low in a glimmering sky that seemed brushed over with a kind of moth-wing dust of gold. Somewhere far down the widening valley a vixen called to her mate, and somehow the sound left the silence empty.

Justin thought, If we are killed tomorrow, the vixen will still call across the valley to her mate. Maybe she has cubs somewhere among the root-tangle of the woods. Life goes on. And the thought was somehow comforting. Flavius had gone down to the Praetorium to get the new watchword and tomorrow's battle-cry; and the rest of the band sprawled about their fire, waiting for his return. Cullen sat beneath the battered Eagle, which they had driven upright into the turf, his face absorbed and happy as he touched almost soundlessly the apples of his beloved Silver Branch; and beside him—an unlikely couple, but drawn together by the bond of their Hibernian blood, as fellow countrymen in a strange land—Evicatos sat with his hands round one updrawn knee, his face turned to the north and west of north, as though he looked away to his own lost hills. Kyndylan and one of the legionaries were playing knucklebones. Pandarus, with the dried wisp of yesterday's yellow rose in his cloak-pin, had found a suitable stone and was sharpening his dagger, smiling to himself a small, grimly joyous smile. 'The bread and onions you ate this morning tasted better than any feast to a man who expects to eat again, and the sun through the grilles overhead is brighter for you than for any man who thinks to see it rise tomorrow,' Pandarus had said once. For himself, Justin found that the knowledge that he was quite likely going to be killed tomorrow was rather a heavy price to pay for his own sudden and piercing awareness of the moonlit world and the faint scent of honeysuckle on the night air, and the vixen calling to her mate. But then I suppose I've always been a coward—maybe that was the real reason I never wanted to be a soldier. It really isn't any wonder father was so disappointed in me, thought poor Justin.

Somebody came by on his way back from visiting outposts, whistling a tune half under his breath, and checked beside them. Justin glanced up and saw a crested helmet outlined against the moon and was on his feet in an instant, as Licinius's voice said, 'It is pleasant up here above the camp; may I join you for a while?'

'Surely, sir. Sit here.' Justin indicated the sheepskin riding-rug on which he had been sitting, and with a word of thanks the Primus Pilus folded up on to it, saying to those of the band who, mindful of old discipline, had risen or showed signs of doing so, 'Nay, go on as you were before. I come only as a self-invited guest, not in any official capacity.'

Justin said after a few minutes, 'Everything seems so quiet. And by this hour tomorrow it will be as quiet again.'

'Aye, and in all likelihood with the fate of the province settled in the time between.'

Justin nodded. 'I am glad the Parthica and the Ulpia Victrix are here.'

'Why so?'

'Because they served under C-Carausius once. It seems right that his own legions should avenge him.'

Licinius glanced at him sideways under his helmet rim. 'When you go into battle tomorrow, will it be for Rome, or for Carausius?'

'I—don't know,' Justin said painstakingly. 'I suppose for the province of Britain. And yet—it is in my mind there'll be a good few remembering the little Emperor, among the men who served under him.'

'So, for Britain, and for one little half-pirate Emperor, and not for Rome at all,' Licinius said. '*Sa, sa,* the greatness of Rome falls into yesterday.'

Justin pulled a bracken frond beside him, and began carefully to strip the tiny lobes from the stalk. 'Carausius said something like that to Flavius and me once. He said that if Britain could be made strong enough to stand alone when Rome fell, something m-might be saved from the dark, but if not—the lights would go out everywhere. He said that if he could avoid a knife in his back before the work was done, he would make Britain as strong as that. But in the end he d-didn't avoid it; and so now we fight in the ranks of Rome again.'

They were silent a while, then Licinius drew his legs under him. 'Ah well, I think that we have been talking treason, you and I. And now I must be on my way.'

When he was gone, Justin sat for a while staring into the fire. His few words with his old Commander had brought Carausius very vividly before him; the terrible little Emperor who had yet thought to write the letter that Flavius carried in the breast of his tunic.

When he looked up again, Flavius was coming towards him through the bracken, 'Have you the watchword?'

'Watchword and battle-cry, they're both the same,' Flavius said. He looked round at the throng in the firelight, his eyes at their most blazing bright under the wild shock of flaming hair. 'Brothers, the watchword for tonight and the battle shout for tomorrow is *"Carausius!"*'

The first light of next morning was shining water pale over the woods, as Justin headed down with Flavius and the rest, through the fern and the young foxgloves that swayed bellyhigh about their horses' legs, to their appointed place among the Auxiliary cavalry of the right wing. The heavy dew of the summer morning was grey on the bracken fronds, and flew in shining spray as they brushed by, and suddenly, though there was no sun as yet, all the air was shining and a lark leapt into the morning, dropping its rippling thread of song above the massing Legions, as the disreputable band sidled their horses into position behind a squadron of Gaulish Cavalry.

After that there was waiting again—waiting.

And then Flavius's head went up suddenly. 'Listen! Did you hear anything?'

Justin listened, his heart racing. There was only the jink of a bridle-bit as one of the ponies moved, the distant bark of an order from the battle-line, and then stillness again. And then, somewhere away below them in the mist that still hung about the lower ground, a faint, low-pitched murmur of sound, like the distant thunder that one feels while it is still too far off to hear. Only a moment, before it was lost in some fold of the land; then, even as they strained after it, the tension running through the massed Cohorts like a wind-ripple through standing corn, here it came again, clearer, nearer: the sound of an advancing host with many horses.

'Not long now,' Flavius said.

Justin nodded, running the tip of his tongue over a dry lip.

Nearer and nearer rolled the blurred thunder of hooves and marching feet; and then, far ahead where the Auxiliary skirmishers held the first line of defence, a trumpet sang, and from further off another answered it, as cock crows defiance to cock in the dawn.

The opening phases of that battle seemed to Justin, looking down on it from above and apart, as Jove might do, to be quite unreal; a thing of the ordered movements of great blocks of men, more like some vast and deadly game of chess than the struggle for a province. A game controlled by the tiny child's-toy figure on the opposite hillside that he knew was the Prefect Asklepiodotus with his staff about him. He saw far away the wavering and billowmg line where the light skirmishing troops of both armies came together; he saw, closer in, the solid, grey-mailed blocks of the Cohorts, each under its own standard, with the Eagle of the Ulpia Victrix in the van. He saw the Auxiliaries, their part played, falling back, slowly, steadily, passing cleanly through the gaps left for them between Cohort and Cohort; saw the gaps closing like a door. And now the trumpets were sounding the Advance, and with a slow and measured certainty that was somehow more terrible than any wild rush, the whole battle-front was rolling forward to meet that other host rolling darkly towards them up the line of the ancient track and far across the ferny hillside on either hand.

Again the trumpets were singing, ringing to the morning sky, Cavalry trumpets now, and the long waiting was over. 'Come on, my heroes; it's our turn now!' Flavius cried; and with the fiery notes of the trumpets still ringing in their ears, the horses broke from a stand into a canter, and they were sweeping forward to guard the flanks of the Cohorts as the valley broadened and the shielding thorn-scrub fell away on either hand. The sun was well up now; far ahead of them it glinted on spearhead and shield-rim, axe-blade and helmet of grey iron, striking sparks of light from the polished bronze of horse ornaments. Justin saw the black boar banners of the Saxons, the swarming squadrons of Cavalry. He could make out the denser massing of standards in the midst of the enemy host, the stiffer lines of marines and legionaries and the gleam of gold and Imperial Purple where Allectus himself rode among his wild barbarian horde. Vaguely in the engulfing turmoil, he was aware of the two battle-lines rolling in towards each other; and his ears were full of a sound that he had never heard before; the clashing, grinding furnace-roar of full battle.

And now, for Justin, the battle whose opening moves had seemed like a game of chess, became a bright and terrible confusion, narrowing down to his own part in it, while all else ceased to have any meaning. For him, the great battle for the province of Britain fought out that fine summer's day, was a snarling, blue-eyed face and streaming yellow hair; it was a coral-studded shield-boss and a darting spear-blade and the up-tossed rolling mane of a horse. It was a thunder of hooves and the wheeling and swerving of wild cavalry through the bracken, and the red stain growing on his own sword. It was Flavius always the length of his horse's head in front of him, and the wingless Eagle in the thick of the press, and the little Emperor's name yelled above the tumult for a battle-cry, 'Carausius! Carausius!'

And then somehow the battle was growing ragged, scattering and spreading out over the countryside, becoming no longer one battle, but a score. And suddenly, as though a bright and raging fever had lifted from his brain, Justin was aware of breathing-space, and the sun away over towards evening in a sky puffed with white summer cloud. And they were far to the north, on the tattered fringe of things; and southward the legionaries were rounding up the beaten enemy as sheep-dogs driving sheep.

He shook his head like a swimmer breaking surface, and looked about him at the Lost Legion. It was smaller than it had been this morning, and several of those who still rode with them had some hurt. Little Cullen, still carrying the Eagle proudly erect, its crown of yellow broom long since torn away, had a gash over one eye; and Kyndylan was managing his horse one-handed, with a useless arm hanging at his side.

Turning back towards what remained of the battle, they came

straggling up a long wooded ridge; and from the crest of it found themselves looking down on the Londinium road.

And along the Londinium road and all across the country below them, like a river in storm spate, was pouring a wild flood of fugitives, reserves and horse-holders probably for the most part; mercenaries breaking back and streaming away from the battle; a broken rabble of barbarians on foot and on horse-back, flying for their lives.

Justin felt suddenly sick. Few things in the world could be more pitiless than a beaten and demoralized army; and only a few miles away the Londinium road ran through Calleva!

Flavius broke the silence that had gripped them all with something like a groan. 'Calleva! It will be fire and sword for the whole city if that rabble get in!' He wheeled about on the men with him. 'We must save Calleva! We must ride with them and hope for our chance at the gates. There's no time to wait for orders. Anthonius, get back to Asklepiodotus and tell him what goes forward, and bid him, in the names of all the gods there be, to send up a few squadrons of Cavalry!'

Anthonius flung up his hand, and wheeling his horse was away almost before the words were spoken.

'Cullen, cover up the Eagle. Now, come on, and remember we are fugitives like the rest until we are within the gates,' Flavius cried. 'Follow me—and *keep together*!'

Justin was at his side as usual; Cullen with the Eagle under his ragged cloak and the spear-shaft sticking out behind him. Evicatos and the old gladiator, and the rest hard behind, a wild-geese skein of flying horsemen, as they broke from cover of the woods and sent their horses downhill, crashing through the fern and foxgloves as though in desperate flight, swinging wide into the midst of the fleeing barbarians.

XVII
Eagle in the Flames

THE flood of fugitives caught them up and swept them on and away. A flood that was desperate—and wicked. Justin could feel the desperation and the wickedness flowing all about him, as he dug his heel again and again into his mare's flank, leaning forward to ease her, in a desperate attempt to force a way ahead, to outride the stream of sudden death pouring towards Calleva, and reach the gates ahead of it.

The gates—if only the gates were shut in time, it might be that the little city would yet be safe, for this wolfish rabble would scarcely spare the time to break them down, with Asklepiodotus and his legions the gods knew how close on its heels. If *only* they had got the gates closed in time!

But when the road lifted over the last ridge, and Calleva lay before them on its gentle hill, Justin saw, with a sickening lurch of the heart, that the gates were open, and the barbarians pouring through. The whole countryside was alive with fugitives by now; with desperate shadows among the trees, fleeing onward and away; and, ever more thickly, that dark stream of men, turning aside from the main flood of their fellows, to the open gate of Calleva and the prospect of loot that was more to them than escape.

Riding neck and neck, with the Lost Legion close behind them, yelling with the rest, Justin and Flavius swept through between the gate towers. The bodies of half a dozen legionaries and townsmen lay within the gates, which they must have sought to close too late. Allectus had withdrawn the rest of the guard.

The wide main street running north from the gate was already jammed with the marauders; some of the houses were on fire, and abandoned horses, terrified by the tumult and the smell of burning, were running loose among the howling mob. But a large part of the rabble had halted to sack the big posting inn just within the gates, which, from its size and air of importance, seemed to promise treasure for the taking.

'Down here!' Flavius shouted. 'Get ahead of them—' and swung his horse right-handed into a narrow alleyway beside the inn. Justin and the rest swung after him; a small knot of Saxons also, but they were dealt with shortly and sharply, and the band pressed on. The narrow ways were deserted; it seemed that most of the people must have fled to the shelter of the basilica. In the gardens of the temple of Sul Minerva, Flavius reined up in full career, and dropped to the ground, followed by the rest. 'Leave the horses here. If the fire spreads they'll have a chance to keep clear,' he panted. 'Kyndylan, come you with me—and you—and you.' Quickly he singled out about a dozen of the band, all men who knew Calleva well. 'Justin, you take the rest, and hold those devils back as long as may be. It looks as though most of the town has made for the Forum already—but we must be sure. Give us all the time you can . . .'

They were heading back for the heart of the town, from which came ever more strongly the reek of burning and the shouts and cries of the Saxons. Justin remembered after, though he scarcely noticed at the time, how Pandarus broke a crimson rose in passing from a bush beside the temple steps, and thrust it into the shoulder-pin of his cloak as he ran. Pandarus and his rose for the Arena!

The lane they were following brought them into a wider one, and they swung left, then left again, the ugly tumult swelling every moment on their ears; and then they were back in the main street. Justin caught one glimpse of the gleaming white colonnades of the Forum at the top of the street, then it was behind him as he headed his little company towards the fight which was now raging lower down.

'Friend! friend! friend!' Justin shouted as they flung themselves into the thin ranks of the defenders. 'Carausius! Carausius!'

There were a few among the citizens who had swords; but for the most part they were armed only with such weapons as they had been able to catch up: daggers and knives and the heavy tools of their trade. Justin glimpsed the purple tunic-stripe of a magistrate, the saffron kilt of a countryman, and in their midst one russet-haired giant swinging a butcher's axe. It was a most valiant defence, but it could not last. Already they had been driven back half the length of the street. The sudden swelling of their ranks by Justin and his fellows with their long cavalry swords checked the fall back for a moment, but it would have taken a couple of Cohorts to hold that mob, maddened now by the wine of the Silver Garland's cellars, so that they forgot the danger hard behind them, forgot all else in the wild joy of destruction. The street was full of the smoke of burning houses, and out of it yelling Saxons loomed to fling themselves like wild beasts on the defenders; while at any moment more of them might find their way round by the side streets—there was nothing to prevent them—and be between the defenders and the Forum.

How long they held up the barbarian flood, slowly giving ground despite all their desperate resistance, fighting back from house to house, from street corner to street corner, Justin had not the least idea. Suddenly they were right back into the open space that surrounded the Forum, and there was no longer any question of holding the barbarians in check, no question of anything but somehow gaining the Forum entrance themselves before they were completely cut off.

And then Flavius was there, and others with him; Flavius yelling in his ear, 'The main entrance—barricaded the rest.'

The arch of the main entrance was overhead, proud and pompous with its marble sheathing and bronze statues, and Flavius was shouting to the townsmen with them, 'Back! Get back to the basilica. We'll hold the gate for you—do you hold the door for us when we come!'

And in the mouth of the deep gate arch, the Lost Legion turned shoulder to shoulder to hold back the yelling horde of barbarians while the townsmen gained the basilica.

Behind him, Justin heard the retreating rush of feet growing smaller across the sun-warmed emptiness of the Forum. Little Cullen was beside him, the battered Eagle raised high amid the reeling press; Pandarus with the crimson rose in his shoulder-pin; Flavius with his buckler long since gone, and his blade biting deep; a rocksteady band of champions to hold back the tide of raging, fair-haired devils that crashed and hurled against them.

It was a short struggle, but a desperate one, and several of the band were down, their places instantly filled by the next man behind them, before the cry went up, 'All clear behind!'

And Flavius yelled, 'Break off! Back to the basilica—now!' and they sprang back and turned to run for their lives.

Justin was running with the rest; running and stumbling with a bursting heart across a seemingly endless expanse of sunlit cobbles, towards the refuge of the great east door that seemed to draw no nearer. They had a few moments' start, for in the very wildness of their rush, undisciplined as they were, the Saxons had jammed themselves together in the gate arch, yelling, struggling, trampling over each other in wild confusion, and the band of desperate men were half across the Forum before Allectus's wolves burst through like a flood released behind them. They were into the shadow of the basilica now, but the barbarians were hard on their heels. The great door was gaping before them; men massed at either side to shield their flanks and draw them in; and on the portico steps the hindmost of the Lost Legion whirled about, buckler to buckler, to do rearguard for the rest.

Justin, his shoulder against Flavius's shoulder, had a confused vision of a wave of barbarians sweeping towards them, winged and snarling heads and the evening light on spear and saexblade and upswung axe. The forerunners of the wave were upon them, and he struck home over the rim of his buckler, and saw a man crumple down the portico steps, even as he felt the top step against his heel, and moved backward and up.

'*Sa, sa!* We'll just do it!' Flavius shouted.

The doors were three parts closed, leaving only room for their passage, as the two of them dropped their points and sprang back. And next instant, with the power of a score of shoulders behind them, the great carved timber leaves crashed shut, and the heavy bars were thrust into place.

Outside in the Forum rose a yell of baffled fury, and a crashing of blows against the doors that echoed in the high, empty places of the vast building above the heads of the multitude huddled there. A tall man with an old uniform sword in his hand, who had been with them through the street-fighting, turned a haggard face to Flavius as he leaned a moment panting against the door. 'In the name of all the gods, who are you?' And then. 'Roma Dea! It is young Aquila!'

Flavius pushed off from the door. 'Yes, sir. We'll give you an account of ourselves later. Just now there's not much time to spare. Help will be here soon, but we've got to hold the basilica till it comes.'

He had stepped, naturally and inevitably, into the Command; and even in that moment of stress, it flashed into Justin's mind with a glimmer of laughter that if they were not all killed in the next hour or so, Flavius would undoubtedly get his Legion one day.

Flavius, knowing the basilica and its weak places as well as anyone there, was posting men to hold the main entrance and the small side doors, and in the Municipal offices and treasure-chambers that opened all down the long side of the hall opposite to the entrance; getting the women and children cleared away from the danger points. 'Back, further back here. We must have more fighting space.' Posting guards in the galleries above the aisle of the great hall, to watch the high windows, in case the Saxons should seek to reach them by way of the colonnade roof.

Justin never forgot that scene. There must have been eighteen hundred souls or more, slave and free, crowded into the basilica. The women and children, the old and the sick, huddled together around the feet of the columns, on the raised floor of the Tribunals at either end where in time of peace the Magistrates sat to deal justice, on the steps of the Council Chamber itself; while the men with their hastily snatched up weapons stood to the barred doors beyond which rose the wolf-pack yelling of the Saxon mercenaries. He saw huddled forms and strained white faces in the shadows; here a mother trying to comfort a frightened child, there an old merchant clutching the bag of jewels he had caught up in flight. There were family pets, too, and small pathetic family treasures. A little dark-eyed girl had a singing-bird in a cage, to which she talked softly all the while, and which hopped unconcernedly about, fluting a few notes from time to time above the yelling and the random thunder of blows against the carved timbers of the entrance.

But Justin had little leisure to look about him. He was Flavius's Second-in-command, but also he was a surgeon; and just now the wounded—there were many wounded—needed him more than Flavius did; and he laid aside sword and buckler to do what he could for them. It was not much; there was no water, no bandage linen, and he must have help. Looking hurriedly round the great hall, his eye picked out a figure huddled in the shadows that he knew for the chief physician of the place. He called to him. 'Balbus, come and help me, man.' Then, as the huddled figure paid no heed, thinking that perhaps the man was deaf, he rose from his knee beside one of the wounded, and went quickly across to him. But when he stooped and set a hand on his shoulder, the other shied away from him and looked up with a face shining with sweat and the colour of lard, and began to rock himself to and fro. Justin dropped his hand and turned away with a feeling of mingled disgust and pity. No help to be found there.

But in the same instant two women rose in his path, and he saw that the foremost was Aunt Honoria and the one just behind her was the enormous Volumnia.

'Tell us what to do and we will do it,' said Aunt Honoria, and it seemed to him that she was very beautiful.

'Tear up your tunics,' he said. 'I want bandage linen; there are men here who will live if the bleeding is stopped and d-die if it isn't. We must get the wounded together, too. Can't see what there is to do, with them scattered all up and down the hall.'

Other helpers were gathering to him before the words were well out; a stout wine-shop woman; a slave from the dyeworks with splashes of old dyes ingrained in skin and garments; a girl like a white flower, who looked as though she had never seen blood before, and many others.

They got the wounded together before the North Tribunal, and at least there was no lack of stuff for bandages now; bandages of the coarsest homespun and the finest flower-coloured summer linen, as the women stripped off their outer tunics and tore them up to serve the need, and set to work with him in their shifts. Most of them knew how to deal with a sword-cut or a broken head, he found, and that left him free to attend to the more sorely hurt. Thank the gods he had his instrument-case!

With the fair girl to help him, he had just finished getting a javelin-head out of the shoulder of one of the Otter's Ford brothers, when the pounding against the main door, which had slackened a little as the barbarians found the money-changers and the wine-shops in the Forum, suddenly returned tenfold. A new yelling arose outside, unearthly in its savagery and insane triumph, and suddenly the smoke-dimmed sky beyond the clerestory windows was shot with fire. The great door shook and shuddered under the new onslaught—not now the mere random thunder of war-axes and light beams torn from the nearby shops, but something infinitely more deadly. The Saxon devils must have got into the timber yard nearby, and found there something to use as a ram.

There was nothing more at the moment to be done for the wounded that could not be done as well by Aunt Honoria and the other women. Justin said to the pale girl, 'Stay here with him whatever happens, and if the bleeding starts again, press where I showed you,' and snatching up sword and buckler, ran for his place among the men at the main entrance. Flavius yelled to him above the rendering thunder of the ram, to get up to the gallery and see what was happening. And a few moments later, scarcely aware of the steep stairs behind the Tribunal that he had taken two at a time, he emerged high above the nave of the basilica. The light was beginning to fade, sulphurous behind the rolling smoke; and when he peered out through the beautiful unglazed lattice-work of the nearest window, the whole Forum seemed a pit of fire. The Saxons, made drunk on the contents of every wine-shop in Calleva, and raging not only for plunder, but for blood, with the savage, wild-beast frenzy of their kind, had dragged bits of timber from the burning buildings to spread the blaze, and were rushing to and fro, their makeshift torches streaming in mares' tails of smoky flame behind them. They were flinging burning stuff against the basilica, heedless of who among their own kind it scorched. The Forum was full of looted gear, running with wine from broken jars and burst skins, the shops falling into red ruin. And below, part hidden by the roof of the portico, part plain to see, a score of men were charging again and again at the main doors, swinging between them the great balk of timber—almost a whole tree trunk—that they had found to serve them as a ram.

Again the knot of barbarians charged forward, again came the crash of the tree trunk against the door. The timbers could not stand long against such punishment; but surely any moment now help would come—help drumming up the road towards them, maybe already at the gates . . .

'It can't be long now,' he said to himself as much as to Pandarus who was on guard at the end of the gallery.

'*Na*, either way, it can't be long now,' said Pandarus; and looking quickly round at him, Justin saw that the old gladiator was happy—happy as he had not been since he won his wooden foil.

For himself, Justin was not at all happy. The fighting over the open downs had been one thing, this was quite another. Somehow the surroundings of polished marble and finely wrought bronze, the whole atmosphere of a place meant for dignity and order and good manners, made what was happening horrible and grotesque, and his old horror of being in any place from which he could not get out at will was jibbering most unpleasantly at his elbow. He made some sort of hurried jest to Pandarus—he was never sure what it was—and turned and plunged down the stairs again.

There was no need, no opportunity either, to tell Flavius what he had seen. The main door was going as he regained the hall; and above the splintering crash of timbers and the sudden clash of blade on blade and the savage burst of shouting as attack and defence came together in the jagged and smoking breach, he heard the cry go up that the Saxons were breaking in from the rear into the main Court room.

And without any clear idea in his head save Flavius was in command at one danger point, and therefore his place was at the other, he found himself heading at the run for the new menace, with a handful of the Lost Legion at his heels.

The outer door of the Court room had gone up in flames, and fiery smoke hung in a drifting haze above the heads of the fighters. And it came to his mind, even as he charged to the aid of the townsmen, that the basilica was now well on fire. Then a giant with bright hair streaming like the flames of the torches made for him, long-handled axe upswung for a mighty stroke; somehow he swerved from the path of the blow, and dived on, young Myron behind him and Evicatos at his shoulder with his great spear drinking deep.

It was a desperate and a bloody business, fought out among the splintered wreckage of the solid Court-room furniture, while ever the smoke thickened overhead and the red glare strengthened on winged helmet and upswung blade. Many of the defenders were down with the first onslaught, while for every Saxon who fell it seemed that two more sprang in through the gaping doorway or down from the torn-out window-holes. And to Justin, struggling desperately for every inch of ground that he was forced to yield, it had begun to seem that they could not hold the barbarians back much longer from the main hall, from the women and the children and the wounded, when above the tumult his ear caught the thin sweet mockery of bells; and Cullen the Fool dived almost under his elbow into the trampling press. And suddenly above them in the rolling murk, blazing red-gold in the light of Calleva burning, was the wingless Eagle.

The gods alone knew what had prompted little Cullen to bring them the Eagle, but the sense of increase was like wine, like fire, running not only through the band but through the townsmen who had not followed that battered standard before; and they steadied as though they had been reinforced by a Cohort of the Legions.

But the next thing Justin saw was Cullen struggling breast to breast with a yellow-haired barbarian for possession of the Eagle! And even as he sprang sideways to the little man's aid, he disappeared completely in the press; and a howl of rage burst from the Saxon, and the white-ash spear-shaft swung aloft, with the cross-piece still intact, but of the Eagle—never a sign.

Something in Justin's mind understood quite coolly that the age-corroded talons must have snapped under the strain upon them. And then, even as a roar of fury burst from his own men, there came a jingle of bells above the uproar, and a little figure sprang clear of the press, leaping for an overturned table, then up again—and Cullen was on the main house-beam above them, and in his hands the Eagle! He scrambled out along the beam on his knees, and crouched there, holding it high, the red light of the flames all about him, the Eagle burning in his hands like a bird of fire. And the cry of fury changed to shout on shout of fierce triumph, as the defenders once more closed their thinning ranks and drove forward.

Next instant a flung spear caught the little Fool in the shoulder. He swayed and seemed to crumple up, like some small gaudy bird hit by a stone, becoming a mere bundle of bright feathers; but by a miracle he clung to his vantage point just long enough to set the Eagle firmly on the flat top of the beam. Then he toppled down into the very midst of the fight.

Justin, with a fighting power he had not known he possessed until that moment, was crashing forward in one more desperate charge, sweeping the rest with him. 'Cullen! Save Cullen!' But it was Evicatos, the swan's feathers of his great spear crimson now, who reached the spot first, ploughing forward into the very midst of the enemy to bestride the little crumpled body while the rest came battling on in his wake.

And in that instant, above the tumult of the conflict, far off and infinitely clear and sweet, they caught the sound of Roman trumpets!

The barbarians heard it too, and swayed back; and with a sound that was almost a sob, Justin drove in his charge; past Evicatos and on.

When all was over, Evicatos still stood astride the body of the little Fool, beneath the Eagle on the house-beam; a great and terrible figure, red with his wounds from head to heel, like some hero out of one of the wild legends of his own people, like a Conal of the Victories.

He steadied himself upright, and with one last superb effort, sent his beloved spear hurtling after the flying foe. But already the sure aim was gone from him, and the great spear missed its mark, and crashing into the stone column beyond the reeking doorway, shivered into fragments of iron and wood and blood-stained feathers on the pavement.

'*Sa.* It is well,' Evicatos said. He flung up his head, and there was a pealing triumph in his voice. 'We go together, back to our own people, she and I.'

And so crashed down headlong among the slain.

Little Cullen had not a mark on him but the spear-gash in his shoulder and a cut over one eye, and was already whimpering back to life as they drew him out from under Evicatos's body.

Justin lifted him—he was so small that he could handle him quite easily—and turned to the inner doorway. Vaguely he heard someone ask about the Eagle, and shook his head. 'Leave it. It has served its hour and must go back to the dark.' And he carried Cullen out into the hall.

The nave of the basilica was full of smoke, and the rafters at the far end were well alight. Here also the fighting was over, and Flavius, with blood trickling from a gashed cheek, was struggling to call off his fighting men like a hunter calling off his hounds. 'Leave them to the Cavalry! *Leave them,* lads; we've our work cut out here!'

Justin carried the little Fool across to the North Tribunal, and laid him down among the rest. Aunt Honoria was beside him as he did so; and just behind her the girl like a white flower still knelt beside the farmer from the Otter's Ford, with his head in her lap.

The basilica was emptying swiftly, as the women and children were passed out into the wrecked Forum, but the roar of the fire was increasing every moment, and the tall man who had recognized Flavius was improvising a bucket chain from the well outside to keep the flames back from the Records Office and Treasury while the city's gods were got out; it was hopeless to think of doing more—the fire had too big a hold. Justin, knotting off the bandage about Cullen's shoulder, said to the physician, who, now that the fighting was over, had pulled himself together and come to his aid, 'It is growing a bit warm. Time, I think, that we got this lot outside.'

There were many willing hands, and the task was soon accomplished, and Justin, who had remained inside himself until the last man was out, was about to follow, when something fell from the gallery above, from which the guards had by now been withdrawn, and landed with a plop beside him, and, glancing down, he saw that it was the crimson rose which Pandarus had picked in the temple garden only an hour or so ago. Instinctively he stooped to pick it up—and the crimson came off on his fingers.

Next instant he was pounding up the gallery stairs, calling the gladiator by name.

He thought he heard a groan, and then he burst out upon the narrow gallery. The western windows across the nave were filled with a mingled glare of fire and sunset that streamed across, turning the smoke to a billowing, tawny fog. The nearest lattice on this side was broken in, and beneath it lay a dead Saxon, his short sword still in his hand, his hair outflung across the stained floor; and beside him Pandarus, who must have lingered behind the rest, leaned on one arm, while his life drained away from a red hole under his ribs.

He raised his head with a twisted smile as Justin reached him, and gasped, 'Habet! It is thumbs down for me at last.'

One glance told Justin that the wound was mortal and the old gladiator could not last many moments. There was nothing he could do for Pandarus, nothing but stay with him through those few moments, and he crouched down and laid the other back against his knee. 'Not thumbs down! That is for a beaten fighter,' he said vehemently; then, as his gaze fell on the dead Saxon, 'Euge! that was a fine stroke.'

The rush of the flames was very near, the heat growing every moment more intense. Smoke billowed across Justin's face, choking, suffocating him; and as he glanced over his shoulder, he saw that the floor of the gallery itself had caught, and the fire was writhing towards him. Below the windows, the roof of the Colonnade was crackling into flame; no going that way if the stairs caught . . . his heart was racing, and he was sweating with more than the heat. Here with a vengeance was the place from which he could not get out. Not while Pandarus lived.

He bent low over the dying gladiator, trying to shield him with his own body from the heat and the fiery cinders that were falling around them now from the burning roof, striving to fan back the smoke with a fold of his cloak. Above the furnace-roar of the flames he thought he heard something else. The beat of horses' hooves.

Pandarus turned his head a little. 'It grows dark. What is this great noise?'

'It is the people shouting for you!' Justin said. 'All the people who have c-come to watch you win your greatest fight of all!'

There was a ghost of laughter in Pandarus's face, a ghost of an old pride. He put up his hand in the gesture of a victorious gladiator acknowledging the cheers of the crowd; and with the gesture half made, fell back against Justin's knee, with his greatest and his last fight fought indeed.

Justin laid him down, and finding that he was still holding the crimson rose, laid it in the hollow of the dead gladiator's shoulder, with a confused feeling that it was fitting Pandarus should carry with him his rose for the Arena.

As he got to his feet, the first ranks of Asklepiodotus's cavalry were swinging into the ruined Forum.

He thought he heard someone calling him. He called back, lurching towards the stair, his head beginning to swim. The narrow stairs were already alight as he plunged down them, one arm upflung to shield his face. The smoke was shot with little torn-off tongues of flame, sucked upward by the draught; the heat poured up the stair-shaft, lapping him round, searing his lungs as he stumbled downward, and near the foot blundered into Flavius with a wet rag over his mouth crashing up to find him.

He heard a gasp of relief, and was not sure whether it was Flavius's or his own. 'Who else is up there?' Flavius croaked.

'No one save Pandarus, and he's dead.' Justin caught a crowing, shuddering breath, and somehow they were at the stair foot, crouching to catch the current of clearer air along the floor. 'Eagle's in—the Court-room roof—all right?'

'All right,' Flavius choked.

The whole basilica was blotted out in rolling smoke, its far end veiled in a roaring curtain of flame; and a blazing beam came down with a crash not a spear's length from them, scattering red-hot fragments in all directions. 'Got to get out! Nothing more we can do,' Flavius was croaking in his ear.

The side door close to the stair-foot was blocked by the blazing ruins of the garland-maker's shop, and they headed at a stumbling run for the main entrance. It seemed a long way off, such a long way, at the end of a fiery tunnel . . .

And then suddenly Anthonius was there, and Kyndylan and others—and they were outside, and there was air to breathe; real air, not black smoke and red flame. Justin dragged it into his tortured lungs, stumbling forward, and finding a burst bale of some kind in his path, sat down on it. He was dimly aware of men and horses, of a great throng of people, of the Forum a blackened shambles, and the sounds of strife in the burning town, and the drum of horses' hooves dying away into the distance as the Cavalry swept on after the Saxon wolves. He heard someone shouting that the traitor Allectus had been captured, but he didn't care. He was aware with surprise that it was still sunset—and that somewhere the little bird in its cage was singing, most sweetly and shiningly, like a star singing. But the whole scene was dipping and swimming round him like a great wheel.

Myron's rat-pointed, anxious face swam into his sight hovering over him, and Flavius had an arm round his shoulders and was holding a broken bowl to his mouth. There was water in the bowl, and he sucked it down to the last drop. A few moments later he was sick with all that he had in his stomach to be sick with, which was not much besides the water, because he had not eaten since before dawn; and the world began to steady.

He pulled himself together, and got up. 'My wounded—must g-go and see to my wounded,' he mumbled.

XVIII
Triumphal Garlands

JUST over a month later, on a sweltering July day, all Londinium was waiting for the coming of the Caesar Constantius. Londinium, decked as for an Imperial Triumph, her crowds in their best and gayest clothes. And all up the broad paved street from the river to the Forum and from the Forum right across the City, men of the legions were on street-lining duty; men of the Second Augustan and the other British legions who had all come in to make their submission again to Rome. A thin line of bronze and russet-red up each side of the street to hold back the holiday crowds, unbroken save in one place—a place of honour—about halfway up from the River Gate to the Forum; where Flavius and Justin and Anthonius stood with the valiant, tattered handful that were left of the Lost Legion.

The three of them still wore the rough barbarian garments that they had worn so long. Flavius's eyebrows, which had been singed off, were only just beginning to grow again; and Justin had lost most of his front hair and still showed on his right forearm the sore-looking shiny pink of new skin. And the little reckless band on either side of them, bearing also the marks of burning Calleva, were as tattered and disreputable as themselves. But in their odd way they were the proudest unit in the streets of Londinium that day.

Justin, leaning on his spear, could glimpse beyond the River Gate, the long timber bridge that carried in the road from Rutupiae and the Saxon coast, the flash and shimmer of the river in the sunlight, and the prow of a naval galley garlanded with green. But all Londinium was garlanded today. Strange to think how very easily Londinium might have been like Calleva—Calleva as he had seen it last, blackened and desolate under the summer rain.

Asklepiodotus had left a company of pioneers to help clear the town, and swept the rest of his force on at full pace towards Londinium. But Saxon fugitives from the battle were well ahead of them, and bands of Mercenaries were swarming in from the forest and the coast-wise fortresses; and the legions, despite all their forced marching, would have been too late to save the richest and greatest city of the province from fire and the sword. But Constantius's missing transports, storm-swept clear round Tanatus into the Thamesis estuary, had forced a way up-river to reach Londinium just as the first wave of Barbarians swept to its walls. And that had been the end of Allectus's wolves.

Yes, Rome had avenged Carausius most fully. Justin remembered the executions that there had been in the ruined Forum at Calleva. Allectus's as it were leading the rest, Serapion's amongst them. He was not of a vengeful disposition, but he was glad about Serapion.—But somehow, looking back on them, they did not seem real; not as the things that went before had been real. He remembered looking up from his work and feeling the heat like the blast from an open oven on his face, and seeing the roof of the basilica sinking inward like blazing canvas; the sudden hush, all the world seeming to wait, holding its breath, and then the rending, shuddering roar of the falling roof, and the basilica a black shell full of fire as a cup is full of wine; and Flavius suddenly beside him, scorched and blackened from head to foot, crying to him above the tumult, 'See there! A fine pyre for a lost Eagle!' That had been real. He remembered the big house close by that had escaped the worst of the fire, where they had carried the wounded. He remembered Aunt Honoria with the paint patchy on her grey face, saying in that jewel-cut voice of hers, when they told her that her house had gone, 'Ah well, I have always had a fancy to live at Aquae Sulis, and now I shall gratify it.' He remembered men who had died that night under his hands, and men who had lived. He remembered them bringing Allectus through the City to the transit camp for safe keeping; and the way the sinking fires of Calleva had seemed to flare up again at his passing, as though they knew the man who had kindled them, and greeted him in mockery; and the glimpse of Imperial Purple rags, and a white, staring face in which the old charming smile had become a set and rigid snarl of rage and torn pride and despair.

He remembered the overset and broken rose-jars in the colonnade of the big house, and a crimson rose-spray outflung on the pavement, caught for an instant in the swinging light of a lantern, that had torn at him with the sudden understanding he had not had time for before, that Pandarus was dead. Pandarus and Evicatos, and little plump Paulinus a year ago, and so many others; but it was for those three that suddenly he had been blind with tears.

A striped wasp whining past his ear made him jerk his head, and brought him back to the present. To the garlanded street that waited for the Caesar Constantius, who, forced to put back into Gesoriacum by the failure of his transports to make contact with him, was now coming in person to take possession of the lost province that was once again part of Rome.

Justin shifted his weight from one foot to the other, and shifting, felt again the thin papyrus roll that he had slipped inside the breast of his tattered tunic. His first letter from home in almost two years. The very first letter he had ever had from his father that had not made him feel a disappointment. 'It is with relief that I receive word of you,' his father had written. 'On the occasion of your last letter, you assured me that you had done nothing of which to be ashamed, and I am rejoiced to find that most fully borne out by a certain report I have had of you from my old friend and your one-time commanding officer, Fulvius Licinius. Believe me, however, that I was never in the least danger of being ashamed of you. There was a time when I was disappointed at your failure to carry on the family tradition, but I have always been perfectly assured that you would not under any circumstances give me cause for shame . . . ' And then further on, 'I trust that when we next meet we may learn to know each other rather better than we have done in the past.'

And Justin, turning the stiff and formal phrases over in his mind, knew that he had quite ceased to be a disappointment to his father; and was glad with a warmth that laughed a little at both of them, but principally at himself, as he could not have done two years ago.

And now there was a stirring, far away across the river; a sound rhythmic as a pulse, that grew and strengthened moment by moment into the ringing tramp of legions on the march. Excitement was running through the crowded streets, where tribesmen in plaid breeks and townsmen in Roman tunics jostled cheerfully for a better view. Now there was a flicker of movement on the bridge—white and bright and many-coloured movement—and the street-lining legionaries linked their arms into a stronger barrier. The head of the advancing column was past the gigantic statue of Hadrian at the near end of the bridge; now it was coming beneath the arch of the garlanded River Gate, and a roar of acclamation burst up from the crowd, as the leading ranks, headed by the chief Magistrates who had met the advancing army a mile outside the City, swung into the broad, paved street.

On they came, the Magistrates in the dignity of their purple-bordered togas, the tramp-tramp-tramp of the Legions' feet swelling into a pulsing crash of sound that could not be drowned even by the roaring of the crowd. The people were throwing green branches in the roadway, surging forward. Justin, leaning back against the thrust that threatened to jerk him into the middle of the road, his arms linked with Flavius on one side and Anthonius on the other, was thumped violently between the shoulders by one excited citizen, while another bellowed blessings upon the Saviour of Britain into his left ear. The Magistrates were past now, and behind them marched the trumpeters, four abreast, the sun glinting on the enormous ram's-horn coils of the Roman trumpets. And then, mounted on a tall black stallion, with his staff and senior officers about him, the Caesar Constantius himself.

Looking up past the black, arched mane, Justin caught a rather startling glimpse of a face under the Eagle-crested Imperial helmet, that was almost as pale as Allectus's had been, and remembered that the troops had bestowed on this man the surname of Chlorus, Green, because of his pallor. Then the Caesar Constantius also was past, and they heard the wave of cheering run before him on towards the Forum. Justin caught sight of Asklepiodotus looking half asleep as usual; and lean, brown Licinius. And then behind them the great silver-winged Eagle of the Seventh Claudian Legion went by, steady as a rock with all its weight of gilded battle honours, upborne with rigid pride by its lion-skinned Eagle-bearer pacing between his escort. And the spread wings bright against the summer sky sent Justin's mind back in a moment of vivid memory to the mutilated stump of a once-proud ensign, beneath which Evicatos had died, the battered Eagle that lay lost for ever under the blackened ruins of Calleva's basilica. And then the memory was swallowed up in the thunderous tramp of the Legions swinging by.

The summer day passed with its drawn-out celebrations. Londinium had been eager to show her gratitude and joy in a great banquet, but the Caesar Constantius had let it be known in advance that he had no mind for a banquet at this time. 'There is over-much work waiting for us in the North, and we march not our fastest on full stomachs,' ran his message. 'Feast us when we return.' And so, when the Magistrates had made their speeches in the basilica and the sacrificial bull had died before Jove's altar, he retired at the day's end to the fort at the north-west angle of the City walls, with his staff and Senior Officers.

Below the fort a vast marching camp had been made ready for the Legions outside the City walls; and in the still summer twilight, by and by, the camp-fires sprang up, and the soldiers made merry on the extra wine that had been issued to them for the occasion. Round one such fire, down towards the horse-lines, the handful that were left of the Lost Legion were taking their ease; all save Justin and Flavius. And those two, summoned from their comrades, were standing in the lamplit Praetorium of the Fort, before a very weary man wearing the Imperial Purple.

The Caesar Constantius had laid aside his gilded breast-plate and the great Eagle-crested helmet that had left a crimson weal across his forehead. He was sitting half turned on the cushioned bench, to speak to Licinius almost behind him, but he looked round as they snapped to attention in front of him, showing a face that, for all its whiteness, had none of that look of a thing bred in the dark that had marred Allectus's features, and acknowledged their salute with a swift gesture of the hand. 'These are the two, Centurion Licinius?'

'These are the two, sir,' said Licinius by the window.

'I greet you. Which of you is Centurion Aquila?'

Flavius advanced the regulation pace. 'Hail, Caesar.'

Constantius turned his gaze to Justin. 'And you are Tiberius Justinianus of the Army Medical Corps?'

'As Caesar says.'

'I sent for you because I have been hearing things concerning a certain band of irregular troops, and wished to meet its Captains, and to thank him for the intelligence and—reinforcements that have reached me from time to time over the past year and a half from this province.'

'Thank you, sir,' said Flavius and Justin in one breath. And Flavius added quickly, 'But it was a one-time secretary of Carausius's who began the work, and—died for it. We took over from him, no more.'

Constantius bent his head gravely, but Justin had a feeling that there was a flicker of amusement behind the gravity. 'Have no fear that I shall give you the credit that belongs to another man . . . Nevertheless, you took over, and to good purpose, and for that the thanks of the Empire are due to you. At a later date I shall demand of you a full account of these past years; it should make a tale worth the hearing. But that can wait.' He leaned forward on his crossed arms, and studied them, first one, and then the other, with a long, quiet scrutiny that made Justin at least feel uncomfortably as though the outer layers of himself were being peeled off like the skins of an onion, that this man with the white, fine-drawn face might see exactly what lay at his core and judge of its worth.

'Yes,' said the Caesar Constantius at last as having seen what he wanted, and made his judgement, and rose, with a hand on the table beside him. 'You have earned a long spell of leave, and I make no doubt that you need it. But the North is bursting into flames again; the very Wall itself is in danger. Doubtless you know all that. It was inevitable, with half the troops withdrawn to fight Allectus's battles. In two days we march north to put out the fires, and—we need men.'

He stood looking quietly from one to the other as though waiting for the answer to a question. And Justin saw suddenly that on the writing-table by his hand lay two sealed tablets on which were written their own names.

It was very quiet in the lamplit room, high above the fort. They heard the challenge of a sentry on the ramparts, and the soft rise and fall of sound that was the voice of the City, like a sea below them, far, far below. Then Flavius, glancing also at those tablets and up again, said, 'Our marching orders, Caesar?'

'Not necessarily. I do not order in this case; I leave the choice to you. You have earned the right to refuse.'

'What happens if we do refuse?' Flavius asked after a moment. 'If we say that we served the Emperor Carausius with our whole hearts, and have not the same service to give again?'

The Caesar Constantius took up one of the tablets. 'Then I open this and soften the wax at the lamp here, and smooth out what is written within. That is all. And you shall be free to retire from the Eagles with all honour. But I hope that you will not say that. I hope it for the sake of this province of Britain, and a little, I find, for my own.'

There was the faintest shadow of a smile in his eyes as he spoke; and looking at him, Justin knew that here was a man worth following.

Flavius took another pace forward, and picked up the tablet with his name on it. 'For myself, I am ready to march north in two days' time,' he said.

But Justin was still silent. It often took him longer to be sure about things than it did Flavius; and he had to be sure, quite sure, about this. And then he was sure. 'For m-myself also,' he said, and took the pace forward, and picked up the little tablet that had his fate on it.

'So. It is good,' Constantius said. He looked from one to the other. 'I am told that you two are kinsmen; but I think you are also friends, which is a greater thing. Indeed, that was told me by the Primus Pilus here. Therefore I hope you may not be ill satisfied to find yourselves once again posted together.'

Justin turned his head quickly to look at Flavius, and found that Flavius had done the same. He realized suddenly how far Flavius had grown—himself too, he supposed—from the boys that they had been when first they found each other before the great pharos at Rutupiae. All that way they had come shoulder to shoulder, and the old bond between them was strengthened accordingly.

'Caesar is very good,' Flavius said.

'It is in my mind that Rome owes you that, at all events,' Constantius said, with that shadow of a smile again in his eyes. He took up some papers from the table. 'I think that there is nothing more that we need to speak of tonight?'

'One thing more, Caesar,' Flavius said urgently.

Constantius lowered the papers again. 'Well, Centurion?'

'Caesar, we have four legionaries and another Cohort Centurion yet with us. They are as much Caesar's men as those that escaped to Gaul.'

'Send them to my Staff Centurion in the morning.' The smile that had been hovering flashed up in Caesar's face, lighting the thin whiteness of it so that he seemed suddenly much younger and less tired. 'And meanwhile, you can bid them—unofficially—also to be ready to march north in two days' time . . . So! It is settled. Go now and draw your equipment and set about disbanding these cut-throats of yours. We shall both be busy in the next hours. I salute you and bid you goodnight.'

Outside, by common consent Justin and Flavius turned aside from the head of the open stairway on to the high rampart walk, the tablets containing their posting still unopened in their hands, and lingered there a few moments, needing as it were a breathing-space between one world and another. Justin thought, We ought to be going back to the band. Only it isn't a band any more, or it won't be after tonight. Just men—free to go their own way.

Save for the sentry pacing his beat, they were alone on the rampart walk. Below them the darkening City was strung with lights—dim amber window squares, and the golden drops of light that were lamps and lanterns in the garlanded streets. Lights and lights and lights away to the misty river. 'Londinium rejoices,' Flavius said. 'Surely there's not a dark house within the City walls tonight.'

Justin nodded, not wanting to talk, his mind turning back to the start of it all: to that interview with Licinius, more than three years ago; the sand-wreathes in the corners of the mud-walled office, and the jackals crying. That had been the night that it began. Tonight was the night that it was over.

Over, like Carausius's brief Empire in the North that had been brought to nothing by the murdering hand of Allectus. Britain was once again part of Rome, safe so long as Rome was strong to hold her safe—and no longer . . . Well, better for Britain to take her chance with Rome than fall to ruin under Allectus and his kind. And tonight, with the lights of rejoicing Londinium spread below them, and the Legions encamped beyond the walls, and the man with the thin white conqueror's face seated at his writing-table in the lamp-lit Praetorium, the idea of a time coming when Rome would not be strong seemed, after all, thin and remote.

And for themselves—they had kept faith with their own little Emperor; and the world of familiar things that they had laid down, walking south from the Wall into that autumn mist of almost two years ago, was waiting for them to take it up again; and life was good.

He was just about to push off from the wall on which he leaned, when something that had been squatting unseen in the shadows uncurled and stood up with a faint chime of bells into the light of a gate tower doorway.

'Cullen!' Flavius said. 'What do you here?'

'I followed my Lords in case, as a good hound should,' Cullen said.

'In case of what?'

'Just in case,' said Cullen, and touched the little dagger beside the Silver Branch in his belt. 'What do we do now?'

'Those of us who are of the Legions march north in the morn's morning,' Flavius said. 'For the rest—the Lost Legion is finished—broke up—free to go its own way.'

'So. I go my Lords' way; I am my Lords' hound,' Cullen said contentedly.

'But you are free now,' Flavius said.

Cullen shook his head vehemently. 'Curoi said that if he died, I was my Lords' hound.'

There was a small silence, and then Flavius said helplessly, 'Cullen, we are not Emperors, nor High Kings of Erin, that we should need a Household Fool.'

'I can be much, besides a Fool; I can keep your armour bright; I can serve you at table, and carry messages, and keep secrets.'

'Would it not be better to be free?'

'Free? I was born a slave, the son of a slave. What is "Free" to me, but being masterless—and maybe hungry?'

They could not see his strange narrow face save as a pale blur in the reflected light of the doorway; but there was something in his voice that could not be denied.

Justin spoke for the first time, across the little man's head to Flavius. 'We have never been masterless and hungry, you and I.'

'Never masterless, at all events,' Flavius said, and Justin knew that the thoughts of both of them had gone for an instant to the man they had left in the Praetorium. There was no disloyalty to Carausius in that, for they knew, both of them, that a man may give his service more than once without breaking faith, but only once for the first time.

Suddenly Flavius flung up his head and laughed. 'Well, it's a good thing we are posted together, or we should have to slice our hound in half!'

'I come with my Lords?' Cullen said. '*Sa*, it is good!'

'It is good,' Justin said.

Flavius laid a heavy arm across his cousin's shoulders. 'Come on, old lad. We must tell Anthonius and the rest how the wind blows, and get some sleep while we can. We shall have our work cut out in the time before we march north.'

They turned back to the rampart stair, and clattering down it, headed for the gate which stood open tonight between the fort and the great marching camp; little Cullen strutting behind them with his hound's tail a-swing at every step, sounding the apples of his Silver Branch triumphantly as he went.

THE LANTERN BEARERS

Contents

I	The Terrace Steps	399
II	Rutupiae Light	410
III	The Wolves of the Sea	419
IV	Ullasfjord	431
V	Wild Geese Flighting	443
VI	The Saxon Wind	454
VII	The Woman in the Doorway	462
VIII	Singing Magic	472
IX	Forest Sanctuary	480
X	The Fortress of the High Powers	492
XI	The Young Foxes	503
XII	Brown Sister, Golden Sister	516
XIII	The Empty Hut	523
XIV	The Honour of First Blood	531
XV	The Hawking Glove	539
XVI	White Thorn and Yellow Iris	548
XVII	'Minnow, Dolphin's Son'	560
XVIII	The Hostage	570
XIX	'Victory like a Trumpet Blast'	579
XX	The Dark Warrior	589
XXI	The Return of Odysseus	599
XXII	The Blossoming Tree	609

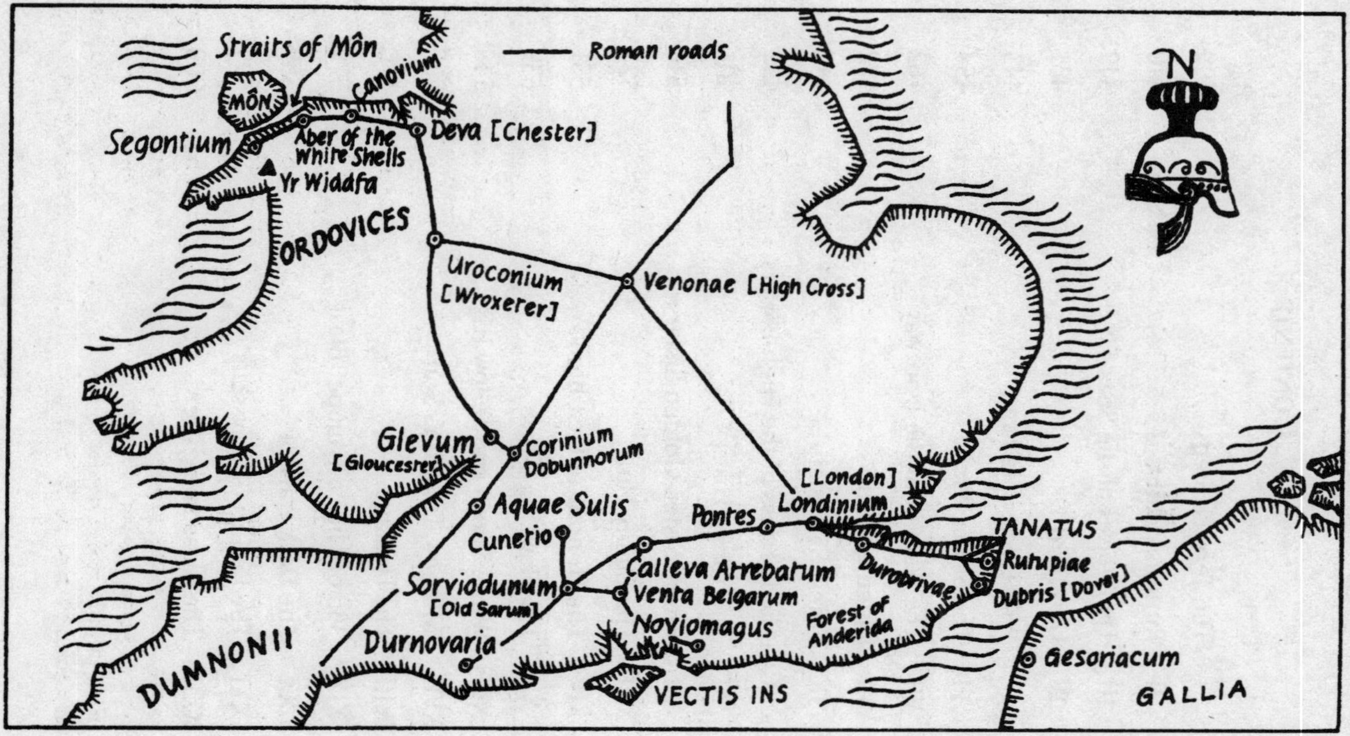

Straits of Môn
MÔN
Canovium
Roman roads
N
Segontium
Aber of the White Shells
Deva [Chester]
Yr Widdfa
ORDOVICES
Uroconium [Wroxerer]
Venonae [High Cross]
Glevum
[Gloucester]
Corinium Dobunnorum
Aquae Sulis
Cunetio
Sorviodunum
[Old Sarum]
Durnovaria
DUMNONII
Calleva Atrebatum
Venta Belgarum
Noviomagus
VECTIS INS
Pontes
[London]
Londinium
Durobrivae
Forest of Anderida
TANATUS
Rutupiae
Dubris [Dover]
Gesoriacum
GALLIA

I

The Terrace Steps

AQUILA halted on the edge of the hanging woods, looking down. Below him he could see the farmstead under the great, bare swell of the downs; the russet-roofed huddle of buildings, the orchard behind, making a darker pattern on the paleness of the open turf, the barley just beginning to show its first tinge of harvest gold, the stream that rose under the orchard wall and wandered down the valley to turn the creaking wheel of the water-mill that ground their corn.

Almost a year had gone by since the last time that he had stood here and looked down, for it was only last night that he had come home on leave from Rutupiae, where he commanded a troop of Rhenus Horse—Auxiliary Cavalry; there had been no regular legions in Britain for forty years now—and every detail of the scene gave him a sharp-edged pleasure. It was good to be home. And really, the place didn't look so bad. It was not what it had been in the good old days, of course. Kuno, who was the oldest man on the farm, could remember when there had been vine terraces on the south slope; you could see the traces of them still, just below the woods here, like the traces of the old fields and the old sheep-runs that had had to be let go back to the wild. It was the Pict War that had done the mischief, so long ago that even Kuno couldn't remember, though he swore that he could, and, when he had drunk enough heather beer, used to tell everybody how he had seen the great Theodosius himself, when he came to drive out the Saxons and the Painted People. But though Theodosius had swept Britain clear, the damage had been done and the countryside had never been the same again. The great houses had been burned, the slaves had revolted against their masters, and the big estates had been ruined. It hadn't been so bad for the small estates and farms, especially those that were not worked with slave labour. Kuno was very fond of telling—and the hearing of it always made Aquila feel humble, though he was sure that it should make him proud—how in the bad time, the Killing Time, when the slaves revolted, the free men of his own farm had kept faith with his great-grandfather.

Because he was seeing his home again for the first time in almost a year, he was piercingly aware of it, and the things it stood for, and aware also how easily it might be lost. Old Tiberius's farm, not many miles further seaward, had been burned by the Saxon raiders last year. When you thought about it, you realized that you were living in a world that might fall to pieces at any moment: but Aquila seldom thought about it much. He had lived in that world all his life, and so had at least three generations of his kind before him, and it hadn't fallen to pieces yet, and it didn't seem likely that it would do so on this rich, ripening day with the powdery whiteness of July lying over the countryside.

There was the sound of flying feet behind him, and a brushing through the undergrowth and Flavia his sister was beside him, demanding breathlessly, 'Why didn't you wait for me?'

Aquila turned his head to look at her. 'I got tired of propping up the wall of Sabra's cot, being stared out of countenance by that yellow-eyed cat of hers, while you chittered inside.'

'You could have stayed inside and chittered too.'

'I didn't want to, thank you. Besides, I wanted to get back here and make sure the farm hadn't run away since breakfast.' It was an odd thing to say, born of his sudden, unusual awareness, and they looked at each other quickly.

'It is queer how one feels like that sometimes,' the girl said, grave for the moment. And then the shadow passed, and she was sparkling again. 'But it hasn't run away—and oh! it is so lovely that you are home again, Aquila! And look, here's honeysuckle with crimson tips; and here's clover, and blue scabious, as blue as a butterfly. I shall make a wreath for myself for dinner as though it were a banquet; just for myself, and not for you or father at all, because men look silly in banquet wreaths, especially if they have galley-prow noses like yours!' And while she spoke, she was down on her knees, searching among the leaves for the tough, slender scabious stems.

Aquila leaned against a tree and watched her, making a discovery. 'You have grown up while I have been away.'

She looked up, the flowers in her hands. 'I was grown up before you went away. More than fifteen. And now I'm more than sixteen—quite old.'

Aquila wagged his head sadly. 'That's what I say. I don't suppose you can even run now.'

She sprang up, her face alight with laughter. 'What will you wager me that I do not reach the terrace steps ahead of you?'

'A new pair of crimson slippers against a silver buckle for my sword-belt.' Aquila pushed himself from the tree-trunk as she swooped up the skirt of her yellow tunic with the flowers in its lap.

'Done! Are you ready?'

'Yes. *Now!*'

They sprang away side by side over the short downland turf, by the level-and-drop of the old vine terraces, by the waste strip at the head of the cornland where the plough team turned, skirting the steading yard on flying feet. Flavia was half a spear's length ahead of him as they reached the steps of the terrace before the house and whirled about under the old spreading damson tree that grew there. 'Well? Can I still run? I can run faster than you can now, and I'm a girl!'

Aquila caught her by the wrist. 'You have sharp, hollow bones like a bird, and it is not fair.' They flung themselves down on the step, panting and laughing, and he turned to look at her. He loved being with Flavia again, he always had loved being with her, even when they were small. She was two years younger than he was, but Demetrius, their Greek tutor, declared that they had been meant to be twins and something had gone wrong with their stars to bring about the two years one must wait for the other. Flavia's hair had come down and was flying about her shoulders; hair as black and harsh as a stallion's mane, and so full of life that she could comb sparks out of it when she combed it in the dark. He reached out and gave it a small, brotherly tug.

'Brute!' Flavia said happily. She drew up her knees and clasped her arms round them, tipping up her head to the sunshine that rimmed the damson leaves with gold and made the little dark damsons seem almost transparent. 'I do love being alive! I love the way things look and feel and smell! I love the dustiness of July, and the dry singing the wind makes through the grass, and the way the stones are warm to sit on, and the way the honeysuckle smells!'

There was something almost fierce under her laughter; but that was always the way with Flavia: the fierceness and the laughter and the sparks flying out of her hair. She turned to him with a swift flash of movement. All her movements were swift and flashing. 'Show me the dolphin again.'

With an air of long-suffering, Aquila pulled up the loose sleeve of his tunic and showed her, as he had showed her yesterday evening, the dolphin badge of their family rather inexpertly tattooed on the brown skin of his shoulder. One of the Decurions at Rutupiae had learned the trick from a Pictish hostage, and during the bad weather, when there was not much else to do, several of them had let him try his skill on them.

Flavia ran a finger-tip over the blue lines. 'I'm not sure that I like it. You're not a Pict.'

'If I had been, I'd have had stripes and spirals all over me, not a nice neat little dolphin . . . It might come in very useful. If I were away from home for a long, long time, and when I came back nobody knew me again, like Odysseus, I could take you quietly aside and say, "Look, I've got a dolphin on my shoulder. I'm your long-lost brother." And then you'd know me again, like the old slave when she found the scar of the boar's tusk on Odysseus's thigh.'

'Maybe I'd say, "Oh, stranger, anyone may get a dolphin tattooed on his shoulder." I'd be more likely to recognize you by your nose, however long that had been away.' She turned to the tangle of honey-suckle and small downland flowers in her lap, and began to arrange them for her garland. 'Are you as glad to be home as we are to have you, even though it is only one year and not twenty, like Odysseus?'

Aquila nodded, glancing about him at the familiar scene. From close quarters one could see more clearly that the farm had known better days: the out-houses that needed re-roofing, the wing of the house that had once been lived in and was now a grain-store, the general air of a place run without quite enough money, without quite enough men. But the pigeons were paddling in the sunlight below the terrace steps, and a flicker of brilliant blue showed where Gwyna was coming up with a milk-pail; and he was home again, sitting on the sun-warmed steps where they had sat as children, talking nonsense with Flavia.

Something moved in the farmyard, and Flavian their father came out from the stable, talking with Demetrius. Demetrius, who never smiled himself, said something at which their father laughed, flinging up his head like a boy; then he turned and came striding up towards the terrace, with Margarita his old wolf-hound at his heels.

Aquila half-rose as he drew near. 'We're sitting on the terrace steps; come and join us, sir.'

And their father came and sat down on the top step, with Margarita between his knees.

'Aquila owes me a pair of crimson slippers,' Flavia said, reaching up to lay an arm across his knee. 'He said I was grown up and couldn't run any more.'

Their father smiled. 'And you aren't, and you can. I heard the two of you skirling like curlews all the way down from the top woods. Mind you keep him up to paying his wager!'

He was fondling Margarita's ears, drawing them again and again through his fingers, and the freckled sunlight under the leaves made small, shifting sparks of green fire in the flawed emerald of his great signet ring with its engraved dolphin.

Aquila twisted on his lower step to look up at him. It was hard to realize that Father was blind. There was nothing to show for it but the small scar that the Saxon arrow had made in his temple; and he came and went about the farm with that quick, sure stride, never seeming at a loss to know where he was or in what direction he wanted to go. Now he turned to his son and asked, 'How does the farm look to you, after a year away?'

'The farm looks good to me,' Aquila said, and added with perhaps a little too much vehemence, 'It looks so sure—as though it had been here as long as the downs have been here, and must last as long as the downs remain.'

'I wonder,' their father said, suddenly grave. 'I wonder how long it will last—just how long any of this life that we know will last.'

Aquila shifted abruptly. 'Oh, I know . . . But the worst never seems to happen.' Yet the worst happened to Tiberius, last year, said something in his mind, and he hurried on, as much to silence it as anything else: 'When Vortigern called in that Saxon war band and settled them in the old Iceni territory to hold off the Picts, five—no, six years ago, everyone wagged their heads and said it was the end of Britain. They said it was calling the wolf in over the threshold; but Hengest and his crew haven't done so badly. Settled quite peacefully, seemingly; and they *have* held off the Picts, and left us free to concentrate what Auxiliaries we still have along the Saxon shore to hold off their pirate brothers. Maybe Vortigern wasn't such a fool after all.'

'Do you really think that?' his father said very quietly, and his fingers checked on Margarita's ears.

'It is what quite a lot of the others at Rutupiae think.'

'The temper of the Eagles has changed since my day. Do *you* think it?'

There was a moment's silence and then Aquila said, 'No, I suppose not, really. But it is more comfortable to think that way.'

'Rome has done too much of thinking what is comfortable,' his father said.

But Aquila was not for the moment listening. He was looking away down the valley to where a small figure had just come into sight on the wagon-way that led up from the ford and the ancient track under the downs. 'Sa ha,' he said softly, 'someone coming.'

'Who is it?' said his father.

'No one I know. A little bent man—looks as though he's carrying a basket on his back.'

He thought that both his father and Flavia were suddenly alert in a way that he did not understand. He thought that there was a feeling of waiting about them. A few moments went by, and then his father asked, 'Can you see yet what it is that he carries?'

'Yes. It is a basket. And something else—a lantern on a pole. I believe he is one of those wandering bird-catchers.'

'So. Stand up and signal to him to come to me here.'

Aquila glanced at his father in puzzled surprise, then stood up and waved his arm above his head until the small, trudging figure saw the signal and flung up an arm in reply. 'He is coming,' he said, and sat down again.

A short while later a small, earth-coloured man with a sharply pointed face like a water-rat's came round the corner of the outbuildings and stood before the terrace steps, swinging the great reed basket from his shoulders almost before he had come to a halt. 'I greet my lord. My lord would like some fine fat quails, only caught this morning?'

'Take them up to the kitchen,' Flavian said. 'It is a long time since you were here last.'

'I have had a long walk since I was here last,' the man returned, and something in his rather hurried voice suggested the reply was a thing arranged beforehand. 'It is all of two hundred miles from Venta to the Mountains.'

As he spoke the words, he glanced aside out of doubtful dark eyes at Aquila, and Flavian, seeming to sense the swift, uneasy glance, said, 'Nay, there is nothing that need make you ill at ease, friend. My son is quite to be trusted.' He took a slim wax tablet from the breast of his tunic. 'The quails up to the kitchen. My steward will pay you. And this to the usual place.'

The man took the tablet without looking at it, and stowed it in the ragged breast of his own tunic. 'As my lord bids me,' he said. He made a wide gesture of farewell that took in all three of them, and shouldering his basket again, turned and trudged off round the corner of the house towards the kitchen quarters.

Aquila watched him go, then turned back to his father. 'And what did that mean, sir?' He thought Flavia knew.

Flavian gave a final pull to the old hound's ear, and released her with a pat. 'It means a message up to Dynas Ffaraon in the Arfon mountains.'

'So?' Aquila said. 'What message is that?'

There was a little silence, but he knew that his father was going to tell him.

'I am going back into ancient history,' Flavian said at last. 'Much of it you will know, but bear with me none the less, it is better to have the whole thing . . .

'When Theodosius came to drive out the Picts that old Kuno so dearly loves to talk about, his lieutenant was one Magnus Maximus, a Spaniard. And when Theodosius went south again, he left Maximus in command behind him. Maximus married a British princess, daughter of the line that had ruled in the mountains of Northern Cymru since before we Romans came to Britain; and owing in part to his wife's blood, years later the British troops proclaimed him Emperor in opposition to Gratian. He marched to meet his fate, taking with him most of the Legions and Auxiliaries from the province; and his fate was death. That you know. But he left behind him a young son in Arfon—Constantine.'

Aquila moved abruptly, the tale suddenly laying hold of him. 'Constantine, who saved us after the last of the Legions were withdrawn.'

'Aye. When Rome could do no more for us, and was herself a smoking ruin—though she has recovered in some sort since—we turned to Constantine of Arfon; and he came down from the mountains with his tribesmen behind him, and led us and them to victory and a sweeping back of the Sea Wolves such as there had not been for twenty years before. For upwards of thirty more, with Constantine holding the reins from Venta, things went well for Britain, and the Saxons were driven back again and again from our shores. But in the end Constantine was murdered in his own hall. A Pictish plot, but there have always been many of us believed that Vortigern, who came out of the West as a mere Clan Chieftain of the Ordovices to follow him in his later days and married his sister Severa, was at the root of it. Maybe he thought that if a wife's lineage could raise her husband to the Purple once, it might do so again. Save that it wasn't the Purple he wanted, but power of another kind. Always he has been the spearhead of the hothead party which sees Rome as the Tribes saw her four hundred years ago, which has learned nothing in the years since, which is blinded by its dreams and sees the danger of the Saxon hordes as a lesser evil than the rule of Rome. So Constantine died, and Vortigern contrived to seize the chief power in the land, though never the full power. But there were still Utha and Ambrosius, Constantine's sons in his old age.'

'Yes,' Aquila said, 'I remember. It caught my imagination because they were not much older than I was, and I must have been about eight when it all happened and they disappeared.'

'They were snatched away by a few of their father's household, back to Arfon, to the safety of the mountains; and for ten years Vortigern has held virtually all power in the province—if power it can be called, when he must rest his weight on a Saxon war band to hold off the Picts, *and* on the hated Auxiliaries of Rome to hold off the Saxons . . . ' He moved a little, putting out a hand to feel for the rough edge of the step beside him. 'Utha died a year or so since, but Ambrosius is now come to manhood.'

Aquila looked at him quickly, realizing the significance of that; that the wild Cymric princeling newly come to manhood among the mountains, to an age to bear his shield, was by right of birth the natural leader of those who held to the ways of Rome. 'And so—?' he said.

'And so—seeing that it was so, seeing also that the General Aetius, he who was Consul two years ago, was campaigning in Gaul, we sent to him, reminding him that we still held ourselves to be of the Empire, and begging him to bring us the help and reinforcements that we need, to rid the province both of Vortigern and the Saxon hordes, and resume it for Rome. That was last autumn.'

Aquila caught his breath. 'And that was the reply?'

'No,' his father said. 'As yet there has come no reply.'

'Then—what was the message that you sent?'

'Merely a short agreed passage from Xenophon, copied out for me by Flavia. About the middle of each month the message goes through, by the hand of our friend the bird-catcher, or one of several others, to make sure that the signal route is still open.'

'"It is all of two hundred miles from Venta to the Mountains",' Aquila quoted. 'That is how you know that it is the right person to give it to.'

His father nodded. 'I wondered whether you would pick on the password.'

'But it was last autumn that the word went out to Aetius, you say? And it is high summer now. Surely there should have come some reply long before this?'

'If it is coming at all, it must surely come soon,' his father said with a sudden weariness in his voice. 'If it does not come very soon, it may well be too late to come at all. Every day adds to the danger that Vortigern the Red Fox will smell what is in the wind.'

The sunlight faded while they sat silent after that, and the twilight came lapping up the valley like a quiet tide, and the sky above the long wave-lift of the downs was translucent and colourless as crystal. The scent of the honeysuckle in Flavia's garland seemed to grow stronger as the light faded, and a bat hovered and darted by, pricking the dusk with its needle-thin hunting cry. Old Gwyna came across the atrium behind them to light the candles, scuffing her feet along the floor just as she had done for as long as Aquila could remember.

Everything just as it always had been at the time of the 'tween lights; but he knew now that under the quiet surface the home that he loved was part of the struggle for Britain, menaced by other dangers than the chance raids of Saxon pirates.

Suddenly he felt the passing moments as something that was flowering and would not flower again. Though I sit here on ten thousand other evenings, he thought, this evening will not come again. And he made an unconscious movement as though to cup it in his hands, and so keep it safe for a little longer.

But he could not keep it. Their father drew his long legs under him and got up. 'I hear Gwyna with the lights, and it is time to change for dinner.'

Even as Aquila sprang up also and caught Flavia's hand to pull her to her feet, he heard the beat of horses' hooves coming up the valley. They checked, listening, and Margarita pricked her ears.

'More comers. It seems that we are the hub of the world this evening,' Aquila said.

Their father nodded, his head at the alert, listening angle that was so much a part of him. 'Whoever it is, he has been riding hard and his horse is weary.'

Something held them there on the terrace, waiting, while the rider came nearer, disappeared behind the outbuildings and reined in. In a little, they heard voices, and the tramp of feet, and Gwyna came along the terrace with a man in the leather tunic of an Auxiliary behind her. 'Someone for the young master,' she said.

The man stepped forward, saluting. 'A message for the Decurion Aquila, sir.'

Aquila nodded. 'So—give it here.' He took the tablet that the man held out, broke the sealing thread, and stepping into the light of the atrium doorway, opened the two wooden leaves and glanced hastily over the few words on the wax inside, then looked up. 'Here's an end to my two weeks' leave then. I'm recalled to duty.' He swung round on the waiting Auxiliary. If it had been one of his own troop he might have asked unofficial questions, but the man was scarcely known to him. 'Is your horse being seen to? Go and get a meal while I make ready to ride. Gwyna, feed him, and bid Vran to have Lightfoot and the bay gelding ready to start in the half of an hour.'

'Now I wonder, I wonder, what this may mean,' his father said, very quietly, as the man tramped off after Gwyna.

No one answered as they moved into the atrium. The yellow radiance of the candles seemed very bright, harshly bright after the soft owl-light of the terrace outside. Aquila looked at Flavia, at his father, and knew that the same thought was in all three of them . . . Could it be that this was anything to do with the appeal to Aetius in Gaul? And if so, was its meaning good—or bad?

'Need you go tonight?' Flavia said. 'Oh, need you go tonight, Aquila? You will get back no sooner in riding in the dark.' She was still holding her almost completed banquet wreath, crushed and broken in her hand. It would never now be finished.

'I can be at the next posting station before midnight,' Aquila said, 'ten miles on my way. Maybe I'll get my leave again soon and be back for our banquet. Put me up some bread and cheese, while I collect my gear.' He flung an arm round her thin, braced shoulders, and kissed her hurriedly, touched his silent father on the hand, and strode out towards the sleeping cell to collect his gear.

For Aquila, though he could not know it, the world had begun its falling to pieces.

II
Rutupiae Light

TWO evenings later, Aquila and the Auxiliary were heading up the last mile of the Londinium road towards the grey fortress of Rutupiae that rose massive and menacing above the tawny levels, with all the lonely flatness of Tanatus Island spread beyond it: Rutupiae, fortress of the Saxon Shore, that had seen so much happen, that had known the last legion in Britain. And what now?

They clattered over the timber bridge that carried the road in through the dark, double-gate arch, answering the sentry's challenge that rang hollow under the archway, and in the broad space below the stable rows Aquila handed over the army post-horse that he rode to his companion, and set out to report to the Commandant.

When he first reported at Rutupiae to join his troops, the great fortress, that had been built to house half a legion, and where now only a few companies of Marines and three troops of Auxiliary Horse rattled like dried peas in the emptiness, had seemed to him horribly desolate. But the hunting and wild-fowling were good, and he was a cheerful and easy-going lad who made friends easily with his own kind. And in the business of learning his job, and his growing pride in his troop, he had very soon ceased to notice the emptiness. But he was once again sharply conscious of it this evening as he threaded his way through the square-set alleys of the great fort, heading for the Praetorium. Perhaps it really was emptier than usual at this hour—though indeed there were sounds of something going on very urgently, down towards the Watergate and the harbour. A troop of horse trotted past him on their way up from stables; but otherwise he saw scarcely a living soul, until he came to the Praetorium buildings, passed the sentry at the head of the Commandant's stairs, and stood before Titus Fulvius Callistus as he sat at his big writing-table, filling in the duty rotas for the day. At least that was just as usual, Aquila thought; but as he cast a passing glance at the papyrus sheets on the table, he realized that they weren't the usual duty rotas at all, but lists and papers of some other kind.

'Reporting back for duty, sir,' Aquila said, with the informal salute demanded by the fact that he was still in civilian dress.

Callistus ticked something on his list, and looked up. He was a leathery little man with a piercing eye. 'Ah, I hoped that you would be back tonight,' he said, and ticked off three more items on his list. 'Any idea why I recalled you?'

'No, sir. Your messenger didn't seem to know anything, and he wasn't one of my men—didn't care to ask him much.'

Callistus nodded towards the window. 'Go and look out there.'

Aquila looked at him an instant, questioningly, then crossed to the high windows and stood looking out. From this room high in the Praetorium there was a clear view of the Watergate, and, between the jutting bastions of the Curtain Wall, a glimpse of the inner harbour and the roadstead beyond. One of the three-bank galleys—he thought it was the *Clytemnestra*—was made fast alongside the jetty, taking on board supplies; he could see the small, dark figures on the gangways. There was a swarming of men about the Watergate, stores and fodder and war supplies being brought down under the watchful eye of a Centurion of Marines. Felix, his particular friend, who commanded another troop of horse, was down there struggling to disentangle a mishap of some kind. He saw him waving his arms in his efforts, as though he were drowning. He heard a trumpet call, and beyond in the roadstead the other galleys lay at anchor, quiet above their broken reflections, yet clearly waiting to be away.

'Looks like making ready for embarkation,' he said.

'Looks like what it is.' Callistus laid down his pen and got up, and came across to join him in the window. 'We are being withdrawn from Britain.'

For a moment Aquila could not make the words mean anything. They were so unbelievable that they were only sounds. And then their meaning came home to him, and he turned his head slowly, frowning, to look at the Commandant. 'Did you say "withdrawn from Britain", sir?'

'Yes,' Callistus said, 'I did.'

'But in Our Lord's name, why?'

'Question not the orders of the High Command. Possibly it is considered that our few companies and crews will die more serviceably under the walls of Rome the next time the barbarians choose to sack the city, than here in the mists of this forgotten province in the North.'

Forgotten province; yes, they were that all right, Aquila thought. They had their answer to that desperate appeal to Aetius, all the answer that they would ever have. He heard himself asking, 'Is it a clean sweep? All the remaining garrisons?'

'I imagine so, yes. Rome is scraping the lees from the bottom of the cask. We have been here four hundred years, and in three days we shall be gone.'

'In three days,' Aquila said. He felt that he was repeating things stupidly, but he felt stupid, dazed.

'We sail on the third evening tide from now.' Callistus turned back to his littered table. 'And since that leaves little time for standing idle, go and get into uniform and take over your troop, Decurion.'

Still dazed, Aquila saluted and left the room, hurried down the stairway and across the parade-ground below the Pharos. The vast plinth, long as an eighty-oared galley and three times the height of a man, rose like an island in the empty space, and from it the great central tower sprang up, crested with its iron beacon brazier against the sky. A few shreds of marble facings, a few cracked marble columns upholding the roof of the covered ways for the fuel-carts, remained of the proud days, the days when it had stood shining in wrought bronze and worked marble here at the gateway to Britain, for a triumphal memorial to Rome's conquest of the province. But they had used most of the broken marble for rubble when they built the great walls to keep the Saxons out. The tower rose up bare and starkly grey as a rock, with the seagulls rising and falling about it, the evening light on their wings. The light was beginning to fade; soon the beacon would be lit, and the night after it would be lit, and the night after that, and then there would be no more Rutupiae Light.

Aquila hurried on, across the parade-ground and up to his sleeping cell in the officers' block. He changed into uniform, obscurely comforted by the familiar feel of leather tunic and iron cap and the weight of his long cavalry sword against his thigh; and went to take over command of his troop again.

Later, much later that night, he scratched a few hasty lines of farewell to his father. He knew that among the men in the great fort who must sail in three days' time, many would be making frantic efforts to arrange for wives and children to follow them, for all men must know that now Britain was doomed. One or two of his own troop had already come to him for help and counsel; a young, worried trooper wanting to get his parents out to Gaul, an old one in tears for a wife who must be left behind . . . He had done what he could, but he felt so helpless. It was no good trying to do anything about his own family. Nothing, he knew, would shift his father from a post of duty, even though it was duty to a lost cause; and even if that had not been so, he would never have abandoned the farm and the farm-folk. And Flavia would remain with their father whatever came. So he wrote his letter, sending them his dear love, and promising Flavia her crimson slippers one day. He gave it to an orderly for dispatch, knowing that there would be no time for any farewell message to reach him in return, and lay down to catch a few hours' sleep before he turned out at cockcrow to early Stables.

During the days that followed, Aquila seemed to be two people; one getting on with the business of making his troop ready for embarkation, the other all the while fighting a battle of divided loyalties within himself. It began after the letter to his father had gone, while he lay wakeful in the darkness with the sea sounding in his ears. One didn't hear the sea much in the daytime, save when there was a storm, but at night it was always there, even in a flat calm, a faint, persistent wash of sound like the sea in a shell. It seemed to be out of that faint sea-wash in the silence that the knowledge came to him that he belonged to Britain. He had always belonged to Britain, but he hadn't known it before, because he had never had to question it before. He knew it now.

It was not only because of Flavia and his father. Lying in the darkness with his arm over his eyes, he tried quite deliberately to thrust them from his mind, pretend that they did not exist. It made no difference; even without them, he still belonged to Britain. How odd! he thought. We of the Outposts, we speak of ourselves as Roman; we think of ourselves as Roman—with the surface of our minds—and underneath, it is like this. And they were sailing in three days' time, less than three days, now.

And presently the three days had dwindled down to a few hours.

He longed to talk about it to Felix, good old Felix with whom he had so often gone wild-fowling on Tanatus Marshes. But he knew that Felix, who was also native born, though his roots were not struck so deeply in the province as Aquila's were, would be having trouble enough of his own. Besides, something in him knew that this was one of those things that must be faced alone.

Only there seemed so little time to think, to be sure. And now the last feverish hours of getting the horses into the transports were over, and the men had been marched aboard while the brazen orders of the trumpets rang above the ordered tumult; and there was scarcely anything more to do. A flamed and feathered sunset was fading behind the Great Forest, and the tide was almost at the flood, running far up the creeks and inlets and winding waterways; and amid the last ordered coming and going, Aquila stood on the lifting deck of the *Clytemnestra*. The stern and mast-head lanterns were alight already, as the daylight dimmed, and any moment now the great fire-beacon on the crest of the Pharos should have sprung to life. But there would be no Rutupiae Light tonight to guide the fleets of the Empire. The last of the Eagles were flying from Britain. Any moment now the trumpets would sound as the Commandant came down from the Watergate and stepped on board, and the landing-bridge would be raised, and the Hortator's hammer would begin the steady, remorseless clack-clack-clack that beat out the time for the slaves on the rowing benches.

Aquila suddenly saw himself going to the Commandant in that last moment, laying his drawn sword at his feet, saying, 'Sir, everything is in order. Now let me go.' Would Callistus think that he was mad or hysterical? No, oddly enough—for there had never been a word between them save in the way of duty—he knew that Callistus would understand; but he knew also that Callistus would have no choice but to refuse. The choice was his. Quite clearly and coldly, in the still moment after the three days' turmoil, he knew that he must make it alone.

He turned to his old, grey-whiskered Optio beside him, who had taught him all that he knew of soldiering, all that he knew of the handling of a troop—he had been so proud of his troop—and gripped his leather-clad shoulder an instant.

'God keep you, Aemilius. I'll be back.'

He turned to the head of the landing-bridge and crossed over, quickly and openly as though in obedience to some last-moment order. No chance to bid goodbye to Felix, none to take leave of Nestor, his horse. He strode by the last remaining figures on the jetty, the native dockyard hands, no one particularly noticing him in the fading light, back through the Watergate into the desolate fort.

Everything in him felt bruised and bleeding. He had been bred a soldier, coming of a line of soldiers, and he was breaking faith with all the gods of his kind. Going 'wilful missing'. The very words had the sorry sound of disgrace. He was failing the men of his own troop, which seemed to him in that moment a worse thing than all else. Yet he did not turn back again to the waiting galleys. He knew that what he was doing was a thing that you couldn't judge for other people, only for yourself; and for himself, he did not know if it was the right thing, but he knew that it was the only thing.

He was scarcely aware of his direction, until he found himself at the foot of the Pharos. The ramp for the fuel-carts led steeply upward to the vast plinth, and at the head of it the mouth of the covered way gaped dark and empty in the gathering dusk. He mounted the ramp quickly and strode forward into the darkness. He was in the square hollowness of the tower foot where the fuel-carts were housed. The carts were there now, ranged side by side, mere blots of darkness in the lesser darkness. The dry, musty smell of baled straw was in his nostrils, and the sharp tang of pitch that had soaked into the stones of the walls. He turned to the narrow stairway that wound up the wall like the spiral twist of a snail shell, and began to climb.

He was only halfway up when he heard, faintly through the thick walls from the world outside, the trumpets sounding the Commandant on board. Any moment now he would be missed. Well, they would have little time for searching. They would not miss the tide for one junior officer gone wilful missing. He climbed on, up and up, stumbling a little, through chamber after chamber, with the sense of height increasing on him, past the deserted quarters where the men on beacon duty had lived like peregrine falcons high above the world. The grey dusk seeping through the small windows showed the dark shapes of the debris they had left behind them—rough wooden furniture and cast-off gear, like the stranded flotsam on the shore left when the tide flows out, as Rome's tide was flowing out. Up and up until the stairway ran out into open air, and he ducked at last through a little low-set doorway into complete darkness, into the 'Immediate Use' fuel store just below the signal platform. Feeling with outstretched hands, he found the ranged barrels of pitch, the straw and brushwood and stacked logs. A gap opened to his questing hand between the brushwood and the wall, and he crawled into it and crouched there, pulling the brushwood over again behind him.

It wasn't a good hiding-place, but the tide would be already on the turn.

For what seemed a very long time he crouched there, his heart beating in slow, uneven drubs. From far, far below him, in another world, he thought he heard the tramp of mailed sandals, and voices that shouted his name. He wondered what he should do if they came up here and found him, skulking like a cornered rat under a garbage pile; but the time passed, and the footsteps and the calling voices came and went, hurrying, but never mounted the stairs of the forsaken tower. And presently the trumpets sounded again, recalling the searchers lest they lose the tide. Too late now to change his mind.

More time passed, and he knew that the galleys would be slipping down the broad river-way between the marshes. And then once more he heard the trumpets. No, only one. The call was faint, faint as the echo of a seabird's cry; but Aquila's ear caught the sad, familiar notes of the call. In one of those galleys slipping seaward, somebody, in savage comment on what had happened, or merely in farewell, was sounding 'Lights Out'.

And now that it was all over, now that the choice was made, and one faith kept and one faith broken, Aquila drove his face down on to his forearm against the whippy roughness of the brushwood bundles, and cried as he had never cried before and would never cry again.

A long while later he turned himself about in his hiding-place, and ducked out on to the narrow stairway, spent and empty as though he had cried his heart away. Dusk had long since deepened into the dark, and the cold moonlight came down the steps from the beacon platform, plashing silvery from step to step. And as he checked there, leaning against the wall, the silence of the great fortress came up to him, a silence of desolation and complete emptiness. On a sudden impulse he turned upward towards the moonlight instead of down into the blackness that swallowed the descending stairway, and stumbled up the last few steps, emerging on the beacon platform.

The moon was riding high in a sky pearled and feathered with high wind-cloud, and a little wind sighed across the breast-high parapet with a faint aeolian hum through the iron-work of the beacon tripod. The brazier was made up ready for lighting, with fuel stacked beside it, as it had been stacked every night. Aquila crossed to the parapet and stood looking down. There were lights in the little ragged town that huddled against the fortress walls, but the great fort below him was empty and still in the moonlight as a ruin that had been hearth-cold for a hundred years. Presently, in the daylight, men would come and strip the place of whatever was useful to them, but probably after dark they would leave it forsaken and empty to its ghosts. Would they be the ghosts of the men who had sailed on this tide? Or of the men who had left their names on the leaning gravestones above the wash of the tide? A Cohort Centurion with a Syrian name, dying after thirty years' service, a boy trumpeter of the Second Legion, dying after two . . .

Aquila's gaze lengthened out across the marshes in the wake of the galleys, and far out to sea he thought that he could still make out a spark of light. The stern lantern of a transport; the last of Rome-in-Britain. And beside him the beacon stack rose dark and waiting . . . On a sudden wild impulse he flung open the bronze-sheathed chest in which the fire-lighting gear was kept, and pulled out flint and steel and tinderbox, and tearing his fingers on the steel in his frantic haste, as though he were fighting against time, he struck out fire and kindled the waiting tinder, and set about waking the beacon. Rutupiae Light should burn for this one more night. Maybe Felix or his old Optio would know who had kindled it, but that was not what mattered. The pitch-soaked brushwood caught, and the flames ran crackling up, spreading into a great golden burst of fire; and the still, moonlit world below faded into a blue nothingness as the fierce glare flooded the beacon platform. The wind caught the crest of the blaze and bent it over in a wave; and Aquila's shadow streamed out from him across the parapet and into the night like a ragged cloak. He flung water from the tank in the corner on to the blackened bull's-hide fireshield, and crouched holding it before him by the brazier, feeding the blaze to its greatest strength. The heart of it was glowing now, a blasting, blinding core of heat and brightness under the flames; even from the shores of Gaul they would see the blaze, and say, 'Ah, there is Rutupiae's Light.' It was his farewell to so many things; to the whole world that he had been bred to. But it was something more: a defiance against the dark.

He vaguely, half expected them to come up from the town to see who had lit the beacon, but no one came. Perhaps they thought it was the ghosts. Presently he stoked it up so that it would last for a while, and turned to the stairhead and went clattering down. The beacon would sink low, but he did not think it would go out much before dawn.

He reached the ground level; the moonlight hung like a silver curtain before the doorway, and he walked out into it and across the deserted fortress, and out through a postern gate that stood open, and away. He had the sudden thought that for the sake of the fitness of things he should have broken his sword across his knee and left the pieces beside Rutupiae Light, but he was like to need it in the time that lay ahead.

III
The Wolves of the Sea

THE posting stations were still in existence, but to use them without a military permit cost money, and Aquila had never been one to save his pay, so it was upward of a week later when he came at last up the track from the ford, on an evening of soft mizzle rain. He saw the light in the atrium window and made for it, brushing the chill, spattering drops from the low branches of the damson tree as he mounted the terrace steps. He crossed the terrace and opened the atrium door, and stood leaning against the door-post, feeling like a very weary ghost.

Margarita, who would have been baying her head off at a stranger's footfall before he was halfway up the valley, had risen, stretching and yawning her pleasure, and came padding across the tiled floor to greet him, with her tail swinging behind her. For an instant he saw the familiar scene caught into perfect stillness in the candle light as though it were caught in amber: his father and Demetrius with the chess-board between them—they often played chess in the evenings, on a board with faint ridges between the ivory and ebony squares; Flavia sitting on the wolf-skin rug before the low fire, burnishing the old cavalry sword that she had taken down, as she often did, from its place above the hearth. Only the look on their faces, turned towards the door, was not familiar; the blank, startled, incredulous look, as though he were indeed a ghost that had come back to them mired with the white chalky mud of his journeying.

Then his father said, frowning, 'Is that you, Aquila?'

'Yes, Father.'

'I thought that the last of the Eagles had flown from Britain.'

There was a little silence. Then Aquila said, 'I have deserted the Eagles.'

He pushed off from the door-post, and came in, closing the door behind him against the rain that was dark on the shoulders of his leather tunic. Old Margarita was rubbing her head against his thigh, and he put down a hand to fondle her, without being aware that he did so. He was standing before his silent father now. Demetrius would not judge him, he knew: Demetrius judged no man but himself; and Flavia would care for nothing but that he had come home. But with his father it would be another matter. 'I belong to Britain,' he heard himself saying; not trying to defend himself, simply telling his father what had happened. 'More and more, all those three days, I found that I belonged to Britain. And in the end—I let the galleys sail without me.'

For a long moment his father still sat silent, with the chess-piece he had been holding when Aquila entered still in his hand. His face, turned full on Aquila, was stern and uncompromising. 'Not an easy choice,' he said at last.

'Not an easy choice,' Aquila agreed, and his voice sounded hoarse in his own ears.

His father set down the chess-piece with careful precision.

'Nothing, *nothing*, Aquila, excuses deserting the Eagles. But since it seems to me very probable that in your place I should have done the same as you have done, I can scarcely pass judgement on you.'

'No, sir,' Aquila said, staring straight before him. 'Thank you, sir.'

Old Demetrius smiled a little under his long upper lip, and shifted his own piece on the board.

And Flavia, who had sat ever since he appeared in the doorway, as though caught in some witch's spell of stillness, flung aside the naked sword and sprang up, and came running to set her hands on his shoulders. 'Oh, Aquila, I'm so glad, glad, *glad* that you did let them sail without you! I thought I should have died when your letter came . . . Does Gwyna know you are here?'

'Not yet,' Aquila said.

'I'll go and tell her, and we'll bring you some food—much, much food. You look so hungry. You look—' She broke off, her eyes searching his face. 'Oh, my dear, you said that I had grown up in a year, but you have grown up in twelve days.'

She put her arms round his neck, and held him fiercely close, her cheek pressed against his; then ran from the room calling, 'Gwyna! Gwyna! Aquila's home again! He has come back to us after all, and we must feed him!'

Behind her, Aquila crossed to the fire that burned British fashion on a raised hearth, at the end of the room, and held his hands to it, for he was cold with the rain. Standing there, he said to his father, only half in question, 'No word out of Gaul?'

'I imagine the withdrawal of our last troops is all the word out of Gaul that we shall ever receive,' his father said. He turned in his chair to follow the direction of Aquila's voice. 'Rome has cut her losses, where the province of Britain is concerned, and what the future holds for the province, or for any of us, God knows. Whatever it is, I am glad that you will be sharing it with us, Aquila.'

Two evenings after Aquila's homecoming, they had a fire again, not so much for warmth as to fight the cheerlessness of the summer gale beating against the walls; and with dinner over and the candles lit—you couldn't get oil for the lamps any more—the atrium had taken on its winter aspect, the sense of safety and shelter within firelit walls, and the storm shut out, that belongs to winter time. Aquila had drawn a stool to the side of the hearth, and Flavia had settled herself on the rug beside him, leaning against his knee while she combed and combed her hair. The chess-board had not been brought out tonight, and instead Demetrius, with a scroll spread before him on the table, where the candlelight fell brightest, was reading to their father from *The Odyssey*.

'"For two days and two nights we lay there, making no way and eating our hearts out with despair and the unceasing labour. But on the third morning bright-haired Dawn gave us clear daylight; wherefore up went our masts and white shining sails . . . Indeed that time I all but came unscathed to my Fatherland, only for the swell and the sea currents and a north wind which united against me as I worked round Cape Maleia and drove me wide to Cythera."'

Aquila heard the familiar sentences above the beating of the wind, and realized for the first time that Demetrius had a beautiful voice. His gaze wandered about the room that he had known all his life, brushing over the small household shrine with the sign of the Fish painted on the wall above it, the couches with their coverings of deerskins and gay native rugs, his father's sword hanging above the hearth, the pretty tumble of women's gear—Flavia had never in her life put anything away. His gaze lingered on his father's face, alert and listening in the firelight, his hand with the great dolphin ring fondling Margarita's head on his knee; on Demetrius's grey and gentle features bent over his scroll. Demetrius had been a slave until their father had bought him to be their tutor, and given him his freedom; and when he was no longer needed as a tutor, he had stayed to be Flavian's steward and his eyes. Demetrius was a stoic, a man to whom life was a discipline to be endured with dignity and death a darkness to be met without flinching. Maybe that was what he had taught himself in his slave days, to make them bearable. It came to Aquila suddenly how terrible it must be to be a stoic: but he did not believe that Demetrius was really like that; he loved ideas and people too much. His gaze dropped to Flavia, combing her hair in the firelight that made a glow all round her. She was looking up at him through the dark, flying strands as she flung it this way and that, sweeping the comb through it. And as she combed, she was humming, so softly that the sound would not reach her father or Demetrius at all; a dark, thin, sweet humming that Aquila could barely catch above the voices of the summer storm.

He bent down towards her, his arm across his knee. 'What are you nooning?'

She glimmered with laughter. 'Perhaps I make a singing magic. What would you say if I told you that I combed my hair—just like this—and made a singing magic, on the evening that the galleys sailed, to call you home again?'

He looked at her with unexpected soberness. 'I don't know. But I do not think that I should ever feel quite the same about you again.'

Flavia stopped combing. 'No,' she said, 'I knew that you would not. That is why I did not do it, though I longed to—you can't know how I longed to—because I knew that if I did, and it worked, I should have to tell you. I don't know why, but I should have to tell you, and I couldn't bear that you should not feel the same about me again.'

'Do you know,' Aquila said, 'I don't think I could, either.'

A few weeks ago he would not have dreamed of saying that to Flavia; he would scarcely have thought it to himself. But now it was different; now, when the present moment mattered so much, because there mightn't be anything to come after.

The wind that was roaring up the valley fell away into a long trough of quiet, and in the hush, faint and far off and infinitely sad, rose the hunting cry of a wolf. Aquila cocked up his head, listening. It wasn't often that you heard the wolves in the summer, they were a winter sound; and hearing the long-drawn howl between gust and gust of the storm, he grew freshly aware of the warmth and shelter of the firelit atrium.

Demetrius checked in his reading, to listen also; and Margarita bristled, growling deep in her throat without raising her head from her lord's knee.

'The Forest Wolves call to their brothers of the Sea,' Flavian said, grimly.

Aquila looked at him quickly, knowing that in the past few days there had been several raids on farms nearer the coast. He had seen the distant glare of one such burning farmstead as he followed the downs homeward. It was for that reason that the farm-hands all slept in the house now.

The wind swooped back. Demetrius took up his reading once more at the place where he had broken off, and the group around the fire settled again. But Margarita continued growling, her ears pricked forward, her coat rising a little. She prowled to the door and back, turned round three times after her own tail, and collapsed at her lord's feet, but almost at once she was up again, still growling.

'Hush now. Have you never heard the wolf kind before?' her lord said, and she licked his thumb and sat down again, but still with raised, uneasy head. A few moments later, Bran the sheepdog barked from the farmhands' quarters, and she sprang up, baying, was silent a moment to listen, then broke out baying again.

'I wonder if it *is* the Wolves,' Aquila said, half-rising as he spoke, his hand going to his sword.

And almost in the same instant a wild cry broke through the storm, and a babble of shouting rose in the night outside.

'Name of Light! What is that?'

Aquila didn't know which of them had asked it, but the answer was in all their minds. They were all on their feet now, Demetrius rolling up his precious scroll as the door burst open, letting in a great swoop of wind to drive the smoke billowing from the hearth and set the candle-flames streaming, and Finn the shepherd appeared on the wings of the storm, wild-eyed and panting.

'It is the Saxons! They are all about us! I blundered into them when I went to see to the sheep.' The others were crowding in after him, old Kuno and the farm-hands, all with their weapons, for in these days men were never far from their weapons; little, shrivelled, valiant Gwyna with a long knife from the kitchen, the other women all with what they had been able to catch up. At least there were no children, Aquila thought, only Regan's baby, that was so young it would know nothing . . .

Flavian was quickly and surely issuing his orders; he must have been prepared so long for this to happen, known so exactly what it would be like when it did. The dogs had ceased their baying, and crouched snarling with laid-back ears, Aquila had crossed in two strides to the open doorway. No point in closing it; better to die fighting than be burned in a trap. He called back over his shoulder as red fire sprang up in the farmyard below and he glimpsed the flanged helmets against the uprush of flame.

'They're questing through the out-houses, firing them as they close in. They're driving off the cattle. Lord God! There must be two score of them at least!'

'So. At all events we have a space to breathe until they finish with the byres,' his father said.

Despite the wind, despite the shouting and lowing outside and the red glare that was beginning to beat up from below the terrace, there was a sense of quietness in the long atrium, where the farm-hands with their hastily-snatched-up weapons stood to their appointed places. Aquila supposed that it was the knowing without any doubt that one was going to die, but he thought also it was something that flowed from his father standing in their midst, a kind of strength that was like confidence. Demetrius carefully returned his scroll to the open scroll chest, closed the lid, and, reaching up, took down a long, slender dagger from among the beautiful weapons on the wall. In the leaping, storm-driven light his face was as grey and gentle as ever.

'I think I expressed to you my gratitude for my freedom at the time,' he said to Flavian, testing the blade. 'I have never spoken of it again. I should like now to thank you for the years that I have been a free man, and—I find on reflection—an extremely happy one.'

'Nay, man, there is no debt that you have not paid; and no time for thanks, on either side, between you and me. Will somebody bring me my sword?'

Aquila, who had turned away from the door, leapt to take it down. He drew it from the worn sheath, and casting the sheath aside, set the weapon naked in his father's outstretched hand.

'There it is, sir.'

His father's strong fingers closed round the grip, and there was a faint smile on his mouth. 'So—it is a long time, but the feel is still familiar . . . They will not know that I am blind. It doesn't show, Aquila?'

'No, sir,' Aquila said, looking for what he knew was the last time into his father's thin, scarred face. 'It doesn't show.'

The shouting was drawing nearer, sounding from all round them now. Flavian crossed with a sure step to the shrine at the far end of the atrium, and laid his naked sword for an instant before the little shielded light that burned quite steadily in the flower-shaped altar lamp.

'Lord, receive us into Thy Kingdom,' he said, and took up his sword again, and turned towards the open door.

Aquila also was standing with drawn sword, his arm round Flavia. She felt light and hard and braced in the curve of it. 'Try not to be afraid,' he said.

'I don't think I am,' she returned. 'Not really afraid. It—doesn't seem real, does it?'

No, it didn't seem real. It didn't seem real even when the shouting and the tumult burst upward into a new savagery and the first Saxon came leaping up the terrace steps to meet the resolute figure of the master of the house, standing with drawn sword in the doorway.

After that, for a while, Aquila knew only a red chaos; a great splurge of shouting in his ears and the snarling of the hounds and the ring and clash of weapons; and Flavia with a high, fierce cry snatching the dagger from his belt as he sprang into the doorway beside his father. The flare of firebrands was in his eyes, and the flash of the fire on leaping saex blades. There seemed flame everywhere, ragged, wing-blown flame, and the bull's-horned and boar-crested warriors thrusting in on them out of the rolling smoke. The rafters were alight now over their head, the flames running along them in bright waves before the wind, and the atrium was full of smoke that tore at the defenders' lungs, choking and blinding them. But there were fewer defenders now; only seven where there had been nine, only six—old Kuno was down, Finn too, and Demetrius. A blazing shutter gave way, and a Saxon sprang in yelling through the high window-hole; and now they were beset from behind as well as before. A man in a great flanged helmet, with the golden torc of a chieftain about his neck, made for Flavian with war-axe up-swung for a blow that there could have been no turning even if the man at whom it was aimed had been able to see it coming. Aquila saw his father fall, and with Flavia fighting like a young fury beside him, hurled himself forward against the leaping saex blades to make a last rallying point of his body. 'To me! To me! Close up!'

Through the red haze that beat before his eyes he saw a snarling face with eyes that seemed all blue fire, and wild yellow hair streaming from beneath the great flanged helmet; he drove the point of his sword in over the golden torc, and saw the man drop his axe in mid-swing and stagger back, clutching at his throat with blood spurting between his fingers; and laughed, knowing that at least his father was avenged.

He did not feel the blow that fell glancing on his own temple and brought him down like a poled ox. He only knew that he had leapt forward in time—how much he didn't know—and everything seemed to be over, and he was still alive, which bothered him because the two things didn't fit. He was being dragged to his feet, which seemed odd too, for he did not remember being on the ground, dazed and half blind with the blood running into his eyes. And then he heard Flavia shrieking his name, 'Aquila! *Aquila!*' and wrenched round in his captors' grasp to see her carried past, struggling like a wild cat, over the shoulder of a laughing, fair-haired giant. He tried to spring towards her, dragging his captors with him, but they were all about him, his arms were wrenched behind his back, and he was flung to his knees, struggling until his heart seemed like to burst and blood pounded like a hammer in his temples. For a moment the world darkened and swam in a red haze about him; Flavia's shrieks died as though somebody had stifled them with a hand over her mouth.

Somehow, fighting still, he found himself thrust to a halt with his arms twisted at his back, before a huge man who stood at the head of the familiar terrace steps under the scorched and shrivelled skeleton of the damson tree. The glare of the wind-driven fire that seemed all about them played on his helmet and yellow hair and beard, and made shifting fish-scale jinks of light on the byrnie he wore. And his face, Aquila saw, was the face of the man he had killed for his father's death. But there was no gold torc round this man's neck, and no red hole above it, and therefore it could not be the same.

He stood with arms folded on his breast, staring at Aquila under down-drawn golden brows. Something sparkled green on one great hand, and Aquila, ceasing to struggle now, gasping and spent, knew that it was his father's ring.

'Aye,' the huge Saxon said after a long scrutiny, 'it is the man who slew my brother.'

Through the beating in his head, Aquila understood the meaning of the guttural words, for he had not served a year with Lower Rhenus troops without learning something of the Saxon tongue. He dragged up his head, trying to shake the blood out of his eyes. 'Your brother, who slew my father on the threshold of his own house!'

'So! And he speaks our tongue,' the huge Saxon said, and he smiled, as a wolf smiles. 'Vengeance for a kinsman is sweet. I also, Wiermund of the White Horse, I find it sweet,' and with a slow deliberateness he drew the stained saex from his belt, fondling it, dandling it in his big hands . . .

Aquila waited, his eyes on the Saxon's face. He heard the roar of the flames, and the cattle lowing as they were rounded up, and under it the quietness, the dreadful quietness, full of only the wind. And even the wind was dying now. He was aware of the bodies that lay crumpled and grotesque in the red glare of the fire, bodies of his own folk and of the Sea Wolves; his father and the Saxon Chieftain lying together in the doorway; even Margarita lying dead at her lord's feet, where she must have crawled to him in her last moment. He did not feel very much about them, because he knew that in a few moments he would have joined them. Flavia was the only one he felt anything about—Flavia.

Wiermund of the White Horse had already raised his saex for the death-blow when, far off, above the hoarse moaning of the gale-torn woods, rose a cry that Aquila had heard once already that night: the cry of a hunting wolf, answered by another from away over towards the flank of the downs.

Wiermund checked, listening. Then he lowered his blade, and the smile broadened and broadened on his face until it was a snarl. 'Aiee, the wolf kind smell blood,' he said. 'Soon they will come following their noses.' He seemed to consider a moment, still fingering his saex blade. Then, abruptly, he drove it back into the sheath. 'Take him out to the wood-shore and bind him to a tree.'

The warriors about him looked quickly at each other, and then uncertainly at their leader.

'Alive?' someone said.

'Alive until the wolf kind come,' said the dead Chieftain's brother simply; and a growl of agreement, a grim breath of laughter ran from one to another of the war band. 'Aye, leave him to the wolves! He slew Wiergyls our Chieftain!—They call the wolves our brothers, let the wolves avenge their kin!'

They half thrust, half dragged him down the terrace steps skirting the blazing farmyard, and away up to the tongue of the woods above the old vine terraces, where he had stood with Flavia looking down on their home so short a time ago. At the last moment he began to struggle again, wildly, desperately. It was one thing to brace oneself for the quick dispatch of the saex blade, but quite another to stand unresisting to be tied to a tree for living-bait. His body revolted at the prospect and went on struggling without anything to do with his will. But all his strength seemed to have gone from him, and he was powerless in their hands as a half-drowned pup. They stripped him naked; someone brought a partly charred wagon-rope from the blazing shed, and with the sound part of it they lashed his hands behind his back and bound him to the trunk of a young beech tree. Then they drew off and stood about him, very merry.

He forced up his head against the intolerable weight that seemed to bear it down, and saw their shapes dark against the glare of the blazing farmstead.

'So, bide there with a good fire to warm you until the wolf kind come,' said the man who had been the Chieftain's brother, and he called off his warriors like a hunter calling off his hounds. Aquila did not see them go, only he realized suddenly, through the swimming confusion in his head, that he was alone.

Only the wind swept up the valley, and below the wind he heard the silence. The fires below were sinking; and there would be no more fires in the valley where the hearth fire had burned for so many generations of men; and the silence and the desolation washed up to Aquila like the waves of a dark sea, engulfing him. Swirling nightmare pictures washed to and fro on the darkness of it, so that he saw over and over again the last stand in the atrium doorway, and his father's death, so that he saw over and over again the hideous vision of Flavia struggling in the hands of the barbarians that set him writhing and tearing at his bonds like a mad thing until the blood ran where the ropes bit into him.

He must have lost consciousness at last, because suddenly the grey dawn was all about him, and the gale quite died away. The wolf kind had not come. Maybe there were too many of their human brothers hunting these hills; for he heard the mutter of voices, and the first thing he saw when his eyes opened on a swimming world were a pair of feet in clumsy raw-hide shoes, and the lower rim of a Saxon buckler. Men were standing round him again, but he realized dimly that though they were Saxons, they were not last night's band, but a new raiding party that had come questing out of the woods to find that others had been before them.

'Nay then, why should you meddle with another man's kill?' someone was protesting in a deep growl of exasperation.

And somebody else was hacking at his bonds with a saex blade, saying through shut teeth, 'Because I have a mind to him, that's why.'

The last strands parted, and Aquila swayed forward. He struggled to keep upright before these new tormentors, but his numbed legs gave under him and he crumpled to the ground, his wrists still bound behind him. The man who had cut him from the tree straddled over him hacking at his remaining bonds, and as the last strands of those also parted, he rolled over and saw, frowning upward through the throbbing in his head, that it was a lad younger than himself, a mere stripling in a ring-mail byrnie, with a skin that was clear red and white like a girl's under the golden fuzz of his beard.

'Get some water from the stream,' said the stripling to the world in general; and it seemed that somebody must have brought it in his helmet, for suddenly the iron rim was jolting against Aquila's shut teeth. Someone dashed the cold water into his face, and as he gasped, a wave of it went down his throat, making him choke and splutter, yet dragging him back to life whether he would or no. As his head cleared, he realized that there were about a score of men standing round him, with laden ponies in their midst. Clearly they had had better luck with their raiding in other places than they had in this one.

'What Thormod the son of Thrand should want with another's leavings is a thing beyond my understanding,' said the voice that he had heard before; and Aquila saw now that it belonged to a bull-necked individual with red hair sprouting out of his nose and ears, 'If you would carry home a slave at the summer's end, let it be one of your own taking.'

The boy he had called Thormod stood over Aquila still, the red of his face spreading over the white from the gold collar he wore to the roots of his yellow hair, though he was yet half-laughing. 'Ran the Mother of storms fly away with you, Cynegils! Must you be for ever telling me what I should do and what I should not do? He has a dolphin on his shoulder, and often Bruni my grandsire has told me how in his seafaring days he knew always when he saw a dolphin that his luck would be good, wherefore he took the dolphin for his lucky sign. And therefore I've a mind to take this other man's leavings for a gift to my grandsire that I reckon will catch at his fancy more than a jewelled cup or a little silver god.'

'As for the dolphin, it is but painted on and will surely wash off,' somebody said, bending to peer more closely at Aquila as he half-lay in their midst.

'Nay, it is pricked in after the manner of the patterns that the Painted People wear. I have seen their envoys.' The boy Thormod spat on his hand and rubbed it to and fro over the tattooing on Aquila's shoulder, then held up his hand triumphantly. 'See, it does *not* wash off!'

Somebody laughed. 'Let the boy take his findings; it is his first raiding summer.'

'Also I am Sister's Son to Hunfirth the Chieftain,' said the boy.

A tall man with eyes that were very blue in a square, brown face reached out an arm heavy with bracelets of copper wire and shining blue glass, and caught him a lazy buffet on the side on the head. 'Not so loud, my young cockerel. No man's word counts more than another's in my ship, saving only my own. Nevertheless, we've room for another rower since Ulf was killed, and you shall take him—and be responsible for him—if you've a mind to.'

And so, still half dazed, Aquila was jerked to his feet, and his hands twisted again behind his back and strapped there. And when the little band of Saxon raiders turned seaward, climbing the long slope of the downs, they carried Aquila stumbling in their midst.

Behind him the valley was left to its silence, and nothing moved save the last faint smoke that still curled up from the blackened ruins of his home.

IV
Ullasfjord

SINCE noon the two longships had been nosing their way between the shoals and sandbanks of a wide firth; and now the sun was westering and the shadows of the fierce dragon prows reached forward, jade and milky across the bright water, as though the vessels smelled their own familiar landing-beach and were eager to be home.

The striped sails were down, and the crews had taken to the oars. The *Sea-Snake* followed in the wake of the Chieftain's great *Storm-Wind,* and beyond the high, graceful sweep of the stern, Aquila, pulling with the rest, saw only the tumbled brightness of the sunset spreading up the sky. Against the blaze of it, Wulfnoth the Captain stood braced and watchful at the steer-oar, his voice coming down to them giving the rowing time to which it seemed that rowers and vessel answered as though they were one living thing.

'Lift her! Lift her!'

To Aquila, used to the slave-rowed Roman galleys, it seemed very strange, this rowing by free seamen, among whom he alone was a slave. He had not resisted when he was pressed into rowing. It would have been useless and pointless to resist. Besides, better have something to do; less time for thinking.

But the trouble was that one could row and think at the same time. He had found that out all too soon. And now, his body swinging to the rhythm of the oars, his mind went dragging and straining back over the long trail; back to that hideous forced march over the downs—there had been harebells up on the high downs; odd that he remembered that now—and down over the seaward marshes to the little dark, deadly longship lying in the hidden creek of Regnum Harbour. Out beyond Vectis they had met the *Storm-Wind,* and together put in to replenish supplies. He remembered the fires inland and the screaming, and the cattle driven down for slaughter on the beach, more cattle than they could eat or carry away, wantonly slaughtered and left on the tide line when the *Storm-Wind* and the *Sea-Snake* spread their wings once more. It was like a waking nightmare in his mind. But it was not so terrible as the nightmares that came to him when he slept; the terrible dreams in which he heard Flavia shrieking his name in unutterable fear and agony, saw her carried by, stretching her arms to him, on the shoulders of a golden horror, half man, half beast, and fought to go to her against the stranglehold of a great tree that wrapped its branches about him with thick, throaty laughter and held him fast.

He never dreamed of his father or the others. Maybe that was because for them the horror was over. For Flavia, too, it was most likely over, but he could not be sure, and the thought of her alive in the hands of the barbarians was at once his greatest torment and the thing that made him go on living himself.

He was aware now, as the firth turned more northerly, of a sudden quickening excitement among the crew. Men began snatching glances over their shoulders, and as the longships rounded a low headland, a triumphant shout went up. Aquila, glancing over his shoulder also as he swung to his oar, made out a distant huddle of turf roofs crowding under the shelter of a great dyke, as ponies huddle under a hedge when a storm blows over, and the low, long spines of boat-sheds above the oyster paleness of the beach. As they swept nearer, he could see that the landing-beach was speckled with people. Clearly they had been seen from afar, and the whole settlement had come crowding down to welcome the longships home from their summer's raiding.

Now the Captain's voice rose into swifter chant. *'Lift her! Lift her!'* And the *Sea-Snake* leapt forward like a mare that smells her own stable, coming round in a great swooping curve in the white wake of the Chieftain's keel. Now she was heading straight for the shore through the broken water of the shallows; and Wolfnoth's voice rang out: 'In oars! Out rollers! Now—run her in, brothers!'

The oars were unshipped and swung in-board, the long rollers caught up from their places beneath the thwarts, and with a shout the Sea-Wolves were out over the gunwales, thigh deep in the cold, white water. Shouting and cheering, they ran her up through the shallows in the wake of the *Storm-Wind*, splashing a yeasty turmoil of surf all about them. The people of the settlement came plunging down to meet them, to set their shoulders to the galley's light sides and man the rollers and run them far up the sloping beach out of reach of the tide, churning the pale sand and shingle as they had churned the bright water of the shallows.

And now, in a score, a hundred places at once, it seemed to Aquila, men were greeting their women-folk and bairns, these men whose name beyond the Great Water was written in terror and fire and sword, loudly kissing their yellow-haired women and tossing up squealing children and thumping younger brothers on the back. Under the watchful eye of Hunfirth the Chieftain where he stood in the bows of the *Storm-Wind* with the flame of the sunset all about him, the booty was being got out from below decks, tumbled overboard on to the shingle, and carried up past the boat-sheds. Aquila, standing beside the *Sea-Snake*, soaked to the waist like all the rest, and with the wet, grey shingle heaving under him with the long North Sea swell, watched the harvest of a whole summer's raiding tumbled in heaps along the tide-line: fine weapons and lengths of rich stuffs, bowls and cups of precious metals, the worked ivory cross from a church, lying among the brown and amber sea-wrack.

Thormod was whistling for him; Thormod, standing straddle-legged and proud from his first season's raiding. Aquila stiffened, making for the moment no move to obey the summons. But rebellion would be merely stupid; and his stomach revolted at the idea of big barbarian hands on him, of being dragged up the shingle and flung down like a shock of oats at the feet of this red-and-white-and-golden stripling to whom it seemed that he belonged as though he were a dog.

He shut his teeth and threw up his head, and walked forward, trying not to sway to the swaying of the shingle under him. Naked save for a twist of cloth about his loins, he was all disdainful Rome in the hands of the Barbarians, as he halted before Thormod.

At Thormod's side a very tall man stood leaning on a staff; an old bent giant with hair and beard as fiercely white as a swan's feathers, and eyes that were mere glints of blue ice almost hidden under the crumpled folds of his lids. 'See, here he is,' the boy said. 'I give him to you, Bruni my Grandfather. I brought him home for you because of the thing on his shoulder.'

'So—that is most curious.' The old man stretched out a huge, gaunt hand and ran a finger with obvious pleasure over the blue tattoo-marks as Aquila stood rigidly before him. 'Aye, I ever counted the dolphin a lucky beast.' The bright, hooded eyes studied Aquila from head to heel and back again. 'He has been wounded. Is that the mark of your saex, Grandson, there on his temple?'

Thormod flushed, as Aquila had seen him flush before.

'Na,' he said unwillingly. 'That was another man's work. I found him bound to a tree close by a house that was gutted by some that came before us. And I saw the sign on his shoulder, and it seemed to me that he had been set there that I might bring him to you.'

'So.' The old man nodded. 'It is good to have a dutiful grandson. Yet nevertheless, when *I* followed the seamew's road for the first time, we took our own captives and booty, and not that which was left by other men.'

'Can I help it if another was before me?' Young Thormod flung up his head in retort. 'If I had come upon him first, I would have taken him just the same. With my naked hands I would have taken him, if need be!'

Bruni looked from his angry grandson to the captive standing before him in the harsh, windy, sunset light, taking in the frowning gaze and the set of his mouth, as Aquila gave him back stare for stare; and for an instant there was a glint of harsh humour in his eyes under their many-folded lids. 'With your naked hands? I doubt it. Nevertheless, it is in my mind that you would have tried, young fool that you are . . . Sa, I thank you for the gift of the dolphin. He shall be thrall to me in place of Gunda, who was slain by the bear last winter.'

And so Aquila, who had been Decurion of a Roman Cavalry troop, became Dolphin, thrall to old Bruni, a thing of less account than a good hunting-dog. Nobody troubled to ask his own name, nor even to think that perhaps he had one, nor did he trouble to tell it. It belonged to another life, not to this life on the tide-swept, gale-torn shores of Western Juteland. Juteland; the land of the Jutes; for though, like the rest of his kind, he had thought of all the raiders from across the North Sea as Saxons, the men into whose hands he had fallen were Jutes.

The settlement of Ullasfjord clustered about the painted Hall of Hunfirth the Chieftain, whose antler-crested gables caught the first light that slid over the moors at the day's beginning, and the last sunlight up the firth from the open sea at the day's end; each farm-house in its own garth with its outbuildings and bee-skeps and few wind-torn apple trees. Beyond them was the cornland and the rough pasture, and beyond again was the wild. The farmstead of Bruni, like most of the rest, was a long, barn-like building, warm under deep turf thatch that was held down against the spring and autumn gales by ropes of twisted heather as thick as Aquila's wrist. From the door at one end an aisle led between stalls for the horses and oxen to the house-place at the far end, where the fire burned on a hearth of cobbles in samelled clay, and the family lived and ate and slept: old Bruni himself, and Aude, who was Thormod's mother, and Thorkel the younger boy, and sometimes Thormod, though for the most part he slept in the Chieftain's hall among the other young warriors. There were hay-lofts above the stalls, and there Aquila slept with the two farm-thralls, smelling their unwashed bodies and the warm breath of the kine, as the autumn darkened into the winter.

Among Thormod's share of the booty from the summer's raiding was a bronze box beautifully and curiously enriched with blue and green enamels. By and by it would be traded with one of the merchant kind who appeared from time to time, but for the present it was stowed in the great kist carved with writhing dragon-twists under the high window. Neither Thormod nor his kin had taken much interest in what was inside it, since it did not seem to be anything of value. But on an evening wild with an autumn gale and the firth roaring like an open sea, Aquila came into the house-place carrying driftwood for the fire, and found Bruni and his grandsons bending together over something that the old man held, the bronze box open beside the hearth, while Aude the mother tended the evening meal of oatmeal porridge, broiled cod and beans.

As Aquila checked an instant between the last of the stalls, Bruni was saying disgustedly, 'Nay, I can make neither stem nor stern of this thing. Maybe it is a magic, and I like it not.'

'Safer, then, to burn it,' suggested Thormod, and the old man nodded, as one giving a deeply considered judgement, and turned to throw the thing he held into the fire of spitting birch logs.

In that moment Aquila saw what it was, and flung down the load of salt-whitened driftwood and strode forward, 'No! Let you not do that! It is not magic—not dangerous.'

Bruni looked at him under the long wrinkles of his lids. 'You have seen this thing before, then?'

'I have seen many others of its kind,' Aquila said.

'So? And what thing is it?'

'It is a book. It is as though the words of a man were caught and set down on a long roll, in those small black marks, so that other men may take them up at another time and in another place—maybe long after the speaker is dead—and speak them again.'

'So it *is* magic,' Thorkel the younger boy said eagerly. 'Like our Runes.'

'You talk foolishness,' said his grandfather. 'The Runes are the Runes, and there is nothing else that is like them. They are the strongest of all magic, bought for men by the suffering of Odin, who hung for nine days on a tree to gain the secret of them.'

'None the less, it *is* magic of its kind,' Thormod said, and he looked up from the scroll in his grandfather's hands. 'But perhaps, after all, there is no harm in it. Can anyone read these dead man's words again?'

'Anyone who knows the signs,' Aquila said.

'Do you?'

'Yes.'

Old Bruni looked up from frowning at the magic marks, and frowned instead at Aquila, thrusting out the scroll. 'So. Then let you speak the words that are here, and maybe we will believe that what you say is true.'

Aquila hesitated for a moment of hot rebellion. Why should he lay the mind-riches of the civilized world before these barbarians who spat on their house-place floor and ate and slept like swine? Then he put out his hand and took the beautiful piece of scribe's work that the old man held out to him. The words looked up at him familiarly as he opened it. It was the Ninth book of *The Odyssey*—a Latin translation, fortunately, for despite Demetrius's patient tutoring he had never found it easy to read Greek. Now he translated again, haltingly, as he read, into the Saxon tongue.

' "My island stands deep in the sea, and nearer to the West than to its neighbours, which—which rather face the dawn and the sun. It is a harsh land, yet it breeds good men. But perhaps in every man's sight there is nothing better than his native land." '

The old man and the boys were leaning forward, their eyes moving from the scroll to his face and back again as though trying to catch the secret in flight.

'And who was it said that?' Bruni asked, when he reached the end of the passage.

'A man called Odysseus,' Aquila said, deciding to leave out the complication of Homer, who had put the words into Odysseus' mouth. 'A great seafarer, far from his own home.'

'So-o.' The fierce old warrior nodded. 'And hungry for his own landing-beach. Aye, aye, we have all known the homing hunger, just as we have known the other hunger that comes when the birch-buds thicken and the seaways call again.' He settled himself more comfortably, stretching his great splay feet to the fire. 'Speak me more words of this seafarer who felt even as I have felt when I was young and followed the whale's road.'

And so, squatting in the firelight that leapt and fluttered across the papyrus, Aquila read on. '"Indeed that time I nearly came safely to my native land, only for the swell and the sea currents and a north wind which united against me as I worked round Cape Maleia and drove me wide of Cythera . . ." '

Suddenly the familiar words were sounding in his ears in Demetrius's deep and beautiful voice; and the roar of the firth outside became the roar of the summer gale sweeping up through a great forest; and he was back in the atrium at home, back in those last, oddly shining moments before the dogs began barking and the end of the world had come. He saw his father's hand with the great signet ring catching and losing the firelight as he fondled Margarita's head against his knee; and Demetrius's grey, gentle face bent over the scroll, and Flavia in the glow of the firelight, combing her hair.

He stumbled over the translating of a word, and the present closed down on him like the clanging shut of a prison door. Still he read on. There was nothing else to do, though something very like despair rose in his throat, and for a moment he was reading from memory, for he could not see the words.

The Lotus Eaters were behind them, and Odysseus and his crew had just reached the island of the Cyclops when Aude turned from the fire, her face flushed. 'Enough of this story-telling. Let you eat before the good food spoils.'

The moment was past, and Aquila let the scroll fly up, and laid it back in its box with the rest of the set, while his masters turned to the smoking food.

'When I was young and a warrior, I had a sword whose lightning none might stand against,' said Bruni, holding out his hand for his horn spoon to dip in the common porridge-bowl. 'Now that I grow old and only the things of the mind are left me, I have a thrall who can speak the words of long-dead men, only by looking at some little black marks. Truly I am still great among my kind.' He took a gulp of smoking porridge, spluttered messily, and spat most of it into the fire, for it was too hot, and gave Aquila a long, hard stare. 'Yet if I could have the strength of my sword hand again, and the lifting deck of a longship beneath my feet, my thrall might lie beneath seven galleys' lengths of sea, for aught that I should care!'

Aquila, closing the lid of the box, looked up. The bitterness and the anger rose within him, and the pain of the few moments when it had seemed that he was back in his own world made him reckless. 'And let you be very sure of this, Old Bruni,' he said breathing quickly, 'that your thrall would be content to lie there, rather than be thrall of yours!'

For a long moment their eyes met, Aquila's dark and young and fierce, and the eyes of the old sea-rover that were mere glints of faded blue light under the wrinkled lids; while the two boys and the woman looked on as though they were watching a duel. Then Bruni nodded, with a fierce shadow of a smile on his bearded lips. It was almost the first time that Aquila had seen him smile. 'Sa, sa, sa, that was a fiery word, my thrall; but a flash of fire is not an ill thing in thrall or free,' and he ducked his head again to his porridge spoon.

From that time forward, few evenings went by that the old man, who seldom went up to the Hall now, did not call Aquila from among the farm-thralls to read to him of the journeyings of Odysseus. And so, evening by evening, crouching in the fireglow while the wind howled like wolves about the door, and the old man and his grandsons sat rehafting a spear or plaiting a bow-string as they listened, Aquila woke the magic of golden shores and distant seas as dark as grapes at vintage. He had never known those seas, any more than his listeners, but the magic was familiar to him, belonging to his own lost world.

On an evening on the edge of winter, Aquila squatted in his usual place, reading by the spluttering light of burning birch logs and the red glow of peat how Odysseus strung his great, back-bent bow, when the dogs sprang up quivering with pleased expectancy, and padded to the door.

'That must be Thormod,' young Thorkel said, for his elder brother was with the warriors in Hall that night. Two sets of footsteps crunched over the half-frozen first fall of snow. Someone was stamping in the fore-porch, the door opened letting in a blast of freezing air and crashed shut again; and Thormod appeared between the stalls, with someone else behind him.

He came into the firelight, shaking himself like a dog. 'See who is here! The *Sea-Witch* is back, and look now: I have brought Brand Erikson to set by our hearth a while.'

The man who had come in behind him looked to Aquila as though Odysseus himself had come among them, save that his crisp, curly hair was sandy-grey instead of black. A man brown as a withered oak leaf and lean as a wolf, with a wily, sideways, sly, and daring face. Clearly he was an old friend, one well used to sitting by this hearth, and the others greeted him with the quick and casual gladness of long familiarity. Aude laid aside her spinning and rose and brought him the Guest cup of beechwood enriched with silver, brimming with the carefully hoarded morat that was made of honey and mulberry juice, saying, 'Drink, and be most welcome.'

The newcomer took the cup and drank, with the customary 'Waes-hael!' and gave it back to her. He drew a stool to the fire and sat down, rubbing the crimson stain of the morat into his grey beard, then looked about him with a cocked and contented eye. 'It is good to sit beside the hearth again, my friends; it is good to be through with the sea-ways until spring.'

'You are late back from your trading,' old Bruni said, huddling closer to the fire, his wolfskin cloak about him. 'We had given you up for this year, thinking that Guthrum must have run the *Sea-Witch* up some other landing-beach for her winter's sleep.'

'Na, na; as to that, the ways of trade may be more uncertain than the ways of the war keels.' The newcomer loosened his hairy woollen cloak and stooped to fondle the head of a hound pup that had rolled against his feet. 'Guthrum was minded to make Hengest's port in the North-folk territory our last trading call of the season. But when we made that landfall, what should we find but that Hengest and the main part of his people were gone south to some new hunting-run that the Red Fox had given them, to the island that the Romans called Tanatus—almost down to the White Cliffs. And our trade gone with them.'

Aquila, who had drawn aside into the shadows and taken up a broken seal-spear to work on, glanced up quickly as the familiar names fell on his ear. The Red Fox: did the barbarians, too, call

Vortigern the Red Fox? And what could it mean, this sudden move of Hengest and his war bands? He was suddenly filled with an almost painful awareness of every word that was being spoken round the fire, as he bent again to his task.

'So south we went, coasting the shores of the Romans' Island—and none so easy at this time of year—until we too came to this Tanatus, and saw the great grey burg that the Romans built, across the Marshes. There we did good trading, and were welcome, so that when our trading was done, the season growing so late, it was in the minds of many of us to winter there at Hengest's camp. But the *Sea-Witch* was hungry for her home landing-beach; and so we set her head to the north-east; and truly a hard voyage we had of it, for half the time she ran before the gale until she leapt and twisted like an unbroken mare, and half the time we saw nothing beyond the oar-thresh but the freezing murk. Yet tonight Guthrum and the rest sit by the Chieftain's fire, and I before yours, before I go inland tomorrow to my own home; and it is good.'

'It is always good to sit by the hearth-fire when the voyaging is over,' Bruni said. 'But better to go down to the boat-sheds and hear again the dip of the oars when the spring comes back.' He looked up, his old face fiercely alert as a hawk's in the firelight. 'And what reason lies behind Fox Vortigern's gift of this new territory?'

But Aquila, his head bent low over the seal-spear, knew the answer to that a leaping instant before Brand Erikson gave it. 'A simple enough reason. The birds of the air brought him word of some plan that the followers of the old royal house had made, to rise up and call in the help of Rome and drive both him and our people into the sea. And Tanatus covers the way into the heart of the Romans' Island.'

'So. It seems that you know much concerning this thing.'

'It is a thing known to all the camp. Vortigern has taken an open enough revenge on any he could reach of those who were betrayed to him.'

The old man nodded. 'Aye, aye, it is a sad thing when there is one to betray his brothers—or was that, too, but the birds of the air?'

'Na, not the birds of the air.' The other cocked up his head with a dry crackle of laughter. 'Indeed, I did hear that it was a bird-*catcher* they had the word from—a little, peaceful bird-catcher with a lantern and a basket. Ah, but be that as it may; the Sea Wolves have been busy, and there's more than one dead man that was alive when that message went to Rome-burg, and more than one hearth was warm enough then, that's cold and blackened now.'

Aquila, sitting suddenly rigid in the shadows, drew a sharp breath; he found that his hands were clenched on the spear-shaft until the knuckles shone white as bare bone, and carefully unclenched them. But nobody noticed the thrall beyond the firelight.

'And since when have we been the Red Fox's hired butchers?' old Bruni asked in a deep rumble of disgust.

The newcomer looked at him sideways. 'Nay, the thing was not done altogether in Vortigern's service. Do *we* want the Roman kind strong again in their old province? It is a rich land, the Romans' Island, richer than these barren shores to which our people cling, and Hengest will be sending out the call for more of us—more from all the tribes of Juteland, and the Angles and the Saxons also, come the spring.'

There was a gleam in old Bruni's eyes under the many-folded lids. 'Hengest—by Vortigern's wish?'

'By Vortigern's wish, or by what he thinks is his wish. Hengest is become a great man with the Red Fox. Aiee, a great man. He sits in his Mead Hall in the misty marshes, while the gleemen sing his praises, and he wears the gold arm-ring of an earl.'

Bruni snorted. 'And he naught but the leader of a war band!'

'Yet others besides his own band will follow him, come the spring.'

Thormod, who had sat listening in eager silence until now, broke in suddenly, his eyes brightening with excitement: 'The Romans' Island is indeed rich! Have I not seen it this past summer? On the downs many sheep could graze to the yard-land, and the corn stands thick in the ear, and there is much timber for houses and for ship-building—'

And young Thorkel joined his own voice to his brother's. 'When Hengest's call comes, why should we not answer it? We shall see Hengest's great camp, and there will be much fighting—'

Bruni silenced them both with a gesture of one great hand, much as he would have silenced the baying of his dogs. 'I also have seen the richness of the Romans' Island, though it was not this summer nor for more than five summers past. But I say to you that it is good to raid where the raiding ground is rich; yet no light thing to forsake for ever the landing-beaches that knew our fathers' fathers' keels, and the old settlements, and the old ways.'

In a while, though the two boys grumbled together with hunched shoulders, Bruni and the newcomer fell to talking of other things, telling one against the other of past raids and past voyages in search of new markets, while Aude spun her saffron wool in the firelight.

Aquila no longer heard them. He sat with his head in his hands and stared at a dry sprig of last year's heather among the strewing fern at his feet, and did not see that either. Somehow it had never occurred to him that the Sea Wolves who had slain all that he loved and left his home a smoking ruin had been anything but a chance band of raiders. He knew better now. He knew that there had been no chance in the matter. His father and the rest had died for the cause of the old Royal House and the hope of Britain. Died because they had been betrayed; and he knew who had betrayed them. And the thing that he was seeing was the little brown, pointed face of the bird-catcher . . .

That night he dreamed the old hideous dream again and again, and woke each time shaking and sweating and gasping in the darkness under the turf roof, with Flavia's agonized shrieks still seeming to tear the night apart.

V
Wild Geese Flighting

WINTER passed, and one morning the wind blew from the south with a different smell in it: a smell that tore at Aquila's heart with the memory of green things growing along the woodshores of the Down Country. The days went by, and the stream that had run narrow and still under the ice broke silence and came brawling down, green with snow-water from the moors inland; and suddenly there were pipits among the still bare birches.

As the spring drew on, a restlessness woke in the men of Ullasfjord. Aquila felt it waking, like the call that wakes in the wild geese and draws them north in the spring and south again when the leaves are falling. They began to go down to the boat-sheds, and the talk round the fire at night was of seaways and raiding. Just before seed time, the call came from Hengest, as Brand Erikson had foretold, and from many of the Jutish settlements, from Hakisfjord and Gundasfjord bands of settlers went in answer. But Ullasfjord still held to the old ways; the raiding summer and the return home at summer's end.

Aquila did not see the *Storm-Wind* and the *Sea-Witch* sail. He found something to do at the inland end of the settlement, and tried, with a sickening intensity, not to think. But afterwards he found young Thorkel disconsolately leaning against the forepost of the lower boat-shed and staring away down the firth; behind him the brown, shadowed emptiness where the *Sea-Snake* had hung from the roof-beam, before him the churned tracks of the rollers in the sand. 'They wouldn't take me,' he said, scowling; 'not for another two years. Don't you wish you were sailing in the *Sea-Snake*?'

Aquila rounded on him with a flash of anger. 'Sailing down the Saxon wind against my own people?'

The boy stared at him a, moment, then shrugged. 'I suppose they may try the Romans' Island, though Brand says that most of the richest parts are held by Hengest now, and so the Frankish lands make better raiding. I had forgotten about them being your people.'

'It is easy to forget an ill when it isn't in one's own belly,' Aquila said. 'Your kind under the Red Fox burned my home and slew my father and carried off my sister. I do not forget.'

There was a moment's silence, and then Thorkel said, awkwardly, as though in some way it was an apology, 'I never had a sister.'

Aquila was staring out along the line of dunes with their crests of pale marram grass brushed sideways by the wind. 'I pray to my own God that she is dead,' he said.

If he could know that, there might be some sort of peace for him as well as for Flavia; yet he knew in his innermost heart that if it were so, he would have lost the only thing that he had to hold to; and all there would be left to hope for in this world was that one day he might meet the bird-catcher again.

Without any word, he walked on, leaving young Thorkel still leaning against the boat-house.

Harvest came, and summer's end brought the men back from their raiding, with their own harvest of booty, without which the sparse, salty fields and poor pastures of Ullasfjord could never have supported its people. Winter passed, and seed-time came, and again it was harvest: the second harvest of Aquila's thraldom. That year the raiding season had gone ill, the *Storm-Wind* had suffered much damage from a pounding sea, they had gained little booty and lost several men, and so the war-keels with their crews had returned to lick their wounds even before the late barley was fully ripe to the sickle.

The harvest of the west coast of Juteland was never rich, but this year the sea-winds that had so nearly wrecked the Chieftain's war-keel had burned and blackened the barley, and it stood thin and poor, and beaten down in the salt fields like the staring coat of a sick hound. But such as it was, it must be gathered, and men and women, thrall and free, turned out sickle in hand to the harvest-fields, Aquila among them.

There was no wind from the sea today, and the heat danced over the coast-wise marshes; the sweat trickled on Aquila's body, making the woollen kilt that was his only garment cling damply to his hips and belly. Thormod, working beside him, looked round with a face shining with sweat.

'Ho! Dolphin, it seems that the women have forgotten this corner of the field. Go you and bring me a horn of buttermilk.'

Aquila dropped his sickle and turned, frowning, and made for the corner of the long, three-yardland field where the jars of buttermilk and thin beer stood in the shade of a tump of wind-shaped hawthorn tree. There he found old Bruni, who had come out to watch the reapers, leaning on his staff in the strip of fallow where the ox teams turned at ploughing time. There was a shadow on his old hawk face as he looked away down the field, that was more than the shade of the salt-rusted hawthorn leaves.

'It is in my mind that there'll be tightened belts and hollow cheeks in Ullasfjord before we see the birch buds thicken again,' he said as Aquila came up. But his voice was so inward-turning that for a moment the young man was not sure whether the old man spoke to him or only to his own heart. Then Bruni looked full at him, and he asked, with a glance back over the field where he had been working, over the brown backs of the reapers, the women with the big gleaning baskets and the poor thin barley, 'Is it often like this?'

'I have seen many harvests reaped, since first I took sickle in hand,' Bruni said; 'but it is in my mind that I have seen but two—maybe three—as lean as this one. We are seldom more than one stride ahead of famine, here on the west coast, and this year I think by Thor's Hammer that it will be but a short stride, and we shall feel the Grey Hag snuffling between our shoulder-blades before the spring comes round again.' The faded blue eyes opened full on Aquila. 'That makes you glad, eh?' Aquila gave him back look for look. 'Why should I grieve that my foe goes hungry?'

'Only that you will go hungry with him,' Bruni growled, and there was a sudden twitch of laughter at the bearded corners of his mouth. 'Maybe that is why you work as hard as any man here, to get in what harvest there is.'

Aquila shrugged. 'That is as a man breathes. I have helped to get in many harvests, in my own land.'

'Your own land . . . Richer harvests than this, in the Romans' Island, eh?' the old man said broodingly, and then with a sudden impatience, as Aquila remained silent, 'Well, answer me; are you dumb?'

Aquila said levelly, 'If I say yes, it as though I cried to the Sea Wolves, "Come, and be welcome!" If I say no, you will know that I lie, remembering the thickness of the standing corn you burned to blackened stubble in your own raiding days. Therefore I am dumb.'

The old man looked at him a moment longer, under the grey shag of his brows. Then he nodded.

'Aye, I remember the thickness of the corn. Once we grew such corn, in kinder fields than these. Our women sing of them yet, and our men remember in their bones. But that was before the tribes of the Great Forests over towards the sunrise started the westward drift, driving all before them.' His gaze abandoned Aquila and went out over the marshes to the low dunes that shut out from here the green waters of the firth. 'All men—all peoples—rise in the east like the sun, and follow the sun westward. That is as sure as night follows day, and no more to be checked and turned again than the wild geese in their autumn flighting.'

It seemed to Aquila that a little cold wind blew up over the marshes, though nothing stirred save the shimmering of the heat.

He took up a horn lying beside one of the jars and filled it with cool, curdled buttermilk, and went back to Thormod. The boy swung round on him impatiently, dashing the sweat out of his eyes.

'You have been a long time!'

'Your grandfather was talking to me,' Aquila said.

'What about?'

'Only the harvest,' Aquila said, but he had an odd feeling that the thing they had really been talking about was the fate of Britain.

The harvest was gathered and threshed. They wove fresh ropes of heather to hold down the turf thatch in the autumn gales, and the gales came, and the wild geese came flighting south, and it was winter. A fitting winter to follow such a harvest. Snow drifted almost to the eaves of the settlement on the weather side, and lay there, growing only deeper as the weeks went by. Black frosts froze the very beasts in the byres; and for no reason that any man could give, the seals forsook the firth that winter, so that the seal-hunters returned empty-handed again and again. The deep snow made for bad hunting of any kind, and that meant not only less to eat now but fewer skins to trade with the merchants later.

There was always a lean time at winter's end, when the meal-arks were low and the fish grew scarce and the hunting bad; but in most years the first signs of spring were waking—a redness in the alders by the frozen stream, a lengthening of the icicles under the eaves—to raise the hearts of men and women for the last grim month before suddenly the promise was fulfilled. This year there was nothing save the lengthening of daylight to show how the year drew on. Indeed, as the days grew longer the cold increased. People's heads began to look too big for their gaunt shoulders, and even the children had hollow cheeks like old men. And still the ice clung grey and curdled along the shore, and under the frozen snow the ground was hard as iron. Ploughing would be a month late this year, and the seed, sown a month late, would not have time to ripen before the heat went from the short northern summer; and so the next harvest too was doomed.

Men began to look at each other, seeing each behind his neighbours' eyes the thought that had been growing in all of them ever since the harvest failed; the thought of their own barren, windswept fields, and the corn standing thick in some sheltered valley of the island over towards the sunset. Hengest still wanted settlers, not only for Tanatus, but for all the eastern and southern shores of the Romans' Island; still sent out the call each spring. Half of High Ness settlement had gone last year . . .

When Hunfirth the Chieftain summoned a council of all Ullasfjord to his great Mead Hall, the whole settlement knew what it was that would be talked of.

Old Bruni had been ailing for many days, but he was set like a rock on taking his place among his own kind at the Council. When the appointed night came, he turned a deaf ear to all Aude's protests, wrapped himself in his best cloak of black bearskin lined with saffron cloth, took his staff, and set out with Thormod over the beaten snow. Thorkel had wanted to go too, only to be told, 'When you are a man, then join with the men in Council. Now you are a bairn; bide therefore with the bairns and women.'

So he bided, scowling into the red heart of the fire, when his grandfather and his elder brother were gone. Aquila also crouched by the fire, rubbing down a new ox yoke against ploughing time—if ploughing time ever came again.

It seemed a long time since the last meal, but he did not feel as hungry now as he had done when the shortage started, which was as well, for he knew that there would be little enough to spare for the thralls, from the pot of thin oatmeal porridge which Aude was tending over the fire, against the men's return.

He worked on steadily rubbing and rubbing at the creamy alderwood, but without any idea of what his hand was doing; for all his thoughts were in the Chieftain's Mead Hall, all his awareness turned towards the thing that they would be discussing there; so that every rustle of falling peat ash on the hearth, every stirring of the beasts in the stalls, every beat of his own heart under his ribs seemed part of the fate of Britain. There was driftwood among the burning peat, white-bleached and salt-encrusted, burning blue and green with the shifting colours of distant seas. Driftwood was the right fire for these people, shifting, seaborn, rootless—for all their planted orchards and tilled fields—as the wild geese overhead.

Footsteps crunched and slithered over the frozen snow, and there was the usual stamping and beating in the fore-porch; the door-pin rattled as it was lifted, and the men of the steading were back, letting in a blast of bitter cold that seemed to make the very flames of the fire cower down, before the door crashed shut behind them. Old Bruni came up between the stalls, with his grandson at his shoulder, and looking at them, Aquila thought it would be hard to say whether the old man's eyes or the young one's were the brighter in their starved faces. Bruni stood looking down at them about the hearth.

'So, it is finished, and it is begun,' he said. 'When the spring comes, Ullasfjord also will answer the call.'

Aude looked up from the bubbling porridge-pot without surprise, for she had known like everyone else what Hunfirth's Council spoke of, and what would be the outcome. 'Who leads?' she asked.

'Young Edric. It is his right as Hunfirth's eldest son.'

'And who goes?'

'This year, the fighting men for the most part, and some of their women and bairns. Later, the rest of the settlement.' The old man glanced about him thoughtfully. 'From this steading, myself and Thormod—ah, and the Dolphin; I am old and need my body-thrall about me. And besides, I am a great man and it is not fitting that I should clean and tend my own war gear.'

It seemed to Aquila, looking up from the fire, with his hand clenched on the ox yoke, that for a long moment everything stopped, even his own heart. Back to Britain! Back to his own land . . .

Then Thorkel sprang up with a furious cry. 'I also! Why should I be left behind? Always—always you leave me behind!'

'Peace, puppy,' Bruni rumbled. 'There will come another year.'

'For those who live through this one,' Aude said into the porridge-pot, while the boy, completely quelled by his grandfather as always, subsided glowering. She looked up at him, kindly, but without understanding. 'Old foolish one, and do you think they will take *you*? They want the young ones, the warriors.'

Bruni stood rocking a little on his heels, and looking down at her; and there was a fire about him that Aquila had never seen before, though his face in the upward light of the flames was the face of a bearded skull. 'There are other things besides the strength of a man's sword arm; and even though that fail me—a little—I have my worth. I have more than seventy summers of garnered wisdom, of cunning in battle. I shall have my place when the long keels pull down the firth.'

'You spoke against the thing once, and now you would go yourself: I do not understand.'

'Did ever a woman yet understand ought beyond the baking of breads?' grumbled old Bruni. 'Whether I go this spring or not, the thing will go on. It is no more to be turned back than the flighting of the wild geese. In a few years this settlement will be dead—dead and hearth-cold; and over towards the sunset, in better farming country, a new settlement will rise.' He looked round on them, contemptuous of their little understanding; and towering there with the smoke fronding about his head and the salty green and blue of the burning driftwood at his feet, he seemed to Aquila taller than any mortal man had a right to be. 'Aye, and before that new settlement rises there will be the fighting. Hengest knows that—a cunning warrior and a leader of men, for all that he has no right to wear the arm-ring. And I—I would take my sword in my hand once more, and smell again the oar-thresh and the hot reek of blood: I who was born a warrior and have lived beyond my fighting days.'

'Well, let you sit down now, before the porridge spoils,' Aude said. 'There will be time enough to talk of swords later.'

He made a great, impatient gesture, his head among the smoky rafters. 'Na, I am for sleep. There are other things than the need for porridge in my belly this night,' and he turned, lurching a little as though suddenly it was hard to hold up his own great height, to the box bed beside the hearth. Aquila, torn by a sudden raw and unwilling pity, laid aside the ox yoke and rose to help him.

That was the last time, save once, that he ever saw Bruni stand upright on his own huge feet; for next morning, when the old man would have risen, his legs would not carry him.

Aude scolded. 'Did I not say so? Going out to the Council when he was fit for nothing but his own fireside. These men, they must be for ever breaking their own bodies and the hearts of the women that are fool enough to care if they live or die!' And she opened the little kist of black bog oak in which she kept her herbs and simples, and brewed a strong, heady-smelling draught that she said would maybe drive out the sickness.

Bruni drank the draught, and by and by the sickness, whatever it was, seemed to go away. But no strength came back to the old man. He lay in the deep box bed beside the hearth, while the last days of the winter dragged by and the icicles began to lengthen under the eaves. Thormod and Aquila tended him, without a kind word between them, for he had never been one to speak kind words nor yet to listen for them. He lay under the wolfskin rug that his gaunt frame scarcely lifted. He seemed to be only dried skin lying lightly over the huge old bones, and the veins at his temples and on the backs of his great hands were blue and knotted like the painted worm-twists on the prow of a longship; and his lips, too, were blue. He had his sword beside him on the bed, and would lie fondling it as a man fondles the ears of a favourite hound; and often he would call for Aquila to read to him of the wanderings of Odysseus, that by now he knew almost by heart.

'A sad thing it must have been for this Odysseus,' he said once, when Aquila had come yet again to the end of the last scroll. 'A sad thing to know that the adventuring was over, and nothing left but his own fireside.' And his great hand moved on the amber-studded hilt of the sword lying beside him. 'As for me, glad I am that there will be one more adventuring . . . When the spring comes, I shall grow strong again, despite these black draughts of Aude's.' And then, as though to himself, 'By Thor's Hammer, I *will* grow strong again!'

But after the first days he ceased to speak of the new settlement, of the fighting that must come before it as something that he would have any part in. He made no complaint, spoke no word against his fate; grim old warrior that he was, he would have held proudly silent if he were being roasted before a slow fire. Yet Aquila knew that in the old man there was a furious rebellion. He could feel it, a high wind of rebellion that seemed to fill the whole steading with a sense of storm, though Bruni himself lay as still under his wolfskin, with his great sword beside him, as the pale snow-light that crept through the high windows at noon; as still as the shortening nights outside, beyond the first drippings of the thaw from the eaves.

They all knew that he was dying.

'One of these nights, when the tide runs out, he will go too, the Old One,' Aude said, and the old man himself smiled harshly at the puzzled look on his thrall's face. 'Aye, your folk can die at one time as well as another; but you have naught to do with the sea. We of the coast and the sea-ways cannot die in our beds save at low tide,' and he raised his sword and shook it. 'But there was a time when I never thought I'd lie in the straw waiting for ebb tide!'

In the grey of the next dawn, a great wind rose, a wild storm wind with sleet on its wings that rattled against the stretched membrane of the window-holes; but there was the smell of the south in it, and the sleet was half rain. Bruni slept most of that day, but about dusk he woke, with a wild, imprisoned restlessness on him that was like fever. But it was not fever, for his eyes under their heavy, crumpled lids were clear, and full of impatient and contemptuous laughter at the sight of the anxious faces about him. The wind was dying down now, and the sleety rain had almost ceased to spatter at the window membrane; but as the night drew on, old Bruni's restlessness seemed to rise like another storm, and blow down the whole length of the steading, making the very cattle stamp and fidget in their stalls.

When the other thralls had crawled away into their own places in the hay-loft, Aquila remained crouching by the bed, held there by some feeling for the old dying warrior that he neither understood nor questioned. Aude was at her loom; he watched her shadow leaping all up the gable wall, the shadow of the shuttle as she tossed it to and fro; but the place was full of leaping shadows from the fire, for there was no seal oil to spare for the lamps. Thormod sat by the fire, his hands round his knees, his face strained and white under the tousled brightness of his hair; and Thorkel slept with his head on a hound's flank.

The fire had begun to sink, and the cold was creeping in. Aquila leaned forward to cast on another peat, and as he did so, and the sparks flew upward, a sudden movement from the box bed made him look round quickly.

Bruni had dragged aside the wolfskin covering and struggled into a sitting position, his tangled mane of hair shining round his head and shoulders, and his eyes full of cold blue light under the many-folded lids, and his great shadow bursting like a giant's all up the wall behind him.

'It is near to low tide,' he said. 'Bring me my shield and helm and my bearskin cloak.'

Aude let the weaving shuttle fall with a clatter, and came running to the bed. 'Let you lie down again and save your strength.'

The old man thrust her aside with a gaunt arm. Indeed there was strength in him again, an extraordinary flare of strength, like the last burst of smoky flame from a torch before it goes out. 'Save my strength? To what end shall I save my strength? I tell you I'll die on my feet. Not a straw death! Not a straw death for Bruni the Wave-Rider!'

She made some other protest, but nobody heard her, for the old man cried out in a great gasping voice, turning from his thrall to his grandson and back again: 'Thormod, Dolphin! My war gear!'

For a moment the eyes of the two young men met, blue gaze and dark gaze; and for the first and only time in their lives there was no feeling of any gulf between them. Then, while Thormod sprang for the black-and-gold buckler with its strange winged beast that hung from the house-beam, Aquila turned to the kist under the window and dragged out the bearskin cloak with its saffron lining and the helmet of bull's horn bonded above the brows with grey iron. The great sword with the amber studs there was no need to bring him, for it was already in his hands.

'Out of the way, my mother,' Thormod said; and while she stood against the wall with her hand on the shoulder of young Thorkel, who had woken at the sudden turmoil, the two of them armed old Bruni as though for his last battle, and supported him as he struggled, swaying, to his feet.

'Out!' Bruni said. 'I must have the wind on my face!'

And somehow, Aquila supporting him under one shoulder and Thormod under the other, they got him to the door and out through the fore-porch into the darkness and the failing storm beyond the firelit threshold.

The grey sky was hurrying overhead and the high-riding moon showed as a greasy blur of brightness, rimmed with smoky colours behind the drifting flocks of cloud. The tide was full out, and the brightness fell in bars of tarnished silver on the wet sandbanks beyond the dunes and the cornland, and the oily tumble of the water beyond again. The wind swung blistering in from the south-west and the sea, with the smell of salt in it and that other smell so long delayed, that was the promise of spring; and the whole night was alive with the trickle of melting snow.

Old Bruni drew in a gasping breath. 'Sa! That is better than the hearth reek and the musty straw!' He shook off their hands and actually took one step forward alone, and stood unsupported, his head up into the wind, as though he waited. Aquila saw the proud old giant outlined against the grey, hurrying light, upheld by that sudden flare of strength, by his own terrible will to die on his feet as a warrior should, instead of woman-wise in the straw.

And suddenly, as he stood there, as though it were the thing that he waited for, they heard the wild geese coming—faint at first, far off in the hurrying heights of the sky, but sweeping nearer, nearer—the wild geese giving tongue like a pack of hounds in full cry down the storm wind.

Old Bruni looked up, raising his sword as though in salute to his kin. 'We also!' he cried. 'We also, in the spring, my brothers.'

The yapping of the geese was fading into the distance, and as it died, so it seemed that the last flare of the old warrior's strength was done. The iron-rimmed buckler crashed to the ground; but he was still holding his beloved sword as he fell back into the arms of the two young men behind him.

VI
The Saxon Wind

WITH Bruni, it seemed that Aquila's brief hope of getting back to his own land died too, and must be laid in the old man's grave, with his sword and buckler. He did not ask Thormod to take him for his shield-thrall in his grandfather's stead. That was partly pride, little as he could afford pride: a hot inability to bow his neck to ask anything of the blue-eyed barbarian kind; partly another thing that he would have found it hard to give a name to: an odd sense of fate. If Flavia was alive, she might be in Britain, but just as likely she might be in Juteland, or any other of the Saxon coastwise lands. No action that he could take, no plan that he could make, would help him find her. If he was to find her at all, his only chance was to bide still, waiting for the wind—a little wind of God to rise and show him the right way.

So he waited, with something of the belief in fate, though he did not realize it, that he had caught from those very barbarians. And as it happened, he had not very long to wait; no longer than the day of the Arvale for old Bruni—the gathering that was at once funeral feast for the dead master of the house and heir feast for the man who came after him. There was little to spare for the feasting, but they spread the trestle tables before the house-place door with food that could be ill spared from the store kists, and brought out the heather beer and the dark, heady morat. And Thormod drank the Heir Cup, standing before all the hollow-cheeked gathering, and swore the great deeds he would do in his grandfather's place, according to the custom.

Later, when all the folk had gone home, he stood beside the cobbled hearth, and looked about him in the firelit quiet that was broken only by the stirring of a beast in its stall and the snoring of young Thorkel who slept already, in his favourite position with his head on a hound's flank, and more heather beer inside him than he had ever had at one time before.

'All this is mine!' Thormod said crowingly. 'The steading and the kine and the apple garth; the cloth in the kist and the honey in the crocks—what there is of it—and the thralls in the hay loft.' He laughed, his eyes very bright. 'And I'm going to kick it behind me, and not come back! . . . No, not all, though . . .' He began to cast up on his fingers, and Aquila, who had checked for an instant by the loft ladder, thought that he was a little drunk, but not as Thorkel was, with heather beer alone. 'I shall take my grandfather's good bearskin cloak, and his amber brooch, and the little kist with the carved worm-knots, and the red heifer to add to the breeding herd. Oh, and I shall take the Dolphin.'

Aquila, who had already turned again to the loft ladder, checked once more, and stood very still. Aude, beside the fire, braiding her hair for the night, looked up. 'Why the Dolphin?'

'For the same reason as my grandfather would have taken him. For my body-thrall, to carry my shield behind me.'

She laughed softly, scornfully. 'Large ideas for yourself, you have. Only the greatest warriors have their shield-thralls behind them.'

The young man laughed too, though his colour rose as always. 'And shall I not be a very great warrior? I am Thormod Thrandson, and my grandfather was Bruni the Wave-Rider, and my mother is sister to Hunfirth the Chieftain. It is fitting that I should have my shield-thrall behind me. And besides, not Hunfirth himself has a shield-bearer that can read the magic marks! Therefore, with the Dolphin behind me, I shall be the greater in the eyes of other men, because I have what they have not!'

Aude looked at Aquila by the loft ladder, seeing more deeply than her menfolk had done. 'And do you think that once landed on his own shore, he will not seek at all costs to escape?'

Thormod shrugged, breathing on his new dagger that had been his grandfather's, and rubbing it up his sleeve. 'It is none so easy to escape from the midst of the Jutish camp. Many of our folk in the Romans' Island have their Roman thralls. But to make yet more sure we will collar and chain him like a hound. I do not know why my grandfather did not put a thrall-ring on him years ago.'

The eyes of the two young men met and held, the moment when they had forgotten the gulf between them for old Bruni's sake now in its turn quite forgotten. Then Aquila turned again to the loft ladder and climbed up to his own place under the eaves. It was a long while before he slept, and when he did, he dreamed the old hideous dream again.

* * *

Spring came, full spring, with misty blue and green weather, and the pipits fluttered among the birches and their alder thickets where the buds were thickening. The bustle of preparation swelled louder and more urgent as the days went by. Every year that thrum of preparation broke out as the time for launching the war-keels again drew near. But this year it was all different, more far reaching, far this year Ullasfjord was making ready not for a summer's raiding, but for a setting out from which there would be no return, and besides the men and their weapons, there were the women going, and the bairns, and a dog here and there, and the kine for breeding the new herds. There were extra stores and fodder to be loaded; the best of the seed-corn in baskets, even little fir trees with their roots done up in skins or rough cloth; and farm tools and household treasures—a fine deerskin rug, an especially cherished cooking-pot, a child's wooden doll . . .

On the last night before the setting out there was a gathering of all the men who were going from Ullasfjord in the Gods' House close by the Long Howe where the tribe laid its dead. And there in the torchlit dark a boar was slain and his blood sprinkled on the assembled warriors and smeared on the altar of blackened fir-trunks; and they swore faith to Edric the Chief's son who was to lead them, on the great golden ring—Thor's ring—that lay there; and swore the brotherhood in battle on ship's bulwark and shield's rim, horse's shoulder and sword's edge.

Aquila, being only a thrall, had no part in the gathering, but he crouched with the other thralls around the open door of the Gods' House, looking in. He was very conscious of the pressure on his skin of the heavy iron ring that a few hours earlier had been hammered on to his neck at Thormod's command. Old Bruni, he thought, would at least have made sure that it did not chafe; but Bruni had been more careful than his grandson would ever be to see that the yoke did not gall the neck of his plough-oxen, nor the collar rub the hair from the throat of his hunting dog. Yet in an odd way the chafe of the neck ring felt good to him. It was a promise, a constant reminder that where he was going it might be possible to escape. The little wind—God's wind—that he had been waiting for was blowing now. Suddenly he was sure of it.

With a confused idea that where other people had worshipped, though their gods were not his, must be a good place to pray, Aquila prayed now, silently and with a burning intensity, crouching heedless of the other thralls, with his hands clenched at his sides and his forehead against the bloodstained, serpent-carved door post of the Gods' House. 'Christus, listen to me—you must listen—Let me find my sister if she yet lives, and let me be able to help her, or die with her if—there isn't any other way for her.'

The next morning the wind blew thin and cold from the east, and the waters of the firth were grey as a sword-blade; but the men laughed as they ran the long keels down over their rollers into the shallows.

'The Saxon wind blows strong; surely it is a good omen,' a young warrior cried, holding up a wetted finger. Aquila laughed too, a little, bitter laughter that strangled in his throat. He had thrown aside his honour, deserted all that he had been taught to serve, so that he might stand by Britain. And all he had done was to fall into the hands of the barbarians himself. He had served more than two years' thraldom on a Jutish farm, and now—he was to take an oar in this barbarian longship, his share in bringing her down the Saxon wind against his own land. The laughter in his throat knotted itself into a sob, and he bent his head between his shoulders and splashed down into the surf with the rest, feeling the galley grow light and buoyant as a sea bird as the water took her.

The cattle had already been loaded into the hold of the *Sea-Witch*, and at last it was over, the remaining stores loaded, the last farewells said; those who were to be left behind stood dry-eyed, for they were a people not used to weeping, on the landing-beach. Aquila was in his place at the oar. After more than two years among these people, he was no longer strange in the ways of boats as he had been the first time he felt the oar-loom under his hands. Wulfnoth the Captain stood at the steer-oar; and behind him, behind the high, painted stern of the *Sea-Snake*, the settlement with its dwindling figures on the landing-beach, and the dark line of the moors beyond, all grew fainter—fainter. Something that was over and done with, sinking away into the distance.

Presently, when they were clear of the shoal-water, Wulfnoth ordered, 'In oars. Up sail,' and the *Storm-Wind* and the *Sea-Snake* slipped down the firth before the light north-east wind, the Saxon wind.

They lost the wind after two days, and had to take to the oars again, rowing almost blind in a grey murk mingling with the oar-thresh, in which they all but lost the rest of the squadron. Some of the young warriors grew anxious, though they made a jest of it, saying, 'Ran the Mother of Storms is brewing, and how may one find the way with so much steam rising from her vats?' But old Haki, the Chieftain's uncle, who was as wise as a grey seal in the ways of the sea, sniffed the mist with his wide, hairy nostrils and said, 'By the smell, children.'

Sure enough, when at last the mist gave them up, and at noon they were able to check their position by the dimly seen sun, with a spar set up on the half deck, they were not much off their course. There were other troubles on the voyage: many of the women were sick; a child was lost overboard; one night there was a sudden panic among the cattle that all but capsized the *Sea-Witch*, and in the morning two of the best heifers were dead and one of the men in charge of them had a badly gored shoulder. But on the seventh day the gulls met them; and suddenly, towards sunset, there was a long, dark line that might have been a cloud-bank on the western rim of the sea, and a distant shout came back to them, thin as the cry of a sea bird, from the look-out clinging to the rigging of the *Storm-Wind*'s mast head.

'Land ho!'

Aquila, craning round to gaze over his shoulder as the galley lifted to the crest of the next sea, was suddenly blind with more than the salt hair whipping across his eyes.

For three days they ran down the coast, drawing in slowly, until, long after noon on the third day, they were nosing in towards the low, marshy shores of Tanatus. The wind had fallen light and they had had to take to the oars again to aid the scarcely swelling sails. They had hung the shields, black and crimson, blue and buff and gold, along the bulwarks just clear of the oar-ports, and shipped at their prows the snarling figureheads that had lain until now under the half-decks, safe from the pounding of the seas. And so, proud and deadly, the little wild-goose skein of barbarian keels swept down on Britain, and their appointed landing-beaches.

Aquila rowed with his chin on his shoulder, his gaze rating the tawny shore-line as it crept by, drawing always nearer, until, afar off, he caught the familiar whale-backed hump with its grey crown of ramparts, and knew as Wulfnoth put over the steer-oar that they were heading in straight for Rutupiae.

Wulfhoth's eyes were narrowed in concentration as he brought the

Sea-Snake round in the wake of the *Storm-Wind*, into the mouth of the winding waterway that cut Tanatus from the mainland. And now the smell of the marshes came to Aquila as he swung to and fro at his oar: the sourness of marsh water, the sweetness of marsh grass—a smell subtly different from the smell of the Juteland marshes, that tore at something in his breast. The sail came rattling down, and was gathered into a bundle like a great, striped lily bud; and Wulfnoth's voice came to them at the oars; 'Lift her! Lift her!' as the tawny levels slipped by on either side. They ran the keels ashore at last on the white landing-beach just across the channel from Rutupiae and sprang overboard and dragged them far up the slope of fine shells, out of reach of the tide.

Aquila knew that beach; he and Felix had used to bring their birding-bows out here after wild-fowl. He knew the wriggling trail of sea-wrack on the tide-line, the dunes of drifted shell-sand where the yellow vetch and the tiny striped convolvulus sprawled. Standing with panting breast beside the *Sea-Snake* as she came to rest, he had the feeling that he had only to look down to see the track of his own feet and Felix's in the slipping white sand. He caught a glance over his shoulder, and saw the tower of Rutupiae light rising against the sunset. There was a great burst of flame above its crest, but it was only a cloud catching fire from the setting sun.

They had lifted the children out over the bulwarks. They were helping the women ashore now, and the man with the gored shoulder. Some of the men had turned already to the bellowing cattle in the hold of the *Sea-Witch*, anchored just off shore.

'Sa, we come to the landing-beach! We are here, my brothers in this land that we take for our own!' Edric the leader said. And he scooped up a double handful of the silver sand, and raising his arms, let it trickle through his fingers in a gesture of triumph.

The stern of a big galley jutted sickle-shaped beyond the dunes round the next loop of the channel, and the gable end of a boat-shed reared stag's antlers against the sky; and there was a faint waft of wood-smoke in the air telling of human life that had not been there when Aquila and Felix shot mallard over Tanatus marshes. It seemed that scarcely were the *Storm-Wind* and the *Sea-Snake* lying above the tide-line with their crews swarming about them, before an enquiring shout sounded from the edge of the dunes inland, and a man came crunching down over the shingle towards them:

a big man with a broad, ruddy face under a thatch of barley-pale hair.

'Who comes?'

'Jutes from Ullasfjord, north of Sunfirth,' Edric said. 'I am Edric, son of the Chieftain.'

'Welcome, Edric, Son of the Chieftain of Ullasfjord.' The man cast an eye over the women and children. 'Come to settle, seemingly?'

'Aye, to settle. The times are hard in Ullasfjord. A bad harvest, a hard winter, and the sons said to find another land to farm. Always it is so. And the word blew to us on the wind that Hengest had room for good men at his back.'

'Umph.' The man made a sound at the back of his throat that was half grunt, half laugh. 'As to room—it is in my mind that if we pack much closer into this island of Tanatus we'll be ploughing the salt sea-shores and sowing our corn below the tide-line.'

'Maybe when we have spoken with Hengest we shall up-sail for some other part of the coast. But in any case'—Edric grinned, and jerked his chin towards the winding waterway—'are the Sea Wolves to lair for ever, this side of Tanatus channel?'

'That you must ask of Hengest when you speak with him.' The man flung up his head with a gruff bark of laughter; and the laughter spread, one man catching it from another. More men had appeared behind the first, and now two young women came running down the shingle, followed by a boy with a dog. Tanatus seemed very full of people, where the solitude of three years ago had been. And new-comers and old-comers together, they set about unloading certain of the stores, and getting the cattle ashore and penned, and rigging the ships' awnings; for it was settled that most of the Ullasfjord men should sleep on board with their gear tonight, while the women and bairns and the man with the gored shoulder were taken up to the settlement.

Later, when the full dark had come, and the men had eaten the evening food that the women had brought down to them, and drunk deep of buttermilk and raw imported wine, and lain down to sleep beneath the awnings, Aquila, lying with the other thralls beneath the stern of the longships, raised himself to look out across the water again towards the Rutupiae Light. The long chain by which he was secured for the night like a hound to a ring in the bulwarks rattled as he moved, and someone cursed him sleepily; but he scarcely heard them, any more than he heard the flapping of the awning in the little wind. Everything in him was straining out towards Rutupiae across the marshes and the waterways and the almost three years between; remembering that last night of all, when he had kindled the beacon for a farewell and a defiance; the night that the last Roman troops sailed from Britain. There was no beacon-light now in the windy spring darkness; even the huddle of the native town below the ramparts was dark. It had come into being to serve the fortress, in the ways that such places always sprang up under the wings of the Eagles; and with the Eagles flown, the little town would have ceased to be.

To Aquila, torn by a sudden piercing desolation, it seemed that he was further from his old happy world even than he had been in Juteland, because there the actual distance of sea between had hidden a little the greater gulf—the gulf that there was no crossing. He felt like a man who had been caught away into another world, and coming back to his own world at last, had found it dead and cold, and himself alone in it.

VII
The Woman in the Doorway

SMALL settlements and single farms still raw with newness were scattered over the low, green land of Tanatus, mingling with the few native fisher villages. The core of this barbarian gathering was the great burg of Hengest, half a day's march northward of the place where the Ullasfjord band had made their landing: a vast camp within its bank and ditch and stockade; a vast huddle of reed-thatched steadings, wattle-and-daub huts, and even ship's awning tents that looked like crouching animals rather than living-places, all gathered about the great painted timber Mead Hall which, with its byres and barns, made up the home steading of Hengest himself. Here and there a line of bee-skeps against a house-place wall, here and there a plot of kale or a clump of ricks, their tops roped down against the wind; fair-haired women coming and going to tend the animals, carrying pails up from the milking, grinding corn in stone hand-querns in the doorways; children and dogs playing in the sunshine; men with their weapons; tethered cocks scratching on dunghills with their hens around them; half-wild spitfire cats in warm corners; cattle lowing, men shouting, the ring of hammer on anvil, the bright notes of a struck harp, the smell of roasting meat, and seaweed, and dung; and over all, the smoke of a hundred cooking fires. This was the great burg of Hengest.

Aquila, on his way to the swordsmith's bothy with Thormod's dagger, which had sprung a rivet, looked about him with a feeling of being a ghost in this huge, thrumming, rootless burg that had grown up in three years; and stepped aside yet again, this time for a cart loaded with grain-sacks coming up from the shore gate of the stockade. It was obvious that Tanatus could never yield the grain for all this horde; it must be tribute from the mainland—tribute paid by Fox Vortigern to the wolf within his gates. Aquila wondered whether the tribute-carts might perhaps be his means of escape when the time came. They came in full; did they carry anything on the return journey? If so, might it be something under which a man could hide?

At first, when they had run the keels ashore three days ago, he had been set on making a dash for freedom at the first chance, but Edric, leaving the women and bairns for the present, had swept his warriors straight up here to Hengest's burg, and there had been no chance to break away. That had given Aquila time to think. Now he understood that it would be foolish to try to escape before he had made sure that there were no tidings to be had of Flavia here in the great camp. So he laid plans for getting away when the time came, but in the meanwhile watched and listened and looked about him with an aching intensity.

He was not quite sure where he was in the vast camp, and checking a moment to look round him and make sure of his direction, he saw a woman sitting in the doorway of a wattle cabin close by: a dark woman in a kirtle of bright blue wool, her head-rail laid aside, her head bent low as she braided her hair, and at her feet a man child of about a year old, playing happily between the paws of a patient, grey-muzzled hound. She had begun to hum softly, to herself or to the child, he was not sure which, a thin, sweet, dark humming without words, at sound of which his breath caught in his throat. He couldn't see her face in the shadow of her hair—hair dark and fiercely alive as a black stallion's mane; the kind of hair that might give out sparks if she combed it in the dark. There was a queer, sick stillness in him; and yet he could not believe, he *would* not believe—until, as she flung out her hair, turning and parting it with her fingers, he caught the green flash of a flawed emerald in the windy sunlight, and knew his father's ring that he had last seen on the hand of Wiermund of the White Horse. And the unbelief that he had been desperately clinging to was torn from him.

He didn't think he made any sound, but she looked up quickly, as though startled; and he saw how all the blood drained out of her face, so that her eyes looked like black holes in the whiteness of it. She got to her feet and stood looking at him. The child pressed back against her legs, staring at him also with round, dark eyes; the old hound raised his head and whined softly in his throat; and it seemed as though all the sounds of the camp died away as the wind dies into a trough of quiet.

For a long moment it was clear that she did not quite believe, either. The time since they were last together had turned Aquila from little more than a boy into a thick-set, brown-skinned man, with dark hair and beard bleached sandy silver at the ends by the sun and the salt winds of Juteland; a man with a frown-line bitten deep between his brows, and a white scar running out of his hair to pucker the wind-burnt skin of his temple, and the heavy iron collar of a thrall about his neck. He saw the uncertainty in her eyes, and had the sudden aching thought that he should pull up the sleeve of his tunic and show her the dolphin . . . ('If I were away from home for a long time, and when I came back nobody knew me again, like Odysseus, I could take you aside and say, "Look, I've a dolphin on my shoulder. I'm your long-lost brother".' And she had laughed and said, 'I'd be more likely to know you by looking at your nose, however long it had been away.') Well, he knew the change that there must be in him, seeing the change that there was in her. She was grown up now, with so much in her face that had not been there in the old days, so much of the laughter gone from it, and she wore a Saxon kirtle of fine blue wool with bands of green and crimson needlework at throat and sleeve; the sort of kirtle that would not be given to a slave. His gaze took in all of that, without seeming for an instant to leave her face, and took in also the small man child clinging to her skirt.

Then, her lips scarcely moving, she said, 'Aquila.'

The blood was beating in Aquila's head, pounding in the old scar. 'Aye,' he said.

'They told me you were dead.'

'It is no fault of *theirs* that I am not,' Aquila said heavily. 'You remember how the wolves were howling that night—too close—too close for summer time. They left me tied to a tree on the wood-shore. The wolves did not come, but instead another band of raiders happened by. I have served nearly three years thraldom on a Jutish farm . . . And you, Flavia?'

She made a small convulsive gesture towards the child, as though that answered the whole question.

The silence hung between them. Then Aquila said, 'Does he—belong to the yellow-headed giant who carried you off across his shoulder that night?'

She nodded. 'You saw that, then?'

'Yes, I saw that. I heard you crying to me for help, and—I struggled to come to you. I've dreamed of that ever since.' He put up his hands, in one of which he still held Thormod's dagger, and pressed them to his face. And his words came muffled. 'I've been haunted all this while by the thought of you in Saxon hands; I've prayed harder than I thought a man *could* pray, for I was never much of a one for prayers, that if you yet lived I might find you again . . .' He lowered his hands and looked at her once more. 'But, dear God! I never thought how it would be!'

'Isn't it always so?' Flavia said. 'The men fight, and after the fighting, the women fall to the conquerors.'

'Some women,' Aquila said bitterly. And then, seeing her flinch as though he had struck her, 'No, I—Flavia, I didn't say that—I scarce know *what* I am saying—'

'If I had known that you were alive, I think that I should have had the strength to kill myself,' Flavia said after a long, dragging pause. 'I thought there was no one left, and I was alone, you see.'

'Yes, I see, I—do see, Flavia.'

She remained a moment longer looking into his face, then, with one of her swift, flashing movements, turned half-away, and sitting down again on the stool, began to braid her hair. 'We must not seem to be talking so earnestly together; even now we may have been noticed . . . Aquila, you must escape!'

'Strangely enough, that idea has been in my mind also,' Aquila said.

'Ah, I know, I know; but don't you see, the thing is more urgent now? Wiermund of the White Horse is dead, but his sons are here, and they saw you slay his brother, and may know you again. If that happens, they will call for the full vengeance for the death of a kinsman.'

Aquila did not care. He felt that he would not care much about anything, ever again. But he tried to force his mind in the direction she wanted it to go. 'Escape is a thing more easily said than done. Thormod, my—my lord, calls for me often through the day, and each night to tend his harness before he sleeps; and I must sleep at his feet just like a hound, with—my thrall-ring chained to the tent-pole.' He spoke the last words through shut teeth.

Flavia was silent a little, braiding the dark masses of her hair. Then she said, 'Listen. Two nights from now there will be a great feast in Hengest's Mead Hall; Vortigern himself is coming to it, and there will be much eating and drinking—mostly at his expense—and by midnight everyone will be too drunk to know whether their thralls are there or not, when they reel to bed—even if they get so far, and do not merely sleep among the rushes. That will be your chance.'

'And the guards on the gate?' Aquila said. He was fumbling blindly with his belt, with some confused and helpless idea of looking as though he were doing something to it.

Flavia tied the end of her hair with a thong and flung the heavy braid back over her shoulder before she answered, 'I will take care of the guards on the shore-gate. Also I will bring you a file to rid yourself of that ring about your neck. Come to the back of the woodwright's shop down yonder; you can't miss it, there's a carved figurehead for a galley just outside, and a thorn tree beside the door. Come when the merry-making is at its height, and if I am not there, wait for me. If I should be the first, I will wait for you.'

He did not answer at once, and she looked up quickly. 'You will come—you will come, Aquila?'

'I will come,' said Aquila.

She caught up the child clinging to her skirt, 'Come, baba, it is time for food,' and rose and would have turned back through the house-place doorway, but Aquila stopped her, asking a thing that he felt was stupid and unimportant, and yet had to be asked. 'Flavia, how did you come by Father's ring?'

She checked, holding the solemn baby high on her arm, her head tipped far back to avoid the small, brown, starfish hand that patted her face. 'I told you Wiermund was dead. The ring came to his eldest son, and from his eldest son I had it for my bride gift.'

Then she was gone. The old hound lay still, head raised and watchful amber eyes on the face of the young man who stood there as though he had struck root. Then he got up and padded into the doorway, and lay down again across the threshold.

Aquila also turned away. He felt completely stunned, like a man so badly hurt that for the moment he feels only a numbness where presently there will be unbearable pain. Confusedly he remembered that he had been taking Thormod's dagger to have a sprung rivet seen to; and he went on his way in search of the swordsmith's bothy, because there was nothing else to do—nothing that would be any good.

Two nights later, Aquila sat on the beggers' bench before the door of Hengest's great timber Hall, with the hood of his rough cloak drawn forward to hide his face and the thrall-ring about his neck, and watched the scene before him. It would have been more sensible to have lain up in some quiet corner until the time came to go down to the woodwright's shop, he knew, but invisible strings had drawn him to the feasting in Hengest's Hall, whether he would or no, and all evening he had been looking for Flavia, with a sick dread of finding her there among the other women. But now the eating was over—odd to see so much food again—and the trestle tables had been taken down and stacked against the gable wall; and he knew that she was not here. At least she was not here, pouring mead for these golden hogs and for the Red Fox.

All evening, too, he had been looking for a man he had seen only once before, the man who had given Flavia their father's ring for a bride gift. But he remembered him as something horrible, something not properly human; maybe, after all, he only looked like a big, blond man—and there were so many big, blond men in Hengest's Mead Hall, he could not be sure.

He still felt numb, and the numbness left him free to look about him, and watch with a kind of remote, hill-top clearness the scene before him: the long hall swimming in heat and smoky torchlight, the women moving to and fro with the great mead jars, the hounds among the rushes, the harper by the fire, the warriors sprawling on the benches with their drink-horns slopping. He saw Hengest's hearth companions, and the darker, slighter, redder men who were of Vortigern's company; Saxon and Briton mingling on the same bench, leaning on each other's shoulders, drinking from the same horn; a joyful scene that sickened him. He knew who most of the great ones were. That big, broad-faced, broad-bellied warrior was Horsa, Hengest's brother. That other with a white, proud face, carrying even in Hengest's Mead Hall a hooded falcon on his wrist, was Vortimer, the King's eldest son. But close behind him lounged a man in a tunic of chequered silk, who caught at Aquila's interest, and to whom he could give no name. He muttered to the little, wizened thrall beside him, 'Who is the man behind Vortimer—the man with a face like a dark dagger-thrust?' And the thrall said, 'A kinsman of the Red Fox, Guitolinus I think they call him. If you want no more of that beer, give it to me.'

Aquila passed the horn pot that he had been holding unconsciously on his knee, and his gaze went on from Guitolinus, whose name meant nothing to him now, though he would know it well enough one day, and returned, as it had done again and again that evening, to the two men sitting side by side in the carved High Seat, midway up the hall.

Hengest was a huge man, huge in more than body, so that to Aquila, remembering the scene afterwards, it seemed that his head was upreared almost to touch the firelit under-belly of the house-beam way up where the firelight ended and the smoky darkness began. A greying-golden giant, whose eyes, turned just now on the harper beside the fire, were the shifting grey-green of a wintry sea. He leaned forward, wide kneed, one hand curved about his drink-horn, while with the other he played with the string of raw yellow amber about his neck—an oddly womanish trick that somehow made him seem yet more terrible than he would otherwise have done.

Beside him, and dwarfed by him in every way, sat Vortigern the Red Fox, King of Britain; a long, lean, red-haired man with a thin beard, with rings on every finger of his narrow hands, rings set with jewels as brilliant as the dark eyes that flickered about the hall unceasingly as he talked with the giant beside him, never resting more than a few moments in one place or on one person. Aquila looked at him with that coldly detached interest that had no feeling in it; wondered what he would feel if he knew that the son of a man he had murdered—for the murder had been Vortigern's, no matter who struck the blow—was watching him from the beggars' bench by the door, watching the place where the life beat in his long throat and thinking how simply it could be let out, with a little dagger, or even with one's naked hands. He was probably a good deal stronger than Vortigern.

What were they talking of, he wondered, those two who were breaking Britain between them? What were they talking of under the song of the harper and the rising and falling surge of voices? What was the real meaning behind this great feast? Whatever it was, it could make little difference now, he supposed. The cause of Rome in Britain and the old Royal House was dead; it had been dead nearly three years; but all the same, he would like to know what they were talking of; what was passing in Vortigern's mind. He was more interested in Vortigern's mind than Hengest's, because Hengest was only the enemy without the gates, but Vortigern was the traitor within them.

Vortigern was also wondering, a little, what lay behind this great feast; but not so much as he had done at first, because of the wine. It was difficult to get imported wines inland in Britain now, but Hengest's wine was good, though they drank it like barbarians from ox horns. Probably it was the fruits of piracy, but still . . . He drained the gold-mounted ox horn so quickly that a little of the thick red wine trickled into his beard, and set it down empty on his knee. As he did so, the girl who had been sitting on the steps of the High Seat rose to pour for him again. A tall, red-gold girl, fiercely proud in her crimson kirtle and the fillet of twisted goldsmith's work that bound her hair. The wine that was as crimson as her gown splashed into the ox horn, and the bubbles rose thickly. Vortigern looked up at her, seeing her through a faint haze, golden as the girl's hair. One heavy braid swung forward and brushed his hand, and as she straightened from her task, she smiled at him, only with her eyes that were the same shifting grey-green as Hengest her father's. Mermaid's eyes, he thought, and was pleased because the thought was pretty—worthy of a poet.

The girl poured for her father also, and then seated herself once again on the step, setting the tall wine-jar down beside her, and Hengest raised his horn again.

'Waes-hael! I drink to you, my King. May the sword of power never fall from your hand.'

'I drink to you,' Vortigern returned, and laughed a little. 'Truly I think that it will not—now that the menace of Rome and of young Ambrosius is past.' He did not usually like speaking of such things openly, but the wine seemed to have loosened his tongue.

Hengest laughed also, looking about him with an air of jovial and slightly drunken contentment. 'For me, and for the men that follow me, that menace of Rome and Ambrosius has been a fine thing, and that I'll no deny. This is a better and a fatter land than our North-folks' territory; and here we are your household men. And yet—'

He let the end of the sentence drift into silence; but Vortigern pounced on it. 'And yet? Man, what else would you have of me?'

'Na, na,' Hengest said hurriedly, and yet with seeming unwillingness, staring into his wine. 'It was but that at times my mind misgives me as to the safety of the King's northern borders. The King set me and my war bands to guard the door of the north against the Picts, and we flung back the Picts, and the Pict menace passed a little; and the King called us south to stand in the southern gateway, against another menace. But sometimes now, I think that if the Painted People should one day swarm in from the north again, there would be a thin defence and no strong leader to withstand them.'

Vortigern was alarmed and wary. 'What, then, is the answer? If I send you and even half of your war bands north again, the other danger may wake once more. While young Ambrosius lives among the mountains, he will always be a possible rallying point.'

'Na, na.' Hengest made a gesture as though to brush something away. 'The thought was but a thought—such as men think in the dark of the night, when the evening meat sits heavy under the breast-bone . . . Yet it might be no bad thing to settle some other leader there with his war bands around him; men bound by loyalty, even as we are, to Vortigern the King whose mead they drink and whose golden ornaments they wear.'

Vortigern looked at him a moment, his nostrils widening, as though just for that moment he caught the smell of a trap. Then he said, 'So? And if this leader were for you to choose, who would he be?'

Hengest stared, as though he had never given the matter a thought, until that moment. 'Nay then, let me think. I should choose—whom should I choose? There is Octa, my son, of course. He has his own war bands, his own victories, across the Great Sea; but if the thing were made worth his while . . . ' He broke off with a wide, impatient gesture. 'Ah, but no matter. Forget what I said, Vortigern, my hearth lord. My tongue ran away with me—it is the fault of wine. And talking of wine—' He frowned round at the girl in the crimson kirtle. 'Hey! my maiden, you neglect your duty! Do you not see that the King's horn is not full? Pour again for your guest and your father.'

She looked up quickly, then rose, taking up the wine-jar, and stooped again to pour for the red Celtic King. 'It is not my duty that I neglect, but my heart's pleasure. I crave forgiveness that I did not see my lord's horn was empty.'

'It is good to have the horn empty, so that it be filled by so fair a maiden,' Vortigern said courteously.

She raised her eyes to his in a flash, then lowered them again before he could see what lay under her golden lashes. 'My lord the King is most kind to his handmaiden.'

Hengest swung round to his gleemen sitting beside the central fire and strumming idly with the air of a man who knows that he is not being listened to. 'Sing up, man, strike that harp and give us "The Battle of Goths and Huns"! What is a feast without harping?'

The man grinned, and flung up his head like a hound before it bays, then broke into the swift, fierce word-music of the old lay, beating out the leaping rhythm on the twanging strings of the little harp. The bright harp-notes flew up like the sparks from the fire into the rolling smoke-cloud overhead, and the man's full, strong voice, half singing, half declaiming, filled the hall so that little by little men who had been arguing, talking, laughing, bragging against each other, grew silent to listen. Vortigern listened, leaning back in the High Seat, one hand playing with the horn on his knee, the other, elbow propped on the carved sidepiece, cupping his bearded chin, his restless, brilliant gaze moving as always here and there about the smoky, crowded, firelit hall.

When the last flight of notes had thrummed away into the silence, and the ragged burst of approval that followed it had fallen quiet, Hengest turned to his guest and asked, 'How does my lord the King like our Saxon harping?'

'It is well enough,' Vortigern said, 'but to my ear harsh, and I can find no tune in it.' He smiled as though to take the sting out of his words; he seldom smiled, and when he did it was a pleasant smile save that it showed too many pointed teeth in the thin red of his beard. 'To every people its own music. I am of another people, and to me the music of my own mountains is sweetest.'

Hengest smote his knee with an open palm. 'The King speaks truly; to every man the songs of his own people! Well, let the King but speak, and it may be that even here he will find singing to bring him the very scent of his own mountains.'

'So? Have you then some Cymric harper among your household thralls?'

'Nay, not a Cymric harper, but one skilled in the harp, none the less.' Hengest made a small gesture towards the girl in the crimson kirtle, still standing beside the High Seat. 'For see now, so deeply does Rowena my daughter long to please you that she has been learning a song of your people, from such a harper as you speak of, hoping that you will let her sing it to you. Say then, shall she sing? If she may give you any pleasure, you will make her very happy.'

Vortigern looked again into the mermaid eyes of Hengest's daughter. 'To look at her, singing or silent, is enough to make any man happy,' he said. 'But let her sing.'

VIII
Singing Magic

THEIR earlier talk, under the cheerful tumult and the gleeman's thrumming, had been private to themselves, but this, spoken into the silence following the close of the ancient Saga, was spoken as it were before every soul in the great hall, and as Rowena, carrying her head as though the goldwork fillet were a crown, moved across to the fire and took the slim, black harp from her father's gleeman, every eye in the place was upon her, even to the frowning gaze of the man on the beggars' bench before the door, who sat with the hood of his cloak pulled so far forward that no man might see his face.

For a great lady to take a gleeman's harp and sing before all her father's crowded Mead Hall was a shameless thing, more shameless even than it was for a Saxon woman to appear with her hair uncovered; and yet Aquila, who had known that she was shameless in wearing no head-rail, forgot that she was shameless in this also. He only knew that she was beautiful, the most beautiful thing he had ever seen, and that he hated her.

She sank down beside the hearth, settling the harp on her knee and into the hollow of her shoulder, and remained a few moments gazing into the fire that seemed to leap up to meet her as though there were a kinship between her and the flames, fingering almost silently the horsehair strings. She looked far remote, as though she had no need to be aware of the mead-flushed faces turned towards her, for she and they were in different worlds. She began to pluck the strings more strongly, conjuring up a strange music of long silences and single, singing notes that sprang up, each separate and perfect as some infinitely small silver bird that leapt up like a lark towards the smoky rafters, and hovered a little, and was gone. Gradually the notes spun closer together until the bright shadow of a melody began to emerge; and then suddenly, still looking into the fire, she was singing.

Aquila, watching her, had expected her voice to be hard and high and clear. It was clear, but with a clearness of depth, not height, a dark voice.

> The apple tree blooms white in the Land of the Living:
> The shadow of the blossom falls across my door stone:
> A bird flutters in the branches, singing.
> Green is my bird as the green earth of men, but his song is forgetfulness.
> Listen, and forget the earth.

British born and bred as he was, Aquila could speak the native tongue as easily as the Latin; and though this was a dialect unfamiliar to him, he caught the gist of the song, and his pulses stirred with a strange magic. And by the light of that magic, it seemed to him that the great firelit hall, the warriors leaning forward on their benches, even the two men in the High Seat were no more than a background for the woman harping beside the fire.

> The petals fall from my apple tree, drifting,
> Drifting down the wind like snow: but the snow is warm:
> And a bird flutters in the branches, singing.
> Blue is my bird as the blue summer sky, over the world of men.
> But here is another sky.

She had turned from the fire now, to look up at Vortigern the King, as he sat forward beside her father, his restless gaze still at last, resting on her face. Watching her under the shadow of his hood, Aquila thought, She is a witch! Surely she is a witch! Flavia used to talk of a singing magic . . . Rowena had risen, and moved, drifting as though on the slow, haunting notes of her song, to the foot of the High Seat, and sank down again, still looking up at the thin, red-haired man.

> The apples are silver on the boughs, low bending;
> A tree of chiming, of singing as the wind blows by:
> But the bird flutters through the branches, silent.
> Red is my bird, crimson red as the life of my heart is.
> Will you not come to me?

It seemed to Aquila that the last, lingering notes clung for a long time to the smoky rafters; that they were still hanging there when the singer rose without another word, without another look at Vortigern, and went, sweeping her crimson skirts after her through the rushes, to set the little harp back in the hands that her father's gleeman held out for it.

Hengest sent one glance after her; it might have been in triumph, quickly hidden under his down-drawn, golden brows. But Vortigern did not see it, for his eyes also were following her. They will always follow her now, Aquila thought, with a sudden flash of clear seeing. She has crossed over in his mind from the Saxon folk, and become part of his childhood and his own hills and the songs his people sing and the beautiful crack-brained dreams they dream.

The silence was torn apart by the harsh scream of a peregrine, as the falcon on Vortimer's fist bated wildly, with a furious clapping of wings. The young man rose, striving to calm the bird. He was whiter than ever as he bowed with all courtesy to his father and his host, murmuring his excuses: 'My falcon—not properly manned as yet, it seems. I crave your pardon,' and drew back into the shadows, making for the upper doorway.

The spell that had bound the whole gathering, holding even the Saxons silent, was broken, and the tumult burst upward again, louder than ever. At the lower fire, Thormod and another young warrior, both very flushed with mead, had started a bragging match that would probably end in a quarrel.

'Once I fought three men one after another, and beat them all!'

'That is nothing. Once I fought three men all at the same time—'

Time to be on his way, Aquila thought. He rose, and stood taking a last look at the scene in the great Mead Hall. All these two days past he had been too numbed really to understand that tonight he was going to try to escape; that in one way or the other, this was the end of his years among the Saxon kind, and by dawn he would be either free or dead. But now, in the moment of setting out, there was a breathless tightening at his heart as he stood by the open doorway, with the smoky torchlight in his eyes and the harp-song in his ears. Then he turned, and slipped out from Hengest's hall into the night.

He had eaten all that came his way, not knowing when he might get the chance to eat again, and drunk little, that he might keep a clear head. But even so, his head seemed full of woodsmoke and the fumes of other men's mead, and he stood for a few moments breathing deeply in the night air to clear it. Then he set off for the woodwright's shop. He was surprised to find how light the world was, for he had forgotten that there was a full moon and it would be up now. A still, white night, with a faint mist rising from the water, glimmering, gauzy between the timber halls and the tents that seemed now more than ever like crouching animals. Behind him the sounds of feasting fell away, and around him Hengest's burg lay quiet between the mist and the moon, for by now all those who did not feast with Hengest and the King were asleep or taking their ease around their own hearth, with house-place door or tent-flap drawn close against the chill of the mist.

Once a cat ran like a striped shadow across his path, and turned to look at him with eyes that were wide and hostile in the moonlight; otherwise he met no living thing until he came in sight of the woodwright's shop close to the shore-gate of the burg. He had made sure of the place in the daylight, a solitary spot in some waste land that seemed to belong to the marshes rather than the burg, though it was within the stockade, and easily recognized from the description that Flavia had given him. The mist was thicker down here, so near the water, wreathing and drifting like wet, moonlit smoke about the hump-backed shape of the bothy and the ancient thorn tree beside it. The dragon-head of a galley prow stood against the thorn tree, its snarling mask upreared as though some living monster were trying to crest the mist like a fantastic sea. For a moment, as he came down towards it, Aquila thought that that was all. Then something else moved in the mist, and he saw that Flavia was there before him.

'You have come, then,' she said, as he halted beside her.

It was such an obvious thing to say, but sometimes it was better to stick to the obvious things.

'I have come,' he said, and sent a swift glance towards the stockade gate, just visible in the mist.

She saw the glance, and shook her head. 'There are none there to overhear us. Did I not say that I would take care of the guards on the shore-gate?'

There was a sudden chill in him. 'Flavia, you don't mean—What have you done to them?'

'Oh no, I am not a poisoner. They will but sleep a few hours.'

'But how—?' Aquila began, but she cut him short.

'It was a simple thing to do. They were glad enough of the mead cup that I brought down to them from Hengest's Hall. See now'—she brought a bundle from under her cloak—'here is some food, and a dagger, and a good sharp file that I stole. With the food, you can lie up for a day or so until you are free of that cruel thrall-ring, before you go among men again.'

Aquila took the bundle from her, mumbling something, he did not know what. They stood looking at each other; and suddenly the ordinary things were no good, after all. Aquila said hoarsely, 'I have seen—I have heard a singing magic tonight, Flavia. The Lady Rowena made it for the Red Fox. But she did not comb her hair. I do not think that she could comb sparks out of it in the dark.'

Flavia caught her breath. 'Aquila, no! It hurts too much. I never made *my* singing magic because I could not bear that you should—that you shouldn't feel the same about me any more; and now . . . '

'Come with me,' Aquila said—it felt like a sudden impulse, but he knew that it wasn't really.

'—and leave the babe?'

Silence again. Then Aquila said, 'Bring him too. We'll find somewhere—a place for ourselves. I'll work for both of you.'

'For the child of a Saxon father?'

Aquila looked down at the hand in which he held the bundle, and forced it to relax from the clenched and quivering fist that it had become. 'I will try to forget his Saxon father, and remember only that he is yours,' he said carefully.

She drew closer, lifting her face to his. It was very white in the moonlight and the wreathing mist; and her eyes had again that look of being mere black holes in the whiteness of it. 'Aquila, part of me would lie down and die tomorrow and not think it a heavy price to pay, if I might come with you tonight. But there's another part of me that can never come.'

'You mean, you can't leave the man either.'

'Our Lord help me! He is *my* man.'

After a few moments she moved again, and held out something. 'You must go. But first—take this.'

'What is it?'

'Father's ring.'

Aquila made no move to take it. 'What will *he* do when he knows that you have given his bride gift away, and in what manner you gave it?'

'I shall tell him that I lost it.'

'And will he believe that?'

'Maybe not,' Flavia said. 'But he won't beat me.' How strange and luminous her eyes were, all at once, in the moonlight. 'I am quite safe, my dear. He is a brave man in his way, but he won't beat me.'

Aquila put his free hand on her shoulder, and looked down at her, trying to understand. 'Is it love, with you, or hate, Flavia?'

'I do not know. Something of both maybe; but it doesn't make any difference. I belong to him.' Her low voice was completely toneless. 'Take Father's ring, and—try to forgive me.'

He dropped his hand from her shoulder, and took the ring, and slid it on to his bare signet finger. The numbness that had helped him was wearing thin, and the black, appalling misery was aching through. Somewhere, hidden at the back of his mind, he had thought until now that she would come with him; he hadn't quite accepted that what had happened was for ever. He said in a voice as toneless as her own, 'If I escape by your help, and take Father's ring at your hands, then I must forgive you, Flavia.'

And without another word between them, they turned to the gateway. The guards lay tumbled beside it in uncouth attitudes, the mead cup between them; and Aquila was struck by a sudden fear. 'Flavia—they'll tell, when they awake, who gave them the mead!'

'No,' Flavia said. 'The moon was not up then, and I took pains to change my voice. They will not know who came.' She had gone to the bar that held the gate; but Aquila put her on one side, and raising the heavy timber himself, drew the gate open just enough to let him through. Then, in the narrow gap, he turned again to Flavia, for the last time; the last time of all. She looked very remote and still in the darkness of her cloak, with the mist smoking about her; and here in the shadow of the gateway he could scarcely see her face at all. At the last moment he made a half-movement towards her; but she made none towards him, and he checked and let his arm fall to his side. 'God keep you, Flavia,' he said.

'And you,' Flavia whispered. 'God keep you always. Remember me sometimes—even though it hurts to remember.'

Aquila made a small, harsh sound that was like a sob, and turned away into the glimmering mist that veiled the boat-sheds and the long keels drawn up above the tide-line. He did not look back, but as he went he heard the soft, heavy creak of the gate being urged shut behind him.

There were some small fishing coracles on the tide-line, but he did not want to leave any trace of his escape-route behind him. The tide was ebbing, and soon there would be no more than a narrow channel between Tanatus and the mainland; and a few miles south towards Rutupiae he knew the channels as a man knows the lines of his own hand. Simpler to swim for it. He turned southward, following the edges of the farmed land, and after some miles walking, came down on to salting that he knew well. The mist had cleared and the wild-fowl were stirring. There was no hint of day as yet in the sky.

On a spit of blown dune-sand and shingle where he and Felix had often run their coracle ashore he stripped, and making his tunic, with the things that Flavia had given him, into a bundle in his rough cloak, tied it on to his shoulders with its own ends, and took to the water. The channel had shifted in three years, but he got across without much trouble, and waded ashore among the mainland dunes, shaking himself like a dog. He untied his bundle and dragged his tunic on again over his wet body; his cloak also was wet in the outer folds, but the thick oiliness of the wool had kept out most of the water, and the food was quite dry. He bundled it up again, scarcely aware of what he did; he was not aware of anything very clearly, simply doing each thing as it came, because it was the next thing to do. And because it was the next thing to do, he set out towards the dark shore-line of the distant forest.

The moonlight was fading and the day was coming fast, the cirrus cloud already beginning to catch light from the hidden sun; and a skein of wild duck went overhead against the high, shining dapple of the morning sky. The cool daylight of marsh country was washing over the levels behind him as he reached the first fringes of squat, wind-shaped oak and whitehorn, where the great forest of Anderida swept to within sight of the sea. He pushed in a little way among the trees, found a clearing among brambles and hazel scrub, and sitting down with his back to an oak tree, untied the bundle of food that Flavia had given him. He ate a little without knowing what it was, then took out the file and set to work to rid himself of his thrall-ring.

It did not take him very long to realize that it couldn't be done, not by the man wearing the thing. You couldn't get any force on the file, and you couldn't see what you were doing. Well, it did not matter much. By and by, when he was well clear of the Saxon hunting runs, he would go to a smith and get it cut off. Meanwhile, that left nothing to do but rest a little before he pushed on again. He thrust the useless file back into the bundle, and lay down, his head on his arm. The glints of sky through the young oak leaves were like a thousand eyes looking down at him; blue eyes, mocking him because he had prayed to God that he might find Flavia, and God had answered his prayer; and he did not think that he would ever pray to God again . . . He had said that he forgave Flavia, but he hadn't been able to make the words mean anything. Just words. And Flavia knew that. He knew that she knew. He felt lost and adrift in a black tide of bitterness, and the last thing that he had to hold to was gone. No, not quite the last thing—there was still the hope of finding again the man who had betrayed his father.

He would have given up that hope for Flavia's sake, if she had come with him, because the quest for vengeance was a trail that no man should follow with a woman and a child dependent on him. But Flavia had not come.

He thought about it coolly and carefully. He would go on westward until he was sure that he was clear of the Saxons' reach, and get rid of the thrall-ring on his neck, and then turn back towards the barbarians again; because most likely, he thought, the little bird-catcher would be found clinging to the hem of the Sea Wolves' garments. At any rate, a Saxon camp was the most likely place to get word of him. And word of him he would get, if it took twenty—thirty years.

Had he but known it, it was to take just three days.

IX
Forest Sanctuary

AFTER a while he must have slept, for suddenly it was long past noon, and the sunlight fell slanting through the branches to dapple the brown of last year's leaves. He got up, ate a little more of the food, and then, wrapping it up again, set off westward.

There were few roads through the forest, but next day he struck one of the native trackways that had been old before the Legions' roads were thought of; and since it led in roughly the right direction, he turned into it for the sake of easier travelling and following it along. By the evening of the next day it had led him into higher and more rolling country, an upland world of long, forest ridges, where the ground was sandy underfoot, and the trees grew taller and more cleanly than the damp oak scrub that he had left behind. The fine spell had broken and soft, chill rain was blowing down the wind. Aquila was wet through and blind weary, for he had scarcely rested since he set out westward; if he rested, the little bird-catcher might draw further away from him; so he kept on—and on . . .

It was already dusk among the trees when, as he came trudging up the long slope of yet another ridge, he caught a waft of wood-smoke on the sodden, forest-scented air, and as he checked, sniffing, the warm saffron flicker of firelight reached him through the hazel and wayfaring trees that fringed the track. He must go to men some time and be rid of the betraying thrall-ring about his neck. Also he must have food. He had finished the last scraps in his bundle at dawn, and the emptiness in his belly drew him towards the fire. Almost without knowing that he did so, he turned to a gap in the wayside scrub, beyond which the faint gleam of firelight beckoned.

Parting the hazel boughs, he found himself on the edge of a little clearing—in daylight it must be full in sight from the track—and saw before him a plot of what looked in the dusk like bean-rows and kale; and in the midst of it a knot of daub-and-wattle huts squatting under deep heather thatch, a wisp of hearth-smoke rising against the sodden yellow of the afterglow, and the firelight shining softly through an open door. He hesitated a moment on the edge of the clearing, wondering whether he was yet clear of all shadow of the Saxon kind. Then he saw, hanging from a birch sapling close beside the huts, outlined against the fading daffodil light of the west, something that could only be a small bell. There would be freedom from the Saxons here, where a Christian bell was hanging.

He walked forward between two dripping bean-rows to the firelit doorway. The fine rain hushed across the clearing behind him, but within the hut a fire burned on a small raised hearth, with something boiling in a pot over it, and the warm, fluttering light flushed the little bothy golden as the heart of a yellow rose. There was a stool beside the fire, and a bench with a pillow of plaited straw on it pushed back under the slope of the roof. Otherwise the place was quite bare, save that on the gable wall hung a small cross of rowan wood with the bark still on it, and before it a man in a rough brown tunic stood with arms upraised in the attitude of prayer. Aquila wanted to say, 'It isn't any good, you know: God only laughs at you.' But the rags of a gentle upbringing made him prop himself, against the door post and wait, rather than interrupt the holy man until the prayer was done.

He did not mean to make any sound, but it seemed that the man before the rowan-wood cross had sensed that there was somebody behind him. Aquila saw him stiffen, but he made no move until he came to the end of his prayer. Then he turned and looked at Aquila drooping in the doorway. He was a small, thick-set man, with immensely powerful shoulders, and the quietest face that Aquila had ever seen.

'God's greeting to you, friend,' he said, as though Aquila were an expected guest.

'And to you,' Aquila returned.

'Is it food and shelter that you seek? You are most welcome.'

Still leaning against the door post, Aquila thrust back the shoulder folds of his wet cloak. 'Those too, if you will give them to me: but firstly, to be rid of *this* about my neck.'

The man nodded, still without surprise. 'So, a Saxon thrall-ring.'

'I have a file. It isn't possible to use the thing on oneself.'

'That, I should imagine.' The man had come to Aquila in the doorway, drawing him in, a steadying hand under his elbow as though he knew better even than Aquila himself how far spent he was. 'Eat first, I think, and we will see to the next thing later.'

Aquila found himself sitting on the stool beside the fire, his wet cloak fallen at his feet, while the man in the brown tunic was ladling a mess of beans from the pot over the fire into a bowl of finely turned birch wood. And in a little he was supping up the scalding hot beans, with a wedge of brown barley bread dripping with honey-in-the-comb waiting on the floor beside him, while his host sat on the bench and watched him with an air of quiet pleasure, asking no questions. It was not until he was more than halfway through that he realized that the bean pot was now empty, and stopped with the horn spoon poised on its way to his mouth.

'I am eating your supper.'

The older man smiled. 'I promise you that in eating my supper you are doing me a kindness. I strive after a disciplined life, superior to the pull of the flesh. But alas! the flesh pulls very hard. It is good for my soul that my body should go hungry, but I fear that I find it hard to carry out that particular discipline unless I can prevail on some fellow man to aid me as you are doing now.' His quiet gaze went to the bowl which Aquila had firmly set down on the corner of the hearth, and returned to his face. 'Let you finish the good work, friend, so that I may sleep with a glad heart this night.'

After a long moment's hesitation, Aquila took up the bowl again.

When the beans were gone, and the bread and honey also, the man in the brown tunic rose, saying, 'I think that you have walked a long way, and you are far spent. Let you sleep now. Tomorrow will be time enough to be rid of that thrall-ring.'

But Aquila shook his head stubbornly. 'I would not lie down another night with the Sea Wolves' iron about my neck.'

The other looked at him searchingly. Then he said, 'So be it then. Give me the file, and kneel here against my knees.'

It must have been close on midnight when the file broke through the last filament of metal with a jerk that seemed to jar Aquila's head on his shoulders. The monk wrenched the thing open, and with a satisfied sigh laid it on the floor, and Aquila lurching to his feet, stiff with long kneeling, drunk and dazed with weariness, stood swaying with a hand on the king-post to steady himself, and looked down at the small man who had laboured so many hours for his sake. The monk looked as weary as himself, and there was a red tear in his thumb, where the file had gashed it as it broke through. Surely his host might sleep with a doubly glad heart tonight.

The other man had risen also, and was looking at his neck, touching it gently here and there with square-tipped fingers. 'Aye, the iron has galled you badly, here—and here. I was expecting that. Bide while I salve it; then sleep, my friend.'

And in a little, Aquila did sleep, lying on the bed of clean fern in a tiny wattle bothy behind the main one, that made him think of a bee-skep.

When he woke, the hut was full of sunlight that slanted in through the doorway and quivered like golden water on the lime-washed wall beside him. He realized that he must have slept through the night and most of next day; a sleep that was a black gulf behind him with nothing stirring in it, not even the old hideous dream that had woken him so often with Flavia's screams in his ears. But he was never to have that dream again.

He lay still a few moments, blinking at the living golden water on the wall, while little by little the thoughts and events from across the black gulf fell into place around him. Then he sat up, slowly, and remained for a while squatting in the piled fern, feeling the galled places on his neck with a kind of dull relief because the pressure of the thrall-ring was gone. But it was time to be away, down towards the coast and the Saxon kind again, while there was still some daylight left for travelling, and before the man in the brown tunic could ask questions. Last night the man had been merciful and asked no questions, but now that his guest had eaten and slept, surely he would ask them; and everything in Aquila flinched from the prospect, with a physical flinching, as though from a probing finger too near a raw place.

He sprang up and went to the doorway of the cell. Yesterday's rain was gone, and the still-wet forest was full of a crystal green light. In the cleared plot before the huts, the man in the brown tunic was peacefully hoeing between his bean-rows. Aquila pushed off from the door post and walked towards him. The beans were just coming into flower, black and white among the grey-green leaves, and the scent of them was like honey and almonds, strong and sweet after the rain. The man in the brown tunic straightened up as he drew near, and stood leaning on his hoe.

'You have slept long,' he said, 'and that is well.'

'I have slept over-long!' Aquila returned. 'I thank you for your food and shelter, and for ridding me of this,' he touched the sore where the thrall-ring had pressed on his neck. 'And now I must be away.'

'Where to?'

Aquila hesitated. What if he said, 'Back towards the Saxon kind, to look for the man who betrayed my father'? Doubtless this little monk with the quiet face would try to make him leave his search, say to him that vengeance was for God and not for man. 'I am not sure,' he said And that was true, too, in its way.

The man looked at him kindly. 'To journey, and know not where, makes uncertain travelling. Stay until you *are* sure. Stay at least for tonight, and let me salve your neck again; it is not so often that God sends me a guest.' And then, as Aquila made a swift gesture of refusal, he shifted a little to lean more comfortably on his hoe, his gaze resting on Aquila. 'I will ask you no question, save by what name I am to call you.'

Aquila looked at him in silence for a moment. 'Aquila,' he said at last, and it was as though he lowered a weapon.

'So. And I am Ninnias—Brother Ninnias, of the little Community that used to be in the woods over yonder. And you will stay here at least for tonight, and for that my heart rejoices.'

Aquila had not said that he would stay; but he knew that he would. He had known it when he told Brother Ninnias his name. There was something about this place, a feeling of sanctuary that stilled a little his driving restlessness. He would take one night from following his vengeance, and then no more until he found the bird-catcher and the debt for his father's death was paid. But he would take this one night. He remained silent, staring along the bean-rows.

The little amber bees were droning among the bean-blossom, and at that moment one fell out of a flower, the pollen baskets on her legs full and yellow. She landed sizzling on her back on a flat leaf, righted herself, and made for another flower. But Brother Ninnias stooped and pointed a reproving finger at her. 'That is enough for one journey, little sister. Go back to the hive.'

And the bee, seeming to change her mind, abandoned the bean-flower and zoomed off towards the main hut. Aquila, following her line of flight with his eyes, saw that against the wall stood three heather-thatched bee-skeps. 'It is as though she knew what you said to her,' he said.

Brother Ninnias smiled. 'They are a strange people, the bees. I was bee master to our little Community before the Sea Wolves came. It is so, that I am alive.'

Aquila glanced at him questioningly, but the bargain to ask no questions must work both ways.

Yet Brother Ninnias answered the question as though he had asked it, none the less; and most willingly. 'I was away in the forest after a swarm of bees that had flown away, when the Sea Wolves came. I was angry with myself for having lost them; but since—I have thought that maybe God meant that one of us should be saved. The bees smelled my anger; bees will always smell anger, and so it was a long time before they let me find them. And when at last I found them—just here, hanging on a branch of the oak tree yonder—and came back to the Community with them in my basket, the Saxons had passed that way, and it was black and desolate, even to the bee-skeps along the wall. Only I found the Abbot's bell, quite unharmed, lying in the ruins.' He broke off to pick a bee gently off his rough brown sleeve. 'It was a common enough happening then. At least we do not see so many burned homes in these years; not in the three years that Hengest and his war bands have been squatting in Tanatus, eating from the Red Fox's hand.'

'It does not suit Hengest to have others despoil the land before he swarms out over it himself,' Aquila said harshly.

'Aye, I have often thought that myself. And when I think it, I pray; and when I have prayed, I go and plant something else in my physic garden that it may perhaps flower, and I may perhaps make a salve or a draught from it and heal a child's graze or an old man's cough before the Saxons come.'

There was a silence, full of the peaceful droning of the bees, and then Aquila said, returning to the earlier subject, 'What did you do after you came back to the Community?'

'I said the last prayers for the Abbot and my brethren, and then I took an axe that I found, and the Abbot's bell, and my swarm of bees in their basket, and came away, back to this place where I had found my lost swarm. And here I built a skep for the bees, and hung the Abbot's bell from that birch tree. And then I gave thanks to God, before I set to building my first hut.'

'Why?' Aquila said harshly.

'That I was spared to preach His word.'

'And who do you preach it to? Your bees and the bush-tailed squirrels?'

'A man might preach to worse hearers. But I have others besides. There is a village of iron-workers down yonder, one of many in the Great Forest, and some among them listen to me, though I fear that they still dance for the Horned One at Beltane. And sometimes God sends me a guest, as he did last evening . . . And if I am to feed more guests, I must finish this hoeing lest the weeds engulf my beans.'

And so saying, he returned peacefully to his task.

With some idea of lessening his debt for food and house room, Aquila began to help him, gathering the raked weeds into a willow basket and carrying it up to the place at the far end of the clearing that Brother Ninnias pointed out to him, ready for burning. From that side of the clearing, the land dropped unexpectedly towards the east, and through a gap in the trees the blue distance opened, ridge beyond ridge of rolling forest country fading to the far-off, misty flatness that might be coastwise marshes, or even the sea. Aquila, straightening up from emptying his basket, stood at gaze. The light was fading now, and the forest ridges rolling into the distance were soft as smoke. He must be looking towards Rutupiae, he thought, towards Tanatus and the Saxon kind, and maybe his vengeance. He had been a fool to say that he would stay one more night in this place, just because it had the smell of sanctuary. He would go back and tell Brother Ninnias that he must go now, this evening, after all. There would be the remains of a moon later, and he could be a few miles on his way, a few miles nearer to finding the little bird-catcher, before he lay down to sleep.

The shadows were creeping among the trees, and somewhere an owl hooted softly as he stooped to take up the basket again.

Brother Ninnias's voice spoke just behind him. 'I used to come out here every evening, just at owl-hoot, to watch for Rutupiae Light.'

Aquila looked round quickly at the square, brown man with the hoe on his shoulder. 'Can you see so far from here?' he asked, startled, because in a way it was as though the other's thoughts had been moving with his.

'Sometimes. It must be upward of forty miles, but I could see it in clear weather. And when there was mist or rain I knew that it was there . . . And then one night it was very late in coming; but it came at last, and my heart leapt up to see it as though it were a friend's face. And the next night, though I looked for it three times, it did not come at all. I thought, "The mist has come up and hidden it." But there was no mist that night. And then I knew that the old order had passed, and we were no more part of Rome.'

Both of them were silent awhile; then Brother Ninnias spoke again. 'It came to me later—news travels swiftly along the forest tracks—that the last Roman troops had already sailed, before that last beacon fire shone from Rutupiae. A strange thing, that.'

Aquila shot him a quick glance. 'Strange enough. What did men believe to lie behind it?'

'Ghosts—omens—all kinds of marvels.'

'But you did not believe that, I think?'

Brother Ninnias shook his head. 'I will not say that I did not believe; I should be the last man to disbelieve in marvels; but I have sometimes wondered . . . It has seemed to me that it may so well have been some poor deserter left behind when his comrades sailed. I have even thought of him as someone I know, and wondered what his story was.'

'Why should a deserter take the trouble to light Rutupiae Beacon?' Aquila demanded, and his voice sounded rough in his own ears.

'Maybe in farewell, maybe in defiance. Maybe to hold back the dark for one more night.'

'To hold back the dark for one more night,' Aquila repeated broodingly, his mind going back to that last night, after the galleys sailed, seeing again the beacon platform in the dead silver moonlight, the sudden red flare of the beacon under his hands. And two days' march away this man had been watching for it, and seen it come. In an odd way, that had been their first meeting, his and the quiet brown man's beside him; as though something of each had reached out to make contact with the other, in the sudden flare of Rutupiae Beacon. 'That was a shrewd guess,' he said.

Brother Ninnias's quiet gaze returned from the distance to rest on his face. 'You speak as one who knows.'

'I was the deserter,' Aquila said.

He had not meant to say it. He did not know that he was saying it until he heard the words hanging in the air. But in the same instant he knew that it did not matter; not to this man.

Brother Ninnias said, 'So,' without surprise, without any questioning, simply in acceptance of what Aquila had told him.

Aquila had been so afraid of questions; but now, because Brother

Ninnias had asked none, because of that odd feeling that they had reached out to each other in the last flaring of Rutupiae Light and were somehow old friends, suddenly he was talking—talking in small, bitter sentences, standing there with the willow basket forgotten in his hand, and his gaze going out over the forest in the fading light.

'You said that you wondered what his story was—the deserter who lit Rutupiae Beacon that last time . . . He found that he belonged to Britain, to the things that Rome-in-Britain stands for; not to Rome. He thought once that they were the same thing; but they're not. And so at last he deserted. He went back to his own place—his own people. Two days later, the Saxons came. They burned the farm and slew his father and the rest of the household. The deserter they bound to a tree and left for the wolves. The wolves did not come, but instead a raiding party found him and took him for a thrall. He served three years on a Jutish farm, until this spring half the settlement came to join Hengest in Tanatus, and among them the man who owned him. So he came again to Britain.'

'And from Hengest's burg, he escaped,' Brother Ninnias said.

'A man helped him to escape,' Aquila said after a moment. And the words caught a little in his throat. To no living soul, not even to this man, could he speak of Flavia in the Saxon camp.

Brother Ninnias seemed to know that he could ask a question now, for he said after a while: 'You spoke of these men who took you thrall, as a raiding band, as though they were different in that from the men who burned your home.'

'The men who burned my home were no mere raiding band,' Aquila said bitterly. 'No chance inland thrust of the Sea Wolves, that is.' He was silent a moment, his hand tightening convulsively on the plaited rim of the willow basket. 'My father was heart and soul with the Roman party who stood behind young Ambrosius. They appealed to Aetius in Gaul for help to drive out both Vortigern and the Saxons. You will know that, as all men know it, now. You will know that all the answer they ever had was that the last Roman troops left in the province were withdrawn. But Vortigern was brought word of the plan, and took no chances. He called Hengest and his war bands down from their old territory and settled them in Tanatus at the gateway to Britain; and he took his revenge on all he could reach of those who were—betrayed to him.'

He was aware of a sudden odd stillness in the man beside him. 'Among them, your father,' Brother Ninnias said.

'Among them my father; betrayed to his death by a little rat-faced bird-catcher.' Aquila almost choked.

Brother Ninnias made a small, quickly suppressed sound, and Aquila whipped round to face him. For a long moment they remained looking at each other. Then Aquila said, 'What did you say?'

'I do not think that I said anything.'

'You cried out—you know something of that bird-catcher. Something that I don't.' His eyes widened in the dusk, his lip stuck back a little over the dryness of his teeth. 'Maybe you know where he is! Tell me—you shall tell me—'

'So that you may be revenged on him?'

'So that I may repay the debt,' Aquila said in a voice suddenly hard and quiet with the intensity of his hating.

'You are too late. The debt has been repaid.'

'What do you mean? You're trying to shield him because of your monkish ideas—but you know where he is, and you *shall* tell me!'

He flung the willow basket aside, and caught the other man by the shoulders, shaking him, thrusting his own distorted face into the one that looked back at him as quietly as ever. 'Tell me! By Our Lord, you shall tell me!'

'Let me go,' Brother Ninnias said. 'I am as strong as you, possibly stronger. Do not make me put out my strength against one who has eaten my salt.'

For a few moments Aquila continued to drag him to and fro; then he dropped his hands, panting. '*Let you tell me where he is!*'

Brother Ninnias stooped and picked up his hoe and the willow basket. 'Come over here,' he said and turned towards the nearest trees.

Aquila hesitated an instant, staring after him with narrowed eyes. Then he strode forward after the broad, brown back. A wild suspicion of the truth woke in him, even before they halted among the first of the forest shadows, at a gesture from Brother Ninnias, and he found himself looking down at a long, narrow hummock of mossy turf under an oak tree.

For a long time he remained, staring down at the grave. All the fury, all the hate, all the purpose had gone out of him. After a while he said in a dead-level voice, and still without looking up, 'Tell me what happened.'

'I told you that sometimes God sends me a guest,' Brother Ninnias said. 'Nearly three years ago—aye, only a few nights after Rutupiae Light went out—God sent me one, sore pressed and very near to his end. A man escaped from the hands of Saxon torturers. I took him in and did for him what I could, but there is a limit beyond which the body cannot be hurt and live . . . For two nights he raved in fever, so that, sitting with him, I learned that he had been one of those who followed Ambrosius, one who had carried messages among the others, passing as a bird-catcher. And again and again he cried out against Vortigern's torturers, that he could bear no more, and cried out that he had betrayed his fellows. On the third night, he died.'

'Other men have died under torture, without speaking,' Aquila said after a moment, in a hard, level voice.

'All men's spirits are not equally strong. Are you sure of the strength of your own?'

Aquila was silent a long time, still staring down at the long hummock that seemed dissolving into the dusk. The grave of the man who had betrayed his father under torture, a man who had died because flesh and spirit had been torn apart by the Saxon torturers, and also, perhaps, because he did not wish to live. 'No,' he said at last. He had lost everything now—all that he had to love, and all that he had to hate—in three days. He looked up at last, and asked as a lost child might ask it, 'What shall I do?'

'Now that you are robbed of an old hate; robbed of the tracking down and the vengeance?' Brother Ninnias said, with a great gentleness.

'Yes.'

'I think, if it were me, that I should thank God, and look for another service to take.'

'I am not one for the holy life,' Aquila said, with an ugly bitterness in his voice.

'Nay, I did not think that you were. If you believe, as your father believed, that the hope of Britain lies with Ambrosius of the House of Constantine, let you take your father's service on you.'

For a long moment they stood facing each other across the bird-catcher's grave. Then Aquila said, 'Is it there to take? Surely the cause of the Roman party was finished nearly three years ago.'

'It is not so easy to kill a cause that men are prepared to die for,' Brother Ninnias said. 'Come back to the evening food now, and eat, and sleep again; and in the morning let you go to young Ambrosius in Arfon.'

Aquila turned his head to look westward, where the afterglow still flushed behind the trees and the first star hovered like a moth above the tree tops.

'To Arfon,' he said. 'Yes, I will go to Arfon, and seek out this Ambrosius.'

X
The Fortress of the High Powers

A LITTLE before sunset on an autumn evening, Aquila was leaning against the trunk of a poplar tree beside the gate of the principal inn of Uroconium idly watching the broad main street, and the life of the city that came and went along it. Inn courtyards were good places; often there were odd jobs to be done for guests and a few coins to be earned. He knew; he had hung about inn courtyards all across Britain in the past few months. A yellow poplar leaf came circling down through the still air past his face, and added itself to the freckled moon-yellow carpet already spread around his feet. But the evening was as warm as summer, with the still, backward-looking warmth that returns sometimes when summer is long past; and the little group of ladies who came out from the Forum gardens across the way wore only light wraps, pretty and fragile as flower petals, over their indoor tunics. One of them carried a late white rosebud, and another sniffed at a ball of amber in her hand, and they laughed together, softly, as they went on up the street. A man came out through the Forum gate, with a slave behind him carrying his books. Maybe he was a lawyer. How odd that there were still towns where the Magistrates sat to administer the laws and discuss the water supply, and women walked abroad with balls of amber in their hands for its delicate fragrance. The town was shabby as all towns were, the walls that had gleamed so white against the distant mountains of Cymru, stained and pitted here and there with fallen plaster, the streets inclined to be dirty. But there were things to buy in the shops, and on the citizens' faces a look of unawareness that made Aquila want to climb on to the mounting-block and cry out to them. 'Don't you know what is happening all round the coasts? Haven't you *heard*?'

'I suppose this is so far inland that they have never felt the Saxon wind blowing. But what hope can there be for us if only our coastwise fringes understand?'

He did not realize that he had spoken the thought aloud, until a voice behind him said in heartfelt agreement, 'The same question occurs to me from time to time,' and he swung round to find a man standing in the courtyard gateway; a big man, with a plump, pale face spreading in blue, shaven chins over the dark neckfolds of his mantle, and eyes that were soft and slightly bulging like purple grapes.

'You speak, I think, as one who has felt the Saxon wind blow somewhat keenly?' said the man.

'Aye,' Aquila agreed.

The full dark eyes moved in leisurely fashion from the white scar of the thrall-ring on his neck, down to his feet bound in dusty straw and rags, and up again to his face. '. . . And have walked far today.'

'I am on a journey, and since I have no money for horse hire, I walk.'

The man nodded, and slipped a hand into his girdle, and held out a sesterce. 'So. This will at least give you a meal and a night's shelter before your next march. I also have little love for the Saxon kind.'

Aquila stiffened. He was hungry, and he had been hanging round the inn in the hope of earning the price of a meal; but earning, not begging. He could not afford pride, but it rose in his throat all the same. 'Tell me what I may do to earn it.'

The other smiled, raising his brows a little. 'Some days ago I left a piece of broken mule-harness to be mended at the saddler's by the West Gate; and since tomorrow I continue my own journey, I am in need of it. Do you go and fetch it for me.'

'What name shall I tell them, so that they will give it to me?'

'Say that Eugenus the Physician sent you to collect his mule-bridle that he left three days ago.' He fished again in his girdle. 'Here is some more money to pay for the mending. Now take the other without hurt to your pride.'

And so, with the price of a meal stowed in the breast of his ragged tunic, Aquila set out for the West Gate.

The saddler had not finished his work, so he got a meal in a cheap cook-shop while he waited; and it was near to dusk when he came again up the broad main street towards the inn, the mended bridle in his hand chiming with every step he took, for the fine crimson leather was hung with tiny bronze and silver bells. He had expected to hand the thing over to one of the inn slaves and go his way, but when he came into the courtyard, the man he spoke to jerked a thumb towards the outside stair that led to a kind of gallery and said with obvious disapproval: 'You're to take it up yourself, he says. It's the first door at the head of the stair; you can't miss it.'

So Aquila went up the stairs, and turned to the first door he came to, and a few moments later, having knocked and been bidden to enter, he stood in a small chamber shadowy with mingled dusk and candlelight, that looked into the inn courtyard. Eugenus, who was standing at the window, looked round as he entered. 'Ah, you have brought it, then.'

'Did you think that I had run off with it? It must be worth quite a handful, with all those little chiming bells.' Aquila laid the gay harness across the foot of the sleeping-couch, and a small bronze coin on the table beside the wine-flask that stood there. 'I would have come back sooner, but it was not finished, and I had to wait. There is a denarius change from the money that you gave me to pay for it'

Eugenus took up the coin, looked at Aquila a moment, as though wondering whether to offer it to him, and then returned it to his girdle and reached instead for the wine-flask and a cup of faintly honey-coloured glass. 'I did not think that you had run off with it, no. I think that you have eaten since I saw you last, and therefore it will do you no harm to drink before you go.'

Aquila was suddenly on his guard, his reason telling him that Eugenus was not the type of man to be asking every chance, dusty wayfarer he met into his chamber to drink with him. He demanded bluntly, 'Why did you leave word that I was to bring the harness up to you myself, and why do you seek to keep me here, now that I have brought it?'

Eugenus poured out the wine before he answered, and pushed the wine-cup across the table. 'For a very simple and a very innocent reason. I am interested in people—in interesting people, that is to say.'

Aquila frowned. 'You find me interesting?'

'I—think so, yes.' The physician lowered himself on to the couch and leaned back, fingering his stomach as gently and sensitively as though it were somebody else's, with a pain in it. But his eyes never left Aquila's face. 'You have a very bitter face, my young friend, and I think that it was not always so. Also there are about you certain contradictions. You are—forgive me—extremely ragged and dusty, and carry what looks very much like the scar of a Saxon thrall-ring on your neck; you are without the price of a meal; yet when I proffer you a sesterce in charity, you stiffen, and give me to understand that if you may earn it, and not otherwise, you will do me the favour of accepting it. And all the while you wear on your hand a signet ring that would pay for many meals.'

'It was my father's ring, and it is not for sale,' Aquila said.

'Your father being dead, I take it? Maybe at the Saxons' hands?'

Aquila was silent a moment, facing the questing interest in the full, dark eyes. His mouth was tight and hard. 'My father was killed by the Saxon kind, three years ago,' he said at last, 'and I was carried off into thraldom. My father's ring came to me again in a way that does not matter to anyone save myself. I escaped from the Saxon camp on Tanatus and now I am on a journey. Does that answer all your questions?'

Eugenus smiled; a smile that was big and slow like himself; but there was all at once a new alertness in his gaze. 'What an inquisitive creature I am. This journey—where does it lead you?'

'Westwards, into the mountains.'

'So. That is a long journey. *It is all of two hundred miles from Venta to the Mountains.*'

Aquila, who had taken up the cup of wine, set it down again with great care, as though he were afraid of spilling it. He felt exactly as though he had been jolted in the stomach, and the memory of the terrace steps at home and the sharp brown face of the bird-catcher sprang out before his inner eye. There was a long silence, and then he looked up. 'Why did you say that?'

'To see if the phrase meant anything to you, and it does, doesn't it?'

'My father was one of Ambrosius's men; it was so that he died by Vortigern's order,' Aquila said harshly. 'What made you guess that the old password would mean anything to me?'

Eugenus made a deprecating gesture of one hand—a plump hand, unexpectedly small for such a big man. 'Oh, it was nothing so definite as a guess. Merely the wildest arrow loosed in the dark, that could do no harm if it missed its target.'

'Who are you?' Aquila demanded.

'I was personal physician to Constantine when he ruled in Venta Belgarum. Now I serve Ambrosius his son in the same capacity, and occasionally, as at present, as a strictly unofficial envoy.'

There was another silence, and then Aquila said, 'Do you believe in blind chance?'

'Meaning, do I believe it was by blind chance that you, on your way, as I take it, to lay your sword—if you had one—at Ambrosius's feet, should fall in with Ambrosius's envoy in the gateway of the Golden Grapevine at Uroconium?'

Aquila nodded.

Eugenus puckered his lips a little. 'Blind chance has about it, somehow, the ugly sound of despair; a world without form or meaning. Let us say that if it was chance, it was a kindly one. For me a most fortunate one; for tomorrow, having completed my mission here, or rather, failed to complete it with any success—as you say, this is so far inland that they have not felt the Saxon wind blowing—I return to Ambrosius in the mountains. And since I am by nature a sociable creature, I shall be delighted to have company on the road.'

The river rushed and sang and dawdled beside the track, and on either side the mountains soared upwards, out of the tawny woodlands into bare, mist-scarfed rock and fading bell heather. The clop of the mule's hooves and the jingle of little bells that seemed out of place in the great solitude nagged at Aquila's ears as he trudged beside the beast on which Eugenus rode. Eugenus sat slumped in the saddle, sighing and snorting. He was soft; one of those unfortunates who never seem to get hardened by the things that harden and toughen most people; but his spirit rose above the flabbiness of his big body: Aquila had learned that in the week and more that they had travelled together.

A week and more that had brought them up from Uroconium among its orchards and water-meadows, into the wild heart of the Arfon Mountains. 'Eryri, the Home of the Eagles,' Eugenus had said when first they saw the distant mass of interlocking peaks against the sunset, with Yr Widdfa standing like a king in their midst, and Aquila thought that the name was a fitting one.

Presently the valley opened before them, and the track dipped to skirt the alder-grown fringes of a lake. Faint mist hung over the water, rising already among the alders, and creeping up the glens and corries of the far mountain-sides that were already blue with the first twilight of the autumn evening. Rising out of the mist, as he looked away southward beyond the foot of the lake. Aquila saw a great, round hill standing boldly out from the mountains behind, as though to close the valley; and caught even at that distance the trace of rampart walls that lay like a coiled snake about and about and about the huge, up-thrusting mass of it.

'Ah-h-h!' Eugenus heaved a gusty and heartfelt sigh of relief. 'Dynas Ffaraon! And never did I see a more welcome sight, for I am saddle-sore from the crown of my head to the soles of my feet.' And then, glancing about him at the mist creeping up over the matted heather and bog myrtle: 'Also I think that we have arrived just in time, for poor, fat, comfort-loving creature that I am, I have no liking for riding blind in one of our mountain mists.'

Aquila nodded, his gaze fixed on the fortress hill that seemed to close the valley. 'And so that is Ambrosius's stronghold,' he said, and there was both wonder and a faint distrust in his tone.

'That is Ambrosius's stronghold from the autumn round again to the spring. It was old before the Legions drove their first road through the mountains to build Segontium on the coast, and has served many princes in its time.' Eugenus gave him a glance of amused understanding. 'You find it not to your liking?'

'Maybe it was well enough for some wild mountain princeling of the old time,' Aquila said.

'But not for Ambrosius the son of Constantine, that last hope of Britain? You must realize that this old hill fortress has always been the ruling-place of the Lords of Arfon, and as such it has a power in men's minds that Segontium of the Legions could never have; though it is to Segontium that he calls his young men for training in the summer. Not for nothing is it called Dynas Ffaraon, the Fortress of the High Powers . . . Also let you not forget that it was from this hill fort that Constantine came down in his day, to drive the Saxons into the sea.'

Aquila looked up at the big, weary man on the mule's back, and asked the question that he had been on the edge of asking many times since Uroconium. 'Will Ambrosius ever come down from the mountains as his father did? Is it a living cause, Eugenus, or a dead one that men serve because they loved it when it was alive?'

'Speaking for myself,' Eugenus said after a moment, 'I think that I might die for a dead cause, but I do not think, I really do *not* think, my young friend, that I could bring myself to ride up and down the world on anything so uncomfortable as a mule, in its service.'

And they went on in silence, the mist thickening little by little about them. Aquila had accepted what Eugenus had said, but his uneasiness remained. He had thought of young Ambrosius as the leader of men like his father, but now he began to realize that the son of Constantine was something very much more complicated than that. Not only the leader of the Roman party, but the Lord of Arfon, a man belonging to two worlds. Was he, after all, only another Vortigern?

Slowly the fortress hill drew nearer until it towered right above them in the mist and the lake was left behind; Aquila saw that it did not after all close the valley, but left a narrow pass through which both the track and the river ran on. A rocky path swung right-handed, rounding some stone-walled cattle enclosures, and took the steep upward slope at a bound; and as Aquila took hold of the mule's head-gear to help the poor brute, suddenly out of the mist that was growing thicker every moment there loomed on either side of them the great, rough-hewn walls of the first defences. The path squeezed its way through, and plunged on upward. In the softer and more level places it was a slithering quagmire, at others it ran out on to bare, mist-wet rock. Other great ramparts, part man-made, part natural outcrop, loomed through the drifting whiteness as the path went leaping and looping upward; and Aquila sensed people near him, and glimpsed the crouching shapes of turf-roofed bothies among the rocks and hazel scrub, for it seemed that all up the slopes of the fortress hill, wherever there was foothold for a bothy, men had their living-places. But they met nobody until they were about halfway up. Then a young man with a couple of huge, rough-coated hounds in leash came round the next corner out of the mist, and stopped at sight of them. 'Sa ha! Eugenus! I thought it must be you when I heard that fairy chiming of mule bells. What news of the outer world?'

Eugenus brought his weary mule to a halt. 'None that cannot wait until I have first seen Ambrosius. What news of the world here, Brychan?'

The other shrugged. 'What news is there ever, here in the mountains? You have come in a good time, though. Belarius has had his thigh laid open by a boar, and that fool Amlodd doesn't seem able to do much about it.'

Eugenus sighed. 'Other men may rest at their journey's end, but so sure as I return weary from distant parts, somebody waits for me with a fever or a gored leg! Where is he?'

'In his hut.'

'I'll go round and take a look at him as soon as I reach the top—if

I ever do. I swear by Æsculapius's Rod, this track grows steeper and longer as the years go by.'

Eugenus was already urging his mule on again: but the young man still stood directly in his path. A very tall young man in a close-fitting tunic of many-coloured plaid, with a smooth cap of darkly golden hair and a laughing, insolent face. He flicked a long finger towards Aquila. 'Who is this that you have collected on your travels?'

'A friend,' Eugenus said. 'Maybe he will tell you his name himself, later, if you ask him.'

The young man looked at Aquila, and Aquila looked back. 'So? I may ask him—some time, if I chance to remember,' the young man said coolly.

The frown that was always between Aquila's brows deepened. 'If you do, I would suggest that you ask in a more courteous manner.'

Again they looked at each other, with a quarrel smouldering between them; and then suddenly laughter won in the young man's face. 'It may be that I will even do that!' He stepped aside, flinging up his hand in greeting and farewell to Eugenus, and went on down the track.

Aquila stood a moment, still frowning, looking after him as he merged into the twilight and the mist, then turned once more to the steep climb as Eugenus, saying blandly, 'Shall we go on?' shook the reins and urged his tired mule into movement again.

The track levelled for a few yards, then swung inward and upward, cutting through the side of a sheer outcrop of black rock, and looking up Aquila saw the innermost ramparts close above him, and a tall man leaning on a spear in the gateway, with nothing but the wet, smoking mist behind him.

A short while later he was walking over the hill crest into that mist, alone, while Eugenus, tumbling from the mule's back like a sack of peat, went to tend his patient.

'Go up to the Fire-hall,' Eugenus had said. 'You can see the roof ridge over the lift of the ground yonder. It must be close on supper time, and Ambrosius may be there already. If he is not, wait for me.'

But the mist had become a dense whiteness, salt tasting on his lips, that wreathed about him like a wet smoke out of which the huts and bothies loomed and were lost in the fading light. The roof ridge of Ambrosius's Fire-hall had dissolved into the mist, as though it had never been. Maybe he had been a fool to refuse when the man who took over the mule had offered to come with him. It had been a friendly offer, and once he would have accepted it gladly. But he turned away from all things that were friendly now. He held on in what he thought was the right direction. There was peat reek in the air, and the tang of horse-droppings and the fat smell of cooking; he heard cattle lowing in the mist, and knew that people were coming and going about their usual business, but saw no one of whom to ask his way. Suddenly the ground dipped beneath his feet, and he found himself on the edge of a little hollow with the gleam of water at the bottom of it. He halted, and as he stood there his ear caught very faintly the struck notes of a harp that seemed to rise from that gleam of water. Through the mist, he made out the crouching shapes of a cluster of huts; and from the doorway of the largest came the faint, amber gleam of firelight. At all events there must be someone down there to tell him where he was. So he turned his steps down into the little hollow.

A few moments later he stood on the threshold of the largest hut, between the swirling mist and the firelight. The fire burned on a raised hearth in the midst of the big, round house-place, and all the place was fragrant with the smoke of peat and wild apple logs that hung in a blue haze under the crown of the roof, and the fluttering flame-light showed Aquila, at that first swift glance, the glint of weapons along the walls and hanging from the king-post, and that for the most part they were the long swords and small, round bucklers of Roman Cavalry. But if the hut was an armoury, clearly it was a living-place as well. On the creamy, spread ram-skins of the bed-place an old man sat with his harp on his knee, his head bent over it as though he slept, and his fingers plucking the shining strings so softly and wanderingly that it was as though he played in his sleep. And beside the hearth a man with a pouchy face and a general air of having run to seed, but something in the set of his shoulders that made Aquila instantly think of the parade-ground none the less, stood looking down at a third who crouched on one knee, tracing something with a charred stick on the flagged floor beside the hearthstone. A slight, dark man, this, of about Aquila's own age, in a rough, home-spun-tunic, and a sheepskin with the fleece inside belted about his waist for a mantle, but a narrow gold fillet round his head, such as Aquila had seen the Celtic nobles wear before now.

'Aye, it is well enough, though the bend of the Tamesis should be somewhat sharper,' the man with drilled shoulders was saying. 'If you make that map many times more, I am thinking that you will be able to make it blindfold.'

'There is always something new, Valarius,' the dark young man said, speaking in Latin with an accent that was somehow just a little too pure, as though it were not quite his native tongue. 'And I must be able to carry it in my head, so that I have but to shut my eyes to see it all here on the hearth, as a Royal Eagle in the sky must see the whole of Britain spread below him.' He looked up, and saw Aquila in the doorway, and rose, the charred stick still in his hand. 'I greet you, stranger. Have you some message for me?'

Aquila shook his head. 'I seek Ambrosius, Prince of Britain, and was told that I might find him in the Fire-hall. But I have lost the Fire-hall in this fiend's brew of a mist—and seeing your firelight and hearing your harper—'

The young man tossed the charred stick into the flames. 'It is early yet, and Ambrosius will not have gone to the Fire-hall. What is it that you want with him?'

'If I had a sword, I should say "To lay it at his feet".'

For a moment they stood looking at each other in the firelight, while the old harper still fingered the shining strings, and the other man looked on with a gleam of amusement lurking in his watery blue eyes. But Aquila was not looking at him. He was looking only at the dark young man, seeing that he was darker even than he had thought at first, and slightly built in a way that went with the darkness, as though maybe the old blood, the blood of the People of the Hills, ran strong in him. But his eyes, under brows as straight as a raven's flight-pinions, were not the eyes of the Little Dark People, that were black and unstable and full of dreams, but a pale, clear grey lit with gold that gave the effect of flame behind them.

'But you have no sword,' the dark young man said.

'I had once.'

'Tell me how you lost it.'

Afterwards, Aquila never knew how it was that he neither questioned the dark man's right to ask, nor guessed the truth about him. Maybe the mist had got into his head—mists were notoriously unchancy things. He came in from the doorway without knowing that he did so, and standing beside the hearth with the fragrant smoke of the burning apple logs fronding across his face, he gave account of himself in a few brief, harsh sentences, much as he had done to

Eugenus. 'So I came west to take my father's service upon me if that may be,' he ended, 'not loving greatly either the Saxon kind or the Red Fox.'

'Not loving greatly either the Saxon kind or the Red Fox,' the dark young man echoed broodingly. 'Yes, there are things easier to forgive than the murder of one's father.' He stood looking at Aquila for a few moments: a long look, a hard look. Then he turned and took down from among the weapons that hung on the king-post a long cavalry sword in a rough, wolfskin sheath. He drew it with a swift, controlled gesture—swiftness and control were in all he did—ran his eye along the brightness of the blade, and sheathing it again, held it out, hilt foremost. 'Here is your sword.'

Aquila's hand moved involuntarily to close round the familiar grip. But in the act, he checked, his head up and the frown deepening between his brows; and then a sudden suspicion of the truth dawned on him. 'Do you usually decide who Ambrosius shall take into his service?'

The dark young man smiled—a swift flash of a smile that seemed to kindle his whole narrow face. 'Usually—I *am* Ambrosius, Prince of Britain.'

Aquila was silent a long moment. Then he said, 'Yes, I should have known that . . . May I serve you as truly as my father did, my Lord Ambrosius.' He put out his hand again, and his fingers closed round the plain, workmanlike bronze hilt.

So Aquila took his father's service upon him. It wasn't as good as love; it wasn't as good as hate; but it was something to put into the emptiness within him; better than nothing at all.

XI
The Young Foxes

ON a day in early spring, Aquila came up from the level valley to the south of Dynas Ffaraon, where the wild, leggy two-year-olds singled out from the horse herds were gathered for breaking. The Celts were all horse-breeders and breakers, and now it seemed that every sheltered glen in Arfon had its herds of brood mares, its long-legged, tangle-maned colts who would one day be the horses of the British Cavalry. Aquila, cavalry trained as he was, had worked with the breakers all winter. If he worked hard enough and long enough, spending mind and strength and skill in the battle with some wild and whirling young stallion, and came back to Ambrosius's Fire-hall so tired that sleep closed over him almost before the evening meal was eaten, it was easier not to think, not to remember.

The snows were melting on the high southern face of Yr Widdfa, and the sound of running water was everywhere, mingling with the wild, sweet, bubbling call of curlews from the high heather slopes above the valley; and the hazel scrub along the skirts of the fortress hill was dappled mealy gold with catkins. The strangeness was gone from the fortress hill, no mist hung above it now save the faint blue haze of cooking-fires, as Aquila looked up at it. It was just a place that he knew, as he knew other places, with people that he knew in it: old Finnen the Harper, and Valarius with his pouchy red face and watery blue eyes, who had been of Constantine's bodyguard in his better days; Fat Eugenus, and the lean and fiery little priest Eliphias, with his prophet's eye; Brychan with his two great hounds—the men, mostly young, who formed a kind of inner circle, a brotherhood, round Ambrosius, and whom he called his Companions.

He headed for the winding cleft in the hill-side where the trickle from the fortress spring in its little hollow came down. It was a climb for goats, but it saved going round to pick up the track on the north side of the hill. There was a thin warmth from the sun on the back of his neck, as he climbed, and a flittering of tits among the still-bare blackthorn bushes that arched over the little thread of water, and the small purple flowers of the butterwort cushioned the wet, starling-coloured rocks. More than halfway up, where the cleft widened and the freshet had worn a tiny pool for itself among rocks and tree-roots, he found a small boy and a hound puppy very intent on a hole under a brown tumble of last year's ferns. He would have passed by without speaking and left them to it, but the small boy sat up and grinned at him, thrusting back a shock of hair the warm, silvery-mouse colour of a hayfield in June, and the puppy thumped its tail; there was something so irresistibly friendly about both of them that he stopped, without meaning to, pointing at the hole.

'Is it a grass-snake?'

The boy nodded. 'We have been watching for him a long while, Cabal and I. He came out yesterday. A monster!' He hooked an arm round the puppy's neck. 'When he comes out again, I am going to catch him and take him up to show Ambrosius.'

Artorius—Artos, most people called him, meaning a bear—was Ambrosius's nephew, bastard son to his brother Utha; and when Utha died, Ambrosius had taken him. From that day, Ambrosius had become Artos's private God.

Suddenly he remembered something which in his concentration on the grass-snake he had forgotten; Aquila saw his eyes darken with excitement in his square, brown face. 'Did you hear the messenger come?'

'No,' Aquila said, his foot already on the next step of the climb. 'What messenger was that, then?'

'From Canovium. His horse was all in a smother. He said that Vortigern has put away his real wife and married Hengest's daughter instead, and given Hengest a *huge* piece of land, that wasn't his to give, for a bride piece!'

Aquila brought his foot down again. 'Since when have Ambrosius's messengers told their news to Artos the bear cub?'

The boy nodded, gravely vehement. 'He didn't tell me, of course. But it is true! All the Dun is buzzing with it.' He sat up straighter, his eyes fixed on Aquila's face. 'They say she's very beautiful—Hengest's daughter.'

'She is,' Aquila said.

'Have you seen her?'

'Yes, when I was a thrall in the Jutish camp.'

'What is she like?'

'A golden witch in a crimson gown.'

'Oh,' said Artos, digesting this. He brushed the hair of the puppy's neck up the wrong way, parting it between his fingers as though in search of ticks. 'It's sad for Vortigern's real wife,' he said gruffly, and then, his excitement quickening again, 'What do you think will happen now? Something is *bound* to happen now!'

'Is it?' Aquila said. He stood silent a few moments, staring at the little dark hole under the ferns, while the boy and the puppy watched him expectantly. 'Yes, I suppose it is . . . Good grass-snake hunting to you.' And he stepped over the puppy and went on up. Rowena had made her singing magic well, he thought; she had caught the Red Fox in a net of her golden hair; and what would happen now? What would the three Young Foxes do about their mother's wrongs? So much might depend on that.

But there was little time for wondering in the days that followed. For with spring running through the glens, Ambrosius was making ready to go down from Dynas Ffaraon to the coast.

The grey stone fortress of Segontium, that crouched on its low hill with its seaward ramparts reflected in the narrow straits of Môn, had been abandoned by the Legions long before they marched from Britain, and the tribesmen had taken from it all of Rome that could be carried off, and left it to the mountain foxes. But now it had been pressed into service again to help defend the coast against the Scots from Erin who swarmed all along the western shores in the raiding season, its broken walls patched up, its fallen roofs replaced with bracken thatch. There was fire again on its cold hearths and horses in its stable rows. Here Ambrosius made his headquarters while spring drew on, and day by day the old grey fortress became fuller of crowding life as the young men of the little standing army that he had been gathering in the last few years came in for their summer training. And in the grain-lands of Môn across the Straits men ploughed, and sowed the barley, while the coastwise guards kept watch westward for the first dark sails of the Scots raiders.

But the Scots were late that year, and still there had been no sign of them, and no more news of the outside world, when Ambrosius went north for a few days, with a handful of his chosen Companions, to Aber of the White Shells, at the place where the northern road from Canovium came down through the mountains to the coast.

On the third day that they were at Aber, they had been out with Dogfael the Chieftain and some of his warriors, trying their horses against each other on the hard, wave-rippled sands that stretched towards Môn: and now they were heading back towards the dunes that fringed the coast. The wind blustered in from the sea, setting the horses' manes streaming sideways, and the gulls wheeled mewing against the blue-and-grey tumble of the sky; and Aquila, riding a little aside from the rest as usual, caught for a moment from the wind and the gulls and the wet sand and the living, leaping power of the young red mare under him, something of the joy of simply being alive that he had taken for granted in the old days. He still wasn't certain how he came to be there, one of the inner circle, one of Ambrosius's chosen Companions; it was a thing that had grown naturally through the winter. But suddenly for that one moment he was glad that it was so.

As they swept inland, a gap widened in the dunes where the stream came down. He could see the bracken-thatched huddle of the village now, at the mouth of the valley that licked like a green flame into the dun and grey and purple of the mountains; and beyond it the Legion's road that came plunging down from the high mountain saddle. And far up that road he could see a puff of dust with a seed of blackness at its heart; a seed which, even as he watched, became a horseman riding at full gallop.

The others had seen it at the same moment. Ambrosius spoke to Dogfael riding beside him, and urged his black stallion into a canter, the rest following. Aquila, driving his heel into the red mare's flank, found himself riding beside Brychan—Brychan of the two great hounds, who could take the harp from old Finnen and charm a bird off a tree with his playing, but whose chief joy in life was the picking of quarrels. Brychan had come to him, a while after their first encounter, and asked his name with an elaborate show of deference, long after he must have known it perfectly well, and Aquila had longed to put the puppy across his knee and teach him manners with the flat of his hand. But he was used to Brychan now, and there was a kind of armed peace between them, within which they got on well enough together. Brychan cast a quick glance at him over his shoulder, and grinned. 'If it is news that must travel at that pace, then surely it is news to melt the snows of Yr Widdfa!'

They lost sight of the road for a few moments among the dunes, and when they swept through onto the landward side, the wild rider was already past the village and coming on towards them at the same tearing gallop. A few moments later he had brought his rough-coated pony to a plunging halt, and dropped from its back; a young, round-faced warrior, looking from Dogfael to Ambrosius and back again, his breast panting.

'My Lord Ambrosius—Dogfael the Chieftain—there is a band of men on the road from Canovium. They were past the Mark Stones when I saw them, and I have galloped all the way to bring you word.'

'It is not the first time that men have come down the road from Canovium,' Dogfael said.

But Ambrosius looked at the panting young warrior. 'What is different about these men?'

'My Lord Ambrosius, the three who lead them carry green branches like an embassy that comes in peace, and the heads of all three shine red as foxes' pelts in the sunshine!'

He checked, almost choking with the hugeness of the thing he had to say. 'My Lord Ambrosius, it is in my mind that it is—the Young Foxes!'

For a moment there was absolute silence save for the crying of the gulls. Then Ambrosius said, 'I wonder if you are right,' and turned to the others about him. 'Well, we shall soon know. Valarius, Aquila, follow me.'

'I also, and some of my warriors,' Dogfael said quickly.

'Neither you, nor any of your warriors, I think.'

But Valarius seconded the Chieftain, his watery eyes full of urgent trouble. 'Sir, you should have more of us with you. It may be a trick!'

Before Ambrosius could answer, Brychan flung up his head and laughed. 'Valarius the cautious thinks maybe of his own skin! Best take me in his stead, sir.'

The old soldier swung round on him with his hand on the hilt of his sword. 'Why, you—you young whelp! Let you say that again—' His face was darkly mottled and he breathed through flaring nostrils with a rage that seemed to Aquila, watching, to be out of all proportion to what had called it up. Surely the fool had known Brychan long enough to understand that this was merely Brychan being himself!

'If you want to fight me, I am most joyfully all yours, when we ride back again,' Brychan said lightly. 'Don't drink any more before then; it makes your sword hand unsure.'

Ambrosius's voice cut quietly into the flaring quarrel. 'Peace, my brothers! I have other things to do than beat up your swords, either now or later. Brychan, your manners grow worse as the days go by. Valarius, have you not sense to make allowances for a half-broken cub?' And while Brychan shrugged, and Valarius sat gnawing his lower lip, he turned to Dogfael. 'If these men come in friendship, I should do ill to ride to meet them with a swarm of armed men about me.'

But it was Valarius who answered, grimly sticking to his point. 'And if they do *not* in truth come in friendship?'

His voice was shaking, and Aquila, glancing at his bridle hand, saw that it was shaking too, and realized that there was something here that he did not understand.

Ambrosius was already wheeling his horse towards the road; he looked round at them. 'One man with a dagger under his cloak would be as like to succeed as three men with a war band behind them . . . If it is God's will that I am to lead Britain, then I shall not die as my father did at a murderer's hand, with my work undone. If I die so, then you and Eugenus and old Finnen with his harp had all your pains for nothing, when you carried me off that night, and after all it is not God's will that I should lead Britain.'

He struck his heel into the black stallion's flank, and the great brute broke forward from a stand into a canter; and he was away, his dark cloak lifting and spreading behind him. Aquila and Valarius heeled their own horses to a canter after him, and so, with only his two chosen Companions, Ambrosius rode up towards the mountain pass, to meet the three red-haired riders.

The road swept on and up, the great mountain mass that thronged about Yr Widdfa towering dark as a gathering thunder storm on either side. Presently they were in a different world from the green valley and the white sands of Aber left far behind: a high, wide-skied, empty world, with no sound beyond the beat of their horses' hooves save the wind through the tawny mountain grasses, and the sharp cry of a golden eagle that hung circling above the crags. Then the road lifted over the mountain shoulder, and the next long, looping stretch lay clear ahead, with a distant knot of horsemen sweeping towards them along it.

'So, here we meet our guests,' Ambrosius said, and striking his heel again into the black's flank, broke forward into a full gallop,

Aquila and Valarius behind him. And so the two knots of horsemen thundered towards each other, with the dust of early summer rising behind them. Aquila saw three men riding ahead of the stranger band; three men whose flying cloaks made points of vivid colour in the pale mountain air, one saffron, one emerald, and one, whose wearer rode at the very point of the arrowhead of wild riders, glowing violet; and the heads of all three shone red as a fox's pelt in the sunshine. Nearer and nearer they swept, until the two dust-clouds were almost one, and Ambrosius reined the black stallion back on its haunches, in full gallop, plunging and snorting, the great round hooves scraping along the ground. There were a few moments of trampling chaos as the sweating horses plunged under their riders, fighting for the heads; and then the dust sank a little, and the two knots of horsemen were facing each other with a spear's length of road between. The man in the violet cloak wheeled his tiger-spotted mount with superb horsemanship, and brought him out from among his companions, almost with a dancing step; and Aquila, still soothing his own red mare as she fidgeted under him, recognized the white, proud face under the flaming crest of hair, and the hooded falcon he carried on his fist, just as he had carried it in Hengest's Mead Hall a year ago.

'I greet you, strangers. Who are you that come over the mountains with green branches in your hands?' Ambrosius asked, as the last of the dust-cloud drifted away.

Vortimer lowered the spray of birch leaves that he held in his bridle hand, and sat for an instant lithe and haughty in the saddle, looking Ambrosius full in the face; and, watching him, Aquila thought suddenly of a purple saffron crocus—the same pride, the same silken sheen. Then he said, 'We three are the sons of Vortigern the High King, and we would speak with Ambrosius Aurelianus, Lord of Arfon.'

Ambrosius, sitting his fidgeting black stallion, looked back with a quieter and cooler pride. 'I am Ambrosius Aurelianus, Prince of Britain,' he said; and then, 'To all who come in friendship, I give welcome; to a kinsman most of all.'

Aquila looked at them quickly. He had forgotten that they were cousins, the dark man and the red ones.

Vortimer bent his head in acknowledgement of both rebuke and welcome. 'My Lord Ambrosius, Lord of Arfon and Prince of Britain, we come to lay our swords at your feet and be your men if you will have it so.'

'Deserting the standard of Vortigern your father, to serve under mine?'

There was a low, angry muttering from the men behind. The two younger brothers stared straight before them, frowning. Vortimer spoke for them again, his head up and the mountain wind lifting the red hair on his forehead. 'My Lord Ambrosius will maybe have heard that our father has put aside Severa our mother, to take in her place the golden Saxon witch who is Hengest's daughter. My lord will have heard also that he has given much land east of Tanatus to the Saxons for a bride gift. Therefore with our mother's wrongs burning upon us we come to lay our swords at your feet. Also we do not come alone and empty-handed. With us here are seven Chieftains who were our father's men; they will bring over their clans; and there are others besides, more than half of those that followed him—for the sake of our mother's wrongs and for the sake of British lands given over their prince's head to the Saxon kind.'

So Vortigern had gone too far, Aquila thought, Hengest, that giant with the shifting, grey-green eyes, had overreached himself. Between them they had split the Celtic party from top to bottom, and sent more than half of them to Ambrosius. If Ambrosius would take them—and Ambrosius must take them; it would be madness to refuse; but they might be a weakness as well as an added strength.

'Are the Saxon kind, then, become yet more hateful to you than Rome has always been?'Ambrosius said levelly.

The silence held for a long moment, broken only by the soughing of the wind through the heather and the jink of a bridle-bit as a horse flung up its head. Then Vortimer spoke again for his fellows. 'My Lord Ambrosius, we are a free people, taking hardly to any yoke; but for us, now, the Saxon yoke is unthinkable above all others. Therefore we stand with you against the menace of the Saxon kind. Let you speak one word and we will ride back with it by the road that we have come, to gather all the fighting men we may. Then, before summer's end, look for our spears against the sunrise.'

'How may I be sure that all this is not a trick to bring an army through our defences?'

'One of us three, whichever you choose, will remain here in your hands as a hostage for our good faith,' Vortimer said proudly.

Ambrosius shook his head. 'Nay, I ask no hostage.' He had come to his decision, and he was smiling. Aquila, close behind him, could hear both the decision and the smile in his voice. 'I speak the word, Vortimer my kinsman; let you ride back with it to those that follow you. But not yet. First there are many things on which we must take counsel together. I have no need of more men here in the mountains, nor space, nor fodder; my need is to know that I can call upon them when the time comes. All that we must speak of. Meanwhile come back with us now, and feast among my Companions tonight, that we may seal the covenant in mead from our mountain heather honey.'

Vortimer looked at him a moment, not speaking. Then he thrust the spray of birch leaves into his belt, and swung down from the saddle, and with the bridle over his arm and the tiger-spotted horse pacing beside him, came to set his hand on Ambrosius's thigh, and take the oath of allegiance on him.

'If we break faith with you, may the green earth gape and swallow us, may the grey seas roll in and overwhelm us, may the sky of stars fall on us and crush us out of life for ever.'

It was an ancient oath, well suited to the mountains and the wild scene. The two younger brothers, who had also dismounted, came and took it after him. They would keep faith, the Young Foxes, Aquila thought; but what of those who followed them? Out of the knot of Chieftains, another face looked back at him, a dark, reckless face as dangerous as a dagger-thrust; Guitolinus somebody had said his name was. His eyes were dark blue, and the sun made raw turquoise flecks in them, the eyes of a fanatic, beyond the binding of any oath.

That evening Ambrosius with his Companions and the Young Foxes with their following feasted side by side in the bracken-thatched hall of Dogfael. The fire cast a web of leaping, tawny light over the ring of alert faces; over fine wool the colour of jewels, and pied and dappled sheepskin, the blink of Irish gold from the hilt of a dagger, the green, unwinking eyes of a hound, the fiercely flecked breast of the hooded falcon secured by its jesses to the back of Vortimer's seat. And all round the long hearth ran a kind of shining, jagged thorn garland, where every man had drawn his sword and laid it before him in full view of all the rest. By ancient custom no man should bring his weapons to such a gathering, but on the coast in these days no man went unarmed.

Aquila's neighbour was a middle-aged man, Cradoc by name, with sandy hair like the ruffled feathers of a bird in a high wind, and a face full of old regrets. He was a Chieftain from further south, and found all things here in the north of Cymru to be less good than in his own mountains.

'In Powys,' he was saying, 'where I have my hall, the turf is richer even at mid-winter than this valley is now; and the soil is red and strong. I have an apple orchard running to the river, and in the autumn every tree in it bows to the ground under its weight of apples.' And then, looking regretfully into his cup, 'Our mead is better than this, too.'

Ambrosius rose in his place, that on other nights was Dogfael the Chieftain's, holding high his golden cup, and turned to Vortimer beside him. 'I drink to our friendship, and the new bond between us.'

He drank, and gave the cup to the Young Fox, who took it from him with a bend of the head, and stood for a moment spear-straight in the firelight with the great cup shining between his hands. Then, almost in the act of drinking, he checked, and his head whipped up, as, clear in the hush that had fallen on the hall from somewhere seaward beyond the village rose a long-drawn cry.

There was a moment's tingling silence, while the men about the fire looked each into his neighbour's eyes, and then a scatter of shouting broke out in the village itself.

'It is in my mind that the Scots wind blows again from Erin,' Ambrosius said, and stooped for his sword.

As though the action had broken a spell of stillness, a splurge of voices burst up in the hall; and every man had sprung to his feet, catching up his weapons, when a man burst through the doorway into the firelight, crying, 'The Scots! They're close in shore, heading for the bay!'

Ambrosius whirled about on them, his light eyes blazing, his sword naked in his hand. 'We are to fight our first battle together sooner than we thought! Come, my brothers!'

The big, silver-fringed clouds were drifting overhead before a light sea wind as they headed for the shore, joined as they ran by every man and boy in Aber of the White Shells, and the moon rode high in the deep blue of the sky between. The tide was in, covering the sand where they had raced their horses a few hours earlier, and out on the tossing, quicksilver surface of the bay three vessels showed dark: low amidships, high at stem and stern like venomous sea creatures with head and tail upreared to strike: many-legged creatures, for the sails were down and they were creeping in under oars.

'Down into the cover of the dunes,' Ambrosius ordered. 'Let them not see you until the ships are fairly beached and I give the word. So maybe there shall be three Scots ships the less to come raiding our shores in another summer.' And the order ran from man to man. 'Get down—keep out of sight!'

As he crouched in the lee of the furze tangle, Aquila's view of the shore was cut off by the shoulder of the long dune where the stream came through, but that made no odds: there was nothing to do but wait until Ambrosius gave the word . . . He found that Cradoc was still at his shoulder, suddenly much happier and with the superiority of the south quite forgotten.

'Sa! This is better than feasting!' Cradoc said softly.

Aquila nodded, shifting his hand a little on the grip of his buckler. Better than feasting; there was not much pleasure for him in feasting, these days; but in that moment of waiting there was a keen, cold pleasure as sharp as the blade in his hand. The moments passed, silent save for the sea wind in the furze and the creamings of the tide beyond the dunes. Then, very faintly, his straining ears caught the dip of oars; and a shiver of expectancy ran through the waiting men. A few moments more, and there came, faint but unmistakable, the light splash of men slipping overboard and the grating of a keel on the beach. A pause, and then the sounds were repeated as the second galley was run up the sand, the third following so close that Aquila could not tell where one ended and the other began. There was a grumble of orders, and a low, daring laugh. He could hear men splashing ashore through the shallows now; and he drew a deep, slow breath, his body tensing under him like that of a runner in the instant before the white garland falls. And then, on the very crest of the dune before him, Ambrosius rose with a yell, his sword above his head.

'Now! With me. my brothers!'

They saw him stand for an instant against the drifting sky; then they rose like a wave and swept after him, across the crest and down over the slipping sand.

The three raiders lay in the shallows, their dark bows on shore like so many stranded sea-beasts, and men were swarming up the beach, the moon on their weapons and the lime-whitened discs of their shields. The sea-raiders and the British—for all those who followed Ambrosius were British at that moment, with no thought of Celt or Roman—came together above the tide-line in the soft sand at the foot of the dunes, sword to sword, shield to shield, in a ragged burst of shouting. The Scots, taken by surprise when they had thought the surprise to be on their side, attacked furiously at first, shouting their battle-cry as they closed buckler to buckler and strove to break through; and for a time the fight hung in the balance, as now one side drove forward and now the other, the whole skirmish wavering this way and that like a banner streaming in the wind. Aquila's ears were full of a great yelling, and the clash and rasp of weapons. The soft, shifting sand clogged his feet and the fine lime-dust from the enemy shields rose white in the moonlight. Cradoc was still at his shoulder, shouting some wild, rhythmic battle-song of his own people that rose and rose above the tumult of the fighting into a kind of triumphant raving that was horrible to hear. From the swaying line of warriors a tall Scot leapt in with war-axe upswung, and Cradoc's war-song ended in a grunt. Aquila was aware of the place at his shoulder suddenly empty, and the moonlit flash of the axe blade raised to finish the work it had begun, and in the same instant he had sprung astride the fallen man, who was already struggling to his elbow among the trampling feet of the mêlée. He took the blow, as it came whistling down, on his upflung buckler, and the axe blade sheared through the bull's hide and beaten bronze, so that it was hacked almost in two. He bore down with all his force on the shield with the axe blade still embedded in it, and stabbed wildly with shortened sword point, and saw the Scot fling wide his arms and stagger back, gaping stupidly, as the blow went home.

He realized suddenly that the Scots were beginning to give ground, the wavering of the fighting line going all one way. Stubbornly, valiantly, fighting for every step before yielding it, they were back into the shallows now, the trampled spray sheeting up all about them in the moonlight, falling back more swiftly: no aim left but to win back to their ships. But around the stranded ships also there was fighting, as more of the British, led by the Young Foxes, flung themselves upon the men who had been left to guard them; and suddenly, from one of the galleys, from another, from the third, yellow tongues of fire shot up, licking about the masts. Someone had brought a fire-brand from the village, and there was to be no escape for this band of raiders. A yell, a howl rose from them as they saw the flames, and they turned as a doomed boar turns at bay, to make their last stand in the shallows about their blazing ships.

The silver of the moon was ousted by the angry gold of the burning vessels as the flames leapt higher, and there was gold in the hollow of every ripple that spread shoreward; gold, and then red . . . It was over at last, and the glare of the blazing galleys shone on dead men lying like sea-wrack along the tide-line; and the sea wind and the hushing of the tide sounded clear again. The British were taking stock of their own dead and wounded, and Aquila knelt over Cradoc, helping him staunch the blood that ran from the base of his neck.

Cradoc looked up at him with a twisted smile. 'Sa! It seems that they teach men to fight under the Eagles! It was a good fight; and that I am here to say so instead of lying in the sand with my head smitten from my shoulders is a thing that I owe to you. Also it is a thing that I shall not forget.'

'In the heat of battle it is no more to ward a blow from a comrade than to ward it from oneself,' Aquila said. 'Hold still or I cannot stop this bleeding. It is not a thing for remembering afterwards.'

A few paces off, in the full glare of the flames that leapt from the snarling prow of the nearest galley, Vortimer, with his gay crocus tunic gashed and stained and sodden about him, leaned on his reddened sword and smiled at Ambrosius as he stood in the gilded foam-fringe, starkly outlined against the flames. 'It is a good covenant, and we have sealed it in blood, which is better than the mead of feasting.'

XII
Brown Sister, Golden Sister

CRADOC had exaggerated the richness of his own valley, Aquila thought, as he rode down from the low saddle of the hills, following the track that the man at the ford in the last valley had pointed out to him. The place was mostly under bracken—bracken beginning to turn now, and patched with bright buttercup gold where it had been cut for litter and not yet carried; and the hall that he glimpsed below him in the bend of the valley, with its huddle of turf bothies around it, was the usual squat, heather-thatched hall of every petty Chieftain, lord of a few mountain valleys, a few hundred cattle, a few score spears. But maybe one's own valley, when one was away from it, was always richer than anyone else's; one's own orchard bore sweeter apples. Maybe even his own valley in the Down Country . . . He reined back his mind from the memory as he might have reined the red mare Inganiad back from a pit in the track before them.

It was almost a year since he had come up with Eugenus the Physician to take service with the Prince of Britain. A year in which he had made some kind of mended life for himself, some kind of place among Ambrosius's Companions, some kind of name for himself—and the name, he knew, was not altogether a pleasant one. The dark man with the scarred forehead and the frown always between his eyes had no friends. He went always in a kind of armour, and a man who does that cannot have friends. They called him the Dolphin, as old Bruni had done, because of the pattern on his shoulder; and they called him the Lone Wolf. Felix could have told them that he hadn't always been like that; Felix, with whom he had laughed, and shot wild fowl over Tanatus Marshes. But Felix was like enough dead by now in the Padus marshes in defence of Rome. They said the Vandals were pressing down Italy again.

Automatically he gathered the mare, steadying her for the stony, downward plunge of the track; but his thoughts went wandering back over the summer that had gone by since the Young Foxes had come in with their Chieftains behind them; the summer that he had spent training men as he had spent winter breaking horses, striving to hammer into wild, mounted tribesmen some idea of what made disciplined cavalry. It was odd to find himself something like a Decurion of Horse again.

Only a few weeks ago they had heard that Vortigern, deserted by his sons and most of his followers, had fled north, to the lands held by Octa and his war bands, and now Ambrosius rode south to hold counsel with his new allies. It was so that Aquila, sent ahead of the main party, was riding down into Cradoc's valley this still autumn day, to warn him that Ambrosius would be there by dusk, claiming lord's shelter for himself and his Companions as they passed by.

The Hall and its huddled bothies was drawing nearer, and he saw the hearth-smoke rising blue against the tawny flank of the mountain beyond, and a few people moving about the kale plots and the cattle-byres. The track swung right hand, towards the village, skirting a small orchard, an orchard cradled in the loop of the river, the apples ripe on the dipping branches of the little half-wild trees; and the bright shadow of a song came into his mind.

> The apples are silver on the boughs, low bending;
> A tree of chiming, of singing as the wind blows by.

But these apples were homely russet, not silver, and no wind stirred the branches; only the still, autumn sunlight slanted through the orchard, casting each tree's shadow to the foot of the next. But there was movement among the trees, a girl's laugh, and the flicker of colours under the leaves, dark red and saffron and tawny, and a deep, living blue like a kingfisher's mantle, and he realized that a group of girls were at the apple-picking.

It seemed that they became aware of the rider on the track at the same moment as he became aware of them. Their laughter stopped, and there was a moment's hush among the trees, and then two of the girls broke away from the rest, and ran back towards the Chieftain's Hall as though to carry word of his coming.

He rode on slowly, the bridle loose on Inganiad's neck. He heard the chink of a smith's hammer on anvil as he came up between the bracken-thatched bothies, and a woman coming from the weaving-shed with a piece of new cloth over her arm, the long threads still dangling where it had been cut from the loom, turned to watch him as he rode by; and a child and a hound puppy were struggling for possession of a wild cherry branch with the coral and scarlet leaves still upon it. Then, as he rode out into the open space before Cradoc's hall, he saw the two girls again, waiting for him in the doorway, and realized that they must be Cradoc's womenfolk and had run ahead to receive him as a stranger should be received, on the threshold of the house.

The taller of the two held a cup between her hands, and as he reined in and dropped from the saddle, she came forward, holding it out to him, saying in a very soft and gentle voice, 'God's greeting to you, stranger. Drink, and forget the dust of the journey.'

Aquila took the cup and drank as custom demanded. It was an ancient cup of flame-grained birch inlaid with gold and age-blackened silver, and the drink was mead; a thin mead with the aromatic tang of heather in it. He gave the cup back into her hands, looking at her for the first time, and saw that her hair was bright in the sunshine, brighter than the gold clasp at the shoulder of her tawny kirtle, and he supposed vaguely that she was pretty.

'God's Grace upon this house. The dust of the journey is forgotten.' He made the customary reply with cold courtesy. 'Is Cradoc the Chieftain here, that I may speak with him?'

'Cradoc my father is out hunting, and the other men with him,' the girl said. 'Let you come in, and be most welcome, while you wait for his return.'

'I will come in,' Aquila said. 'But since my business cannot wait for Cradoc's hunting, it seems that I must tell it to you. Ambrosius, Prince of Britain, is on the road here, and sent me ahead with word that he will be on your threshold by dusk, claiming lord's shelter for the night, for himself and eight of his Companions.'

The girl's eyes widened. 'Ambrosius? Tonight? Oh, then we must kill the pig.'

'Must you so? You have my sympathy,' Aquila said, with a flicker of contemptuous laughter.

The girl blushed scarlet, and he saw her gathering her dignity about her as though it had been an embroidered mantle. 'We must indeed. But that need not concern you. Let you come in now, and I will bring you warm water, for you are dusty and must be weary besides.'

'What of my mare?' Aquila asked.

'I will take your mare and tend her,' another voice answered him, a harder and lower voice, and looking round, he saw that the other girl had gone to Inganiad's head. He had forgotten about the other girl; a little fierce, nut-brown creature who seemed even browner by contrast with the kingfisher blue of her kirtle. Seeing his look, she smiled, but her gaze was challenging. 'I am used to horses, and I promise you that I am quite trustworthy.'

Aquila's hand tightened on the bridle. For the golden sister to bring him the Guest Cup in welcome, to bid him in and promise warm water after the dust of the journey, was no more than the duty of the mistress of the house towards the stranger within her gates; but, in some odd way, for the brown sister to take his mare and rub her down seemed a more personal thing.

'Cannot one of the men take her?' he said.

'Did you not hear Rhyanidd my sister say that our father and the men have ridden hunting?'

'All the men of the village?'

'All who are not busy in other ways. Shall I call Kilwyn from his shoeing, or Vran from his own hut where he nurses a broken ankle?'

'Ness, how *can* you?' the elder girl put in in soft distress, but neither paid any heed to her.

'I will take and tend her myself, if you will tell me where I may find the stable,' Aquila said.

'And let it be said that in my father's house a stranger must stable his own horse at the journey's end? This is so poor and outlandish a place that we must kill a pig to feed the Prince of Britain—though I daresay that pigs have been killed for him before—but at least no guest need tend his own horse.'

He realized that she was angry with him because he had laughed at her sister about the pig—no, not because he had laughed, because of the *way* he had laughed—and he liked her the better for that. Her hand was beside his on the head-stall now, and he had no choice but to let his own hand drop.

'Then it seems that I can only thank you and give you your will,' he said stiffly.

He stood a moment watching as she led the red mare away, then turned back to Rhyanidd. She was still flushed foxglove pink, and he wondered if she were going to make some sort of apology for her sister. But she did not. She said only with gentle dignity, 'And now come you in and rest, while we make all things ready for Ambrosius.' They were loyal to each other, those two.

At cow-stalling time, Ambrosius and the hunting party arrived almost together. And that night there was feasting in Cradoc's hall, and next day they rode out after wolves—Cradoc was proud of the hunting in his runs—and brought home three grizzle carcasses to be shown to the women and hung up for trophies in the hall before they were flayed and the meat given to the hounds. That night, when the feasting was over and the time came for sleep, Ambrosius sent for Aquila to attend him, instead of his armour-bearer, who, being young and weak-headed and proud of his part in the wolf hunt, had drunk too much of the thin, heather-flavoured mead, and was asleep under one of the hall benches.

The guest place reminded Aquila of the little beehive hut of Brother Ninnias, where he had slept with the gall of the Saxon thrall-ring still smarting on his neck. Only there were fine roe-deer skins on the bed-place, and feather-stuffed pillows of blue and violet cloth; and someone had set a bowl of apples on the stool beside it; apples whose smooth gold was flecked and feathered with coral colour, and the scent of them mingled with the aromatic breath of the herbs burning in the white, honeywax candle.

Ambrosius, sitting on the bed-place, had taken an apple from the bowl, and sat turning it in his hands, examining the delicate flecking and feathering of the skin. 'What a beautiful thing an apple is. One so seldom notices . . . ' He looked up suddenly at Aquila, where he stood against the central king-post, rubbing up the bronze boss of the light wicker hunting shield that his lord had carried that day. 'Does it seem very strange to you, this life among the mountains, Dolphin?'

'Yes,' Aquila said, 'but not so strange as it did a year ago.'

'It is so familiar to me. The only life that I have known since I was nine years old.' He had returned to the apple in his hand, turning and turning it. 'It seemed strange enough to me then . . . I was brought up to wear a Roman tunic and read with a Greek tutor. I remember the baths at Venta, and the high, square rooms, and the troops of Thracian Horse trotting down the street looking as though all the world were a bad smell under their noses. It is an odd thing to belong to two worlds, Dolphin.'

'But a thing that may be the saving of Britain,' Aquila said in a moment of clear seeing. He breathed on the bronze boss and rubbed harder to get out a spot of wolf's blood. 'A leader who was all Britain, or all Rome, would be hard put to it, I'm thinking, to handle such a mixed band as we are, when the day comes for fighting.'

'When the day comes for fighting,' Ambrosius said broodingly. 'It is in my mind that next spring comes all too soon.'

There was a sudden silence. Aquila raised his eyes quickly to Ambrosius's face, finding there a white gravity which startled him, after the harp song and the easy merriment in Cradoc's hall. His hand checked in its burnishing.

'Next spring?'

'Aye, with the Saxons already beginning to hum like a swarming hive, we daren't delay an attack any longer.'

Aquila's heart was suddenly beating a little faster. So it was coming at last, the thing that they had been waiting for so long. But something that he sensed in the other man puzzled him, and he frowned. 'Daren't? Why do you wish to delay longer?'

'I suppose I sound as creeping cautious as an old man.' Ambrosius looked up again. 'Dolphin, I am as eager to be at the Saxons' throats as the wildest hothead among us. But I have to be sure. If Aetius in Gaul had sent us one legion, we could have done it; when Rome failed us I knew that it must be years before we were strong enough to take up the fight alone . . . I have to be sure; I can't afford to fail once, because I've nothing in reserve with which to turn failure into victory.'

'Have the Young Foxes not bettered things by coming over to our standard?' Aquila said after a moment.

'If I could be sure of them, yes,' Ambrosius said. 'Oh, I'm sure of the Young Foxes themselves, their personal loyalty. For the rest—I don't know. I am seldom quite sure of my own kind; we dream too many dreams, and the dreams divide us . . . That is why we must make closer ties between ourselves and these new friends of ours.'

'What sort of ties?'

Ambrosius set the apple back in the bowl with the air of coming to a decision. 'Dolphin, let you take one of Cradoc's daughters for your wife.'

At first Aquila thought it was a jest, and then he realized that it was not. Along with the rest of the Companions, he had been waited on by Cradoc's daughters; he had spoken a few words with them, but that was all.

'I have had no thought of taking any woman from her father's hearth,' he said after a moment.

'Think of it now.'

There was a long silence. The two men looked at each other levelly in the candle-light.

'Why should Cradoc give me a daughter from his hearth?' Aquila said at last. 'I am a landless man, owning nothing but my horse and my sword, both of which you gave me.'

'Cradoc will give you his daughter if you ask, because you are of my Company, and because he would have died at Aber of the White Shells, if you had not turned the blow that was meant for him.'

Aquila said, 'If it seems to Ambrosius good that there should be such ties between his folk and Vortimer's folk, then surely it is for Ambrosius himself to take a wife from the hearth of some greater prince than Cradoc.'

Ambrosius raised his head slowly, and there was a look in his eyes as though he were seeing something at a great distance. 'To lead Britain is enough for one man; with a whole heart and no other ties.'

Aquila was silent. Because of Flavia he wanted nothing to do with women, ever. They were dangerous, they could hurt too much. But he hoped that if Ambrosius had asked him to walk out of the candle-lit guest place to certain death, because in some way his death could help to bind Britain together and drive the barbarians into the sea, he would have done it. Had he any right to refuse the lesser thing?

Ambrosius smiled a little, looking into his eyes. 'Rhyanidd is very fair—cream and heather-honey.'

Aquila never knew what made him say it, hanging the hunting shield from its peg on the king-post with great care as he did so. 'Cream and heather-honey may grow to be a weariness. If I must take one, when I want neither, I'll take the little brown sister.'

XIII
The Empty Hut

NEXT morning, with the bustle of preparations for departure already beginning to rise, Aquila sought out Cradoc the Chieftain and asked him for Ness, that he might take her with him for his wife when he rode north again. He did not quite believe, even while he asked, that Ambrosius had been right. But when he had finished asking, he found that Ambrosius had been perfectly right. There was no escape.

When he and Cradoc had done talking together, and everything was settled, he did not at once go to join the rest of the Companions. He should have gone, he knew; they were already gathering, the horses being walked up and down, but he had to be alone for a little. He turned aside into the orchard and walked to and fro under the trees, with his sword gathered into his arms. The gold was gone from the orchard, even the apples had lost their warmth of colour, and the branches swayed in the small, chill wind that turned up the leaves silvery against the drifting, sheepswool sky. He turned at last to go back to the others—and found Ness standing at a little distance, watching him.

He went towards her slowly, and they stood and looked at each other. 'What is it that you do here, Ness?' he asked at last, in a tone as grey as the morning.

'I came to look at you. I must be forgiven if I am a little interested, seeing that I am to go with you among strangers and live the rest of my life in the hollow of your hand.'

'Cradoc your father has told you, then?' Aquila asked.

'Oh yes, my father has told me. That was kind of him. It makes no difference in the end, of course; but it is nice to be told these things at the time, not left to find them out afterwards.' She looked at him with the cool challenge in her eyes that had been there the first time he saw her, but without the smile. 'Why do you want to marry me?'

If it had been the golden sister, Aquila knew that he would have had to make some kind of lie for kindness' sake, but not for Ness; only the truth for Ness. 'Because unless we can become one people, we shall not save Britain from the barbarians,' he said. It sounded stiff and pompous, but it was the truth, the best he could do.

Ness studied him for a moment, and there was a twitch of laughter at the corner of her mouth. 'So it is by Ambrosius's order! And to think that we killed the pig for him!' And then, suddenly grave again, she asked curiously, 'Then if it does not matter which of us it is, why me, and not Rhyanidd?'

'I don't know,' said Aquila simply.

There was a little silence, and then Ness said, 'I wonder if you ever will. How long have I, to make ready for my wedding?'

'We shall be in the south upward of a month. Be ready to ride with me when we pass this way on the road north again.'

Ness took her eyes from his face for the first time since he had turned and found her watching him, and looked about her, back towards the thatched roof of her father's Hall, up through the shivering apple branches to the dark lift of the mountains against the sky. And her look hurt him sharply with the memory of a valley in the Down Country with the trace of old vine terraces on the southern slopes.

'I have known this orchard for sixteen years,' she said. 'And now there's only a month left.' But she was not talking to him.

Aquila realized that the prospect of the marriage must be far more overwhelming for her than it was for him, because for her it meant being torn away from all that she knew and loved. But he shut his mind to that thought quickly. Once he began to feel sorry for the girl the whole thing would become unbearable. And he also had been torn away from all that he knew and loved, and more harshly than this.

He heard one of the others calling him. 'Dolphin! Hi! Dolphin! Are we to wait all day?' and he turned without another word, leaving her standing under the dipping branches of the apple trees, and strode back to rejoin his fellows.

When Ambrosius and his Companions returned to their winter quarters at Dynas Ffaraon, Aquila no longer had his regular sleeping-place among the young men in Ambrosius's Hall, but was lord of a turf-roofed bothy below the western rampart, where Ness spread fine skins on the bed-place and fresh bracken on the earthen floor, and cooked for him when he chose to eat at home, and spun wool by herself in the firelight, in the long winter evenings. Aquila was not often there. In this last winter before the great attack there was so much to do, so much to think about, that for most of the time he managed to forget about Ness altogether. She seemed as far away from him as though she had never ridden up from the south in the curve of his bridle arm; and he found it quite easy to forget her.

Winter passed, and spring came to the mountains, the snipe drumming over the matted bog myrtle at the head of the lake, and the purple butterwort in flower among the rocks of the cleft where the little stream came down. Dynas Ffaraon was humming, thrumming with preparations for the march; and all the broad valley below the Dun was an armed camp.

On a close, still evening Aquila sat beside Valarius at supper in the Fire-hall, his legs outstretched beneath the table on which he leaned, his platter of cold bear ham almost untouched before him. The great hall, crowded with leaders from the camp, was hot, despite the earliness of the year; too close and airless to eat, with the heavy, brooding closeness of coming storm. Also there were things in his stomach that came between him and food. Only a few hours since, he had ridden in with his squadron from Segontium, and all evening he had been with Ambrosius and his captains in council. Everything was settled now, as far as it could be in advance. The Cran-tara had been sent out days ago, the stick dipped in goat's blood and charred at one end, whose summons no tribesman might disobey. They were to host at Canovium, four days from now. That was for northern Cymru. Powys and the south were to join them later on the line of march. Aquila glanced again at the strangers sitting beside Ambrosius in the High Place, men in Roman tunics and with clipped hair and beards. They too had ridden in only a few hours since, bringing Ambrosius word from the Roman party of the support that waited for him in Venta and Aquae Sulis, Calleva and Sorviodunum, the cities of his father's old lowland territories. Bringing also word of another kind from the world beyond the mountains; word that for the second rime Rome had fallen.

They had known for years that there was no more help to be had from Rome, that they were cut off. But now they were not merely cut off, but *alone*—the solitary outpost of an empire that had ceased to exist. Aquila's thoughts were suddenly with his old troop from

Rutupiae garrison, the men of his own world whom he had known and served with; the old optio, who had taught him all he knew of soldiery and whose teaching he was now sweating in his turn to hammer into his wild mountain tribesmen; Felix, dead under the blazing walls of Rome. He jibed at himself for a fool; Felix and his troop might have been dead any time these four years past, they might have been drafted to the Eastern Empire, and be feasting safe in Constantinople tonight. But still the sense of loss was with him.

A woman bent over him to refill the cup that stood empty by his hand. He looked up, vaguely expecting it to be Ness, for the women generally poured for their own men in Hall, but it was the wife of one of the other captains; and when he came to think of it, he had seen no sign of Ness in Hall this evening. The woman smiled at him, and passed on. He realized suddenly that men were beginning to leave the Hall, rising as they finished their meal, and taking their weapons and going. There was so much to be done; no time for sitting and staring at nothing. The waiting time was over.

He began to eat again, hurriedly.

'Sixteen years we have waited for this coming down from the mountains,' Valarius said beside him, rather thickly. 'Sixteen crawling years since Constantine was murdered.'

Aquila looked round at him. 'You were one of those who got Ambrosius and his brother away to safety after that happened, weren't you?'

Valarius took a long, loud drink from his mead cup, and set it down a little unsteadily, before he answered. 'Aye.'

'That must be a proud thing for you; now that the waiting time is over and he comes down to take his father's place.'

'Proud! I leave pride to the other two—to old Finnen with his harp and Eugenus with his draughts and stinking salves.'

There was a kind of raw, jeering bitterness in his voice, under the thickness of the mead, that startled Aquila, and he asked quickly, 'What do you mean?'

'Eugenus was Constantine's physician, Finnen was Constantine's harper; not to them the shame,' Valarius said dully after a moment. '*I* was one of Constantine's bodyguard—yet Constantine died at a murderer's hand.'

There was a small silence. Aquila was suddenly remembering the scene of Aber of the White Shells, remembering that rage of Valarius's that had seemed out of all proportion to Brychan's jibe. Odd, he thought, how little one knew about people. He had lived and worked with Valarius for more than a year, and never known anything about him but that he drank too much and was the ruins of a good soldier, never known that for sixteen years he had carried shame with him as a man might carry a scar, a bodily hurt hidden from the eyes of other men. Maybe it was because the waiting was over and they stood on the edge of a great struggle and that somehow loosened things, maybe it was because of his own feeling of loss for Felix, something in him reached out to the older man, stiffly, rather painfully because it was so long since he had reached out to another human being, and he said with unaccustomed gentleness, 'Assuredly Ambrosius has not thought of the thing in that way.'

'But I have,' Valarius said. And it seemed that there was no more to be said.

Aquila finished his own meal quickly, and went out into the dusk. He went first to make sure that all was well down at the horse-lines and with his troop; then made for his own bothy. The skin apron was drawn back from the doorway and there was fresh bracken on the floor; a tallow candle burned low and guttering on the carved kist that held Ness's clothes, and his own; everything in readiness for him, but no sign of Ness here either.

He stood for a while with his hand on the door-post and his head ducked under the lintel, thinking. He was bone weary, and on any other night he would simply have slipped his sword-belt over his head and flung himself down on the piled fern of the bed-place, to sleep. But tonight, because Rome had fallen and Felix was dead, because of Valarius's shame, the empty hut seemed horribly lonely, and there was a small aching need in him for somebody to notice, even if they were not glad, that he had come home. That frightened him, because it was only as long as you did not need anybody else that you were safe from being hurt. But after a few moments he pinched out the candle and went in search of Ness, all the same.

He thought he knew where to find her: in the little hollow of the bush-lined cleft where he had once found Artos and his hound watching for a grass-snake. He had found her there once before, and she had told him, 'It is a good place. It looks south, and if I close my eyes to shut out the mountains in between, I can see the apples budding in my father's orchard.'

It was full dark now, though the flat-topped clouds massing above the pass to the coast were still touched with rose-copper on their under-bellies. The air was without freshness, lying like warm silk over one's face, and the stars were veiled in faint thunder-wrack. Certainly there was a storm coming, Aquila thought, as he made his way round the curve of the hill below the inner rampart, and plunged into the twisting cleft among the rocks. The thin, silver plash of the water under the ferns sounded unnaturally loud in the stillness, and the faint honey scent of the blackthorn breathed up to him. Looking down as he scrambled lower, he saw the pale blur of the blossoms like foam on dark water, where the thorn trees leaned together over the little hollow in the rocks—and the pale blur of a face suddenly turned up to him.

'Ness! What are you doing here?' he demanded, slithering to a halt just above her. 'There's going to be a storm.'

'I like storms,' said Ness composedly.

'And so you come down here to meet this one, instead of being in Hall this evening?'

He could not see her face, save as a paleness among the cloudier paleness of the blackthorn blossom, but he heard the old challenge in her voice. 'Why should I be in Hall? I have not the second sight to know that my lord would ride in tonight.'

'But you did know it, didn't you, before you came out here? You left all ready for me in the bothy.'

'What is it, then, that you complain of? Did no one feed you?'

'A woman brought me cold meat and bannock and kept my winecup filled,' Aquila said, coldly angry now, and not quite sure why. 'And when I looked up, it was Cordaella, Cenfirth's wife, and not you.'

'I wonder that you noticed the difference.'

Aquila leaned down towards her over his bent knee. 'There is a simple reason for that,' he said, repaying her in her own coin. 'Cordaella smiled at me, so I knew that she could not be you.'

Ness sprang up to face him with a movement as swiftly fierce as the leap of a mountain cat. 'And why should I smile at you? For joy that you took me from my father's Hall?'

'You know why I took you,' Aquila said after a moment.

'Yes, you told me. For the strengthening of a bond between your people and mine.' She was breathing quickly, the fierce white blur of her face turned up to his. 'Oh, I know that you did not want me, any more than I wanted you. The thing was forced on both of us. It was not that you took me, but the *way* that you took me—' She began to laugh on a hard, mocking note that made him long to hit her; and as though her wild laughter had called it up, and there was some kinship between her and the coming storm, a long, dank breath of wind came sighing up the cleft, thick with the smell of thunder and the thin, honey sweetness of the blackthorn flowers, and a flicker of lightning played between the dark masses of the mountains. 'It was not that you laughed at Rhyanidd about the pig, but the *way* that you laughed. It is never the things that you do, but the way that you do them. You took me from my father's hearth as you might have taken a dog—no, not a dog; I have seen you playing with Cabal's ears and gentling him under the chin—as you might have taken a kist or a cooking-pot that you did not much value. Did you never think that I might have knifed you with your own dagger one night, and been away in the darkness? Did you never think that there might have been someone of my own people whom I loved, and who—might have come to love *me*?'

There was a long silence, filled with the soft uneasy fret of that swiftly rising wind. Aquila's anger ebbed slowly out of him, leaving only a great tiredness behind. 'And was there. Ness?'

The fire had sunk in her also, and her voice was spent and lifeless. 'Yes,' she said.

'I am sorry,' Aquila said stiffly, awkwardly.

'Oh, it doesn't matter now. He is dead. He was killed hunting, nine days ago. Rhyanidd sent me word by the messenger for Ambrosius that came up yesterday.'

'I am sorry,' Aquila said again. There seemed nothing else to say.

He knew that she was looking at him intently, as though for her the darkness was daylight. 'I wonder if you are,' she said at last. 'I wonder if you have it in you to be sorry about anything—or glad . . . '

'I had once,' Aquila said harshly. He made a small, helpless gesture. 'We march against the Saxons in two days' time, and maybe you will be loosed from me soon enough. Meanwhile, come back to the bothy before the storm breaks.'

She drew away a little. 'Let you go back and sleep dry in the warm deerskins. I like storms; did I not tell you? This is my storm, and I am waiting for it. It will be bonnier company than you are to me.'

The wind was blowing in long, fitful gusts now, the blackthorn branches streaming like spray; and a white flicker of lightning showed him Ness with her unbound hair lifting and flying about her head as she crouched against the rocks behind her. She looked like something that belonged to the storm; and how he was to deal with her, now that he had lost his anger, he simply did not know. But deal with her he would; the determination not to be worsted by her rose in him, mingled with a kinder feeling that he could not leave her here to be drenched and beaten by the storm; and he reached out and caught her wrist. 'Come, Ness.' He pulled her towards him and caught her other wrist, not at all sure that if he left it free she would not indeed try to knife him with his own dagger.

She struggled wildly for a moment, and then suddenly it was as though all her fighting was spent. She was leaning weakly against him, and if it had been Rhyanidd, he would have thought that she was crying, the quiet crying of utter desolation. But surely Ness would not know how to cry. The first low rumble of thunder was muttering among the mountains. 'Come, Ness.' he said again. He released her one wrist, and still grasping the other, turned back to the steep climb; and with a little harsh, exhausted sigh, Ness came.

But he had no feeling of victory.

XIV
The Honour of First Blood

IN front of Aquila the main street of Durobrivae ran uphill, deserted in the evening sunlight. The town must have been growing emptier for years, falling gradually into decay, as happened to most of the towns nearest to the Saxon country, until now, before the threat of the Saxon inrush, the few people who were left had streamed away westward. The utter, heart-cold emptiness made Aquila think suddenly of Rutupiae on the night the last of the Eagles flew from Britain. Nothing left alive in Durobrivae but a half-wild yellow cat sitting on a wall; a stillness so complete that the shadow of a wheeling gull sweeping across the cobbles seemed important.

That was in front. Behind Aquila and the knot of champions who stood with him at the town end of the bridge was the ring of axes on heavy timbers, and a hoarse shouting of orders; all the sounds of desperate activity, of labour against time. Time. Aquila sent a swift glance over his shoulder to see how the bridge-felling was going forward. Men were swarming over the long, timber-built bridge, townsmen and Celtic warriors labouring side by side. He saw the bunk of axes in the evening light, as they rose and fell, crashing into the bridge timbers; and Catigern, the second of the Young Foxes, standing in the midst of his men, directing operations, the sunset turning his red hair to the colour of fire. It was a wild sunset, beyond the low, wooded hills, touching woods and marshes and mudflats with its own singing gold and kindling the water to flame. It seemed to Aquila, in that one swift glance before be turned face forward again, somehow fitting that they should fight with the sunset behind them.

The road that led back from the bridge climbed slowly, gold-touched like all the rest, over the brow of the hill, and into the brightness beyond; and Aquila, facing the Saxon lands again, was aware of it behind him, leading back and back, to Deva, to Canovium, to the ancient fortress among the mountains of Arfon. At Deva the three Young Foxes had come in to the hosting. And there, knowing that

Hengest would have word of their advance almost as soon as it was begun, and therefore speed was all important, Ambrosius had divided his host in two, and unloosed his swift-moving cavalry and mounted archers under the Young Foxes directly against the barbarians, while he himself, with the slower foot-soldiers, swept south to Glevum and on through his father's old territories, gathering the troops that waited for him there, on his line of march. That was the last that they had heard of Ambrosius; the last that they could possibly hear for many days. And meanwhile it was for them to hold the river line.

The Saxons, already on the move themselves and fully warned (for news always travelled faster in wild places than a horse could gallop) of British hooves drumming towards them down the Legions' road from Deva, had come swarming out to finish with the British cavalry before the main host could come up with them, if that might be: at all events to reach the river line before the British reached it. Durobrivae River, cutting its broad valley through the downs, had only two crossing places between its estuary and the place where the almost impenetrable forest of Anderida closed its own barriers to friend and foe alike. How often Aquila had seen its course drawn out with a charred stick beside the hearth in Dynas Ffaraon. His mind went to the hurried council of war this morning, in the lee of a dripping hazel copse, with the British leaders gathered about the little dark forest man who had foundered a stolen pony to bring them word of the Saxons' nearness.

'A day's march from the river,' Catigern had said, his face full of reckless laughter. 'Well, so are we, but horses march quicker than men.'

'We cannot hold the river at both points, however many hours we may be ahead of them,' Vortimer said; Vortimer for once without a falcon on his fist, and looking strangely incomplete without it. 'Look at us—we are a meagre handful!' And then with a sudden resolve. 'But if we can be in time to cut the bridge at Durobrivae, it is in my mind that we can hold the upriver ford.'

So they had split forces again, and while the main band, with the little forest man for their guide, had struck off through the scrub for the ford six or seven miles inland, where the ancient track under the North Chalk crossed the river, the smaller squadron had followed Catigern, forcing their weary horses to one last desperate burst of speed, down the road to Durobrivae.

And now, with the Saxons God knew how near, Aquila and his knot of champions stood their guard on the Saxon bank, while their comrades strove desperately against time to cut the bridge behind them.

'How many men do you want?' Catigern had demanded when he had volunteered for the task three hours ago. And Aquila had said, 'Horatius is supposed to have done it with two, but that leaves nothing in reserve. Give me nine—nine who choose to stand with me.'

He had meant men from his own squadron; and indeed the men of his own squadron had been quick enough to come crowding round him, Amgerit and Glevus and grim little Owain and the rest, many times nine. But before he could make his choice from among them, Brychan, of all unlikely people, had come shouldering through the press, crying, 'Hai, hai! Make way for your betters, my children!' to stand beside him.

It was odd, that. There had never been any warmth between them from their first meeting on the track up to Dynas Ffaraon, yet now Brychan came as though by right to stand with him at the doomed bridgehead, and he, Aquila, had accepted his coming as something that fitted as a well-worn garment fits. He glanced aside at the young Celt now. Brychan looked very happy. He came of a people of whom fighting was the very flowering of life. Aquila, coming of another people, could not feel that, only a cold, knife-edged sense of waiting, but something leapt between them all the same, binding them for the moment into a brotherhood.

Steps pounded along the quay, and a man came into sight, running as though all the hounds of hell were behind him. He was shouting as he ran; they could not hear what, but there was no need.

'So, I think they come,' Aquila said, and drew his sword with quiet deliberation. He caught one more glance over his shoulder. The bridge had a lopsided look, and the whole fabric shuddered and jumped with every stroke of the axes. It could not hold much longer, he judged, but the Saxons would be here before it went.

The scout was right upon them now, and checked, panting. 'The Saxons are out of the woods.'

'How many?' Aquila snapped.

'Only an advance party, but more than we are, and; the rest will be hard behind.'

Aquila nodded. 'Get back and report to Catigern.'

As the man plunged on, his feet drumming hollow on the crazy bridge timbers, the ten resolute men at the Saxon end of it closed up shoulder to shoulder, their drawn swords ready in their hands, their eyes turned in the direction from which the enemy must come. Behind them the ring of axes took on a redoubled urgency. In the tumble of bright clouds above Durobrivae a lake of clear sky shone blue, a faded harebell colour with the shadow of dusk already upon it, and the gulls swept and circled by with the sunset on their wings. And then, from away south-eastward beyond the silent town, a Saxon war-horn boomed.

Aquila braced himself, tensing like an animal ready to spring. He felt the slight movement run through the men with him, the tautened body and the softly indrawn breath.

'Brothers,' he said, almost wonderingly, 'whoever, in the years to come, strikes the last blow in this fight for all that we hold worth fighting for, to us—to us ten—is the honour of first blood.'

Behind him he heard a panting shout of orders, and the splintering crash and splash as one of the huge timbers went down, and the bridge shuddered under his feet like a live thing in torment. And now there was shouting before them as well as behind, and the yellow cat streaked along the wall with tail bristling, and the stillness was gone from Durobrivae, as the advance guard of Hengest's host came pouring down the quay, the last fiery light of the sunset jinking on iron helmet and spearpoint and ring-mail byrnie. At sight of the bridge, the foremost checked an instant, then they broke forward, yelling as they ran, storming down upon the little knot of champions who waited grimly to receive them.

As the fight joined, Aquila, who had known only that cold, knife-edged sense of waiting in the moment before, suddenly caught fire. He had known more than one skirmish with Scots pirates in the past year, but this was the first time since Wiermund of the White Horse had burned his home that the man at the other end of his sword had been a Saxon; and for Flavia's sake he hated every Saxon with a sickening hate; a hate that seemed now to spread wings within him and lift him up and fill him with a terrible red delight as each blow went home. Twice a man beside him was struck down, and twice somebody sprang into the empty place, but he was not aware of that, not aware of anything but the faces of the Sea Wolves that thrust upon him, blue-eyed and snarling, behind their bright blades. His own blade was bright, too, and growing red. Aquila killed that day, killed and killed again: and each time his sword struck home, sweeping aside the guard of a Saxon blade or thrusting under the rim of a buckler, his heart cried out within him that this was for his father, that that was for Demetrius, for Kuno, for Gwyna, even for the old hound Margarita. But though it was Flavia who had put that tempest of hate in him, he did not give her name to any of the blows he struck that sunset.

Someone was shouting to him. 'Fall back! In the Christus' name fall back! The bridge is going!' And he woke to the world around him again, and to the fact that he was not there simply to kill Saxons so much as to hold them back while their line of march was cut. He took one long step back, two steps, and the others with him—those that were left of them—their chins tucked down into their shields, their blades biting deep as the Sea Wolves came thrusting after them. The whole bridge felt lax and limber under his feet, swaying above the water as he moved back, and back. Swaying more wildly . . . He heard a voice above the tumult shouting to his comrades to break off the fight, and never knew that it was his own. There was a whining and rending of timbers, as the others lowered their blades and sprang back, and for one splinter of time that seemed to broaden into an eternity, he stood alone in the face of the Saxon flood. Then he had a sudden sense of a gulf, an immensity of nothingness opening behind him; the hills and river and ragged, darkening sky seemed to heel over in a vast half-circle, and with a shout of triumph he sprang back and down.

A falling beam caught him on the temple just over the old scar, sending jagged splinters of light through his head. He was aware of a great falling and crashing down, a rending uproar, and the shock of cold water that engulfed him and closed over his head. Then there was darkness—no, never true darkness; a kind of rolling cloud of confusion that never quite shut out the world.

It lifted at last, and he realized dimly that he was lying on his side on grass, and had just vomited up what felt like about half the river. The river must be tidal at Durobrivae, he thought, for the taste of it was still salt in his mouth. He rolled further on to his face and propped himself up a little on his hands, remembering after a while to open his eyes. He found himself staring down at his own hands in a pool of sharp golden light, one spread-fingered on the rough turf of the river bank, one still cramped about the hilt of his sword, which he must have clung to throughout. In the almost acid radiance every grass-blade stood out distinct and glowing, and a tiny yellow-banded snail-shell was a thing to marvel at, living a life of its own and casting a shadow that was as complete and perfect as itself.

'Sa, that is better,' said Brychan's voice above him; and he made a great effort and got a leg under him, and Brychan helped him to his knees. The world swam unpleasantly in the light of a torch that someone was holding above him; there was a numbed aching behind his forehead, and he hoped vaguely that he wasn't going to be sick again. But after a few moments the world began to steady. It was dusk now, dusk full of movements. He saw other torches, and men moving about him, and horses. A group of men already mounted went past him in the crowding shadows, and he had a confused impression of the black, stark lines of the bridge running out into the cold paleness of the water, jagged and driven askew, and ending in a skeleton tumble of beams, and then nothing. A vague impression also of flames springing up on the farther bank. The barbarians had fired Durobrivae.

'How many of us got—back?' he demanded thickly, with an arm on Brychan's shoulder to steady himself. Brychan was dripping with river water, too, and something in Aquila registered the fact that it was probably Brychan who had hauled him out of Durobrivae River.

'Five. You and I, Struan and Amgerit and Owain. But Amgerit is about done for. They've taken him up to the fisher huts with the rest of the wounded. Anyway, we accounted for a fine lot of Saxons, what with the fight and those that were swept away when the bridge went.'

Aquila said after a moment, 'Five—six out of ten. Well, I suppose that is not a heavy price for the bridge.' He realized for the first time that somebody else had checked beside them. He looked up and saw that it was Catigern himself; and with a hand still on Brychan's shoulder, he lurched unsteadily to his feet. 'First blood to us!'

Catigern nodded. 'First blood to us! That was a most noble fight, my friend . . . Can you ride yet?'

'Yes,' Aquila said.

'So, ride then. We head for the ford now,' and he was gone, swinging his cloak behind him.

Someone brought him a dry cloak to fling round him over his dripping tunic, and someone brought Inganiad. She whinnied, pleased and calling to him, when she caught his smell. He groaned as he hauled himself into the saddle. There had been a few hours' rest for the horses, none for the men.

He knew, when he came to think back over it later, that they pushed on up-river through the short spring night and reached the ford and the British camp before dawn; that there were a few hours' rest, and then more fighting, as the Saxons, baulked of Durobrivae Bridge, swept inland to attack the ford: the first full battle of the long struggle for Britain, and at the day's end the first British victory; to be remembered long after the cutting of Durobrivae Bridge was forgotten. But to Aquila it was all no more than a dream; something seen dimly through the aching numbness in his head, moving like a painted curtain with the wind behind it.

It was not until the fighting was over and sunset came again that reality broke in on him once more, and he found that he was in a charcoal-burner's bothy, twisting a piece of filthy rag round a deep gash in his forearm, and looking down at Catigern's body lying where it had been carried aside from the battle in the full flood of wild sunset light that streamed through the open doorway.

Vortimer and Pascent were there; and Vortimer turned away to give some order to the men who crowded about them, beating his clenched fists together as he did so. 'If I had a thousand men, I'd follow them up; as it is there's nothing that we can do but guard the river line until Ambrosius comes up. Post scouts across the river to bring me word if they show any signs of trying again further up. Calgalus, send men up to the village; it is going to be a wild night and we must get the wounded into shelter.'

But Pascent, the youngest, kneeling beside his brother's body, only went on staring blindly down at it. 'They say that Horsa is dead too. Somebody said that he was lying by the ford with a whole company of Hengest's household warriors about him,' he said. And then, through shut teeth, 'I hope his death is a stone in Hengest's belly tonight!'

They held the river line until nine days later Ambrosius and the rest of the host came out of the woods behind them; lean and mired, footsore and red-eyed with forced marching. Longbowmen from the mountains, men wearing old Roman harness and carrying the short sword and the pilum; old soldiers and the sons of old soldiers from Venta and Aquae Sulis and Sorviodunum and a hundred villas and villages and little towns between.

And then at last they swept forward after the Saxon kind.

When winter came, putting an end to fighting for the next few months, the Saxons were back to the territory from which they had swarmed out in the spring; and settling the better part of his host in winter camps at Durobrivae and Noviomagus, Ambrosius marched the rest back to Venta Belgarum, that had been Constantine's old capital and would now be his.

He rode in through the streets of Venta in a sleet storm, with a bitter wind blowing; and all the city seemed cold and grey and falling derelict. Aquila, riding through the streets that he had known when he was a boy, saw how far the grass had encroached into the road ways in five years. He saw faces that he knew among the crowds, though none of them knew him, and it seemed to him that on them also the grass had encroached. But there was warmth in Venta that day, for besides the Magistrates and chief citizens who had met them at the city gate, there were many to cry a welcome to Ambrosius; a child threw a branch of glowing winter berries under his horse's hooves, and an old man called out to him, 'I knew your father, sir! I served under him in the old days!' and was rewarded by the swift smile even more than by the coin which the slight, dark man on the black stallion tossed down to him.

'You are at home among your own people here, as surely as ever you were at Dynas Ffaraon,' Aquila said to him later that night, when the Magistrates and the chief citizens had departed, and a few of the Companions stood together round the fire in a small side chamber of the old Governor's Palace.

Ambrosius turned his cold hands before the fire, spreading them so that the light shone through between his fingers. 'At home.' He looked up to the high, dark window; and Aquila knew that through the darkness of the sleet-spattered glass in which the reflections of the firelight danced, he was seeing the remote crests of the Arfon skyline, the snow corries of Yr Widdfa; smelling the sweet, cold air of the mountains, and saying his farewells. 'Yes, at home, and among my own people. I even saw certain faces that I knew among the crowds today—and they remembered me for my father's and my grandfather's sakes. One day they may remember me for my own.'

XV
The Hawking Glove

WHEN spring came, Aquila was in the mountains again, sent up with an escort of cavalry to bring down the women and children. Little, grim Owain, riding beside him in the rear of the long, winding cavalcade, had been angrily disgusted when Aquila chose him for his second in command of the escort. It was one thing to stand beside the Dolphin to keep Durobrivae Bridge from the Saxons, quite another to follow him away westward when the fighting was just about to start again. He had gloomed all through the lowlands, his narrow, weather-burned face shut like a trap; but the thin mountain air, the wild, free tang of spring among his own hills had lightened his mood little by little until now he was whistling to himself softly as he rode; and the whistling rose small and clear as a distant bird-call above the soft beat of hooves and creak of harness-leather, the wheel-rumble of the ox carts and the cries of the carters.

Aquila did not whistle, and kept most of his thoughts for the business of getting the ox carts through the soft places. But in him, too, something answered to the blackthorn breaking into flower beside the way, and the plover calling. It was almost a year since he had ridden down from Dynas Ffaraon behind Ambrosius, almost a year since he had seen Ness. He was not sure what he felt about seeing her again, but he wondered a little how it had gone with her through the months between.

'Ah-ee! There it stands against the sky, as though we had been but an hour away,' Owain said, breaking off his whistling, and spitting with satisfaction between his horse's ears.

And Aquila realized that he had been riding without seeing anything for the past mile.

They had sent one of their number on ahead with word of their coming, and men were waiting for them in the cattle enclosures at the foot of the fortress hill. There were hurried greetings, and leaving the tired oxen and the carts in charge of the men who had come to meet them, they set off up the steep track to the inner gateway. In a little while they were clattering between the huge, square-cut gate-timbers; weary men dropping from their saddles, suddenly the centre of a little crowd of women, for the most part, for there would be few men in the Dun at this hour of the day, with the sun still high in the sky; women asking for news of sons or husbands, and small, excited children who must be scooped back out of danger from the horses' hooves; and a swarm of half-grown boys led by young Artos and his hound Cabal, who had come running from sword-and-buckler practice at sound of the escort's arrival. But in all the crowd there was no sign of Ness. Aquila, watching the horses fed and rubbed down and picketed, glanced round for her more than once, but he was not really surprised at not finding her there. Ness had always been good at not being there when he returned from a time away, and it was not likely that she would change now.

He could not bring himself to ask any of the women for news of her, but so much could have happened in a year, and he began to feel vaguely anxious in spite of himself. 'See to the rest of the picket lines,' he said suddenly to Owain, and, taming, thrust out through the little throng towards the gateway and the bothies below the rampart. Some of the women looked after him, and glanced at each other smiling after he had gone. But he did not know that.

His own bothy was partly hidden from this side by an outcrop of rock, so that one could not see it clearly from a distance, but came upon it suddenly. And when he did so now, what he saw pulled him up short, with a feeling of having walked into complete unreality. Ness sat in the bothy doorway with something kicking in a nest of deerskin at her feet. She was bending down to look at the thing, and singing almost under her breath; a fainter, huskier singing than the one that Flavia had made when he found her in the Saxon camp, but with a like crooning note in it. Something seemed to catch Aquila by the throat, making it for the moment hard to breathe. But at least she was not combing her hair. She was spinning, the brown of the crotal-dyed wool on her distaff as deeply rich as the velvet of a bee's back, and the whirling spindle singing its own small, contented song in a kind of undertone to hers.

Then, as he took another step forward and his shadow fell across her feet, she looked up. 'I heard that you were come,' she said, as though he had been gone a day instead of a year.

Aquila looked down at the babe in the deerskin, and then at Ness; he felt stupid, woolly headed, as though for the moment he could not properly understand. Ness had not told him before he went away; maybe she had not known herself, or—maybe she would not have told him anyway.

'Ness—is it mine?'

She laughed, on that hard, mocking, wild bird-note of hers, and laid down spindle and distaff, and stooping, caught up the little creature still muffled in its deerskin, holding it close against her. 'Oh, my lord, look then! Do you not see that he has your eagle's beak for a nose, though there is no blue dolphin on his shoulder?'

Aquila looked more closely. The babe did not seem to him to have much nose at all, but he supposed that women saw these things differently. It had a little dark down on its head, like a curlew chick, and out of its small face two solemn, dark eyes frowned up at him, wandering a little, as the eyes of most very young things do before they have learned to focus.

'He even frowns as you do!' Ness said. She was still laughing, mocking him, but there was less harshness in her mockery than there had used to be.

Aquila put out a bent finger and brushed the baby's cheek with his knuckle. It felt extraordinarily soft and alive. A son, he thought, and there was a queer, rather painful stirring deep down in him. This small, living creature frowning up at him out of the soft folds of deerskin was his son; what he had been to his father.

'Have you given him a name?'

'Nay, that is for you to do.'

There was a little silence filled with the living sounds of the Dun and the warm droning of a bee among the cushions of wild thyme that clung to a ledge of the outcrop close by. Then Aquila said, 'I shall call him Flavian.'

'Flavian?' She seemed to be testing the name on her tongue. 'Why Flavian?'

'It was my father's name.'

Another silence, longer than the first. 'So. I have learned two things about my lord,' Ness said at last. 'My lord had a father, and his name was Flavian . . . Na, three things—' Her voice had lost its mocking note; and looking up, he found her watching him with something of the air of one making a discovery. 'My lord loved his father. I did not think that it was in my lord to love anyone.'

Before he could answer, a pad of feet and a clear whistle sounded above, and Artos came leaping down the outcrop with the great hound Cabal at his bare, brown heels, full of questions about the return journey and demands to be allowed to ride with the escort. And for a while Aquila had no more time for his own affairs.

The next morning Aquila saw his wife and son into the foremost of the ox carts, along with the other women and children going to join their men. She settled herself in the tail of the cart, drawing her cloak forward about herself and the baby in the crook of her arm; and as Aquila stowed her bundle in after her, an older woman with three children clinging about her leaned forward from the interior of the cart, to help her settle, saying as she did so, 'The little one grows fatter now. Has he a name yet?'

'Yes,' Ness said, 'he has a name. He is Flavian.'

'Flavian.' The other woman seemed to be testing the name as Ness herself had done. 'What a man's name, and he so small! Nothing but a minnow.'

Ness looked down at the little creature bundled in her cloak, pressing back the dark green folds with her free hand. 'Minnow,' she said, and then a surprising thing happened, for her eyes went to Aquila, sharing the little warm laughter of the moment in the way that she had never shared anything with him before. 'Minnow, Dolphin's son.'

Aquila touched her foot briefly in acceptance of the laughter; then turned away to mount Inganiad at the head of the escort.

He was very proud because he had a son; and for the first time in six years, as he led the long, winding convoy of horsemen and ox carts down the road to Canovium, the time ahead seemed to hold something for him.

Young Artos rode between Aquila and Owain on his own pony, with the great hound Cabal loping alongside. They had listened to his demand to be one of the escort, and he rode with his pride shining about him like a scarlet cloak, and his hand on his hunting-knife as though the familiar glens of Arfon through which the track wound were suddenly overnight swarming with Saxons.

'I go to help Ambrosius,' he said, not shouting it, but speaking head up into the mountain wind. 'Soon we shall drive the Sea Wolves back into the sea!'

* * *

But it was not to be so simple as that, for despite their hopes last spring, the British were not strong enough to drive the Sea Wolves into the sea. Again and again in the next two years they hurled the Saxons back into the south-east corner of the province, only to have them come swarming out once more as soon as their own thrust was spent. And with the war bands strengthening all the while under Octa in the north, and more coming in down every Saxon wind like the wild geese in October, the menace remained as deadly as ever.

'If we could have one great victory!' Ambrosius cried. 'One victory to sound like a blast of trumpets through the land! Then we should gather to our standard not merely a gallant handful here and there, but the princes of the Dumnonii and the Brigantes with their whole princedoms behind them. Then we might indeed have a Britain whole and bonded together to drive the Sea Wolves into the sea!'

Meanwhile they struggled with the age-old question of how to fight any kind of war with an army that wanted to go home in mid campaign to harvest its own fields, and when it came back, if it did come back, had mostly forgotten its training; struggled also to make one host, one heart, out of lowland Roman and mountain Celt; and so far as the Celts were concerned, it was uphill work.

With the men of Arfon it was well enough; the unbreakable tie between the Chieftain and his warriors bound them to Ambrosius, who was the very heart of the whole movement; but with those who had come in following the Young Foxes, it still seemed to Aquila that one could not be sure.

He spoke of his doubts to Eugenus the Physician, towards dusk of a winter's day, as they walked back together from the baths.

'Ye-es, I have long carried a somewhat uneasy mind on that score myself,' Eugenus said, his words muffled by the folds of his cloak that he had huddled almost to his eyebrows, for in spite of his fat he felt the cold. 'Despite all Ambrosius's efforts, despite the friendships—and the marriages—that have sprung up between us, I believe, most sadly, that the only thing that really holds the Celts to our banner is Vortimer. One man's life is a perilously slender thread. It's a solemn thought, my friend.'

Aquila glanced aside at him as they walked. 'There's young Pascent. He'll keep faith, I'll swear.'

'Aye, but he's no leader—he's too good a follower.' There was a smile in the other's voice, for, like everyone else, he liked Pascent. 'He is the stuff that the very best household warriors are made of, brave as a boar and faithful as a hound; but it is not in him to hold the Celtic party, as Vortimer can.'

They walked on in silence, each busy with his own unquiet thoughts, through the winter dusk.

As they walked, the dusk that rose like quiet, grey water in the shabby streets of Venta was rolling in blue and faintly misty over the high northern moors that Octa and his war bands had over-run. And a woman with red-gold hair and eyes that were the shifting grey-green of shallow seas was bending over the fire in a stone-built hut where the blackened heather swept to the walls. She was holding a big leather hawking glove turned inside out, and as she bent forward the firelight darted on the short, bronze pin projecting from the stitching of the thumb. There was a wisp of sheep's wool in her other hand, and she dipped it again and again into the few drops of some thick, greyish fluid in a bowl among the hot ashes, and painted the bright sliver of metal with infinite care, as one handling a viper's fang. All the while she crooned softly, words in a tongue much older than the Saxons' tongue. Many things had gone to the making of those few drops of greyish fluid, and there were charms for them all, to make them do their work more surely. Each time, she let the stuff dry, then painted it again, until the brightness of the bronze was dimmed and darkened as with a grey rust. Then, with the same infinite care, she turned the glove right side out—it was a beautiful glove of honey-pale mare's skin, embroidered with hair-fine silver wires and silk as deeply blue as the hooded flowers from whose root the woman had distilled her chiefest poison—and laid it aside. She burned the wisp of wool, and broke the little earthen pot and dropped the pieces into the red heart of the fire.

Better for both Hengest and for Vortigern her lord (whose good, in this thing, was Hengest's good) that the Young Fox should be out of the way. But she had not told Vortigern what she did. He was a dreaming fool whose purpose always broke under any strain, and he might shrink from his own good. Later, when the thing was done, and maybe Ambrosius's following had fallen apart like a rotten apple, she would tell him what he owed to her, and watch him writhe.

* * *

A day came when they were ploughing on the downs above Venta, and the alders in the water-meadows were brown and woolly with catkins, and Ambrosius's host was mustering again for the fighting that would come with summer, as it came every summer now.

On the evening of that day, Vortimer, going to his sleeping-quarters in the old Governor's Palace, found lying on his clothes chest, where the light of the candle fell full, a hawking glove that was certainly not his. A honey-pale mare's-skin glove, fringed and exquisitely worked with deep blue silk and fine silver wires. He summoned his armour-bearer, and asked where it had come from.

'A slave brought it this evening, from the Lord Ambrosius's chambers,' the man said.

'For me? You are sure that it was for me?'

'The slave said that Ambrosius had noticed your old one was all but worn through.'

Vortimer had picked up the glove, a little puzzled. 'It is a pretty thing—more like a woman's gift.' He looked up, laughing, at his hooded peregrine on her perch. 'Too fine for your sharp talons, eh, beloved?'

He slipped his hand into the loose glove; and snatched it out again with a curse. 'Ah! the thing has talons of its own! Whoever made it has left the needle inside!' And he sucked the jagged scratch on the ball of his thumb, half laughing, half angry, and rather more puzzled.

By midnight he was dead, as a man dies who has been bitten by a poisonous snake.

In a few hours the news was all over Venta, spreading out through the newly gathered host like a dark stain. And Ambrosius, with a face that seemed to have set into stone, was himself heading a ruthless search for the slave who had brought the glove to Vortimer's quarters.

It was all quite useless; the slave would never be found, Aquila was thinking that evening down by the river, watching the water riffle round Inganiad's muzzle as she drank with the other horses of his squadron. And he saw, not the misty grey-and-amber shadows under the budding willows and the blink of oyster light in every spreading ripple, but Rowena in Hengest's Mead Hall, singing; a golden witch in a crimson gown. He did not know why he was so sure that Rowena stood behind that poisoned hawking glove, but he was sure. And with the dusk creeping up the valley, the foreshadowing of evil to come seemed to rise also.

What happened a few days later surprised nobody, for it grew directly out of what had gone before. Several of the Companions were gathered with Ambrosius about the table in the room where he kept his lists and records of men and horses, his pay-rolls and the old Roman itineraries that told him how many marches it was from one place to another and so helped him in the planning of his campaigns; they were going over plans for the summer's fighting, so far as one could make any plans in advance. Seeing him now, his dark, fine-drawn face caught out of the shadows into the candle-light as he leaned forward to point out something on the unrolled parchment on which the old map so often sketched with a charred stick was drawn in ink, Aquila thought how little of the mountains seemed left in him. It was not only that he looked older, nor that he wore a Roman tunic and his dark hair was clipped short; it was something deeper, a turning back to the world that he had been bred in until he was nine years old. Only the flame that had burned in the Lord of Arfon burned in the Roman leader also.

They heard footsteps coming along the colonnade, heard the sentry outside challenge, and a quick word in answer; and Pascent was standing in the doorway, with the courtyard quenched in the green spring twilight behind him. Looking towards him with the rest, Aquila thought, So it has happened.

Pascent came forward to the table. His face was white and haggard in the candle-light, and little beads of sweat shone on his forehead beneath the heavy lock of foxy hair. He looked at Ambrosius across the table, and they saw his mouth work for a moment as he tried to speak and could not. Then he said, 'My Lord Ambrosius, I cannot hold them.'

'So,' Ambrosius said, and let the map roll up, very slowly and carefully. No need for it now, there could be no carrying the war into the Saxons' country this year. 'I had been more than half expecting that, I think. What reason do they give for deserting my standard?'

Pascent made a small, helpless gesture. 'So many reasons. They say that Vortigern my father is after all their lord, and I am only his youngest son. They say that the Saxons will never reach to Central Cymru (that is, those who *come* from Central Cymru), and what is the rest of Britain to them, when all things are said and done? They say that my Lord Ambrosius has forgotten his own people to carry a Roman sword, and that they are weary of obeying Roman trumpets and leaving their fields to be harvested by their women.' He broke off, and stared down at the table before him, then dragged his gaze up again. 'They say—some of them say—that the slave who brought my brother his death said that he brought it from the Lord Ambrosius; and that maybe the slave spoke the truth.'

Ambrosius's face was suddenly very cold. 'And why, in the Name of Light, should the Lord Ambrosius be sending death to the chiefest of his allies?'

Pascent's hands were clenched on the table, and in his face there was an agony of shame. 'Because Guitolinus my father's kinsman has put it into their hearts that the Lord Ambrosius was jealous, fearing that Vortimer might gain too much power.'

There was a long silence, flat and hard. No one moved about the table. Then Ambrosius said in a quiet, curiously smooth voice—a voice as smooth as a sword-blade, that Aquila had never heard from him before—'Let you bid all the chiefs that have yet gathered here to meet me in the Forum, tomorrow at the third hour.'

'It will make no difference,' Pascent groaned.

'That I know well. Whatever I can say to them, they will go. But they shall not desert my standard and the standard of Britain without telling me face to face that they do so—and why.' Ambrosius was silent a moment, his gaze never moving from Pascent's haggard face. 'And you? Do you go with your own people?'

Pascent said, 'I am Ambrosius's man—since the day that I swore faith, I and my brothers.' His eyes clung to Ambrosius's like a dog's. 'I am ashamed with my people's shame; so ashamed that I do not think I want to live. I will serve you living, with a whole heart, or if you ask for such a payment, I will go out of here and fall on my own sword tonight. But either way, I am Ambrosius's man.'

It might have sounded hysterical, but Aquila knew that it was not. It was a simple offer. Pascent felt the shame of what his people were doing so keenly that he was perfectly prepared to pay for it with his own death, if his death seemed any sort of recompense to Ambrosius.

Ambrosius looked at him for a moment, still in silence, and then the white coldness of his face gentled suddenly. 'Not to you the shame, my kinsman. Nay, then, you are of more worth to me living than dead.'

XVI
White Thorn and Yellow Iris

'I am Ambrosius's man, since the day that I swore faith; I and my brothers.'

The words were still sounding in Aquila's inner ear next noon, as he made his way from the Basilica; not as he had heard them spoken in defeat last night, but as he heard them spoken in proud defiance, less than an hour since, in the thin spring sunlight of the Forum court. The scene was still sharp-edged and vivid in his mind; he could see Ambrosius standing on the shallow steps before the great Basilica door, his face a white mask of scorn: Ambrosius, wearing what he scarcely ever wore, a mantle of the Imperial Purple, the straight folds burning in the sunlight with a living depth of colour that drained into itself all the colour from the world around him. A very lonely figure, for he would have none of his officers with him, though they waited in the shadow of the colonnade. And below him, gathered on the grass that was still tawny with winter, the princes and chieftains of the Celtic party; foremost among them, those dark-blue fanatic's eyes of his blazing with triumph, Guitolinus, who had taken it upon himself to act as spokesman for the rest.

It had been over quite quickly, the talking and the shouting and the brandished fists and the shame that seemed to wash to and fro about the stillness of the purple-clad figure dominating the scene from the portico steps. And when it was over, Pascent had walked deliberately out from among his own people, and turned at the foot of the steps to cry to them in fury, 'You have listened to Guitolinus the Traitor, and not to me. You have broken your faith. So be it; you are curs that run back to your own dung-heap. But you shall run without me!' And without another glance at them, he had mounted the shallow steps to kneel at Ambrosius's feet with the proud submission of a hound, and set his hands between Ambrosius's hands.

Afterwards, Cradoc, his father-in-law, who had come in to the muster five days ago, had been waiting for Aquila in the shadow of an archway. They came together so suddenly in that shadowed place that Aquila's hand flew to his dagger. But the other stayed him. 'Na, na, my lad, I am Cradoc, and no robber. I was waiting for you.'

'Why?' demanded Aquila uncompromisingly.

'Only for this. To say to you that I have not forgotten how at Aber of the White Shells you turned the blow that was meant for me.' Cradoc's face was more deeply lined than usual, more full of old regrets. 'Therefore I will not go to Ness before I leave Venta with my spears. I will not seek to persuade her to come back to her own people.'

Aquila stared at him a few moments, with a feeling of sickening shock. 'As to that, she must go or stay as she chooses,' he said at last, very slowly, and turned away into the street.

He heard the disturbed hum of the city as he walked. He knew the full tragedy of what had happened. He knew that in the years to come it might make the difference between victory and defeat for Britain. But for the moment all that was a dark background to trouble of his own.

After Flavia, he had felt that whatever happened to him, he had nothing to lose. It was a very safe feeling, a kind of armour, and he clung to it because he had been afraid to go unarmed. But now he had something to lose again, and all too likely he was going to lose it. Once he could have kept Ness against her will if need be, and risked her knifing him as he slept. The irony of the thing was that that had been in the days when he did not want her. It was different now, though he had only just realized it. He did not want Ness to go; and so he could not keep her against her will.

He came to the great house beside the old Governor's Palace that he shared with Eugenus and three other officers with their families, and went in, past the porter dozing in the doorway. The atrium, the central room of the house, was shared by all the families that lived there. But today it was deserted; no women chattering in the doorway, no children and hounds tumbling about the cracked tessarae of the floor. Another cube of pink sandstone had come out of Ganymede's face, he saw, as he crossed to the colonnade door and went out into the sunlit courtyard. The children prised them up to play games with. It must have been a lovely and gracious house once; it was gracious still, but with the sad graciousness of decay; and today he noticed the decay as he seldom did, for he had grown used to it in two years. One couldn't get the fallen plaster and crumbling stonework put right in the winter, and in the summer there were always the Saxons. There was grass along the foot of the walls, and green moss creeping here and there up the foot of a column. The stone basin in the centre of the paved court had nothing in it but a little green slime and a few crumbled last-year's leaves and a pigeon's feather; and the dolphin on the rim no longer spouted water from its open mouth, for the water supply, like the drains, was not what it had been. Only a few days ago Ness had held the Minnow—he was still Pilcod the Minnow, his greater name kept for state occasions and when he was in disgrace—up in her arms to pat the gaping creature, saying, 'See, it is like the blue creature on Father's shoulder.' And watching them as he sat on the half-wall of the colonnade, cleaning a piece of equipment, Aquila had been absurdly pleased, without stopping to wonder why.

He crossed the courtyard, and turned into the colonnade beyond, heading for the rooms that were his and Ness's. And when he came into the inner court, Ness was sitting in the sunlight beside the little postern door that gave into the court of the Governor's Palace. The damson tree that grew beside the door was thickening into bud, the shadows of its branches stirring and dappling on the old sunlit wall and over Ness herself. But nothing else about her moved. Her spindle and distaff lay beside her on the stone bench where she had abandoned them, and she sat with her hands linked round her knees. Close beside her Flavian and a hound puppy lay tumbled together, sound asleep on the grass. The puppy's coat was brindled in bars of black and amber, shining in the sun, and the small boy, in a once-bright blue tunic, faded with many washings, lay with his dark head on the puppy's flank; together, Aquila thought, they were supremely good to look at. But Ness was not looking at them, only staring straight before her.

She looked up as he came out from the colonnade, but she did not greet him, only sat watching him out of that waiting stillness.

He came and stood leaning his shoulder against the wall beside her, as though he were very tired. And still she watched him, though she had to look sharply upward now, to do so.

'What is it, then, that brings you home at this hour of day?' she asked at last.

'I came to tell you that your people are leaving Ambrosius's standard,' Aquila said heavily. 'In a day or so, maybe before tonight, they will be gone.'

Her face never lost its waiting stillness. 'I know. All Venta hums with that news.'

'I—spoke with Cradoc your father a while since. He said that because I once turned the blow that was meant for him, he would leave you free to choose for yourself, Ness.'

'And you? Do you also leave me free to choose for myself?'

'If you choose your own people, I will not hold you,' Aquila said.

She rose from the bench and stood facing him, her eyes full of the old challenge. 'And the child?'

Aquila did not answer at once. The words seemed to stick in his throat and choke him. He looked at the small boy and the hound puppy. 'Take the Minnow too,' he said at last, and his voice was hoarse and strained. 'He is so little, he needs you more than me. Only—let him come back to me when he is of age to bear his shield.' He pulled himself up. 'No, you cannot promise that; it might be to send him to fight against his own kind. Take him and keep him, Ness.'

'A strange man you are, my lord,' Ness said. 'Three autumns ago you took me from my father's hearth as though I were a mere piece of household gear that you did not much want. And now you will let me go—you will let the child go—because, I *think* you would fain have us stay.'

Aquila nodded, wordlessly. He knew so little of Ness, scarcely anything at all; certainly not enough to guess what was going on behind her thin, brown face.

She stared at him a long moment, then flung up her head and began to laugh, on the old clear, wild bird-note, waking the Minnow so that he sat up blinking, puzzled at finding his father suddenly there and startled by his mother's wild laughter; he clutched the puppy against him for comfort. But her laughter broke in the middle, and she bent her face into her hands. 'I used to dream night after night of being free; free to go back to my people—my own people . . . But it is too late. I belong to you now, I and the child.'

It seemed to Aquila that there was suddenly a great quietness all about him. 'They will say that you betrayed your own people to stay with me,' he said.

She lifted her face from her hands, with the look of accepting something. 'I *am* betraying my own people—my own world—to stay with you.'

And suddenly out of the quietness he seemed to hear Flavia's voice sounding behind Ness's; Flavia's pretty voice made hoarse and toneless by grief. 'Our Lord help me! He is *my* man.'

It was not the same thing. He was not the enemy, as the Saxons were the enemy; he was not one of a band that had killed Ness's father. Yet he knew that deep down at the heart of things Ness's choosing and Flavia's choosing sprang from the same kind of seed. He had a sudden longing, which wasn't a bit like him now, though it was like the person he had been before the Saxons burned his home, to give Ness things; to bring them and heap them into her lap. New songs and the three stars of Orion's belt, and honey-in-the-comb, and branches of white flowering thorn at mid-winter; not only for her sake, but for Flavia's sake as well.

He heard himself giving her the only thing that he had to give in that way; his own voice, hoarse and a little stumbling, begging her to understand and accept what he gave. 'I had a sister once, Ness. She was carried off by the Saxons when they burned our home. I thought—I prayed—that she was dead, until I found her again years later in the Saxon camp. I would have taken her away with me, but for her also it—was too late, by then. Her name was Flavia.'

It was the first time that he had spoken of his sister in all those years.

Ness made a small gesture with her cupped hands, as though she received a gift into them. 'Poor Aquila—and poor Flavia—and poor Ness.'

Then a party of horsemen passed cantering up the street beyond the house, and she dropped her hands; and the world outside was back with them again.

Aquila hitched at his sword-belt, thrusting his own affairs into the background. 'I must be away and see to sending up some of our men to take over the outposts that Vortimer's people were to have manned.'

He said 'Vortimer's people' not 'your people' now, and did not even notice that it was so. Ness noticed, and there was a faint smile on her mouth, bitter and sweet together, like the juice of the crab apple, as she watched him go striding back to his man's world. Then she turned herself to comfort the Minnow, who, thoroughly upset by all this, had burst into tears.

Somehow Aquila had felt that the desertion of Vortimer's troops must bring the long struggle to a head, and the future down on them like a tide when the seawall goes; and he strode out past the dozing porter into the street again with his hands instinctively making sure that his sword was loose in its sheath, as though he expected already to hear the Saxon war cry rise beyond the walls of Venta, and the clash of weapons at the gates.

Instead, all that summer there was a long, uneasy hush, while the weakened British host waited under arms, to guard their borders from an attack that somehow never came. In the nerve-racking hush, as summer dragged by, news filtered through to them now and again from the rest of Britain. With his followers returned to him after his son's death, Vortigern was striving to make a stronger stand than he had done of old, striving to make firmer treaties with the Saxons.

'The fool! The fool!' Ambrosius said. 'Of what use to make bargains in the Fire-hall with the Wolf that you have welcomed in over the threshold.' And he set himself and his Companions with yet grimmer urgency to the task of making an army, and hammering the territories of Calleva and Venta, Aquae Sulis and Sorviodunum into one, after the years of being left to their own devices that had broken them down into separate status and turned their Magistrates, whose forebears had been petty princes, back into petty princes again.

They heard that there was to be a great gathering of the Saxon and Celtic leaders at Durnovaria to make a treaty that would fix for ever the Saxon frontiers in Britain; and they laughed with a small, grim laughter around their watch fires. 'When the last Sea Wolf is dead, then the Saxon frontiers in Britain will be fixed for all time, and not before.'

At summer's end, they heard how that gathering had ended.

It had a name by then; the name of 'The Treachery of the Long Knives' by which it was to be known for generations to come. In accordance with the usual custom that no man should carry weapons to the council circle, Vortigern and his men had gone unarmed to the gathering. But Hengest's house carls sitting with them on the same benches at the feasting which followed the council, a Saxon and a Celt alternately, had had each his dirk concealed inside his sleeve ('Well may the Saxons wear long sleeves' and 'Never trust a man with long sleeves,' said the British for a thousand years). At a given signal each man had ripped out his dagger and stabbed the man on his left. More than a hundred of the Celtic nobles died at that council, but not Vortigern himself. Vortigern, who styled himself High King, had been kept to pay head ransom for his life; and Vortigern had paid it, with the last rags of his pride torn from him, with a dagger at his throat under the thin red beard, and a scribe to write the whole thing down in fair Latin that it might not be denied afterwards; paid it in huge grants of land in the Great Forest and the Down Country and up the Tamesis almost to Londinium.

After that a few of the Celtic party returned to Ambrosius like beaten hounds with their tails between their legs, but for the most part they simply melted away back to their own mountains. Lacking more support—even having to send back some of the troops he had left to help strengthen the western coasts against the Scots pirates—all that Ambrosius could do was to hold his father's old territory as a kind of island, a fortress within its own frontiers. So almost another year went by, and it was full summer again.

The brown floor of the woods dropped gently away before Inganiad's hooves; the trunks of the ash trees rose straight and pale on either hand, and the light under the high canopy of leaves was palely green, so that Aquila seemed to be moving under water as one does in an ash wood. He heard the faint jingle of the patrol coming down behind him; no sound of voices, for they were men used to riding quietly in the woods. Young Artos, riding at his side, with Cabal loping along before, cocked up his head suddenly, caught into swift delight.

'Look, Dolphin—squirrel! There on that branch—Ah, look, there he goes.'

Aquila followed the direction of the boy's gaze, and saw a streak of reddish fur flicker out along the limb of a tree a little to their right. It clung an instant in the crotch where two branches met, chittering at them angrily, then darted on, out on to the slender, swaying, tipmost spray and, scarcely seeming to spring, was in the next tree, floating and lilting through the branches as though it had no more weight than a wind-blown flame. Then it was gone, only they heard it still chittering in the distance. Artos chittered back, then, laughing, took up the alarm call of a jay.

Silence fell on them again, as they rode on, the reins slack on the horses' necks, through the woodland ways.

Presently Aquila glanced again at the boy riding beside him. Young Artos was fourteen, with still a year to wait before Ambrosius judged him ready for battle (if it ever came to open battle again), but he had been like a restive colt all that spring, so that Ambrosius had finally sent him up to Aquila, keeping watch on the northern borders, to get the smell of the camp into his nose and begin to be a man. Artos the Bear. In some ways the name suited him, Aquila thought, for already his body under the leather tunic showed signs of great physical strength, and he had something of the clumsiness of a bear cub in his movements, though not when he was on horseback. Artos on horseback was beautiful with the beauty that comes of a thing's absolute fitness for the purpose for which it was created: a longship at sea, a bird in flight, Artos on horseback.

They were dropping down towards the trackway, the ancient track under the North Chalk, on which, four years ago and forty miles towards the sunrise, Vortimer had held the river line against the host of Hengest. They were out of the straight green aisles of the ash wood now, into the thickets of hazel and alder and crack willow that bordered the track, brushing through the undergrowth with the warm smell of sunshine and open country in their nostrils. Then Artos's head went up again. 'Listen.'

Aquila heard it too; the rumble of wheels and the pelting hooves of cattle on the track; and a few moments later they glimpsed through the twig-tangle of the scrub about them a pathetic little convoy coming into sight: a few lean cattle herded by boys ahead of the rest, a couple of ox carts loaded with gear and women and children, several men on ponies, or on foot, two herd dogs. Aquila had seen many such little bands of refugees in the past year, as the Saxons with their new land grants spread further over the south-east of Britain.

'More of the poor devils,' he said over his shoulder to the men behind him, reining Inganiad to a halt. 'Let them go by before we cross.'

Among the scrub of the wood-shore they sat their horses, waiting. The cattle went by, white to the belly with dust, hot and weary, with low heads and the strings of slime hanging from their soft muzzles; the first ox cart drawn by its patient, wide-horned oxen, its load of sad women and children and kitchen pots and poultry.

'Those poor people! And Vortigern sitting safe and full fed in his stronghold of Geronwy!' Artos said fiercely.

Aquila looked at him again, and saw his face white and pinched, and his fists clenched on the reins. Artos was very angry; but it wasn't anger alone in his face, it was misery. That was always the way with young Artos; a horse or a hound or a man in pain or trouble, and Artos seemed to feel the ache of it in his own belly. It would make life hard for him, harder than it would otherwise have been; but it would also, Aquila thought, make him very much beloved. He turned his attention back to the fugitives on the track. The men on their ponies were spread out on either side, brushing through the meadowsweet that grew thick along the open verge. In the second cart, surrounded by all her household gear, an old woman sat dozing under a great hat of dock leaves, on a rough wicker crate of poultry. In the back of that cart was a heather-thatched bee-skep, carefully wedged in position. And behind the cart, the last of the convoy save for a footsore dog with a frilled wet ribbon of tongue drooling from its open jaws, trudged a man with a bundle on his shoulder; a small, strong man, clearly as footsore as the dog, in a rough, brown tunic powdered white with dust.

Something about him tugged at Aquila's memory with a kind of half recognition such as one may feel for a figure seen afar off, that begins, as it draws nearer, to take on the look of a friend.

He turned abruptly to Artos. 'Take the troop back to camp—and see the horses fed and picketed if I have not come by then.'

'Why—what—?' Artos began.

'I go to speak with one of the men down there—an old friend. Take over command, Artos.'

He saw the anger that had been in the boy's face lost in the sudden pride of his first command, and cast a quick glance over his head to the grim little weather-beaten man behind him; Owain would see that all went well. Then he lifted the reins, sending Inganiad down slantwise towards the track, out of the scrub, parting the creamy surf of meadowsweet that swayed together again behind him, sending up its thick sweetness of scent to mingle with the rising dust. The folk at the rear of the convoy had seen him coming now; they were startled, beginning to huddle as sheep huddle, having seen maybe too many armed men lately. He shouted to them reassuringly; there was nothing to make them afraid; he would speak with the Holy Man, that was all; and he brought Inganiad out on to the track beside the small man with the bundle on his shoulder.

'Brother Ninnias, is that your bee-skep?'

The man, who had not looked round with the rest to watch him coming, turned to him now with no more show of surprise than he had made at their first meeting; and with the same serene courtesy. Clearly at first he did not recognize him.

'God's greeting to you, friend. You know my name and my bees. Forgive me, and grant me but a moment to remember you.'

His quiet gaze was on Aquila's face, and Aquila, bending in the saddle to receive the scrutiny, smiled a little, seeing the recognition wake slowly in the small man's eyes.

'Ah—' His gaze took in the tall, flame-red mare and the iron-bound helmet swinging at the saddle-bow, the stained and greasy leather tunic which Aquila wore, and the long cavalry sword at his hip; and returned to his face. 'You are somewhat changed, my friend, at any rate in your outward seeming. It must be five or six years since you helped me gather the raked weeds from my bean rows.'

'It is seven,' Aquila said, and slid from Inganiad's back. 'You are footsore and I am fresh. Let you ride awhile.'

Ninnias cast an eye at the tall mare beginning already to dance a little with impatience at the slow pace. 'I thank you, no. It is in my mind that I shall travel more safely on my own sore feet.'

There was truth in that, for Ninnias had not the look of a horseman. Aquila laughed, and they walked on at the tail of the little convoy in companionable silence, save when from time to time Aquila spoke quietingly to the mare. One or two of the men glanced back at them now and then, but without curiosity; they were too dazed for curiosity.

After a while Aquila said, 'You follow the westward drift with the rest, I suppose?'

'Aye,' Ninnias sighed. 'If it had been Brother Drusus that the Lord saw fit to save, instead of me, when the Sea Wolves burned out our little Community, he would have stayed in the face of this new Saxon flood, to die a martyr's death . . . If any Christian among the iron folk that I used to serve had been left in the old village, I would have stayed with them—I hope and believe that I would have stayed with them. Brother Drusus would have stayed, anyway, and maybe carried Christ's word to one Saxon before they killed him. Of such are the Kingdom of Heaven. *I* have not the missionary fire; I should not be able to carry Christ's word to even one Saxon. If it were bees it would be another matter. I can be of more use among the poor folk who have lost their homes to the Saxons. So I packed some roots from my physic garden and gave my bees their freedom, save for this one hive that Cunefa most kindly found space for in his cart; and took the Abbot's bell again—I have it here in my bundle—and came away.' He glanced again at the sword Aquila wore. 'And you? It seems that you found your service to take.'

'I found my service to take,' Aquila said.

'It is, I think, not greatly to be wondered at that I did not know you again,' Brother Ninnias said reflectively.

'Seven years are apt to change a man.'

'There are things that change a man even more than seven years.' The other looked fully round at him. 'When you came to my hut you were lost in a great bitterness, empty of everything save your thirst for vengeance, and when you left me, even that was lost to you.'

'And now?' Aquila said.

'I think that at least you are not empty any more.'

There was a cuckoo calling somewhere among the trees; a rich and sleepy sound, the very voice of summer. Aquila said, 'I have a cause to serve, and a horse and a sword to serve it with. I have a woman and a child down in Venta.'

'You are rich, my friend,' Ninnias said quietly. And then, as though in answer to something in Aquila's tone, 'And yet even now the wound is not healed?'

Aquila was silent a moment, staring ahead into the dust-cloud of the little convoy. No, he thought, it wasn't quite that; the thing had healed all right. The old black bitterness that he had known because of Flavia had gone—Ness had taken it away when she chose to stay with him. But he had lost something—lost it so completely that he did not even really know what it was, so completely that it was only now, with Ninnias, that he knew he had lost it. He knew that he was a different man from the one he would have been if Flavia—if it hadn't been for Flavia.

'Nay, it is healed well enough. Maybe the scar still aches before rain,' he said lightly; and his tone warned the other from any question.

They walked on in silence until they came in sight of the place where a bridle-path branched from the main track, running upward through the gently rolling woods. They had fallen some way behind the rest, so that when they came in sight of the path, the foremost of the cattle were already past it and going on down the main track. Aquila realized that when they came to the branch he would go one way and Ninnias another, and their meeting would be over.

'My way lies up yonder,' he said suddenly. 'I have my summer camp below the village up there. Come my way and preach Christ's Word to us in the war hosts of Britain.'

Brother Ninnias shook his head. 'Nay, I shall be of more use to the poor homeless folk than I should be in a war camp.'

'How much further do you mean to go? Is there any place in your mind?'

'I do not know how much further; there is no place in my mind,' Ninnias said. 'It may be that I shall stop when Cunefa and his people stop; it may be that I shall stop before, or go further. God will tell me when I come to the right place.'

'But I shall not know where that place is,' Aquila said, suddenly saddened by the quickness with which things passed. Things, and people.

'Does that matter so much?'

'Yes,' Aquila said simply.

They had reached the parting of the ways now, and checked. The cuckoo was still calling in a distance that was blue as wood-smoke, and in the marshy ground beside the track the dense mat of iris leaves still showed a few yellow flowers, proudly upheld like lamps among the cool green sword-blades of the leaves. Brother Ninnias stooped and touched one of the flowers without picking it. 'Three petals has the iris, see—a wise flower that carries the number of the Trinity in its head. Father, Son, and Holy Spirit; man, woman, and child; yesterday, today, and tomorrow. Three is the number of perfection and the perfected pattern. Do you know, my friend, I have the strongest feeling that for us two the pattern waits for a third meeting, to attain perfection. But how and when it comes about must lie in God's hands.' He hitched at his bundle. 'Until then—God keep you, Aquila.' He turned and trudged away in the wake of the others, hurrying now to catch up with the cart that had his bee-skep in it.

Aquila stood looking after him, where the two ways branched, his arm through Inganiad's bridle, until the bend of the track hid him from view. Then he mounted, and set off at a canter up the path through the woods. But after a time he slackened rein and walked the mare, to give young Artos time to have finished seeing the horses picketed before he came.

XVII
'Minnow, Dolphin's Son'

NEWS of Vortigern's death reached Venta in the spring; and with it news that Guitolinus the trouble-maker had taken his place as leader of the Celtic party. Bad news for the British cause, for Vortigern had been a shamed and broken man, but Guitolinus was young and fiery and something of a fanatic, one maybe to light the Celtic fires again. And in the years that followed, Ambrosius was to have his hands full enough with the Saxon kind, without having to guard against a Celtic knife in the back. For the hordes of Hengest were on the move, not as a swift, forward thrust this time, but as a slow, inflowing tide. They were moving down from the fens of the old Iceni territory, and up from the bride-gift lands of the south-east towards the upper Tamesis Valley, while others from the lands that had already taken their names of North folk and South folk were pushing westward to cut Cymru and the north completely off from the rest of Britain.

Ambrosius and the British host hung on their southern flanks like mastiffs to the flank of a bull, thrusting in on them wherever chance offered, harrying them by every means in their power; but still, year by year, the Saxon wedge drove westward splitting Britain in two. And so six summers went by and a seventh winter came.

Aquila had become one of Ambrosius's captains now; captain of an Aela, a great cavalry wing; for cavalry was beginning to form a larger and larger part of the war hosts of Britain. That was young Artos's doing; Artos, who had begun to gather to him all the best and most gallant of the young warriors; Artos, who rode like a flame in battle, a superb leader of mounted men and a rebel against the old-established order. 'Aye, I know that the Legions depended on their Foot and not their Horse; is that any reason why we must do the same?' he had countered Valarius's protests and head-wagging. 'The Saxon kind pour in, numberless as the wild geese in October, numberless as the sands of the sea, but we who are of the mountains, we who have been

Roman Cavalry, we know how to use the horse in battle, and by God's Grace that shall give us the victory.'

And so, as that seventh winter drew towards spring, Aquila's hands were even more full than usual, his time divided between the council table and the water-meadows where the cavalry were in training. But he found time to keep an eye on young Flavian's breaking-in, all the same. The Minnow was nine years old now, and went to the school which a Christian priest had started in the colonnaded court of one of the big houses.

Ness had no patience with such schooling. 'So long as he learns to speak the truth and use a sword and ride a horse, what else is there he needs to learn?'

'Among other things, he needs to learn to read,' Aquila had said.

She had laughed on the old scornful note. 'Read? What use shall reading be to him? This is a world in which only the sword matters, not books any more.'

That had seemed to Aquila a terrible thing to say, and all Demetrius's teaching cried out against it. He had used the only argument he could think of that would seem good to Ness. 'It was because I could read that Thormod my lord brought me with him to Hengest's camp. If I had not been able to read, I should have died a thrall in Juteland.' He did not think that she had been convinced, but she did not say any more. And Flavian went to school. That is to say, he went when he could not help it, for Flavian also had little use for books.

A day came that was not spring as yet, but poised on the edge of spring; and the water-meadows around Venta were becoming already one vast camp. Aquila and his kind had been working all that day on some raw levies from the Cymric border, trying to teach them something of ordered movement, at least to recognize the trumpet calls that they must obey in battle. In some ways it was like the cavalry manoeuvres that they had used to put on at Rutupiae, Aquila thought, walking Inganiad back from the far end of the practice ground, with the shadows lying long on the turf and the bloom thick on the distant hills as the bloom on a bilberry. His inner eye was still full of the beautiful, constantly changing patterns of the day, the wings and squadrons of cavalry sweeping this way and that, obedient to the voice of the trumpets; the jewel brilliance of the long, lance-head serpents that the squadron leaders carried, streaming, like flames in the wind of their going, beautiful and gallant against the pollen-dusted sallows and the meadows shaking off their winter greyness. And as though she, too, were remembering the day, Inganiad whinnied softly. Aquila patted her warm, moist neck. The mare was fifteen now; after this year, he thought, he would not use her in battle any more. He wondered which of them would hate that the most.

Artos, with several of the Companions, had just ridden off the field after the last sweeping charge, and turned beside a knot of sallows to watch the horsemen gathering into their own squadrons again and trailing off towards the horse lines and the evening cooking-fires; and Aquila caught through the fuzzy golden green of the budding branches the crimson gleam of a cloak and the wave-break curve of a white stallion's neck, and heard the stir and stamp of a great round hoof, and the jink of a bridle bit, a burst of laughter—and then Flavian's voice.

When he rounded the low, whippy, pollen-dusted mass of branches, there was his son, who should have been at his evening lessons, standing at Artos's stirrup, feet apart and hands behind his back, gazing up at him, while the young man leaned forward in the saddle to return the look. The first thing Aquila felt was a half-amused exasperation, for it was not the first time that Flavian had run from his lessons to the cavalry training. But something in the boy's look, a kind of joyful and eager worship that showed even in his back view, and sounded in his small gruff voice, 'Well, then, when I'm *fourteen* will you let me? I can ride very well already—when I'm four*teen* will you let me ride with you?' hurt Aquila sharply. It was he who had taught Flavian to ride, making time when there was so little time to spare; but the boy had never spoken to him like that.

Right at the beginning, nine years ago, he had hoped that he and the Minnow might be friends; the sort of friends that he and his father had been to each other. But somehow it had not worked out like that. He didn't know what had gone wrong; it was not often that he noticed that something had gone wrong at all, but when he did notice, it hurt him. Maybe it was something to do with the thing that he had lost . . .

Flavian was so taken up with his eager desire to be one of Artos's followers that he was deaf to the soft fall of Inganiad's hooves on the turf behind him. Aquila brought the mare up, saying with cold lightness, 'Ah, Flavian. I had assumed that you would serve in my wing when you reach the age to carry your shield. Am I, then, deserted?'

Flavian jumped at the sound of his voice, and spun round, and the shining eagerness in him went out like a light. 'Father—I—I didn't know you were there.'

'No,' Aquila said, 'I imagine that you did not. However, that does not particularly matter. Your future plans are for the future; at the present moment you should be with Brother Eliphias, learning to read words of more than one syllable. You are over-fond of playing truant.'

His tone was more blighting than he had meant it to be. He saw the Minnow's face suddenly white and forlorn, with the pride about it that he wore like a garment when he wanted to cry. He saw Artos make a sudden movement as though to lean down and touch the boy's shoulder, and then check himself. Suddenly he knew that whatever happened, he must make amends. He forced a smile, and said quickly, 'Nay then, we'll forget that part of it. Since you *are* here, you can make yourself useful and ride Inganiad back for me. I want to try Falcon's paces on the way home.'

He knew that for a long while past Flavian had been desperately eager to ride Inganiad, and so he looked for a quick flare of joyful excitement. For a moment, delight did leap in the boy's face, but only for a moment, then it was gone again, and Flavian said, 'Yes, Father. Thank you, Father.' But it sounded more dutiful than anything else. Aquila, pretending not to notice as he dismounted and called to one of his men to bring up Falcon, his spare mount, wondered what the trouble was now. He swung the small boy up into the saddle with a 'There you are. Hold tight,' which sounded falsely hearty in his own ears, and set to shortening the stirrup ropes. And as he did so, he understood what was wrong. For so long Flavian had longed for the day when he would be deemed worthy to ride Inganiad; it should have been a great occasion, a time of trumpets. But he had made it only a lump of honeycomb after a smacking. (It is never the things that you do, but the way you do them. It was not that you laughed at Rhyanidd about the pig . . .) Would he never learn? He could have groaned. Well, too late to do anything about it now. Still keeping a firm hold on Inganiad's reins, he mounted Falcon, and wheeled both horses towards the distant walls of Venta, with the rest of the group who were already moving off.

Flavian looked very small on the tall, flame-coloured mare as his father glanced aside at him. He was sitting very upright, his eyes shining; he was a man riding among men. Maybe it hadn't been such a very bad mistake after all. Aquila saw and understood the appeal on the boy's face. Flavian wanted him to let go the reins. He hesitated, but Inganiad was quiet after her day's work; she had known and loved Flavian all his life and was used to his climbing about her back in stable. She would be gentle with him. Aquila took his hand off the reins.

A very short while later, if there had been any time for cursing, he would have been cursing himself by every name under heaven that he had done so. The thing happened so quickly, that it was over almost before it was begun. A white owl, early on the hunting trail, flew out of the alder brake on silent, ghost-soft wings almost under Inganiad's nose; and the mare, startled, and missing her lord's strong and familiar hand on the bridle, shied violently and went up in a rearing half-turn. Aquila had an instant's sight of the Minnow's white, terrified face that stayed with him afterwards as though it were bitten into his mind. He shouted to the boy to hold on, even as he flung himself sideways in his own saddle to catch the reins, but he was too late. The next thing he knew was that Flavian was on the ground and he was kneeling over him.

The boy lay unmoving, with blood trickling from the great broken place in his head where it had struck a sharp alder root. With a cold sickness rising in him, Aquila set his hand over the Minnow's heart. It was beating, though very faintly, and he drew a long, shuddering gasp of relief. Artos was kneeling beside him, and he heard quick, concerned voices all around, but he didn't hear what they said. He was feeling the Minnow all over with desperate urgency. Nothing seemed broken; there was only that terrible blow on the head. With infinite care he gathered him into his arms, and stood up; the child felt very light, as though his bones were hollow like a bird's. Someone must have caught the horses, and someone brought him Inganiad, still trembling and wild of eye. He shook his head; to ride back he would have to let Flavian out of his arms while he mounted. 'I'll walk,' he muttered.

He walked back to Venta, carrying the small, unconscious body; and Artos walked with him, leading his own horse. What had happened to the rest, he neither knew nor cared. Once inside the city gates he said to Artos, 'Go ahead and warn Ness.' And when Artos had mounted and gone clattering away on his errand, he walked on alone.

He carried Flavian up the street and in at the door where Artos's horse was tied to the hitching-post, and across the courtyard where the stone dolphin still gaped senselessly in its broken fountain. Ness met him as he reached the inner courtyard, Artos behind her. She was as white as the boy, and held out her arms without a word to take him, but Aquila shook his head. 'Better not to change him over. I'll put him on his bed . . . I let him ride Inganiad and a white owl startled her.' He forgot that Artos would have told her that already. The door of Flavian's sleeping cell stood open and he carried him in and laid him down on the narrow cot; then, as Ness slipped to her knees beside it, he turned to Artos, big and anxious in the doorway. 'Go across to Eugenus's quarters and get him quickly.'

The daylight was going fast, draining out of the little lime-washed room as it might so easily be that the life was draining out of Flavian's small, still body. 'If the boy dies,' Aquila said, 'I've killed him.'

Ness looked up from the work of her hands as she pressed back Flavian's dark, feathery hair and laid a piece of soft linen against his temple to staunch the slowly trickling blood.

'Get the lamps lit so that Eugenus has light to work by,' she said. 'Then go and bid one of the slaves to bring hot water.'

There was an agonizing delay before Eugenus came, for he had just gone out to a supper party, and it was some time before Artos could find him, but he came hurrying at last, still wearing his banquet wreath of early white violets and bringing with him a faint scent of wine. He felt Flavian all over much as Aquila had done, examined and bathed and bound his head, felt his heart and listened to his breathing, and pulled up his closed lids to look into his eyes.

'A bad blow, a cruel blow, but I think that the skull is not cracked,' he said. 'I will come again in the morning. Meanwhile keep him warm and do not move him. On no account try to bring him back to his body before he is ready to come. That may take several days.'

'But he—will come back?' Ness said, still kneeling by the bed with the child's head between her hands.

Eugenus looked from her to Aquila standing at the bed-foot and back again; and his dark, bulging eyes were extraordinarily kind under the ridiculous banquet wreath. 'I hope and pray so,' he said.

In the next three days Aquila went about his duties as usual, but training ground and council chambers alike seemed quite unreal.

Only the nights were real, when he kept watch by Flavian while Ness got a few hours' sleep. The other wives in the big house would have helped her gladly, though she had made close friends with none of them, but she would not leave the boy for more than a few moments to anybody but Aquila. He would bring work with him—horse lists that needed checking, some problem of transport to be worked out—but he made small progress with them. Sometimes he dozed a little, for he was very tired, but never deeply enough to lose consciousness of the narrow cell, the glow of the shielded lamp thrown upward on the limewashed wall, and Flavian's small, still face on the pillow, so like Flavia's, so incredibly like. It was odd that he had never realized before how like to Flavia the boy was.

For three nights there was no change, and then, halfway through the fourth night, Flavian stirred. He had stirred before, flung his arms about and muttered: but it had been a kind of blind stirring, as though it were not Flavian himself, but only his body showing that it was ill at ease. This time it was different: Aquila knew that it was different, even as he laid aside the tables he had been working on and strained forward to look into the boy's face. Flavian stirred again, a little shiver ran through him, and he was still once more. But his breathing was growing quicker, he shifted his bandaged head from side to side on the pillow; his mouth was half open and his eyelids fluttered. He looked like someone trying to wake from a sleep that is too heavy for him.

'Flavian,' Aquila said quietly. 'Minnow.'

Eugenus had said that they must not try to bring him back into his body until he was ready to come; but now he was ready, he was trying to come, needing help. He didn't know if Flavian heard him, but he made a kind of whimpering, and a little groping movement of one hand on the coverlid. Aquila put his own hand over it. 'It is all right. It is all right, Minnow, I'm here.'

Flavian drew a long, fluttering breath, and then another; and then he opened his eyes and lay frowning up at his father.

'It is all right,' Aquila said again. 'Nothing to worry about. Lie still.'

Flavian's gaze wandered off unsteadily to blink at the lamp, and returned to his father's face. 'Have I—been ill?'

'No,' Aquila said. 'You hurt your head, but it is better now.'

There was a moment's silence, and then Flavian turned his hand over to cling to Aquila's. 'I fell off Inganiad—didn't I?' he mumbled. 'I'm sorry, Father.'

'Inganiad threw you,' Aquila said. 'A white owl startled her and she threw you. If I had been on her back, she would like enough have thrown me.'

Flavian smiled. It was a very sleepy smile, and Aquila smiled back; and just for the moment they were very near together, with the wall that had grown up between them dwindled quite away. But Flavian was a little anxious; there was something else his father must understand. 'It wasn't Inganiad's fault, Father—really it wasn't. It was the white owl.'

'It was the white owl,' Aquila said. 'Go to sleep again, Minnow.'

Flavian scarcely needed telling, for his eyes were already drooping shut; and in a little while he was sleeping quietly, his hand still holding Aquila's. Aquila sat for a time, watching him, then he dropped his head on to his forearm on the edge of the cot. He had not prayed for Flavian's life, he hadn't prayed for anything or about anything, since the day that he lay under the oak tree after his parting with Flavia, and decided that it was a waste of time. But there was a deep rush of gratitude in him, now.

He did not go to rouse Ness; she was asleep and needed the sleep desperately. And besides, the Minnow still had him by the hand.

When Flavian woke up again in the morning, he drank some broth and managed a shaky grin for his family. But the old barrier was up again between him and his father—though maybe not quite so high as it had been before.

Having begun to mend, he mended at a gallop, and not so many days later Aquila, with an hour to spare in the morning, wrapped him in a striped native rug and carried him out to sit on the bench in the inner courtyard. There was beginning to be some strength in the sun, and the old wall at their backs was faintly warm as they sat side by side. It was just the two of them, and Argos, who had been a fat, brindled puppy when Ness chose between Aquila and her own people, lying outstretched at their feet, dignified as a stone lion. The violets that grew against the wall were not out yet, but there was a faint scent of them from their leaves, and a cock chaffinch was flirting to and fro in the branches of the damson tree. Aquila had a feeling of 'home' on him. You couldn't really call this great, decaying house that they shared with so many other families 'home', but it was the place where he lived when he was in Venta with Ness and the Minnow;

it had been for nearly nine years, and every stone of it was familiar. To Flavian, he supposed, it must be home; it would be the first place that he remembered. No orchard below the mountains, no downland valley for Flavian.

He looked round at the boy beside him. The Minnow was sitting gathered in on himself like a ball, with his feet drawn up inside the striped rug and only his head sticking out. He had been allowed to leave the bandage off for the first time, and his thin, eager face was more than ever like Flavia's.

'Let's look at your head,' Aquila said, and then, as the boy scuffled round on the bench, cocking it obediently to one side and screwing up his eyes, 'Yes, it's mending . . . I'll tell you a thing. Minnow; you're going to have a scar on your forehead to spoil your beauty, exactly like the one I have on mine.'

Flavian's eyes flew open. 'Truly?' he said, as though it were something to be much desired.

'Very truly,' Aquila said, and there was a sudden warmth of laughter in him, because he had not thought of it like that. They looked at each other for a moment in silence, and in the silence it was as though, very hesitantly, they reached out a little towards each other.

'Minnow—' Aquila began, without any clear idea of what he was going to say. But in the same instant he realized that the Minnow was not listening. He had craned round to listen to quick footsteps that were coming across the court of the Governor's Palace towards the little postern door under the damson tree. He saw the pin lift, the door opened, and Brychan came striding through. And the moment was lost.

Aquila got up quickly to meet the newcomer. 'Brychan, what is it, then?' But he thought he knew. They had been waiting for the final order, almost on the edge of marching for days now.

Brychan had halted at sight of them; he was bright with the special flame that always woke in him at the approach of fighting. 'The scouts have just come in. Hengest himself is encamped this side of Pontes and we march at noon in advance of the rest. I came through this way on my way down to the horse lines, to bring you the word.'

They looked at each other for a moment, both on the edge of going their separate ways, both aware that what was coming was something different from the harrying of the past summers.

'I have almost forgotten the smell of full battle,' Brychan said.

Aquila said abruptly, almost as though some grey shadow of the future had reached out to touch him, 'Have we left it too long?—We had something once, something that wins battles. Have we got it still?'

'Too much wine last night?' Brychan drawled. 'Or just an encouraging thought on the eve of the battle?'

'Just a thought,' Aquila said. He was hitching already at his sword-belt.

For a moment Brychan's face had neither its usual insolence nor its usual laughter. 'We have got Artos,' he said, almost gravely.

'Yes, we've got Artos.' Aquila looked up from his sword-belt. 'I only have to pick up my saddle bag and say goodbye to Ness. I'll be down at the horse lines close behind you.'

Brychan nodded, and in the act of turning away, flicked a long finger towards Flavian, round-eyed with excitement on the bench. 'How is the boy?'

Flavian answered for himself. 'I am almost mended, and I shall have a scar on my head like my father's!'

'Sa, sa! my young fighting cock!' Brychan stood looking down at him an instant, laughing again, his darkly golden head seeming very far up among the twisted branches of the damson tree. 'What it is to be a son, and what it is to have one!' and he swung on his heel and went with his long, lazy stride across the court and disappeared into the shadows of the colonnade.

Aquila looked down at his son. If only they could have had a little longer, he thought, they might have begun to know each other. Now maybe there wouldn't be another chance. Even if he came back, it would probably be too late, and the time would have gone by. He saw suddenly how the buds were swelling on the damson tree, and it came to him that he had never seen the damson tree in flower. The Saxons came before the buds broke.

'Back to bed with you,' he said, and picked up his son, very silent now, and carried him back into his sleeping-cell and set him down on the bed.

'What did you begin to say, before Brychan came?' Flavian asked.

'Did I begin to say anything? I have forgotten.' Aquila gave him a hurried and awkward hug, and strode out, shouting to one of the stable slaves to bring round Inganiad; then went to pick up his saddle bag and find Ness.

XVIII
The Hostage

A FEW days later, on the fringe of the Tamesis Valley, the British and Saxon war hosts met in battle; and five days later still, terribly, shamefully, unbelievably, the leaders of both sides met in the Basilica at Calleva, to discuss an agreed peace.

The Basilica at Calleva had been burned down, like most of the town, in the troubles that ended the reign of Emperor Allectus a hundred and fifty years ago, and, like the rest of the town, rebuilt on its own blackened rubble. Standing with the other British leaders at the council table that had been set up on the tribunal dais, Aquila could see by the clumsier workmanship where the new walls joined on to the old ones; even the stain of the burning, reddish as a stain of almost washed-out blood, showed up in the dusty sunlight that fell through the high clerestory windows of the vast hall. Odd how one noticed things like that—things that didn't matter, when the Lord God knew that there were things enough that did, to think about . . .

What had happened five days ago? How had it come about, this grey state of things between defeat and victory? The slackening of an army's fibre through too many years of waiting? 'Have we waited too long?' he had said to Brychan when the order came to march. 'We had something once—something that wins battles. Have we got it still?' And Brychan said, 'We have got Artos.' That had been a true word; they had got Artos, whose crashing cavalry charges had wrenched a drawn battle out of what would otherwise have been a British defeat. He glanced aside, and saw the tall, mouse-fair head upraised above the heads of the other men round Ambrosius's chair. Ambrosius was one whom men followed for love, into the dark if need be, but Artos was already one whom men would feel that they were following into the light; a great burst of light that had somehow the warmth of laughter in it as well as the sound of trumpets. But not even Artos had been able to drag victory out of that battle five days ago. Aquila's eye went for an instant in search of Brychan, before he remembered that

Brychan was dead, like Inganiad. Not for the red mare the old age in quiet meadows that he had planned for her . . . Strange, the tricks that your mind could play, so that you forgot for a moment, as though it were a light thing, that your sword brother was dead.

He looked at Hengest, sitting on the far side of the table with his leaders about him. He was a little more grey, a little less golden than he had been on the night that Rowena made her singing magic, a little broader and heavier of body, but with the same shifting, grey-green light in his eyes; the same womanish trick of playing with the same string of raw amber round his neck as he sat sideways in his chair, his other hand on the narwhal ivory hilt of his sword, and watched Ambrosius under his brows.

Ambrosius was speaking levelly and a little harshly, putting into a few words the thing that they had been arguing about, it seemed to Aquila, for hours. 'Assuredly it goes as hardly with you as with us, to speak of an agreed peace, O my enemy. Yet weakened as we both of us are by the battle that we have fought, we must both of us know that there is no other road that we can take. You cannot sleep secure in your new settlements, knowing that we may be upon your flanks at any hour, and that we are too strong for you to crush us out of existence. We, alas, are not strong enough to drive you into the sea. And so the matter stands.'

The heavy creases in Hengest's wind-bitten cheeks deepened in a ferocious smile. 'And so the matter stands.' His eyes never leaving Ambrosius's face, he leaned forward, and dropping his hand from the amber about his neck, made on the table the unmistakable gesture of a man moving a piece on a chess-board. 'Stalemate. It remains only, O my enemy, to draw a frontier between us.'

Ambrosius rose, pulled his dagger from the crimson scarf knotted about his waist, and bending forward a little, he drew a long curved line on the table, crossing it with a straight one, then another, the sharp point of the dagger scoring cruelly deep into a fine, polished citron wood with a sound that set one's teeth on edge. Ambrosius, the last leader of Rome-in-Britain, was very quiet, very controlled, very civilized; but the searing, screeching line of the dagger's wake, white on the precious wood, showed his mood clearly enough. Aquila, watching, saw the familiar map beginning to take shape, the map that he had seen drawn so often in charred stick beside the hearth at Dynas Ffaraon, now scratched with a dagger on a polished table-top, for the making of an agreed frontier with the barbarians.

Hengest, who had been frowning down at the thing growing on the table-top, bent forward suddenly with a grunt. 'Sa! A picture of a land! I have seen the country so—spread out—when I lay on the High Chalk and looked down as an eagle might.'

'A picture of a land,' Ambrosius said. 'Here is Aquae Sulis, here Cunetio, here runs the High Chalk, and here'—he stabbed downward with the dagger and left it quivering in the table between them—'we stand in the Basilica at Calleva Atrebatum, talking of a frontier.'

They talked long, very long, and heavily and hotly, before at last the matter was talked out; and Ambrosius plucked up his dagger and drew one great, jagged furrow screeching across the map, from agreed point to agreed point, making of Calleva almost a frontier town. He drew it with careful precision, but so deeply that Aquila saw his wrist quiver.

'So, it is done,' Hengest said. 'Now swear,' and took from the breast of his ring-mail byrnie a great arm-ring of beaten gold, and laid it on the table, midway across the frontier that Ambrosius had drawn.

Ambrosius looked down at it, shining in the cool, greenish light of the great hall. 'On what am I to swear?'

'On Thor's ring.'

'Thor is not my God,' Ambrosius said. 'I will swear by the name of my own God, and in the words that have bound my people for a thousand years. If we break faith in this peace that has been agreed between your people and mine, may the green earth open and swallow us, may the grey seas roll in and overwhelm us, may the sky of stars fall on us and crush us out of life for ever.'

Hengest smiled, a little contemptuously. 'So, I accept it. And now I swear for my people on Thor's Ring.' He rose as he spoke, his great hand was on the ring. 'Hear me, Thor the Thunderer, hear me swear for my people, that we also keep the faith.'

There was a silence, echoing in the high emptiness of the hall; then Ambrosius said, 'And now all that is left is to choose the men from either host who are to trace out the frontier.'

Hengest's eyes narrowed a little. 'One thing more.'

'So? And what is that?'

'The question of hostages.'

That time the silence was a long one, broken only by a quick and furious movement from Artos, instantly stilled. Then Ambrosius said, 'Is a most sacred oath, then, not a thing to be relied upon?'

'A hostage who is dear to his lord makes it yet more to be relied upon,' Hengest said, inexorably.

Ambrosius's hand on his dagger-hilt clenched until the knuckles shone white as the scars that he had made on the polished citron wood. He looked at Hengest for a long moment, eye into eye.

'Very well,' he said at last; and the words, though icily clear, sounded as though his lips were stiff. He turned his head, and looked consideringly into face after face of the men about him. Artos looked back, smiling a little from his great height; Pascent's face was wide open to him, both of them offering themselves. But his dark gaze passed them over and came to rest on the pouchy, slack-lined face of the man who had been one of his father's bodyguard. 'Valarius, will you do this for me?'

Aquila saw an odd look in the older man's face, as though the blurred lines grew clearer, saw his head go up with a new pride. 'Yes, sir, most joyfully I will do this for you,' Valarius said.

One or two of the Saxons muttered together, and Hengest said, 'Who, then, is this man that you offer as hostage?'

'Valarius, one of my father's bodyguard, to whom I owe my life,' Ambrosius said, 'and my friend.'

Hengest looked from the Prince of Britain to the old soldier and back again, studying both faces under his brows, and nodded. 'So be it, then. For my own hostage—'

Ambrosius cut him short, in that voice as smooth as a swordblade that Aquila had heard only once before. 'I ask no hostage in return. If Hengest is not bound by his sacred oath, I do not believe that the life of one of his hearth-companions will bind him. Therefore I accept his oath alone, though he does not accept mine.'

If he had hoped to reach some kind of chivalry in his enemy, the hope was a vain one. Hengest merely shrugged his great shoulders, his flickering stare still on Ambrosius's face. 'It is for Ambrosius to do as he chooses,' he said. But the flickering gaze said as clearly as could be, that if Ambrosius chose to be a fool . . .

Aquila stood leaning on his spear beside the gap in the bank and ditch where the road came through, and looked away north-eastward. Almost from his feet the land began its gentle, undulating fall-away to the smoke-blue distances of the Tamesis Valley: wood and pasture and winding water, all blurred over with a blueness that was like smoke. It might have been the smoke of burning cities, but the Saxons had not burned the cities. They had looted sometimes, but for the most part, having no use for town life, they had simply left the cities alone to live as best they could, to grow emptier and poorer, and fall more and more into decay, until the few people left in them drifted out at last to the Saxon way of life. It was all Saxon land down there now.

Summer was nearly gone, the sixth summer since Hengest and Ambrosius had faced each other across the council table at Calleva Atrebatum; and the goldfinches were busy among the silk-headed seeding thistles in the ditch, and the hawthorn bushes of the slopes below were already growing red as rust with berries, though there were still harebells in the grass of the bank beside Aquila, where the turf was tawny as a hound's coat. Five years ago that bank had been bare, chalky earth, raw with newness; a dyke cast up to mark the frontier between two worlds where it crossed the open downs and had nothing else to mark it; now it looked as old and settled in its ways as the downs themselves.

A faint waft of woodsmoke came to Aquila on the evening air, mingling with the warm, dry scent of the turf, and a horse whinnied, and somebody began to sing, and he heard the rattle of a bucket from the huddled bothies of the guard-post behind him. They had not had guards along the downs at first, but the years of peace had grown more strained and uneasy as they went by, and the simple line had become little by little a guarded frontier. Aquila, who had spent much of those five years on the frontier, thought sometimes that he knew something of what it must have been like on Hadrian's Wall in the old days; the long waiting with one's eyes always on the north; not enough to do, yet never able to relax. And behind the frontiers, as those five years went by, Ambrosius, with Artos at his shoulder, had been at the old struggle to keep their fighting men together, to make some kind of oneness with their neighbours, against the time when the war hosts of Britain and the barbarians crashed together again. For, despite oaths and hostages, all men knew that that time would come one day. Last year there had been so much unrest along the borders that they had thought it was upon them. But this year had passed more quietly again; and now the campaigning season was almost over.

The light was beginning to fade, and he was on the point of turning away to go down to the guard-post for the evening meal, when his eye was caught by a movement among the bushes lower down the slope.

He checked, instantly alert, watching for it to come again. For a long, waiting moment nothing moved down there save an indignant blackbird that flew scolding out of a hawthorn bush; and then the movement flickered again under the turf-tangle of the autumn scrub. Something, someone was working his way through the bushes towards the road. Aquila's hand tightened automatically on the shaft of his spear, his frowning gaze following the small, stealthy movements as they drew nearer—nearer—until, between one instant and the other, a man broke from cover of the whitethorn scrub on to the open turf. An oldish man, for his head was cobweb colour in the fading light: a man who ran low, swerving and zigzagging as a snipe flies, but with none of the lightness of a snipe, for he stumbled and lurched as he ran, as though he were far spent, with unmistakably the look of a hunted man putting on one last, heart-tearing burst of speed to reach the bank that marked the frontier before the hunt was upon him. Aquila's mouth was open to shout for his men, but he shut it again. He could see no sign of pursuit, and if the fugitive had for the moment shaken off whoever it was that he ran from, to shout would betray him. Aquila took a long step forward, poised for instant action. The fugitive had stumbled out on to the road now; he was very near the gap in the bank, so near that for a moment he looked as though he might make it. Then a kind of snapping hum sounded behind him in the bushes, something thrummed like a hornet through the air towards him, and he staggered and half fell, then recovered himself and ran on. Aquila sprang forward, yelling to the men behind him in the guard-post as he ran. Another arrow thrummed out of the bushes, but in the fading light it missed, and stood quivering in the roadway. Aquila cast his spear at the bushes from which it had come, and heard a cry as he ripped out his sword, still running. A few moments later, with his own men already pounding down towards him, he reached the reeling fugitive just as he fell, and saw the short Saxon arrow in his back: saw also, with a feeling of shocked unbelief, who the man was. The hostage had returned in a strange manner to his own people.

Aquila was kneeling over him in the road, his men all around them.

'It's Valarius,' he said. 'Get him back, lads. The devils! See what they have done to him!'

They took the old man up and carried him back through the gap in the dyke that he had so nearly gained, and on the British side of it, in the safety that was too late for him now, made to lie down on his face. But somehow he got to his knees, looking up at Aquila with a twisted and sweating face that yet smiled a little.

'Ah, the Dolphin! Five years is a long time, and it is good—to be—among friends again,' he said, and sagged forward into Aquila's arms.

'Keep guard, in case they try to rush us,' Aquila said to his men. 'Valarius, in Our Lord's name, what has happened?'

'They won't rush you—won't—risk any sort of frontier trouble—not now,' Valarius gasped. 'I hoped to lie up till—dark before trying—to get across, but they—routed me out too soon.' And then, as he felt Aquila's hand near the wound, 'Na, let be! There's naught to be done, and—if you meddle with that—I shall die—shall die anyway, but—must talk—first.'

Aquila also knew that there was nothing to be done, not with an arrow deep-driven in that position. He eased the old soldier over, holding him with an arm under his shoulders so that no weight came on the barb, and propped him with a knee, listening to the harsh, agonized words that he gasped out with such desperate urgency. 'Hengest has made—an alliance with Guitolinus—the Scots too, some Scots settlers from southern Cymru—going to invade—invade—'

'When?' Aquila snapped.

'In—half a month, by the—original plan. That leaves them—clear month's campaigning time—maybe more. Gambling on Ambrosius—not expecting anything so—late in the year. But knowing that I'm—slipped through their fingers with—maybe breath for a few words left in—my body, I think they'll—come sooner.'

'They swore on Thor's Ring,' Aquila began stupidly.

'To the Saxon kind—an oath between friends is binding—to the death. An oath between—enemies is made to be kept until—the time comes for breaking it.'

'Are you sure of all this?' Aquila demanded.

'I have been a hostage among them for five years—oh, my God! Five years!—Nobody troubles to keep a hostage in the dark. I know these things—beyond all doubt.'

'Where will the attack fall?'

'I—do not know.'

'Do you know anything more?' Aquila pressed him with merciless urgency, for it seemed to him that Valarius was beginning already to drift away from them. 'Anything more, Valarius?'

'Na, nothing more. Is not that—enough?'

Aquila looked up, singling out one from among the men around him. 'Priscus, saddle up and ride like the hammers of hell for Venta. Tell Ambrosius that Hengest has made an alliance with Guitolinus and the Scots settlers in Cymru and intends invading, certainly in half a moon, maybe sooner. Tell him that Valarius has returned to us, and in what manner. Repeat after me.'

The man repeated his orders, and swung away, striding downhill towards the horse-lines. Aquila shifted a little, trying to find an easier position for Valarius.

'Water,' Valarius whispered.

'Go and get it,' Aquila said to the man nearest him.

Valarius lay looking up at the sky, from which the light was beginning to fade. Little clouds that had not showed when the sun was up made a flight of dim, rose-coloured feathers across the arch of it. The green plover were crying, and a little wind, cool after the heat of the day, stirred the grass along the crest of the bank. The men of the guard-post stood round in silence, looking down.

'It is good to come back,' Valarius said with a deep contentment. 'The Saxon kind promised—that when the fighting joined, and the time for secrecy was done—I should be free to—come back to die with my—own people, but I was always—an impatient man. Is the—water coming?'

'It will be here very soon,' Aquila said, wiping away the stain of blood from the corner of Valarius's mouth. 'Is there any word that you would have me carry to Ambrosius?'

'Tell him—I rejoice to have redeemed my debt.'

'He has never thought of any debt,' Aquila said. 'I have told you that before.'

A queer little smile twisted Valarius's mouth. 'But I have—and I have told you that before . . . Tell him, all the same. Even if he has—not thought of it so—he will understand and be—glad for me.' His last words were scarcely to be heard at all. He turned his head on Aquila's arm, and began to cough, and more blood came out of his mouth; and the thing was over. So Valarius died with more dignity than he had lived for many years.

The man who had gone for the water came running with it in his leather helmet, and knelt down beside Aquila. 'Is he—am I—?'

Aquila shook his head. 'You are just too late.' He felt under Valarius's body, and snapped off the projecting arrow-shaft, knowing that there was no more harm the barb could do him now, and laid him down at the foot of the bank among the long, tawny grasses and the late harebells that looked almost white in the dusk.

XIX
'Victory like a Trumpet Blast'

A FEW evenings later the British war host was encamped within the turf banks of the ancient hill fort a few miles east of Sorviodunum, knowing that tomorrow's battle was for life or death.

Aquila, checking just below the crest of the great western rampart on his way down to the horse-lines, saw the slow heave of the downs westward like a vast sea in the windy dusk. Below him, below the encircling rampart on its isolated hill, the shallow valley dipped away, rising again to the wave-lift of downs on the far side. As he looked away north-westward along the line of them, he could just make out, even now, the gap in the hills where the road from Sorviodunum came through on its way to Calleva; the gap beyond which, somewhere, the hosts of Hengest were encamped, waiting, as the British were waiting, for dawn. Behind the ancient turf fortress the land fell gently, dark-furred with thorn scrub, as were all the skirts of the downs, to the low flatness of reed and willow and alder brake, the stray gleam of water where the river marshes crept in among the hills. Ambrosius had chosen his position well: the marshes and the thorn scrub and the hill slopes to guard the British flanks, the road from Venta to Sorviodunum a few miles behind for their supply line.

Only three days ago, the whole frontier had gone up in flames. The break-through had come just below Cunetio, and Hengest with Guitolinus and the Scots had swept like a flood through a broken dam down the road south, hurling back the British skirmishing bands sent up to clog their advance and slow them down while the main defence made ready. A few hours since, and a few miles short of Sorviodunum, they had swung south-eastward for the gap in the downs where the Calleva road passed through. Once through that they would be free to march on Venta itself, or, more likely, sweep down the broad river valley the last few miles to the head of Vectis Water, so cutting Ambrosius's little kingdom in two. Free, that is, save for the British standing in the way, the hastily gathered host of lowland foot-soldiers and mountain cavalry, the bowmen of Cymru and a few untrained late-joined companies from the nearest fringes of the Dumnonii.

Ambrosius had called in almost the whole of the British host, staking everything on this one great battle; for Ambrosius, as well as Hengest, knew how to be a gambler. If they were beaten now, that was the end. 'I can't afford to fail once,' Ambrosius had said, years ago, 'because I've nothing in reserve with which to turn failure into victory.' It had been a curb then, holding them back; now it was become a spur. An odd change, that, Aquila thought, listening to the confused hum of the camp behind him. Five years ago the mood of the British camp had been somehow deadened with long waiting. It should have been worse now, worse by five years, but it was not. Maybe it was a kind of desperation, the knowledge that this time there could be no agreed peace, that nerved them. But whatever it was, Aquila had felt the change of mood at once when he rode in at noon with his own men; had felt something rising like a dry wind through the whole host. Unaccountable were the ways of men, and still more unaccountable the ways of hosts that were quite unlike the ways of the men from which they were made.

Aquila turned and went on his way. The whole camp was throbbing like a lightly tapped drum as he went down through it. Men came and went, horses stamped, he heard the ring of hammer on field anvil where the armourers were busy on last-minute harness repairs; arrows were being given out from the fletches' wagons, and the smoke of cooking fires spread and billowed across the darkening hill-top before the rising wind.

There was a fire down by the near end of the horse-lines, and some of his own men gathered about it. And there, standing a little uncertainly on the edge of the firelight, he found Flavian.

Flavian was wearing a weather-worn leather tunic too big for him across the shoulders, and he must have been to the armourers' wagons, for a long sword in a plain wolfskin sheath hung at his side. The wind was blowing his dark, feathery hair sideways across his forehead like a pony's forelock, and the five-year-old scar showed white in the wind-driven firelight. To Aquila, stopping abruptly in his tracks at sight of him, he looked very surprisingly like a man.

'Flavian! What do you suppose you are doing here?'

'I came out to take my part against the Saxons,' Flavian said, and came a step nearer into the firelight. He was as tall as his father already; a tall, grave boy with level eyes. 'They were saying in Venta that every man who could carry a sword would be needed.'

'Every *man*, yes,' Aquila said.

'You always said that I should have my shield when I was fifteen, Father.'

'You have miscounted. You are not fifteen yet.'

'I shall be in a month's time,' Flavian countered, quickly.

There was a small silence, and then Aquila asked, quietly, because he did not want to shame the boy in the hearing of the men round the fire, 'You did not come without word to your mother?'

Flavian shook his head. 'No, sir; Mother sent me.'

Again there was silence. They looked at each other through the smoke of the windy fire, through the barrier that had always been between them. They had never got back to where they had been in the sunny courtyard five years ago. The whole summer had gone by before Aquila returned to Venta again, and by that time it had been too late. Just for the moment Aquila had thought that the boy had come to him of his own accord. But Ness had sent him . . .

'Very well, then,' he said, with no softening of his stern manner. 'I take you. Did you ride Whitefoot?'

'Yes, sir, but—'

'Where have you picketed him?'

'In the same row as Falcon, sir, for the moment, but—'

Aquila's brows snapped together. 'For the moment?'

'Yes; you see—' Flavian hesitated, and his father saw him swallow. 'Sir—when I got here, they told me you were in council with Ambrosius, and I had to picket him somewhere until I could see you and ask your leave. Sir, I want to take my sword to Artos and ask him to let me ride in his wing.'

Aquila was wincingly aware of his own men gathered about the fire and looking on, listening. 'At least this time you have thought fit to ask my leave in the matter,' he said coldly. 'I suppose that I should be gratified by that.'

'Then I may go to Artos?' Young Flavian was already poised to be away in search of his heart's desire.

'No,' Aquila said, 'I am afraid not.'

'But, sir—'

'I am afraid not.'

For an instant Flavian seemed about to fly out at him with some furious protest, but he choked it back, and asked in a tone as quiet as his father's, 'Why, sir?'

Aquila was silent a moment. He was letting this tall, almost unknown son of his go into battle before the time that he had meant to, but at least he would keep him close to himself. It was not jealousy, it was a feeling that he would be safer there. He knew that that was confused thinking, a Saxon arrow was as likely to find him in one part of the battle as another; but somehow he felt that he owed it to Ness, who had sent him his son on the eve of battle.

'Possibly one day I may give you my reasons,' he said at last. 'For the present, I fear that you must accept blindly the fact that I forbid you to take that sword that you have come by to Artos.' He waited for an answer, and then as it did not come, said sharply, 'Understood?'

Flavian stared straight before him, no longer looking at his father. 'Understood, sir.'

'Very well. You had best join yourself to Owain's squadron; tell him I sent you. You will find him by the lower fire down yonder.'

Flavian drew himself up stiffly in the Roman salute that he had seen some of the old soldiers give; and turned without another word, and walked away. Aquila, watching him disappear in the dusk, thought suddenly and painfully of all the things he would have liked to say to the Minnow before his first battle.

In the darkness before dawn, suddenly a spark of red fire woke on the black crest of the downs, signalling to the watchers in the British camp that the Saxons were showing signs of movement. The hosts of Ambrosius rose and shook themselves, and turned themselves to the business of the day. Dawn, when it came, was a wild one, a fiercely shining, yellow dawn that meant storm and tempest; and the wind that had been rising all night was sweeping like a winged thing down the valley; and overhead the great, double-piled clouds racing from the west were laced and fringed with fire. And from the topmost spray of the whitethorn that grew high on the ancient ramparts a storm cock was singing. His song, fiercely shining as the morning, was sometimes scattered by the wind, sometimes came clearly down to the waiting cavalry on the slopes below.

Aquila heard his song, a song like a drawn sword, cutting through the formless sounds of a gathering army. From here on the slopes of the fortress hill he could see the whole battle line strung across the shallow trough of the valley; the main body of spears in the centre, where in the old days the legions would have been, the long-bow men behind them, and on either side the outspread wings of cavalry and mounted archers. The wild, changing light splintered on spear-point and helmet-comb, picked out here the up-tossed mane of a horse, there a crimson cloak flung back on the wind, and burned like coloured flame in the standards that the wind set flying: Pascent's standard, a mere flicker of blood red above the far cavalry wing; his own with the silken dolphin that Ness had worked for him when first he came to command a whole wing; and away down in the midst of the host the great, gleaming, red-gold Dragon of Britain, where Ambrosius in battered harness and cloak of the proud Imperial Purple sat his huge black stallion with a knot of his Companions about him.

Artos, with his standard flying above the flower of the British cavalry, was out of sight round the flank of the fortress hill, waiting for his moment to come. He was all the reserves they had; and save for him, the whole hope of Britain was strung across that shallow downland valley. Aquila wondered suddenly whether Flavian minded desperately being with him instead of with Artos, and glanced round at the boy sitting his horse just behind him. Flavian looked rather white. He was smiling a little, but the smile did not touch his eyes; and as Aquila looked, he ran the tip of his tongue over his lower lip as though it were uncomfortably dry. It was the look that Aquila had often seen before in the face of a boy going into battle for the first time. Flavian caught his eye and flushed painfully, as though his father's look made him ashamed, and stooped to fiddle with Whitefoot's harness. Aquila looked face-forward again. Amid the whole British host, he suddenly felt very much alone.

The day had fully come—a day of broken lights and grape-coloured shadows racing across the tawny hills—when a darkness that was denser and slower than a cloud shadow came into view, creeping towards them along the fringe of the downs. Knowing that it would be hidden as yet from the main battle line, Aquila flashed his sword from its sheath, and rising in his stirrups flourished it in great circles above his head, and from the knot of horsemen about the golden dragon, far off and small and bright with distance, he saw Ambrosius fling up his own sword arm, and knew that his signal had been received; he felt in himself the kind of ripple that ran down the long curve of the battle line like a deep-drawn breath. The dark swarm of the advancing host drew nearer. When the cloud shadows sped across it, it was merely a dark mass, but when the sun touched it, it woke to a kind of pulsing, beetle-wing brilliance with here and there a blink of light from a bronze shield-boss or the curved top of a Chieftain's helmet. A faint haze of white chalk-dust hung like a cloud above the rear of the Saxon host, for it had been a dry summer; and behind them, north-westward, the sky and the hills seemed to darken as they came, as though they trailed the storm like a cloak behind them. And away over the downs, for a jewel in that sombre cloak, Aquila saw the ragged, torn-off end of a rainbow brightening against the gloom of the massing stormclouds.

He pointed. 'Look, lads! Already the Rainbow Bridge is run out for the Saxon kind. Surely they make ready to welcome Hengest in the Valhalla tonight!'

There was a laugh behind him, and little fierce Owain, who had stood with him to hold Durobrivae Bridge fourteen years ago, cried out, laughing also, 'Na, na! It is but the stump of a bridge. They have cut through Bifrost to keep him out!'

The Saxons were so near now that he could see the white gleam of the horse's head borne on a spear-shaft that was Hengest's standard, and hear plain above the wuthering of the wind in his ears the formless smother of sound that was the voice of an advancing host. A Saxon war-horn boomed, and was answered by the higher, brighter note of the Roman trumpets; challenge and answering challenge tossed to and fro by the wind. The Saxon war host came rolling on, not fast, but remorselessly, shield to shield, with Guitolinus's light cavalry scouring on either side. They seemed appallingly strong, but Aquila, sitting with his bull's hide buckler high on his shoulder, and the flat of his drawn sword resting across Falcon's neck, saw that though they outnumbered the waiting British by upward of two to one, they were for the most part a foot army, and had nothing to compare with Artos's great hidden cavalry wing.

They were within bowshot now, and there came a sudden flicker of movement among the knot of archers behind the British spearmen, and a flight of arrows leapt out over the spears to plunge into the advancing battle-mass of the Saxons. For a few moments the enemy ranks had the look of a barley field hit by a sudden squall, as men staggered and dropped in their tracks; but the rest closed their torn ranks and pressed on, yelling. The British long-bow men got in one more flight, before the Saxon short-bows came into range; and after that the deadly hail of arrows was a two-way thing, tearing its gaps in the British ranks as it had torn them in the Saxon. And in the midst of the killing hail, the two hosts rolled together, seeming at the last instant to gather themselves like two great animals, then spring for each other's throats.

A few moments later, without ever taking his eyes from the reeling press below, Aquila said to the man beside him, 'Now! Sound me the charge!' And the dull roar of battle and the storm cock's shining song were drowned in the ringing *tran-ta-ran* of the cavalry trumpet. Falcon flung up his head and neighed, adding his defiance to the defiance of the trumpet, not needing his rider's urging heel in his flank as he broke from a stand into a canter, from a canter into a full flying gallop. Aquila heard behind him the hoof-thunder of the cavalry wing sweeping down the hill-side into the teeth of the westerly gale. He was yelling the war cry, 'Constantine! Constantine!' And he heard it caught up in a great rushing wave of sound. Guitolinus's cavalry wheeled about to meet them, and as they thundered down upon each other, Aquila's sight was full of a wild wave of up-tossed horses' heads, the dazzle of the stormy sunlight on shield-rim and swordblade, a nearing wall of faces with staring eyes and open, yelling mouths. He caught the glint of gilded bronze and the emerald flash of a wind-torn silken cloak where Guitolinus rode among his men. Then they rolled together with a shock that seemed as though it must shake the very roots of the fortress hill.

Guitolinus's cavalry crumpled and gave ground, then gathered again for a forward thrust. And for Aquila the battle, that had been clear in view and purpose as he sat his horse above it such a short while ago, had lost all form, become a sheer, blind struggle. He had no idea of how things were going with Pascent in the left wing, or even what was happening along the centre; all he knew was the cavalry struggle going on around him, the shock of charge and counter-charge, until at last, above the roar of battle, his ear caught the sound that all the while it had been waiting for: the sound of a hunting-horn ringing like the horns of the Lordly Ones from behind the shoulder of the fortress hill. It was like Artos to sweep his men into action with the gay notes of a hunting-horn. The sound rose above the battle din, high and sweet and shining as the song of the storm cock in the whitethorn tree. A great warning cry went up from the nearest ranks of the enemy, and snatching one glance over his shoulder, Aquila saw the flower of the British cavalry sweeping towards them along the tawny slope. There was a swelling thunder of hooves in his ears, and the wild, high song of the hunting-horn as the great arrow-head of wild riders hurtled down upon the battle. At the shining point of the arrow-head, Artos swept by, his great white horse turned for a flashing moment to silver by the burst of sunlight that came scudding down the valley to meet him, the silver mane streaming over his bridle arm, and the sods flying like birds from the great round hooves. His huge wolfhound, Cabal—son to the Cabal of his boyhood—bounded at his side, and half a length behind him galloped Kylan, his standard-bearer, with the crimson dragon streaming like a flame from its upreared spearshaft. Just for the one instant they were there, seen out of the corner of the eye, with the white, fierce brilliance of figures seen by lightning; then they were past, and the following cavalry thundered after, to hurl themselves into the cavalry of Guitolinus—into them and through them, scattering them as dead leaves scatter before a gust of wind, and on.

Aquila swept his own men forward into the breach that Artos had made.

'Constantine! Constantine! Follow me!'

He heard the hunting-horn again, and again the wild riders were sweeping towards them. They circled wide to charge from the flank, hurling Guitolinus's cavalry back in confusion on to the Saxon shield wall. Ambrosius's hard-pressed centre, relieved for the moment from the deadly thrust against them, drove forward again, cheering wildly, into a charge of their own. From the far wing also, from Pascent's cavalry, the cheering had begun to rise. Aquila, charging again and again at the head of a wedge of his own men, knew nothing of that; he knew only that there was no longer a solid mass of cavalry before him, but isolated knots of desperate horsemen. Indeed, the whole battle seemed breaking up, disintegrating, while in the midst of the spreading chaos the core of the Saxon host strove desperately to form the shield burg about the white-horse standard of Hengest.

Shouting to his men, Aquila drove his heel into Falcon's flank and rode straight for the half-formed shield burg.

Under his barbaric standard, Hengest stood head and shoulders taller than any of his house carls, wielding his great war-axe at arm's length, blood striping the hair under his bull-horned helmet, blood on his shoulders and crimsoning the downsweeping blade, and in his berserker's face the eyes full of a grey-green flame.

But it was not Hengest's wild features that started out at Aquila as the shield burg reeled and crumbled. It was the face of a young warrior glaring up at him over a broken shield-rim. A dark, fine-boned face, distorted now with rage and hate, that was yet as like to Flavia's face as a man's can be to a woman's.

Only for an instant he saw it, for a jagged sickening splinter of time; and then a half-naked Scot sprang in under Falcon's head, his reddened dirk stabbing upward under Aquila's buckler. He wrenched sideways half out of his saddle, and felt the blow, that should have ripped up his belly like a rotten fig, gash through his old leather tunic, nicking the flesh like a hornet sting. Falcon reared up with lashing hooves, but he brought him down again with a blow of his shield-rim between the ears, and thrust in, in his turn, above the Scot's buckler; and the man was gone as though he had never been, under the trampling hooves of the mêlée.

The young dark warrior also was gone as though he had never been. The battle had closed over between him and Aquila, and he was no more to be seen. Maybe he, too, was down now under the trampling horses' hooves and the red welter of the breaking shield burg.

By noon the storm had broken, and the white, lashing swathes of rain were sweeping across the downs before the gale. The great battle of the Dragon and the White Horse had scattered over a score of downland and marshy miles, into a score of lesser battles; and there were dead men and horses lying in the little chalky stream and scattered grotesquely over the hillsides and down the wide valley. Guitolinus lay dead, his emerald cloak darkened and sodden with the driving rain, under a whitethorn bush on whose tossing and streaming branches the berries were already the colour of dried blood. The storm cock was still shouting his shining song over the battlefield. And Artos and the British Cavalry were hunting the tattered remnant of Hengest's war host over the bare, chalky uplands north of Sorviodunum.

For Aquila, riding on the wing of that ruthless hunt, there had been a time of sickening anxiety when he realized that the Minnow was no longer with his squadron. It had not lasted long, for when he had demanded of Owain what had become of the boy, that grim little man had laughed, jerking his head sideways. 'The last I saw of him he was riding half a length behind Artos and yelling like all the fiends in hell!'

Now he was merely angry, and that with only half his mind; for the other half was twisted and tangled with the dark young warrior he had seen for one jagged instant of time as the shield burg crumbled.

XX
The Dark Warrior

FAR up towards the old frontier below Cunetio a great villa, and one that had been rich in the old days, stood with its cornland and orchards spread below it in a bay of the wooded downs. Its people had fled before the Saxon break-through, and Hengest's host, sweeping southward, had found it empty, plundered it and set torch to it in passing. But for some reason the fire had not spread through the whole three-sided range of buildings, and the main house-place had stood deserted with its one burnt-out wing, until, two days after the great battle for Britain, Artos had called off the chase some miles north of Cunetio, and drawn his men back into British territory. Now, in the light of a wild sunset, the place was thrumming with life again, though not the life of its own people.

Men slow and half blind with weariness dropped from horses as weary as themselves in the pale gold of the stubble-field below the garden wall; there were makeshift horse-lines in the lee of the orchard, and in the wide greenness of the garden court, campfires began to echo the colours of the windy sunset.

Aquila, riding in with his men, late from their scouring of the hills, found the whole bay of the downs between the woods and the river already turned into a great camp. And almost the first person he saw as he reined in below the orchard where the apples were gold and russet on the wind-tossed branches, was Flavian plodding up from the horse-lines with a saddle on his shoulder.

The boy caught sight of him at the same instant, and Aquila saw him hesitate, and brace himself for whatever might be coming. Then he changed direction and came to meet his father. He halted at Falcon's shoulder, and stood looking up.

'I hope that you had good hunting with Artos,' Aquila said formally, after a moment.

Flavian flushed scarlet, but his eyes never wavered. 'I am sorry about that, Father. It—it just happened.'

Aquila nodded wearily. He had been very angry, but now he felt too weary to be angry any more, too weary to be anything very definite. 'Things do—just happen, in the heat of battle,' he said, and saw the quick relief in his son's face.

Flavian put up a hand to caress Falcon's neck. 'Sir, I was close behind you—I mean—I was *still* close behind you when you charged the Saxon shield burg. I'm glad I didn't miss that; it was magnificent!'

Aquila did not answer at once. He was wondering rather desperately why he could not remember that charge and the shield burg crumbling without seeing again and again a dark face that was so like Flavian's, so like Flavia's, starting out at him from the press. All these two days past he had been looking for that dark Saxon warrior, looking for him in every live Saxon he saw, and every dead one. Again and again he had told himself that he was a fool, that the thing had been no more than a chance resemblance; that whatever it had been, the man was surely dead back there under the ramparts of the old green hill fort, and he would look for him no more. But he had gone on looking.

'I rejoice that it won your approval,' he said briefly at last. Then, turning away from the thought of the crumbling shield burg, 'Is Artos up at the house?'

'Yes, Father.' Flavian dropped his hand from Falcon's neck, as though it were the horse that had rebuffed him. 'He has made his headquarters in the main block.'

Aquila nodded, and swung himself stiffly out of the saddle. 'Do you know where they are dealing with the wounded?'

'Up at the house too. Somewhere in the north wing, I think. The Saxons have burned the south one.'

'So.' Aquila turned round on the weary and battered men who had dropped from their horses behind him. 'Take over, Owain; send Dunod and Capell, and whoever else needs it, up to get their wounds tended. I'll not be long.'

'I'll see to Falcon,' Flavian said a little breathlessly, as Owain saluted and turned away to carry out his orders. 'There's a sheltered spot at the other end of the orchard, and we've got some fodder—'

So the Minnow was trying to make amends. Aquila smiled suddenly. 'Thanks, Flavian,' he said. He gave Falcon into the boy's charge with a pat, and then turned away to find Artos and make his report.

The fires of the sunset were dying over beyond the high downs, and the fires in the wide green court flowering brighter as the daylight faded. The rain had passed, but the wind that had sunk for a little while had risen again, though not so high as before, and all the place was full of side-blown smoke and the remains of sodden, burned thatch that flapped along the ground and whirled up in corners like singed birds. Some of the men had rounded up a few sheep on the hill pastures, and driven them in for slaughter; others were questing to and fro through the house and out-buildings and among the ruins, in search of anything that the barbarians had overlooked; they must have unearthed a secret wine-store, for two men staggered by him, grinning, with a huge wine-jar between them, and he passed a red-bearded tribesman sitting with his back to a column and his long legs stuck straight before him, with the lap of his tunic full of apples and a wine-flask of jewel-coloured glass in his hand. When it came to damage, Aquila reckoned that a British host could do nearly as well as a Saxon one.

He threaded his way through the fringes of the shifting throng, heading for the main house-place across the far end of the court. But before he reached it a tall figure whose hair—he had taken off his helmet and it hung at his shoulder-strap—shone mouse-fair in the windy firelight, turned away from the knot of men about a fire that he was passing, and saw him.

'Sa ha! Dolphin! You have come in, then.'

'Reporting back,' Aquila agreed. 'My Lord Artos.'

Artos had come out to join him, his great footsore hound stalking at heel, and they turned aside together into the shadow of the burned-out colonnade. He cast a quick glance over his shoulder, to where the house-place door glowed dim saffron across the terrace, and said almost apologetically, 'They lit a fire for me in the atrium, and three candles. But it is so desolate in there; the house is dead, and I want to be with my own men tonight.' They stood together on the fringe of the firelight, greeting each other, but without words. Presently they would be triumphant, knowing their share in the triumph that was already roaring through the crowded camp and would sweep like a forest fire through Britain; but now they were still too close to their victory for any outcry. Then Artos said very quietly, fondling Cabal's pricked ears as the great hound sat against his knee, 'A good hunting?'

'A good hunting.' Aquila said, as quietly.

'What of your losses?'

'Until we rejoin the main host I cannot be sure; but I think not too heavy. Several of the men who rode in with me are wounded, and I have sent them up to the north wing for tending—if there is anyone there to tend them.'

'We have routed out a few women,' Artos said. 'There's a village up yonder over the downs, safe out of the Saxon's path . . . Anything else to report?'

'Nothing save what every captain who comes near you tonight will have reported already. That Hengest is safe away with the rags of his war host.'

'Aye: I think that not many men could have pulled back even the rags of an army from—what it was like on the Sorviodunum road, two days ago,' Artos said, with slow and considered admiration for his enemy. 'They are foes worthy of each other, Ambrosius and Hengest, and they are not done with each other yet.' He laid a great arm across Aquila's shoulder with one of the warm, faintly clumsy gestures that were so much a part of him. 'We ride a long road, old Dolphin, and this is only the beginning. Even here in the south it is only the beginning; and in the north, where Octa and his war bands still hold the land unchallenged, the thing is not yet even begun. But by Our Lord, it has been a beginning for men to tell their grandsons of, in the years ahead!' He was looking out over the fires and the shifting crowd, far out into some distance of his own beyond the windy twilight. 'When I was small, I remember Ambrosius crying out for one great victory to sound like a blast of trumpets through the land . . . '

'A blast of trumpets through the land,' Aquila said. 'Aye, we have that now: and so in a while we may have a Britain standing together against the Saxon swarms at last.'

'Bonded together under one King,' Artos said. 'It is in my mind that we shall see Ambrosius crowned High King in Venta Belgarum this winter.'

A long pause fell between them, full of the voices of the makeshift camp and the long-drawn hushing of the wind along the ruined colonnade. Aquila wondered suddenly what it meant to Ambrosius, who would be crowned High King this winter, that the tall, slow young man who could lead men like a flame, who was son to him in all but face, was base born and could not rule Britain after him. He wondered what it meant to Artos himself, and scarcely knowing that he did so, looked round at his companion. Artos turned his head at the same instant, and the light of the nearest fire showed them each other's face.

'For myself, I don't mind very much,' Artos said, as though the thing had been spoken. 'By and by I shall lead Britain in war, and that is enough for me. I do not want to rule Britain in peace. I do not want the loneliness.' He had turned back to his distance beyond the fire-light and the dusk; and Aquila, still looking at him, thought suddenly of the way he had come out from the atrium to join his men about the fires. Ambrosius would have known that his place was solitary in the atrium with the three candles that had been lit for him; Artos wanted the cooking-fires below the terrace, and the touch of other men's shoulders against his. 'I should like to be Ambrosius's son, of course,' Artos said after a little, very simply. 'But only because I should like to be his son, bastard or no, not for any other reason.'

'To be father and son does not always bring any kind of nearness,' Aquila said harshly; and it was Artos's turn to look round quickly. There was a rather painful silence.

'I am sorry about young Flavian,' he said awkwardly. 'One may so easily be carried away in the heat of fighting, without any idea afterwards of how it came about.'

Aquila's mouth curled into a wry smile, though the old frown lines were still bitten deep between his brows. 'I said as much to the boy himself a while since. There's not much need that you should defend him to me, Bear Cub.' Then, deliberately, he changed the subject, as he had grown used to doing whenever it drew too near to his own raw places. 'We have just won a battle that may save Britain from the dark. Does it seem to you at all strange that we stand here talking of our own affairs?'

'Not really,' Artos said. 'Our own affairs are small enough for words; the other thing is too great.'

It was full dusk now, and the scene in the wide court was a confusion of armed men and firelight under the rising moon that came and went, blurred silver through the scudding cloud-drift. They had killed the sheep, and the carcasses, hacked into rough joints for quicker cooking, were already scorching and sizzling over the flames. Round one of the fires the men had begun to sing, some wild and haunting victory song of their own mountains that they took up one from another, tossing it to and fro. And between gust and gust of the wind, between fall and rise of the singing, suddenly from the dark woods above the house a cry leapt into the night; a cry that rose and rose high and agonized and only part human and ended as though it were cut off with a knife, leaving the night again to the wind and the mountain men singing.

Some of the men about the fire glanced at each other, some grinned or cocked their heads in the direction from which it had come, but not all. It was nothing unusual.

'Another Saxon straggler,' Artos said. 'He and his kind would have done as much and more for any man of ours, if the victory had gone the other way. Nevertheless, this is a part of victory that I do not like,' and his heavy arm slipped lightly enough from Aquila's shoulder.

Aquila, with that ghastly cry still seeming in his ears to tear the night apart, was staring into the heart of the nearest fire. But he did not see it. He saw the darkness of the wind-lashed woods, and a flurry of desperate movement in the undergrowth, the white blink of moonlight on a dagger blade, and shapes that closed in as men close in to finish a deer that the hounds have brought to bay. He saw the face of the quarry turned up for an instant to the whitening moon, snarling as it had snarled up at him over a broken shield-rim, two days ago . . . He pulled himself together with an angry jerk, and saw the fire again. Fool, fool that he was, and fanciful as a green girl!

A fox-haired man was making his way towards them from the gateway, and he pushed himself off from the column against which, without knowing it, he had been leaning. 'Yonder comes Pascent to report that Hengest is safe away. And I must go back to my own men.' He put up his hand to Artos in a way that was half salute and half a gesture between friends. 'It was a good hunting, Bear Cub.'

He strode down the shallow steps, exchanged a quick greeting with Pascent, and continued on his way.

He went down to the horse-lines and made sure that all was well there; saw his men in a fair way to being fed, spoke with Owain about guard duty and arrangements for the night. Then he sat himself down beside one of the fires to eat stolen mutton. But though he was wolf-hungry, he could eat little, and the men about him—even Artos, moving from fire to fire among his beloved fighting men—looked at his dark, inward-turned face, and left him to himself. In a while he got up and looked about him as though he were a little lost. There was nothing more that he could do but go now and find some corner out of the wind, and crawl into it like a tired dog and sleep. But something in him dreaded lying down to sleep; something that he could give no name to, that was to do with the face that he could not stop seeing. There was a wild unrest in him, a sense of urgency, something to be done that would not let him rest, though his body ached and his eyes were hot in his head with the need for sleep.

He raised his arms above his head, stretching until the small muscles cracked behind his shoulders—and caught his breath at the sudden twinge and smart of the gash in his side that he had carried out of battle. He had almost forgotten about it; it was no more than a shallow cut along the ribs. But now it was an excuse for something else to do. He would go up to the north wing, where they had dealt with the wounded, and get some woman to bathe it and put on a smear of salve, and that would hold off for a little longer the time when there was really nothing to do but to lie down.

He made his way through the camp again to the north wing, and dragged his feet up the three shallow steps to the open colonnade that ran the length of the place. The rooms beyond seemed to be mainly farm workshops, wool stores, and chambers for drying corn. He turned to a door through which smoky lantern-light shone, and found himself on the threshold of a long chamber half filled with wool-sacks and other stores, whose tessellated floor, cracked and damaged now, showed that it must once have been a living-room, and a beautiful one. Some women were moving about, water was heating in an iron cauldron propped over a fire in the centre of the floor that was half filling the place with smoke; and a few of the men who had come in to have wounds dressed still lingered, sitting or sprawling on wool-sacks round the blaze. In the light of a lantern hanging from the rafters a man stood wiping his hands and arms, who turned to look enquiringly towards the door. A small, strong-shouldered man in a brown tunic, the loose sleeves rolled high, with a deeply tanned, intensely quiet face, and a fuzz of hair round his head that shone in the pool of light from the lantern like the seed-silk of the wild clematis, or the silver fringe round a cloud with the sun behind it.

For the first moment that silver fuzz put Aquila off; and then he remembered that it must be twelve years since their last meeting, on the track below the ash woods.

'Brother Ninnias! So here is our third meeting that you promised me.'

The little man watched him with a look that was more a warmth than an actual smile, as he came forward into the fireglow, then strode to meet him, tossing aside the piece of rag on which he had been cleaning his stained hands. 'And a third meeting should surely be the richest. God's greeting to you, Aquila my friend.'

'So you remember me this time,' Aquila said.

'This time my eyes were open because I was already looking for you. When word was brought to me that Ambrosius's cavalry was descended upon this valley, and I gathered a few salves and came down to see what help I might be to any who rode in with wounds upon them, I was wondering whether I might find you among those that rode with Artos the Bear.' He smiled. 'But it is you that have found me. Do you bring me a wound for salving?'

'The merest scratch, nothing to the gall of a Saxon thrall-ring that you salved for me once before.'

'Show me.'

Standing by the fire, Aquila tugged free the buckles, pulled off his old leather tunic, and slipped his woollen under-tunic down to the waist, laying bare the shallow gash along his ribs, reddened a little by the rub of his harness that would not let it heal in peace. Ninnias looked at it, then called to one of the women to bring warm water from the cauldron. He made Aquila sit down on some of the wool-sacks, leaning sideways, and bathed the place and set about salving it with the same salve that he had used that other time. Aquila leaned his elbow on the wool-sacks, and looked down, his head swimming a little in the smoky air and the smell of the fleeces and men's hurt bodies, watching the firelight play with the figures in the cracked tesserae, the figure of a girl with a flowering branch in one hand and a bird in the other. Maybe it was supposed to be Spring. It was odd, he thought, how little of surprise there seemed in this meeting with Brother Ninnias; as little as there was in putting on a familiar garment. Quietness rose within him, easing his wild unrest as the salve was cooling the smart of his gashed side. But that was always the way with Brother Ninnias, the quietness, the sense of sanctuary were things that he carried with him.

'So it is among these woods that you found your halting place at last,' Aquila said, when the salving was finished, pulling up his tunic again.

'Aye, I and my bees; north-westward into the next valley.' Brother Ninnias helped him with the stiff leather harness-tunic. 'Leave that lower buckle slack, or you will start the thing chafing again . . . I have my bee-skeps and my bean-rows and my physic garden, all as I had them before. And now I am away back to them again, for you are the last man to call for my leech-craft tonight, and there is no more need of me here.'

Seeing again the place where the track forked below the ashwoods, and himself going one way and Ninnias the other, Aquila got up, saying urgently, 'I will come back with you for a while.'

'You are tried, my friend, and need sleep.'

Aquila rubbed the back of one hand across his forehead. 'I am tired; but I need your company tonight more than I need sleep. I—' He checked and dropped his hand and looked up. 'Let me walk with you, Ninnias, rather than walk the camp all night.'

They faced each other, quite oblivious of the watching women and the men about the fire; and for a moment Aquila was afraid that there might be questions coming. But it seemed that Brother Ninnias still had his old gift for not asking questions. 'Come then, my friend,' he said at last, and that was all.

And so in a little while they left the camp together and struck away north-westwards, uphill through the hanging woods. The wind through the trees made a roaring like a high sea all about them, and the silver light came and went as the ragged clouds raced across the sky, and the storm had strewn the woods with fallen branches to catch at their feet in the darkness below the undergrowth where the moonlight never reached. But Brother Ninnias walked through the turmoil as a man walks on the clear path that leads home. They crossed the broad saddle of the downs and came down into the next valley; and the sudden waft of wood-smoke on the wind and the barking of dogs told Aquila that they were near a village. Maybe the village of which Artos had spoken. 'Do these folk also dance for the Horned One at Beltane, as your iron folk did?' he asked.

'Aye,' Ninnias said, out of the darkness ahead. 'But they listen to God's Word between whiles, as the iron folk did.'

They came to a little swift chalk stream coming down in spate with its hair full of alder leaves, and turned up beside it, Brother Ninnias leading, Aquila following where Brother Ninnias led. Soon the woods began to fall back, the dense masses of oak and yew giving place to elder and whitethorn, hazel and crack willow that would soon give place to the open hillside.

And then Brother Ninnias stumbled on something and half fell. Aquila, coming up behind him, heard him give a low exclamation, and demanded, 'What is it?'

'A man—a man's body,' Ninnias said, kneeling over something among the brambles and the dry hemlock stalks.

'Saxon?'

'Most like. For the moment I know no more than that it is flesh and blood.' Ninnias was turning the body over, and a pale blur showed in the darkness. Almost in the same instant, the moon, that had been behind a hurrying cloud, swam out into a lake of clear, and light flooded down between the hazel scrub, turning all the turmoil of the night to silver. And the pale blur became a face surrounded by a tangle of dark hair, the face of a young man in Saxon war harness. It was not snarling now, as Aquila had seen it snarling up at him as the shield wall crumbled; it was quite still, as full of quiet as a face carved on a memorial stone, but it was the same face.

Aquila had a moment of blinding shock, and after that it was as though he had known all along what he was going to find here. Only for that one moment he had the odd impression that the wind had died away and the woods were quite still.

XXI
The Return of Odysseus

NINNIAS'S hands were busy about the young man's body. In a little, he looked up. 'Not dead; but his shoulder is all but hacked in two. He'll come back to himself in a while—so much the worse for him maybe.'

And as though to give point to his words, far off in the darkness of the woods there rose again the cry that Aquila had heard earlier that evening as he stood beside Artos in the light of the cooking fires. The hunt was still on.

His head straining over his shoulder in the direction from which the cry had come, Aquila dropped to one knee beside the young Saxon's body. The moonlight jinked on the pummel of a Saxon sword, and he caught it up, slipping the sword-belt clear, and sent the whole thing spinning into the stream. The alder roots would keep it safe. Then he got hold of the boy to lift him. All the unrest, all the vague and formless urgency of the past hours gathered itself into an arrow-head of purpose within him.

'How near is your hut? Quick!'

'So near that if I had not smoored the fire before I came out, you could see the firelight from here,' Brother Ninnias said. 'Give him to me now, and go away and forget you walked with me tonight.'

Aquila shook his head, not even taking in what the words meant, and lurched to his feet with the unconscious Saxon hanging a dead weight in his arms. 'Show me the way. I'll be close behind you.'

Brother Ninnias looked at him a moment, very strangely in the moonlight. Then he got up and moved into the lead again, holding aside a branch to clear the way. 'Come, then.'

Aquila lurched after him, stumbling under the weight of his burden. In only a few paces more the elder and hazel scrub fell back, and open turf glimmered ahead of him, dim-silver in the moonlight, darkly islanded with furze. And less than a bow-shot away he saw the squat, comfortable shape of a bracken-thatched bothy sitting in its cultivated plot like a hen in a warm dust-patch.

'Wait here while I make sure that all is well. Come when I whistle,' Brother Ninnias said; and then Aquila was alone among the hazel bushes, watching the small, broad-shouldered figure dwindle away between the furze-bushes until the dark doorway of the bothy swallowed him. Three bee-skeps stood beside it, he saw, with a sense of greeting old, familiar things, nestling against the bothy wall like chicks under the hen. It would be thyme honey here, he supposed; pale thyme honey instead of dark, tangy honey of the heather country, but just as sweet.

A low whistle reached him, and already firelight was brightening in the bothy doorway. Aquila had crouched down, managing to take some of the weight of the young Saxon on one knee, but had not laid him down, because he was unsure, spent as he was, of his ability to take him up again without rough handling that might do further damage to his shoulder. Now he lurched upright, and struggled forward again, through the scattered furze and up between the dark wreck of the summer's bean rows, towards the brightening gleam of firelight. He reached the doorway, gasping for breath, feeling again the dark prickle of blood from his own wound under his harness tunic. The inside of the small, round hut was golden and still after the storm-driven black and silver of the night outside, and he lurched over to the bed of piled bracken against the wall, and set his burden down.

Brother Ninnias had already turned from waking the fire on the central hearth, and was taking fresh salves and other things that he might need from a couple of high shelves against the wall. He came without a word to kneel beside Aquila, and together they loosened the leather byrnie with its hacked and stained shoulder, and eased the unconscious man out of it, revealing a blood-soaked woollen kirtle and a mass of sodden and stiffened rags—maybe part of a dead comrade's kirtle—that he must have stuffed inside his harness to try to staunch the wound. Aquila eased off the sodden mass that left red stains on his hands, and flung it vaguely in the direction of the fire, and laid bare an ugly wound between neck and shoulder, and the shoulder itself hanging down, collapsed into the boy's body as happens with a broken collar-bone. It was not bleeding much now, but clearly before it stopped the young warrior had bled almost white.

'Collar-bone hacked through; and the wound two or three days old, by the look of it,' Brother Ninnias said, his blunt, gentle fingers exploring the surrounding area. 'He will have been trying to make his way back after the rest, I suppose. Hold him for me—so . . .' They worked together over the battered body without another word between them until the wound had been cleaned and salved and the grating collar-bone set, and Brother Ninnias had brought strips of an old cloak to bind it in position—he had used what linen he had in the British camp. And then at last he spoke again, his quiet gaze lifting from the work of his hands to rest on Aquila's face. 'I am a priest, and not a fighting man. As no man is beyond God's mercy, so none can be beyond mine, but it seems to me a strange and an unlikely thing that you have done tonight, my friend.'

It was the nearest thing to an uninvited question that Aquila had ever heard from him.

Aquila looked down at the fugitive's face, drained and bloodless so that it seemed all but transparent in the firelight, seeing the old-man hollows at cheek and temple, the bruise-coloured smudges under the closed eyes; and more clearly than ever, that startling, unbelievable likeness to Flavia. But it was something else, over and above the likeness, something in himself that made him sure beyond all doubt of the boy's kinship. As he looked, the faintest quiver of movement woke in the still face. For an instant he thought that it was only the firelight, before he knew that it was the first flicker of returning life.

'Wait: he is coming to himself,' he said, letting the half-question lie unanswered.

A little later, with startling suddenness, the Saxon opened his eyes with a groan and glared about him. 'Where—what—?'

'Softly now,' Brother Ninnias said, fumbling a little with the Saxon tongue. 'There are none but friends here.'

But the young man's eyes had thrust past him to find Aquila dark against the firelight. 'Friends, is it? Friends in Roman harness!'

'Friends, none the less,' Ninnias said.

And Aquila leaned forward, speaking, not in the Saxon tongue as Ninnias had done, but, scarcely realizing that he did so, in his own. 'What is your name?'

The other frowned up at him with black brows drawn close, and mouth set like a stone; but Aquila thought there was a flicker of startled puzzlement in his eyes. And after a few moments he answered in the same tongue, though with the broad, guttural accent of his own people, flinging the words at him with a reckless bravado. 'I was called Mull by my mother on the day that I was born, if my name is a thing that has to do with you!'

'Mull—a half-breed. And you speak my tongue. Was she British, this mother?'

'She came of your people,' the other said after a moment. And then proudly, disdaining to seem as though he asked for any mercy on that score, 'But I carry my shield among my father's kind—and my father was first son to Wiermund of the White Horse!' He tried to struggle up on his sound arm, to fling some defiance at the man who bulked so dark and still between him and the firelight. 'Ah! I have seen you before—when shield burg went. That was a good time for you, wasn't it? But it will not always be so good! You will not stop the Sea People flooding in. We shall overwhelm you in the end! We—' The breath went out of him in a groan, and he fell back on to the piled fern.

'Maybe it would have been as well to wait till he had some stir-about in him before asking him his name,' Brother Ninnias said, without condemnation.

Aquila let out a long, gasping sigh, like the long breath of relief from pain or almost unbearable tension, and rubbed one hand across his scarred forehead. He heard very clearly, in the sheltered stillness under the wind as it roared over, the flutter of flames on the central hearth and the rustle of some small living thing in the thatch. And another sound, out of the windy night, the sound of a voice upraised in a snatch of song.

For an instant the stillness in the hut became brittle as thin ice, and in the stillness the two men looked at each other above the unconscious body of the third. Aquila got up, and stood listening, more intensely than he had ever listened in his life before. The sound came nearer, the snatch of song was caught up by other voices; there was a drunken splurge of laughter and a burst of swearing as someone maybe caught his foot in an alder root. They were coming up the stream side; any moment now they would be clear of the trees.

'Make ready your stir-about, but even if you have to put him out again, for God's sake don't let him make any sound,' he snapped, and strode to the doorway.

Pray God they were not some of the newly joined Dumnonii who had ridden under Pascent's banner and would not know him by sight! He ducked out of the low doorway into the hurrying night, and stood with hunched shoulders reaching almost to the lintel, his arms akimbo so that the heavy folds of his cloak spread wide to shield the doorway. Firelight spilled out in a golden stain about his feet but unless a man lay on the ground to get it, there would be no clear view into the hut behind him. He realized that his own leather tunic was stained with Flavia's son's blood where he had carried him, and the stains showed black in the moonlight; but he had a wound of his own to account for that. Men were coming up through the tangle of sloe and elder and the dark furze beyond the bean-patch. He saw the movement of them, caught the spark of moonlight on a weapon, heard their voices and their thick, reckless laughter.

They broke cover in a ragged knot, checked at sight of the hut and the man in its doorway, and then came on, giving tongue like a small, unsteady hound pack. And as they drew nearer an almost painful relief stabbed through him as he realized that they were a bunch of Artos's wild lads, and well enough known to him. But clearly they had been at the wine that had escaped the Saxons; they were not very drunk, but drunk enough to be dangerous; in a reckless mood, looking for whatever mischief they could find: more wine to drink, another Saxon fugitive to kill.

Aquila stood, lounging a little in the doorway, and watched them come.

They were all around him before they checked again, their mouths loose and laughing, their eyes fiercely bright in the moonlight.

'Why, it's the Dolphin!' someone said. 'It's Ambrosius's old Lone Wolf. What's doing here, Lone Wolf?'

'Getting a gashed flank salved by the Holy Man,' Aquila said. 'What do you, for the matter of that? Lost your way back to camp in the haze from a wine-jar?'

A tall, fair-haired youngster with a gold torc round his neck laughed, swaying on his heels. 'We been hunting. *Good* hunting! We killed three times, and now we're thirsty again.'

'The stream is yonder; if that's not to your liking, best be getting back to camp and look for whatever else the Saxons have overlooked.'

Another man cocked his chin at the thatched skeps against the wall. 'Bees,' he said thickly. 'Might be heather beer in this doghole—or even mead.'

'There might be,' Aquila agreed. 'But in actual fact there's naught but salves and colic water and a little barley gruel.'

'Under the hearthstones, perhaps,' a third man put in. 'Let's turn the place upside down and see!'

Aquila did not move from before the door. 'You've enough vine leaves in your hair without adding bee bloom to it,' he said. And then more sternly, 'Leave robbing the church to the Saxon kind. Go back to camp, you fools, or you'll be in no state to ride south in the morning.'

His tone of authority seemed to sober them a little, for they had, after all, begun to be used to discipline. The tall stripling with the golden collar, who seemed to be a leader among them, shrugged. 'Maybe you are right.'

'I am very sure I am right,' said Aquila cordially. 'God speed you on your way back to camp, my heroes.'

They were a little uncertain, looking all ways at once; then the tall stripling made him a flourishing salute, and swung on his heel. 'Come away, lads; he doesn't want us. It's my belief he's got a girl in there.'

And with that parting shot, howling with laughter at their own wit, they turned back the way that they had come.

When the last sound of their going had died away, Aquila sat down on the threshold, his hands hanging lax across his knees and his head low between his shoulders. In a while a hand came on his bowed shoulder, and Brother Ninnias's voice said, 'That was very well done, my friend.'

'How is the boy?' he said muzzily, without looking up.

'Asleep. It passed into sleep; and the longer before he wakes, the better. I am going to begin burning his rags now; the byrnie I shall take out and lose, later.'

Aquila nodded, and leaned sideways with a little sigh to prop himself against the door-post. He did not feel the Holy Man's hand leave his shoulder. It was in his mind to keep watch, there in the doorway; and part of him did remain on guard, but part of him slept, while the last of the three-day storm blew itself out around him.

It was not far from dawn, and the night full of a soft, wet, woody-scented hush after the storm, when he came fully back to himself, and realized that life was moving again in the bothy behind him. He lurched to his feet, stood a few moments looking about him, and turning, ducked into the firelit hut again. Flavia's son was awake, and strained up on to an elbow at his coming, flinging back the wild black hair from his eyes, as he glared up at him. 'My sword! Where is my sword?'

'In the stream yonder,' Aquila said, 'with the alder roots to hold it under.'

'So! You have taken pains that I should have no weapon against you!'

'You fool, do you really think that I felt it needful to disarm you in the state you are in at present?' Aquila said wearily. 'It isn't healthy to be found with a Saxon sword in these parts.'

Mull began to laugh, taunting, furious, weak laughter that seemed to buffet him as though it were a wind outside himself. 'I do not doubt that you have a vast care for my health! Ah, but of course, fool that I am! It is your own skin that you look to!'

'Easy, my son,' Brother Ninnias said from the further shadows. 'It so chances that he cared enough for your skin to carry you here last night and doubtless reopen a gash in his own skin doing it. And you have him to thank you were not later dragged out of this hut like a badger out of its hole, and knifed on the threshold by a pack of wine-lit British soldiers in search of more wine or Saxons.'

Mull's rage fell still, and his laughter with it. For a long moment he lay looking at Aquila, catching his lower lip between his teeth, as Flavia had done when she was puzzled.

'I do not understand. Why did you do that?' he said at last.

'For your mother's sake.'

'My mother? What can my mother be to you?'

'My sister,' Aquila said levelly.

'Your—sister.' Mull spoke as though he were testing the words. His frowning gaze moved over Aquila, over the fine workmanship of his sword-belt and the long Roman cavalry sword, and the bronze-and-silver brooch that held his weather-worn cloak, and returned to his dark, harsh, hawk-nosed face, taking in something that had gathered to him during twenty years of commanding men. 'A great man among your own people,' he said slowly. 'A bitter thing it must be for you to have a kinsman among Hengest's war host.'

'It is,' Aquila said. 'God knows that it is. But not quite as you mean it.' He straightened his shoulders, turning to the more practical side of things. 'We shall be riding south in a few hours, and there should be little enough risk for you now, while you lie up here.' He never questioned whether Brother Ninnias would accept the charge and the risk that there was; he had too sure a faith in the little brown man for that. He turned to him now. 'Nevertheless, the sooner he is away, the better. When should he be able to travel?'

'Not for two or three weeks.' Brother Ninnias looked up from the bowl in which he was preparing barley stir-about. 'Two or three weeks for me to take joy in another guest that the Lord has sent me. But for his own sake he shall go in the first hour that I judge him strong enough.'

Aquila was thinking quickly: 'How long a march from here to the nearest point on the border? Ah, but there isn't a fixed border any longer. How far to the nearest of his own kind, I wonder?'

'That is a thing that there is no means of knowing,' Brother Ninnias said. 'But I know the forest northward of this for a good way, and can set him far on his road.'

Aquila nodded, settling down on to one heel. He pulled his purse from the breast of his stained leather tunic, and tossed it down on to the bracken, where it fell with a faint click. 'There's a little money—all I have by me. It's not much, but it will help. Get him a tunic, Ninnias, one that doesn't shout "Saxon" by its cut and long sleeves.' Then he took out his tablet and stylus, and while the other two watched him, hurriedly scratched a few words on the wax. He looked for a moment at what he had written, then returned his stylus to his folded girdle, and put the tablet down softly and precisely beside his purse. 'You will pass well enough for British, until you open your mouth. Therefore you must pretend to be dumb. If you run up against anyone, show them this pass. Signed by the Commander of Ambrosius's Second Cavalry Wing, it should get you out of any trouble. Understand?'

'I—understand,' Mull said after a moment. He swallowed. 'There seems nothing more, but—that I should thank you.'

'One thing more.' Aquila pulled the battered signet ring from his finger. 'This was my father's ring. When you come to the fringes of your own people, you must find means to send it back to Brother Ninnias here. Brother Ninnias will find means to get it back to me: and I shall know that you are safe away.'

'Safe like a beaten cur that runs with its tail between its legs,' Mull said with a sudden furious bitterness.

Aquila looked at his drawn face, proud and bitter and sullenly ashamed, the boy's eyes were much too bright. Probably he had some fever from the wound. Well, Ninnias would see to that. 'Hengest did not die when the shield burg went; he is safe away with the rags of his host,' he said abruptly. 'You're not deserting a dead leader, you're following back a living one. There's no shame in that.'

'A gentle enemy!' Mull said jibingly.

'No, I am not a gentle enemy. I loved your mother, my sister; that is all.'

They looked at each other in silence for a moment; and then—it was as though he laid down his weapons—Mull reached out and took the ring from Aquila. 'Even after she—even after *that* happened.'

'I once wagered her a pair of crimson slippers that she could not run faster than I,' Aquila said with careful lightness. 'She won, and I—never had the chance to pay my debt. You must tell her that I send her son back to her, in place of a pair of crimson slippers.'

'If I—when I see her again, is there any other word that you would have me say to her?' Mull asked.

Aquila was staring into the fire, his arm across his knees. What was there to say to Flavia, after their last meeting, and the years between? And then he knew. He put up his hand and freed the shoulder-buckle of his leather tunic, and pulled it back; he dragged up the loose woollen sleeve beneath, to bare his shoulder, and leaned towards Mull in the firelight. 'Look.'

Mull strained up higher on his sound arm, and looked. 'It is a dolphin,' he said.

'A friend did it for me when I was a boy.' He let his sleeve fall and began to refasten the buckle. 'Ask her if she remembers the terrace steps under the damson tree at home. Ask her if she remembers the talk that we had there once, about Odysseus coming home. Say to her—as though it were I who spoke through you, "Look, I've a dolphin on my shoulder. I'm your long-lost brother".'

'The terrace steps under the damson tree. Odysseus coming home. "Look, I've a dolphin on my shoulder. I'm your long-lost brother",' Mull repeated. 'Will she understand?'

'If she remembers the steps under the damson tree, she will understand,' Aquila said. He got up, and turned to the dark doorway. He looked back once, at Mull still propped on one elbow and staring after him, then ducked out into the first paling of the dawn.

Brother Ninnias came with him to the end of the bean-rows, and there they turned towards each other in parting. Aquila had half expected that the monk would say something about what had happened, about the part of the old story that he had not known before. But, tipping up his head to look about him with a wide, quiet, all-embracing gladness, he said only, 'The storm is over, and it is going to be a glorious day.'

And Aquila, looking about him also, saw that the moon was down; but the dark had paled to grey, and the grey was growing luminous. The eastern sky was awash with silver light, and somewhere down by the stream a willow wren was singing, and the whole world seemed poised on the edge of revelation, about to spread its wings . . .

'Do you believe in blind chance?' he asked, as he had asked it once of Eugenus the Physician, long ago. 'No, I remember that you believe in a pattern of things.'

'I also believe in God, and in the Grace of God,' Brother Ninnias said.

Aquila stood quite still, his face lifted to the light above the wooded valley that was setting the east singing like the willow wren. At last he stirred. 'I must be away to my men. Give me your blessing before I go.'

A few moments later he was striding down the stream side towards the camp and his men and the long, long battle for Britain. He knew that he would not see Brother Ninnias again.

XXII
The Blossoming Tree

SLEET whispered against the high windows of the old house in Venta, and in the living-room of Aquila's quarters the little mean wind of early winter made icy draughts along the floor and teased the flames of the candles in the bronze lampholder. The last of the daylight was fading, and the light of the candles was taking over. Aquila stood in the glow of warmth from the brazier where apple logs were burning on the charcoal, buckling his bronze-bossed crimson belt over a fresh tunic, while his cast-off daytime garments lay at his feet. It was so cold in the sleeping-cells that he had snatched up his festival clothes spread ready for him, and brought them in here to change beside the fire.

Earlier that day, Ambrosius Aurelianus had been crowned High King of Britain; crowned with the same slim, golden circlet that he had worn for so many years, with his Companions and the leaders of his fighting men there to see the thing done, before he went out to show himself to his people from the Basilica steps where once he had confronted Guitolinus and the Celtic party. The roar of their acclamation was a thing that Aquila thought he should never forget. And this evening, in the banqueting chamber of the old Governor's Palace, he was feasting with the men who had seen him crowned. Aquila reached for his best cloak, where it lay in a tumble, dark as spilled wine, across the foot of the low couch, and flung it round him, hastily settling the shoulder-folds. He was late, for there had been some trouble down at the horse-lines over the new Cymric steeds that he must see to, and the feast would have begun by now; this crowning feast for a new High King who was the hope of Britain. He stabbed home the pin of the great bronze-and-silver shoulder brooch, and when he looked up again, there seemed to be all at once more warmth in the room, and more colour; for Ness stood in the inner doorway in a gown of thick, soft wool the colour of the apple flames. Roman in so many things nowadays, she had never taken to the pale colours that the Roman ladies wore, and suddenly he was glad of that.

'I feel as though I could warm my hands at you, in that gown,' he said.

She laughed; something of the old mockery in her laughter still, but the sting gone from it. 'My lord learns to say pretty things in his old age!' She came forward into the inner circle of warmth and light about the brazier. 'A man has just left this for you,' and he saw that she was holding out something that looked like a little ivory ball.

He took it from her, and realized that it was a ball of white honey-wax, and instantly knew the sender, though no word was scratched on the smooth, creamy surface. 'Is the messenger still here?'

Ness shook her head. 'He was a merchant of some sort and wanted to get on to his trading in the town. He said that the man who gave it to him said there was no answer to wait for. Should he have waited?'

'No,' Aquila said. 'It was just that I thought for a moment it might be somebody that I knew.' The wax was brittle with cold. He broke it open between his hands, and spilled his father's ring into his palm.

For a little time he stood quite still, seeing it lying there among the creamy flakes and fragments of broken wax; watching the green spark wake and vanish in the heart of the flawed emerald as the fire-light flickered. So the boy was safe among his own people again. He tossed the wax into the red heart of the brazier and slipped the ring on to his bare signet finger. It was good to feel it there again. Good to know that he was free now to take what he had done to Ambrosius and abide by the consequences. With long thinking about it, he had reached the stage of not knowing how right or wrong the thing was that he had done. He only knew that it had been inevitable, and that now Mull's safety no longer hung on his silence, he must lay it bare to Ambrosius. Maybe tonight, after the banquet . . .

Ness's voice broke in on him. 'But it is your ring! Your ring that was lost! I do not understand—'

Presently he would tell Ness too. But Ambrosius first. 'You shall, by and by,' he said. 'Not now. I am late enough as it is.' He half turned towards the colonnade doorway, then back again, realizing that he would probably not see Ness again until after he had told Ambrosius. 'You look so pretty in that gown. I wish this wasn't an all-male banquet.'

She let the question of the ring go by. 'I am sure that the Princes of the Dumnonii and the Lords of Glevum and the Cymru would be outraged if they found themselves expected to follow the Roman fashion and sit down to feast in the same hall with women, on such a state occasion as this!'

'Your people,' Aquila said, and was struck by a sudden thought. 'Ness, do you see that it has come full circle? The Princes of the Cymru feast their High King. Tonight Ambrosius will confirm Pascent as lord of his father's lands and his father's people. Tonight your people and mine are come together again!'

'Yes, I do see,' Ness said. 'After twelve, nearly thirteen years.'

Aquila felt that he had been stupid in pointing that out to her as though it were a thing that she might not have noticed, when it must be so much nearer to her than it was to him. He wondered whether she had regretted the choice that she had made, almost thirteen years ago, but could not find the words to ask her.

And then Ness came and put her thin brown hands on his shoulders and said, as though she knew what he was thinking, 'Have *you* regretted it?'

'Why should I regret it?' Aquila said, and put his hands over hers.

'I'm not beautiful like Rhyanidd—'

'You never were, but it was you I chose, in my rather odd way.'

'And maybe I've grown dull. Contented women do grow dull; I've seen it happen.' She began to laugh again, and this time with no mockery at all. 'But at least I haven't grown fat, as some contented women do.' She gave him a little push, and dropped her hands. 'Go now to this splendid all-male banquet of yours, before you are later than you are already.'

He went across the inner court, huddling his chin into his cloak against the thin, icy wind and the sleet that was turning to snow, opened the postern door under the damson tree, and passed through, letting it swing to behind him. In the wide court of the Governor's Palace a lantern swayed in the wind, setting the shadows running all along the colonnades, and there was a great coming and going in the early winter dusk; young men gathered in knots by lighted doorways, cooks and servants and younger sons hurried to and fro; a man passed him with a couple of great wolf hounds in leash, making him think of Brychan in the early days. He turned into the north colonnade, weaving his way through the shifting, noisy throng, until he came at last to the ante-room where men stood on guard, leaning on their spears; and then he stood on the threshold of the banqueting chamber itself.

In the daylight the banqueting hall of the old palace was as shabby, crumbling, and faded as the rest of Venta Belgarum. But in the warm light of many candles, the dim colours of the painted garlands on the walls glowed with an echo of the colours of living flowers, and cracked marble and blackened gilding lost their starkness behind the twined and twisted ropes of ivy, bay, and rosemary whose aromatic scent mingled with the faint waft of wood-smoke from the braziers—for here, too, braziers were burning, though the chief warmth of the place rose from the hypocausts under the floor.

The hall was thronged with men seated at the long tables that seemed to swim in honey-thick light; men with clipped hair in the loose, formal tunics of Rome; men with tunics plaid and chequered in the deeper and more barbaric colours of an older Britain, with flowing hair, and river-washed yellow gold about their necks.

The first course of hard-boiled duck eggs and strong cured fish and little cups of watered wine was already being brought in, and Aquila, casting a quick glance among the boys and young warriors bearing in the great charges, saw Flavian moving through the throng with an air of serious concentration as he tried to avoid spilling any drop from his wine-cups. In these days of shortage of slaves and servants, they had begun to use their sons and younger brothers as servers and cup-bearers, much as the Tribes had always done. Passing over his son, Aquila's gaze went up to seek the High Table, where Ambrosius sat, with the faithful Pascent beside him, and big, clumsy Artos, whose wild-wind cavalry charge had done more than all else to gain them this first great victory; and the Princes of the Dumnonii and the Lords of Glevum and the Cymru, who had held back all these years, come in at last to swear their fealty to the High King. And suddenly he was remembering the first sight that he had had of the dark young Prince of Britain, by the hearth in a mountain fortress, with the salt mist wreathing beyond the door, and the same narrow gleam of gold round his head. They had ridden a long road since then, and the gold fillet was become the High King's crown; and he saw with a sense of shock that Ambrosius's hair looked as though grey wood ash had been rubbed into it at the temples.

Somebody brushed against him with a wine-jar, bringing him back to himself, and he walked forward between the long, crowding tables, up the hall. Ambrosius, who had been sitting half-turned to listen to a long-nosed princeling beside him, glanced up and saw him, and his dark, narrow face kindled as it always did at a friend's coming. 'Ah!

Here he is at last! Why, man, you're late; and tonight of all nights, when I must have my brothers about me!'

Aquila halted before the low step of the dais, putting up his hand in salute. 'Let you forgive me, Ambrosius the King. There was some trouble down at the horse-lines, and it is so that I am late.'

'I might have known that nothing but a horse would keep you away from me,' Ambrosius said, with something that was half laughing and half serious in his voice and eyes. 'Is all well now?'

'Aye, all well now,' Aquila said.

And at that moment Artos leaned forward, exclaiming, 'Why, Dolphin, this is surely a night of fortunate stars! You have found your ring again!'

For a moment of time no longer than a heart-beat, but it seemed long to him, Aquila did not answer. He could let it go at that for now, and still go to Ambrosius later with the true story, with a fumbled and shamefaced explanation of why he had not spoken out now, in this moment. But to do that would be in a queer way to deny Flavia; to deny something more than Flavia, that had no name to it, a faith that all men must keep within themselves. He must speak out now, before these strangers, and before the men among whom he had grown great, or break some faith that he had not broken before, even when he went wilful missing and let the galleys sail without him, all those years ago.

'My ring was sent back to me,' he said, his voice level and deliberate. And though the answer was for Artos, his eyes met and held Ambrosius's across the gold-pooled candlelight of the High Table. 'After our victory in the autumn, I gave it to a certain one of Hengest's warriors, along with money and a pass to help him on his way, that he might send it back to me for a sign when he was safe among his own kind again.'

Never in his life had he been so aware of silence as he was in the few moments that followed—a silence that reached out and out all down the long room behind him, as men, caught by some sudden sense of drama at the High Table, broke off whatever they were saying or doing, and turned to watch and listen. Never in his life had he been so aware of faces: the faces of strangers and of brothers-in-arms, all turned full upon him. Yet his own gaze never wavered from the still, dark face of Ambrosius, who seemed to sit at the very heart of the silence.

Then Ambrosius said, 'If the Dolphin, of all men, has had dealings with the barbarians, then it is in my mind that the reason must have been a strong one. Who and what was this certain one among the Saxon kind?'

Aquila stood braced as for a physical ordeal, his head up, his hands clenched under his cloak until the nails bit into his palms. 'My sister's son.'

Something flickered far back in Ambrosius's eyes. 'I never knew you had a sister.'

'I—have not spoken of her, these past years,' Aquila said. He drew a harsh breath. 'The Saxons who burned my home and slew my father and all our household carried her off with them. In three years I found her again in Hengest's camp while I still wore a Jutish thrall-ring. She helped me to escape, and I—hoped that she would come with me. But she was not free as I was free, who had only a thrall-ring to hold me. There was a child to bind her to her new people—and a man . . . So I came away alone, and did not speak of my sister any more.'

Ambrosius bent his head. 'Go on.'

'After our victory in the autumn, it was put into my hand to find her son among the fugitives of Hengest's host. How the thing came about is no matter—I found him, and I did what there was to do, to send him back to her. My Lord Ambrosius, there is no more to tell.'

The silence closed in over his words, and in it Aquila felt horribly alone. Then the silence was broken by a sudden movement among the group of young men standing against the wall, and the Minnow thrust out through his fellows and came across the chamber to his father's side.

Into the chill of his loneliness, Aquila felt a sudden rush of warmth. The Minnow, whom he had never properly known, who had disobeyed him to follow another leader in his first battle, had come running his neck into trouble to stand with him now. He felt him standing there, bright-eyed and defiant; felt the warmth of his loyalty like a physical touch.

'Keep out of this, you young fool,' he muttered. 'Nothing to do with you.'

The Minnow did not move, stubborn in his loyalty to his father and his determination to share with him whatever was coming. 'It is only nothing to do with me because I did not know about it,' he said, and the words were for Ambrosius as much as for his father. 'If I had known, I'd have done anything—all that was in me—to help!'

Nobody said anything, but Artos made a small gesture with the hand in which he held his wine-cup, as though he raised it to drink with the boy.

Ambrosius was studying Aquila's set face as though it were the face of someone he had never seen before. 'Why do you choose to tell me all this?' he said. 'Your ring was lost, your ring is found again. Why not let it sleep at that?'

Aquila did not answer at once. He had not expected that particular question, and though his reasons were clear in his own mind, he had no words for them. 'Because I have not broken faith with you before,' he said at last. 'Because I have done a thing, and I am prepared to pay the price. Because I—do not wish to carry shame under my cloak.' There were other reasons too, reasons that had to do with Flavia; but they were between Flavia and himself.

For a long, long moment Ambrosius continued to sit studying his face with that odd look of questioning and testing and discovery. 'A strange, and an uncomfortable thing is honour,' he said reflectively; and then suddenly his own dark face lit with the old, swift warmth. 'Nay, man, the years and the Saxons have torn gaps enough in the ranks of our Company. Let you sit down now in your own place, for I can ill afford to lose any more of my Companions.'

Aquila drew himself up still further, and made a small, proud gesture of acceptance and salute.

So it was done and over; no shame, no disgrace for Flavian to share with him—but Flavian hadn't known that when he came out to share it. The boy was standing a little uncertainly now on the point of turning away. Aquila brought a hand down on his shoulder and gripped it in passing. 'Thanks, Minnow.' It did not seem much to say, but it covered the situation, and he was not very sure of his own voice just then.

The Minnow said nothing at all, but he looked at his father, and both of them were satisfied.

But it was Artos thrusting Cabal further under the table to make room, and pushing his wine-cup towards Aquila as he swung a leg over the cushioned bench and slid into place beside him, who spoke the last words on the matter, very loudly and for all men to hear: 'I never had a sister; but if I had, I hope I'd be as true to her after twenty years.'

Much later that night, when the feasting was over, Aquila walked home with Eugenus the Physician. The snow had stopped, the thin wind had fallen away, and the sky above the whitened roofs of the old palace was full of stars; but the fresh snow in the lantern-lit courtyard was already becoming churned and trampled, broken up into chains of tracks by the crowding feasters heading for their own quarters in the city or in other wings of the palace. Eugenus had been asking questions—all the questions that Brother Ninnias had never asked. But Aquila found that they no longer made him flinch as they used to do; and there was freedom in that, too. Now, as they turned for an instant in the shadow of the postern doorway, and looked back, there was another thought in both their minds.

'There has not been a night quite like this for Britain before,' Aquila said, 'and there will not be a night quite like it again.'

'It is wonderful what one victory in the hands of the right man will do,' Eugenus said musingly beside him. 'With a Britain bonded together at last, we may yet thrust the barbarians into the sea, and even hold them there—for a while.'

Aquila's hand was already on the pin of the door behind him, though he still watched the thinning, lantern-touched crowd in the courtyard. 'For a while?—You sound not over-hopeful.'

'Oh, I am. In my own way I am the most hopeful man alive. I believe that we shall hold the barbarians off for a while, and maybe for a long while, though—not for ever . . . It was once told me that the great beacon light of Rutupiae was seen blazing on the night *after* the last of the Eagles flew from Britain. I have always felt that that was'—he hesitated over the word—'not an omen: a symbol.'

Aquila glanced at him, but said nothing. Odd, to have started a legend.

'I sometimes think that we stand at sunset,' Eugenus said after a pause. 'It may be that the night will close over us in the end, but I believe that morning will come again. Morning always grows again out of the darkness, though maybe not for the people who saw the sun go down. We are the Lantern Bearers, my friend; for us to keep something burning, to carry what light we can forward into the darkness and the wind.'

Aquila was silent a moment; and then he said an odd thing. 'I wonder if they will remember us at all, those people on the other side of the darkness.'

Eugenus was looking back towards the main colonnade, where a knot of young warriors, Flavian among them, had parted a little, and the light of a nearby lantern fell full on the mouse-fair head of the tall man who stood in their midst, flushed and laughing, with a great hound against his knee.

'You and I and all our kind they will forget utterly, though they live and die in our debt,' he said. 'Ambrosius they will remember a little; but *he* is the kind that men make songs about to sing for a thousand years.'

There was a long silence in the shadow of the postern door; then Eugenus shook his plump, muffled shoulders, and turned with a puff of a sigh and a puff of laughter. 'For you this has been a good night, in more ways than one; but if you wish to stand here and sing songs to the stars like a hound puppy, you must do it alone. I am a very old man with a belly that cannot abide as much wine as it used to do, also my feet grow cold. Therefore I am away to my bed.'

Aquila laughed, and opened the small, deep-set door, and stood aside for Eugenus to go through before him.

A good night, yes. He lingered a little, fastening the doorpin while the old physician scuffed away towards his own quarters. There was a feeling of quietness in him, a feeling of coming into harbour. He had spent half his life fighting the Saxon kind, and he would go on fighting them, he supposed, until he found his death from a Saxon sword or grew too old to carry his own. 'No more to be turned back than the wild geese in their autumn flighting,' old Bruni had said of the Saxon kind. And Eugenus's words of only a few moments ago echoed old Bruni's in his mind: 'We may thrust the barbarians into the sea; and even hold them there—for a while.' No respite in this war, and maybe only darkness at the end of it. But for himself, now, in this present moment, he seemed to have come to a quiet place in which to rest a little before going on. He had all at once a feeling of great riches. Ness had chosen to forsake her own people to be with him; and the Minnow had come out before all men to stand beside him in the face of possible disgrace, which was probably, he thought, the best thing that had ever happened to him; and in some way that he neither understood nor questioned, he had found Flavia again.

He looked up at the old damson tree, and saw the three stars of Orion's belt tangled in the snowy branches. Someone, maybe Ness, had hung out a lantern in the colonnade, and in the starlight and the faint and far-most fringe of the lantern glow it was as though the damson tree had burst into blossom; fragile, triumphant blossom all along the boughs.

ROSEMARY Sutcliff was born in Surrey, the daughter of a naval officer. At the age of two she contracted the progressively wasting Still's disease and spent most of her life in a wheelchair. During her early years she had to lie on her back and was read to by her mother: such authors as Dickens, Thackeray, and Trollope, as well as Greek and Roman legends. Apart from reading, she made little progress at school and left at fourteen to attend art school, specializing in miniature painting. In the 1940s she exhibited her first miniature at the Royal Academy and was elected a member of the Royal Society of Miniature Painters just after the war.

In 1950 her first children's book, *The Queen's Story,* was published and from then on she devoted her time to writing the children's historical novels which have made her such an esteemed and highly respected name in the field of children's literature.

She received an OBE in the 1975 Birthday Honours List and a CBE in 1992.

Rosemary Sutcliff died at the age of 72 in 1992.